A BREED APART

Set against the world of international horsebreeding and the opulence of immense wealth, this is the story of Geri-Jo Lockley, a beautiful woman with the courage and will of a champion who rises from poverty to command the jet-set society of those who breed winners.

Jeanne Day Lord

A Breed Apart

CORGI BOOKS

A BREED APART
A CORGI BOOK 0 552 13043 5

First publication in Great Britain

PRINTING HISTORY
Corgi edition published 1987

Copyright © 1987 by Jeanne Day Lord

This book is set in Plantin

Corgi Books are published by Transworld Publishers Ltd., 61–63 Uxbridge Road, Ealing, London W5 5SA, in Australia by Transworld Publishers (Aust.) Pty. Ltd., 15–23 Helles Avenue, Moorebank, NSW 2170, and in New Zealand by Transworld Publishers (N.Z.) Ltd., Cnr. Moselle and Waipareira Avenues, Henderson, Auckland.

Printed and bound in Great Britain by
Cox & Wyman Ltd., Reading, Berks.

This book is dedicated to the thoroughbreds – human variety – in my own stable: Max, Daisy, and Con. With love and thanks for all your winning ways, and for keeping me in shape for the race.

BOOK I: *THE GATE*

Eastern Kentucky — Autumn, 1959

CHAPTER ONE

The rusting schoolbus drove along the steep mountain road, lurching and whining whenever the driver changed gears. At the wheel, Perry Drummond struggled to shift smoothly, but the worn clutch always engaged with a jolt so violent that the children were thrown forward in their seats.

Damn army surplus, Drummond thought. Even before the County had bought the buses they'd been shot to hell ferrying troops around in Korea. Every time he took this run he expected a breakdown. What worried him most was a failure in the steering or brakes that might send the big rattletrap crashing down the mountain with all these kids inside . . .

A few drops of water spattered onto the windshield, and the driver glanced at the sky. Only a couple of clouds floated in the broad expanse of blue, and the sun still shone brightly. Maybe it hadn't been rain, just some moisture shaken from the leaves of trees beside the road. Sometimes the rain in late October could pour down suddenly, flooding out the roads. Nothing to worry about today, though. The run would be finished soon, just the MacKittrick boys to let off at the turn a mile ahead, and, lastly, the five Lockely kids who went on a few miles to the hollow.

The grade tilted up again. Drummond shifted into low with a shuddering jolt, then turned to look over his shoulder at the frail blond girl in the front window seat across the aisle. As always, she had her face pressed right up against the glass.

'Sit back, Geri-Jo. All the bumpin' around we're doin' in this tincan, you'll get some headache if you bang agin that windah.' The girl sat back a little, though Drummond guessed it wouldn't be long before she'd creep forward again. She always pressed herself against the window as if she wanted to pass through it, fly off into the sky. Riding back and forth every day to the two-room schoolhouse was her only chance to see a bit of the world outside the small settlement between steep hills where she and her family lived — 'the hollow', as the mountain folk called it. The driver thought this girl seemed to be the one kid in the whole bunch who spent all her time thinking about what lay beyond these Appalachian hollows — planning someday, somehow, to see whatever was on the other side of the horizon.

Or did he only *hope* she had such dreams, the driver wondered — because when he looked at the pure sweet beauty of her face, those bright aquamarine eyes and the milky skin and silken hair, he hated to think of the way it would all be aged and spoiled long before its time. Too much work and too little food and no time or money to spend on doctors and cures took a toll on all of the people here sooner or later. At twelve years old Geri-Jo Lockely still looked her age; thin and pale, maybe, but still fresh. At twenty, though, she'd look closer to thirty; and at thirty closer to fifty; and at fifty, if she was still alive, she'd look more than ready to die. That was the way with the women in these hills. No place in this whole damn country, Drummond thought, was life as hard as it was here in this corner of Appalachia.

A light shower of droplets began pattering onto the window. Drummond turned on the wipers, and lifted his eyes again. The sun was still up there.

'See that, Perry?' said the girl across the aisle without turning from the window. 'The devil must be beatin' his wife.'

'Reckon he is, Geri-Jo,' the driver said with a laugh. It was a common saying among the local people: if the sun shines when it's raining, then the devil's beating his wife.

'Perry,' Geri-Jo said after a moment, 'why'n they say that?'

'Just a sayin' is all. Sun and rain together means something good's happenin' same time as something bad. Same as with the devil beatin' on his woman.'

'I don't see no good part there.'

Drummond tossed another glance at Geri-Jo Lockely. She had turned from the window, and her wide eyes sparkled at him like the blue-green gemstones that were sometimes found in the mountains. Stymied by her inquisitiveness, it crossed the driver's mind to issue the standard warning on the dangers of children asking too many questions. Then he decided her curiosity ought to be protected. She would be scolded often enough for questioning, that was the custom among the mountain people: no sense asking for explanations of so many things that could never be changed.

'Well, I s'pose it's good that Satan's got trouble with his wife,' he answered, ''cause that means he won't get no lovin' tonight.'

'Don't see nothin' good there neither,' Geri-Jo Lockely persisted. 'Y'got to think about ol' Mrs. Satan — what it's like for her.'

Drummond laughed again. 'She's a devil, too, Geri-Jo. Deserves what she gets.'

'She's just his woman, Perry,' Geri-Jo said feistily. 'And ain't *no* woman deserves gettin' beat on!'

A shout came from the rear. 'Geri-Jo, leave off your pesterin'. Way this rain's comin' down, Perry best pay full mind to keepin' this junkpile on the road.'

It was the voice of her brother, Ethan. He was just a year older, but always bossing her around, acting like he knew everything. Whirling towards the back, Geri-Jo spotted him sitting next to the eldest, Zeno, who was also grinning sassily. She stuck out her tongue at both of them. Then, turning away she caught the eye of her thirteen-year-old sister, Lucy, sitting with Lucy's twin brother, Coy. Lucy gave an encouraging wink, and Geri-Jo returned her gaze to the window.

Gray clouds had smothered the sun at last. The bus stopped. Geri-Jo thought it had gotten stuck in the mud, but then the door hissed open, and the McKittrick boys clattered down the steps. The bus jumped forward again, heading up toward the hollow.

11

A minute later, the rain started to come down in sheets, blurring the driver's view. Here and there, the rear wheels began to spin, the rear end skidded sideways.

Drummond halted again and opened the front door. 'Got to let y'all out here,' he called. 'Coupla miles still to go, but this dirt keeps gettin' softer we could get a slip that'd take us all down with it.'

'Oh shoot, Perry,' Zeno said as he came up the aisle. At fourteen, he was tall and gangly, and given to wise-cracks. 'Don't make like you worried 'bout us. It's the bus you're thinkin' to save.'

'Well now, why not?' Drummond answered lightly. 'County's got to scrape for a new bus, but new kids bein' made here by the carload ever' day. See y'all tomorrow.'

Geri-Jo was the last out of her seat. As she fell in behind her brothers and sisters, Drummond noticed that her hand-me-down cotton was frayed through in several places from too many washings. He reached under his seat and pulled out the old Army sweat shirt he kept handy to wipe fogged windows. As the child went down the steps, he quickly slipped the shirt down over her shoulders. 'There, Geri-Jo. Give ya some extra cover 'til ya get home.'

'Thank ya, Perry. Give it ya back after Mama washes it.'

Zeno, Ethan and the twins were already slogging away in a group toward the hollow. Geri-Jo jumped down to the muddy road and hurried to catch up.

For a while the children walked in uncomplaining silence. A two-mile walk was no hardship. Until a year ago, when the County had finally bought the buses, they had walked the whole nine miles to school.

'Reckon Pa's already fightin' to keep the crop from floodin' out,' Zeno said abruptly, and started throwing his long legs out with bigger strides. 'C'mon, all of ya,' he shouted through the roar of the rain. 'He'll need us . . .'

The other children scurried to keep up with him, and Geri-Jo soon felt out of breath.

'. . . can't hurry so, Zee . . .,' she whimpered.

But the rest kept marching ahead.

12

Geri-Jo didn't complain again. Her throat burned and her heart was pounding, but she knew Zeno was right. The only land they had planted was on the hill above their house — some greens and root vegetables they depended on for food, and a small cash crop of tobacco. All of it might disappear in the storm. When the steep hillsides got soft, slides were always a possibility. Shivering, Geri-Jo hunched down into the sweat shirt. The rain was coming so hard and fast now that it hurt as it pelted against her skull. The furrows of the road were ankle-deep in water. Streamlets, red-brown with loosened soil, coursed along every rocky gulley on the hillsides.

'It's gettin' badder!' Zeno screamed suddenly. 'I got to be helpin' Pa.' Throwing down his school-books, he bolted up the road. Shocked, the others paused for a second and watched him. Then Geri-Jo stooped to pick the books out of the mud. As she stood, the others piled their books and writing tablets into her arms.

'We'd best light a shuck for home, too, Geri-Jo.' Ethan said. 'You carry those so's we can run.'

Geri-Jo's arms could barely contain the heap of heavy school-books, still she tried to keep up with her brothers and sisters, spurred on less by the thought of the emergency at home than by her terror of the dark surrounding woods. Often, sitting around the stove of the big room where her family ate and slept, she'd listened to her Pa's old great-aunt, Gran' Parsons, telling tales about the evil spirits that haunted these mountain forests. The stories would be reinforced by the warnings Gran' gave not to stray too far if the children went out hunting for wild herbs or mountain laurel or anything else they could pick to make extra money when the men from the hollow traveled up to town to sell to the florists or the pharmacies. For there were all kind of evil spirits about, the children were told — some that stole young 'uns out of their beds at night, and others that stole people's teeth while they slept, and others that got into the heads of the women at full-moon time and made them crazy so they did something Gran' Parsons called 'fornicatin'.'

As she scurried along the road, Geri-Jo searched the woods

at the side. Behind the dark vibrating curtain of rain, the forest was alive with movement. Evil shining eyes seemed to peek out from between bushes. Were those bright purple dots the blossoms of a redbud tree, or the noses of wood demons?

As she reached the last steep stretch of road before the turn into the hollow, she could already see evidence of the damage wrought by the storm on the little settlement ahead. Runoff from the hillsides turned the road into a cold river that tore at her thin legs as she pushed forward. Bobbing everywhere in the rushing water were plants that had been swept from gardens, pieces of wood cut for winter fires, clothing that had been torn loose from washlines. A length of firewood came swirling down and banged into her shins. Geri-Jo yelped and tears sprang to her eyes. Yet at the same moment she was distracted from her pain by the sudden comprehension of how horribly serious things were. She realized that her father and mother and eight brothers and sisters and all the other kin that lived in the hollow were caught in a battle with nature that threatened to take away everything on which they depended to survive.

'I'm comin'!' she shouted desperately to no one and tried to run. But the rising water knocked her off balance, and after a couple of steps she stumbled and pitched forward. As she plopped down, the armload of school-books was swept out of her arms. She watched one float away, pages riffling open, then the splash of cold water against the side of her face made her snap forward again. Just beyond a clump of redbud trees, she caught sight of the first house in the hollow. Struggling to her feet, Geri-Jo pushed ahead.

Her family's cabin stood near the base of the bowl of hills around the settlement. As she hurried up, Geri-Jo saw the three youngest children huddling on the porch. Her four-year-old brother, Caleb, was sucking at a bottle of sugar-water, his eyes showing confusion and fear. But her eight-year-old sister, red-headed Molly, hovered in the doorway, looking more curious than concerned as she faced toward the hillside behind the house. Nine-year-old Lorene cried out as soon as she saw Geri-Jo.

14

'Oh, Geri-Jo, what we gon' do?' Her brown hair had been longest in the family until a week ago, when parasites had been found on her scalp. Now, cut to short spiky strands that stuck up all over her head, she looked especially pitiful.

'Be all right, Lor',' Geri-Jo answered, knowing it was what her mother would say. 'Just stay put there with Mol' and Caybie.'

She went on past the porch. In the driving rain everything looked fuzzy, as if actually submerged beneath an ocean. The air was so heavy it was difficult to breathe. Pausing at the foot of the slope, she scanned the cleared area higher up. She could see Lucy and Coy and Ethan in the garden, scrambling along the rows, plucking vegetables and stuffing them into bushel baskets. Off to the side and higher up, in the tobacco patch, Ma and Pa and Zeno were gathering in leaves before they got too torn for anyone ever to buy. And Geri-Jo could vaguely discern two more figures farther up — her eldest brothers who had already left school — digging channels to divert the run-off.

She started climbing toward the tobacco patch. Not that she cared more about saving the cash crop than the food, she just thought she'd feel better working alongside Pa and Ma. But then she heard her mother hollering down at her.

'Go back, Geri-Jo! See to the little 'uns.'

Geri-Jo looked up at her mother, standing with her knees sunk deep in mud. 'Lorene's there, Ma,' she shouted. 'I'll help with the pickin'.'

'Quit yer darn sass, girl!' her mother bellowed hoarsely. 'You'll be where I need ya!'

Geri-Jo turned and strutted down angrily, her feet slipping on the wet incline. Need? They didn't need her anywhere if they thought she wasn't big enough or strong enough to do anything but stay with the little 'uns. With her pride dampened, the real effects of the rain suddenly seemed insignificant.

Lorene came eagerly down the steps when she saw Geri-Jo returning to the house.

'Get back in,' Geri-Jo snapped, adopting her mother's hard tone.

Lorene retreated, but now four-year-old Caleb waddled down the steps, and when Lorene made a grab for him, he fell instantly into an undeclared game of tag.

'Caybie!' Geri-Jo shouted, running after him through the mud. But pursuit only confirmed the game. Oblivious to the rain, he giggled and scampered toward the steep slope. Lorene, already wet, came down off the porch and joined in the chase. With a lunge, Geri-Jo scooped her little brother into her arms and started back to the house. As she reached the steps, she noticed Lorene lingering at the foot of the hill.

'Lor!' Seeing her sister turn and nod, Geri-Jo went inside. In the big, bare front room, Molly sat in a chair near the metal stove, passively fiddling with her long red hair. Geri-Jo felt a rush of pique that her sister had stayed there warming herself instead of helping chase after Caybie.

'Hist yerself outta that chair,' she ordered sharply, 'and get Caybie somethin' dry to put on.' Molly made a face, but she got up to shuffle across the room as Geri-Jo set her brother on the empty chair and started to remove his wet clothes.

Just then there was a low booming noise outside the house. Not thunder, not something in the air. There was a solidity to this sound, a bit as if a heavy foot had thudded on the porch. Could that be Lorene coming in? Geri-Jo glanced back through the open door just as the noise came again, a soft rumble.

Alarmed, Caleb looked up and questioningly uttered his own name for her. 'Jejo . . .?'

Edging toward the door, Geri-Jo looked out at the porch. Empty. Where was Lorene? Her eyes darted to the hillside, where she saw her sister starting to clamber up the slope. Geri-Jo leaned forward, about to order Lorene to return. But then she saw, too, that none of the others on the slope were working. They had all stopped to look uphill, as if they had also heard the noise and thought it came from near the top. Something about the line of figures spread across the hillside — their absolute stillness, the way their hands were poised as though to fend off some pouncing beast — gave Geri-Jo an odd tingly feeling. She had never seen her father stand coiled up quite that way. Then she noticed that he had dropped the shovel he'd been using.

At that instant it came to her — what the noise was. And a feeling went through her like her heart tearing loose as she made a move to run from the porch. To go and save them.

But then it gave. The wet brown skin covering the whole mountain started to slip. Huge rocks that had always been solidly moored shuddered and began to tumble loose. The air was filled with the cracking of trees as they tore from the earth, and the raucous cawing of birds fluttering up out of the branches in droves.

Paralyzed by astonishment as much as fear, Geri-Jo watched. She felt the porch begin to sway under her, heard it creak as the ground beneath trembled. Yet, oddly, it seemed to her that the line of figures across the slope was the one thing that hadn't moved at all. Her brothers and sisters, Pa and Ma, all were frozen in place, their feet rooted in mud — though, strangely, they also seemed to be coming closer. Suddenly, with a gasp, Geri-Jo realized that the whole section of the hillside where they stood was sliding down in one piece, a huge raft of earth on which they were all riding. Then she saw Lorene, farther down the slope, scrambling toward the house to escape the piece of mountain that was chasing after her.

'Lor'!' Even as Geri-Jo started to run toward her sister, she saw the wall of earth come rushing up right behind Lorene, knock her over . . . and then plough on past, burying her in an instant grave.

Geri-Jo tried to cry out, but she couldn't find her voice. Suddenly she felt nauseous. She wanted to race to the spot where she had seen her sister buried, and dig and dig and dig and dig. But in the blink of an eye she could no longer tell where the spot was, for the earth kept rushing down, bringing with it trees and rocks and bushes in a boiling brown stew.

She became aware now of the screams of the others. The huge island of earth on which her family had all been trapped was breaking up. Wide cracks rippled across the center, gigantic clods of soil split away from the edges. As Geri-Jo stared, a new crack shot like an arrow toward where Zeno's legs were planted. Then the crack reached him and he fell into the fissure. The sick sensation mushroomed inside her, but she could only go on staring dumbly, trying to take in the enormity of the nightmare. There was her mother, half sunk in the rushing muck as if swimming in a river — and, even as Geri-Jo watched, an enormous tree came tobogganning down the hill and went right over the place where her mother had been.

Everywhere she saw someone running, scrambling, sinking. Ethan was down, rolling like a log. Pa was on his knees, hands pawing at the mud. The twins, Coy and Lucy, were up to their hips, arms windmilling as they fought to keep from being dragged deeper. The mountain was going to take them all!

'Jejo!'

The shrill cry broke through her daze. She looked down at her side. Caybie was there, clutching at her dress. The mud was rising up over his ankles — and, she realized now, her own.

In an instant the sick feeling was gone, replaced completely by a terrible certainty that there was nothing she could do to save the others, but that if she had any hope of saving Caybie and herself then she had to do it now.

Holding her little brother's hand tightly, Geri-Jo tried to turn and run but her thin legs were stuck in the mud's slimy grip.

'Go, Caybie,' she screamed, letting go of him. 'Go t'house!'

'Scared, Jejo. Take me.'

The rumbling was growing louder, she could feel a warm rush of air as if the mountain was a beast breathing right down her neck. Her arms shot out and grabbed her brother around the waist as she wrenched and twisted her legs free and headed for the house. Each step was a strain, but the farther they got from the base of the slope, the firmer the ground became. If they could reach the road out of the hollow, they might not be buried. The ranks of big trees on each side would act as a break against the sliding earth. At last Geri-Jo decided it would be safe to set Caybie down; they could move faster running side by side.

But at once Caybie veered off toward the cabin, his own

symbol of safety. Geri-Jo chased after him, and snagged his shirt just as he was clambering up the porch steps.

'No, not here, Cay —' Her voice caught as he turned, and she saw his wide eyes darken with the shadow of something looming behind her. Geri-Jo swung around. Only yards away, the huge moving dam of earth was surging toward them. She scooped up Caybie and dashed through the door into the big room. The roof alone would not hold, she thought; they'd need something more above them. Her eyes darted around the room, taking in the wardrobe and the big trunk in the corner, the long, stout table in front of them. And there, too, at the end of the table was Molly, still sitting in the chair, looking oddly calm and unconcerned. Had she even looked out the door, seen what was happening to all the others?

'Mol'!' Geri-Jo shouted. 'It's comin' down. Get t'cover!'

But her last word was drowned out as the slide slammed into the porch and the underpinnings splintered and were swept away. The whole cabin listed like a sinking boat. A moment later there was a sound like thousands of tiny chimes as all the windows exploded inward. Geri-Jo dove under the table with Caybie still wrapped in her arms. Boards from the roof clattered down onto the table top as the house collapsed.

Caybie screamed and Geri-Jo held him firmly. 'Pray, Caybie,' she whispered urgently. 'Pray, else we don't get t'heaven.'

Tons of earth broke through the roof, and piled up around them. Caybie whimpered. She hugged him tighter and then began to recite as much as she remembered of the prayer she liked best.

'The Lord'll be My Shepherd, I won't want for nothin'.'

A leg of the table gave, then another, and the top began to press down on her, harder and harder, while the earth spilled down around its legs. If she could just keep praying . . . but her breath was gone, and she could barely whisper it.

He takes care of my soul and comforts me.

Crushed by the table, she could say it only in her mind. *He makes me lay down near cool* — Water? She didn't like thinking

19

of that. The slurry of mud was seeping into her dress, the cold creeping into her bones.

But then the coldness left her body. There was only the tremendous pressure on all sides, and silence.

And, finally, though she knew it was much too soon, she was walking into the valley of the shadows.

CHAPTER TWO

On the fourth Sunday of every July, the mountain people gathered basketfuls of the summer blossoms rioting over the hillsides and brought them to decorate the graves of their kin, untended the rest of the year. The hard life in Appalachia left little time to worry about the needs of the dead, and trips to the cemeteries were further discouraged by their location, usually on one of the highest mountain tops, a long hard climb from the settlements.

When Geri-Jo had made the trip in October to see her mother and six of her brothers and sisters buried, she had asked her father why the mountain folk put their cemeteries so high up.

'I reckon,' he'd said, 'it's so God won't have to waste too much time lookin' for our souls. The way He treats us while we're livin', He might just forget our dead altogether if we didn't plant our bones right up here in plain sight.'

Geri-Jo remembered the answer as she and Caybie and Mol' trailed Pa into the cemetery on this hot July day. She didn't agree with him, though. It was beautiful up here, she thought; it gave the living an idea of what paradise might be like so they could feel closer to the ones they'd lost.

Looking out from the mountain top you could see far away to where the land leveled off, and even beyond that to the purple line marking the horizon where the sun had just risen. The cemetery itself was a grassy plateau surrounded by a dark

21

dense forest of high pines. Dark as the forest was, Geri-Jo no longer feared its evil spirits. Even if there were such things as goblins and wood demons, she had learned that their threat was small compared to the harm that could be done by the accidents of life itself. The breeze that swept through the pines at this time of morning filled the air with a fresh tangy smell.

It was so much nicer up here than in the hollow, Geri-Jo thought, especially since the slide had devastated the houses and most of the people had moved away. She wished Pa had wanted to leave, too, instead of building another crude cabin with lumber from the other abandoned ruins. She had asked him why they couldn't leave like the others.

''Cause I don't hist one foot 'til the other's settin' flat,' he had said.

She guessed he meant that he didn't want to leave behind whatever he had until he was sure he'd have as much somewhere else. But how was it possible to have less than they had here? The only time the mountains looked good to her was from up here on top, when the hollow was hidden far below in the trees.

'Don't stand there gawkin' at nothin', Geri-Jo. Put them flowers where they belong so's we can be leavin'.'

Pa's voice cut into her reverie. 'Leavin'? Pa, I want to hear the prayers and hymns.'

'There's nothin' in that for us, Geri-Jo.'

'Then why'd we come?'

Her father didn't answer, but kept marching ahead through the ranks of headstones toward the family's corner plot. Geri-Jo's heart started to beat faster. She had spent days trying to prepare for what she was about to see, but it didn't matter. As they came to the group of seven stones, Geri-Jo relived it all again, saw Lor' running up the hillside, had a vision of Ma sunk in the mud up to her knees. She felt faint as she stopped before the largest grave marker and stared at the chiseled lettering:

CHARLENE MILLER LOCKELY

1925 — 1959

If she stared hard enough at the name, would it help

somehow to bring back more about her mother? So much had already faded from her memory. There had been a couple of old photographs taken at a fair, Pa said, but they'd been lost in the mud. Now when Geri-Jo tried to picture Ma in her mind, it was as though a dusty window covered the image. She could see a figure moving around behind the window, cooking or shouting at one of them to do some chore. And she remembered some nice things, like the way Ma had held her once after a nightmare, and Christmastime when she'd handed out sweet things to eat. But no matter how hard she tried, Geri-Jo couldn't see her mother's face clearly anymore. It made her wish that she had spent more time just looking at Ma.

Molly and Caybie had begun to lay flowers on a couple of the other graves. Geri-Jo knelt, placing her own basket beside her, and started to work, laying down a carpet of shasta daisies and mountain laurel and blue cornflowers, weaving the stems over one another. As she laid down the flowers, Geri-Jo stole a glance at her father. He was posed stiffly against one of the listing headstones of an old plot nearby, staring vacantly at the ground. Dressed in his only suit, the same rough black wool he had bought to wear to the autumn funeral, he was perspiring heavily. Rivulets of sweat poured down across the leathery skin of his gaunt face from under the fringe of his dark brown hair.

Even with Pa right in front of her, Geri-Jo had a feeling that he had faded from her memory, too. There had been a time when he liked to laugh, and play his dulcimer, and take all the children on trips in the jalopy he'd built out of spare parts. But she could hardly remember what his smile looked like. He scowled all the time now, and spoke very little, and never sang.

'Done, Pa,' Molly crowed, and tossed her long red hair back smugly when Geri-Jo looked over.

But Geri-Jo saw that Molly hadn't so much decorated a couple of the graves as merely dumped her baskets over them. Damn ol' Molly, Geri-Jo fumed inwardly, never doing a bit more than the least. Hell, the way she'd sat in that chair calm as you please doing nothing the day that mountain fell down!

If she'd stirred her butt the tiniest bit, if she'd just grabbed Caybie and started running with him, then maybe —

But there was no point in thinking about maybes. Not today of all days.

Geri-Jo turned to her younger brother. He was laying out the flowers one by one, his hand sometimes jerking aside with a spastic movement. He saw her watching, and gave her his slow, lopsided smile.

'Good, Jejo?'

'Beautiful, Caybie.'

He sounded more like a baby now than he had almost a year ago. It wasn't only forming words that gave him trouble, he had difficulty remembering, and he also dragged one leg when he walked. For weeks after they'd been rescued, Geri-Jo had believed Caybie's condition would improve. How could the injury be serious when there was no outward sign of it at all? But finally Pa had passed along what he'd heard from the doctors at the county hospital. The problem came from not getting enough air during the time he'd been buried in the mud under the table. Caybie might look fine, but part of his brain had died.

Other families had begun to arrive. After all the graves had been decorated, there would be a prayer service and singing. Geri-Jo hoped Pa would change his mind and stay for that. She lingered over her task, and when she was done began to help her brother with the flowers left in his basket.

Then, as she glanced around the cemetery, she noticed the Millers — Ma's kin, her father and three brothers — lined up in front of their own family plot near the middle of the cemetery. They made a fearsome sight. Though Abel Miller was much older than Pa, with a gray beard that hung down nearly to his stomach, he was big and broad with heavily muscled arms. His three sons were taller and stronger still. They weren't praying or laying flowers, they were just glaring fiercely at Pa.

At the funeral, too, Geri-Jo remembered, the Millers had stayed to themselves and scowled at Pa. There had never been any closeness with them — they had never come to visit Ma at

24

the house — so Geri-Jo hadn't made much of their unfriendliness. But today she was frightened. From the heat in their gaze, she could almost imagine that lightning was going to shoot straight out of those eyes. Others in the cemetery had also sensed the electricity in the air, and they stopped working over their graves to look at Pa and the Millers.

Geri-Jo realized now that it must be Pa's desire to avoid bad blood that explained why he didn't want to stay for the hymns. Taking Caybie's hand, she fell in quickly behind Pa and Molly as they started walking between the headstones, back toward the edge of the clearing.

Suddenly a voice roared out. 'Blasphemer!'

Geri-Jo halted in her tracks, but Pa kept marching ahead, so she jumped forward to catch up. Then she saw the huge figures hurrying up alongside, and before she could shout to warn Pa, Abel Miller had run into his path and grabbed him with his huge hand.

'Where you goin', Garrett Lockely? You sent my daughter to her death, and now you ain't decent enough to say a prayer for her?'

'Said my own,' Garrett Lockely said, shaking loose from Abel Miller's grip. 'Now stand aside, Abel. We got no cause to quarrel.'

Luke Miller pushed up beside Pa. He was the largest of the sons, a giant several inches over six feet. 'Charlene's dead,' he said hotly. 'I call that cause for more than quarrelin'.'

Geri-Jo listened in confusion. Was Pa being blamed for Ma's death? But he had tried to save her, dug through rocks and mud until his hands bled.

Other families started to drift over, forming a circle around them. Geri-Jo saw that they were all grim and accepting, regarding Pa with their own frowns of disapproval.

'Nature done it,' Garrett Lockely said. 'Ain't no way to help that. Now get outta my way.' He straightened his arm to push Abel Miller aside, but the giant Luke reached out and grabbed Garrett's arm, forcing it down.

'Nature's just another name for God,' said Abel Miller. 'It's his wrath that brought the mountain down, ever'body knows

25

that. And we all know what He was payin' back. Sins, Lockely, your foul sins! Started the day you got back from the war — tellin' people how bad we got it here, sayin' there ain't no such thing as God's will and if there was a god — *if*, you dared say — then He forgets us.'

Miller wasn't speaking only to Pa now, Geri-Jo noticed, he was playing to the crowd. His deep powerful voice echoed across the whole meadow as he shouted out his damnation of Pa.

'Your pride and ingratitude,' he went on. 'That's what brung the mountain down. But even now you don't stop. My boys hear that whenever you been up to town gettin' a few drinks into ya, you're still spoutin' the same line. Bringin' one disaster down on us ain't enough, you're like to make it happen all over again.' He flicked a glance toward Geri-Jo, Molly, and Caleb. 'You'd let what's left of your family get took.'

Murmurs of accord rippled through the thickening crowd.

Geri-Jo wished now they hadn't come at all. Moving to her father, she tried to grab his hand and pull him away. But he stepped abruptly out of reach, clearing a space between himself and Abel Miller as he whirled to make his own speech to the crowd.

'Goddamned fools! All of ya! Can't get a bad break — can't suffer livin' the way we do — without lookin' to the same old crazy excuses and superstitious claptrap. It's God's will, you say! Pure is pure, our hunger is His will . . . and He'll strike us down anytime we dare to think we deserve better. Shit! All that is nothin' but a bunch o' goddamn lies we tell ourselves. And if there's a God, He knows it as well as I do!'

His blasphemy sparked a flurry of angry whispers from the bystanders. Abel Miller seemed pleased that Garrett Lockely was getting the crowd worked up. He smiled, and signaled restraint when his son Luke took a threatening step toward Garrett.

Geri-Jo's stomach turned over as Pa went on shouting. He was going to get himself lynched for sure.

'I seen the way it really is, I know better than all of ya!

Between here and fightin' a war, I seen where the folks live who run the companies that keep us down — companies that own all the good land they cut for timber, and gouge for coal, while we're stuck back up in these hills. I seen all the chances they got to earn and learn. And I seen there's a divide between their world and ours that just ain't right, and that we ain't never gonna get across if we're forever leavin' it to God to decide when we rate a little bit more! If you want to know the goddamn truth, that's been my one sin: to go on believin' I had to listen for His word on what I deserve. 'Cause He ain't never spoke, and He's never goin' to.'

Geri-Jo gawked at her father. Never before had she heard him string so many words together. Even more amazing was his talk about wanting more, wanting chances to — how had he put it? — earn and learn. If only he had told her all these feelings sometime when they were alone instead of here, in front of everyone, she could have asked him to explain. If he felt this way for so many years — since he'd come back from the war, almost her whole life — then why had he stayed in the hollow?

But there was no chance to ask now. The crowd surrounding them had grown still darker with anger and resentment at her father's defiance. Abel Miller and his sons had formed into a line like a row of judges. The fists of the young men were clenched again, their arms crooked as if eager to strike.

'Pa!' Geri-Jo cried out. 'Don't say no more. Just take us down, I don't care about the hymns —'

'Hear the way he's raisin' 'em?' Abel Miller addressed the crowd. 'Got another blasphemer in the makin'.'

Geri-Jo stepped up to him. 'I ain't a blas . . . one of those. And Pa ain't done no harm. Now let us go!' She thrust her hand against his enormous stomach to push him aside.

He didn't budge. 'Oh, we'll let you go, child. Our Charlene's got to be stayin' with us, but you and your Pa and all your kind can go.' He turned to Garrett, his jaw jutting so his long gray beard billowed away from his body. 'We don't want you 'round here anyway. You're a blight on the hollow. Our life may be hard, but when God hears the likes of you talk,

He can only make it worse. So you go, Lockely. But just don't you stop goin'. You hear? Get off this mountain, out of this valley. Get out, or we'll carry you out!'

For a long moment, Garrett Lockely glared back at Abel Miller and his sons, his face red with anger. In the crowd around them there was absolute stillness. Geri-Jo sucked in her breath and held it, praying that Pa would have the sense to walk away without saying another word. She knew that if he couldn't be moved, then the righteous anger that had been limited to heated words would explode in violence. She also knew better than to plead with him herself; if she said anything, he'd just do the opposite. Pa was like that.

It was Caybie, not knowing better, who finally broke the silence. 'Come, Pa. Don't be killed.'

For a moment Garrett Lockely went on glaring at his enemies. But at last he turned and continued along the path leading out of the cemetery.

Looking at her father's rigid back as they made their way down the mountain, Geri-Jo couldn't stop wondering about him. She had thought once that he was simply the loving father who liked to tell her stories about faraway places he'd seen when he was a soldier, a man who knew how to smile. When he had become so mute and brooding after the slide, she believed the sweeter man went on living inside and would someday return. But now she accepted that she didn't really know him at all. For years he had hated his life here, for years he believed it was a doomed place where people foolishly accepted their lot. Yet she had never known.

So who was Pa? Why, if he felt that way, had he stayed here, even when so many others had gone?

CHAPTER THREE

As the eldest of the children, it fell automatically to Geri-Jo to become the caretaker of the household in the wake of her mother's death. She cooked the meals, did the washing and the mending, nursed Caybie when he was sick, and picked up after Pa. She was used to work, and none of the new chores were any harder than the ones she'd done in the past, but being in Ma's place bothered her. She felt as if part of her life had been stolen away before she'd been ready to lose it. She was doing the work of a woman, and that seemed to make her one. Pa even looked at her sometimes in a way that was too much like the way he used to look at Ma before they went off to make love, his eyes sweeping over the new curves in her body, or resting too long on her face.

At thirteen, Geri-Jo was already beginning to evolve into a spectacular beauty, though she had little reason to be aware of it. Her hair had grown long, but she kept it crudely bunched up as Ma had done so it wouldn't get in the way of her work; her wide blue-green eyes were often narrowed and shadowed with fatigue, and her finely sculpted face smudged with soil or flour or laundry soap. The clothes she'd inherited from Ma were faded and baggy and overlong, concealing her lithe developing figure and slim legs. Of course, if the hollow had remained inhabited by many other families, there would have been boys around to make her conscious of herself. Girls of thirteen were married off sometimes. But almost everyone else

29

was gone, and Geri-Jo was glad. She didn't want to be paired off yet. She wasn't ready to be a woman.

Still, Pa needed someone to do the chores, and there was no choice about that part. She begged him to let her continue with school, but he forbade it saying Caybie couldn't be left alone, and he had no time for it himself. There were plenty of kids in the mountains, he reminded her, who gave up learning at twelve or thirteen to work and bring in some money to help the family.

For a while, Geri-Jo accepted what Pa told her. But her thinking began to change after she heard her father's outburst at the cemetery. If he hated it here, then why shouldn't they leave? Couldn't they find a place where Pa might have a chance to earn money himself — enough to buy food instead of sweating so hard to grow their meager crop, enough to pay for a place to live instead of having to rebuild it from logs he cut and split himself? There, maybe she could continue with school. She worried, too, that if they didn't pull up stakes, the Millers might make good on their threats against Pa.

Geri-Jo kept looking for the right moment to talk to her father about it, to try and answer the mystery of why they stayed, but in the days after their trip to the cemetery, he was even more silent and inaccessible than usual. He rose at dawn, and went out to clear the rocks and trees that had been scattered over their land since the slide. With only an axe and a pick for tools, it often took a week to dislodge a large boulder, and sometimes twice as long for a stout tree. At the end of each day he hauled logs down the hillside, then at last he would come into the small shed he had raised quickly after the slide. He would eat the food Geri-Jo had left for him after feeding Caybie and Molly, and then go straight to bed, or else march out the door and drive off in the jalopy. Hours later, Geri-Jo might wake to hear him stumbling drunkenly into the dark cabin, cursing as he bumped into the furniture until he found the bed.

The more she saw her father sweating to reclaim the place he had admitted hating, the more Geri-Jo yearned to ask him to explain the things he'd said at the cemetery. But his silence was so grim and constant, he seemed to exist in a bubble of solitude that would explode violently, damaging everything, if she pricked it with her curiosity.

Then, one summer night, she rose out of sleep to an unfamiliar sound, not the thumping and cursing, but Pa's voice — raised in song, a melody Geri-Jo had never heard before. He wasn't in the house, but somewhere outside, so that the words of his song were indistinct. She got out of bed and went to the door of the cabin. By the light of a three-quarter moon, she saw her father's angular silhouette, reeling across the open ground where other houses had once stood, a whiskey jug held in one hand as he sang at the top of his lungs. And now she could hear the words — though she still couldn't understand them. Meaningless nonsense, she thought, and the frightening idea seized her that Pa wasn't merely drunk, he had also gone crazy.

She walked to him, thinking he ought to be helped home. Even from several yards away, she could smell the reek of liquor overwhelming the gentler night fragrance of wildflowers.

'C'mon, Pa,' she said, 'I'll get you to bed.'

He was gazing up at the moon, but he stopped singing and turned to her. He stared at her for so long in an odd way that Geri-Jo thought he didn't recognize her. 'That you, Jo?' he said at last.

'Sure, who else?' she answered, though he had never before called her Jo. It was always Geri-Jo, short for Geraldine-Josephine. The double name had resulted from a disagreement over naming her when she was born. Ma had insisted the first new girl in the family after the war should be named for her only sister Geraldine, who'd died when the hospital ship on which she served as a nurse was sunk by a Japanese torpedo. Pa, with no less stubbornness — and for no given reason — had insisted on 'Josephine'. The argument had raged until they compromised at two names — hooked together with a dash. 'Don't want it to be no middle name that just gets dropped off,' Garrett had insisted. So that was the way the baby had been christened, and she had become Geri-Jo.

Now she went forward and hooked an arm around Pa's waist to help him walk to the house. 'C'mon. Let's go to bed.'

'Oh Chris', Jo,' he murmured then. 'Us together. That's the way it should be. Been so goddamn long since I had you . . .'

That didn't make any more sense than the words she'd heard him singing before.

'That song you was singin',' she said. 'What was it?'

He laughed. 'Forgot, didja? Hell, I learnt it from you.'

Geri-Jo glanced at her father in astonishment, but the impulse to disagree died on her lips. By the bluish light of the moon she could see the glaze on his eyes, and she realized he was lost in some kind of waking dream.

She helped him into the house, laid him out on his bed, and helped him off with his boots and overalls. As she reached to unbutton his shirt, he seized her arms and started pulling her down over him.

'Josefina,' he whispered hoarsely, his eyes fixed on her. 'You're so damn beautiful . . .' Then he lifted his head to kiss her, but it was a rough demanding kiss, and Geri-Jo struggled to free herself. Only then, as she felt the lengthening hardness thrusting at her below, did she understand how confused he was.

'No, Pa!' she yelped as she exerted all her strength to tear loose from him. 'Leave off,' she went on in an urgent whisper, fearful of waking Mol' and Caybie, whose beds were just across the room. 'It's me, Geri-Jo . . .'

'Josefina,' he murmured again, his eyes closed now. His hands reached out and groped the air languidly, but after a moment his arms dropped back on the bed. Two seconds later he was snoring.

Still shaking from the incident, Geri-Jo went back outside and took a deep breath of air. Looking up at the night sky, she wondered if maybe moon-fever had something to do with her father's strange behavior. But after she'd gotten back into bed and lain awake until the birds started their dawn twittering, she knew it wasn't that simple. It was all part of the same mystery, all the secrets her father had kept. And if she couldn't get the answers, she thought, the secrets might destroy what was left of their family. Because maybe it was true, what her mother's kin had said; maybe Garrett was being punished for his sins.

Geri-Jo waited into the next afternoon, while Molly had taken Caybie off for a wash in the creek at the bottom of the mountain, before she climbed the hill to where he was preparing some new ground for tobacco. As she approached, he turned his back to rake a far corner of the patch. Geri-Jo stood silently for a while, hoping he might be the first to speak. It would be easier then. But he said nothing, and as the silence went on the lump of sadness in her throat seemed to swell and harden until she could hardly breathe. How different it had been when she was younger! Then if she came up to work beside him, he would smile at her, or pause with her to listen to a bird-call. Or, while they went back and forth along the rows he would tell her stories about the time he'd been the other side of an ocean so big it took days and days to get across in a giant boat, and of cities he'd seen filled with palaces and churches where the windows were made of glass the color of rubies and sapphires. And about how he'd stood once in the middle of a big round stadium where a long time ago — so long that Jesus hadn't even been born yet — crowds had gathered to watch races of two-wheeled chariots pulled by horses, or to see warriors known by a special word (she couldn't remember the word exactly, but it was something like 'gladiolas') fight against lions!

But all that had been before the day of the slide.

'Got to talk, Pa.' The words burst forth as it struck her that this might be a last chance to keep their dreams from dying.

He kept raking at the same steady pace, giving no sign that he'd heard.

She raised her voice. 'About last night . . . the way you went after me . . .'

'Sorry.' The word was so low it was barely more than a grunt. He didn't stop raking.

But she was encouraged. 'Who's Jo, Pa? You was callin' me Jo . . . Josefina. You said she taught you that crazy song. What's it all about, Pa . . .?'

33

He stopped raking and lifted his head to look straight off toward the woods, though he didn't turn around. 'No call for you to know.'

'I think there is. 'Cause you named me for her, didn't ya, Pa? Feels to me like maybe knowin' who I am could take knowin' who I'm named for. And that ain't all. Feels to me like there's a lotta stuff you kept inside you . . . and it's keepin' you from thinkin' straight since Ma's gone. I got to know what it is, Pa, So I can help . . .'

He bent over his rake again and gave it a long pull through the soil, then tossed it down and turned to look at her. There was a glimmer of that gentle light she had not seen in his eyes for nearly a year. 'Don't see how it can help,' he said. 'But I suppose it couldn't hurt you to know either. Maybe you'd see then why leavin' here just ain't no use . . .'

He sat on a rock in the shade and told it in a tired, toneless voice — as if he had told it a thousand times instead of just this once — while she leant against a tree nearby, listening so intently she never moved.

It had happened when he was a soldier, fighting in a country called Italy. There had been lulls in the fighting sometimes, allowing the troops to stay in once place and sample some small taste of a normal life, a stroll through a town, or an afternoon swim in a cool river. He had gone for such a swim alone one day when a woman had come down to the river bank to wash some clothes. She was young and very beautiful, he said, though dressed all in black which showed she was a widow.

As Geri-Jo listened to her father describe the woman — 'hair as fine as the floss on a dandelion seed,' he said, 'and skin the pale gold of tobacco when it's just turnin' ' — she had no need to be told about how deep his feelings ran, then or now. She knew that Pa had been married at the time to Ma, knew it was ruled a sin for a man to go outside of marriage to love another woman; yet the way Pa talked about this woman from the past, it was hard to think he had done anything wrong.

Somehow it didn't shock her when Pa admitted he had gone on seeing the woman every chance he got, traveling many miles after his unit moved on. And it didn't surprise her to hear that the woman's name had been Josefina. But then Pa began to tell a part of the story that, while not unexpected, still made her feel restless and uncomfortable while she listened.

'Hadn't ever been a feelin' between me and your Ma like there was with Jo. In the hollow, we got married 'cause there was nothin' else to do. Before I'd gone off to war we'd already had the first five kids. To tell the truth, half the reason for my goin' to war was to get away from all the noise and the mess. So after I met Jo, I didn't see no sense in ever comin' back here. If I had any doubt, it left me when I found out she was gonna have our baby. O' course, I knew the day would come when the army'd wanta ship me home, but I was gonna disappear before then, run off to the middle of nowhere with Jo . . .' He fell silent, staring into the distance.

'But you did come back,' Geri-Jo prompted.

When he resumed, his voice was no longer flat and dry. It trembled and cracked in a way Geri-Jo had never heard before. He had come back, Pa said, because in the end there was no reason not to. His Josefina had been the widow of a man who had been an officer in the army of the Italian leader, Mussolini — the enemy. Although the Italian people had followed their leader into war, when it was over they blamed him for the ruin of their country. In the frenzy that followed the liberation of Italy, his followers were hunted down and killed. Upon travelling back to Josefina's village to tell her he was planning to defect from his army, Garrett Lockely had learned that she was dead. Because her husband had been one of Mussolini's officers, other women had roused their husbands to march to her home and drive her out. When she proudly refused to leave, they had set fire to her house — and she had burned to death.

At the end of the story, very softly he added, 'When you were born, first one after I came home, I always sorta figured that maybe a spirit found its way to you. Hers maybe . . . or the baby's. Made it easier for a while . . .'

Geri-Jo wasn't sure how long she had been listening to her father, but the sun was much lower in the sky and it glinted against the wet streaks that she could see now on his cheeks, even though he was partly turned away.

At the bottom of the hill, they could see Mol' and Caybie straggling back up the road toward the cabin.

Pa rubbed his hands quickly over his face and stood up. Geri-Jo saw his expression begin to set again into the hard stoney mask. It was too soon for the confession to end, she thought. She had learned some of the secrets Pa had kept; she even knew why he had come back to a place he had hated. But she still didn't understand why they had to stay. As Pa took a step forward, she reached out desperately and grabbed him.

'You still ain't made me see, Pa. You hated this place so you left it; you found a dream and you were gonna stay where it was, and when it died you came back. I reckon all that. But if it's dead here now, too, why are we stayin'? There's got to be somethin' better. And you got the folks here wantin' to chase you out. So why can't we go, Pa?'

''Cause it just ain't no use,' he said. 'Is that so hard to understand, Geri-Jo? Doesn't matter where I go, my luck'll follow me. I'm a cursed man, that's all. A cursed man . . .'

And with that he tore loose from her grip and began stalking down the mountain.

When he went outside after dinner and started cranking the jalopy, Geri-Jo knew he was going off to get drunk. He had done it often enough, but she had a premonition that something terrible was going to happen tonight, that he was never coming back. She ran out of the house intending to plead with him to stay, but he was already driving down the road, and he never heard her over the rackety sputtering of the jalopy's engine.

'What you so raggedy about?' Molly said later, when Geri-Jo kept going to the window, listening for the sound of the motor coming back.

Geri-Jo wished she could tell her sister everything she'd heard from Pa earlier, but confiding in Molly never made her feel better. If she admitted to missing Ma, or to being sad for Caybie, or worried about what was going to happen to all of them, Molly only shrugged and told her it was no good worrying or mourning anyone or shedding any tears. Things were how they were, Molly would say, and nothing could change that.

Geri-Jo had never been able to understand why Molly had always been so cool and quiet and uninvolved. Tonight, though, it occurred to Geri-Jo that maybe it had something to do with what Pa had told her about believing she was a 'reborn' of that woman he'd loved or the baby. Molly had been the next girl born after her, and if she'd grown up noticing Pa treated Geri-Jo different, she could've got the idea somehow that she didn't belong. Maybe not caring about anything or anyone was her way of getting even.

Geri-Jo was still awake when the sky began to grow light, and Pa still hadn't returned. She kept straining to hear the faint sound of the jalopy coming up the mountain road, but there was only the birds waking up and the rustle of leaves. Suddenly there was a loud thump outside. Was it Pa coming home? Had he left the car somewhere and walked? She waited to hear him dragging himself up the porch, waited to see his shadow in the doorway.

But the next thing she heard was a groan, and she could tell from the strangled expulsion of breath that it came from someone in pain. She leapt out of bed and ran outside.

Pa was lying on his back a few yards from the house. A splotch of blackened blood was caked around one eye, and his face was a mass of purple bruises. In several places his shirt was torn, and there were large stains where blood had either dripped onto his clothes or seeped through from beneath.

'Pa . . .!' she cried out.

His eyes were open, and they followed her as she bent over him.

'Oh God, Pa, what happened to ya? I knew I shouldn'ta let you go!'

He said nothing, but tried to push himself up off the ground again. Geri-Jo threw an arm around him, and steadied him as he staggered into the cabin, and lurched to his bed.

'You drove off the road . . . that it?' she asked as she helped him get comfortable.

37

'Wasn't no accident,' he whispered painfully. 'The Millers done me.' Then he groaned once more and rolled over.

For the next week, Geri-Jo nursed her father. A high fever was sapping his strength, keeping him to his bed, and the smashed bones in his cheek and jaw made it difficult for him to take in the nourishment that might restore him.

Geri-Jo recalled that many times her mother would treat fevers in the children by feeding them a soup made with some green herbs and a gnarled brown root found high in the hills that mountain people called 'sang'. She also remembered Ma saying that sang was good for curing a lot of ailments — and that Chinese people, who had it in their country, too, believed it could make anyone who took it regular live much longer. They didn't call it sang, though, they had a word for it that started with 'gin'. Gin-sang, was that it?

She sent Caybie and Molly to dig for some of the root, then made the soup, and — since she might have remembered wrong, and gin was part of the cure not the word, but there wasn't any gin in the house — she laced the soup with whiskey and sat spooning it into him. He could open his lips only enough to make a thin slit, so it took almost an hour to feed him each bowlful. To help heal his bruises, she applied another local remedy, poultices of kerosene and lard that she strapped to his cheek and jaw.

The morning after the first whole night her father had slept peacefully and without fever, Geri-Jo went to the old dresser containing all of her clothes and Molly's and Caybie's. Choosing out the items that had the most wear left, she made bundles, tying the clothes inside sheets.

She had started to pick through the things in the kitchen when her father shuffled blearily around the partition.

'What ya doin'?'

'Fixin' to go.'

He stared at her a moment. 'Waste of time, Geri-Jo. We ain't goin' nowhere.' He turned and went back to bed.

She tied a few pans together, and threw some knives and forks and enameled metal cups and plates into a left-over potato sack. She took the flour and rice and salt off the shelves and put it into pots with lids, or packed it into orange crates her father brought home to break up for kindling.

In a while, Caybie and Molly woke up and Geri-Jo explained that they were leaving. After giving them breakfast, she had them help carry the belongings outside. Then she told them to sit on the steps and wait. Both obeyed quietly, Molly with a slight smile on her lips.

At last, Geri-Jo went to her father's bed. 'Done now, Pa.'

He was propped up awake, staring out a window. 'Ain't goin', Geri-Jo. Told you that once. Ain't no use.'

She reached over and laid a hand on his forehead. It was cool. 'You're fit. Ain't no reason to stay.'

'Nothin' waitin' for us anywhere else,' he said. 'That's all the reason I need.'

'I listened, Pa,' Geri-Jo said. 'Heard all you were sayin' over Mama's grave. *Here's* where we got nothin', wasn't that the gist? Anywhere else we might have it better. I ain't gonna let you keep us back from that. I know it's hard leavin'. It's been home, and it's where —' She didn't know exactly what she had planned to say, but even before the thought was formed fully in her mind it filled her with an unbearable sadness and her throat closed so she couldn't speak.

But if she gave in to the sadness, Geri-Jo knew, then she could never help her father defeat his own, so she swallowed to open her throat, and she shook her head as if the tears could be shaken off as simply as a dog dries his coat after the rain.

Her father had seized the silence to speak. 'No good dreamin', child. We can't make it out. Folks like us, wherever we go we'll get beat down, don't ya see. We ain't got the —'

The scream burst out of her, like a fire exploding from within the sadness. 'No! We can have what any folks has, and we'll keep movin' 'til we find it.' She grabbed at the bedclothes covering him and tore them away. 'Darn ya, Pa, get up! We're only gonna get beat if we just lie down and let it happen. And if you're so far gone you ain't got the gumption to try then . . . then, by God, I'm takin' Cayb' and Mol' and I swear I'm goin' off down that road without ya!'

She started carrying the blanket and sheets away to pack

39

them. But then she paused and looked back, half afraid he might be lungeing after her to give her a hiding. How had she dared to mouth off at him like that? Go off alone? Where? She'd never get farther than the front door before stopping cold.

When she turned he was already reaching slowly to unhook his overalls from the bedpost where they'd been hanging since he got the beating. Suddenly she had a bad-funny feeling, as if she had stolen something from him. But, not knowing what it was, she didn't know what she could say to give it back.

She walked around, picking up some of the small decorations her mother had bought at a five-and-ten up in town and that they'd managed to save after the slide. The green ceramic vase she used for wildflowers, the ashtray with a silver dollar suspended in the glass bottom. She wrapped them in some clothes, and stuffed them in a crate.

Soon her father appeared, carrying his loaded army duffel. He looked once around the small cabin, and went out the door. She started to follow him, then realized he hadn't taken his dulcimer. She glanced toward the high peg by the firehole where it hung, a narrow stringed instrument, shaped like a starving guitar. If she brought it, would he ever play it again?

What else had given her a hunger to get out? The hope of hearing him sing again, seeing him laugh.

With a jump so she could reach it, Geri-Jo yanked the dulcimer off the peg and charged out of the cabin as if she were running for her life.

BOOK II: *THE FIRST TURN*

Lexington — Spring, 1964

CHAPTER ONE

'. . . in Washington,' said the voice on the radio, 'it was announced that more U.S. troops are being sent to Vietnam, bringing the total to nearly seventy thousand. The Pentagon stated that the situation is now contained and there will be no need for any further troop commitment. Also in Washington . . .'

Looking up from the desk where she sat writing up a bill for a five-thousand-mile check and oil change, Geri-Jo repeated the word softly to herself. 'Washington . . . Washington . . .' Not Washin'ton, she instructed herself. The 'ing' sound, that made all the difference. If she was ever going to stop being pegged as a poor dumb mountain girl, she'd have to be sure to say the *whole* word. Learning to speak better, Mr Parker had said, might open doors, help her get a good job after high school.

'In sports —'

There was a snap and the radio went dead. Geri-Jo whirled to look across the small windowless room where she'd been given a desk amid the file cabinets full of automobile sales contracts. Standing by the radio that stood atop one of the cabinets was Alma Hubble, the sinewy chicken-necked spinster who was personal secretary to Ed Parker, the owner of Parker Chevrolet and Cadillac.

'Mr Parker told me I could listen,' Geri-Jo protested. 'Put that radio there so's I could improve my speakin'. Speak*ing*,' she tacked on quickly.

'All well and good when business is draggin', but you're not paid so you can sit talkin' to yourself while a customer's expected any minute. I want that bill ready when Mr Follett gets here.' Miss Hubble marched out.

'Washington,' Geri-Jo whispered defiantly to herself in place of a curse. She wondered why Mr Parker hadn't told his secretary to listen to the radio; Alma Hubble dropped enough 'g's' to fill a bushel.

She finished the bill and brought it to Miss Hubble, whose desk stood next to Mr Parker's in the large front office. As Miss Hubble checked over the invoice, Geri-Jo gazed through the glass partition separating the office from the showroom. Beyond the large showroom windows out front, a shipment of cars was being unloaded. A gleaming fire-engine-red Corvette was just coming down the ramp from an auto-transporter. The sun glinted off the chrome and the shiny body. Gosh, it was beautiful, Geri-Jo thought. Where did people get so much money they could spend it on a car that didn't even have room for more than two people!

Miss Hubble inked the total onto the bill and looked up. Seeing the focus of Geri-Jo's interest, she grabbed a stack of folders off the corner of her desk. 'Ain't paid neither to stand around gogglin' at auto*mo*biles.' She pushed the papers at Geri-Jo and told her to file them, and when that was done to stamp and address envelopes for the new truck brochures, and then clean the front bathroom used by customers. 'And if there's any time before closin', unpack those boxes of new stationery. Otherwise, start with that tomorrow.'

'Saturday tomorrow, Miss Hubble. I'll be working for my Pa.'

'Then you'd best get everything done tonight.'

Geri-Jo brought the files back to her desk. As she put them away, her thoughts drifted to what she would have been doing in the hollow on a warm May afternoon like this. There would be hard chores, no doubt, harder than anything she had to do here; but they'd be done in the outdoors, not in a small musty room.

The move had been meant to give them new possibilities,

but had anything changed for the better? Pa earned a bit more, but it also cost more to live. There wasn't time or place to plant their own food, so it all had to be bought. She and Molly couldn't get by at school with the kind of faded hand-me-downs that had always been good enough when the other kids' clothes were no better. Even with the extra money from the job at Parker's, and from Molly working nights ushering at the moviehouse, there were often things they needed that they couldn't afford. In the hollow nobody else had had more, no one could look down on others who had less. Here, it was different. There were a lot of kids at school who had much more, lived in nice houses. Without the right clothes, without time when she wasn't working to mix with the other kids, Geri-Jo always felt self-conscious and isolated. It didn't help that Pa was more moody than ever, and Geri-Jo sensed that if ever she brought a friend back to the gas station he would embarrass her. So she stayed to herself, and acquired the reputation of being a loner.

Maybe it was seeing that red Corvette that had done it — made her feel how hopeless it was to expect more from life — but today she felt more strongly than at any time since they had come from the hollow that maybe Pa had been right to think it was no use to leave.

They had driven out of the mountains along the road that headed south and west. While Caybie sat in the cab up front, the only room for Geri-Jo and Molly was riding with the boxes and furniture on the jalopy's rear flatbed. There were no railings on the rear — Garrett Lockely had assembled the vehicle himself, and simply put together some flat boards to haul cargo — so if the truck hit a bump too fast, the girls might be jolted off. Forced to go slowly, they had been on the road most of the day without travelling even two hundred miles.

Then, just after they had crossed the Licking River and passed a sign saying they had entered Bourbon County, the land levelled out and they were able to drive faster. From her place in back, perched on a bundle of sheets, Geri-Jo could see across a broad span of land to a distant horizon, crisply outlined by the lowering sun. They had arrived, she guessed,

45

in that part of the state which people back home still talked about as 'The Great Meadow'. The phrase had lasted since pioneer days, when adventurous hunters had first moved westward — out of the mountainous region of dark forests they had come to know as 'The Dark and Bloody Ground' — and had discovered a more hospitable landscape, with longer summers and shorter winters, and vast well-watered plains that sustained thriving herds of buffalo and deer. Gazing across the broad expanse of green land, Geri-Jo felt her hopes rise. Where men struggling for survival had found it in the past, Pa ought to find it now. Clearly, the rolling fertile lands of The Great Meadow had already served as the foundation for fortunes. Driving on mile after mile, Geri-Jo saw many enormous red-brick pillared mansions set back amidst groves of tall trees, each house surrounded by a number of neatly painted barns and hundreds of acres of grassy pasture criss-crossed by long, long lines of snow-white fences. As the sun dropped lower, the tracery of white lines and their echoing shadows that tapered over the smooth breast of the land looked like a gigantic mantle of the most delicate lace.

And, most beautiful of all to Geri-Jo, in the open spaces of the white webs, she saw sleek horses running together in groups or grazing quietly by themselves.

Suddenly, she became aware of something that excited her so much she started hammering on the roof of the jalopy's metal cab to get her father's attention. The jalopy braked to a quick halt on the shoulder, and Pa jumped out of the cab. He ran to the rear and swept a glance over the road behind them, before turning to Geri-Jo.

'Wasn't you shoutin' about somethin' that blew off the truck?'

She laughed. 'No, Pa! I was tellin' you it's *blue*!'

'What's blue?'

She pointed to the pasture beside them. 'The grass, Pa! Don't ya see? Ain't just plain green at all. The grass got blue in it. You see it, don't ya, Mol'?'

Slouched against a sack she was using for a pillow, Molly barely bothered to look. 'Don't matter a hoot what color

46

anythin' is but the money,' she said. 'We can't live eatin' grass like them stupid critters.'

Garrett stared across the field and shook his head. Of course, he had heard The Great Meadow talked about as 'bluegrass country'. You couldn't be a Kentuckian and not hear that one. He guessed Geri-Jo must have picked it up in school, and was seeing what she'd been told to see.

'Gettin' toward evening,' he said, putting a foot up on the running board to climb back behind the wheel. 'The eye plays tricks.'

'I see it, I swear. Why don't we stay 'round here, Pa? There's magic in this place, I feel it! You see them houses . . . and the horses? Ain't never seen a place so beautiful. It's like bein' in a dream . . .'

'This is horse country, girl. Full of rich folks raisin' animals to run 'em in races so's they can win more money. It's a dreamworld, all right, and I don't reckon it's the best place for me to find work.' He shut the door, started the motor and pulled the truck back onto the highway.

Geri-Jo's heart sank. If ever she'd seen a place that looked like her idea of paradise, this was it. But Pa kept driving, heading for his own idea of a future.

The road passed through the fringe of a small city named Lexington, and soon they were on the other side, back in open country. More sprawling horse farms lined both sides of the road, and as the long shadows faded in the glow of twilight, the mansions and the barns and the horses in the fields looked even more idyllic to Geri-Jo. If she could make just one wish in her whole life, she thought, it would be to stay here.

And barely a minute after she'd thought it the jalopy passed a gas station beside the road and Geri-Jo caught sight of a large piece of cardboard taped in a window of the little stucco building behind the pumps, hand-lettered with the words: MECHANIC WANTED. She pounded again on the roof of the cab.

Pa half-leaned out the window. 'I see the damn grass,' he shouted back. The twilight had deepened to purple now, and the grass really did look blue.

''T'aint that, Pa. I see'd a job for you!'

'Job?' he called over his shoulder.

'Back at that last bend. Gas station had a sign for wantin' a mechanic. That's right for you, ain't it?' She knew he'd worked maintaining trucks and jeeps in the army. That was where he'd gotten the know-how to fix up their truck out of spare parts.

She wasn't surprised when he kept his foot on the gas; she knew he didn't want to live where he felt so out of place. Yet, now that she'd been here and seen it, Geri-Jo couldn't imagine being happy anywhere else. Unless they settled here, where the horses grazed on blue grass, she would become like Pa, permanently disappointed and hopeless.

'Don't be crazy, Pa! Stop!' she screamed into the wind. 'A job, first day out and it's waitin' for ya!'

'Give up on this place, Geri-Jo,' Molly said. 'You wouldn't never get near the nice parts, anyway . . .'

She couldn't give up, though. 'Please, Pa!' she shouted against the wind as the truck sped faster down the road. She thought then of what he'd said about when she was born — how he believed she might be the reborn spirit of the Italian woman he had loved so much. 'This is where we got to be, don't ya see? Feels to me like an angel put that job right there . . .'

It was only another moment before he took his foot off the gas, and veered off the road to turn around.

The filling station was closed when they drove back. With a second look Geri-Jo wondered if she'd done right to push him into coming. It was a ramshackle place, a small central hut behind the pumps with stucco walls that were cracked and flaking like stale cake, and a garage with two bays that smelled strongly of grease even with the doors pulled down. Discarded tires and rusted fenders were heaped in a huge mound at one side. The best thing about it was the setting. It stood on an empty stretch of flat road, with a field behind it and a brook running alongside the other side of the road, no other stations or stores in sight.

They parked the jalopy in front and slept that night on the rear flatbed. In the morning a boy arrived to open the place,

48

and he directed Garrett back to Lexington to see Harold Parker.

A tall thin man with lank brown hair that flopped down across his forehead like a farmboy's, Parker owned one of the largest auto dealerships in Lexington, and three Mobil gas stations in the surrounding area. The son of a local blacksmith, he was a Korean war vet who spoke proudly of building his success on a foundation of business courses paid for under the G.I. Bill.

When Garrett appeared in front of Hal Parker's desk, the businessman regarded him dubiously. He had noticed the makeshift truck parked out front with the job applicant's three ragtag children. But Parker was a polite man, and he took the trouble to ask Garrett's background and qualifications. When he heard that Garrett Lockely was also a war veteran, and learned of the hardships that had brought him down from the mountains, Parker was moved to provide more than just a job. He owned an old Airstream trailer in which he and his wife had taken trips during the early years of their marriage. The trailer vacations had been discontinued, and the silvery Airstream had since stood parked in a corner of the dealership's outdoor lot. Parker offered it as a home for Garrett, and had it towed out to a flat meadow behind the gas station. Not simply out of kindness. With a man living there, Parker figured, the gas station could be run single-handed — with a bit of help now and then from the kids.

For a while the job gave them all a sense of having improved their lives. The gas station itself wasn't a very pretty place, and it was tedious when she had to help Pa — not the work so much as sitting and waiting for the cars to come in. Geri-Jo liked living in the trailer, though. The way everything fit so cleverly into small spaces made it feel cosy and safe. She didn't mind, either, that their home stood on wheels in a large flat field: no mountain of mud could ever slide down and bury them here.

Though Molly and Geri-Jo were taken in at the local school, Caybie couldn't qualify. So while Garrett did his work, he let Caybie stay in the trailer or sit in a corner of the garage tinkering with tools and screws and bits of metal. Then one morning Garrett was working on an old car that needed a new steering rod. The part was no longer supplied, so he started to shape a new rod with a blowtorch and callipers. Interrupted to tend a car at the pumps, he was outside when Caybie wandered over to the lighted torch that had been left hissing on a workbench. The boy began aiming the flame at one thing and another — until he idly turned it around . . .

The screams brought Garrett running but Caybie's flaming clothes had already caused third degree burns over half his body.

When the circumstances behind the accident came to the attention of state authorities concerned with child welfare, a prim woman case-worker arrived to inspect the garage and the trailer, then informed Garrett that the child's 'best interests' would not be served by allowing him to return home.

Garrett raged against the authorities and prepared to fight them, until Hal Parker advised him against it. If it came to a court, Parker said, Garrett might be declared an unfit father, and he might lose the girls as well. In the trailer one evening, Geri-Jo listened as Mr Parker sat at the small fold-down table and advised her father. 'Let him go, Garrett . . . your son should be where he can get special care, and be trained to deal with his handicaps . . .'

Geri-Jo had always thought Mr Parker was smart, but nothing had ever impressed her so much as witnessing how he had cracked through Pa's hard shell of stubbornness without ever once raising his voice. After that she wanted more chances to watch and listen to Hal Parker; to learn how to speak softly, and yet be able to persuade someone tough-minded like Pa. She went to his auto showroom and asked for a job there.

'Doesn't your father need you, Geri-Jo? Working for him comes first.'

'I know, sir. But there's time after school when he could spare me.'

'Can you use a typewriter?'

'No. But I'm up for learnin' anything you're up for teachin'.'

Mr Parker smiled. 'Well you've already got the most

important thing, Geri-Jo: attitude. Keep that attitude, and you'll go far.'

He offered to take her on for three afternoons a week. The job meant giving up time when she might have participated in more school activities, or expanded her social life, but Geri-Jo didn't hesitate to accept. There were boys who wanted to date her, and chances to be a cheerleader or join one of the girls' teams herself, but she couldn't think of anything more important than going to work, improving herself. Earning some money to buy more of her own clothes wouldn't hurt, either. She always felt self-conscious in the cheap, drab outfits that Pa picked out as most practical and durable.

Parker let Geri-Jo do every odd job he could think of — and, unfortunately, any that Miss Hubble could think of, too. Filing, sweeping, licking envelopes. There was little to be learned from the work, she found — though, as she had hoped, being near Mr Parker did add to her education. Hearing her answer the phone now and then, Mr Parker had finally suggested that she ought to spend some time listening to the way people spoke on the radio. 'They have to talk very clearly, Geri-Jo, so that everyone can understand. That might help you, too.'

'Never had no folks complain 'bout understandin' me.'

'I'm not complaining either. But the better you speak, the more places you can go — and the more people you can speak to — without losing touch.'

'I don't see myself ever goin' to many places, Mr Parker.'

He gave her a smile, and then told her to sit in the chair beside his desk. 'I know what you've been through, Geri-Jo. From the way you've handled it, I'd say you've got an extra share of heart and courage and brains. And one more thing that, for better or worse, means a lot in this world: you're very pretty, Geri-Jo — and someday, I'd venture to say, you're going to be beautiful. Fact is, if my wife and I could have had a daughter, you're just about everything we'd have wanted her to be . . .'

Mr Parker's words were the nicest anyone had ever said to her. She murmured a 'thank you' and he went on.

'The point is, you've got a chance at having a special life. But you've got to do things to help yourself along. And one of the most important is to be sure wherever you go, whoever you're with, that you can communicate.'

She went away from the conversation and did what Mr Parker advised, listening to the way people talked on the radio as often as she could. There was no radio at home — a luxury they didn't need, Pa said — and she was able to listen only by going to an appliance store in town. The hours of standing there listening to news programs, along with the way she began speaking — in slow careful imitation, at first, of Northern speech — got her a reputation at school of being a little strange and stuck-up, and the other kids left her alone. Seeing Molly always surrounded by boys, Geri-Jo felt a little jealous. But she didn't want to change her ways. Within her was a terror that, if she didn't improve herself, someday she might find herself forced to return to the hollow. And she never wanted to go back there.

Mr Parker encouraged her in every way he could. When he ran into Geri-Jo one day in the appliance store and learned that she had no radio at home, he brought one in to work.

She had been doing the job more than half a year when Mr Parker asked if she would be willing to spend one afternoon a week working at his home instead of at the agency. 'My wife could use some help,' he explained.

Geri-Jo liked to do whatever Mr Parker asked — yet she was a little frightened by the prospect of meeting his wife. From a few gossipy phone conversations she had overheard Alma Hubble having with her sister when Mr Parker wasn't around, Geri-Jo knew that Letitia Parker was a strange and difficult woman. She never left her house, never had company, and she collected dolls which — according to Miss Hubble — she was no less attached to than if they were children. At times she scolded the dolls furiously.

Mr Parker seemed to anticipate Geri-Jo's qualms, because on the first afternoon that she was to work at his house, he had her come to the agency first and then drove her there himself. As they pulled into the driveway, Geri-Jo gasped with admiration. The house was not a grand mansion like the ones that went with the horse farms along the Versailles Pike, but to her mind it was even nicer. It sat behind a broad expanse of flat green lawn bordered with rosebushes, a snow-white colonial with green shutters and gables — like a giant version of the dollhouse she'd longed for when she used to leaf through Ma's Sears catalogue.

Before getting out of the car, Mr Parker hesitated. 'I expect you've heard people talk about my wife, Geri-Jo . . .'

'Yes, sir.'

'Remember, what people see when they look at someone from the outside isn't the whole truth. Lettie's had a hard time of it.' He paused a moment. 'We wanted children, see. Three times she lost them before they were born, and after that she wasn't able. Being hurt over and over, has made her afraid of . . . of everything. So she stays where she feels safe. Do you understand . . .?'

'I think I do.' Geri-Jo guessed the hurt of losing a person you *planned* to love wasn't so different from losing one you'd already seen and known.

When they went inside, Mrs Parker was sitting in a chair in the front hall as if she had been waiting there for a very long time. She was a thin woman, with small brown eyes set in a long face, and hair the color of sun-burnt grass that was waved and lacquered so that it didn't move at all. She was wearing the sort of clothes Geri-Jo imagined might be chosen to go to a birthday party, a dress of some thin flowery fabric that billowed as soon as the woman stood up and came toward them.

'How lovely to meet you,' she said when Mr Parker introduced Geri-Jo, and extended her arm languidly for a handshake. The whole scene felt very odd to Geri-Jo. Wasn't she coming only to do the cleaning? Yet Mrs Parker was all dressed up and shaking hands as if they were meeting outside of the church.

But Geri-Jo didn't do any maid's work, after all. After Mr Parker returned to work, his wife took Geri-Jo into the kitchen and gave her cake and milk while asking questions about

53

school. Then she brought Geri-Jo upstairs and showed her a room filled with dozens of elaborately dressed dolls. There were dolls from all over the world, Mrs Parker explained, and some more than a hundred years old. She picked up a few to show Geri-Jo, and handled them very gently. But Geri-Jo didn't see Mrs Parker treating any as if they were alive. Delighted by the dolls, Geri-Jo spent a long time looking at them.

And then Mrs Parker said a strange thing. 'Geri-Jo, you've got lovely hair. Would you mind if I washed it for you?'

Getting paid sixty cents an hour to have a shampoo was certainly better than going back to the showroom to be nagged by Alma Hubble.

Mrs Parker took her into a large bathroom, with a little mirrored table in one corner covered with bottles of perfume and colored liquids, and told Geri-Jo to take off her clothes so they wouldn't get wet.

At first, Geri-Jo didn't like being treated as though she were a little girl. But having someone else gently shampoo her hair made Geri-Jo think of her mother. Ma had always been more quick and rough about it, still the memory was a nice one, and Geri-Jo felt warmly toward Mrs Parker for bringing it back.

When she was done, Mrs Parker held her at arm's length a moment, looking at her, and then abruptly pulled her into a tight hug and kissed her on the shoulder. Geri-Jo felt oddly as if she had been turned into one of the dolls.

She went again a week later. The afternoon was almost the same except they spent less time looking at the dolls, and before the shampoo Geri-Jo helped Mrs Parker with her garden. While they dug and planted, Mrs Parker kept up a stream of chatter about herself, her background. Once her family had been very rich, she said, and had lived in a big beautiful white house in 'the real South' — as she called it — with lots of servants. But then they had lost everything in the war.

'Must've been real hard for you to make a change like that,' Geri-Jo said.

Only after Mrs Parker explained there had been no change

because it had all happened long before she was born, did Geri-Jo understand that the servants Mrs Parker had spoken about were slaves, and the war must have been the one in which the North had fought the South a hundred years ago.

As the visits continued, and Mrs Parker began giving her gifts of clothing and perfume and a silver-backed hairbrush, Geri-Jo came to realize then what she had to give in return for all the kindnesses, and why Mr Parker had wanted her to come to the house in the first place. She was to play the part of the child that the woman hadn't been able to have. As she matured herself, the idea bothered Geri-Jo more and more — yet Mrs Parker seemed so sad and well-meaning that Geri-Jo couldn't bring herself to refuse. For month after month, it continued — one afternoon a week, playing with the dolls and letting Mrs Parker wash her hair and hold her — and sometimes an evening when the Parkers took her out to a restaurant. Often at the evening dinners, Mrs Parker would correct her table manners in a hissing whisper. 'Don't wipe your soup bowl with your bread, Geri-Jo! How many times must I tell you that's *common*?'

Eventually Geri-Jo felt that playing along with the lie of being Mrs Parker's child was allowing a part of her real self to be chipped away as surely as a stick being whittled into another shape. She suspected, too, that all the promises made to her of a wonderful life that would be hers someday — all the Parkers' talk about the difference it would make to speak better, and dress better, and develop better manners — were only part of their dream of a daughter that would have been special.

So now hope was fading. She thought often of the day she had first seen the blue grass country, and the horses that seemed to her the most beautiful part of the landscape, the essence of the magic she sensed in this paradise. Since then she had learned more about the horses. When Pa had mentioned they were used for racing, she hadn't realized how valuable that made them. But she had come to know that only the richest people, here in Lexington and elsewhere in the world, owned these animals. They were always so coddled and protected that she would never get near any one of them. Now the horses were no longer a symbol of the magic that might reshape her life, but a constant reminder of the impossibility of her dreams. Geri-Jo saw the white fences everywhere in the countryside around Lexington not so much as a barrier to keep the animals in, but the bars imprisoning her in a cold narrow life. The horses looked as unreal and distant to her now as figures in a tapestry that hung on some palace wall glimpsed occasionally through a small window.

And if they were going to remain forever out of reach, she felt, then she would be better off back in the hollow. At least the people there had never forced her to play strange unwanted roles in their own pretending, had never played up to her simply to soften her up for their own ends, had never asked her to be anything but what she was.

CHAPTER TWO

The moment that her life turned around seemed the same as any other, at first, only another beat in the long steady march of tedium. It was the end of a late spring day and she was sweeping the showroom, when a slender blond boy dressed in jeans and a sweatshirt with frayed, cut-off sleeves came through the door. For the past few weeks the red Corvette had been displayed in the big center window, and there had been a lot of cocky hotrodders coming in. They liked to run their hands along the car's sleek finish, and — if nobody stopped them — to get behind the wheel and flip the knobs on the dash. Mr Parker or one of the two regular salesmen usually got to them before they could leave any finger smudges on the polished paint, but this one had nearly reached the car. Geri-Jo glanced around. Miss Hubble and the salesmen had already gone home, and Mr Parker had evidently stepped out to the service area. She propped her broom in a corner as the boy began caressing the finish along the top of the door. 'Don't touch, please.'

He looked around sharply, and she saw now how good-looking he was, almost pretty. His blond hair was very pale and silky, and he had a narrow face with gray eyes shaped like a cat's. His skin was slightly tanned, and so smooth it was hard to tell if he had started shaving yet. He was taller than she by a few inches, but she guessed he wasn't more than a year or two older.

As she came up, he tossed his head, flipping a lock of the fine hair out of his eyes. 'I like it,' he said. 'What's on it?'

She almost confessed that it wasn't her job to know. But that would rob her of all authority. 'Everything,' she said, a fair assumption.

He reached for the door handle.

'You can't touch,' she said firmly.

He was already sliding into the driver's seat. 'Where's the key?'

Geri-Jo looked around nervously, wishing help would arrive. 'I don't know. Now look, you'd better climb out of that car —'

'What's your name?' He took hold of the steering wheel as he looked up at her.

'Geri-Jo,' she answered, and then felt foolish for responding. 'Listen here, if you don't —'

He slapped the horn button, blasting it once. 'What about the engine, Geri-Jo? Is it the big one — the three-forty?'

The steady gaze of his gray cat-eyes unsettled her. 'I don't know,' she mumbled, losing the hold on her pretense.

'Goddamn! What kind of dumb little bitch are you? Engine's the whole thing in a buggy like this!'

Now she lost the rein on her temper, too. 'Listen to me, you foul-mouthed snotnose, I got more rights here any day than a piece of walkin' horse-pucky like you with nothin' better to do than put on big-spendin' airs.' Her fury unleashed, she couldn't stop herself from grabbing the collar of his sweat-shirt. 'Now just get out of that car and shoo out from under this roof before I show you what happens when I *really* get mad!'

As always when she blew off, she realized within a second it was a mistake. The boy was big enough to do more than resist; he could hurt her as well. Fortunately, he let her tug him out of the car without saying a word.

When he was standing beside her, he gave her another glance. She perceived then that if he had obeyed her, it wasn't because he was meek and fearful. From the glint in his eyes and the confident tilt of his smile, she knew that this boy was simply amused by withholding his strength — not mere physical strength, but some hidden power great enough to give him total confidence.

When he turned abruptly and left the showroom, Geri-Jo sighed aloud, 'Thank the Lord!' But she found herself seized by a strange combination of relief and disappointment.

A minute later he sauntered in again through the door from the service area wearing a smug expression with Mr Parker following just a step behind. Geri-Jo stared in amazement as her boss ushered the boy over to the Corvette, and opened the door for him as he called out loudly, 'Geri-Jo! Get the keys for this wagon off the pegboard in my office.'

She dreaded facing the boy again. He was *somebody*, all right. She kept her eyes on Mr Parker as she walked up and held out the keys.

'No, no, Geri-Jo,' Mr Parker said. 'Give them to Mr Mitchell. They're *his* now.'

Her arm felt as stiff as an iron rod as she handed over the keys.

'Thank you kindly, Geri-Jo,' he said, smiling again — though this one wasn't all smug like the last one. Then he climbed straight into the car — without opening the door.

Mr Parker asked him not to start the engine until the big sliding showroom windows had been opened, and told Geri-Jo to help with the task. A minute later the boy drove out, right off the showroom floor.

'Well, that's a nice day's work,' Mr Parker said, laying a hand on Geri-Jo's shoulder. 'And you've earned yourself a twenty-five-dollar bonus for selling that car.'

She spun toward him wide-eyed. 'I didn't sell it.'

'That's not what I heard from Bard Mitchell. When he got me out of the shop, he said the salesgirl had already convinced him to buy the car, he had just one or two more questions . . .'

Hiding her astonishment, Geri-Jo turned to watch the tail of the vanishing car until it had swerved around a far corner.

Overcoming her shyness, Geri-Jo asked a girl in one of her classes if she knew anything about someone named Bard Mitchell. The girl replied that she had never met him, but she knew about his family. The Mitchells had been in Lexington 'forever', she said, and had 'all kinds of money'. Every part of the boy's full name — Barden Clay Mitchell — stood for a connection to some ancestral line that went deep into Kentucky tradition.

That was enough to reinforce what Geri-Jo had warned herself as the red car drove away from the Parker agency — that her path and the boy's weren't likely to cross ever again, and there was no point letting him take up any space in her mind.

Of course that wasn't the only reason it seemed just as well not to hope the boy came around again. There was Pa to worry about, too . . .

Of all the disappointments for Geri-Jo, the worst was that Pa hadn't gotten better at all. With each passing day he seemed more dark and quiet, his face set more firmly in an angry scowl. The steepest dive in his mood had come after they had all gone up to Frankfort to put Caybie into the state home. The institution was situated in pleasant grounds, but the drab hallways, dormitories full of metal beds with sagging mattresses and rough gray blankets, and the staff of gruff men and women, induced a feeling that Caybie had been put away in something more like a prison than a place where he'd get special care and education. When they were leaving, Caybie cried and asked to come home. 'Someday,' Pa said. But they all knew it would never happen.

Now that only she and Molly were left with Pa, he seemed more locked inside himself, and more explosive on those rare occasions when he did emerge from his shell. He seemed especially skittish whenever it came to her being involved in any way with boys. As the weather got warmer and more joyriding hotrodders took to stopping at the station, she became particularly aware of it. The only time he'd let her wait on any boys was because he was down in the grease pit or out on a tow. She had managed it always without incident — until a Saturday, a few weeks back when a group had come in headed home from a day of swimming and drinking beer at Taylorsville Lake. One of them had grabbed a gas nozzle, and begun waggling it in front of Geri-Jo suggestively. The boisterous laughter of his friends had brought Pa charging straight out of the garage, brandishing a crowbar. As soon as he reached their car he started swinging — busting the windshield, the headlights, denting the hood. The boys made no move to prevent him. There was murder in his eyes, none of them doubted it. When he told the boys to get in their hotrod and never come within a mile of the station again, they were gone in three seconds.

Then he rounded on her. 'What'd you do to give 'em the idea they could fool with ya like that . . .?'

'Nothin', Pa!'

But he hadn't listened. 'I catch you again makin' eyes at any one of these punks,' he vowed, 'I'll give you so much strappin' I can be sure you won't get on your back for anyone ever!'

She had believed, at first, that his strict conditions came only from a desire to protect her; wrong-headed and overheated, maybe, yet understandable in the light of what had happened to the rest of the family. But on a couple of evenings recently when she had been alone with him in the trailer, after Molly had gone off to her usher's job and he had stayed at the table drinking beer, he had begun rambling softly.

'You know how much I love ya, Jo . . . I just want to keep you safe . . .'

When he called her 'Jo', she knew at once that he was confusing her again with his memory of a woman from another time and place, a ghost of love. It made her shiver to remember how he had kissed her that moonlit night in the hollow, yet she didn't know how to cure him of the confusion. But if she didn't, she sensed, it was only going to get worse. As much as she loved Pa, she was also becoming more and more afraid of him — afraid of the kind of love he had for her.

On a Saturday, two weeks after she had first seen Bard Mitchell, the red Corvette came wheeling into the gas station. The top was down, and he was driving. With Pa in the grease pit doing a transmission, and Molly gone to usher the matinee at the movie house, Geri-Jo was on the pumps.

It took an effort to walk up to Barden Clay Mitchell as if he was any customer. 'What'll you have . . .?'

'High-test. Fill it up.'

His gray eyes held hers for a moment. She felt warm suddenly, intensely aware of herself, her body, in a way she never had been before. She wrenched her gaze from his, went to the rear of the car and put the nozzle in the tank. 'That was nice what you done with Mr Parker,' she said. 'Worked out well for me. Thank you.'

She was surprised when he didn't answer right away. He seemed to take her appreciation as though it was due to him.

Then he said, 'How about cleaning my window?'

She noticed a breathiness to his voice, and felt he was toying with her, luring her to the front again. But she set the catch on the nozzle that kept the gas flowing and picked up the squeegee. When she leaned across the windshield, he said, 'You're one damn pretty number, Geri-Jo. How about coming out with me?'

She glanced up at him, speechless. Then, hiding her surprise, she looked to the place next to him in his car and it seemed to her like the way to ride into a whole other world. She longed to say yes to him, but so many other thoughts and questions began jamming up in her mind. How could she think of entering his world, a place of mansions, and fine clothes? Or would she ever even see that part? What did he want with her, anyway?

And there was Pa to worry about, too. After the way he'd warned her about boys, what would he do if she went out with Bard Mitchell? He seemed wound up so tight these days, she didn't want to do anything to make it worse.

'I . . . I don't think I can,' she said at last.

'Sure you can. Just don't tell your old man about it.'

She shot a glance at him, surprised that he understood her problem.

'Oh, I know about your father, Geri-Jo. First thing I heard when I started asking 'round about you was what a terror your old man is anytime someone gets too near you or your sister. Word has it he damn near killed some guys who were in here a few weeks back and started fooling with you . . .'

She kept rubbing silently at the windshield, overwhelmed to hear that he'd been thinking about her, too, asking questions.

'So will you come out with me?' he asked again.

She looked at him again. 'That story about my Pa don't worry you none?'

He smiled. 'A little maybe. But looks to me like you're a girl worth taking a chance for.'

Then, almost as though it was someone else talking, she heard herself say that she went to Mrs Parker's on Tuesday afternoons, and if she could get off a little early she might have some time with him before her father expected her home.

'Okay,' he said, 'I'll be on the corner near Parker's house at three o'clock next Tuesday . . .'

She heard the catch on the pump click, signalling his tank was full, but for a second she couldn't stop staring into his eyes.

Suddenly a voice boomed out behind her, shattering the fragile mood. 'You done with that car, Geri-Jo . . .?'

Turning, she saw Pa standing in the garage's open bay, a large wrench in one hand. 'Yes, Pa,' she called obediently.

'Then there's plenty else needs tendin'. To start, you can get to the restrooms and give those filthy toilets a real good swabbin' out.'

She flicked a helpless glance toward Bard Mitchell, but he had already looked away and started the engine. And when he handed her the money for the gas, he kept his eyes averted.

He wouldn't be on the corner Tuesday, she realized as he drove away. Pa had reminded them both that there was a gap that couldn't be bridged. The rich boy wasn't going to want a girl who cleaned public toilets sitting next to him in his nice clean expensive machine.

CHAPTER THREE

Geri-Jo studied the reflection of the woman at her shoulder in the dressing-table mirror, her face so intent on the hair she was brushing. Was this a good moment to ask? Geri-Jo wondered. Mrs. Parker — Lettie, as she liked to be called now — was so fond of their time together. But it must be close to three o'clock. If she didn't speak up she'd never get away.

'Oh my, Geri-Jo, you do get lovelier all the time.' Lettie sighed. 'You'll be breaking hearts any day now . . .'

'I hope not. I don't ever want to be the cause of anyone getting hurt.'

'Dear girl,' Lettie said, 'it won't always be a matter of choice. But you must've begun to learn that. Goodness, you'll be out of high school in a year, ready to get married. There must be boys already trying to get close to you — and they can't all be to your own liking.'

Their eyes met in the mirror. The woman standing behind her smiled, and Geri-Jo felt suddenly that it might be no co-incidence the topic of boys had been raised. It wasn't the first time Lettie Parker had shown an uncanny sensitivity to secret thoughts. In fact, Geri-Jo believed that Lettie understood her better and was more sympathetic to her than anyone else had ever been. She had never seen a sign of the terrible temper Alma Hubble gossiped about. Over the months their conversations had become deeper and more personal. Often she found herself being led into discussions of things that had been

64

weighing on her mind. On a day when she might be particularly upset by Pa's strictness, Lettie would tell about her own father and his moods in a way that somehow sent Geri-Jo away with a greater reservoir of forgiveness.

'You know how my Pa is about boys,' Geri-Jo said. 'There's *none* to his liking, so I hardly get the chance to know which ones might please me.'

'It's difficult for a man with a daughter like you, Geri-Jo. You're like a jewel; he doesn't want to see you go off with anyone who doesn't know your value.' She paused in her brushing. 'My father was like that, too. Of course, I wasn't such a prize as you, but I was still a jewel to him — no boy good enough. He was forever telling me what good stock we came from, the big houses we'd had and all . . . going way back, you know, to before we'd lost our labor, the blacks, and saw it all dwindle . . .'

Watching Lettie in the mirror, Geri-Jo saw the distant look in her eyes. Though Lettie had been born generations after the time she was referring to, she often talked as though she had lived on a plantation and owned slaves herself.

At last, Geri-Jo could contain herself no longer. 'There is a boy,' she said. 'He asked me to meet him at the corner — today at three. Though I'm not sure he'll be there. Pa may have scared him off already.'

'Oh, he'll be there,' Lettie said, fondly smoothing down Geri-Jo's hair with her hand. 'For you, child, they'll always be there.' Slowly she moved around the stool to look at Geri-Jo directly. 'You like this boy, too?'

'I don't know. That's what I'm saying: I've never had a chance to be with him. I never will, if it's left to Pa . . .'

Lettie cocked her head. There was no missing the pleading tone in the girl's voice. Emphasizing her delight at joining a conspiracy, she lowered her voice to a near whisper. 'He's a nice boy, is he . . . good family?'

Expecting she would know the name, Geri-Jo told Lettie it was Bard Mitchell.

Lettie's eyes widened. 'Well, Geri-Jo, we've got to capitalize on an opportunity like that.'

'Oh, Lettie, do you mean it? I was so worried you might be mad . . .'

'Why should I be mad, child? You look so lovely, it'd be a shame not to let this boy see you in all your glory.'

Geri-Jo sat still as Lettie finished touching up her hair, brushing a couple of big waves into the front, and added a dab of perfume behind both her ears. By then it was only a couple of minutes before three, and Lettie went downstairs with her.

At the front door, Lettie stopped Geri-Jo for a warning. 'Remember one thing, Geri-Jo. Folks like the Mitchells think they can own anything and anyone.' Abruptly she grabbed Geri-Jo by the wrist. 'Swear to me you won't . . . do anything to disgrace yourself. I truly couldn't stand it if you ever did anything to make me ashamed.'

Geri-Jo winced at the surprising intensity of Lettie's grip. 'I swear . . .' she said. Only then Lettie released her to run through the door.

She had never felt as happy and excited as when she saw Bard Mitchell already waiting at the corner, standing beside his car. As she reached him and smiled, his eyes swept up and down in frank approval.

'Mmmm-mmm,' he purred. 'Don't you look good enough to eat.'

Though she tried not to show it, his reaction embarrassed her, and when he opened the door she slid quickly into the front seat.

The road he took south out of Lexington was one she had never been on before, but the beauty of the landscape was not unfamiliar. Rolling velvet green hills stitched everywhere by snow-white fences that boxed in fields full of horses. As the car whizzed along, Bard supplied a commentary on some of the horse farms they were passing — farms that belonged to friends of his family, which had bred big stakes winners. Geri-Jo sat back and let the wind stream through her long hair, trying to luxuriate in the experience of riding in the snazzy red sports car. Yet she couldn't help feeling nervous. Was she dressed well enough? She had worn her best blouse, a white cotton with an elastic neckline that pulled down low around the shoulders, and a flared pale blue skirt she'd saved weeks to buy. But she knew that girls from families like Bard's had much prettier things, and she was painfully conscious that he had given her no compliments on what she was wearing, only a leering appreciation of her face and body. Perhaps it didn't matter to him what clothes she had on — perhaps he hadn't even noticed. What could he want with her anyway? she asked herself for the hundredth time. He must have his pick of belles from the best families.

Her concern about his intentions was heightened by the fact that when she'd asked where they were going as soon as she got in the car, he had refused to answer. 'Someplace you'll have no worries,' was all he would say. 'I know you don't want anybody telling your Pa we were seen together.'

Could he be taking her off to some isolated spot where he could make demands on her? Lettie's warning echoed in her mind.

At last Bard swerved the car into a wide driveway that passed under a high wooden portal with raised brass letters across the top spelling out SKYEVALE. For a minute or two they raced along a broad avenue of elm trees that ended finally at one of the largest and most beautiful white mansions Geri-Jo had ever seen, fronted by a portico reached by two wings of curving steps and supported by four soaring fluted pillars. Bard braked to a stop on a wide circle of gravel so white and shiny it looked like crushed pearls.

Geri-Jo realized now where he had brought her, and suddenly the torture of being forever kept at a distance seemed oddly preferable to the horror of being confronted with a place where, she knew beyond the smallest doubt, she didn't belong. 'Oh Bard, I just didn't expect this. I would've planned more . . . what to wear, what to say. Now I'm going to come on dumb as a coot and your folks won't be any more pleased seeing me with you, than my Pa is about —'

'Settle down, Geri-Jo. You won't be seeing my folks. They're away for the Preakness.'

'What are the . . . Preakness?'

Bard laughed. 'It's a single thing, a famous horserace . . . up in Maryland. So we've got the place all to ourselves.'

Assured that they would be alone, Geri-Jo relaxed enough to let Bard lead her up the steps of the portico. As they reached the top, the front entrance was opened by a butler with skin almost as black and shiny as the varnish on the door. 'Good afternoon, Mister Bard,' he said in a deep bass voice. 'And Miss . . .' He bowed slightly toward Geri-Jo.

'Hi, Little,' Bard called over his shoulder as he went in. 'That's Miss Lockely . . .'

Over the threshold, Geri-Jo stopped to stare. The large entrance hall had marble floors, and was bare of furniture except for a couple of chairs and a table on which stood a vase bursting with flowers — enough, thought Geri-Jo, for two dozen graves on a Decoration Sunday. High overhead hung a chandelier that looked as if it was made out of a million diamonds, and the stairs that circled up to a mezzanine brought to mind the sort of stairway she imagined her mother's soul must have climbed to heaven. Standing in the foyer, several times the size of the whole trailer in which she and Pa and Molly lived, Geri-Jo felt very small. Too small to deal with Bard, or any of the giants who inhabited this place.

'Can I get anything for you or Miss Lockely?' the black butler addressed Bard.

'We'll be going down to the pool, Little,' Bard replied. 'Bring us something to eat there . . .' Then he bounded up the stairs.

She followed automatically. Catching up with Bard, she whispered, 'You said we'd be alone.' She nodded over her shoulder toward the butler.

'Little's a servant, Geri-Jo. There's always a few of them in the house . . . even when it's empty.'

He guided her to an enormous bedroom off a mezzanine, all done in shades of pink. It belonged to his older sister who was away at college, Bard explained, as he rummaged in a dresser drawer and pulled out a little wad of yellow fabric which he tossed onto the bed.

'You can use one of Caroline's bathing suits, you're about

68

the same size. Meet you in the hall in a couple of minutes and we'll go down to the pool . . .'

He was gone before she could mention that she'd never had a chance to learn how to swim. She knew, though, that she shouldn't say anything to disappoint him. She grabbed the bathing suit . . . and the yellow bundle separated into two narrow bands of thin cloth. She could hear her father's voice proclaiming what would be said about a girl who exposed so much of herself, but she locked the door and put on the bikini.

Standing at a mirror, she studied herself. Wearing only the two skimpy pieces of the suit, her body was even more exposed than in the bra and panties she had removed. She felt nearly naked, timid about facing Bard this way. Yet it was also exciting, the sense of skirting along the borders of the forbidden. She had to admit, too, that she looked all right in the suit. Forced to be modest around Pa in the confines of the trailer, she rarely paused before a mirror to take stock of herself, avoided nudity. But now she felt proud of her body, her long legs and slim hips, flat stomach and full rounded breasts, unblemished skin. For a moment, filled with a realistic appreciation of herself, she felt resentment toward Pa for making her feel ashamed and scared of becoming a woman — and, at the same time, eagerness to explore this new experience with Bard.

When she went into the corridor, he was leaning against the balcony railing, wearing only a lowcut brief of black elastic material and a towel slung around his neck. For a long moment they stared at each other. He had a narrow build, she saw, but his arms and torso were well-muscled. Unthinkingly, her glance went lower, but she checked it as she found herself looking at the fine line of blond hair that went down the center of his abdomen. She lifted her eyes to his.

'My sister,' he said, 'never looked half so good in that . . .'

Suddenly self-conscious again, she rubbed her hands together to screen her body. 'Which way?' she said.

They went downstairs and out through a passage to a broad flagstone terrace from which more stairs descended to a patio

69

and a long, shimmering aquamarine pool bordered by lush flowerbeds.

Flinging aside his towel, Bard ran straight to the pool and dived in. He swam to the other end in smooth powerful strokes, then called her to join him. She approached the edge tentatively, and when he called again, she confessed:

'I don't know how, Bard . . .'

'Then I'll teach you. C'mon . . .' He swam to the shallow end near her and held out his hand. She took it and jumped in, her skin tingling at the contact with the cool water.

Soon he had coaxed her into floating. Standing alongside her, he supported her in his arms, holding her on her back. He was a good teacher, patient, giving constant encouragement. When she relaxed a little, he turned her over on her stomach and instructed her in how to kick and stroke the water. As he supported her now, she was acutely aware of his palms against her bare skin, one on her stomach, the other under one of her thighs. Even in the cool water, her skin where he was touching her felt hot.

Finally, he left her at one side of the pool and moved to the other. 'Now swim to me,' he said. 'Try it . . .'

She gulped a little water, but managed to keep her feet off the bottom until she had reached him. Then he caught her, and pulled her up close to him.

'We're a great match, Geri-Jo. I'm a good teacher, and you're one hell of a fast learner. There's a lot more I could teach you . . .'

With her skin cooled by the water, it was a moment before she felt his hand move down inside the skimpy pants of the suit, cupping her buttocks, then probing between her thighs. Frozen with shock, she did nothing as he kissed her. And then, while his warm lips rested lightly on hers and his tongue slid into her mouth, a tide of pleasure rose within her. She clung to him for an instant, her palms sliding down his back, until she felt his fingers enter the soft cleft, massaging her so that a sudden sharp thrill bolted up through her stomach and to the tips of her limbs. She reeled back as though hit by a bolt of electricity and wrestled him away.

Then the angry words poured out — not really what she wanted to say, but words planted there by Pa's threats and Lettie's warning. 'Wouldn't be so damn bold with a rich girl, would you? You can move on me because I'm just nothin' but poor trash to you. Right? You figure it's all I'm good for . . .'

'No, Geri-Jo. Don't make it something bad. You turn me on, that's all. There'd be something wrong with me if I didn't want you . . .'

They separated as a black maid appeared from a door under the terrace pushing a cart loaded with silver and glassware, crystal pitchers of iced tea and lemonade, and more food than five people could eat — sandwiches and fried chicken, a large salad in a silver bowl, a plate of sliced meats, lemon tarts and chocolate-covered cookies. Bard pointed to a far corner of the patio near a white fence thickly overgrown with trailing pink and red roses. The maid wheeled the cart there and raised its two wings, converting it to a table. After placing two pool chairs beside it, she left.

They climbed out of the water, and dried themselves, then Bard led Geri-Jo to the table and pulled the chair for her. She was about to sit, when she glanced to the side of the table. Suddenly, she straightened again, her gaze held by the vista beyond the nearby fence — the rest of Skyevale's sprawling property, a small village of immaculate white stables with red doors and shutters standing amid groves of trees, all surrounded by pastures intersected by more miles of fencing. Off to one side there was a large oval track, around which a horse was galloping, his distant hoofbeats riding the warm air as softly as a cricket's chirp, and here and there Geri-Jo saw other horses being sponged off as they stood beneath the trees, or being led slowly along paths by black men holding ropes, or grazing in the pastures.

She had walked into her heart's dream, and she had to fight back tears at the prospect of her inevitable waking. She felt the same mysterious certainty at this moment as she had the first day she had seen the blue-grass country — that these beautiful animals were part of her destiny.

Too excited now to be hungry, but thinking that she might

never have a chance at a meal like this again, Geri-Jo wished she could sweep the food into a bag and take it all home. But, with a glance at Bard, she did exactly as he did. She unfolded a white linen napkin and put it across her lap and helped herself to a piece of fried chicken and a little salad. For a while she picked at her food. Having seen the horses, she wanted nothing so much as a chance to get closer to them, touch one, make it real, not just a figure in a beautiful view. But to earn that chance what did she have to do for Bard . . .?

The question burst into the open. 'Look, I'm no better off than the folks you've got cleanin' up, you know that. So what the hell is it you want with me if it ain't just . . . to use me? All the rest you can have with girls who are more your kind, all those country club girls in their long white dresses!'

'I'll let you in on a secret, Geri-Jo. There's plenty of those debs who go around buck naked under their fluffy ball gowns. So if all I want is an easy lay, I don't have to go far.'

'Then why —'?

'Because you *are* different.' He put down a chicken leg and wiped his hands on the napkin. 'You've got something I never saw in a girl before, Geri-Jo. That day I walked into Parker's, I saw it right off, something that sets you apart. It's like . . . when some men around here look at racehorses, they can pick out the winners, the ones that have the spirit to push out in front of all the rest. They may talk a lot about pedigree, but when the time comes to judge a horse — say, a yearling that's never raced — the old horsemen have their own standard. Never mind the bloodlines, never mind where that horse was bred or what his price is, if they can spot a certain look in a horse's eye, they know it's got the spirit to be a winner. They've got a phrase for it, this glitter in the eyes of a great horse. They call it "the look of eagles".' He leaned closer across the table. 'That's what makes me want you, Geri-Jo. The first second you passed in front of me, I saw it in you — the look of eagles.'

She didn't take it seriously, but it was flattering to have him spend his cleverness on her. 'You know it all, don't you, Bard? How to talk like a movie star . . . how to get a girl all worked up?'

'Not all, Geri-Jo. I plan to keep on learning, though, for at least another fifty years.'

She had to smile. 'But how does it come so easy? You're not shy at all about the things that seem to keep plenty of boys tied in knots. Men, even . . .'

He shrugged. 'Maybe I learned it from the horses.'

'I'm being serious.'

'So am I. I been wandering around these barns since I was knee-high. You watch enough of these animals being bred, the mystery goes out of it. The first thing you see is that nothing happens without both the mare and stallion being good and ready. I've never been afraid of revealing exactly what I wanted . . . since I learned I'd pretty much always find a mare wanting it just as much.'

His first comparison with horses had been a compliment, but this one annoyed her. She had also seen farm animals coupling when she was a child, but it had never occurred to her that sex between people was the same. Much as she was attracted to Bard herself, she felt he was too experienced for her, that he could use his cleverness to bend her to his own desires before she could be certain that she shared them. She wanted now to get away from being confined with him at the table, to get back into her clothes.

'Could we go and see the horses?' she asked impulsively.

He looked genuinely surprised. 'Well, sure, if that would amuse you. We might even take a couple of ponies and go for a ride.'

She bounced straight up from her chair. 'Oh, could we really . . ?'

He laughed as he stood up. 'I've got to confess that we've always had so many horses around here — always being talked about and pampered and worried over — that I'm at the point where the big dumb beasts bore me silly. But if it's your idea of fun . . .'

'Oh it is, Bard. It's all I want.'

As they started toward the house, she let him put his arm around her bare waist. She wondered why it didn't seem important to mention that she'd never ridden a horse before.

She wanted to stroll slowly around the barns, inhale the smells, stamp it all in her memory to have in case Bard never asked her to come again. But after they had changed, Bard headed briskly along a flower-lined path toward the stable area. Along the way, he offered only one or two dry comments on the surroundings. 'That's our newest barn,' he said pointing out one of the red and white buildings. 'That's the breeding shed,' he said as they passed another. He showed no interest in the horses himself; his only reason for going near the stables was obviously to please her.

There was less activity around the red and white barns than she had seen earlier from the terrace. Only a couple of horses were standing in the shade of the tall trees, being sponged off by a couple of elderly black men. Noticing how tenderly one of the men treated the sleek brown horse he was washing, Geri-Jo paused to watch and heard the black man maintaining a constant patter to the animals. 'Now don't you flinch like that, mister . . . I'll have you all clean in a minute . . . and when those fillies see you comin' they'll be dancin' and snortin' to get near ya . . .'

Bard went into one of the barns, arranged to have a couple of horses saddled, and returned.

'Do you think he understands?' Geri-Jo asked. 'I mean, the way that man is talking to him . . .'

'Some of these old grooms make noises just to keep the horses settled. But they could croon any mumbo-jumbo and it would have the same effect. Horses are dumb animals, Geri-Jo. Some are good to look at, and a few are good to bet on. But they're plain stupid. They don't do what they do to please us, or even because they like to win. Thoroughbreds run because it's in their blood, because they have no choice, because it's all the critters know how to do.'

She turned to Bard, who was regarding the horse with contempt. What set him against the animals? she wondered. Weren't they part of his family's tradition, a source of their wealth and importance?

'Here's our ponies,' Bard said as the saddled mounts were led out of the barn. They looked too big and powerful to be the

74

'ponies', but when Geri-Jo remarked on it, he explained that all horses used for riding around thoroughbred stables were called ponies or 'hacks'. They were generally racehorses that had performed poorly on the track, and had been judged of low breeding quality.

But the fact they had raced at all must mean they were fast and high-spirited, Geri-Jo thought. She couldn't understand why nervousness had yet to strike her. Wasn't it crazy *not* to be afraid?

If there was even a flutter of anxiety, it vanished in the thrill as the horses came nearer. They were the sleekest and most beautiful she had ever seen, one a pale silver gray, and the other a reddish brown with a blaze of white on its head and a white streak in the center of its mane. Distracted by the horses, it took a moment before Geri-Jo focussed on the strange old man who was leading the animals by the reins. His spine was so bowed over that he was forced to look at the ground unless he arched his neck back, yet he chose to restrict his view further by wearing a battered felt hat with a broad brim pulled low.

He came up to Bard, and the horses stopped behind him. 'There they are,' he said in a hoarse whispery voice. 'But I'm reminding you once more, Mister Bard —'

'Never mind, Henry. I know my father's instructions. But he's away, and I'm sure he'll be glad the gray got exercised.' He reached over, and took the reins for the pale silver horse. 'Now, hold for Miss Lockely while she gets up.'

The old man craned his neck back revealing a face as weathered and cracked as earth breaking up after a long drought. His eyes were mere slits through which Geri-Jo could see glints, small as chips of mica in stone. 'If you got any influence with him, Miss,' he said, nodding to Bard, 'you ought to keep him off that gray. If big Mister Mitchell hears —'

'Shut your mouth, Henry!'

Bard's sudden ferocity alarmed Geri-Jo. Glancing over, she saw his hand raised to dangle the reins in front of the old man as though preparing to use them as a whip. Geri-Jo's pity was aroused, but the bent old man seemed unconcerned for himself.

'Left leg into the stirrup now, Miss,' he urged her. 'I'll hold him steady . . .'

Geri-Jo thought she saw him wink as he held out the stirrup, and directed her which foot to use. It struck her then that somehow, in his one canny look, he had sized up her inexperience. 'Thank you, Henry,' she said, following his directions. While Bard was busy mounting his own horse, the old man laid the reins quickly into her hands so that in one deft movement he had threaded them through her fingers for the correct grip.

'His name's Peacepipe,' old Henry said as he adjusted the straps to raise the stirrups to the proper length. 'When he raced they used to say he was a pipe that never smoked, but he's just fine for a saddle pony. A light pull stops him, and he'll turn with just a touch of rein on his neck whichever side you want him to go . . .'

Geri-Jo nodded her appreciation, and the old man scuttled back beside a tree. 'Have a nice ride, Miss,' he called, as Bard kicked his horse into a walk and Peacepipe automatically followed. 'And you be ginger with that gray, Mister Bard.'

Straight paths of neatly raked soft earth passed between all the stable buildings. At first, Bard kept the animals to a walk, and Geri-Jo settled back in the saddle, her assurance growing. For the first time in her life, she had a sense that she possessed some kind of . . . control. The creature under her was large and strong, many times stronger than a man. Yet she believed that she was attuned to the mood of the animal and could exercise power over it. It was almost intoxicating, this change from feeling powerless and weak . . . a small creature herself to be steered by the whims of others.

Soon they reached a fence separating the stables from a broad open field. Leaning down from the saddle, Bard opened a gate in the fence, and after his horse and Geri-Jo's were through, he closed it again. 'Want to let 'em run?' he asked.

'Let's . . . take it easy a while longer.'

Bard gave her a sidelong glance, but proceeded to walk his

horse alongside Peacepipe. 'Not afraid are you, Geri-Jo? I mean, with all that talk of old Henry's about The Ghost.'

'. . . Ghost . . .'

'My mount, that's his name. Henry makes him sound like a terror, doesn't he? He's got an idea that he'll run away with anyone but my father in the saddle. It's bullshit though. My father just likes to keep everyone thinking he's the only one who's man enough to do anything . . .'

It made her feel closer to Bard to hear that, like her, he had some confused feelings about his father.

They rode along a ridge. The fences of other pastures stretched away below and, beyond those, there were other farms extending as far as the horizons. The countryside hadn't seemed so beautiful to Geri-Jo since the day she had first seen it. 'It's paradise,' she blurted out. 'Don't you feel it, Bard . . .?'

He gave her one of his thin smiles. 'Tell me often enough, Geri-Jo. You're the one person who could make me believe it. Now let's see what it feels like to fly through paradise . . .' Suddenly he kicked his horse hard. At once it took off in a gallop.

In the next instant, her horse followed automatically. Jolted backward, one of her feet slipped from the stirrup, and her hands flew up, fingers automatically splayed so that the reins pulled loose. She slid sideways in the saddle, and felt herself falling . . . but then she flung her hands forward, caught the horse's mane, and pulled herself upright again. As she clung on blindly, she was consumed by panic. She had risked too much. She was going to die, as all the others had died — be thrown from the back of this racing animal and crushed just as she had seen her brothers and sisters thrown to their death from the skin of a mountain gone wild.

But as her memory replayed the vision of all of them going under, she resolved to survive. By God, she wasn't going to let herself be shaken loose. She was going to hang on to power over this animal . . . over her fate. Winding her hands tighter into the mane, she hunched down, pressed herself against the back of the horse, making herself a part of it, starting to anticipate its movements and respond with adjustments of her weight and muscle. And then the fear was gone. Her control was sure, she knew, not an illusion. And she was where she belonged, reveling in the speed, exulting in the synchrony of her body with the animal beneath her. She felt comfortable enough now to risk making a grab for the flapping reins. But even when she had gathered them in, she didn't pull back. She didn't want the sensation to end. She couldn't catch Bard, though. The Ghost was going extremely fast, galloping over ground that looked uneven in places. Perhaps it was only the result of all the warnings she'd heard back at the stable, but she had an impression that the horse was going headlong at his own pace and Bard had surrendered control. Suddenly she felt afraid for him.

'Bard!' she called urgently. 'Slow down . . .!'

But he was moving too fast to hear. They went the length of the ridge, the gap widening between them until The Ghost finally came to a stop. As she approached the place where Bard was waiting, sitting calmly in the saddle, Geri-Jo noticed his eyes were abnormally bright, like someone with a fever.

'Weren't you scared?' she asked. 'I thought you were going too fast.'

Bard laughed. 'No such thing as too fast for me, girl.'

He seemed sincere, yet she sensed that he had been scared, too. All at once, Geri-Jo understood that toying with self-destruction was a game for him. The horse he was riding might be more than he could handle, yet he enjoyed balancing on the edge of disaster. Perhaps that explained, too, his interest in her; what drew him to her was the danger of inciting Pa's wrath or his own father's angry disappointment.

So as long as she wanted Bard and all the opportunities he offered, Geri-Jo realized now, she might have to stay right on the edge with him, share in his dangerous games.

But a day like today, she didn't think it was too high a price to pay. And when he challenged her to race him back to the stables — even though she had seen enough of the other horse to know she had no chance at all to win — her instant answer was to spur her own mount into a galloping headstart.

CHAPTER FOUR

Over the next couple of weeks Geri-Jo went several times to Skyevale. The Parkers let her leave work early so that she could see Bard without her father finding out, and Hal Parker even paid her for all the lost hours. 'Your father counts on that money,' he said when Geri-Jo objected to being paid for work she hadn't done. 'Don't want him asking why your pay is short, do we?'

She could only promise to make it up to him someday.

'Nothing to repay,' Hal Parker said. 'You're like our own, Geri-Jo. Lettie and I could do no less . . .'

He stuck up for her, too, when Alma Hubble began to resent Geri-Jo's special treatment. 'You could say it's none of my business, Mr Parker,' the spinster secretary complained as Geri-Jo was leaving early one afternoon, 'but we got too much to do around here for you to be playin' Cupid for that girl.'

'You're right, Alma,' Hal Parker said. 'It is none of your business.'

Each time, Bard picked her up either at the showroom or near the Parker home, and at the end of the day he drove her back to a spot around a bend from the gas station, a few hundred yards away. There was a side road there that led to an old dump, and Bard would turn off there, and they would sit in the car for a few minutes and kiss and fondle each other. Geri-Jo was always excited by Bard, she liked him to touch her; away from him, she spent more and more time daydreaming about what it might be like if they stayed together, got married someday. She would imagine herself living at Skyevale, having a horse of her own.

Yet reality would always shatter the dream: she was a poor girl from the mountains, he was rich and well-educated, already planning to go off to some big Eastern college next year. If he had any interest in her, she felt, it had to be linked to sex more than anything else. That made her wary of giving too much — being an 'easy lay', as he'd called some of the rich girls. Though Bard kept asking her to spend the whole night with him at Skyevale sometime when his parents were away, it was a relief to be able to say that her father would never permit it.

And it was enough for her to be at Skyevale during the days. That was the best time to see the horses, and learn more about them. With each day she spent around the stables, she became more interested, too, in the activities around the big track in a flat meadow off to the side of the stabling area where horses were being trained to race.

Despite Bard's own lack of interest in his family's thoroughbred operations, he let Geri-Jo spend all the time she wanted at the stables, and he explained whatever he knew himself about the training and breeding process. With the busy summer racing season approaching, there was constant activity around the barns and the training track, and all of it fascinated Geri-Jo. She saw colts being given their first work-outs by young, lightweight riders called exercise boys. For the younger horses, the work-outs consisted mainly of running them around the oval training track in an easy loping gallop called a 'breeze'. For the two- and three-year-old horses, already veterans of at least a few races, the exercise sessions lasted longer and were more rigorous, with the horses sometimes being run at full speed. Some of the horses being exercised, Bard said, were being prepared to be shipped to races where the winners received prizes of more than a hundred thousand dollars. With the spring racing season almost over, the best thoroughbreds had already moved on from the great Kentucky tracks — Churchill Downs and Keeneland — to compete in events at Belmont in New York,

Pimlico in Baltimore, Arlington Park in Chicago, and many other tracks.

Hearing about the prize money, Geri-Jo decided that if there was any hope of ever getting such a fortune of money as a hundred thousand dollars, she would do it somehow through the horses. Leaning on the rail of the training track, watching one of the thoroughbreds go breezing by, she tried to fathom what element of muscle or spirit provided the edge that made a winner, what went into the process of refining those qualities.

But the answer eluded her. All she saw were horses being ridden around a track. Or was there anything more to see? Perhaps the result of what happened when a racehorse finally bolted out of a starting gate and headed toward a finish line came down to nothing more than pure luck. Though, if there *was* anything more to the art of training, after spending several afternoons at Skyevale's training track Geri-Jo was pretty sure who could teach it to her.

He was a thin man with a plain weathered face masked by wire-frame spectacles and further shielded by a plaid woolen hat he always wore tilted down low over his eyes. Despite the increasing heat of the late spring days, he usually had on a tweed jacket with leather elbow patches over his plain gray slacks and blue denim workshirt. He never moved from a position by the gate that led onto the training track, and Geri-Jo noticed that before each horse took its work-out, the rider would stop beside the man and lean down to consult him for a minute or two. When the horse made its first circuit of the track, the man watched intently. From the taut set of his body, Geri-Jo could tell that every bit of his attention was focussed on the moving animal. Occasionally, he hunched across the guardrail, or seemed to reach out to grab a handful of air, and Geri-Jo would feel that he was somehow expressing an energy that came directly from the animal, or was calling on his own energy to send some silent message of encouragement. At last Geri-Jo asked Bard who the man was and what he was telling the riders.

'That's Oakie Whitten, our head trainer.' Whitten, Bard went on, was in charge of educating the horse to race, and bringing out its maximum potential. His instructions to the riders were geared to that aim. 'Don't ask me what they are, though. He could be saying abracadabra for all I know.'

One afternoon, when a training session had just ended, Geri-Jo asked Bard to take her over to Oakie and introduce her.

As they shook hands, the trainer gave her a penetrating look with eyes she could see now were the palest blue. 'I've noticed you hangin' around quite a bit, Geri-Jo,' Oakie Whitten said in a slow resonant drawl. 'Seems you've got a powerful interest in what we're doin' here . . .'

'There's sure a lot I'd like to know,' she answered. 'I'm always trying to figure out what you do. I mean, the winners are born, aren't they, made better? So what's your part . . .?

Oakie smiled. 'Well, you're right: there is a limit to what I can do. But it ain't nothin'. Nobody ever made a bad horse good, but there's things that'll make a good horse run his best. Can't learn it out of books, though. If you want to know the secrets, you'll just have to keep hangin' around and keep your eyes open.'

'I intend to.'

'Think you'd like to make a life in horseracing?'

'I sure like the horses . . . but I don't know if I can approve of the part that has to do with gambling. I mean, maybe these horses have to be run too hard for the sake of people chasing after money.'

Oakie laughed. 'Plenty of folks have that reservation. For my own part, I love every part of the game, training 'em, and betting 'em. Stay with it, Geri-Jo, and you'll come to feel as I do — that a bad day at the races is still better than a good day anywhere else.' He tipped his plaid woolen hat to her, and excused himself to go back to the barns.

She longed to stay with the trainer, watch more of what he did. But when Bard said he wanted to go for a swim, she gave in. She came prepared these days, with a suit of her own.

When she started to descend the steps to the pool, Geri-Jo saw a small party in progress around the pool. In the past, with Bard's parents away, and his sister still at college, she had always been alone with him. But today a bar and buffet was set up, with Little waiting behind it, and two dozen guests were already gathered, some sunning themselves on chaises, some in the water, others eating and drinking around the tables. Seeing a mix of younger and older people, Geri-Jo realized Bard's parents must be there. The thought of confronting them made her so anxious that a sharp cramp tore at her insides, and she turned as if to run back up the steps. But Bard had been holding her hand and he pulled her back.

'What's wrong?'

She couldn't tell him the truth. It was too close to admitting that she didn't feel good enough to be with him. And damn it, why *should* she feel that way. As she straightened up and looked back to the crowd, she swore to get over the idea that anyone could look down on her just because she had been born with less money.

'I . . . tripped on the step,' she told Bard, and forced herself to keep descending to the patio.

'Come meet my folks,' Bard said right away, heading for a table where two couples sat. Geri-Jo picked them out at a glance, from the way they looked her up and down. Bard introduced them as 'my mother and father', and the other couple as a Mr and Mrs Harkins, who owned the farm across the way.

Geri-Jo thought Mrs Mitchell had to be one of the most beautiful women God ever created. She had luxuriant dark brown hair, large golden hazel eyes, and skin as smooth and white as piano keys. Her high cheekbones and a nose that was very slightly upturned, gave a feline quality to her face, the origins of Bard's cat-like eyes. The hand that emerged from the folds of her green silk pool-kimono to shake Geri-Jo's had long tapering fingers, with nails at the end as lustrous as jewels.

'It's so nice you could join us, Geri-Jo,' she said in a low husky voice, and looked across the table to Bard's father. 'Isn't it, Eldon? Isn't it nice that Bard's brought Miss Lockely?'

Geri-Jo noticed another quality now, something she had never encountered. A tilt of the mouth, a lilt in Mrs Mitchell's tone, combined to make it seem as if she might be on the point of breaking into laughter, and that nothing she had said was to be taken seriously. Yet, as long as she didn't reach that point, it was hard to doubt that she was sincere. Listening to her, Geri-Jo felt simultaneously foolish for allowing herself to be mocked, and ashamed for nursing unkind suspicions of someone so lovely.

Eldon Mitchell remained seated, but it was easy to see he was a large man. He had a massive head set on broad shoulders, and long whitish hair that had no doubt once been the same color as Bard's. The wide muscular chest that bulged between the open lapels of his black velour robe was covered with iron gray hair as thick and wiry as chainmail.

'Yes indeed,' he replied to his wife. 'I'm delighted to meet Miss Lockely.' He turned to Geri-Jo. 'So you're the young lady my son likes to impress by racing around on *my* horse. Well, now that I've seen you, I can forgive both of you. Fact is, I'll forgive a pretty girl just about anything — short of riding *me* too hard and fast.' The Harkinses laughed, but Geri-Jo felt Bard tensing beside her.

Gwenn Mitchell jumped in again. 'Bard, push up a chair and I'll get to know your young lady while you go over to the buffet and fill a couple of plates.'

A look of defeat passed across Bard's face as he dutifully seated her beside Gwenn Mitchell and then went to the buffet.

'Tell me, Geri-Jo, how did you and my son meet . . .?'

During the few minutes Bard was at the buffet, Geri-Jo felt her whole life's story being drawn out by Bard's mother. How and why and when she came to Lexington, and where she went to school, and what her father did. Often Gwenn Mitchell reacted to a reply by looking across at her husband and echoing it.

'A gas station,' she said, after Geri-Jo told about her father's work. 'Well, it's always good to have friends in the oil business, isn't it, Eldon? And what work did you have in mind for yourself, Geri-Jo . . .?'

'Since coming here, I've wondered if I might somehow earn a living out of the horses.'

'It certainly has been good to us. Hasn't it, Eldon? Do you

84

think horses might have a place in Geri-Jo's future?' Her tone kept that constant balance between sincerity and camouflaged ridicule.

Though Mr Mitchell was more blunt, Geri-Jo began to like him better. She felt he meant to advise her well when he said, 'Horses are one hell of a tough business, Geri-Jo. It may look pretty, but there are always a lot of heartbreaks. You pour yourself — and your money — into a horse, and more often than not he'll end up going nowhere. Isn't that right, Clem?' He glanced to Mr Harkins, who nodded. 'I'd have to say for someone in your position, Geri-Jo, you probably ought to find something else.'

Bard came back, but Mrs Mitchell didn't tell him to pull up another chair. 'I've had a lovely chat with your young lady,' she said. 'Now, I'm sure, you want to be alone.'

Gwenn Mitchell was finished with her, Geri-Jo realized. She had been judged — not so differently from a horse: her pedigree, her potential. There was no sign that she had been picked as a winner.

Later a tall well-tanned girl came up and introduced herself as Bard's sister, Caroline. Geri-Jo sensed again that the purpose was simply to get close enough for a thorough inspection. Among these people, a poor girl was evidently an oddity, a freak. But Geri-Jo fought against the temptation to retreat, and after a while she felt growing pride in her ability to shrug off their subtle intimidations. After mingling with the Mitchells and their friends, Geri-Jo appreciated Bard more. It took some strength, she realized, for him to bring her into his world.

'Seems like you're the only one who can see it,' she said to him when he was driving her home.

'See what?'

'The look of eagles. I don't get the feeling the rest of your family thinks much of me.'

'My mother said you're always welcome, didn't she?'

Geri-Jo had seen enough of Gwenn Mitchell to know she was not the kind to fight openly with her son. For now, perhaps, she wouldn't mind Bard experimenting with a girl from the wrong side of the tracks; but when she wanted it to end, Bard wouldn't be able to fight her.

Still, he was the one who had opened doors. Whether or not they would stay open, Geri-Jo had seen things that would always be with her, had inspired her to form new ideas and plans. When he pulled up at the place he always let her off, she leaned toward him, and when he kissed her, she gave herself to it completely, letting his hands slide up and down her body, her excitement mounting as he undid the buttons of her blouse and began to caress her breasts, then to kiss them, lightly sucking at her nipples in a way that embarrassed her and hurt very slightly, yet aroused her even more.

'God, you're so beautiful, Geri-Jo,' he moaned. 'I love you.'

Love. Hearing the word thrilled her, and she clung even harder to Bard. Had anyone ever spoken of love before, even Ma or Pa? The feelings might be there, but they were never spoken about.

Suddenly she became aware of Bard's hands moving away from her body and unbuckling his own pants. She drew away sharply, and gathered her blouse around her.

He stared at her. 'What's the matter? Seemed like you wanted me . . .'

'I . . . I think I do,' she stammered. 'But I . . . I want it to be special, I guess. To be sure it's special for you. Otherwise . . .'

'Otherwise what?'

'Maybe you wouldn't want me after . . .'

He eased back and gave her one of his charming smiles. 'Sure, I'll want you. I said I loved you, didn't I? I just can't stand not to let you know it . . . in every way I can . . .' He reached for her again, and she was reminded then of how smooth he was, and how well he had been taught to understand animal desires — he said — by watching the horses.

'I can't . . . stay here any longer, Bard. Pa's gonna wonder where I am . . .'

Bard hesitated a moment, then fastened his pants again, switched on the ignition, and started the engine, revving it up to a roar. 'That's it, then. You better be running home.'

She got out, wounded by his abrupt dismissal. But then she turned back.

'When will I see you again?'

He paused only a second. 'Soon. But let's make sure there's time to be alone together. Maybe you could spend a night at Skyevale . . .'

Before she could answer, he plunged his foot down on the accelerator and the car roared away.

Watching the car vanish around a turn, she wondered how much longer she could go on refusing him before he gave up on her?

As she tried to make sense out of her feelings, Geri-Jo wished she and Molly had a sisterly alliance so they could share secrets, exchange opinions. Many times she had seen Molly at school walking with boys, smiling and flirting with them. Even though she was two years younger, Molly seemed to know how to handle herself. Geri-Jo thought her sister might have some answers for her.

But most of the times they were together, Pa was also there. On the few occasions they were alone, Geri-Jo was too afraid Molly might mock her — say that these tales of being taken up by a rich boy were just empty bragging — or that, if Molly believed her, then she might be bitterly jealous.

It was a relief, therefore, when she entered the trailer this evening and Molly herself raised the subject at a moment when Pa was still out in the garage. She was sitting in the dining niche, one foot propped on the table as she brushed a vermilion polish onto her toenails. It was the first time Geri-Jo had noticed Molly painting the nails on her feet, and she sat down to watch.

'Don't you think you're a little young to be painting yourself up in strange places . . .?' she said after a minute.

Molly's intense blue eyes peered up from under the bangs of her bright red hair. 'If I'm too young for that, then God help me for all the other things I've done. And in strange places, too.'

'What things?'

Molly smiled coyly as she dipped the brush back into the

bottle of polish. 'Oh now, Geri-Jo, you know what a girl's got to do when it's spring and the moon is full . . .'

Geri-Jo stared at her younger sister.

'And don't go playin' dumb,' Molly added. 'I've been hearin' about you and this Mitchell boy, and I'm sure he ain't the kind that would take to you just 'cause he thinks your conversation is so witty and entertainin'.'

'Where'd you hear —?'

'Oh, some boy told me, can't even remember which — I talk to so many when I'm workin' down at the movie house. Sure came as a surprise, though. Never a word from you about it.'

'Well, you know . . . Pa wouldn't like it.'

Molly laughed, tossing her head back. 'Oh, I know that, all right.'

'Then you've got a boyfriend, too?'

Molly's reply was another sly smile.

The sharing of similar secrets sparked the sisterly feeling Geri-Jo had been longing to discover with Molly. 'I don't know what to do, Mol'. I like being with Bard Mitchell. But I'm not sure if I like him enough to . . . to do whatever he wants.'

Molly stopped stroking the brush across the nail of her big toe and looked up in surprise. 'Been holdin' out on him?'

'I don't think of it that way. It just seems to me that I'm not ready for . . . for everything.'

Molly stared another minute, and then she laughed. 'Holy shit, Geri-Jo. You don't know what it's about yet, do ya? Hell, I pity that poor Mitchell boy for meetin' you first. Just let him say he'd like to spend time with me, and I'd show him a good time.' She gave Geri-Jo a sly leer. 'I might just pass the word along that he's been lookin' in the wrong direction . . .'

Stung by Molly's taunt, Geri-Jo couldn't bring herself to answer at all. She glared at her younger sister a moment, but even that was ineffective since Molly had gone back to concentrating on her big toe. The brief blossoming of sisterly feeling was over, perhaps gone forever.

That night Geri-Jo lay awake for a long time thinking about Bard. Unless she gave him whatever he needed to hold out

against the very different wishes of his mother and father —
then it wouldn't be long before she lost her foothold in
paradise. Yet she didn't want to be like Molly, trading feelings
for favors. No matter how much she hungered to save her
access to the horses, she wouldn't let her body be the price of
admission. She didn't want to be sneaking around Pa
anymore, either. Maybe she didn't get near a church anymore,
but she knew there were still rules in the scripture she wanted
to live by. A good life had to be built on truth, not lies.

CHAPTER FIVE

Bard called her at work the next day to ask if she would come out to Skyevale the following afternoon. 'I've planned a special treat,' he said.

She wanted to accept right away, but aware of Alma Hubble sitting nearby, she said, 'I've got to ask Mr Parker if he'll let me off.'

'Oh, he will,' Bard said. 'Especially when he hears my dad's about to buy two new trucks — and I'm recommending Chevvies.'

The remark rekindled Geri-Jo's fear that her own choices were getting lost in too many other people's interests. She resolved to tell Bard when she saw him that as much as she liked him, she wouldn't be rushed into sleeping with him. But on the ride to Skyevale the next day, Bard kept grinning at her, full of secret pleasure at his planned treat, and she couldn't bring herself to say anything that would dampen the mood.

As soon as they arrived at the farm, he hurried her along one of the paths that led toward the stables. Near the building that Bard had once told her was the breeding shed, a big trailer-van was just being backed up near a door at one end, watched by half a dozen stable workers.

'There's a mare coming in to be bred,' Bard explained. 'It's always quite a show. I've seen it a few times myself, but the way you've taken to all this horse nonsense, Geri-Jo, I knew you wouldn't want to miss the fireworks.'

It crossed her mind that he wasn't planning this purely to indulge her curiosity, but as an object lesson. He was right, though: she was eager to see what went into the process.

As they reached the shed, a ramp at the rear of the truck was just being lowered. Inside the padded van a horse stood, steadied by several ropes. A couple of stable hands boarded the truck, untied the horse, and started to lead it down the ramp. Just then it began to buck and rear, and the handlers had to fight to bring it under control before leading it into the shed.

'It's the first time for this mare,' Bard said. 'Makes her a little finicky. She has to be coddled, given a little more time. All females seem to have that in common at the start . . .' He gave her a meaningful glance as he steered her inside.

The interior of the building was not what she had expected. Instead of stalls and hay-covered wood floors in a dim place smelling of grain and manure, it was bright with overhead fluorescent lights. The floor wasn't merely damp earth or cement, but a layer of bluestone chips, and along the walls there were tables covered with instruments and glassware of a kind that reminded Geri-Jo of her school's science labs.

Brought to the center of the open floor, the mare was carefully surrounded by a group of men who threw a large leather blanket over her flanks. As they circled busily around the horse, Bard quietly explained the activities of these men — whom he called the stud crew. The blanket was to keep the mare from being hurt by the stallion's hooves when he mounted her. There were 'hobbles' being put on her rear legs, to prevent the mare from kicking out and causing an injury if she wanted to repel the stallion who would be brought to her. The tail was being wrapped in tape so it would be kept more easily out of the way. And a 'twitch' — a loop of chain attached to a short wooden pole — was being wrapped around the horse's upper lip; tightening the twitch around the sensitive lip by twisting the pole could quickly restrain a horse that might be moving around too much.

For the next hour Geri-Jo remained with Bard in the breeding shed. Though the mating arranged for today was to a stallion named Roman Candle, another horse was brought to the mare first. This animal — called 'a teaser', Bard said — was used to excite the nervous mare so she would be more receptive at the point that the chosen stallion arrived. Teasers were also exposed to mares at other times to test the level of receptivity and thus allow the breeding cycle to be determined. Impregnation did not occur because the teasers were docile animals who could be taken away whenever the handlers wanted.

Finally Roman Candle was brought in. As soon as the powerful-looking coal-black horse appeared, Geri-Jo detected a change in the atmosphere. The men on the stud crew began to move even more slowly and carefully, talking to each other only in soft voices. When the stallion stood away from the mare without showing interest, the stud crew also stood back and watched.

Bard whispered to Geri-Jo. 'Some stallions come right in and "bam", it's done in a minute. The Candle takes his time. Now and then he'll go to a mare right off, but most of them he's got to look over a while, work up some interest . . .'

'Why not just breed him to the ones he likes?'

Bard gave Geri-Jo an incredulous glance. 'You serious, girl? There'd be no breeding business at all if the idea was to run a lover's lane for horses. We're trying to do one thing here — the same thing every time: make the fastest damn racehorse that ever was. Finding horses that *like* each other has nothing to do with making that happen!'

'Then what does?' she asked, intent on learning. 'Why are these two being put together?'

'First off, because the owner of this mare has paid two thousand dollars to my Daddy for a P.T.B. and second —'

'Not so fast. What's a P.T.B.?'

'Privilege to breed. It's a right to bring a mare during each breeding season.' Geri-Jo nodded, and Bard went on. This particular mare had been chosen for this breeding opportunity, because the owner believed that her qualities when combined with a different set of attributes from Roman Candle would produce a horse at least as good as either one, and possibly better than both. 'The Candle is a winner, and built for speed,' Bard said. 'But he's on the small side for a stallion; he had to retire as a three-year-old because he was delicate and had an early injury. Now look at that mare. She's got good bones and more length to her body; she could add strength to the mixture and make a horse with more staying power.'

Geri-Jo gazed at the horses. The stallion didn't look small or delicate to her, the mare didn't look much larger or slower. How long would it take, she wondered, to be able to recognize the distinctions Bard talked about?

He saw her intensely studying the animals. 'Here's the main thing to remember, Geri-Jo,' he said, leaning close and putting an arm around her. 'Breeding like to like isn't necessarily the best way. It can be smart sometimes to take a male who's real fine and sleek, and breed to a female who's . . . sort of the opposite, maybe even a little tough and coarse . . .'

When Bard winked at her, Geri-Jo suddenly understood the deliberate innuendo in his explanation of mixing well-bred males and 'coarse' females. Now she was all the more determined to tell him that she wouldn't let sex be the price of admission to his world. But for the moment she was held by observing the process that was at the very heart of creating a racing stable.

Roman Candle was still standing quietly off to one side. The handlers and men on the stud crew all looked on passively. A long time went by without either horse showing any interest in the other. At last one of the men on the floor walked slowly over to the stallion, and took hold of a leather halter it was wearing. The man stood by the horse, patting its neck, murmuring softly. Like Oakie Whitten, Geri-Jo thought, he seemed to have some inborn affinity with the animals.

'Who's that?' she asked Bard.

'Doc Kimball, one of the vets. He may be able to move things along . . .'

Geri-Jo studied Kimball's face — lean and boney, with dark brown eyes, and curly brown hair cropped short, as if he couldn't be bothered brushing it. To learn more, she might want to find him again, too.

After pacifying the stallion for a minute, the veterinarian led it up behind the mare, and then prompted it to rub its head against the mare's flanks. It did this for a minute, then abruptly the stallion reared to raise its forelegs onto the back of the mare, and moved up behind it.

The mating was over soon. The stallion was led from the breeding shed, back to its own barn.

'That's it,' Bard said, guiding Geri-Jo out of the shed. 'With any luck, Roman Candle just made dear old Dad another two thousand bucks.' He asked her if she wanted to swim or ride, and of course she chose the horses. They walked along a path toward another one of the barns.

'You really get paid two thousand dollars every time one of your stallions breeds with a mare?' Geri-Jo asked.

Bard laughed. 'Not every one, Geri-Jo. We get that for a cover by Roman Candle because he won a lot of races, and he's been a successful stallion — a fair percentage of the horses he's sired have also won some money. But we don't collect unless the mare gets pregnant and delivers a live foal.'

Geri-Jo shook her head. Two thousand dollars earned in a couple of minutes. At thirty-five bucks a week, Pa didn't earn much more in a year of working hard sixteen hours a day.

'What did you call it just now, a cover . . .?'

Bard nodded.

'How many covers will that stallion do in a year?'

'Ten or fifteen every week in a breeding season — that's the six months from the middle of February on — well, you figure it out.'

She did the calculations in her head, and then did them again, sure she'd made a mistake. Was it possible that, in just half a year, the Mitchells were paid more than half a million dollars for the breeding services of just one of their horses?

'It's hard to believe,' she blurted out.

'Well, that's the business,' Bard said.

'I don't mean about the horses. I meant . . . you and me. I can't believe you want me for anything but . . . well, like what you said back in the shed. You think there's some point in putting the fine and fancy together with . . . the coarse.'

94

He stopped on the path. 'Still think that's all I care about, eh? Still think I'm just tryin' to get into your pants?'

'I don't know, Bard. I just keep wondering how long you'll want me around if it can't be on your terms . . .'

He stared at her another few moments. Suddenly, his hand shot out and grabbed hers.

'I know you've got a birthday in a few weeks,' he said, yanking her along the path toward one of the barns, 'and I was going to wait 'til then. But damn, you've got to be taught now, girl, just how much I really care!'

She tried to wrest her hand free. From what he'd said, he was taking her into the barn to attack her. All the warnings she'd heard from Pa and Lettie had been right. But his grip remained tight and firm as he pulled her into the cool recesses of the big airy building.

It was the ponies' barn, Geri-Jo realized. Inside, old Henry was sitting on an overturned metal tub, turning the pages of a tattered magazine by the scant light of a bare overhead bulb.

'Afternoon, Geri-Jo,' he said, rising to his feet.

'Henry,' Bard said. 'I believe you're keeping something here that belongs to Miss Lockely . . .'

At once, the bent old man shuffled away into the shadowy corners at the rear of the barn. A moment later, Geri-Jo heard the *clopping* of a horse being led out of its stall. Then the animal emerged from the shadows, his lustrous dark brown coat catching even the dim light. His only markings were a small white star between his eyes, and white bands directly above the hooves that gave the amusing effect of the horse wearing socks. Geri-Jo stared at the horse as old Henry brought it to a halt.

'Henry told me the old horsemen have a rhyme about a horse like this,' Bard said. 'Let's hear that poem, Henry.'

Peering up from under his battered hat, the old man recited:

 'One white foot, keep him not a day
 Two white feet, give him soon away
 Three white feet, sell him to a friend
 Four white feet, ride him to the end.'

'Sounded to me,' Bard said, 'like he might be just good

enough for you, Geri-Jo. He's just a two-year-old. With his pedigree, he should've gone to last summer's sales at Keeneland, but he got a bowed tendon and that meant he could never be raced. So we kept him . . . and I asked Dad if he could be yours. He'll stay on the farm, but you'll be the only one to ride him. One of the exercise boys has already given him a little saddle training . . .' He broke into a grin. 'Happy birthday, Geri-Jo.'

To be *given* the very thing she most wanted! In her experience, life took away; it did not give. But here it was, the answer to an unspoken wish — a prayer. She threw her arms around Bard and kissed him, then spun away and ran to the horse. Old Henry gave her the reins.

Staring up into the animal's face, Geri-Jo ran her hands over the smooth coat of his neck. 'What's his name?'

'Hasn't got a name yet, that's for you to provide. How about taking him out now?'

While she saddled her own horse, Bard brought out The Ghost. Henry looked on, but he had been put down too often to protest again. Geri-Jo thought twice about doing it herself, but at last she had to remind Bard that he was risking his father's wrath. She recalled that Eldon Mitchell seemed to hold her partly responsible for Bard's violation of the rule against using his personal mount.

'He thinks you do it to impress me, Bard — that's what he said. He forgave it once, but next time he's going to be almightily ticked, and then he might —'

'Damn it, Geri-Jo!' Bard erupted. 'Don't you start nagging at me like everybody else. If I was going to do everything the way my folks told me, you wouldn't even be here.'

The reminder stunned her to silence.

Bard made no apology, but her hurt and anger were forgotten as soon as she was mounted on the back of her horse, and Bard was riding beside her, cantering with her away from the stable area and out into the rolling pastures of Skyevale. He really did care about her, she thought, he wanted her dreams to come true. She could forgive him anything. 'Dream,' she said finally, 'I'm going to name him Dream. Is that all right?' She was just slowing to a trot after taking the horse for the first time at a full gallop, racing against Bard. The motion had been so fluid that staying in the saddle seemed no harder to her than sitting in a chair.

'Call him anything you want,' Bard said. 'He's yours . . .'

It seemed to Geri-Jo that they traveled for many miles, sometimes walking the horses, or trotting, sometimes racing at full gallop. It was all part of Skyevale, Bard said. Beyond the many fenced pastures of cropped grass, there were vast meadows of unmown hay, and patches of forest that grew up the sides of hills. At one point, they rode into a large field where dozens of felled trees lay scattered about, and the ground was pocked with deep holes where stumps had been pulled up. A new pasture was being created, Bard explained, Skyevale Farms was expanding.

'Take it slow through here,' he warned. 'If Dream puts a leg into one of these holes, that could be the end of him.'

At the farthest edge of the property, the dividing line was marked by a rushing stream with willows growing along the edge.

'This is a good spot to rest and water the horses,' Bard said. He dismounted and led his horse to the edge of the stream.

As Geri-Jo got off her horse, she saw Bard walk to one of the biggest willows, and pull a picnic basket from behind it. Obviously, he had planned the ride earlier, and cached a picnic. Kneeling to open the basket, he removed a large red-and-white checkered cloth which he spread on a shady patch of ground near the stream. Then he brought out a couple of glasses, a thermos, and packages of food that he unwrapped.

'People need to cool off, too,' he said.

She led her horse to drink, then looped the reins over a willow branch as Bard had done, and finally sat down by the cloth. As she eyed the rushing water nearby, an image flashed through her mind of that day when the rain had poured down into the hollow . . . but at last the pain was balanced by evidence that God was doing something to make it up to her.

Bard had poured some golden liquid from the thermos into a

glass and was holding it out to her. 'What shall we drink to?' he said, as he poured a glass for himself.

She shrugged, unfamiliar with the custom.

'Don't you have a wish?' he asked.

'I had one,' she glanced at the horse. 'It came true.'

'Is that all — just one?'

'A couple more, maybe.' She was shy about admitting it, afraid somehow she might be punished for wanting too much. She remembered Abel Miller denouncing her father for being dissatisfied with his lot.

'Well, this is another way of making a wish. Say what you want — whatever you want most — and take a sip of wine.'

She held the glass out in front of her. 'This is wine?' The only alcohol she had ever tasted was the corn liquor made by the moonshiners near the hollow; sometimes, when she was sick, Ma would give her a spoonful to help her sleep.

'Got to be wine for this purpose, Geri-Jo. C'mon, what else do you want . . ?'

'Oh golly,' she burst out, 'I guess . . . I want to hear Pa laugh.'

'All right then — to hearing your Pa laugh.' He leaned over to clink his glass lightly against hers, and then drank down all the wine in one swallow. Geri-Jo watched and did the same. She liked the taste of the golden liquid, fruity and tangy, and the fresh chill that took all the dryness from the back of her throat.

Bard refilled their glasses and held his aloft. 'Now, I want to make a wish: To you and me, Geri-Jo — to being together for a long time.' The crystal rang as one glass clinked against the other.

If it could only happen just from drinking a glass of wine, Geri-Jo thought, as she drank until her glass was empty.

'Any more wishes?' Bard said, pouring more.

The wine didn't burn at all the way corn liquor did. It went down so easy, she was sure she could drink a lot of it. 'Well, I've got a horse to ride,' she said, 'but I suppose I'd like to have one to race someday — a horse that wins.'

'To Geri-Jo owning a winner,' Bard said.

As she lowered her empty glass this time, there was a sudden rush of heat through her body, and in the next second an odd hollow feeling, as thought the center of her had fallen out like an apple losing its core. It was an uncomfortable sensation, but it lasted only a moment and was replaced by a lovely illusion — that she was floating very slightly above the ground. The things she had been worried about for days, weeks, years, seemed smaller, farther away — part of that heavy core that had fallen out. She didn't worry about what Bard wanted from her, or what Pa wanted to deny her.

Was this all part of being rich, too — these magical floating feelings, this freedom from worry? How many more new wonders would there be if she and Bard could stay together.

'Lie back, Geri-Jo,' he said.

Lying down was just what she wanted to do, and when he stretched out beside her and kissed her, she realized that this, too, was exactly what she wanted. It was Pa that made her feel bad about it, only Pa. But he wasn't anywhere near this cloud that was ascending higher and higher. The kisses traveled from her mouth, along her neck. Then Bard opened her shirt, and kissed her breasts and her stomach. He unbuttoned her jeans, and pulled them lower, and kissed her thighs. She kept her eyes closed, enjoying the light tickling sensation of his lips and breath on her skin. She missed it when he stopped for a few moments, but then she felt him over her again, the warm bare skin of his chest and stomach and legs touching hers. When he put his hand between her thighs and pushed them wider apart, she groaned with pleasure, wanting him now, believing that it was right, that he loved her as no one else ever had or would, that as young as they were they would stay together. That she would be his wife someday. Her arms encircled him, pulling him closer.

All at once he thrust down into her, and a bolt of pain shot up from her belly. She cried out, and tightened her arms as though it would keep her from falling into a fire that would destroy her, and just a second later the pain was gone. There was only wave after wave of pleasure as he rose and fell over her, sliding in and out and then again deeper into her. She wanted him to go on and on . . .

But soon she felt him shudder and then he pulled back and rolled off to one side.

Without him inside her, with the abrupt end of the incessant thrill, she felt strangely empty and alone. The cloud on which she'd been floating seemed to fall to earth with a bump, and suddenly she was filled with regret for having given herself to him. Tears came to her eyes, and she turned away so that he wouldn't see them, oddly thinking that her sorrow was too private to be shared with the same person who had just taken her virginity.

'There now,' Bard said quietly. 'Easier than you thought, wasn't it? It'll be even better when you can spend a whole night with me . . .'

She sat up and dressed herself, unable to tell him that she was ashamed and filled with regret. But at first he took no notice. He dressed himself, too, and started to gather up the picnic things. Finally, he looked over at her. 'You okay . . .?'

She stood up. 'I was wrong to do that, Bard,' she said. 'I . . . I love you, I think . . . but we weren't ready . . .'

He gave a short hooting laugh. 'Hell, if we weren't ready then nothing would have happened. It's just natural, Geri-Jo. You should've learned that from what we saw before . . .'

'Darn you, Bard,' she sputtered, infuriated by the reminder that there had been an ulterior motive in his visit to the breeding shed. 'This isn't a matter of someone paying for a . . . a P.T.B. This is about something only *people* can feel — love.'

'I told you I love you,' he said plainly.

'Then you should care about how I feel.'

'And you don't want to see me anymore . . .?'

'I didn't say that! But I . . . we can't do this again. Not for a while. I need more time.'

'Time for what?'

'To believe that everything you've given me is real — that it's all not going to vanish . . .'

'Why should it?'

'I don't know, Bard. I'm just afraid that nothing lasts. It's been that way in my life . . .'

He gazed at her a moment, and she thought that he had

100

understood. But then she saw the flame in his eyes, getting hotter. Suddenly, he whirled away and began gathering the picnic things, tossing them into the basket helter-skelter. When at last, he threw the wine bottle in on top of the glasses, Geri-Jo heard the crystal shatter. Cursing under his breath, Bard slammed the top down on the basket, and then on a sudden furious impulse he hurled the whole thing into the stream. Silver knives and forks, left-over food, everything went riding away on the current. Geri-Jo stared after it until it sank, her memory swirling with images of other objects being taken by water. Then she became aware of Bard untethering The Ghost. She hurried after him.

'Bard, I told you I care —'

'Then what the hell is so strange about showing me?' He pulled the reins of The Ghost loose, then turned on her. 'And don't give me any of that shit about how your father's brought you and your sister up to be so damn pure. You think I haven't heard about all the guys *she* takes on in the back row of the theatre . . .?' He swung himself up into the saddle.

His callousness brought tears to her eyes again. 'I can't help that,' she said, 'but it's not the way I am.'

He smiled down at her thinly, but there was no forgiveness in it. Suddenly he snapped out a gruff command. 'Mount up, Geri-Jo . . .'

'We don't have to go,' she said, a last plea for a chance to reach an understanding.

'Get on the damn horse!' he shouted, his frustration boiling over. 'We're gonna have a race.'

She shook her head, unable for a moment to follow the leap Bard had made from their argument to this challenge. But then she realized it was all the same to him. He needed a total conquest — of one kind or another, it made no difference.

'Can't have everything on your terms,' Bard went on, 'got to learn that. So I'm not going to let you keep that horse — not unless you win him. We'll race back to the stables. Get there first, and we'll go on together, on your terms . . .'

'And if you win?'

'You can keep the horse,' he said. 'But only on my terms.'

She wanted to refuse, to reject the idea as absurd and pointless. But looking at Bard, his eyes burning and his face flushed, she knew that nothing would dissuade him. And she couldn't bring herself to renounce all the treasures he offered. Not just the horse. Some belief in herself, some hope for the future — so newly discovered — also seemed to be rooted completely in this world of privilege. If she was banished, she would lose it all.

She untethered her horse. 'Hold still, Dream,' she said as she mounted, using the name for the first time. As she settled into the saddle, Bard began to peal off a nasal announcement, mimicking the voice that might be heard coming through the loudspeaker at a racetrack. 'The horses are in the gate . . . they're under starter's orders . . .' He paused to give her a challenging glance. 'And they're off!' he cried, sending The Ghost into a gallop with a switch of the reins. For another fraction of a second she waited, unwilling to play his game. But then, by reflex more than thought, she kicked her legs into the side of her horse and sent him plunging toward the horizon. She stayed low, standing slightly in the stirrups, and felt herself fall into the rhythm of the horse. The Ghost pounded ahead of her at tremendous speed, but soon the gap narrowed.

And then she saw something ahead of the gray horse that sparked a reflex to pull back on the reins. Beyond a dip at the end of the broad field of hay they were traversing now, lay the span of felled trees and uprooted stumps where a future pasture was being prepared. Bard was galloping straight for it, but Geri-Jo didn't see how any horse could race safely across so much rutted ground.

'Bard!' she screamed. 'Stop! You can't make it through —'

When he looked back over his shoulder, she thought he might have heard her. But he gave his horse another lash with the reins, and plummeted ahead even faster, down the dip and into the field of stumpholes and toppled trees.

She went right up to the edge before reining in sharply. 'Bard! Stop, for God's sake! You'll kill yourself . . .!' But he was already more than halfway across, deftly threading a path between the obstacles. He'd make it; after all, she guessed, he had planned his dangerous route knowing it guaranteed him victory —

The squealing neigh that rose suddenly from across the field was awful, an injured animal's scream of pain and terror. In the distant whirl of movement as Bard's horse went down, Geri-Jo could see him being thrown high into the air and tumbling down out of view behind a log. Impulsively, she spurred her horse to rush to Bard's aid, then pulled back sharply on the reins, slowing the horse to a walk to avoid a similar accident . . .

The horse was thrashing on its side when she reached it, legs wildly pedalling the air. It was still making pitiful sounds, throaty rumbles, mixed with high-pitched whines and wheezes. The Ghost had been brought down, Geri-Jo saw, by putting his foot into the deep stumphole not far from where he had fallen. But where was Bard? Jumping to the ground, she began to dart from one fallen tree to the other. 'Bard? Talk to me, for God's sake . . .!'

He heaved into view, obviously dazed. There was mud on his face and in his hair, and his clothes were dirty and torn. Still, he looked better than Geri-Jo had imagined possible, no blood on him anywhere.

'Thank God!' she gasped. 'I was thinking you might be dead.'

Wordlessly, he pulled himself slowly over the fallen tree and, moving with a slight limp, headed for The Ghost.

She caught up with him. 'God damn . . .' she heard him saying between gulps of air. 'God damn . . .' Then she realized his words weren't being punctuated by gulps, but sobs. Shuffling up to the horse, he knelt down.

'What can I do to help?' Geri-Jo said.

He remained oblivious, so she stepped back, waiting to be told.

All at once, he leapt up and grabbed the reins of her horse. 'Wait here. I'll ride to the stables for help.'

When she argued that it would be better if he rested and she went, he wouldn't listen. He could get it done faster, he knew exactly where to get what was needed. 'If you want to help,' he said as he mounted the brown colt, 'see what you can do to keep that animal quiet.' He started away, riding not much slower than before.

The Ghost was no longer neighing so loudly, but it was still writhing on the ground, flailing its legs in what appeared to be futile efforts to rise again. Remembering the black groom she had seen washing a horse, crooning to keep him still, Geri-Jo began a stream of soft chatter. In a minute, she had the horse's head cradled in her lap. As she stroked its neck, the animal subsided into labored breathing and stopped flailing.

She had no idea how much time passed before she heard hoofbeats and turned to see only one horse coming toward her over the brow of the nearest hill. Bard had brought no help at all!

It wasn't until he rode up that she saw the shotgun lashed to the back of his saddle. 'What's that for?'

The pain of his bruises was apparent as he dismounted gingerly, and began to untie the gun. 'The horse has a broken leg,' he said quietly.

She hadn't realized before the kind of injury the animal had sustained, and she didn't know enough about horses to know it couldn't be made whole again. 'Nobody's even looked at him yet, Bard. Doc Kimball, that vet, shouldn't you bring him out here first?'

'No, I . . . I can't do that.' He finished removing the gun, but stood with it in his hands, not moving toward The Ghost. 'Doesn't matter, anyway. This is the only thing to do.'

'Without having him checked,' Geri-Jo insisted, 'you can't —'

'You don't know about this!' Bard roared. 'So just shut the hell up. Horse breaks his leg, it's got to be shot. There's no choice. No damn —' His voice broke, and he just shook his head. Then he tore away from Geri-Jo and moved toward The Ghost.

She watched mutely as he cracked the barrel of the gun, and took a shell from his pocket. When his hand came up it quaked so badly that he had difficulty jiggling the shell into the barrel,

104

but at last he managed. He appeared so exhausted by the small feat, though, that it was a moment before he snapped barrel and stock together again. Watching his shaking hands, Geri-Jo feared the gun might go off accidentally at any second. She took a step toward him, intending to help, but he spun away and went to The Ghost, positioning himself by the horse's head. Planting his feet, he lifted the barrel, trying to point it at the narrow bridge between the animal's eyes. But his hands wavered, his aim sliding from side to side.

'I can't do it,' he wailed at last. 'God damn . . . it's *his* horse, see . . . he'll never let me forget it . . . never . . .'

She understood then. Bard's collapse was all tangled up with feelings about his father. To ride the animal was to prove himself as much a man; to fall with it — to the point of having to destroy it — was the ultimate failure.

He gave Geri-Jo a beseeching look. 'Be easier maybe,' he said, 'if I shot myself . . .'

She ran forward and grabbed the weapon out of his shaking hands. Having seen his aborted efforts, she had no doubt about what she had to do. She placed the muzzle of the gun to the boney forehead between the eyes, and her finger curled around the trigger.

She hesitated a second. What penalty would she pay for killing the animal? she wondered. Or would Bard defend her against his father's fury?

He loved her, he said. He wanted to marry her someday.

The horse whined pitifully and Geri-Jo fired the gun.

CHAPTER SIX

When a few days went by and there was no contact from Bard, she told herself it was understandable. Of course, they had to let a little time pass. Bard had warned Geri-Jo that it would take his father a while to forgive the death of his favorite horse.

Right after the shooting, he had brought her back to the stables, riding behind him on Dream. Though her clothes and hands were spattered with blood, Bard had hurried her straight to his car, insisting that they didn't want to arouse any curiosity around the farm. On the drive home, he said he would take care of everything, explain the accident to the stables foreman, arrange to have the animal's corpse removed from the field, and then figure out how to deal with his father.

'Maybe it'd be easier if I talk to him myself,' Geri-Jo had said. 'Seems only right. I'm the one who did the shooting —'

'And I'm the one who rode that horse into the ground. No, I've got to set things straight first, or they'll never let you get near Skyevale again.' When he left her at the usual place, he told her again to be patient. They made no plans for their next meeting.

Two weeks passed before she realized at last that it was over. The Mitchells had probably forbidden Bard to see her again, and he no longer had the will to fight them. Or had she really lost him because she refused to go on sleeping with him?

Hurt as she was, the rejection didn't really surprise her. She hadn't expected her happiness to last, after all.

As her life returned to its monotonous routine, the hours she had spent at Skyevale became ever more brilliant in memory — a flash of lightning that had illuminated a rainy night. Sitting on the step of the gas station's dingy office hut, passing the hours waiting for another car to drive in, she daydreamed ceaselessly about that brief hour when she had owned a horse named Dream. She knew there was no hope of reclaiming it now.

Pa showed no awareness that anything had changed for her. Of course, he had never known about her idyllic days in another world; even on the evening she had returned with the horse's blood staining her clothes she had been able to get into the trailer and wash without him becoming any the wiser. But the loss of everything else that had given her a taste of happiness made Geri-Jo grieve all the more at his cold silences. Awaking once in a cold sweat from a nightmare in which she saw the head of a horse exploding, blood thick as rain falling around her, she went to the door of Pa's compartment and stood for a long time, desperately wishing she had a father she could wake for solace.

Molly, too, had moved even farther out of reach. She went to work each day at the laundromat, and at night she had a new job waitressing at a drive-in hamburger stand a mile up the road. She brought home more money, which made Pa willing to let her stay out later hours, though he kept the same close watch he always had on Geri-Jo.

In the absence of any other source of sympathy, she responded more to Lettie Parker's desire to mother her. She didn't lean on Lettie, yet she felt more vulnerable to her advice.

'What happened with that Mitchell boy?' Lettie asked on the first Tuesday Geri-Jo resumed spending afternoons with her.

'Didn't amount to anything,' Geri-Jo said simply. She didn't want to relive again the story of how it had ended.

'I might have known,' Lettie sighed. She was washing Geri-Jo's hair, always a time she liked to gossip or spout opinions. 'I prayed so hard it would be good for you, Geri-Jo. But I knew it couldn't work out. People like the Mitchells, they don't really make room for anyone a step down. Even my Ed, with all he's accomplished, he's still a common working man far as all these blue-grass bluebloods are concerned. Mind me, this experience with the Mitchell boy should be a lesson for you. Don't overreach. Ed and I can help you up some — we can work on your manners and your speech and your dress — but there are limits. Folks like us can climb so high and no higher . . .'

It was curious, she thought, that on the surface the Parkers could seem to be so different from her father, and yet when it came to the most crucial idea of all they were just the same. For a long time, she had refused to accept the impossibility of escaping from the patterns into which you were born. But hearing the hopeless message repeated over and over from all sides, she began to think it was time to surrender.

Returning home from Lettie's that Tuesday, Geri-Jo saw the gas station closed, the garage door pulled down. As she walked around to the trailer, she noticed the tow-truck parked beside it. Now she was worried. The only time Pa ever closed early was when he went out on a tow or to get a part, and then the truck wouldn't be here. She stepped warily into the trailer, sensing that something must be wrong. 'Pa . . .'

There was no answer, but she knew he was here. On the table she'd left clean this morning, an empty tumbler sat in a pool of spilled amber liquid. She hadn't seen the signs of heavy drinking since the few days after they'd put Caybie into the state home. What had set him off this time? When she looked into his sleeping compartment he was sitting on the one small chair beside the bed, head bowed. The shades were pulled down over the small windows.

'Pa . . . what's wrong?'

'Thought I could count on you,' he said without looking up. 'Nobody else was worth a good goddamn, but you were special, that's what I thought. You'd be the one who never turned from me, always played straight.' He speared her with a furious gaze. 'Now I hear you were lyin' to me all along . . .'

Molly had told him about Bard, she guessed. Out of

108

jealousy, no doubt, not knowing there was no longer any reason to envy her. 'I wanted to tell you, Pa. There's so much I've wished I —'

'Don't need to tell me nothin' now,' he broke in. 'I heard it all. How you been trashin' yourself, playin' me for a fool right along.'

'No, Pa, it wasn't that way at all —'

'Don't give me your shit, Jo!' he shouted, lurching up out of his chair.

That name again. Remembering the other times he'd used it, she took it as a warning. Her pulse began to race as she took a quick step backward.

But the hint of escape only inflamed him, made him rave on. As he came at her, his face twisted with anger, he seemed to be a stranger. She saw the scars across his cheek left from the terrible beating the Millers had given him, but she couldn't take them as reassuring marks of identification. They only reminded her of all the bad things that had happened in the hollow, all the things that had damaged his mind and soul so that he might be capable of anything. 'Think I don't know exactly what's been goin' on behind my back?' he screamed. 'That Hubble woman told me ever'thin', said I had a right to know . . .'

So it hadn't been Molly . . . but that jealous, vicious *Alma*! Then he hadn't even heard the truth, only a version of things that had been whipped up out of the spinster's spite and envy. 'Listen, Pa, please! You've got to give me a chance to —'

'Chance!' he bellowed, seizing her roughly. 'Chance to trick me! Chance to go away and fuck that candy-ass rich boy! Goddamn, Jo, if that's what you want, there's no need goin' to him.' His grip loosened, and he pulled her closer, put his arms around her, and began to murmur. 'Oh, baby, I wanted to save you, protect you, you were all I ever really loved. Didn't you know that, Jo?' He was grinding his body against hers.

'No, Pa, no,' she cried. 'It isn't right . . .'

He thrust her out in front of him, and growled. 'You gonna tell me what's right, eh? While you lie and open your legs for him because he comes from the power around here and I'm nothin'? Well, you gotta be taught. I ain't *nothin'*! I got all kinds of love, good as anyone . . .'

Keeping a hold on her with one hand, he used the other to unfasten his belt and started pulling his trousers down.

'Pa!' she shrieked. 'Stop it, Pa! For God's sakes . . .!' She flailed her fists to keep him away, and the edge of her hand caught him on the cheek. For a second he pulled back, startled. She used the moment to dart out of his grasp, and scramble quickly out of his compartment, into the small bathroom. He raced after her, but she had time to slam the door and lock it just ahead of him.

He was too insanely enraged, though, to be stopped by any barrier. Geri-Jo cowered within as he started pummeling the door, and one of his fists smashed through the thin partition. 'Please Pa,' she wailed. 'I'm beggin' ya! Think of what you're doin'.'

'If it's what I got to do to keep ya, Jo,' his voice came back, 'then I don't care if I go to hell . . .'

She looked at the small bathroom window wondering if she could possibly escape through it. Then the door crashed in off its hinges. When he grabbed for her, and started tearing at her clothes, she made a blind reach for the bathroom shelf and her hand closed around a bottle of mouthwash. She swung, and as it connected with his temple, he froze. For a second, Geri-Jo thought he had been jolted out of his crazed pursuit. But suddenly he retaliated, bringing his fist around into her cheek. She reeled back, overcome with dizziness, and he started tearing at her clothes.

Once more she screamed, and the shrill siren of her own voice cut through the dizziness, rousing her again to a defense. With all her strength she levered her arms between their two bodies, and thrust him backward with such force that he reeled through the open door of the bathroom. Already unsteady from the alcohol, he tumbled to the floor. Geri-Jo darted through the unguarded door, jumped over her father's sprawled form, and went running from the trailer.

She didn't stop until she had reached the road. There she looked back and saw that he hadn't chased her. She staggered a few steps down the road, then stopped, uncertain of her next move. Pa had come out of these fits before. Perhaps he was hurt, needed her help . . .

But she was too afraid to go back. She kept walking along the shoulder of the road, not certain where she was going, not even sure of her direction. To Lettie's, maybe, though then there would have to be explanations. And what would happen if she ever told anyone what Pa had done? Would one of those prim ladies from a state agency arrive and recommend that Geri-Jo and Molly be sent someplace they could be 'better looked after' as Caybie had been?

She didn't want Pa to get into trouble, and she didn't want what was left of the Lockelys to be split up any more. That must never happen. She and Molly and Pa were all that were left. They had to stay together, no matter what. If they didn't, that would really be the final death of their family.

CHAPTER SEVEN

As she slogged aimlessly along the side of the road, dozens of cars passed by, passengers turning occasionally to peer through a window at her torn clothes and tear-streaked face. Several times a driver slowed as if to offer help, but she waved each of them on, unwilling to answer any questions.

Then a battered station wagon heading in the other direction circled around to drive up beside her and stop just ahead on the grass verge. Geri-Jo gestured the driver to leave her alone, but a man got out of the car. 'Geri-Jo, isn't it?' he asked, hurrying toward her.

She recognized the veterinarian Bard had pointed out that day in the breeding shed — 'Doc' Kimball. As he came within a step, she stared at him wordlessly, afraid to give Pa away by anything she might say, yet grateful for the compassionate look she saw on his face.

'My God,' he said, 'what's happened . . .'

Suddenly a wave of relief swept through her, turning everything in her body that had been tense and stiff — holding her on her feet, keeping her going — into water. She started to fall, and the vet leapt forward to catch her. Supporting her in his arms, he walked her to his car and settled her in the passenger seat.

'What happened, Geri-Jo?' he asked again, as he touched a finger very gently to the bruise on her face, the kind of exploratory probe a real doctor would make.

She rolled her face away, too ashamed and afraid to answer. Kimball lingered another moment by her side, then closed the door on the passenger side and came back around to the driver's side.

When Geri-Jo heard the engine start, the pool of relief in which she'd been wallowing went suddenly dry. 'Where're you taking me?'

'You've been attacked, obviously. I want to get you some medical attention. And then the police ought to be —'

'No!' she cried. 'I can't do that, can't tell anyone.'

'Geri-Jo, you need to have —'

'No!' she screamed again, her hand going to the door handle.

His hand shot out to hold the door closed. 'Okay, okay, we'll do whatever you want. But don't decide yet. The important thing now is to give you a little tending to, and a chance to relax. Okay?'

Geri-Jo looked closely at him, his face etched by an expression of concern. 'No police or anything . . .?'

He nodded agreement. 'I could take you to my place,' he said. 'Unless you'd rather go home . . .'

'No,' she said, making an effort not to let him hear her alarm. 'I . . . I don't want my Pa to see me this way . . .

'All right. You'll come with me . . .'

She swept her eyes over him once more, gathering in every hint of whether or not she could feel safe with him. She liked his face. He looked something like that old movie star who was always playing shy, decent men — Gary Cooper, wasn't that the name? — except that Kimball's brown hair was very curly, just going to gray. He was in his late thirties or early forties, she guessed, and every year showed. His warm brown eyes somehow conveyed a sadness, a hint of some unshakeable tragedy in his own past, that made Geri-Jo feel an automatic kinship. The air of poignancy was accentuated by his rumpled seersucker suit, although the reassuring style of an old-fashioned gentleman remained in the blue polka-dotted bow tie worn at the neck of a plain white shirt with a threadbare collar. Geri-Jo supposed that Kimball must earn a good living — being involved with the Mitchells, who made millions —

but he didn't show any outward signs of affluence in either his clothes or his old Ford station wagon. He could be trusted, she decided. As he turned the car around, headed again in the direction he'd been going before he stopped, she leaned back in the seat and didn't even look out the window. After a little while, he spoke again.

'Feeling better?'

'Yes, thanks. Lucky you came along, Doc . . .'

'I was on my way home after delivering a foal.'

'Out at Skyevale?' The regret for lost chances tinged her voice.

'No, I work other places, too.' There was a pause. 'You're interested in the horses, aren't you? That day you were in the breeding shed, the way you watched everything that went on. I got the idea that you were keen to learn . . .'

'You could tell that?'

'When the sightseers come to a breeding, they get embarrassed by the whole thing. The men make wisecracks, the women blush and giggle. You were different, watching almost like an old hand — all business — studying everything, asking Bard questions.'

She was pleased that he had realized the truth. 'Bard brought me there just because he thought it'd get me . . . warmed up.'

He glanced over at her, his eyes narrowing with speculation. 'Was it Bard who attacked you?' he said, looking back to the road.

'No,' she said quickly.

'You shouldn't protect him if it was, Geri-Jo. He's been in trouble before, you know. Bard's a kid who thinks he should have everything his way . . .'

She didn't know what to say. It would be so easy to go along with the vet's mistake, let Bard take the blame. Hurt at the way he had cast her off, she wanted to wound him, too. And she wanted to protect her father. He hadn't meant to hurt her, she knew; it was part of the craziness that came from his being hurt so badly himself.

She couldn't tell such a lie, though; she could see the chain

114

of complications that would follow. Yet if she planted some doubt in Kimball's mind then maybe Pa could be kept safe, too.

'Look, Doc, you were kind to stop and help me, I really appreciate that. But you said I could handle this my way. So don't ask me about it, please. It's over, and it's my business. If you're going to keep at me about it, then you'd better let me out right here.'

He gave her a smile, a small one that didn't dim the sadness in his eyes. 'Lie back again, Geri-Jo,' he said. 'I won't ask any more questions.'

They drove on a few more miles and then turned onto a dirt road. Silhouetted against the candy-striped sky of sunset, Geri-Jo saw a series of small shacks on either side, laundry hanging from clothes lines, here and there a yard littered with old lumber or a washing machine or a bathtub. Some of the windows glowed with lamplight, and Geri-Jo heard a baby crying, the *clack* of a screen door slamming. A woman's voice rose into the still evening air summoning a child home for dinner. Enough of an accent came through the few words for Geri-Jo to tell the woman was black.

The vet had brought her to one of the backwoods shantytowns where black folks lived, she realized, and for a moment she reviewed her decision to trust him. Why would he bring her here?

The road dead-ended at a grassy strip beyond which stood a small white house. It could have been called a shack, too, except that, unlike the others, its paint wasn't peeling, the porch didn't sag, the roof had all its shingles in place and there were no broken panes in the windows. The yard was clean and neatly mown, and planted near the house were beds of flowers. The evening air brought out the sweet fragrance of the petunias.

'Here we are,' Kimball said, as he shut off the engine and opened his door.

She looked after him in amazement as he walked toward the house. Hadn't he said he was taking her to his home? But *he* couldn't live here, in this neighborhood. Warily, she followed him. Inside it was dark, but Geri-Jo could see the front room they had entered was clean and nicely furnished.

'Chel?' Steve Kimball called loudly as soon as he'd closed the front door behind him. 'Chel, you home?' I need you out here . . .!' He turned to Geri-Jo. 'She's a nurse,' he explained. 'Worked the graveyard shift last night, so she'll be taking a nap . . .'

That explained it. He knew a black nurse, so he'd brought her here to get the treatment he had said she needed. They went through to a rear kitchen where he turned on the light. Copper pots hung from a rack over the stove, and the dark wood table in the center of the room was oiled to a satin finish. Kimball opened a cabinet and took out a pot.

'Soon as Chel's up, we'll get you clean, with something warm to wear. Meantime, I'll start on something to warm your insides. Like some soup? Or would you rather have oatmeal and some eggs . . ?'

'Anything at all,' Geri-Jo murmured. Watching him pour milk into the pot she became aware of how hungry she was.

He was crossing to a cupboard when he paused abruptly and looked past Geri-Jo. 'Sorry to break into your rest, babe,' he said, 'but we've got a situation here that could really use a woman's touch.'

Geri-Jo spun around. In the doorway stood a tall black woman in her mid-twenties drowsily buttoning on a man's white shirt. The plain white of the shirt contrasted so sharply with the black of the woman's skin that it seemed to produce a glare beyond which Geri-Jo could discern no detail.

Moving to the door, Steve put an arm around the young woman and gave her a kiss, quick, but lingering just long enough to convey the electricity passing between them. Now Geri-Jo understood that this was where *he* lived, too.

'Geri-Jo,' the vet said, 'this is Rachel Dennison.'

'How 'do, Ma'am,' Geri-Jo said politely. She couldn't help staring. She had never seen black and white together this way. She'd heard rumors about it, of course, and she knew that there'd been black women in the cathouses white men visited in the mountain towns near the hollow. But this was different;

this was seeing for a fact that a white man lived with a black woman, a good-looking white man who spent time among the best people and earned enough money to have any kind of woman he wanted. Seeing the vet in front of her with his arm around this black woman, Geri-Jo felt every idea in her head about men and women and sex, and even about laws and the little she knew about politics, turning topsy-turvy.

Rachel gave her a sympathetic smile, as if she understood how strange and uncomfortable Geri-Jo was feeling. 'Hi, Geri-Jo.'

'Found her on the road this way,' Steve explained. 'It'd be good if you take her and —'

'You think you need to tell me, Doc?' Her voice was sweet and clear. She moved to Geri-Jo and put an arm around her shoulder. 'Just leave us two women alone while you get back to your man's work — at the stove! We'll want a good meal on the table soon as we return.' She guided Geri-Jo out of the kitchen.

Kimball laughed, and called after them, 'Yes, Ma'am!' It was a revelation to Geri-Jo that a black woman could talk so boldly to a white man — and that any man and woman could live together and still sound as if they had fun. But more astonishing than anything was the vet being with this woman. Poor as they had been in the hollow, Geri-Jo had been brought up to believe they'd always be better off than the blacks.

The bathroom was as clean and nice as everything else in the house. Chel ran hot water into the tub, adding epsom salts and something that made the surface mount up with white bubbles. While the tub was filling, there was a knock on the door. She stepped outside, and Geri-Jo heard the low hum of conversation from the other side of the door. In a minute Chel returned. She gave Geri-Jo two aspirin, and then poured some clear liquid onto a piece of cotton and dabbed at the bruise on her face where Pa had punched her.

When Geri-Jo was immersed in the foam, Chel knelt by the tub, and rolled up her sleeves. With a natural sponge as big as the ones the grooms used on the horses, she washed Geri-Jo's bruised body. Circling the sponge lightly over Geri-Jo's back, she began to hum softly. As the bath soothed her body, the sweetness of the black woman's voice seemed to wash the bad memories out of Geri-Jo's mind.

Chel began to speak in short bursts. 'Steve's mentioned you a couple of times since he noticed you around the farm. He was a little worried about you being tied up with that Mitchell boy.'

At the mention of Bard, Geri-Jo guessed that the reason Steve Kimball had summoned Chel out of the bathroom was to report his suspicions. She ought to correct the mistake, Geri-Jo thought, but again she worried that suspicion would then shift to Pa.

'Geri-Jo,' Chel said when she finished with the sponge. 'I understand you don't want to talk about what happened . . . but I can help you best if I know one thing. Whoever was responsible for this . . . did he penetrate?'

'Ma'am?'

'Were you raped? Did a man force himself inside you . . . and come to orgasm?'

Timid about hearing the words, much less saying them, Geri-Jo couldn't bring herself to answer. Remembering what had happened was painful enough, talking about it would be even worse.

Chel continued to coax softly. 'Geri-Jo, I'm a nurse at one of the local hospitals; I know how to help you. But you've got to tell me what was done . . .' Gently, she put a hand to Geri-Jo's face and turned it around so they were looking directly at each other.

As dark as her eyes were, Geri-Jo thought, they were so clear and warm. 'Nothing, Ma'am,' she said at last, barely above a whisper. 'I mean, he didn't put himself inside.' As she remembered, a sickness mushroomed inside of her, and she started to sob.

'All right, honey, easy now.' Chel said, 'I don't need to know anything else. Just relax. And call me Chel, not Ma'am. If you're a friend of Steve's, then you're a friend of mine.' She smiled. 'That is, if you want to be . . .'

All at once, Geri-Jo was able to see past the color, and she realized how exquisitely beautiful Rachel Dennison was. Her eyes were as black as midnight, yet they shone with all the light and color of everything surrounding her. Her hair was jet black, too, but Geri-Jo caught highlights that seemed to be the color of the sky. And as Chel moved, the surface of her face and her slender arms and the full breasts showing beneath the loosely buttoned shirt danced with flashes of gold and blue and deep reds. Geri-Jo was reminded now of a teacher in her high-school science class saying that black wasn't really a color all its own, like blue or red or yellow, but was made of every color mixed together. Chel was fine-featured, her hair long and loose about her face, but the real source of her beauty seemed to come not so much from the way she was made, as the way she composed herself. The set of her mouth, or the way her eyelids were half-drawn down across her eyes like the curtains over the windows of a fancy room, gave her a look of confidence that Geri-Jo admired. Geri-Jo already felt she wanted to be like this black woman, to have her soft humorous way, and her amazing air of belief in herself.

After the bath, Chel handed her a towel, then went out to fetch some clothes. When she returned she had changed into jeans and a jersey, and had brought a similar outfit for Geri-Jo.

The minute they entered the kitchen, Steve started putting food on dishes and bringing it to the table. Oatmeal with brown sugar melted in, scrambled eggs, bacon, toast with three flavors of jam, and cocoa. Geri-Jo gaped at the food as it was set in front of her.

'You made all this?' she asked Steve in disbelief. No man she knew had ever cooked a thing, certainly not Pa.

He laughed. 'You know, Geri-Jo, I'm more than just a pretty face . . .'

Soothed by the bath and the warm kitchen and the kindness of the two people who were tending her, Geri-Jo could almost feel glad about what had happened with Pa if only because it had brought her here. She gobbled the food ravenously, until she became aware of Chel Dennison and Steve Kimball watching her. Then she stopped in embarrassment.

'Dig in, girl,' Chel urged her. 'No reason to be shy with us.'

119

But there *was* a reason, Geri-Jo thought, as she avoided looking at them, and concentrated on her food.

'We've thrown a lot of questions at you, Geri-Jo,' Steve said at last. 'Anything you'd like to ask us . . .'

She shrugged, and took another gulp of cocoa.

'I know there are things that might be . . . confusing.'

It occurred to her then that perhaps the vet could understand better than anyone else how she felt entering the world of the Mitchells and then being cast out — what it was like to want things you could only have by entering a place you would never belong. Suddenly she was anxious to know how he and Chel had dared to make the choice they had.

'You two seem so happy,' she said timidly. 'How do you do it? I mean, being . . . like you are, it's just got to be so godawful hard!'

They smiled slightly at each other, then Steve gave Chel a little nod as though gesturing her to go first through some invisible door. 'Being like we are, Geri-Jo,' she said, 'is exactly what makes it possible. Because we are the kind of people who can put what we want ahead of everything else . . . as long as we live up to one rule.'

'What rule?'

'That nobody else gets hurt.'

Geri-Jo nodded, recording it in memory as carefully as she might write a rule of geometry on a tablet. Until now, she'd known only part of it, not to hurt others. But the training she'd been given by Pa — emphasized by Lettie Parker — was that you *couldn't* have anything you wanted. The way Chel and Steve Kimball put the lessons somehow took the chains off the idea of wanting, and she was determined never to forget it. You could strive for anything, absolutely anything . . . as long as taking it didn't harm anyone else.

'Though beware, Geri-Jo,' Steve went on. 'It can be a complicated business to decide if and when you're breaking that rule. There's plenty of people Chel and I don't even know and who never heard of us — people who live a thousand miles from here — who believe with all their hearts and minds that *they're* getting hurt if she and I love each other.'

'But how can they . . .?'

'Their rules are being broken, that's all they have to know. Then it comes down to which rules are fair. If they feel as strongly about theirs as we do about ours, it gets very hard to decide who's right. The fight over that has been going on for a long time in this part of the country. I guess you know they even went to war over it a hundred years ago — and Jefferson Davis, the man who led the South, was born right here in Kentucky.'

'I suppose a fight like that might never be settled,' Geri-Jo said. 'So it's best to do what you think is right and just try to forget what other folks think.'

'No, that's not the best thing,' Steve said. 'What's better is to teach people when their rules don't make sense. We work on that a little all the time.' He leaned toward her, and looked at her squarely. 'I've got to admit, I'm working on it a little right now.'

Geri-Jo looked down sheepishly, recalling that when she'd first seen them together she had felt somehow as if their choice threatened her. Funny how the opposite was really true. Understanding them helped her feel freer. She wanted now to learn everything about love like theirs, love so strong and certain that, stacked up against it, things that ought to be terrible problems didn't amount to much. At last she was emboldened to ask how they had met.

After a moment, Steve responded. It had been a very bad time in his life, he said, so bad that he had even thought of suicide, but he held a certain reverence for humanity itself that forbade him to destroy any life that might be saved, even his own. Unfortunately, he explained, every person had a secret self that could sometimes carry out wishes unconsciously. So when he took his car out on a late call one night and he fell asleep at the wheel, it was not exactly an accident. In the emergency room where he had been taken — and where his heart had stopped beating — Chel had been the swab nurse whose job it was to stand by and blot up spilled blood so others could work. When his blood pressure had fallen and his heart had stopped and the doctors had been ready to give up, Chel had argued that it was too soon, and had shamed the whole emergency team into staying at the table. Later, when he was recovering in the hospital she had made a point of visiting him, and that had been the beginning.

Geri-Jo thought she understood now why Steve was so committed to being with Chel. She had done no less than save his life. But then he went on:

'That was the best piece of luck I've ever had — and one of the worst. It's a blessing she came into my life, but everything would've been easier if I'd only met her at any other time and place.' He leaned over to Geri-Jo, as if confiding something he was reluctant for Chel to hear. 'I was unconscious when they brought me in. Hell, ten minutes later I was *dead*. But the moment I woke in a bed the next day and saw this woman standing across the room, I loved her. Loved the way she talked, and looked at me, and the sound of her voice, and the way she —'

'This is going to my head,' Chel said lightly.

'The goddamn trouble was she wouldn't believe it. Kept telling me it was just all mixed up with thinking I owed her my life. Held me off the best part of a year with all her damn doubts. That's a year of love I wouldn't have lost if we'd met any other way!'

He sounded angry, but Geri-Jo realized he was pretending when he put his hand across the table and Chel took it.

'I was a fool, Geri-Jo,' Chel said. 'Full of pride . . . and, I guess, prejudice. After I gave it a chance, I discovered that when it's right, you forget the differences . . . and, in a way, you save each other's life a little bit every day.'

She watched them holding hands, and wished again that she would know that kind of love someday.

Then Steve sat back, and Chel rose to get more coffee. 'Well, Geri-Jo, much as I like having you around, we've got to decide our next moves. Have you thought again about reporting what happened to the police?'

She looked down. 'I can't. Please don't make me.'

'I'm not going to force you to do anything you don't want. Now what about going home . . .?'

'Couldn't I wait a while longer? It's just my Pa' there, see — my mother's dead — and I can't face him yet, I mean having him ask where I got these clothes . . . or who hurt me . . .'

'It's all right if you stay the night,' Chel said.

'I couldn't do that. But if I could just wait a few hours . . .' Pa would be asleep then, she thought, and she could take the chance of returning. The spell of wanting her — of imagining she was his 'Jo' — hadn't lasted long in the past; she was sure it would pass again.

Steve told her to take a nap and then he would drive her home afterward. Chel pulled the curtains in the parlor and laid a blanket over Geri-Jo as she stretched out on the couch. Geri-Jo noticed that the beautiful black woman was humming again; the tune stirred a memory.

'My mama used to sing me to sleep with that song,' Geri-Jo said.

Chel smiled and sat on the edge of the couch. Without being asked, she began to croon the words softly. 'Hush little baby, don't you cry, Mama's gonna sing you a lullaby . . .'

As the grip of shock relinquished its last hold on her nerves, Geri-Jo closed her eyes on the vision of the beautiful black woman, and dozed off with her mother's voice in her ears.

In the car when he was taking Geri-Jo home, the vet came back to talking about her interest in the horses.

'Maybe you'd like to come around with me sometime, see more of what I do . . .'

'I sure would,' she said, but then she had an afterthought. 'I'd be afraid of going back to Skyevale, though.'

'Nothing to be afraid of if you're working with me. But I told you there's plenty of other places I work for.' After a pause, he added, 'It's wrong for you to have to hide from anyone, though. Forgive me for harping on it, Geri-Jo, but if you're afraid of seeing Bard because —'

'It's nothing to do with what happened tonight,' she said, guilty about misleading him anymore than she already had. 'And it isn't just seeing Bard that worries me. I don't imagine Mr Mitchell wants me coming around, either, not after what I did to his horse . . .'

There was a short puzzled silence before Kimball tossed his head back with sudden comprehension. 'Oh yes . . . you were out riding with Bard that day.'

'That's right,' she muttered. She wondered if her new friendship with the vet might also suffer from the confession. Wasn't it part of his job to keep horses alive?

'I don't think you should blame yourself for what happened,' Kimball said. 'Bard knows that terrain much better than you do, and he's probably more experienced with high-spirited horses. If he'd just guided you around a safer way there wouldn't have been an accident. Hell,' he added crossly, 'letting you gallop The Ghost in that field it was asking for trouble. The way I see it, if Bard had to end up shooting that horse, he was no less responsible . . .'

It was a moment before the significance of the vet's words came through and she understood the lie Bard had told to cover himself. Then she drew her breath in sharply, freshly pained by the betrayal and loss that had been her reward for helping him. She said nothing, though, only turned to the window, hiding the bitterness she felt.

But Kimball wasn't blind to her reaction. 'Isn't that what happened? You asked to ride The Ghost and ran him too fast . . .?'

'That's what Bard told you?'

'It's what he told his father. But if it's not the truth, I want to know. Anything that affects the horses physically is my business, and I like to have the facts.'

It was done, she thought, let it go. Revealing that Bard had altered the facts would gain her no reprieve. 'If he says it was my fault, that's the way it was.' They were nearing the gas station. Geri-Jo pointed to the road ahead. 'You can let me out right there . . .'

Steve Kimball braked the car to a stop. 'Why do you want to protect someone who's hurt you?' he asked before Geri-Jo could open the door.

She thought: why should she? Maybe it was because the worst hurt had been done by nature years ago; there was nothing that could be done about that, so she had learned early just to take it and go on. And compared with that hurt, every other knock life gave her seemed small. 'I don't believe in revenge, maybe,' she said. 'I don't have the stomach for it — and I don't have the time, not if I'm going to pull myself up and get some better things done with my life.'

Kimball gave her an admiring nod. 'Then suppose I lend a hand so you don't have to do all the pulling alone. You'll come out with me when I make rounds at the different breeding farms.'

'I can't do it all the time.'

He opened the glove compartment, took out a small card and handed it to Geri-Jo. 'Just call whenever you want.'

She looked at the card, printed with his name, followed by the letters D.V.M., and a telephone number that she guessed must be his home. 'What's that mean,' she asked, 'D.V.M.?'

'Doctor of Veterinary Medicine.'

Grasping the card tightly — her ticket of admission to the second chance at a dream — she thanked him, asked him to thank Miss Dennison, and got out of the car.

When she entered the trailer it was dark and she could hear Pa snoring loudly in his compartment. She looked over at the tiny bathroom and saw that he'd already patched up the wooden door and put it back on its hinges. He'd be back to normal tomorrow, she was sure. Brooding and strict, but not the monster he had been for those few minutes earlier tonight. She wouldn't have to be terrified of him. Not for a while, anyway.

In bed, she lay awake thinking about her new friends, the vet and his woman, struck again by the curious way fate worked. If Pa's craziness hadn't sent her fleeing, she probably wouldn't have gotten the chance she had now.

At the moment she drifted finally into sleep, she was wondering how her own name might look someday printed on a little card . . . followed by three letters.

CHAPTER EIGHT

As soon as summer recess from school began, Geri-Jo responded to Steve Kimball's offer. By phoning him at home or agreeing on future meetings whenever she was with him, Geri-Jo set up a schedule of sharing in the vet's rounds two or three times a week. Fascinated by his work with the horses, she started cutting back on the number of hours she put in at Hal Parker's showroom and slipping away more often from the gas station.

Since the beating, there was no problem getting away from Pa. He didn't object when she left, didn't ask where she'd been when she returned. He kept his distance in a way that made it seem he regarded her as having wronged him and he was withholding forgiveness. The situation pained Geri-Jo, but she didn't know how to change it. Trying to approach him, acting soft and friendly, might arouse his confused ideas about her again. In any case, she didn't want to do anything that would interfere with the freedom his indifference allowed her.

From making rounds with Steve Kimball, Geri-Jo quickly began to collect a great deal of miscellaneous knowledge about thoroughbred horses, and about the indispensable place of a veterinarian in the racing world. A breeding process which concentrated on developing animals for speed, Steve explained, could not pay equal attention to selection based on which animals were the hardiest and most disease resistant. The latter qualities were not completely ignored, of course, but they were inevitably subordinated to the question of how fast a horse could run. And, to some degree, honing the horse physically to make him faster also took risks with its health. The animals were conditioned to be hungry and high-strung, so there wasn't an ounce of extra fat, and a kind of fire in the nerves that might be translated into a will to win. Thus while a thoroughbred line might produce horses that were faster and faster, it could also continuously yield animals with physical problems that were intensified in each generation. Weak bones, breathing difficulties, allergic tendencies, even problems of disposition, had troubled many of the fastest and most famous horses. It was also true, Steve pointed out, that even the strongest horse might suffer an injury under the stress of racing. There were hundreds of moments in the course of each headlong gallop, when a horse had only one of its feet touching the track, and its full weight was pounding down on the bones of that one leg.

'Breeding in weaknesses . . . and then putting them under that much pressure,' Geri-Jo remarked, 'that makes the whole thing seem kind of cruel.'

'You can't look at it that way, Geri-Jo. It's just the price these animals have to pay for being what they are. To be the best in one way, the fastest, they have to make sacrifices. But don't we all . . . if we want to be something special?'

Before long, she wasn't only accompanying Steve, but assisting him. Observing that he often pepped up certain horses after their daily work-out with intravenous injections of electrolyte solution, Geri-Jo noted which bottles among the large assortment Steve carried in the back of his station wagon held the electrolyte, and as he emptied one, she would run for another. Racehorses also received many vitamin supplements, sometimes mixed with the electrolyte. By paying close attention Geri-Jo soon learned to fetch, without being asked, the mix of ingredients Steve wanted to administer.

She helped in other ways, too, holding a horse's head still while it received an injection — given usually through the jugular vein in the neck — or while the firing iron was applied to a leg. 'Firing' was a common procedure, she learned from

Steve, an old-fashioned but still effective way of treating leg injuries. With the stress placed on its leg bones when a thoroughbred galloped over a hard surface at full speed, there was a high incidence of fractures. But these were not always disastrous injuries; a bone that was not actually splintered could heal to the point where the horse could race again. This healing process was aided by 'firing', in which a glowing red hot iron was applied to the horse's leg at the point of the injury. This caused a swelling, and the additional blood and fluids flowing through the swollen area helped promote the formation of new bone, usually leaving the healed leg stronger than it had been before the injury. The first time she had witnessed the procedure, Geri-Jo had thought it was barbaric. But Steve assured her that it was often essential to keeping cracked bones from developing into more serious injuries that could require a horse to be destroyed.

Though Steve had been effectively making rounds for years without any assistant, whenever Geri-Jo was with him he gave her the feeling that she made the job much easier, and he patiently supplied instruction and kept expanding her responsibilities. The time she spent with him taught her about more than horses, too. The first couple of days she had gone on rounds with him, he had made so many calls at different farms that Geri-Jo wondered if there could be more than one or two other vets in Lexington. But as Steve introduced her to others, explaining that he was often called in to consult or supplement the treatment of the 'resident' vets, she began to understand the system and his place in it. Almost all the larger, more successful racing farms had a veterinarian who was a regular part of its operation. With sixty, eighty, or even a hundred horses to look after, each of these farms needed a man who would deal only with its animals and no others. Sometimes this regular vet would be away, travelling with a horse that had been sent to a race; thoroughbreds often had a problem that was serious enough to need the constant attention of a doctor, yet not so serious that it wasn't worth sending the horse onto a track to run for under two minutes on the chance it could win fifty thousand dollars. Other times, an owner would want a second opinion on the condition of an animal worth half a million dollars. Steve was also sub-contracted by the regular vets to lighten the load of routine work.

From hearing the way trainers and owners and other vets talked to him and asked his opinion, Geri-Jo soon realized that Steve was regarded as one of the best. 'How come you don't work for one farm?' she asked him one afternoon as they finished their call at one of the biggest stables. Seeing that the resident vet was given a beautiful house on the property as part of his job, Geri-Jo couldn't imagine that Steve wouldn't appreciate receiving the same benefits.

'I wouldn't mind,' he replied.

'Well, then why don't you get the word around? Must be half a dozen places'd take you in a minute.'

'They'll take my opinions about the horses,' he said grimly. 'It's my opinions about other things they can't live with. They don't want to hear 'em . . . and, even more, they don't want to see 'em.'

She understood then. Wherever Steve lived he'd want Chel with him, and she was an opinion you couldn't miss seeing. No matter how good a vet Steve was, his choice of a woman consigned him to being a kind of veterinary handyman.

She wondered if other people might have their minds changed if they could spend time with Steve and Chel as she did, if they could see how much they laughed together, how kind they were to each other. Now that Pa had taken the reins off her, Geri-Jo often went with Steve after making rounds and had her evening meal at his house. With Chel, they would talk and laugh around the table, and afterward she might stretch out with one of the many pamphlets about horses lying around, and Chel would pick up a piece of sewing, and Steve would do his accounts. Pausing in her reading, Geri-Jo would listen to the silence in their home and marvel at how happy even that could be, how different from the hard tense stillness around Pa.

Growing still closer to Steve, it became natural to talk more about the situation at home. Driving between one barn call and another, she found herself opening up about Pa, his strict rules, his wrong-headed idea that she was a slut. She stopped short of confessing that he was the one who'd attacked her, yet she was tempted even to reveal that. The way Steve listened and reacted always evinced a kindness and concern Geri-Jo had been yearning for long before tonight. He wanted to know how long things had been bad at home, and how much and how often her father drank, and also if Geri-Jo had trouble sleeping, or had problems with her appetite. He spoke to her, she thought, almost as if he was a regular M.D., not merely a horse doctor.

From the time she confessed to the problems with her father, Steve would never see her without asking about the situation at home. Geri-Jo sensed that if ever she said things were very bad, he might even offer her a refuge.

There were signs that Pa was changing for the worse. At the station one day, she heard a man who'd had some engine work done complain that the idling was rough. Pa erupted instantly in a white-hot fury: 'You don't like what I done, customer, then I don't need ya! Take your goddamn junk somewhere else . . .' Grabbing up a hammer, he chased the man back into his car, forfeiting payment for a half day's work he'd already done. It struck Geri-Jo as crazy, since the idling could have been smoothed out with a minor adjustment of the carburetor.

That evening, she took Molly aside. 'You noticed Pa? I think he's getting worse . . .'

'Seems fine to me,' Molly replied.

'But haven't you been watching at all, Mol'? His temper's shorter than ever, and he doesn't eat half the time, and he'll go off and leave the station now and then in the middle —'

'He's the same,' Molly cut in. 'Except for one thing . . .'

'What?'

'He's gone off you, Geri-Jo, that's all. You're not the sun and the moon for him anymore. To you, maybe, that'd be a sign that he's sick. Personally,' Molly added with a gloating smile, 'I take it to mean he's finally gettin' normal.'

The next time Steve asked about things at home, Geri-Jo admitted she was worried, and reported the incident with the customer.

'Sounds like your father ought to get some professional help,' Steve observed. 'He's kept a lot of things bottled up for too long — about how much it hurt when your mother and so many of his children were killed, what it's been like to let Caybie go, and raise you and your sister, all by himself. Getting all that out in the open, talking about it to someone who understands the pressures, could help him a lot . . .'

Steve started ticking off questions then. How much was her father sleeping? What did he eat? Did he ever make any reference to 'giving up' — anything that hinted he might be suicidal? Again it struck her how much like an ordinary medical doctor Steve sometimes sounded. Geri-Jo replied that once or twice lately Pa had muttered some remark like 'it might be better if I was dead' — though it made her jittery to think of trying to push Pa into getting help. Recalling his reaction to getting professional help for Caybie — and how sadly that had turned out — she told Steve she was absolutely certain that Pa would never go to a psychiatrist or the like. 'I've just got to hope things turn around,' she said. 'Just the way he went downhill, maybe he'll start going up again.'

'It doesn't usually work that way,' Steve said regretfully. 'In fact, I'm worried about you.' If a man reached the end of all hope, he explained, there was no telling what he might do. He could turn against himself, or he could strike out against others — or he might take himself down, and everybody with him.

As he spoke, Geri-Jo remembered that Steve had confessed to having self-destructive impulses in his own past. Perhaps they had provided him with special insight.

'I don't like to frighten you, Geri-Jo,' Steve continued, 'but I think you'll have to be careful around your Pa. And if anything he does makes you at all afraid or suspicious, promise me you'll walk straight out and come to me and Chel. Okay? You can stay with us as long as you like.'

She couldn't help thinking about the attack, yet there had been nothing that bad since, and she couldn't imagine anything so bad happening that she would be ready to give up on Pa and leave him for good. Still, knowing that Steve and

Chel did care enough to spare her a corner of their happiness gave Geri-Jo a feeling of being protected.

She had avoided going with Steve anytime his rounds included Skyevale, but a great deal of his work was there, and as the summer passed he encouraged her to believe that, whatever had happened with Bard, she could feel free to accompany him. 'Dozens of people pass through the stables all the time,' Steve said, 'and Bard never shows up himself anymore. I don't know if you picked up on it, but he doesn't have any real love for the horses . . .'

In August, finally, she started returning to the stables at Skyevale. As Steve had predicted, there was no sign of Bard. But she saw old Henry, and she stopped into the ponies' barn and saw the horse that had belonged to her once for a few hours. She looked for Oakie, too, still interested in picking up any pointers she could about training, but the first and second time she risked going to Skyevale, he wasn't there. She learned then from Steve that whenever a horse was sent to an important race, the trainer went along, and Oakie was away at the Northern tracks where the Mitchells had entries in some of the big summer races.

Toward the end of August, however, he reappeared, and whenever Geri-Jo could find him around the stables, he was no less willing than Steve to answer her questions — though he persisted in saying there was little to tell in the way of cut and dried facts when it came to training racehorses. Each horse was different, and what he did to bring the best out of each one was simply a matter of getting to know the animal, feeling it out, using trial and error, going more on guesswork than past experience. Again and again he would tell her that if she wanted to learn, she just had to keep hanging around, and watching . . . and, yes, asking questions, because there was no way to know which ones he might be able to answer, and which he couldn't.

But like Steve, Oakie never lost patience with her, and even when he wasn't able to sum up much about how he worked, he kept her amused with what he knew about the history of racing, and characters he had known. One day, when Geri-Jo was slightly exasperated with him for remaining so vague about his area of expertise, she expressed a doubt that the sport would survive if the important and basic tasks involved in training couldn't be more clearly formulated and taught.

Oakie merely laughed. 'Don't you worry,' he said, 'the only thing that'll ever stop racing in this country is if there's nothing left to eat but the horses. In fact, that's the only thing that delayed it from getting started. Bet you didn't know that way back more than three hundred years ago, when some of the first settlers sailed over to America from England, they made sure to bring six racehorses along. They knew how they wanted to spend their Saturdays, Puritans or not. Trouble was they had a hard first winter, and so the whole racing card ended up on the dinner table.'

After she had been around them enough, Geri-Jo realized that Steve and Oakie represented opposite poles in their approach to the horses. The veterinarian used science to make sure the horse delivered his best, and Oakie used — what? — a kind of sorcery. The mix was all through the sport. Breeding certainly required scientific and medical knowledge, yet Oakie had mentioned that horse breeders also paid close attention to phases of the moon, believing that some were more propitious for the conception of a great horse than others; a leading breeders' journal published a moon-phase and astrological chart each month. Geri-Jo came to realize, too, that there were other people employed around the stables — old Henry was an example — who were valued for having an ability to understand and communicate with horses that was judged to be almost magical. As Steve Kimball told the story, there had been a period when Roman Candle became listless, and suddenly began to lose races after a series of spectacular wins, and yet no medical problem could be found. Then Old Henry had decided Roman Candle was simply bored, and had brought an old wind-up Victrola to the horse's stall, and begun playing him some old records of banjo music for a couple of hours a day. The horse had gone to his next race and won by eight lengths, and had a string of victories thereafter until he was retired due to injury.

What made racing fascinating, Geri-Jo thought, was embodied in the collaboration of people like Steve with others like Oakie and Henry. It was a situation in which the logical and illogical uniquely depended on each other. The science was worthless without the sorcery, knowledge was pointless without luck. But given enough of both, you might win the moon.

CHAPTER NINE

As she returned to high school for her senior year, she went on giving a lot of her spare time, evenings and weekends, to making rounds with Steve. On a sunny Saturday late in autumn, when they were walking across a pasture after checking a new colt, he asked if she had started making any plans for the future. 'You're good with the horses, Geri-Jo. You could stay with it after you graduate. Have you thought about going on to college and vet school . . .?'

She shrugged. 'I couldn't afford it.'

'There are scholarships. I might be able to help you get one . . .'

She had thought Steve might let her go on assisting him, but it had never occurred to her that it might be possible to go to school just as he had. She was so grateful that she threw her arms around Steve and gave him a hug. The feeling of safety in his arms was such a welcome novelty, that she held on for a few extra moments, her face pressed against the shoulder of his tweed jacket. At last he eased her away.

She couldn't help blushing as Steve looked down at her, and then went on quickly, as if to erase the awkward moment: 'But there's another part of your education, that's already overdue, and I think we should do something about that first. With everything else you're learning about thoroughbreds, it's about time you saw what's at the heart of the whole damn racing business.' The two-week October meeting would be starting at Keeneland in a few days, Steve said, and he wanted to take her to the races. Keeneland in Lexington was one of the nicest courses in the country, a place where you could see horse-races run as they had been a hundred years ago, in a leisurely atmosphere, without the hurlyburly and beer vendors of the big Northern tracks. Steve suggested that Geri-Jo come to his house on a Friday evening, spend the night, then go with him when he went to the track the next morning — there were always calls he had to make on horses scheduled to race.

'Chel and I have to be away this coming weekend. But we'll all go to Keeneland the Saturday after . . .'

A few days later, when Geri-Jo went to the garage and mentioned to her father she'd be out overnight on the coming Friday, he simply grunted consent.

'Lately, Pa,' she blurted, 'you act like you don't care much if I live or die. Aren't you worried where I'll be?' He glanced over, and for a moment she thought his expression softened, and it seemed he was going to apologize, provide an opening for the rift between them to be healed. But then he said, 'Don't matter no more, does it? Ain't we finished, Jo . . .?'

She was tempted to try breaking through again, tell him about the new friends she'd made — even considered jolting him with the news that her friends were lovers of different colors. But if his reaction to that was as dead as to everything else then she would feel herself and the friendship diminished.

Walking up the road to Steve's house late on Friday, Geri-Jo was embraced by a feeling that she was not just arriving for a visit, but coming home. When she let herself in through the never-locked door, she was instantly comforted by the warmth from a log-fire in the living room, and delighted by the smells wafting from the kitchen. A dining table at one end of the living room had been set with a vase of flowers at the center, and shining wine glasses stood at each place.

'Hi there, hon',' Chel greeted Geri-Jo when she entered the kitchen. She turned from the stove, and held out an arm. Without hesitation Geri-Jo gave her a hug. She never thought about Chel's color now.

Steve was still in the shower, Chel explained, having just returned from a barn call. As soon as he was out they would eat. While they waited, Chel gave her a preview of the food simmering in pots on the stove and warming in the oven — shrimp creole, broccoli with hollandaise sauce, and chocolate eclairs. As usual they were things Geri-Jo had never eaten before, but she knew that whatever Chel cooked would be delicious.

At last they heard Steve emerge from the shower — still singing — and Chel started transfering the food from pots onto the dishes. Geri-Jo took a plate in each hand and carried them to the table. She was just walking back to the stove to get another plate, when an explosive noise froze her in her tracks. At first she couldn't tell exactly what had happened. There was a sharp cracking sound, and glass breaking and a dish falling from Chel's hand — but which had come first?

Suddenly Chel staggered backward. Now Geri-Jo saw the spot of red burgeoning on her shirt near the arm, and the small hole in the kitchen window, and in the next instant there was a second shot, and the vase on the dining table beyond the kitchen doorway was blasted apart with such force that the flowers all flew up into the air.

'Someone's shooting!' Geri-Jo screamed. Without thinking, she flung herself at Chel, knocking her to the floor just as a third bullet slammed into the wall — on a line right behind where she had been standing.

Steve came charging in from the bathroom, still shirtless and his hair dripping. Only a second after he came through the door another shot was fired, the bullet splintering the doorframe. He dropped to his knees and crawled over beside Chel. Her eyes were open, and she smiled up at him faintly.

'Don't worry, love,' she murmured. 'I'll be all right. Just don't wait too long to call the hospital . . .'

'Stay with her,' Steve said to Geri-Jo. He crawled quickly to the front door and locked it, then scuttled to the phone.

They kept thinking a fifth shot might come at any second, but there were no more.

At last they heard sirens and two police cars and an

ambulance pulled up in front of the house. Steve ran to open the door, and then Geri-Jo heard him shouting. It sounded like an argument. Then he came back into the room, trailed by some policemen and ambulance attendants dressed in white, and Geri-Jo could make out his angry words.

'What difference does that make now? She's been shot, for chrissakes!'

'That's why she needs an emergency treatment,' said an intern from the ambulance as he knelt beside Chel. 'And we've got to go to a hospital that'll take blacks in emergency.'

'No, damn it!' Steve roared, grabbing the doctor by his collar. 'That's not the nearest and we'll be losing —'

A policeman stepped up to Steve and pulled him away from the doctor. 'That's the way things have to be done, mister. You'll only be losing more time if you don't back off so they can get your girlfriend out of here.'

Geri-Jo could hear the nasty edge in the white policeman's tone when he referred to Chel as Steve's girlfriend.

With a defeated shrug, Steve moved to a corner and watched as Chel was put onto a stretcher and carried out. The police kept him and Geri-Jo for a while, while they asked questions and searched the area around the house for a sniper. Then a police car brought them both to a hospital on the other side of Lexington.

Amid all the activity, the police and doctors asking questions, the hours were such a blur of faces and voices that Geri-Jo wasn't sure whether she had wakened from a dream or lapsed into one when at last she found herself seated alone in a small waiting area outside an operating room where Chel was in surgery. Steve had gone off to get a medical report.

When he returned at last, she jumped up. 'She's going to live, isn't she?'

'She'll be good as new,' Steve replied. 'The bullet went in just under the shoulder, missed anything that could've really hurt.' He glanced at his watch. 'Shouldn't take long to get it out.'

Geri-Jo started to cry and Steve sat down beside her. 'You all right here? Maybe I could find you a bed to lie down —'

138

'No. I want to stay.' A second later the apology came, bubbling up from thoughts that had plagued her from the moment the shooting ended. 'Oh, Steve, I'm so sorry . . .'

'Sorry? What the hell for?'

'I keep thinking . . . if it wasn't for me, then maybe it wouldn't have happened . . .'

'You?' Steve shook his head. 'Honey, how can you think it's got anything to do with you?'

He stared at her, waiting. Saying the answer, she felt almost as if she was confessing for herself. 'Seems like . . . it must've been Pa. I can't imagine anybody else crazy enough to do such a thing, and the only reason I can see is to hurt me, to take away what I love. Don't you see? He could do it . . .'

Steve smiled at her sadly, then pulled her against him. 'Not a chance, Geri-Jo. Your father's trouble has more to do with hating himself, than hating me or Chel. That's what this is about . . . and, unfortunately, there's a lot of people crazy enough to feel that way.'

She could tell from the way he spoke that he was absolutely certain. 'You know who did it . . .?'

'Not by name. But I know more or less the kind of person . . .'

'How?'

He went suddenly to the water cooler across the room, drew a cup of water, and drank it at a swallow as though to extinguish some inner fire. 'Our trip last week,' he said. 'I didn't want to make too much of it, but I'd guess that's where it started. Chel and I went to a march, down in Alabama, a gathering of a lot of people to protest the segregation laws. There's a man down there, Geri-Jo, a man named Martin Luther King, who's been leading a fight against all the laws that don't make sense — the kind of rules that can allow Chel to be a nurse in a hospital where she can't get emergency treatment when she needs it. A lot of people think those laws should be changed, so when King marches, huge crowds line up behind him. They come in buses, Geri-Jo, tens of thousands of them, all the way from up North. We wanted to be there, too. And I'm glad we were.' He paused, and when he resumed his voice had a darker, wearier tone. 'But maybe somewhere in the crowd that didn't march, were people who just watched and shouted — people who would've liked to stop us if there hadn't been an army of police between them and us — maybe there was someone who fastened his eyes on me and Chel and didn't like what he saw. Maybe it was someone from around here who was also there and recognized us. Or someone from there who drove clear out of Alabama and across Tennessee, just to follow us. When people get stirred up over these things, no telling how far they'll go. Either way, he didn't like us being there. One of the angry kind you and I once talked about . . . who doesn't know me and Chel, and still wouldn't mind fighting a war to keep us apart.' He threw the water cup into a wastebasket — a gesture that somehow conveyed as much violence as if he had tossed a grenade into an enemy foxhole — and walked to the window of the waiting room, looking out as if checking to see whether the phantom might still be lurking. 'A couple of days after we were back we got a letter, an awful thing, hate pouring out of every word. And there were threats to kill us, too. It mentioned the march, but we didn't make too much of it. We've always gotten a certain amount of hate mail — that's just something we've had to get used to. You can't stop living the way you want because someone writes a letter threatening to kill you. If that's all it takes to destroy what you love and believe in, then you're half dead already.' He came back to sit beside her. 'So don't you go blaming yourself one bit. If anything Chel owes you her life. If you hadn't moved so fast, that second bullet would have done a lot more damage than the first.'

A doctor came in, dressed in his green surgical smock, a mask he had pulled from his face still draped around his neck. He smiled reassuringly, and told Steve everything had gone well. Chel would be in the recovery room for a couple of hours while the anesthetic wore off, and could receive a short visit anytime after that.

'That gives me time to take you home,' Steve said to Geri-Jo when the doctor had gone. He would be busy all night with police and news reporters, he explained. The F.B.I. might enter the case, too, since it could involve interstate violation of

140

Federal civil rights statutes. 'No reason for you to be mixed up with all of that, and I can't allow you to go back and stay at my house alone . . . '

She would have begged to stay at the hospital, but for once she was anxious to go home. Not, however, because she needed the comfort of familiar surroundings.

As she got out of Steve's car down the road from the gas station, he said, 'I'm sorry about the races, Geri-Jo. But as soon as things are back to normal we'll go. All of us — I think it's about time I took Chel, too.'

She realized he had been putting it off rather than let all the owners and trainers 'see his opinions'. Now he no longer cared.

Before entering the trailer, Geri-Jo stopped by Pa's truck, pulled up nearby. She went to the front and held her hand by the grill to see if any heat was radiating from the motor. Of course it had been hours since Chel was shot, so it proved nothing to find that the motor was cool. Yet if Pa had done it, she didn't think he would have driven straight home; he'd probably have gone on a bender.

It surprised her slightly to see that no lights were glowing through the trailer windows. It was only a little after ten o'clock, and Pa often sat up drinking, but he could have turned in early. Molly wouldn't be back yet from ushering the Friday night show.

But as soon as she pulled open the door, Geri-Jo heard a sound that she recognized as Molly's voice, a low moan that reminded her of the sound Chel had made after being shot. A bolt of fear went through her. Had Pa gone berserk, hurt Molly, too? Suddenly her mind was full of Steve's warnings, and the fear of what she might find in the trailer almost sent her fleeing back into the night. Yet she couldn't go, couldn't leave Molly if she was hurt . . .

She took another quiet step in the dark and heard the moan again, coming from behind the door of Pa's compartment. Suddenly, with a desperation stoked to white heat by having lost so many others, she rushed ahead and burst through the door, determined to be the savior, not to fail again.

141

At the sight that greeted her, she stopped and then doubled over as if she had been impaled, her mouth open in a soundless scream. It was there, yes, a picture complete in every detail, the two tangled figures on the bed. But still her brain rejected it, refused to take it for real. It must be an hallucination — the after-effect of shock from the shooting at Steve's . . .

But then Pa pushed himself up, and Molly unlocked her arms and legs from around his naked body, and they both turned to her. Molly's stare of defiance, and his look of guilt mixed with a wild-eyed stare, were not the faces of a mere dream. Geri-Jo reeled back and lurched dizzily into the tiny bathroom, slamming the door. Nausea, hot and heavy as molten lead, dragged her down to her knees and she retched into the toilet.

For a long time she couldn't find the will to move. It must have been going on for a while, she thought. Would she ever have known if not for her unexpected return — hurled by one ugly act into something even more grotesque? What were her choices now? At last she hauled herself up to the sink, pumped it full of cold water and spashed a few handfuls onto her face. A moment later, Molly pushed in. As Geri-Jo unbent from over the sink, she saw her sister in the mirror, red tousled hair of a waif framing the pretty face hardened by an unrepentant stare. The robe she had thrown on hung open, revealing her still immature body, the downy clump of red pubic hair neatly shaved to a perfect triangle.

'What're you gonna do?' Molly asked.

Geri-Jo pulled her hands from under the cold water and stared at the floor. 'Go to someone. Get help. He's in a bad way, Mol'. It's a crime, making you do that.' She turned around. 'Why? How'd it happen . . .'

Molly shrugged.

The tiny gesture blew the pressure. Geri-Jo's hands flew up and seized her sister by the arms. 'All your life you've ignored everything,' she cried at her, 'acted like you can brush it all away like . . . no more than a drop of rain, a little speck of mud! But not *this*, goddamn it!' She jostled Molly violently, trying to shake loose her feelings. 'Why? Tell me! Why?'

Molly stared back dully. ''Cause it's always been you he wanted, that's why. 'Cause if he wanted *me* for once, even like this, it was better than nothin'.'

Geri-Jo's hold loosened and she shrank back. Molly had charged her with being an accomplice, and in some way only vaguely understood Geri-Jo felt she couldn't claim complete innocence.

'You think I didn't see how it was?' Molly went on harshly. 'I could've been buried with Ma and the others for all he cared. As long as he had his precious Geri-Jo, nothin' else mattered. Right up 'til he needed something and he couldn't get it from you. Then he turned to me. He took me, and he didn't need you anymore. And I didn't mind a damn, not if it was the only way to take your place.'

The hatred Geri-Jo saw in Molly's fierce grimace appalled her. How did she begin to set straight such twisted ideas? 'I never wanted to hurt you, Mol'. Just seeing you hurt yourself cuts me in half.'

'Good sweet Geri-Jo,' Molly snarled contemptuously. 'Save all your pretty words. All we want to hear is that you're not gonna stir up any trouble.'

'It's wrong, Mol', all wrong. He's got to know that — got to have help to see it. You, too . . .'

'So you say! I'll look out for myself, and Pa don't want any of those high-minded little ladies from the state comin' 'round either.'

Geri-Jo searched her sister's implacable expression for a hint of doubt or remorse. The absence only made it all the more apparent that Molly was lost, could only be saved by getting away from Pa. She was just fourteen; a child, for all her tough poses. If her spirit had broken in the tide of catastrophe, as Pa's had, still she wasn't so old it couldn't be mended. Geri-Jo shoved past her. Pa stood in the narrow passage outside wearing only a pair of his greasy overalls. She studied his face, a mask some stranger had put on.

'I'm sorry,' she said. 'I've got to do something about it . . .'

'Can't let ya,' he growled, seizing her roughly. 'Can't stand still for it, girl. They won't understand, and I'll be put to rot in prison. Can't let you do it to me, Jo . . .'

She remembered more of Steve's warnings. 'It doesn't have to be like that, Pa. There are people who'll listen and help. You just need to talk to the right person, someone who knows you're sick.'

'Sick? I ain't sick. And I ain't talkin' to anyone. You won't, neither.'

Peering into his eyes, she caught a glint of intention that sparked a new shaft of paralyzing terror. This was the danger Steve had foreseen, that Pa would lose all control, all sense of right or wrong. 'Let me go, Pa,' she whined, struggling to get free of him.

He shoved her roughly ahead along the passage into the wider open area of the lounge, kept a tight hold on her as he scanned the room, evidently searching for something.

'Pa!' she screamed, as though to wake him from a trance.

Molly came up behind him and leaned against the trailer wall watching, as she had always watched, with cool detachment. Keeping one hand viced around Geri-Jo's wrist, Garrett Lockely used the other to yank the wire of a lamp from its socket, and then whipped the wire free of the lamp base.

Oh Lord, was he going to strangle her? She tried to break his grip and couldn't. ''Mol'!' Geri-Jo appealed to her, 'for God's sakes, don't you see? He's gonna *kill* me!'

'Shut your fool mouth,' he said. 'Ain't gonna hurt ya, just make sure ya don't go nowheres 'til you see the light. C'mere, Mol', slip this wire around her hands.'

Molly hesitated a second, then pushed herself off the wall and moved toward Geri-Jo. The cruel smile that rippled across her tight moist mouth made it look like a small pink worm. She reached for the electric cord.

It was inconceivable that they would actually hurt her, Geri-Jo thought, Pa's fury would pass as it had before. Yet there was a time when the scene she had witnessed only minutes ago in Pa's bedroom would also have been inconceivable.

With a sudden wrench, she freed herself from her father's grasp and spun toward the door. He tried to grab Geri-Jo again, but in the confines of the trailer there was no room to maneuver. When Molly also made a lunge for Geri-Jo, she blocked his path.

By then Geri-Jo was outside, scrambling across the field toward the gas station and the road beyond. Glancing over her shoulder she saw her father jump through the door. Her headstart had been only seconds, he wasn't more than ten yards behind. His long legs — and the fuel of his madness — were propelling him so much faster, Geri-Jo realized he would catch up to her before she got near the road and could flag down a passing car. Rounding a corner of the garage, she prayed it wouldn't be locked. Often he left one of the bays open, and went back to work after dinner. If she could get in there, she could get to the phone or find a place to hide . . .

Thank God, the door to one of the two bays had been lowered but not to the ground. She ducked under it and looked around. A grime-encrusted skylight cut the darkness just enough for her to see that the pneumatic lift in the bay she had entered was raised up with a car standing on it. The other bay was empty. There were fewer places to conceal herself than she had expected.

His running footsteps arrived outside. She scuttled behind a couple of oil drums in a corner just as he pushed the door up all the way. Peering through a narrow gap between the cylinders, Geri-Jo saw his looming figure step into the garage. The pulse in her head sounded almost as loud as a hand pounding on one of the hollow drums.

'Know you're in here, Jo.' The sweetness of his voice — as if they were merely playing a childish game of hide and seek — was horrifying. But this was *Pa*! How could she be hiding from him, running for her life? She almost stood up to plead again. But then his shadowy figure moved to the workbench, and she heard clinking sounds as he rummaged among his tools. Then he turned and she saw his silhouette — his arm raised, holding a mallet. He glanced toward the door connecting the garage to the office hut. Did he think she'd gone for the phone? If he went in there she could get back outside —

But he went instead to pull down the garage door, closing off the bay, trapping her. And now he advanced directly toward the corner where she was hiding. Had he seen her? Suddenly she realized her mistake. On the wall, right above the corner where she'd planted herself was a switchbox — and he was coming over to turn on the lights.

Throwing her weight against one of the big metal drums, she darted to the corner farthest from him. Garrett Lockely laughed and sidestepped the toppled cylinder as he kept moving toward the switch.

She froze in the blaze of light. Pa walked slowly toward her, tapping the mallet in his palm. 'I never wanted nothin' but to love you, Jo. Was that so wrong? Been punished for it, though . . . one thing after another, grindin' me down, breakin' my heart over and over. I'd rather die now . . . have some peace that way. Give us both some peace . . .'

The closer he came, the more she could see the crazy gleam in his eyes. 'Pa, you never lost me,' she pleaded. 'I still love you. That's the whole reason I want to get help for you!'

'The only help I ever needed was to get *out*. I can't take it no more . . . can't . . .' He started to close in. The hand gripping the hammer came up. For one more moment she stared in disbelief. He *did* mean to use. Where was Molly? Geri-Jo wondered fleetingly. Gone for help . . . or was she waiting calmly outside, letting Pa do his worst?

He leapt at her, and she dodged aside. He went after her, and she kept running, staying to the periphery of the garage. A flicker of an old story crossed her mind, the gladiator and the lion. How had they ended here themselves, fighting to the death in an arena?

For a few minutes their aimless dodging went on. Then Geri-Jo recalled that the gladiator used to be given a net as an advantage. She glanced everywhere, wondering if there was something like that she could drop around Pa to immobilize him without hurting him. There wasn't a net, of course, but she did spot the pneumatic lift. As he criss-crossed the garage diagonally in pursuit of her, he kept passing under the metal tracks that supported the car — ducking under with only an inch or two of clearance. Geri-Jo knew that when the lift descended it dropped down the first two or three inches in a quick fall before the mechanism engaged to bring it down slowly the rest of the way. It was her only hope, she decided. At a moment when she was near the switch and he was passing beneath the lift, she could bump it down on him. He wouldn't be more than momentarily dazed, she was sure, but that would give her an edge — or maybe jar him back to his senses. She wouldn't run, of course, if he was too stunned to move. The way Pa's lift worked, you couldn't stop it mid-way once it started down; the ramp was raised by compressed air, and when the compression discharged, you had to wait for it to build up again. Meanwhile, the lift would continue down to the ground very slowly. Pa would have plenty of time to get out from under, though; and if he hesitated, she'd be prepared to help him.

A chance came soon, as he ran diagonally across the garage. But she let the first one pass, hoping that Molly might have summoned help. Then, so out of breath she could hardly run, she could put it off no longer. She circled along the wall to a point near the switch, and stopped moving.

He lumbered toward her, passing under the lift, one of the metal ramps just above his head. Her hand darted out to pull the handle that released the compressed air. There was a hiss, and the heavy mechanism dropped. She had timed it just right. The metal track clipped the side of his head, and he fell to his knees. The mallet slipped from his hand and clattered on the concrete floor. At once, Geri-Jo jumped away from the switch.

'C'mon, Pa, get outta there . . . ' Looking into the shadow under the lift, she saw him still on his knees. He gazed back at her dully, then rolled his eyes up to look at the underside of the car coming nearer. A thin trickle of blood began to ooze down the side of his head. He wasn't going to move by himself, she realized. Without hesitation, she sidled under the slowly descending lift, slipped her hands under his arms, and began to tug. 'Pa, there ain't much time. Please!'

He pitched over, unconscious.

She glanced up. Still time, plenty of time, she told herself. Hadn't she thought it out, prepared for this? Pulling his arms out straight she grasped his hands to slide him out. She hadn't expected the weight, had never imagined he would be this heavy. But she braced herself and heaved, and his body slid an inch or two —

— in the time that the lift came down the same distance.

Summoning all her strength she heaved again, and his prostrate form slid a few more inches, bringing his head and shoulders to the point they'd be clear of the track. But more than half his body was still in the path of the descending metal ramp, and now it was only a couple of feet off the floor.

'Molly!' Geri-Jo screamed for help while she continued to exert all her strength, no longer even pausing to check the progress of the lift. No answer came, but Pa's body slid steadily toward her.

And then the lift slid down into her sight. She was aware of it while perched there on the ground, but still she kept tugging at her father's unconscious form, refusing to accept what her eyes should have told her — until the blood began to seep through his overalls, and the picture was finally too vivid to blot out. His legs were pinned beneath tons of metal. She screamed loudly once, then backpedalled to the switch and reversed it; in a minute or two the compression would build enough to lift the ramp again. She was about to run to the office phone and call for an ambulance when the pounding began on the garage door. She raised it quickly.

Molly stood outside. She didn't move, but simply glanced over the scene, then brought her cool impenetrable gaze back to Geri-Jo.

Words of damnation formed on Geri-Jo's lips, but before she could speak, the sound of a siren yowled faintly from somewhere down the pike, growing gradually louder.

CHAPTER TEN

The cell stank of urine from the seatless toilet in the corner and the sweat of a few thousand hopeless nights soaked into the mattress on the iron cot. Scrawled across the cinder block walls with markers and nail polish were the angry mottos and obscene dares of other men and women who had been locked away here before.

As horrible as Geri-Jo had imagined it would be in jail, the reality was worse. As she had been led down the cellblock, a couple of prisoners in other cells along the block had stood at the bars to watch her go past, and the look in their eyes, half pity and half lust, had made her flesh crawl.

When the door clanged shut behind her, she whirled back to the policeman, the plea forming on her lips as he turned the key. *Wait. Please . . . !* But she choked back the words, and the bolt slammed home into the lock. Scared and desperate as she was, she couldn't change her story, not yet . . . not while things could still be turned around without making them worse.

An accident. If only she stuck to the story, the police would have to accept that it had been nothing more. They couldn't possibly believe she would want to murder Pa.

Through five hours of questioning after they had brought her and Molly back to the police station — ignoring her pleas to ride in the ambulance with Pa — she had never revealed that he had been chasing her in a homicidal rage. To admit that much would have prompted the police to ask what had caused his temper to boil over, and then she would have had to tell about Pa and Molly . . .

Maybe Pa was mentally sick and needed help, but having already done so much to hurt him, Geri-Jo couldn't think now about forcing him to be treated as a criminal. And if the whole story were told, wouldn't Molly suffer, too — be forced into some hell-hole like that place Caybie had been sent? No matter how far apart she and Molly had drifted, Geri-Jo couldn't give up on her. The rest of the family had been decimated. She couldn't be responsible for the final destruction.

So she had told the police nothing about Pa and Mol' — had admitted only that there had been a quarrel in the garage after she arrived home late, and she had bumped into the lift switch. Molly had gone along with that version, of course, but still the police had doubts. Near midnight they had ended their questioning and asked Molly for the name of someone who might shelter her as an alternative to the youth hostel. While Ed Parker was called and Molly waited for him, Geri-Jo had been detained.

At least her imprisonment wouldn't last more than an hour or two. When Mr Parker came, she assured herself, he would arrange to have her released as well. Both he and Lettie knew all about her problems with Pa. Once someone spoke up for her, the police would have to let her go. Wouldn't they . . .?

She felt weak suddenly, unable to stand, and slid down onto the cot. As she stared at the cement wall, and the sour smell of the mattress rose into her nostrils, the reality of what had happened — what she had done — struck her afresh. She started to sob.

'What'sa matter, cutie?' a voice rasped from somewhere along the cellblock. 'Homesick?' A nasty laugh followed.

She clamped her arms over her ears and muffled her sobs, turning her face into the mattress ticking, accepting the awful smell as just punishment.

An hour or two went by, she didn't know how long, but still Mr Parker didn't come. Had there been a hitch? She leapt to the bars and called out a few times for the policeman who'd locked her in. Eventually the door at the end of the jail corridor opened and the guard came to stand outside the bars. 'I'm waiting to see Mr Parker . . . the man who was picking up my sister . . .'

'He came and went hours ago, kid.'

She clutched at the bars, feeling how cold and solid they were for the first time. 'Why wouldn't you let me see him? He would've got me out . . .'

'Don't know about any of that, sweetheart, not my department.' He leaned closer. 'But it's just possible he didn't try.'

The guard turned and sauntered out of the cellblock.

He wouldn't leave her, not Mr Parker. How could he . . .?

All at once she realized the story Molly could have told him. Geri-Jo stopped pacing the cell and slumped back defeatedly onto the cot. It crossed her mind to try calling Steve, but then she realized he was probably still at the hospital keeping a vigil for Chel. Anyway, as soon as she was off her feet Geri-Jo felt too weak and nauseous to do anything but lie back.

Oh God, she cried inwardly, she had hurt Pa so badly. Perhaps by now he was dead; no one had told her anything about his condition, though she kept asking.

She rolled herself into the rough blanket on the cot and tried to shut out everything around her, to forget where she was and how she had come to be here. But she couldn't erase the vision of Pa as the lift came down, crushing him . . . She was horrified by what she had done, and kept going over and over her choice, asking herself if there had been any other way to save herself.

Perhaps, Geri-Jo thought as she stared at the wall where someone had scratched the words 'born to lose', she was right where she belonged.

In the morning, after a breakfast of cardboard eggs and watery coffee, a policeman took her from the cell to a bare meeting room. She expected to find Ed Parker waiting, but the man seated at one end of a long table was a stranger. For a minute after the guard left, the man at the table kept riffling through an open file of papers in front of him. His face was unlined, but he had snow-white hair brushed straight back, and he wore a pair of odd spectacles, with only one lens of clear glass, the other a smokey dark gray. At last he stood and Geri-Jo saw that he was a few inches shorter than she, though his compact build was encased in a very well-fitted dark suit that made him appear very strong. He put out his hand, and she shook it automatically.

'How do you do, Miss Lockely. I'm Delbert Conroy, County Prosecutor. Kindly be seated.' He spoke with the mellow lulling drawl of a traditional Southern gentleman, inducing an air of cordiality despite his brisk manner. Geri-Jo murmured a 'thank you' as he glanced up and gestured to a chair at the opposite end of the table, 'I am regrettably afflicted with weak vision, Miss Lockely, but I don't think I've failed to see anything important in these reports filed by our excellent local police.' He showed his clamped teeth so quickly it could have been a smile or a twitch. 'You'll have to excuse me if I say that, from what I've read, I'd give odds longer than a Kentucky mile that you are a shameless liar.'

'No . . .,' Geri-Jo murmured, not a denial as much as an apology.

But he rolled right on. 'This was no accident. Accordingly, when you are arraigned later today, I will present a writ charging that you knowingly and maliciously subjected Garrett Lockely to grievous bodily harm with potentially fatal consequences.' He paused as though to give her a chance to protest again.

But now she could only shake her head, confused about whether to defend herself by revealing everything, or wait and hope that someone would appear to defend her.

'To put it more simply,' Conroy went on, 'I shall be seeking an indictment against you . . . on a charge of attempted murder.'

The impact of his words was almost physical, leaving Geri-Jo breathless as if hit by a body blow. At the same time, she was curiously relieved. The form of the charge was the first assurance she'd had that Pa was still alive.

Before she could recover her breath, he resumed. 'I don't

like to think of what's ahead of you, Miss Lockely. Under the penal code of this state, you will receive no concessions as a minor for this offense. Even a one-eyed man can see you're a very pretty young girl . . . but a conviction will put you behind bars all the best years of your life.' Again, he flashed his awful twitch-smile. 'Let me heartily encourage you, therefore, to tell me everything. A confession to the charges, taken as evidence of a desire to repent, might earn you a reduced sentence.' He leaned back, hands folded. His spectacles, with that dark lens blocking out one eye, imparted the deceptive aspect of a kindly man giving her an encouraging wink.

Geri-Jo sat forward. 'Mr Conroy,' she said, 'I swear with all my heart, I love my father. I never wanted to hurt him so badly . . .'

'I'm not saying you meant to hurt him,' the prosecutor said unmercifully. 'I'm saying you meant to *kill* him. As for love . . . if people who truly loved each other never tried to kill each other, two-thirds of the killings each year could be wiped from the records. Now, why don't you come clean about when and why you got this fool idea to murder your Daddy?'

'I never meant to,' she cried out. 'Nothing would have happened if —' She stopped herself.

'If *what*?'

She shook her head again, wanting to speak, tempted to tell of her father's past attacks on her, the tragedy that had driven them out of a simpler if poorer life, the whole history that had affected his mental attitude . . . and yet silenced by an unbreakable personal promise to the ghosts of their ruined family to save the little that was left. She'd hurt Pa so badly already, she couldn't turn everything else against him, couldn't bring herself to accuse him of being the one with murder in his heart, and of corrupting Molly.

For the next hour, Conroy went on drilling into her resolve with his cold-blooded courtesy, but she stood up to him, unwilling to admit any more than accidentally injuring her father in the course of an argument. If she could just hold on, it would turn out all right. Another few hours, another day. That much time in jail she deserved. But she wasn't a murderer. They'd have to realize their mistake.

At last, Delbert Conroy folded up his papers and told Geri-Jo that he would see her next in the courtroom.

Before being returned to her cell, she was advised by the guard that she still hadn't taken advantage of her right to make a single phone call. 'To call a lawyer,' he explained.

'I don't know any lawyers,' she said.

'Never mind, then. You'll get one, anyway, provided free. Maybe you ought to call a friend . . .'

He took her to a public phone on a stairway landing and gave her a dime. Before dropping the coin, she wondered whether to try Steve or Mr Parker or Lettie. At last she decided against Steve, not only because she didn't want to disturb him at a time he had other worries, but because she was ashamed to have him know of her predicament. She called the Parker home and Lettie answered.

'Aunt Lettie,' she forced out the words, 'this is Geri-Jo. I'm calling from —'

'I know exactly where you're calling from,' Lettie cut in quickly. 'Ed will be coming to see you very soon, don't you worry. Meantime, Molly's safe here with us . . .'

Geri-Jo tried to think of a way to convince Lettie Parker that she had kept the oath she had made one day at her door — that she would never do anything to disappoint her. 'Lettie,' she began, 'I hope you can believe —'

But there was no point in going on: the line had already been disconnected.

Lettie Parker's haste to get off the phone was the clearest signal yet that others beside the police and Delbert Conroy were thinking she might have deliberately tried to hurt Pa. Back in the cell, she started to cry again, then clenched her fists and forced herself to regain control.

Later in the morning, she was taken again from her cell. The stranger waiting for her this time was slightly pudgy, with red cheeks and fair hair, and he wore a sky-blue suit with a pale pink shirt and a maroon tie. He introduced himself as Charlie Hoyt, the public defender appointed to her case. Geri-Jo thought he looked too young to know very much, and she was further put off by his clothes. Would a serious lawyer wear so much color? Her first inclination was to tell him no more than she'd told the prosecutor.

'Geri-Jo,' he implored her finally, 'Delbert Conroy is one of the shrewdest, meanest sons-o'-bitches that ever stood at the Kentucky bar. Give me more to work with, or I can't get you off.' He spoke softly and sympathetically, but again she gritted her teeth and held to her story. Whatever second thoughts she'd had about telling the truth were always cast aside when she considered the consequences. Pa would either be punished, along with Molly — or, when they asked him to verify the details, he'd deny them and she'd be worse off, accused of telling even more lies.

If anyone was going to be swayed to her side, Geri-Jo began to realize, it couldn't be done without Molly to back her up — and maybe an admission of what had really happened with Pa. She wasn't sure whether she could ask Molly to do that, though. And even if she did, whether Molly would cooperate.

'Mr Hoyt,' Geri-Jo said as the public defender started to collect his papers, 'I haven't seen my sister since . . . the accident. Before I can say any more, I need to settle things with her . . .'

'That might be hard to arrange,' Hoyt said thoughtfully. 'Your sister's a minor — and a valuable witness already in protective custody — so her guardians will have to consent. Even if they do, Conroy might block our access on the grounds that collusion between you and your sister could alter essential testimony before the trial.'

The last word was a fresh shock. Things were moving so fast. 'Trial?' Geri-Jo asked shakily. 'When'll that be?'

'A few weeks, I expect. The prosecution moves fast when they think it's cut and dried.'

'Mr Hoyt, you get Molly here soon, all right? There doesn't have to be a trial if you can do that . . .'

Ed Parker finally arrived at the end of the day. He was brought to the cell and locked in with her. 'They're saying it couldn't be an accident, Geri-Jo. And with what they're

155

hearing about the feuds between you and your Pa, about Bard and all —'

'Who gave Bard's name to the police?'

'Lettie thought it'd be in your interest to have them know how rough your Pa made things for you.' He paused. 'She would have come with me, Geri-Jo, but she's been terribly shaken. Even before this, you know, Lettie didn't have an easy time going out in the world.'

The hint that she could expect no strong support from Lettie Parker concerned Geri-Jo less than the news that Bard Mitchell's name had now been brought in. That meant he and his family would probably be questioned by Delbert Conroy, and she couldn't see any good coming from that. Eldon Mitchell, believing she had been responsible for the death of his favorite pony, was already angry at her. Bard himself would say anything to protect his past lies.

'And Molly,' Geri-Jo asked, 'what's she been saying?'

'Nothing . . . except that she can't imagine what got into you.'

She came close now — much closer than with either lawyer — to baring the truth. But then a voice called along the corridor to Parker that only a minute of his visiting time remained, and he rose from the cot. 'I'm told that the public defender assigned to your case is very good,' he said. He paused to clear his throat, then he added, 'I want to go to bat for you, Geri-Jo. But unless I know you're being totally honest with me, I don't think I could ask anyone I know to take over your case.'

'Do what you have to, Mr Parker, I won't blame you. But just promise me one thing. You'll bring Molly down here. I can't make this come out right without talking to her.'

The footsteps of a guard were approaching along the corridor. 'I don't know if I can promise that, Geri-Jo. But I'll do my best.'

The next morning she was brought to a court room. Conroy and Hoyt each stood up to make quiet speeches, then the judge asked Geri-Jo if she had anything to say. She muttered only that the charges were wrong.

Afterwards she was photographed and finger-printed, and then had to trade her own clothes for a drab khaki denim shift. Wearing her jail uniform, she was taken for a short conference with Charlie Hoyt. He told her she would not be released on bail because there was no acceptable relative to guarantee custody.

'I tried to arrange that meeting with your sister,' Hoyt added then, 'but the Parker woman who's got custody won't give consent.'

'Why not?'

'Well, she's just being kind of motherly, I guess. Wants to protect Molly from an upsetting situation.'

Geri-Jo's hopes sank further as she realized that Molly had moved in to fill the vacuum in Lettie's need for a substitute child.

She turned away, hiding the tears of desperation that were welling in her eyes. Hoyt came and put his arm around her. 'Listen, Geri-Jo, whatever there is between you and your sister, can't you just tell me? If it's going to get you out of here . . .'

Her inclination to trust Charlie Hoyt had grown. She didn't know if he was a skilled lawyer, but he seemed genuinely sympathetic. The terror of being found guilty was growing now and she wished the bond of family loyalty that held her in silence would break — but still, in spite of everything, it held. 'I can't, Mr Hoyt,' she said. 'Do one more thing for me, though.' She told him about her friendship with Steve Kimball, and asked him to arrange a visit for Steve.

But by the third morning, neither Molly had come — nor Steve. She worried then that something might have happened to him. He and Chel had been stalked by an unknown maniac. Would a person fanatic enough to follow them from another state give up after only four shots?

When she was taken once more from her cell, she dared not assume it was anything but another bit of jail routine. And indeed the first man she saw when she entered the dingy meeting room was another stranger. Then she noticed Charlie Hoyt, seated at the end of the table, and, at a window beyond,

Steve. She had never felt such a rush of emotion. She ran to him, and he embraced her and held her while she sobbed against his shoulder. In his arms, she finally felt there was hope.

'Forgive me for taking so long to get here, Geri-Jo. I went straight down to Alabama to help the F.B.I., so I didn't know —'

'It's me you've got to forgive,' she broke in. 'With all your trouble, I hate to pull you into mine. There just isn't anyone else.'

'All the more reason I'm glad to be here.' He helped her into a chair. Then he gestured to the man Geri-Jo hadn't met. 'This is Sidney Ross, Geri-Jo. He's from Frankfort, a lawyer like Charlie. I asked him to come because he's a specialist in defending people accused of serious crimes.' Steve crouched beside her, and looked directly into her eyes. 'Geri-Jo, I know you must be holding back about what really happened — as I know there have been times in the past you protected others at your own expense. But all the facts have to be known this time, or we can't get this straightened out. Please, talk to Mr Ross.'

The lawyer from Frankfort carried the chair from the opposite end of the table and placed it next to Geri-Jo. He sat on it side ways, she noticed, the way old men in the hollow had perched on chairs when they would all gather around a stove on a cold evening. But Ross didn't look like any old cracker from the hollow. He had a narrow angular face with skin the color of young tobacco, jet-black hair, shrewd penetrating dark eyes, and a large nose that hooked down.

'You have a very good friend in Dr Kimball, Geri-Jo,' Ross began. 'I'm here because he told me that he'd never met anyone less likely than you to inflict pain on another person, unless given the strongest provocation. I can imagine reasons it would be hard for you to tell. But as long as you don't trust us, Geri-Jo, you're not just the accused, you're also being your own judge and jury — and your own jailer.'

Could she really trust this exotic-looking man? Geri-Jo looked to Steve. If only she could talk to him first, tell him alone. Steve was the only one she could really trust.

158

But she thought then of the reservations she'd had about Chel the first time they'd met. Finally, her voice breaking, she began. 'I never wanted to hurt Pa — and I'd swear, in his right mind, he'd never have wanted to hurt me. But you see, he's never really been right since the slide, and it just kept getting worse and worse . . .'

With help from Steve and Charlie Hoyt, Sidney Ross went to work trying to build defense. He spent two or three days a week in Lexington, traveling back and forth constantly from Frankfort where he had many other cases in his busy practice. It occurred one day to Geri-Jo that, if he was really the best at this kind of work, then his fees must be high, and his expenses must be mounting up. She understood then that Steve must be paying for everything.

'I can't let you go broke on my account,' she told him the next time he came for a visit. 'Mr Hoyt could do the job. I've got enough to feel guilty about without taking so much from you.'

'Listen, Geri-Jo,' Steve said forcefully. 'You know that I want to be free to make my own choices, love who I want. But I'm not free yet, not really — because the choice I've made breaks some old rules. So I'm helping you because it helps me, too. Because as long as people here turn a blind eye to injustice of any kind, it's that much easier for all kinds of stupid unfair rules to stand. So let me spend my money. Okay?'

For all the effort and expense, though, nothing changed. Sid Ross asked permission to question Geri-Jo's father in the hospital to try confirming her story. But Garrett Lockely was in critical condition, dosed with such heavy pain-killers that the doctors at first deemed him incapable of giving reliable answers. Later, when Ross was finally given access, Lockely said he couldn't remember clearly exactly what had happened on the night he'd been injured. Learning of this from Steve, Geri-Jo didn't believe her father was deliberately concealing the truth. Wasn't it possible he might forget the hateful things he'd done when not in his right mind?

But without corroboration from Pa, the chance for a fair trial still rested on Molly. Delbert Conroy continued to fight

159

Sidney Ross's attempts to take statements from Geri-Jo's younger sister on the ground that she was his only eye-witness and ought to be protected from any undue influence to change her testimony, but at last Sidney Ross obtained the right to depose Molly in the office of the County Prosecutor with Conroy and members of the county welfare board in attendance. By now, Ross had gathered some background on Molly's character to cast doubt upon her reliability as a witness. However, when he raised the subject of Molly's reputation among local boys for being available for random sex in the back of the theater where she worked as an usher, Molly broke into tears and Conroy cut short the deposition. 'Petting in the back of a movie theater,' the prosecutor declared, 'is not abnormal behavior for teenagers, and shouldn't be taken as any indication that this child would be capable of committing incest.'

It wasn't until the eve of the trial, nine weeks after she had been arrested and charged with attempting to murder her father, that there was finally a break in Geri-Jo's favor.

Both Charlie Hoyt and Sidney Ross had continued pressing the court to grant her relief from the ordeal of staying in the county jail. If she was to be tried under the same code applying to an adult, they argued, then she ought to be similarly granted the right of release on bail prior to conviction. At last, with Steve Kimball unconditionally guaranteeing responsibility and paying a bondsman to post a bail of $100,000, the judge agreed to release Geri-Jo into his custody.

As Geri-Jo climbed into Steve's station wagon outside the jail, she asked to be taken first to the hospital where Pa was recovering.

'I'm sorry, Geri-Jo,' Sidney Ross told her. 'While the charge stands against you, there's a court order that forbids access.'

'I just want to see him,' she cried, 'tell him I'm sorry and that I don't blame him for anything he's done or said.'

'You'll have to wait for that chance . . .'

'Until when?'

'Until we win.'

CHAPTER ELEVEN

The case that Delbert Conroy presented to the jury suggested that Geri-Jo's anger at her father's strict rules against dating had finally exploded in a homicidal rage when he learned of her 'affair' with Bard Mitchell and ordered her to end it. As a series of prosecution witnesses came to the stand, nothing seemed to contradict this theory. There was no doubt of course that Geri-Jo had pulled a switch to bring tons of metal crushing down onto her father. When Hal Parker appeared in the witness box, and Conroy led him into describing the many lies Geri-Jo had told so that she could continue her clandestine dates with Bard, that gave a firm foundation to the prosecution's case.

The greater damage was done, however, by the appearance of Bard Mitchell. Dressed in a plain dark blue suit, his hair freshly cut, he was the image of a responsible scion of a prominent family. The jury listened attentively as he described how they had met, and admitted to initiating what Delbert Conroy characterized, at first, as 'teen-age romance'.

'Now Mr Mitchell,' the prosecutor asked then, 'it sounds to me like you would've been quite pleased if your romance with Miss Lockely had continued . . .'

Bard smiled ingenuously. 'I had visions of marrying her,' he said.

Conroy paced thoughtfully in front of the witness box, allowing some suspense to build. 'Yet quite suddenly you stopped seeing each other. Was that because you had reason to be angry with Miss Lockely?'

'No sir. Not at all.'

'But isn't it true that it was because of Miss Lockely that one of your father's favorite horses had to be destroyed?'

'Yes.'

Geri-Jo bolted forward on her chair, not certain how this was to be used against her, but sure that Bard would have to repeat the story he had invented to cover himself. Sidney Ross put a restraining hand on her arm. She had already given him all the details about the sudden end of her friendship with Bard.

Conroy instructed Bard to describe the incident with the horse, and Bard gave the same version Geri-Jo had heard from Steve: she had ridden the animal carelessly, causing an injury that required Bard to destroy it. Geri-Jo had to grab the arms of her chair to prevent herself from springing to her feet and denouncing him as a liar. But Sid Ross had counseled her against such displays in several, vigorous pre-trial training sessions.

'So Mr Mitchell,' Delbert Conroy went on silkily. 'If Miss Lockely was forgiven for . . . causing that damage, what other reason could there be for the end of your . . . friendship?'

Bard looked brazenly toward Geri-Jo. 'I never knew for sure,' he said. 'I wanted to see her again, but suddenly she wouldn't talk to me. I figure her father found out that she'd —'

Abruptly Bard broke off, and looked down.

Conroy finished for him. 'That he'd found out you were sleeping together . . .?'

'Objection!' Ross shouted. 'Prosecution is leading the witness.'

The judge instructed Conroy to rephrase his question, and the prosecutor duly obeyed.

'Master Mitchell, is it true that you had intercourse with Miss Lockely?'

Geri-Jo bowed her head, mortified as she heard Bard reply, 'Yes, sir.'

'And this happened once — and immediately before Miss Lockely suddenly stopped seeing you?'

'That's correct, sir.'

'No more questions, your honor.' Delbert Conroy sat down.

Sidney Ross stood. 'No cross-examination, your honor.'

Geri-Jo was dismayed by her lawyer's announcement; she had told him all about the way The Ghost had died, the real reason Bard had broken off with her. Didn't Ross want to bring out the truth?

Later, during a recess, the lawyer explained why he had allowed the lie to stand. 'I don't want to give the court a picture of you as a violent or impulsive person, Geri-Jo. Even if what you did when you shot that horse was humane, that might not be what stays with a jury when they hear that you grabbed a gun out of Bard's hands and used it to kill a living thing.'

'If even the truth can't help me,' Geri-Jo said despairingly, 'what chance have I got?'

'We're a long way from the end,' Ross said. 'I've lined up plenty of witnesses who'll tell about your father's temper, and attest to your character —'

'You know that won't be enough. We've got to get Molly to tell what really happened,' Geri-Jo insisted. 'That's more important than anything . . .' She had not yet been allowed to meet with her sister, although Ross had petitioned constantly.

'I'm still working on it,' the lawyer said. 'But if they want to protect her testimony by keeping you two apart, that may not be a bad thing. It means she's getting on the stand. Once she's there I've got the ammunition to destroy her credibility.'

'Get us together before that happens, Mr Ross. Please. Let me persuade her to tell the truth.' She didn't want to see Molly publicly destroyed if it could possibly be avoided.

When they returned to the courtroom, Conroy introduced a parade of technical witnesses — doctors who described the extent of Garrett Lockely's injuries, engineers who talked about the workings of pneumatic automobile lifts. Their testimony left the impression that Geri-Jo still should have been able to save her father after he had been struck, if she had wanted to . . .

Geri-Jo hoped that Molly wouldn't be called before the end of the day so that there might be a chance to talk with her first.

Each time Delbert Conroy rose to announce his next witness, she held her breath.

But suddenly Conroy announced, 'No more witnesses, your honor. The prosecution rests.'

As the judge called for an adjournment so the defense could open its case the following day, Geri-Jo cast an astonished glance at Sidney Ross. Had Molly refused, after all, to testify against her?

Later, as Steve bought her dinner in a coffeeshop while they conferred with Ross and Charlie Hoyt, the prosecution tactic was explained to her. 'Perhaps Conroy realized that Molly's story was soft,' Ross said, 'and I'd take it apart. Or else he decided to keep your sister off the stand to send a message to the jury that he doesn't believe the whole incest story, it's just something you made up to cover yourself.'

'It won't help Conroy, though,' Steve put in reassuringly. 'We can still put Molly on the stand,' Steve said.

Ross sighed. 'I'll have to, I suppose. Trouble is, it's not the same as coming at her after she's been used for the prosecution. If *I* put the little sister up there only to rip her story apart, it might only generate sympathy for her . . .'

Geri-Jo shook her head and turned away, not wanting to hear any more, wishing she could wake and find it was all a bad dream. How had it come to this, being part of a war council that spoke about ripping her only sister apart, denying her sympathy?

Steve seemed to read her reaction. He put his arm around her. 'Geri-Jo,' he said, 'we're in a tough fight, remember that. Lose it, and you'll lose anywhere from five to twenty years of your freedom.'

'Then find some decent way to win.' She turned to Ross. 'Even if you keep me out of jail, I won't ever be free from knowing what I've done to Pa. I can't help that now. But if I've got to destroy my sister, whatever freedom I win out of it won't be worth a damn. So you get us together, that's the only way it can work. Let me talk to Molly, let me explain it all so she can go up there and tell the truth and whoever hears it will understand she wasn't a tramp and a liar . . . but just a victim . . . and then this will end right.'

Ross rolled his eyes at Steve before answering. 'I suppose the judge has to grant our petition now. He can't let Conroy block it anymore on the grounds that he's protecting necessary prosecution testimony . . .'

But as the defense case opened, there was still no ruling on whether Geri-Jo would be allowed to meet privately with Molly. The judge had said he wanted to give the matter 'due consideration' — which, Sid Ross explained, could mean that he took a day or two to come back with a decision.

In the meantime, Ross produced a number of the customers and hotrodders to whom Garrett Lockely had exhibited violent behavior, several of them willing to testify that it was no exaggeration to say they had fled in fear of their lives. They were followed by character witnesses for Geri-Jo, teachers, and people she had waited on regularly at the gas station, or others she met on rounds with Steve — all willing to attest to her customary respect and politeness and pleasant disposition.

Then Steve was called to the stand. The original purpose had been for him to tell about the night he had picked up Geri-Jo on the roadside. She had since explained to Steve and Sid Ross that it was her father who had beaten her that night, and the lawyer felt that bringing this out would strengthen the implied need for Geri-Jo to defend herself by any means in the subsequent attack. But after this part of the testimony, Ross changed direction.

'Dr Kimball,' he said, 'there was some testimony earlier from Bard Mitchell that tended to support the belief that Garrett discovered his daughter's romance with the young man and broke it up. If that was true, then perhaps she did indeed resent it. But do you know of a reason that Bard Mitchell might, in fact, have lied to this court about why he stopped seeing Geri-Jo . . ?'

Geri-Jo pulled forward on her seat. With the absence of other ammunition for his defense, Sidney Ross had apparently decided to attack Bard's story, after all. But Geri-Jo had to fight down the impulse to cry out and silence Steve. She knew the sacrifice he was making. The society of horse breeders was tight-knit; the whole business depended upon one member of its elite being supportive of another. By publicly discrediting Bard Mitchell — even though the Mitchells would be awakened to their own son's deception — Steve risked being branded spy and traitor by all the people who employed him. Defending her, Geri-Jo thought, had cost Steve his career.

After Steve told what he knew about the true circumstances of the horse's death, Sidney Ross sat down. He had brought the story out well, stressing the humane aspect of Geri-Jo's actions, and from the faces of the jury it seemed that they had been positively impressed.

Delbert Conroy began his cross-examination: 'Doctor Kimball. You've told us that you came to know Geri-Jo somewhat more intimately after stopping to help her one night when — if we're to believe her — she was attacked by her father. Is that the story she told you that night?'

'No . . .'

'What did she tell you that night?'

'She gave me no details.'

'So it might have been anyone who attacked her. Or . . . it might not have been an attack at all.'

'She was in tears, her clothes torn . . .'

Delbert Conroy paused thoughtfully, leaving the jury to wonder if there weren't other conclusions to make about her appearance. 'Now, Doctor Kimball — excuse me, is that correct to address you as Doctor? I know you're only a veterinarian. Perhaps only horses are entitled to call you by that title . . .'

The jury and spectators laughed, but Steve bristled at being mocked. 'Doctor will do,' he said.

'Very well, Doctor, let us return to the night when you became friendly with Miss Lockely. Coming upon this damsel in distress, you say that you took her to your home. Under the circumstances as you understood them, wouldn't the natural thing have been to bring her to a hospital — or even to the police?'

'She begged me not to go to the police. Since she was in a mild state of shock, I chose not to aggravate her condition by disregarding her wishes. I knew I could supply the treatment she needed.'

'Did you? But as an equine veterinarian, sir, aren't you qualified only to diagnose and treat *horses*?'

Steve pulled himself forward and looked as if he might erupt. But after Ross made a quick gesture with his hand, Steve settled back in the witness chair.

'Of course,' Conroy went on in his genial drawl, 'you would have felt any gaps in your own medical judgment might be covered by the woman with whom you live. Is that right, Doctor Kimball? Miss Rachel Dennison is, I believe, a nurse in a local hospital?'

Steve looked back at Conroy with narrowed eyes, as if straining to see down a long dark tunnel.

'Answer me, please, Doctor. The woman with whom you are currently domiciled — I believe the more colloquial phrase would be "living in sin" — is a nurse?'

Ross's outraged objection to Conroy's critical aside was sustained, yet too late to erase the impression left with the jury that Kimball was not to be taken as any judge of moral or immoral behavior. This was only the beginning. Conroy asked next how Steve could believe his home was really the best place to provide a safe, calm atmosphere for a young girl in shock? Wasn't this the same home into which a madman had recently fired four rifle shots? Could a white man living with a black woman fail to be aware of the constant potential for such danger?

As deftly as an artist bulding an image with fine brush strokes, Conroy applied his smears to portray the witness in a new light for the jury. This animal-doctor who had brought a young girl to his home was not a good samaritan, but an audacious libertine whose defiance of professional obligations and social norms marked him, at best, a poor judge of morality — and, at worst, a depraved sinner. Beneath the grubby surface of innuendo lay a buried suggestion that Steve was no less likely than Garrett Lockely to engage in a perverse sexual relationship with Geri-Jo, perhaps even a triangle that included his black girlfriend. Having broken one tabu, would there be any perversions of which Kimball was not capable?

Ross kept up a barrage of increasingly indignant objections, and most were sustained. But of course it made no difference.

Prior to the mid-day recess, the judge announced he wanted to see counsel for both sides in his chambers. While Ross went off to the conference, Charlie Hoyt took Geri-Jo to the conference room set aside for the defense team. Steve and Chel were there when she entered.

'Oh Steve,' Geri-Jo cried as she went to them, 'why'd you let yourself in for that . . .?'

He shrugged. 'If there was the least chance it would help . . .'

'But it was for nothing,' Geri-Jo said desolately. 'You've lost everything, and it didn't help. Conroy turned it all around.'

Steve mustered a stoic smile. 'We forget how ruthless some people can be — the same damn mistake decent people always make. But I'd do it again. I'd have to try . . .'

Ross strode suddenly into the room. 'The judge has granted our petition. Geri-Jo and Molly will be allowed to meet. There's a catch, though. The judge wants supervision. He's allowing Molly's *de facto* guardian, Lettie Parker, to be present.'

There was a gloomy silence. The stipulation put more pressure on Geri-Jo, would make it harder to convince Molly.

'There's more bad news, I'm afraid.' Ross turned to Steve. 'After your crucifixion this morning, the judge got a call from the child welfare people. They want Geri-Jo removed from your custody.'

Geri-Jo gave a low cry as Chel grasped her hand.

Ross had fought the move with the judge; it would prejudice the case, virtually certify that all of Conroy's worst insinuations were fact. 'The judge might stall it for a day or two. But in the end I think he'll say a minor has to be protected even where only the tiniest doubt of an improper relationship exists.'

'They protect her as a minor, and punish her as an adult,' Charlie Hoyt sneered.

A numbness came over Geri-Jo, as though she was already

adjusting to the hard conditions. 'It'll only be a few days extra,' she said. 'Looks like I'm going get locked up anyway.'

'No!' Ross exhorted her harshly. 'It's too soon to give in. Just get through to Molly, Geri-Jo, that's all you have to do. Make her tell the truth and everything else the jury has heard will be meaningless.'

The bailiff took her to the judge's chambers, a room off a long hallway behind the court with walls of dark panelled wood, kept dim by venetian blinds on the windows. No one else was there. After cautioning her not to touch anything, the bailiff went out, closing the door. Geri-Jo remained standing stiffly in the center of the room, imagining that someone might be observing her from concealment. There were two other doors — closets she supposed — until one opened and the bailiff showed Molly in with Lettie right behind her. The door closed and the three of them were alone.

The silence seemed to last an eternity. Molly kept staring off toward the window, Lettie stood beside her, an arm around her shoulder. Geri-Jo noticed that Molly's long red hair had been cut and set in a new style and glistened with being freshly washed. She was wearing a new outfit, too, a pale green pinafore with frills over a white blouse. She was Lettie's 'daughter', now, and she seemed to have no qualms about playing the role.

'Well, say your piece, Geri-Jo,' Lettie commanded at last. 'We've been ordered to come in here and give a listen.'

Geri-Jo struggled to find her voice. She looked from Molly to Lettie Parker, uncertain of where to direct her plea. Finally, she took a step toward her sister.

'Mol'. . . that night . . . when everything happened, I didn't talk about you and Pa because . . . I didn't want to make things worse. If I wasn't sure you'd come out okay now, maybe I wouldn't even ask you to speak out. I don't know . . . What I do know — what you've got to realize, too — is that unless every-body understands what really happened, I could lose this . . .'

Molly kept gazing off at the slatted view of a bright day beyond the covered window.

Geri-Jo was torn between rage at her sister's callousness, and the need to persuade her. 'Listen, Mol',' Geri-Jo said, her voice rising. 'If I lose, my life's over. You've got to let it all out. Once they understand the way Pa really was, all his problems, I'd be free and you wouldn't be blamed for anything you did . . .'

Molly turned slowly from the window. 'I can't do it, Geri-Jo. I'm sorry, I hate to think of what's ahead for you, and I wish I could stop it. But I can't. It's asking too much if you want me to lie for you.'

'Lie?' Geri-Jo reached out, extending her hands in a plea, and Lettie pulled Molly back a step as though to protect her from being struck. 'I just want you to tell the truth,' Geri-Jo wailed. 'Tell about you and Pa, how I found you together, the way he —'

'That's enough, Geri-Jo!' Lettie snapped. 'I'm not gonna let you drag this child down to save your own skin.'

Geri-Jo turned to Lettie. 'It happened, I swear to you.'

'I don't hold much by your word anymore, Geri-Jo. I put all my trust in you once, but you didn't deserve it, you took me in. Disgraced yourself with that Mitchell boy, too. I can see now that all along your father was just doing his best to straighten you out before it was too late.' She paused, and stroked Molly's hair. 'He failed. But I'm not gonna fail with this child. I've come to love this girl, and I know it's not too late for her. C'mon, dear, we've done what we had to.' Her arm tight around the girl, Lettie Parker swept her toward the door.

'Molly!' Geri-Jo screamed. A door burst open and a bailiff leaned in, looking as though he was prepared to break up a fight.

'Molly,' Geri-Jo repeated, fighting to control herself. 'Don't leave it like this, I'm begging you . . .'

'I'm sorry, Geri-Jo,' Molly said, and turned to Lettie. 'Can we go, Mama?'

They started to move through the door. Geri-Jo shouted after them. 'I'm just gonna pray, Mol', oh God how I'm gonna pray that I can forgive you! Because otherwise I'll hate you the rest of my life, and I don't like what hate does to people!'

'You don't have to pray for nothin',' Molly called over her shoulder. ''Cause there just ain't nothin' to forgive.'

When Geri-Jo returned to the courtroom, it was with the expectation that she would appear on the stand. Her last chance, Ross had said, would be that she could persuade the jury herself.

But the lawyer had just risen to call Geri-Jo, when a policeman burst through the doors at the rear of the room followed by a wedge of newsmen, and hurried up to the prosecution table where he leaned over and whispered to Conroy. Put off by the disturbance, Ross waited until the policeman had finished and retreated. Before he could resume, Conroy pulled himself up and addressed the bench.

'Your honor, I have just received information that profoundly alters the course of these proceedings — indeed, requiring the prosecution to consider withdrawing its charge of attempted murder. Before that, however, I would like to request an immediate adjournment to make certain our next moves are not taken too hastily.'

A ripple of whispers was already sweeping from the back of the courtroom toward the front, the news traveling through the crowd. Geri-Jo flashed a hopeful look at Ross. Molly had gone away and relented, perhaps. Or Pa had changed his story.

'It's near the end of the day, Mister Prosecutor,' the judge said, 'so I have no objection to granting your request. Before adjourning, however, I wonder if you can share this new information.'

'By all means, Your Honor,' Conroy replied in his exceedingly courtly manner. 'Forty minutes ago in Bourbon County Hospital, as a result of long-term complications directly related to injuries sustained at the hand of his daughter three months ago, Garrett Lockely was pronounced dead.'

'No!' Geri-Jo screamed, a futile cry of denial, a refusal to believe the nightmare was becoming still more horrible. Conroy glanced over and gave her a look, withering in its skepticism. Then, as Geri-Jo went on sobbing quietly at the defense table, Conroy turned back to the judge. 'In view of this development, your honor, the prosecution intends to upgrade the charges against Geri-Jo Lockely . . . to murder in the first degree.'

Waking at a touch, she saw Steve's shadow perched on the edge of the bed, the sleeves of his white shirt still rolled up as they had been when she had slipped away from the kitchen table, unable to listen anymore to him and Charlie and Sid Ross talking defense strategy. Conroy could fight virtually the same case all over again and be sure of winning, they agreed. If he hadn't rammed a new writ through this very day, it was only to give Geri-Jo and her advisors one more night to contemplate the inescapable and soften them up for a plea bargain — a few years off the sentence in exchange for an admission of guilt.

Even before listening to their discussion Geri-Jo had been drained of all resistance. Running from the courtroom to a car had been like swimming upstream against a torrent. Newsmen, welfare people, crowds of curiosity-seekers, all seemed more hungry to punish her now that she had been redefined as a murderer. At Steve's she had spent the first hours crying uncontrollably. Only when it seemed there were no more tears left had she spent a while listening to the discussion of her defense. But all that did was make her wonder if she deserved to be defended. Pa was dead. She had killed him.

'What time is it?' she asked drowsily.

'Not quite midnight,' Steve said. 'The others have gone.'

Staring at his silhouette in the dark, his head bowed, she sensed that he had finally given up. 'It's all right,' she said. 'Nobody could've given more. Whatever they do to me now, I —'

'Nobody's going to do anything to you, Geri-Jo — nothing you don't deserve.' The tremor in his voice conveyed a conviction so fierce that, though she might be the beneficiary, it frightened her. He went on quickly, unfolding his intentions with so much furious determination that, although there were a dozen places Geri-Jo wanted to protest, she could only be

172

silent as he ran through the plan he and Chel had conceived as soon as Ross and Hoyt were gone. Chel was at a neighbor's right now, borrowing a car in which they could travel a few hundred miles without its being traced to them. There was no way to freedom but this, they were sure. Bail would be terminated tomorrow. For all they knew, Conroy had already arranged for police to arrive with papers early in the morning. So tonight — this moment — was her only chance.

'We'd better get started on your disguise,' he said, motioning her to rise from the bed. 'I want you across two or three state lines before the sun comes up.'

The mention of disguises and traveling across state lines crystalized what lay ahead if she fled, became a fugitive. 'I can't run,' she said.

'Please, Geri-Jo,' his voice softened, anger transmuted to another kind of passion. 'Stay and the law will bury you. Twenty-five years at least, Sid thinks. But law and justice aren't always the same thing. At times you have to defy one to find the other.'

Twenty-five years. She would be forty-two at the end, the precious years of youth forever gone. Her resistance ebbed. Still, she argued: What would happen to him afterward? He had guaranteed her bail.

It would be difficult to press charges against him, he assured her. If she appeared to have fled on her own — as they would contrive — he could not be held responsible. As for covering the bail money, he simply stated flatly that it wouldn't be a problem.

Spurred by Steve's insistence, she went at last to the bathroom and stood passively in her nightgown while he scissored her hair to a boyish length, then colored it with a can of oxblood shoe polish. He combed it in masculine fashion and, while the polish dried and stiffened, went to get a pair of jeans, a man's shirt, and a couple of bulky sweaters belonging to Chel. 'These will make you appear heavier,' he said before going out so she could change.

When she had dressed, she looked at herself in the mirror. Now even her own face, like Pa's, had been transformed into a stranger's. If she really took this path, when would she ever be herself again? She threw open the door. Steve was standing in the darkened room. He had put on a windbreaker.

'Where can I go?' she asked. 'You'll have to leave me somewhere, won't you? Then what will I do? Who will —'

'Trust me, Geri-Jo. You'll be taken care of. But it's better if I don't tell you more now. I don't want the names of the friends who are helping to be brought in . . . I mean, just in case we're stopped along the way . . .'

There was a soft tapping on a window pane. Steve opened the window and Chel climbed through. She had apparently been staying off the roads. There were brambles stuck to her clothes, a couple of tiny shrub leaves tangled in her hair.

'Got the car,' she said.

'Any sign the house is being watched?'

'No. But I went to the end of the road, and there's a police cruiser at the turn.' She had told the young man who was loaning the car to drive it a few hundred yards past that point and wait for them there.

There was a pause. Then Chel embraced Geri-Jo. 'Take care, baby. I know this is right.'

Geri-Jo hesitated. She was ready to run, but not to leave these two people.

But Steve gave her no chance to retreat. 'Sorry to break this up,' he said, pushing her to the open window, 'but right here in the bail jumper's manual, Rule One says get an early start . . .'

Geri-Jo managed a smile as she broke from Chel and let Steve help her through the window.

They travelled toward the same mountains where she had been spawned, and on through into the rugged Appalachian ridges stitched across a corner of Ohio, and soon after that across the Ohio River and into West Virginia. The rusted ten-year-old Chevrolet lent by a young black neighbor didn't look as though it had many miles left in it, but in fact all the machinery under the ugly exterior had been finely retooled, and the car drove quickly and smoothly. Stopping only for gas, they kept going, mile after mile in the dark, the change in regions marked by nothing except the different kinds of music coming through the radio. Country and western to blue grass to rhythm and blues. Though Steve stayed off main roads, which slowed them a little, the sun still hadn't broken above the horizon when he said, 'Pennsylvania,' with a lilt of elation that made Geri-Jo think she must already be somewhere near her final haven.

Stopping for breakfast in a small diner, Steve explained there was still some traveling to do. 'It'll be another couple of hours before anybody knows you're gone, but there's a chance of an interstate police bulletin asking for a watch on all cars with Kentucky plates. To keep you in the clear, I'd like to be almost all the way home before that goes out.' He would stay with her another two hours, he concluded; so that he could arrive back home before dawn — and make it appear he had not been away all night — he would leave her in Johnstown, and she would take a bus the rest of the way.

The rest of the way to where? she wanted to ask. But Steve obviously intended to hold that back, too. He had already gone up to the counter to pay the bill.

At Johnstown, he parked the car around the corner from the bus company's storefront office, and told her to wait while he checked the schedule and bought a ticket. He returned quickly. 'We're in luck. In ten minutes a bus for Harrisburg comes through. You'll transfer there.' He handed her a ticket, then took out his wallet and extracted several bills. 'That'll cover the second bus ticket, a taxi when you arrive at the other end, and some meals.' He folded the money and pressed it into her hand, then pulled a pen and his prescription pad from a pocket.

He spoke rapidly as he wrote. 'This is the name, address and phone number of a woman who'll be waiting to take you in. Get a taxi after you leave the bus and show them that address.' He tore the piece of paper from the pad, and shoved it into the hand where she still clutched the money. 'Don't lose that,' he added firmly.

She crammed the contents of her hand deep into her pocket without checking them. To count money, or read an address,

175

was to squander all the time remaining with the person who meant most to her in the world — who had given her a reason, she realized now, to care about surviving. She watched him intently as he closed his notebook and stuck it in his shirt pocket. 'I don't want to leave you,' she said.

'It's scary to be alone, I know. But you'll be fine where you're going. I promise.'

Was it possible that he really didn't understand what she meant, what she felt? At the moment of parting from him, she finally understood how important he was to her — feelings she had denied only because she had cared so much for Chel, too.

'I love you,' she said.

'I know. I love you, too, Geri-Jo.'

She started to put her arms around him, and press her body against his, but Steve caught her and gently pushed her back. 'No, Geri-Jo. That doesn't belong between us. That's a different kind of love, and you know I have that with someone else.'

She shook her head, as if it might shake the jumbled thoughts back into some kind of order. 'But then what am I to you? You're not kin. Why have you done so much for me?'

'Because you needed help, and I never met anyone who deserved it more.'

'But how do I love you back?' she pleaded. 'You have the answer, Steve, you've got to. Because I've seen the way you love people — you don't let anything stop you from giving all you've got. Well, all I've got is . . . what Bard wanted, and even Pa . . . and you don't want that. I don't have any other way to pay you back for . . for loving me.'

He hesitated, then pulled her close again and caressed her head as she rested against his chest. 'Some people,' he said, 'get paid back just by being needed. You've done a lot for me that you can't see, and I can't explain. But it's real. Because I've known you, and because I've helped you, every day of my life from now on is going to be easier for me than it was before . . .'

Could that be? Everything he'd done should have only made his life harder? Yet the ring of absolute truth came through the

176

quavering intensity of his voice. As his arms tightened around her, she simply took his love as a child would, without questions, and without debts.

When the time came, he didn't go with her to the bus. It would be best, he said, if no one could later remember seeing any girl of her age with an older man.

Aboard the half-empty bus, she found an isolated seat, where she could cry without disturbing anyone. As the bus pulled away from the small terminal, taking a turn onto some anonymous dark street, the terror of being cast adrift suddenly struck her. She remembered then the slip of paper on which Steve had written her destination — his prescription for a future. She pulled it from her pocket and peered at it through the darkness: a name and an address. But they gave her no comfort. When she saw where she was going, how far from everything she knew, the terror only became greater.

Huddled into her seat, she looked out hopelessly at the highways of the night, until the fatigue building through hours of escape overtook her and she fell into a restless sleep.

BOOK III: *DRIFTING WIDE*

New York City — 1966

CHAPTER ONE

The November wind that gusted along the city street made Geri-Jo shiver inside her thin coat as she stood at the edge of the sidewalk and looked at the building in front of her. She felt so utterly exhausted, so fearful of entering an unknown situation, that she was tempted to go back into the park she had seen not far away, crawl under a bush and sleep like an animal. She glanced down again at the slip of paper she had been holding crumpled tightly in her hand. Cold as she was, anxiety had made her palms moist, causing the ink on the paper to run. As she scanned the blurred name and address Steve had provided, she wondered if she'd misread his handwriting:

Mrs Sylvia Balkin
32 East 74th Street
New York, New York

Perhaps what she'd taken for a '7' was a '1' . . ? Again she examined the building in front of her. It was a wide limestone townhouse, guarded by an imposing fence of black iron grillwork with a gate at the center that led up a few stairs to a pair of bronze doors. The number '32', outlined in gilt paint, was worked right into the filigreed iron of the gate. The house had five floors, leading up to a slate mansard roof, with a balcony on the second floor and a large bow window on the third. Could anyone willing to harbor a fugitive be attached to a place that looked so respectable? Who was Sylvia Balkin? Conscious of her makeshift disguise and ashamed of her fugitive status, Geri-Jo worried that this unknown woman would not only reject her, but — once it was clear exactly who and what had been sent by Steve Kimball — might turn her over to the police.

Perhaps she would be better off trying to survive on her own in some quieter place; she might get a job waitressing or pumping gas. The few hours she had so far spent in the city had already made it seem a cruel, hateful place. Within minutes of getting off the bus, she had experienced its dangers. As she had walked in a daze through the noisy crowded terminal, a nice-looking young man had approached to offer help since she appeared lost. She had accepted an invitation to get something to eat, and as they strolled he had begun talking about how she might work for him. When she realized the kind of work he was proposing and tried to leave, he had grabbed her and forced her to turn over the suitcase and all her money before vanishing into the crowd. Her impulse to call a policeman hadn't lasted more than an instant. The thief, she reflected bitterly, couldn't have chosen a better victim than a bail-jumper.

Without money, she had been forced to walk to the address on the paper, and everything she saw along the way only added to her hopelessness. Rivers of humanity flowing between slabs of concrete and steel so high they blocked out the sun; the noise of jackhammers raising up still more buildings; hot winds that swirled up from stairways leading down to some netherworld below the streets. Why had Steve sent her here? There must be a better place . . .

But wherever it was, she didn't have enough strength or hope left to go looking for it. As twilight came on, the November chill sliced even deeper into her flesh and Geri-Jo felt that if she didn't get into a warm place soon, she would become ill. She opened the black iron gate marked by the number 32, walked up the steps, and pushed the button beside the big bronze door.

It was opened a few moments later by a plump elderly woman dressed in a plain gray uniform with starched white collar and cuffs.

'Are you Sylvia Balkin?' Geri-Jo asked tentatively.

'No.' The woman raked her eyes up and down once and then added briskly, 'Come in. I'll tell Mrs. Balkin you've arrived.' She instructed Geri-Jo to wait in the large entrance hall, then went away up a wide flight of stairs.

Standing in the middle of the huge foyer, Geri-Jo revolved slowly, taking it in. Large pictures hung on the walls and, standing on pedestals around the carpeted floor, were big pieces of sculpted stone and structured metal. Some of the pieces reminded her of work she'd seen on posters in high-school art class. The place must be some kind of museum, she thought. She was sure one of the paintings was by the famous Picasso; and another, a huge canvas covered with dripped and splattered paint, was also by someone famous whose name she couldn't remember. She looked closely at the splotchy picture, trying to find the painter's signature.

'Do you like it?'

At the sound of the cool strong voice behind her, Geri-Jo spun around. Halfway down the stairs, a woman stood with her hand on the polished mahogany bannister. She was dressed in a plain black suit and white blouse, but the proud set of her head, the way her arm rested gracefully on the railing, brought to mind the image of a queen posed beside her throne. Adding to the impression was a diamond nearly the size of a walnut that sparkled on one finger. Having been raised in the hollow among too many young women who looked old, Geri-Jo was not a good judge of age — but the iron gray of the woman's hair, and the elaborate way in which it was styled, certainly indicated she wasn't young. Anywhere from fifty to seventy, Geri-Jo guessed.

'Don't you have an opinion?' the woman said, moving down the stairs again. Awed by the queenly woman, Geri-Jo was still staring speechlessly. 'I may as well warn you, we're not going to get along if you don't have opinions. I like people who say what they think, even if they disagree. Jules — my husband — always used to say that if two people agree on everything, one of them is unnecessary.' Reaching the bottom of the stairs, she paused again and nodded at the picture behind Geri-Jo. 'Well, what *do* you think . . .?'

It was as though she was being tested, Geri-Jo thought, her opinion might determine whether or not she was permitted to stay. She glanced back to the picture, and forced herself to speak the feelings it inspired. 'Looks kind of messy, at first. But the way all that paint is thrown on there, all those different colors banging into each other, I can't help thinking how much the man who did it must have had to dance around. So while I'm looking I can almost feel his movement, and then the colors still seem to be flying through the air and . . .' She heard a sound nearby, and turned to find the woman at her shoulder, regarding her with an imperious stare. 'Well, I mean, yes, I do like it,' Geri-Jo concluded timidly. 'Is that . . . right?'

The woman scrutinized her for another moment. 'It was an opinion,' she said. 'That's all I asked for.' Abruptly, she moved to press a small button set in a doorframe. 'You're hungry, I imagine. We'll do something about that, but first things first. A young woman shouldn't sit down to eat looking as you do.'

The housekeeper reappeared.

'Margaret,' said Sylvia Balkin, 'take this young lady upstairs, and do whatever is necessary to send her back to me looking as much like her real self as possible — and suitably dressed for an informal supper. I'm sure some of Alice's old things will fit well enough until we have a chance to go shopping.' With a wry glance at Geri-Jo, she added, 'And see that she doesn't take too long. I must admit to being a little impatient to learn more about this new philanthropy I've taken on . . . thanks to my son.'

They took an elevator to an upper floor, where the housekeeper showed her into an enormous marble bathroom with a tub set into the floor amidst tall green trees and flowering shrubs. While Geri-Jo stripped off her clothes, gaping all the time at her surroundings, Margaret filled the tub with steaming water.

'Get in,' the starchy housekeeper commanded, 'and wash all that awful muck out of your hair. Goodness, what is it . . .?'

'Shoe polish,' Geri-Jo said.

184

'A disguise, eh?' said Margaret. 'Mr Steven's idea, I suppose . . .' She seemed to have shared with Sylvia Balkin whatever information had been provided about Geri-Jo. As the housekeeper left the bathroom, she was chuckling softly.

Soaking in the tub surrounded by live plants produced the illusion of swimming in a warm jungle pool. For the first time, Geri-Jo felt some of the tension begin ebbing away, replaced by a light-headed sense of disbelief. Last night she had been running for her life; now she was in the most luxurious place she had ever seen. The change was so extreme that she warned herself to beware another sudden change. At any moment, she might find herself cast out again, alone, without a cent. At the thought a wave of despair swept over her. Warm tears ran down her face and dropped into the water, sending out ripples like rain in a pond. If only, if only, she wished silently, things could be undone, Pa could be alive again . . .

Then, resigning herself to the reality, she wiped her face and began to soap herself. At least, she was safe here for as long as she was allowed to stay. Sylvia Balkin was obviously a woman of immense wealth. And with wealth came power and influence.

As she finished soaping herself and reclined in the warm scented water, Geri-Jo thought again about Sylvia Balkin's amazing last words. Could Steve Kimball truly be this woman's son? Why would anyone born into such splendor leave it to live so humbly? The greatest mystery lay in Steve's desire to hide his identity, twisting Balkin around to become Kimball. From whom, or what, might Steve want to hide?

The housekeeper returned and said it was time to dress. After drying off, Geri-Jo went into an adjoining bedroom even larger than the ones at Skyevale. Laid out on the bed were silk underwear, a pale blue silk skirt, and a silk pastel print blouse. When she stood back, staring at the lovely clothes, Margaret urged her forward.

'Go on, go on. They're for you . . .'

She had never worn such fine things, and after putting them on, she stood in front of a full-length mirror simultaneously admiring the way they looked on her, and ashamed of her crudely shortened hair, the reminder that she was running from the law. Could Mrs Balkin really know the seriousness of the charges against her?

When she entered the downstairs room to which the housekeeper led her next, Geri-Jo felt almost as if she had stepped into a garden. There were flowers in the paintings on pale yellow walls, chairs upholstered in yellow silk embroidered with tiny flower designs, and arrangements of real flowers bursting from vases that stood on a sideboard and on the center of a small round dining table set beside a fireplace where a few logs blazed. China plates and soup bowls with gold rims and gold utensils were laid at two places on the table.

Margaret pulled a chair at one place for Geri-Jo, then went away. As she was waiting, Geri-Jo inventoried all the dishes and utensils in front of her, and tried to remember all the pointers on manners and etiquette she had been given by Lettie Parker.

Sylvia Balkin strode in and Geri-Jo jumped up by reflex — so quickly that her chair pitched over backwards. Mrs Balkin said nothing, but the display of clumsiness left Geri-Jo so embarrassed she didn't raise her eyes after she had righted the chair and sat down. The uncomfortable silence lasted while a maid brought in a tureen and ladled a pale pinkish soup into each bowl. And still longer until Geri-Jo had picked up the large spoon — copying her hostess — and tasted the soup. She realized she was being watched every second.

'What do you think . . .?' Sylvia Balkin asked finally.

Another opinion called for. Was it going to be like this all the time? 'I'm sorry,' Geri-Jo said, daring at last to look up. 'I know you like people to say what they think. But I've never had anything like this before. I'll have to taste it a few more times before I know if I like it or not.'

Sylvia Balkin studied her with pale blue eyes that seemed a few degrees warmer than they had earlier. 'I do like opinions,' she said sternly. 'But I didn't say I like them half-baked. I can quite understand if you take your time to sort out what you think about this or anything else. This is lobster bisque, by the

186

way. It's a favorite of mine, but many people find it too rich.' She dipped her own spoon into her soup, swallowed a mouthful, then shot another sharp look at Geri-Jo. 'And now you might appreciate hearing an opinion of mine: I think my son was right about you . . .'

Over the rest of the meal Geri-Jo answered Mrs Balkin's questions about her background, the origins of her friendship with Steve, and finally about the crime she was charged with committing, the trial, and her feelings about her father's death. By the time she was served a dish of billowy chocolate mousse — another 'first', but one she didn't have to taste twice to approve — she felt there was no more about herself to tell.

Mrs Balkin's direct no-nonsense manner made Geri-Jo uncomfortable at first, but as she grew accustomed to it, she decided it had certain advantages. As long as she was straightforward and truthful herself, Geri-Jo felt, she would always know exactly where she stood with Sylvia Balkin.

They sat quietly while a second maid, in a different kind of uniform, cleared the dessert plates, and then brought a silver coffee urn and a single cup which she set in front of Mrs Balkin. 'You don't drink coffee, do you . . .?' Sylvia Balkin asked. When Geri-Jo said she didn't, the maid was dispatched. 'Now,' Sylvia Balkin announced after a sip of her coffee. 'It's your turn: I can imagine there's a great deal you'd like to ask me . . .'

Geri-Jo hesitated. Would she still be welcome if she was someone who pried too deeply into the secrets of as rich a family as this? 'You've a right to know about me,' she answered. 'You're going out on a limb, and you need to know what you're getting into. But I don't expect you to tell me anything more than you want to.'

Sylvia Balkin gave her a patient smile. 'Evidently you've deduced that we have some skeletons sleeping in the family closet, and you think I'd prefer to tiptoe around them rather than wake them up and rattle their bones . . .?'

Unaccustomed to repartee, Geri-Jo had to ponder this talk of skeletons before she understood. 'If Steve wants to keep certain things quiet, that's his right. I'm just more than glad to have a place to stay for a while, but I don't intend to take advantage. I'll try to be off your hands as soon as I can find —'

'There's no need for that,' Sylvia Balkin interrupted. 'It was Steve's intention when he sent you to me that you should have a home. I agreed to take you in with the understanding that I'd take full responsibility and care for you completely.'

It wasn't easy for Geri-Jo to comprehend such total generosity. 'Why?' she said.

Sylvia Balkin smiled again, softly, the way a teacher might condone the impetuous curiosity of a good student. 'Suppose I just tell you a little more about my son,' she said. 'That ought to explain everything.' She took another sip of coffee, using the moment to gather her thoughts. 'Steven is the youngest of my children,' she went on, setting her cup down. 'I have another son and a daughter. But from the time he was a boy, Steven was the one who'd climb a tree to get a stranded cat, or fetch an aspirin if his father mentioned having a headache after coming home from the office. So it didn't start with you, my dear, this concern for helping others. It's so much a part of him that I've thought at times it could be a genetic trait — I might even say a birth defect, to the extent he's suffered so much because of it. My other children aren't like that, not at all . . .'

It was because of his desire to help people, Sylvia Balkin continued, that by the time he went to college, Steve had decided to be a doctor. With the family money behind him, he had gone on to Harvard Med, always near the top of his class, and graduated to a residency at one of the best hospitals in Boston. After deciding on his specialty, he had moved to New York to practice. It was hardly a surprise that he picked an area of specialization that required him to deal with people who were most in need, in the worst pain, facing the most difficult ordeals. Not that it brought out the best in him.

'Only a few years out of med school,' Sylvia said, 'he was one of the most sought-after oncologists in the city.' She caught Geri-Jo's puzzled look. 'You thought he'd always been a vet?'

'I wasn't sure. Plenty of times he'd sound like a real doctor. But that word you used — the kind of doctor . . .?'

'An oncologist,' Sylvia explained, 'is what they call a cancer specialist, a doctor who usually works on cases where the disease is advanced and treatment calls for special therapies.'

An extremely difficult case had come to him, she went on. The patient, the sort of man who'd thought he was indestructible, had simply waited too long to get help. 'You see,' Sylvia observed, 'he was very wealthy; being able to buy anything can sometimes fool us into thinking we can *have* anything. Some things, however, are beyond anyone's power. By the time the patient came to Steve, his condition was hopeless. Yet Steve went to work, determined to help him.' Sylvia shook her head thoughtfully. 'He never worked harder to save anyone, tried every new kind of treatment. But finally the disease defeated him. The man's pain got worse and worse, unendurable — though he stayed in a hospital and was kept alive day after day by machines. At last, Steve couldn't stand to see his patient suffer any more, and he did things . . . used certain medicines that ended it . . .' The reflection of firelight in Sylvia Balkin's eyes had grown a little brighter and deeper. 'Mercy-killing, some people call it. But perhaps the death of a rich and powerful man is harder to think of as merciful because it parts him from so much. This man that Steve' — her breath caught — 'killed, he'd even given millions to build a new wing at the very hospital in which he died. So what Steve did to spare him pain — to hasten the inevitable — wasn't so easily forgiven. That, too, was called murder.'

Sylvia Balkin took a long slow sip of coffee before continuing. Unlike what had happened to Geri-Jo, Steve's case had not gone to court. With the money to hire all the right lawyers, he had been able to avoid being tried as a criminal. But his medical license had been revoked, his career ruined. He had gone through a long bout with despair, turning to drink and even drugs, tortured by having no release for his passion to help others.

'But then one day, he decided there might be some salvation in trying a new career, a kind of medicine that might not be closed to him. Jules and I had owned a racing stable since Steve was a boy. We'd often take him and the other children with us to the track, no doubt that seeded the idea. But the thing that pushed him, finally, was the realization that a certain sanity existed in the treatment of animals that had been denied him when he dealt with people. If you put a suffering horse out of its misery, it's seen as an act of kindness; but to save a human being a day of unnecessary pain was regarded as a crime.'

After receiving his veterinary degree, Mrs Balkin concluded, Steve had gone to Kentucky because it offered the opportunity of quickly building a practice in equine medicine, and because helping in the civil rights struggle gave some further outlet to his altruistic drive. And going away allowed him to escape the notoriety that still clung to him, to his name.

'Do you see now, my dear?' she said to Geri-Jo. 'Steve felt he hardly had a choice but to help you, because you'd both done the same thing. And he sent you here, because he knew that I also needed a second chance.'

Geri-Jo found Mrs Balkin gazing at her intently, as though it was truly important that everything be perfectly clear before she could fully accept Geri-Jo into her house.

'I don't really understand,' Geri-Jo confessed. 'I mean, saying what we did was the same. Or about a second chance . . .'

'For me to support him,' Sylvia Balkin said, 'to back him up. I didn't do it the first time, you see. I called it murder, too, and said I could never forgive him.' She smiled once more at Geri-Jo, but this was a smile of infinite sadness. 'But, then . . . I had loved Jules so very much.'

Still puzzled that their conversation seemed to be ending before all her questions had been answered, Geri-Jo watched Sylvia Balkin fold her napkin and push her chair back from the table. 'Now, you must be terribly tired, my dear,' Sylvia Balkin was saying. 'I'll have Margaret show you up to your bedroom . . .'

Only as Geri-Jo rose automatically to follow Sylvia Balkin from the table did the realization sink in — the way in which what she and Steve had done were the same, the reason he could feel the depth of her pain and guilt as no one else could.

If only, Geri-Jo thought, she could have the comfort of knowing that killing her own father had been an act of mercy.

CHAPTER TWO

Opening her eyes, she saw the hands of a bedside clock standing at a few minutes before three, and bright sunlight slanting in through drawn curtains.

She had slept in the same room where her clothes had been laid out the night before. Decorated in shades of ivory and rose with floral-patterned wallpaper, drapes and bedspread, and a deep pile rug in a shade of pale lilac, it was exactly the kind of room she had dreamed of having as a child — if only she could be rich. As she got out of the wide canopied bed, she saw that someone must have entered while she slept. A vase of fresh white tulips stood on a dressing table and another change of clothes — a woolen plum-coloured skirt, and a white silk blouse — was laid out across a chaise near the window. Lined up at the foot of the chaise, were three pairs of flat-heeled shoes in different sizes.

After dressing, she wended her way down the broad staircase, looking for Mrs Balkin as she went from floor to floor. She saw no one until, following the aroma of baking pastry, she arrived at an enormous kitchen in the basement where a buxom, stout-armed woman in a white apron was rolling dough. She stopped the moment Geri entered. 'Ah, the friend of Mr Steven! I am Helga, the cook. Tell me, what can I fix for you . . .?'

'Nothing. I ought to wait for Mrs Balkin.'

'Nonsense. You are hungry after such a long sleep, yes, and

Mrs Balkin is out for the day. Margaret is shopping, too, but she said to feed you whatever you wanted . . .'

Famished from the moment she had gotten out of bed, she told the cook that anything at all would be welcome.

The cook set aside her rolling pin and went through the door of a walk-in freezer at one end of the kitchen, emerging in a moment with a slab of fresh bacon from which she sliced off several strips. Through the door of the freezer, Geri could see racks hanging with whole sides of beef. The kitchen, she realized, was on a scale that might serve a hotel.

In a few minutes, a meal had been assembled on a tray: orange juice, eggs and bacon, a small steak, home-fried potatoes, milk, a salad, and a bowl of fruit. 'Excuse me for not serving you upstairs,' said the cook. 'You could eat here, but I must be baking for tonight so it will be hot, and there are so many nicer places . . .'

Geri would have been most comfortable in the kitchen, but at Helga's urging she carried the tray back upstairs, looking for the cheerful yellow room where she had eaten last night. The house was so big, however, that she couldn't find it, and the rooms she kept peeking into looked too grand and filled with polished furniture to be suitable for breakfast eaten off a tray. A couple of times, she caught sight of maids silently dusting.

On the second floor, she came to a library, its walls lined from floor to ceiling with shelves of books. Scores of framed photographs were placed across a fireplace mantle and on shelves, and numerous magazines lay fanned out on different tables, making the library seem homier and less stiff than the perfectly neatened rooms for formal entertaining. Geri went in and ate sitting on a leather davenport, the tray balanced on her lap. As she ate, her eyes roamed across the photographs. Many showed a man and woman standing by a horse with a jockey perched on its back. The woman with jet-black hair was obviously Sylvia Balkin years ago, the husky mustachioed man at her side evidently Jules Balkin. In some of the pictures, Geri recognized young Steve, along with another boy and girl — his brother and sister. And she was astonished to recognize many other famous people posed with the Balkins in situations that were both formal and extremely casual. Jules Balkin, dressed in white tie and tailcoat, in a small group of people that stood around President Roosevelt in a wheelchair. President Kennedy in a sweater holding the tiller of a sailboat — with Mr and Mrs Balkin seated near him in the cockpit . . .

Only now did it truly dawn on her that the world she had entered was far above and beyond the one she had once thought was at the pinnacle of wealth and society. A rejection by the Mitchells was meaningless compared with acceptance by the Balkins.

After eating, Geri browsed among the bookshelves. Soon she came upon a whole section of books, magazines, and scrapbooks relating in one way or another to Jules Balkin. She made a selection which she intended to bring to her room after returning the tray to Helga. But when she turned from the shelves, she saw that the tray had already been whisked away by one of the silent maids.

She spent the rest of the afternoon in her room poring through the material about Steve's father. Some of the magazines contained stories of his death, focussing sensationally on his son's role in it, and Steve's indictment for murder. Then, in a book entitled *American Midas,* Geri skimmed through the story of Jules Balkin's life. The son of Russian immigrants, he had come to this country toward the end of the last century and obtained work on Wall Street as a runner. Investing all the money he earned in stocks, he had amassed several hundred thousand dollars before he was twenty. Eventually he had joined with another young man, a German immigrant, to start a firm that had grown into the investment banking house of Balkin-Weill. The book ended by detailing his extensive involvement in the arts and civic betterment and improving international relations. He had given money — often anonymously — to hospitals, museums, liberal political campaigns, and civil rights causes. Having compiled a fortune estimated at four hundred million dollars, it was said that Jules Balkin had given away more than half.

Riffling at last through the scrapbooks, Geri discovered

them filled with clippings about the Balkins' racing activities. There were many more pictures of them holding horses in the winner's circles of various high-stakes events — the Kentucky Derby and the Preakness which she had heard of, and many others she hadn't. But the stories were always printed on yellowing paper, from publications dating back twenty or thirty years. Apparently the racing stable had been given up long ago.

The light outside had faded, and she had just switched on a lamp when there was a soft knock at the door. She opened it and Sylvia Balkin came in. 'Good evening, my dear. How are you feeling?'

'Fine, thank you.' She saw that Sylvia Balkin was eyeing the books and magazines spread out on the bed. 'I've been reading about Mr Balkin. I'll put them all back . . .'

'I don't mind if you're curious and eager to learn. I'm sure it's one of the things Steve liked about you, too. In fact, I came to extend an invitation that could add to your education. May I sit down?'

'Yes, sure . . .' It startled Geri that a woman should ask permission to sit in her own house — an insight into manners that went far beyond any of Lettie's lectures. She sat on the edge of the bed, opposite the chair Sylvia had taken.

'I'm having a party tonight,' Sylvia said. 'People come to dine with me often, their conversation is one of my greatest pleasures. I want you to know you're welcome to join us, Geri-Jo. You might learn a great deal; there will be some fascinating people here tonight — writers, diplomats, educators.'

The invitation terrified her. Recalling the photographs she had seen downstairs, she could imagine the kind of people who would be dining at Sylvia Balkin's table. She couldn't possibly sit among such people and not make a fool of herself. Wasn't it likely, too, that she would be spotted as a fraud, a runaway from a criminal past? Didn't Mrs Balkin realize that? Geri-Jo was about to provide some excuse about not feeling well, but Sylvia Balkin spoke first.

'I can understand if you'd rather relax in your room. But remember, as long as you are in my house that you are always invited to my table, to sit among my friends. I shall never want you to be uncomfortable, though, so it will be up to you to decide when you're ready to accept my invitation.' She paused. 'Now, we have to make some plans for your future. This can't be just an endless holiday. I'll expect you to meet certain standards, and that's going to mean hard work.'

'Of course, Mrs Balkin, it's only fair to work for my keep. I can do anything, help with the cooking or clean —'

Mrs Balkin held up her hand. The small gesture carried such authority that Geri-Jo was instantly silent.

'The work I'll insist on isn't for me, Geri-Jo, but for yourself. You must study, my dear, to be educated and properly prepared. I'd happily send you to school, but in your present situation I think it's best to reduce the number of questions you have to answer about yourself. Accordingly, I'm making arrangements to have you tutored. Do you have any objection?'

'No, ma'am.'

'Good — and you must call me Sylvia.' She stood up. 'I'll have dinner sent up to your room tonight.' She moved to the door.

Geri-Jo rose. 'Thank you, ma'a . . . Sylvia.'

Sylvia turned with her hand on the doorknob. 'On the subject of names, by the way, we must do something about yours — to cover your tracks a bit, you see. Since there's a matter of freedom involved, I thought it might be rather appropriate if we changed the 'lock' to a 'key'. What do you say to that, Miss Lockely? Do you mind presenting yourself hereafter as . . . Miss Keyes? And your present first name stands out a bit too much. I don't think anyone will look for you here, but suppose we make you a "Geri" to help you blend in. That's rather more ordinary. Then we'll add a few details about where you came from — sent to me by a distant cousin in Oklahoma, her daughter in need of straightening out under my firm hand, that sort of thing . . .'

Geri-Jo nodded acceptance.

'Now have a good dinner, and get a good night's rest. Tomorrow the hard work begins.' She pulled open the door.

Though she felt an impulse to give Steve's mother a grateful embrace Geri-Jo held back, sure that it would seem presumptuous. For all Sylvia Balkin's kindness, nothing had changed the initial perception that she was somehow unapproachable, a queen reigning above every other woman Geri-Jo had ever met.

That night, after getting into bed, she lay awake thinking about her name — Geri Keyes. In some mysterious way, it helped her to feel that she was actually stepping into a different body, becoming a new person, escaping some of the guilt and shame that had plagued her through the months of being tried as a criminal.

'Geri,' she murmured to herself several times in the dark as she drifted into sleep. She was Geri Keyes now, sent to New York by a distant cousin of Mrs Balkin's from Oklahoma.

What Sylvia Balkin had described as hard work started out seeming more like a grand prize won on some quiz show.

When Sylvia escorted her from the house the next morning, a wine-colored Rolls-Royce was standing at the curb. Chauffeured by an elderly English gentleman named Hinchingham, they drove down Fifth Avenue, past soaring apartment houses on one side and the green park on the other, then between rows of luxury stores. Seen through the faintly rose-tinted glass of the windows beside the plush back seat of the smooth-riding limousine, the city looked to 'Geri Keyes' like a totally different place than the one she had seen two days ago. No longer a hateful dirty metropolis of cold stones, but a fantasy world with a thousand gleaming spires, and windows along the streets filled with treasures.

The ride ended at Elizabeth Arden, where Sylvia gave instruction for Geri's hastily cropped hair to be styled into something less makeshift. For two hours, she was fussed over as never before, given a facial and a massage and a shampoo even before the hairdresser went to work. Then, after she emerged from the drier, she was brought into a small private room where a young woman sat her down at a make-up table and, while applying the lightest touches of eye shadow and blush and lipstick, gave her some basic instruction in — as the instructor called it — 'maquillage'.

At the end of the morning, Geri was waiting in the reception area to be collected. She glanced up from a fashion magazine just in time to see Sylvia enter and stalk past her to upbraid the lady at a reception desk. 'I'm Mrs Balkin. I would have thought the young lady I left earlier would be done by now —'

Geri jumped up and called tentatively, 'Here I am . . .'

Sylvia spun and stared at her wide-eyed. 'I'm sorry, my dear. I thought you were one of the gaggle of models who are always flocking in here.' She stood looking at Geri for another moment before adding, 'I'm bound to say that you really are one of the most extraordinarily beautiful young women I've seen . . .' Then she gave an annoyed twitch of her head. 'But I shall hate myself for telling you if it goes to your head. Now come, my dear, our work has only begun. We've got to do something about your wardrobe . . .'

For the rest of the day, she was ushered through the grand department stores of New York. Bloomingdales. Saks. Bonwit Teller. She gaped at the splendor and size of the stores, the miles and miles of counters. She marveled at the selection of clothes and jewelry and perfumes available, and, since each store seemed capable of supplying every need, she was confounded that Mrs Balkin usually moved on after buying only one or two items. 'We're done with Bergdorf's' she would say, having purchased only a trim woolen coat, 'we'll go to Bendel for your shoes.' And there was a different store, too, for underwear, and yet another for sportclothes, and still another for dresses, and sweaters. It seemed an inexplicable waste of time to Geri, and when she caught an occasional glimpse of a price tag, she also thought a tremendous amount of money was being unnecessarily spent. Finally, as Hinchingham drove them to yet another place — 'I think you'll like the sweaters at Aquascutum,' said Sylvia — Geri couldn't help declaring that she didn't need nearly so many clothes, and she would have had no objection to getting them all in one place where they wouldn't be so expensive.

'The only expensive things,' Mrs Balkin replied firmly, 'are those not worth the cost. Always buy the best, my dear, and buy enough to spread the wear; that's really the most economical way.'

For all of Sylvia's authoritative pronouncements, however, she made no attempt to exercise total control. If she was tyrannical about anything, in fact, it was in constantly demanding that Geri express her own tastes and feelings. 'If you don't approve of that, my dear,' she would say as a salesperson confronted Geri with a selection, 'choose something else. Get what you like. You're the one who has to wear it.'

By the end of the day, Geri had been outfitted with everything from underwear to a heavy winter coat to a couple of so-called mini-skirts that were, said the salesgirl at Bloomingdales, the latest thing in from London's Carnaby Street. Sylvia's willingness to indulge tastes other than her own was apparently stretched to the limit by this latter choice. 'You certainly have the legs for it, my dear,' she said. 'But I do hope you won't wear those to dinner.'

'I don't have to get —' Geri started to back down from her choice.

But Sylvia cut in, smiling. 'No, no. Don't be put off by my prejudices. We must always make room for . . . "the latest thing".'

By the end of the day, journeying back to the Balkin house with a car full of packages, Geri knew what Sylvia had meant when she said shopping for a wardrobe was hard work.

She would have slept late again the next morning, but at nine o'clock Margaret came in, threw back the curtains, and jolted her awake as effectively as an alarm clock with a loud announcement. 'Get up. Your teacher is waiting downstairs.'

When she went down, Margaret directed her to the 'small dining room', as she had learned the cheerful yellow room was called. Sylvia Balkin was already seated at breakfast across from a young man with a lean angular face, olive skin and thick, straight black hair that fell across his forehead. A pair of spectacles perched on his straight nose gave him a studious look, accentuated by penetrating dark eyes behind lenses cut in a traditional, unfashionable shape. He stood up as Geri entered, and she saw he was quite tall and rail thin.

Sylvia said good morning, then introduced her: 'Geri Keyes, this is Anthony Novello.' As they seated themselves around the table, Sylvia went on. 'Tony is the tutor we spoke about, Geri. I've been discussing your schedule with him. We thought you could study with him for five hours three times a week, and weekends as well. Do you think that will be too much?'

She glanced at Anthony Novello who gave her a shy smile that somehow communicated he felt no less under the total domination of Queen Sylvia than she did. The tutor looked like an easy person to spend time with. 'It sounds fine.'

'Then suppose you get started right now.' Sylvia pushed back her chair. 'Excuse me for leaving so quickly but I have to be at a meeting of museum trustees at ten. Goodbye, Tony, and thank you . . .' She swept out.

Left alone so abruptly, there was an awkward moment before Tony Novello said, 'I hope you'll be patient with me, Geri. I haven't done this kind of work before . . .'

'Well, I've sure never had a tutor, so I'm not going to be hard to please.'

He smiled. 'It's Sylvia I have to please. She told me she's expecting me to do a lot for you.'

Geri wondered momentarily what else Sylvia might have said to explain the need for a tutor, then remembered the story she'd suggested the night before. Before Tony Novello could ask any more about her background, she diverted him to talking about himself, asking how he had happened to take this job.

It took the rest of breakfast for him to answer, and by the end Geri not only felt the beginnings of a friendship with Tony Novello, she realized that they had a great deal in common.

Until a few months ago, Tony said, he had been a graduate student in higher mathematics at M.I.T. — 'the Massachusetts Institute of Technology,' he explained, when Geri asked about the initials, 'probably the best place for math in the country.' Studying there had been a tremendous achievement for him, he admitted, since going to college wouldn't have been possible except on full scholarships. 'My parents are Italians — immigrants — and neither one of them ever went past the eighth grade. When I first started school I didn't even know there was such a thing as college. But along the line, I had some teachers who noticed I had a knack for numbers, and they encouraged me. Once I got into learning, I liked it . . . and it turned out I had what they call a photographic memory, so getting the grades was easy . . .'

Tony Novello clearly didn't mean to be boastful, but he could hardly relate his story to her without revealing that he had been a brilliant student. After going through M.I.T. in three years, he had been given a special grant to do graduate work in theoretical mathematics. He had kept at that two years . . . until four months ago when he had received his draft notice from the Army. 'That's how I came to know Mrs Balkin,' he said.

'What's she got to do with the Army?' Geri asked.

Tony chuckled. 'Not a damn thing. But you see I refused to go because I'm against this crazy war the country's fighting in Vietnam. That got me into a lot of trouble, and an adviser at school steered me to a group that Mrs B. has given a lot of money to keep going — a group that helps draft resisters like me. Mrs Balkin heard about me and offered some special help.'

Geri studied him thoughtfully. 'I didn't know you could refuse to fight with the Army.'

Tony smiled. 'It isn't standard procedure. But there are a lot of people who think that all wars are wrong, and this one in particular — and if you believe that deeply enough then how can you do anything but refuse to fight?'

'Are you still in trouble?' Geri asked.

'Not out of the woods, but the group I mentioned supplies lawyers to fight cases like mine. At the moment, I'm free until my case goes to court. Then . . .' He shrugged.

'I hope you stay free,' she said.

'Well, I've got to now, haven't I? Mrs Balkin's expecting me to teach you some French, math, history and English lit — high-school level, of course — also a little art appreciation, and in general sharpen you up all around. Maybe I'll throw in a little Italian, too — eh, *ragazza*? I'll never get through all of that unless you and I have plenty of time.'

Geri felt that everything Tony had told her about himself

200

had forged a bond between them. He'd had some of the same struggles, come to the same crossroads. She was looking forward to the time she'd spend with him. 'Well,' she said, 'I'm ready for school.'

Over the next few days, there were many times Geri paused suddenly in the middle of whatever she was doing and wondered if she wasn't lost in a dream. One day she had been poor, on the point of going to prison for years, now she was living in a palace, all her needs taken care of, choosing her clothes each day from closets that never seemed to stop yielding up some item she couldn't remember seeing before. Most amazing, she was being given the endless gift of knowledge. Sometimes, remembering the twist of circumstances that had brought her here — and filled with fresh remorse for causing her father's death, self-defense or no — she felt so undeserving that she thought of running away, even going back to Lexington and accepting punishment. But Sylvia seemed to sense her low points, and she would find a moment to offer assurances that Steve had never done anything more sensible than sending her here.

On the other hand, Sylvia never showed any outward sign of growing affection. From the first she had been friendly and fair and encouraging, yet she remained regally aloof. As Geri's appreciation of Mrs Balkin's kindness grew, so did her fondness for her. At times, having tea with Sylvia by a fire in the cheery drawing room, Geri had an impulse to walk across and hug Sylvia, express her gratitude for all she'd done. But the invisible barrier of formality that Sylvia erected around herself somehow made it plain that such an act would be out of bounds. Though she came to feel less and less out of place in her luxurious surroundings, Geri could never feel that this was truly her home. Denied any emotional tie to Sylvia, Geri felt she would never be more than one of Sylvia's philanthropic projects.

As she spent more time in the huge house on 74th Street, Geri-Jo became aware that the largesse Sylvia had extended by taking her in was not simply a special favor to her son. It was part of an extensive involvement with helping many people

201

and causes, both as a sizeable contributor of funds and a dynamic generator of ideas. Three or four nights a week there would be some kind of gathering at the house. A great crowd of people might arrive early in the evening, and after having cocktails in the downstairs rooms, they would sit down to hear someone make a plea for contributions to a political campaign, or some new committee to right old wrongs. From the story told by Tony Novello, Geri had realized that one of Sylvia's major concerns was trying to end the war in Vietnam.

Not all of Sylvia's gatherings were aimed at raising money for causes, however. There were small parties, too, groups of eight or twelve or sixteen who would arrive later in the evening, dressed in more formal clothes, and sit in the cheerful yellow room talking late into the night. Geri had not yet dared to accept Sylvia's open invitation to join the guests, but from her room on the third floor, she would often hear voices raised in lively argument or bursts of hearty laughter rising up through the house as the guests ate or sipped coffee after dinner. Or there would be music; Sylvia frequently invited Van Cliburn and Isaac Stern and other concert artists, and often they would sit in her large living room and give informal recitals. Listening to it all, Geri wished she could summon the nerve to leave the security of her room. But even if she had overcome the fear that anyone would uncover that she was an illegal runaway, she still felt unprepared. At the Mitchells, she had felt herself separated by a lack of money and manners. Now she felt it was her mind that was lacking.

But once aware of the lack, she applied herself vigorously to her studies. Being tutored, she thought, was an easier way to learn than going to school. For one thing, she liked Tony, liked pleasing him — and he was always so satisfied when she finally grasped some mathematical principle he had spent hours trying to convey, or when she reached the point of being able to argue with him over some theory of history. Their hours together were not merely stiff classroom sessions, with information being learned by rote from a blackboard. Tony augmented his instruction in the French language by bringing her to subtitled French movies, and made history come to life

202

by taking her through some of the city's great museums — showing her the collection of armor in the Metropolitan when he taught her about the Middle Ages — or taking her on a boat ride around Manhattan Island when he talked about the early settlement of New York by the Dutch.

He had also made her aware for the first time of the issues that were being hotly debated in the country, not only among lawmakers, but being carried into the streets in angry demonstrations. One Saturday he had taken her to a mass rally of students at Columbia University opposed to the war in Vietnam, then he had spent hours with her explaining the political and historical origins of the war. Geri couldn't grasp all of it, but she realized how blind she had been to the complexities that affected the fate of the world.

Returning one afternoon after her first tour of the Museum of Natural History with Tony — an adjunct to his teachings in evolution — Geri was met at the door by Margaret and told to join Mrs Balkin for tea in the small sitting room on the second floor. As she neared the door, Geri could hear Sylvia's cool voice in conversation with a couple of others that sounded more agitated. Lingering outside rather than intrude on what might be personal business, Geri heard a man's voice rise above the others:

'This is insanity, Mother. It's one thing to be a do-gooder, but what you're involved in now is something else.'

Another unfamiliar voice chimed in, a woman this time. 'Phil's right. In a case like this, you're making yourself liable for —'

Sylvia's commanding tone interrupted. 'Now, that's enough. I think I owe this to Steven — we all do, in fact. But if you object, frankly I'm not concerned. I believe I have the ability — and the responsibility — to protect this girl. And even if there should be consequences, I'll accept them.'

The talk ceased, and there was silence broken only by the rattle of teacups.

Geri had all but forgotten Sylvia's earlier mention of her other children, but obviously they had come to call and Sylvia had felt it necessary to inform them of the guest she had taken

203

in. Evidently she had also told them enough of Geri's situation to have earned their strong disapproval.

It was even harder now for Geri to enter the room, but she decided there would be just as many complications if she snubbed the invitation to join them for tea.

The moment she stepped into the doorway, all eyes were directed at her. Seated with Sylvia in the sunny bow-windowed room were a chunky young woman of about thirty whose broad face was accentuated by too much eye make-up and lipstick, and a tall severe man with a receding hairline and spectacles whom Geri judged to be a couple of years older than Steve. Whatever their private feelings toward Geri, their hostility was held in check by Sylvia's outward support and they remained cordial in her presence. The son, Phillip, asked her impressions of New York; the daughter, Alice, reminisced fondly about what it was like to grow up in this house.

But when she excused herself later, Geri had no sooner taken a few steps down the hall than she could hear a low hiss of criticism break out. Though interrupted again by some cool admonition from Sylvia, it was clear to Geri that she could never expect to be welcomed by Alice or Phillip Balkin.

The day before Christmas, Sylvia threw open her house to underprivileged children and had presents for all of them under a twenty-foot tree in her formal dining room. At Sylvia's request, Geri helped at the children's party along with Tony, so she was there when other friends began to arrive toward evening. Normally she would have felt nervous, but in a crowd, at least, it was possible to remain relatively anonymous. Even the arrival of Phil and Alice Balkin didn't spoil Geri's own holiday spirit; they both gazed past her with no more than a cool smile, and left early.

Now that she had begun to read the newspapers — Tony demanded it as background to teaching her about politics and current events — Geri recognized the important politicians and corporate leaders as well as famous writers and actors who began to fill Sylvia's house. She would have fled upstairs, except that Tony urged her to stay.

'Talking to some of these people can be an education in itself.

They're movers and shakers, Geri. Mingle with them . . .'

With his encouragement, she tried sallying forth into the crowd. A couple of times, she was stopped by men, one an actor in a Broadway musical to which Tony had taken her. But the inevitable questions asked by strangers required her to lie, and she eventually retreated to Tony's side.

When a band began playing at one end of the large dining room, other couples took to the floor and she began to wish Tony would ask her to dance. But, while he kept hovering beside her protectively, he remained content to watch the others. She couldn't imagine that he didn't know how to dance — his photographic memory made him wise in so many other things — and decided at last that he must feel it was necessary to maintain a certain distance in his role as her teacher. Eventually she was asked by a couple of other young men, but their questions again made her uncomfortable and after that she declined all requests.

Toward the end of the evening, the guests gathered around the tree where a collection of presents had been placed for Sylvia's friends. Geri hung back until Sylvia came over to her.

'There are some for you, too, my dear . . .'

Still, she waited until all the guests and Tony had gone. Going at last to the tree, she found that the only gifts left were all marked with her name. Along with a cashmere scarf and some blouses and a portable radio and dictionary, there was also a gold wristwatch. Engraved on the back of the case were the words, 'Sooner or later. Love, Steve.'

There had been nothing else from him, no calls or letters, though she knew from Sylvia that, after her escape, the police had questioned him rigorously before deciding there wasn't enough evidence to press charges against him for helping her jump bail. Not communicating with her was necessary to protect them both, she understood, and she took the inscription on the watch as his oath that they would soon meet again.

The vow was her best Christmas present, and she resolved to stay safe with Steve's mother until it could be fulfilled.

CHAPTER THREE

Through the cold New York winter, with snow in the streets that turned quickly to dirty slush, Geri felt little inclination to leave Sylvia's house and explore the city. She spent her time virtually in hiding. If she wasn't with Tony or Sylvia, she would be alone, usually sitting by a fire in one of the many rooms of the huge house, reading some book Tony had suggested.

But with the first warm days of spring came the inevitable lure to get outside, walk in the park, find some small adventure. Geri began to feel more keenly the loss of the true freedom she would have had if she were not a fugitive. She longed for the companionship of other girls that would have come easily if she could have gone to school; she wanted the license to speak freely about who she was, and what had happened to her, without which she felt it was senseless to try and make friends.

Tony could fill only a small part of the gap. He took her out for meals and to movies and for walks in Central Park, through the zoo or along the lake, and she enjoyed his company. But always the conversation would center around something he wanted to teach her. They never talked about themselves. She could never admit that everything he believed about her was a lie, and she guessed that her own reluctance to reveal anything personal sent a signal that she wanted no more from him.

Spring also heightened the yearnings of her body. At her

next birthday she would be twenty. By that age, she reflected ironically, most of the women in the place where she'd been born would have been married and on their third baby. Of course, that was a result of ignorance and poverty, she understood now. But the situation was also created out of a basic natural drive that existed in all human beings. What had happened with Bard and Pa had made her glad, at first, to retreat from acknowledging that part of herself. But now she worried that it had warped her in some way, left her incapable of loving if and when the right opportunity came along.

Perhaps the opportunity was already right in front of her and she was denying it. Tony. Couldn't they be lovers? If she told him the truth about herself, might some barrier fall . . .?

She began choosing her clothes with more awareness of what might please him, taking note of any time he complimented her on what she was wearing. He liked the more casual 'peasant' look, she found, long print skirts rather than the more popular minis, and he usually made a point of telling her how nice she looked on days when she wasn't wearing any make-up. She tried to promote a mood in which intimacies might be shared, suggesting that with all the excursions on which he'd taken her — to Chinatown, and a dozen museums, and shows and baseball games — he had never taken her out to a restaurant for a candlelight dinner.

But, as if he understood her goal and needed to discourage it, he always made some excuse to avoid seeing her in the evening. She suspected then that he might be put off by the same awe of social differences that had once paralyzed her. He had been poor — and for all he knew she was related to the wealthy Balkins. She was tempted to reveal the truth, but she felt that by accepting Sylvia's protection she had made a contract not to compromise her in any way.

As the nights grew milder, however, she spent more time wondering what it might be like if she and Tony could be lovers. So at breakfast with Sylvia, one sunny Saturday before she was to go art-gallery hopping with Tony, Geri asked permission to explain how and why she had come to live in the Balkin house.

After listening to Geri's request, Sylvia spent a moment straightening the silver on her plate. 'Why do you feel it's important to tell him?' she asked at last.

'To be myself. I want him to know who I really am . . .'

'My dear,' Sylvia argued mildly, 'whatever details about your past he does or doesn't know, what you show to the world is still what you *are*. A bright, intelligent, attractive, caring —'

'But he . . . he doesn't know how much we have in common!' Geri burst out with an urgency that surprised her.

Sylvia's eyes widened. 'Ah,' she said, nodding slowly. 'Forgive me for being such a fool, my dear. Of course, I should have anticipated that a lovely young woman would need . . . a man who could be more than just a friend. But Tony . . . he isn't the one for you, dear girl.'

'Why?' Geri demanded, upset at being so quickly denied. 'Because he's poor? I'm no different.' She pulled at her fine clothes. 'This is just a costume . . . everything I see around me is like . . . props on a stage —'

Sylvia leaned across the table, her pale blue eyes flashing. 'It has nothing to do with money,' she cut in forcefully, 'you should know me better than that. I make no apologies for being wealthy, but I don't think it's a standard for establishing a person's worth. Jules was an immigrant, too, like Tony's parents . . .'

'Forgive me,' Geri said, on the point of tears. She knew she had been unfair to Sylvia. 'But then why shouldn't I . . . hope for something more with Tony?'

Sylvia took a sip of coffee and then stared down into her cup for a long moment. 'Tony is gay, my dear.'

Geri shook her head, uncomprehending, before Sylvia continued, explaining what the word meant in the context she had used it. At first, it was hard for Geri to understand. Whatever sophistication she had acquired in the past few months, this wasn't something she could be open minded about. Except that Sylvia wouldn't let her simply reject it as unnatural; she went on patiently explaining, enumerating the many creative geniuses of past and present who had been homosexual, affirming the importance of making room for all kinds of personal choice — as long as they were choices that did not hurt others.

Hearing the echo of the liberal philosophy Steve had once espoused, Geri felt her rejection of Tony and what he represented begin to wane.

'Is that the real reason he didn't want to go in the Army?' she asked when Sylvia had finished.

Sylvia smiled tolerantly. 'There are gay people in the Army and the police and everywhere else, Geri. Someday, perhaps, they won't have to be as secretive about it as they are now. But while they may have a different need from ours, that doesn't mean there's anything they can't do. I'm sure Tony could have been as good a soldier as anyone else. He didn't go because his conscience wouldn't allow him to fight for something he didn't believe in.'

Once she understood, Geri found it was easier rather than harder to be with Tony. She didn't expect more from him than what he could give, and she didn't feel that she was betraying the friendship they did have by keeping her own secrets.

But now, when she lay awake on balmy spring nights, she could only wonder if ever she would find a man with whom the secrets — and the nights — could be shared.

Aside from romance, one other pleasure was missing from her life. During all her time in the city, she had not been near a horse except briefly on two occasions. Once, she and Tony had been walking outside the Plaza Hotel where the horsedrawn hansom cabs waited to pick up tourists. Observing her affection for the animals in the way she stopped to stroke them, Tony had offered to take her for a ride. But she had declined. She didn't like seeing the horses yoked to carriages, no matter how elegant; it made them seem more like beasts of burden than the majestic creatures she believed them to be. It was different when a rider was mounted on the animal's back; there was a kind of equality then, a partnership in jockey and horse racing together.

After she explained her passion, Tony had tried again to satisfy it by taking her to ride a saddlehorse at the Claremont Stables. Again the experience was unfulfilling. There was no thrill in controlling the spiritless mounts that had been tamed to accommodate hundreds of different customers, many of them careless or even abusive.

It was Sylvia, finally, who answered a dream of Geri's that had remained unfulfilled.

'We're going to the races today,' she announced crisply at breakfast one warm Saturday in April. When Steve had asked her to harbor Geri, she said, he had mentioned Geri's passionate interest in thoroughbreds, and his judgment that she possessed an innate ability to care for and handle them. Still regretting that his promise of a day at Keeneland had been deferred, and that this disappointment coincided exactly with the beginning of a series of far more serious hardships for Geri, Steve had told his mother that he believed fulfilling his promise to take Geri to the races might somehow set her whole life back on the right course.

When she went after breakfast to dress for her day at the track, Geri found a new, very smart ivory linen suit and a broad-brimmed straw picture hat laid out over the bedspread. A card stuck into the brim of the hat read simply 'For a Winning Day — Sylvia'.

Later in the morning, the Rolls collected them for the ride to the track. Geri had grown accustomed to being driven around the city by Hinchingham, but this was the first time she had headed out of the city across one of the bridges that spanned the East River. The sun glinting through the massive webbing of steel high above the water brought a rush of excitement, reminding her again of how far she had come from a backwoods valley a thousand miles away. Overflowing again with gratitude, she looked at Sylvia and wished she could express it. But she had already tried to thank her for the gorgeous new outfit, and Sylvia had cut her short.

'Please, my dear, you needn't thank me all the time. Whatever I do for you is simply a debt I owe to Steven.'

In the car, Sylvia soon began to talk about horseracing. Her years as the wife of a man who had owned a thriving thoroughbred stable had made her knowledgeable, and Geri eagerly pumped her for the smallest details. The track to which they were going, Sylvia said, was called Aqueduct. It was the smaller of two racecourses near the city, the other being Belmont Park which was viewed by most racing enthusiasts as the very center of the sport, the premier track in the nation. Traditionally, the season opened at Aqueduct, then moved after several weeks to Belmont. The two tracks were never open simultaneously, and both were closed during the month of August, when the racing moved to a third track owned and operated by the same organization behind both Aqueduct and Belmont, the New York Racing Association.

'Where's the third one?' Geri asked.

'At Saratoga — a small town upstate.'

'Why leave here to go to a small town?'

'There was racing in Saratoga a hundred years ago, my dear, decades before there was ever a race in this metropolis. So they still go — the best horses, and of course the best people — they go simply because they always have. For those who love this sport, tradition has always been one of the moving forces.'

Tradition. From the way Sylvia said the word, it was obvious she thought traditions were important, too. If ever she found her way into greater contact with the sport, Geri thought, she would also try to respect tradition.

They had been travelling less than an hour when Sylvia nudged Geri and pointed ahead through the window. Beyond a line of traffic lay the racetrack's grandstand building, a looming structure of brick and yellow concrete. Soon the car drew up to a gate in the shadow of the grandstand, and Hinchingham stopped to show a pass to a uniformed guard. Sylvia told Geri that the gate they were entering led to the restricted area known as the owners' enclosure.

'Then you still own a racing stable?' Geri said.

'Not on the same scale as when Jules was alive. I didn't have the heart to keep it going myself. But Phillip enjoys dabbling, and so he's kept a few horses.' In fact, Sylvia said, he had an entry in the feature race this afternoon.

That meant Phillip would also be here, Geri guessed. The prospect of seeing him or Alice ordinarily dampened her spirits, made it impossible to enjoy anything. Though they came rarely to Seventy-fourth Street, she knew that Sylvia occasionally met her son or daughter for lunch, and she was certain that in her absence these two went on pressuring Sylvia to remove her protection. Whenever she thought about this constant sniping, Geri fell back into wondering if she didn't owe it to the woman who had already given her so much to move on and spare her this constant battle with her own children.

Today, however, she was too caught up in the excitement of seeing her first horse race to worry about anything else. Stepping out of the car into the air of the racetrack, she heard for the first time the faint buzz of the huge crowd gathering inside.

They went through a special entrance marked by a sign that specified it was for 'Jockey Club and NYRA Members Only', and walked along a path past beds of flowers, shaded by huge trees. The track and the grounds surrounding it must be as beautiful as any palace, she thought. After passing through an entrance, a short elevator ride took them up to the clubhouse.

A headwaiter met them, bowing low to Sylvia. 'Mrs Balkin,' he crooned, 'it's been too long since we've seen you . . .' He led them into a huge balcony restaurant with descending tiers of tables that faced out over the track through a broad open wall; it was packed for opening day, and as the headwaiter led them to a large table which looked directly down on the finish line, people at other tables waved or nodded to Sylvia. She acknowledged each one with a queenly nod.

Already waiting at the table alone was Alice Balkin. She rose to kiss her mother on the cheek, and acknowledged Geri with no more than a frosty smile. But Geri barely noticed, her attention fixed on the sprawling oval track surrounding an infield of lush green grass set with two small lakes. Thousands of people milled beside the track and in the seats of a grandstand next to the clubhouse, sending up a noise that sounded to Geri like the hum of a titanic generator.

The first time she had climbed on the back of a horse, she had felt that the skill to control the animal was part of her destiny. Now she was seized by the same intuitive certainty that she had found the world in which she belonged. Here, in the midst of tens of thousands of strangers, she was more at home than she could ever be anywhere else. For a moment, she was puzzled by her wholehearted response: there wasn't a horse to be seen yet. But then it dawned on her that the attraction to this place wasn't solely an extension of her basic love of the animals. Looking down at the oval of naked earth where they would run, she understood that the point here — the thing that caused the track to exist, the animals to be bred and raced, the crowds to come and bet and cheer — was to *win*. It was all about winning, being the best — breeding or buying the best animal, riding the best race, making the best bet. Standing above the arena where all that human desire to win could be expressed, Geri recognized as never before the powerful consuming hunger that had been building within her over a lifetime. For as long as she could remember, she had fought against the message — muttered aloud by Pa, delivered silently by the hollow — that the circumstances of her birth gave her no chance to be anything but a loser. The prophecy had come close to being fulfilled. Now — still, when all was said and done, on the run from her past — it was as if her very right to exist had become linked to proving the future would be different, that she could be a winner. And here was a place that offered a chance to do it in many ways — as bettor, or rider, or trainer, or owner, or simply as a *believer*. And to do it again and again, hour after hour, day after day, week after week . . .

She waited in a veritable trance of anticipation for the horses to appear for the first race. A waiter came to take orders for lunch, and Sylvia suggested some food to Geri, who nodded without really hearing or taking her eyes from the track.

'We have some time before our lunch comes,' Sylvia said. 'Would you like to visit the paddock, Geri?' She explained that the paddock was an area where all the horses in each race paraded before going onto the track. 'Many bettors make their choice based on how the horse looked in the paddock right before the race.'

'Then maybe I should save that for the time when I start to bet,' Geri said.

213

'Why not start now? What's a day at the races without making a few wagers.' Extracting a couple of fifty-dollar bills from her purse, Sylvia offered them for betting money.

But Geri turned the gift politely aside. She already received a weekly stipend of pocket money that she had never found sufficient occasion to spend. 'I brought ten dollars with me. If it comes to placing any bets, I don't want to lose more than that.'

Alice Balkin gave Geri a sidelong glance which subtly conveyed her opinion that this pose of frugality was too good to be true. Then she turned to her mother and, referring to their programs, they began discussing their choices in the first and second races. Geri started turning the pages of a program, too, idly noting the names of the horses, and the details provided to help bettors — the odds, the weight carried by the horse, the name of the jockey and the trainer and the owner. From the conversation she heard between Sylvia and Alice — apparently experienced handicappers — the jockey or trainer was as much a factor as the pedigree of the horse.

'Look, Mother,' Alice was saying, 'that new young jockey Cordero is riding in the first. I'm going to back him. He's been the top winner lately . . .'

'But he's running against the California-bred trained by Charlie Whittingham. I wouldn't want to bet against one of Charlie's horses . . .'

Having made their choices, Sylvia and Alice fished some money out of their bags and called over a boy who had been circulating among the tables, writing bets on a pad.

As Geri went on browsing through the program, one name suddenly leapt out at her: Oakie Whitten — listed as trainer of a horse named 'Since When' in the fourth race. Her pulse began to race. If Oakie was here running one of the Skyevale horses, then the Mitchells might be as well; they had always travelled to wherever their horses were running — and no doubt they would view the race from the clubhouse. Of course if they recognized her, they would waste no time informing the authorities.

Slumping in her seat, pulling her face down against the lapels of her suit, Geri glanced around gingerly. As her eyes passed from one face to the next, she began to relax. The Mitchells were nowhere to be seen. Checking her program again where Oakie's name had been printed, she noticed that the owner listed for 'Since When' was not Skyevale Stable, but an individual, 'Mrs C. P. Beecher'. It seemed that Oakie was no longer working for the Mitchells. Checking further, Geri saw that no Skyevale horses were running today.

She wished she could see Oakie again, but she realized it was probably best to avoid him. He had been fond of her, and was unlikely to turn her in — yet he was an honorable man, and knowing her whereabouts could also compromise him with the law. Fortunately he wasn't in the clubhouse either; probably he would watch his horse run from the same place he liked to watch them train — down by the rail.

When the races finally began, Geri found herself lifted to a new level of excitement. From the thrill as the horses burst suddenly out of the starting gate, to the quickening drama of shifting patterns as one challenged another for the lead around turn after turn, until the moment of elation — or, for some, of surrender — as the whole field of charging, galloping animals finally swept under the finish line, she had never before felt herself propelled so quickly through such an intense series of emotional highs. Though she had no stake in the outcome, she felt like cheering for the winner. But she was held in check by the staid atmosphere of the clubhouse restaurant. The excitement openly displayed by any of the middle-aged well-dressed diners at the surrounding tables was at a very low level. 'Well, all *right*! I got that one,' Geri heard a man say at the next table, and a couple of others holding winning tickets applauded briefly. For all the comforts of this privileged setting, Geri would have preferred to be in the grandstand, where she could see people jumping up and down as their horse won, and where the whole crowd had been roaring its head off during the race.

Finished with their meal by the end of the fourth race — in which Oakie's horse had come in second — the Balkins and Geri moved out of the restaurant to an open box of six seats. It was a 'family box', Sylvia told Geri, held on subscription ever since Aqueduct had opened. 'So there will always be a place for you, my dear, whenever you want to come to the races again.'

They had just taken their seats when Phillip arrived. Usually, he wore dark suits and ties that emphasized his stern countenance, but today he was a rakish sportsman, dressed in a blue madras sport jacket and a colored tie.

'How's our southern cousin?' he greeted Geri after kissing his mother and sister. The tone was flippant but not cruelly mocking, and Geri answered evenly that she was fine.

His mood at the moment was buoyed by the visit he had been having with his jockey and trainer. Both had agreed that Maccabee, the four-year-old he had entered in the fifth race, was at the peak of condition. A winner of several races as a two-year-old he had not done well last year, and only now was he coming back on form. 'His workouts have been excellent,' Phillip said. 'If he wasn't coming off a long losing streak, he might be the favorite. As it is, he'll probably go off at low odds.'

'How low?' Alice asked.

'The morning line was six-to-one.'

'Not bad odds for a near-favorite,' Sylvia observed. To Geri she explained that the morning line gave the odds on all horses as estimated by an official handicapper at the track. Then she turned back to Phillip. 'Sounds like a very good bet at six-to-one.'

Which made it sound like a good bet to Geri, too. She had noticed that after two of the first three races, the 'bet boys' who had taken Sylvia's money at the table had returned to pay off her winnings, once on a horse that had come in first, the other time on a runner-up 'place' horse that had come in second by no more than a nose. Sylvia's reading of the program, and a newspaper she showed Geri called *The Racing Form,* seemed to be all she needed to know about the horses.

At Phillip's insistence, they all went down to the paddock to see his horse. Sylvia urged Geri to come along.

In a tree-shaded area outside the grandstand building, the horses were walking around a fenced-in ring, led by their

216

grooms. The jockeys, small men dressed in their brightly colored silks, looked curiously uncomfortable as they rode by — for they were seated on their mounts during this slow procession, but their saddles had been designed to make standing in the stirrups a more natural position. Geri remembered Oakie explaining to her that this moved the center of gravity forward, which made it easier for the horse to carry the weight of a jockey during a race.

'He does look very good,' Sylvia said when Phillip pointed out his horse.

Geri thought so, too. The stallion was a large, powerfully built bay, and he was prancing lightly as he passed, not skittish but projecting a sense of energy waiting to be tapped.

As she lingered by the paddock, however, Geri's attention was attracted to another horse that followed several places behind Phillip's. He was smaller, and less appealing because his color was a drabber brown. But she could see the taut muscles rippling under his coat, and as she studied the animal's walk something else she'd once overheard Oakie say came back to her. The trainer had been commenting to an exercise boy on a similarly small horse. 'It ain't how tall he is that counts,' Oakie had said, 'it's how far he can stretch those legs.' Then he had gestured to the hoofprints left in the dirt when the little horse came onto the track, pointing out that as the horse walked, the mark of his left hind shoe always came down in front of the imprint left by the left front shoe that had touched ground before it. It was an indicator of a good stride, Oakie had said, always worth watching for. Geri could see now that the small horse walking several places behind Maccabee had this same trait. She watched it walk all the way around the paddock and she could see with every step that he was putting his hind feet down well ahead of the point where the front feet had just touched. And there was something else that told her the small horse could be a winner, nothing she could put her finger on, but the belief came from the same well of intuition that told her she was standing on ground where she had always belonged.

She noted the large black '9' on the white number cloth

draped behind the saddle, and then followed Sylvia and her children into the clubhouse.

Back in their box, Phillip personally collected money for the bets he would place. Geri watched as Sylvia took a one-hundred-dollar bill from her purse and handed it to her son, with an instruction to bet it all 'on the nose'.

'Now what about you, "cousin"?' Phillip said, after he had taken some more cash from Alice. 'We've got a sure thing this time. Aren't you ever going to bet any of your . . . hard-earned money?'

His tone this time was unmistakeably snide. Sylvia noted her disapproval by flashing a peevish glance at him.

Usually, Geri refused to be baited by Alice or Phillip. But today for some reason it wasn't enough to sit back and let Sylvia hold them in check. 'I'll make my own bet,' Geri answered Phillip curtly. 'And on my own sure thing.'

Sylvia lifted an eyebrow and then smiled very slightly at Geri, as if approving her response.

Phillip looked disconcerted. 'Is that a fact? So you're an expert on racing now?'

'An expert on running, anyway,' Alice murmured.

Sylvia reared back and glared at her daughter, but Phillip went on goading Geri. 'Of course, there's really no reason for you to bet with us, is there? You don't have the same sentimental attachment as we —'

'Enough, Phillip,' Sylvia cut in sharply. 'For the sake of sentiment I might toss a penny into a wishing well. But when I bet a hundred dollars it's because I expect a horse to come in first. Don't make this into anything more than a difference of opinion.' She turned to Geri. 'Which horse do you favor, my dear?'

Geri glanced quickly at one of the programs where the horses were listed next to the number of their gate position and recited the name beside number 9: 'Postage Due.'

Both Phillip and Alice scanned the track below where the horses were walking in a file toward the starting gate.

'Look at him,' Alice hooted. 'He's the runt of the litter.'

'Fifteen-to-one,' Phillip said, referring to the big totalizator

218

board where the odds, and the amount of money in the betting pool were displayed in constantly changing electric figures.

Sylvia had not taken her eyes from Geri. 'You have any reasons for this choice?' she asked. 'Or is it just a wild guess?'

'I have reasons,' Geri said. She was about to give them, and admit, too, that part of it was a hunch — which was not really the same as a wild guess.

But Sylvia didn't ask. She had already turned to Phillip. 'I've changed my mind. Put mine on Postage Due.'

Phillip's face reddened. Alice, too, shot a fiery look at her mother, before subsiding into a resentful pout. Sylvia's way of warning her contentious children that she could tolerate no more of their unkind opposition to Geri had obviously escalated the game of betting from a simple matter of preferences to a question of loyalties.

'You'd take her opinion over mine?' Phillip demanded heavily. The terms of his question gave it an importance that went far beyond the moment.

'It's her own,' Sylvia replied, 'that's what I like about it. You've only passed along what others told you.'

Phillip hesitated another second, then stood abruptly and stalked out of the box.

An announcement that the horses were approaching the starting gate came over the public address system. Geri started to get up, but Sylvia lightly took hold of her arm.

'Never mind, my dear. You keep your money. If something good happens, I'll share my luck with you.' Geri suspected now that Sylvia didn't really believe her selection had a chance, had made the bet only to make a point.

Phillip came back clutching a fistful of tickets. It looked as if he had bet several thousand dollars, goaded by his mother's defection into risking more than originally planned so that the vindication of his own knowledge and wisdom would be that much more satisfying.

The tense silence in the box lasted until the track announcer's cry of 'They're off!' came through the loud-speakers, and the army of bettors in the stands exploded with their shouted prayers.

219

The contest between Maccabee and Postage Due wasn't even close. Phillip's horse started well, and held the lead around the first turn, but then started to fade. Meanwhile, the small horse Geri had thought might have a big stride came surging through a jam of five others around the last turn.

The well-heeled subscribers to other family boxes around the Balkins' had continued to hold their seats, and utter only the most restrained encouragement to their own bets. But Geri could no longer contain herself. Primed by the background of cheering that came from the nearby grandstand, she shot unthinkingly to her feet and started to shout:

'Let's go, Postage Due . . . let's go! You can do it! Keep on coming . . !' And, as if the little horse could hear her, with each moment his stride seemed to lengthen, pulling him closer to the front.

The staid occupants of other boxes turned to glare at Geri for a moment, but then a few became infected by her fever, and rose to their feet to urge on their own horses. As the pack of horses shot past the clubhouse, even some of the elderly matrons like Sylvia were shouting as raucously as the fans in the grandstand.

Coming under the finish line, Postage Due led by half a length. Maccabee had finished sixth.

Sylvia had kept her seat and remained silent throughout the race. 'Very good, my dear,' she said as the noise around her subsided. 'You must tell me someday exactly what your reasons were.'

Phillip slammed his thick deck of worthless tickets down on the ground. 'I can tell you now,' he erupted. 'Blind stupid luck, nothing else, no *good* reason. My horse was ready, today was *his* day. He was jinxed, that's all.' The thought had bubbled up from his unconscious, the irrational product of anger and disappointment. But the moment it was out it took hold. Superstition was as much a foundation of any bettor's logic as fact. 'Yes, that's all that really got in the way,' he went on, staring hotly at Geri. 'A goddamn jinx. And as long as you're around, I'd give odds we haven't seen the end of our bad luck.'

'For pity's sake, Phillip,' Sylvia hissed. 'Stop this at once. And apologize!'

'I'll be damned if I will.' Leaning closer to his mother, he kept his voice low to avoid being heard in the other boxes, yet the tremor of his rage came through. 'What am I supposed to be sorry for? Wishing you'd come to your senses? Trying to keep you from getting in trouble with the law? Keeping this little tramp and letting her sponge off you? It never made sense for you to go along with this crazy idea of Steve's.'

'My God, Mother,' Alice leapt into the discussion. 'If any-one learns who she really is — *what* she is —'

Sylvia sat erect in her seat. 'I shall ask you only once more: cease this insulting discussion, and apologize. Both of you.'

There was a pause. Phillip and Alice looked in tandem from their mother to Geri.

Geri had to struggle to hold her head up and try to tell them with her own open unflinching gaze that she had done nothing wrong, wanted no one hurt, and would willingly leave if it would save them all from this battling. She wished she could speak it, too, but an odd combination of pride and shame forbade her from either yielding or defending herself.

'I think you're asking too much,' Phillip said. 'I have nothing to apologize for.' He stood and turned to Alice, silently soliciting her vote.

'I can't admit to something I don't feel,' she said, rising to her feet as well. She shot a fiery look at Geri. 'She should go!'

Sylvia turned from her children to look straight ahead at the view. 'If those are your feelings,' she said quickly, 'then I don't wish to see you again. Never . . . unless and until you recover your manners, and a proper respect for my wishes.'

Phillip opened his mouth as if to speak. Geri looked at Sylvia, too, ready to sacrifice herself rather than cause such a rift. She knew what it meant for a family to be torn apart.

But sitting poised and calmly composed, Sylvia Balkin projected a regal aura that discouraged any hope that she might change her mind. The queen had issued an edict. After a moment, Phillip whirled, hooked his arm through his sister's, and they hurried away.

'I'm sorry,' Geri said quietly.

'You? You did nothing . . .'

'I came between you and your children. They meant well. It's true that my being here could make trouble. It might be best if I —'

Sylvia didn't need to hear the words to finish the thought. She spun toward Geri, and gripped her wrist with her fine strong hand. 'I won't hear of it, do you understand? I gave my word to Steve to keep you safe, and nothing will change my determination to uphold that vow.'

'If your children want to get rid of me,' Geri said, 'you know they really don't have a big problem. There are certain people who'd like to know where I am. There'd be trouble for you, too, if Phillip and Alice tell them where to find me . . .'

Sylvia's neck stiffened. With the slow deliberate rhythm of bullets being shot from a well-aimed gun she fired off just three words. 'They wouldn't dare.'

Geri believed then that they wouldn't. Still, didn't she owe it to Sylvia to remove herself as the cause of dissension?

Detecting Geri's doubts, Sylvia's hand tightened again on her arm. 'Please,' she said. She was not a woman accustomed to pleading, and as if to erase even this one small slip, she went on quickly. 'Now, my dear, we mustn't let ourselves be distracted anymore from enjoying the day. We've a big winning ticket to cash in, and the horses for the sixth are probably in the paddock, and it's time we looked them over so you can make a choice.' She rose and moved into the aisle, then paused to stretch out her hand to Geri.

'You know,' Geri said, 'that *was* beginner's luck. I don't think I can do it every time.'

Sylvia gave a laugh, as bright and girlish as Geri had ever heard. 'We'll see,' she said as they headed for the paddock. 'We'll just see . . .'

CHAPTER FOUR

'I've had some wonderful news,' Sylvia said at breakfast one Sunday morning in May. 'Steve called late last night. He's coming for a visit in two weeks . . .' Geri was so overcome with delight that she leapt up and threw her arms around Sylvia, who flinched under the abandon of accustomed formality. 'Unfortunately,' she went on, after Geri sat down again, 'he can't spend much time with us. He's raising money for the civil rights movement, and he'll be traveling around the colleges, organizing Northern students to go South for the summer and help with voter registration. Then he'll go back to Mississippi to get the campaign started. He's there now, doing some preliminary groundwork.'

Geri's exposure to the intellectual atmosphere of the Balkin house had enlightened her about the civil rights struggle. She was aware of the massive effort that had been planned to educate Southern blacks to their democratic rights, and get them on the rolls to vote in the November election that would choose a President for '68. With Lyndon Johnson already retreating from the campaign in the face of growing anti-war opposition, the election seemed wide open to bring in a conservative Republican who might undo many of Johnson's 'Great Society' programs. Achieving fair policies for uneducated minorities, Geri understood, involved not only blacks, but people of all kinds who lived in poverty — like those in the mountains where she had been born.

'Maybe I could go with him and help him this summer,' she said.

'That wouldn't be wise, my dear. Fighting for freedom is a worthy cause, sometimes even at the cost of jeopardizing your own. But it's too soon, too dangerous, for you to be traveling in the south . . .'

Lately, Geri had felt so safe with Sylvia that her unresolved problem with the law could slip from her thoughts. She knew from a file of official papers and news clippings Sylvia had paid to have privately compiled that while her whereabouts had remained unknown the authorities had turned their attention to more pressing and easily resolved cases. Nevertheless, it was true that she would be instantly arrested and tried for murder if recognized in a southern jurisdiction.

'I can still help Steve in other ways,' she replied to Sylvia, 'do some organizing right here.' Sylvia nodded in approval. After a silence, Geri added, 'What about Phillip and Alice? You'll let them know about Steve, won't you?'

Since their day at the races a month ago, the family rift had gone on, unbroken by a single word of contact. Though Geri didn't miss seeing Phillip or Alice, she blamed herself for being the catalyst in the rupture among the Balkins. She worried, too, that if Steve arrived to discover a schism in his family, he might feel she had betrayed his faith in sending her here. After being away so long he would want to see his family united in welcoming him back.

But when Geri expressed her concern, Sylvia remained adamant: 'Phil and Alice behaved abominably toward you, my dear. I can't forgive them unless they apologize.'

'I can. Isn't that enough?'

'There are absolutes of decent behavior. I can't say I've never breached them myself; there was a time I didn't stand beside Steven when I should have. But I don't forgive myself easily for that, and that makes it hard for me to excuse others. An apology is little enough to ask for.'

Sylvia's position didn't soften in the days ahead. As Steve's visit drew nearer, she made no effort to inform Phil or Alice of their brother's homecoming. Increasingly anxious that Steve

224

should have no reason to regret sending her into their midst, and eager to ease any difficulties in Sylvia's life, Geri decided at last to take the initiative.

When the door of the apartment swung open, Geri was startled to see not a maid staring back at her — Sylvia never opened her own door — but Alice Balkin herself. For a long moment Alice regarded her coldly, as if slamming the door again was actually under consideration. Then she motioned Geri to enter with an exaggerated sweep of her hand, and led her across a foyer tiled in black marble, past the staircase of the duplex apartment to an immense double-height living room with an eagle view of the East River. At first glance, the modern furnishings around the room struck Geri as being perfectly suited to Alice Balkin's personality — all sharp edges, and hard shiny surfaces.

Geri stood immobilized by the impressive view until Alice Balkin pointed her to a long low couch upholstered in midnight-blue silk. Feeling jumpy and vulnerable in Alice's overbearing presence, Geri didn't feel like sitting down. All she wanted was to present her case, and escape as quickly as possible. But she knew it was important to hide her nervousness. Alice was the kind of woman who would pounce all the more quickly at any sign of weakness or vulnerability.

She settled onto the couch and tried to seem relaxed as Alice leaned over a coffee table surfaced in stainless steel, and picked up a gold cigarette lighter and a cigarette from a crystal box, all the while eyeing Geri suspiciously.

'Your call,' she said after lighting the cigarette, 'was one of the more intriguing novelties of my week. If I had to make a list of people I'd never expect to hear from, you'd be at the top.'

'Look . . .' Geri said softly, 'we don't have to go into how we feel about each other. I know you don't like me, and . . . it's true that doesn't make me want to know you any better. But this visit isn't something I'm doing for myself . . .'

'Oh? Then exactly what is the reason for all this cloak-and-dagger bullshit?'

On the phone, Geri had refused to explain the reason for her request to meet. Alice could have more easily avoided her then, or might have wanted Phillip present. Though Alice was outwardly cynical, and played up to her hard fearless image with rough talk and daring clothes like the broad-shouldered paratroop-type black jumpsuit she had on now, Geri sensed there was a better chance of reasoning with her if they could talk alone. 'Steve is coming to visit in a few days,' she said. 'I thought you should know . . .'

Alice raised her eyebrows. 'Is this news just for little old me . . .?'

'No, I hoped you'd pass it along to Phillip.'

'Easy enough. Anything else you wanted?' Alice asked coyly, clearly aware there must be.

Geri paused to choose her words. 'I wanted Steve's homecoming to be a happy occasion . . . But it can't be if he arrives and finds that you and Phillip are on the outs with your mother. I guess I thought . . . if you patch things up before Steve gets here, it would be nicer all around. Sylvia insists, though, on your apology to me.'

'So you've come to collect . . .?' Alice's cold eyes drilled into her.

Geri met her gaze head-on. 'No. I don't give a hoot about apologies for myself, only to smooth things over for Steve and your mother. I just had the idea it might be easier for you somehow if I let you know that I'm not the one making a point of it. The fact is, I understand how my staying with your mother can be difficult for you. I guess . . . I can't blame you for worrying about the trouble Sylvia might get into for giving me a home.'

'Can't you?' Alice lowered herself into a chair. 'Then if you really want to make it easy on everyone, why don't you just go away?' She made a small movement with her fingers, as if simply flicking away a piece of dust.

'I've thought about it.'

'But no decision . . .'

Geri fought to keep steady and unemotional in the face of Alice's openly hostile challenge. 'I'm safe here, and I'm very happy. I have chances I never had before. And Sylvia's told me that doing this is important to her — for Steve more than for

226

me. Aren't those reasons enough to stay?'

Alice gave her a grudging smile. 'Well, well . . . quite the little diplomat, aren't you? Full of schemes for making peace. Since dear mother still expects you to get an apology . . . so be it. But if we apologize in front of her, you'll — what? — agree not to take it seriously, pretend it never happened?'

'Look, this isn't for me,' Geri repeated. 'Can't you use this homecoming as chance for you and your mother to get back together?' Having seen her own family destroyed and torn apart, Geri couldn't bear to play any part in the Balkin rift. She pleaded with genuine passion for a resolution.

But Alice appeared unmoved as she took a puff on her cigarette. 'Touching, this concern for our togetherness. Is it really as simple as that?'

Geri gazed silently at Alice, perplexed.

'And this devotion to dear Steve? What's all that about? Does my black sheep brother sometimes lie down with other little lambs — who aren't black . . .?'

Still unaccustomed to this kind of nasty repartee, it took Geri a second to get the double dig against both her and Chel. An angry reply started to boil up, but then she realized they would wreck her effort at peacemaking. 'Steve has been good to me,' she said simply, 'that's why I care about him. He saved my life.'

'Oh yes,' Alice said, 'you'd be in jail now if it wasn't for him. In fact, you'd be in jail *tomorrow* if you didn't keep all of us in line — keep a roof over your head. Isn't that what this is *really* about? Making things sweet again before dear Sylvia has to make a choice between us and you — keep her busy pulling those golden strings, keep the hush money being passed along to the right people?'

'Hush money? What are you talking about?'

'Only a guess,' Alice said with a sly look at Geri. 'But covering your trail might involve paying off someone, somewhere . . .'

Geri shook her head. 'I don't know anything about pay-offs. Please believe me, this isn't about what I need. It's just for —'

'Sylvia,' Alice cut in, 'and of course Steve — dear darling

Steve, anything for him. All right. Let's suppose Phil and I make it a gala homecoming, one big happy family gathered around the fireside.' She leaned forward, and her voice fell to a purr. 'Then don't you think you should do us a favor in return?'

'How?'

Alice blew out a stream of smoke. She watched it swirl away through the bright sunlight before giving her answer. 'Disappear.' Her steady gray eyes came back to Geri.

Geri was stunned almost as much by the cruelty behind the woman's casual tone as by the demand itself. 'I know you want to protect your mother, but she's prepared to take the risks to help me — and she knows they get smaller every day.'

Alice shook her head. 'I often wonder. Are you really as much of a sweet little hick as you pretend to be? Do you really not understand?' Her tone got brassier. 'This isn't about the risks of helping you, mountain-girl. My well-connected mama can spread enough influence around to make those very small. There are other things at stake . . . much bigger things.'

'What?'

'Dollars,' Alice said flatly, 'and cents.'

For just a moment, Geri thought that the money begrudged her was merely the amount that had been spent on keeping her, clothing her, paying a tutor. But as she stared back at Alice Balkin's hard expression, the truth came through. The money that Sylvia's children were so anxious to protect was their inheritance.

'You're crazy to worry about that,' Geri erupted. 'I'm not trying to take anybody's place with your mother . . .'

'Oh, you don't have to try, dearie. You just have to be what you are — an adorable little underdog. The mongrel breed has an irresistible appeal for mother somehow, as it had for my father. Steven takes after them, too. They all like to throw the underdog a few bones now and then — it adds up to a couple of hundred millions' worth of bones so far. It's all very noble, of course, and Phil and I haven't minded as long as we knew we were . . . provided for. But if you stay around long enough, who knows what mother might do? You're the kind of needy

228

pup who just might give her the idea of dishing out a whole dog's dinner.' She stood up, only to assume a higher vantage point. 'Maybe you've fooled my mother into believing you're innocent, but from my own reading of your troubles with the law, I'd say there's a good chance you've got larceny as well as murder in your heart. And if you can't take mother for a ride, you think you might get money from Steve' — a tight smile curled her lips again — 'by staying close and wagging your adorable little underdog's tail.'

A surge of fury pushed Geri to her feet, yet she worked to force it down. If she walked out, it would end any hope of accomplishing what she had come for. 'Please believe me, I don't want to take anything from you or anybody else. I just . . . want to stay free. I never did anything wrong . . .'

'Then why did you run away?' Alice Balkin came back. A harder edge came into her voice. 'If you really want to do a favor, then do it for yourself. Move on. Clear out soon. Because any day Phil and I are going to lose our patience . . .'

Geri had no doubt about the meaning of Alice Balkin's threat. She spun away to the window, hiding from the vicious look of triumph she saw on Alice Balkin's face. But as she stared out at the view — the sprawl of poorer sections of the city that lay across the river — Geri realized that she could no longer feel safe with Sylvia. She had been living in a dream and now it was over.

Turning on her heel, she walked to the front door. Crossing the marble foyer, she heard Alice close behind her.

After pulling open the door, Geri stopped. 'I'll want to stay until after Steve has come and gone,' she said quietly, still facing away from Alice.

'But of course, Phil and I would want that, too,' said the voice at her shoulder. 'My goodness, if Steve didn't find you here, he'd be heartbroken.'

The next day, Phillip Balkin called Sylvia. He and Alice did realize they had behaved badly, he said, and they hoped to have the chance to atone.

It never occurred to Sylvia that Geri could have had a hand in the rapprochement. She assumed that Alice and Phil had learned, through one of the trusted family lawyers Steve kept abreast of his plans, that he was to visit, and they had been prompted to repent because of their own desire to see him. Sylvia invited them to the house so they could make their apology to Geri.

They arrived together the next evening, both bearing gifts. Alice brought an overnight bag from Mark Cross — relishing the secret humor of presenting Geri with travel accessories — Phillip brought the current annual edition of the American Racing Manual. Riffling through its fifteen hundred-odd pages, he showed Geri that it contained virtually every significant fact relevant to the American racing scene — records of every horse running, lists of leading money-winning horses, leading breeders and their animals, diagrams of all the racetracks in the country, records of the yearling sales, and much more. The book delighted Geri; she only wished it could have come from someone she liked.

She accepted both gifts and apologies graciously, however. For Sylvia's sake, she was resolved to match Alice and Phillip's convincing performance of a real desire to turn over a new leaf. Sylvia was clearly gratified at being reunited with her children — and on her own terms. She brought out champagne at dinner, and spoke happily about the huge party she was planning for the dual purpose of welcoming Steve and raising money to aid the voting drive. 'I spoke to Dr King this morning, and he's agreed to come and talk. And I thought we might put Count Basie's orchestra in the big dining room and have dancing, and someone told me about these wonderful girls from Detroit, The Supremes, I'll get them to sing . . .'

She was asking Alice what friends of Steve's from his college days he might still like to see when Margaret entered and quietly informed her that a man was waiting on the phone to speak with her.

Sylvia was openly annoyed. 'Goodness, Margaret, you should know I never accept calls during dinner.'

'Of course, Mrs Balkin. But you see, this man insisted . . . and he's with the police.'

Sylvia shot an alarmed glance at Geri. 'I'll take it in the

230

library,' she said, and rose to follow Margaret from the room.

Geri's heart began to pound, and the silver fork in her hand seemed suddenly as heavy as a sledgehammer. Had Alice or Phil given her away? Yet what sense was there in doing it now? She had agreed to go. Even if they wanted her punished, they wouldn't have risked Sylvia's wrath — and surely if they had tipped the police Sylvia would find out. The mystified looks that Phil and Alice were exchanging also seemed genuine.

When Sylvia reappeared after ten minutes, she was ashen, her normally brisk stride brittle and unsteady. She sat down again, and stared down vacantly at the place in front as she delivered her explanation. 'The call came from the State Police in Mississippi . . . Yesterday evening Steve left one town where he'd been recruiting some help for the voter registration to drive to his next stop. Four people were with him, all involved in the same work — one of them, I'm told, a black woman he'd known for some time. They never arrived at their destination. As soon as they were missed, their co-workers began a search. This morning they found Steve's car by a roadside, empty. There was a bullet hole in one of the windows, and some blood on a back seat. Right now, that's all the police have.' After a moment, she added, 'So they say.'

The feelings that had plagued Geri just a minute ago suddenly seemed preferable to the sorrow and dread she experienced now. 'You think there's something they're not telling you? You think they already know that Steve is . . . hurt?'

It hadn't been the word that was in her mind. Yet she couldn't bring herself actually to say the other. Steve had to be alive. If she lost him, she would lose her last anchor to belief in her future.

'For all we know,' Sylvia said heavily, 'there may be police involved.'

'Is there anything we can do?' Phillip asked.

Sylvia shook her head disconsolately.

'Are they sure it's related to this civil rights thing?' Alice asked. 'Perhaps someone found out who Steve really was and went after him for a ransom . . .'

No one bothered to answer. Sylvia seemed to sink even deeper into some morbid reflection.

Since that first moment Geri had seen her on the stairs, she had not thought of Sylvia's age. Always full of ideas and plans, bristling with energy, Sylvia seemed ageless. Now all at once she looked like an old woman, weak and withered. Obviously she had already given up hope for Steve.

After being buttressed so often by Sylvia's strength and optimism, Geri was thrown by seeing her reduced to helplessness. As pained and upset as she was herself by the news, Geri felt that she had to be the strong one this time. She reached across the table and laid her hand over Sylvia's.

'He'll be all right,' she said, her voice emerging in a fervent hush, a prayer rising out of her own need. 'I know he will . . .'

But Sylvia didn't answer, didn't look at her. Her hand under Geri's remained as cold and lifeless as stone.

Geri looked to Phillip and Alice for help. But they sat impassively, watching the scene between Geri and Sylvia unfold as if they were simply curious as to how it would end.

'Let me take you upstairs.' Geri rose, and moved closer to help Sylvia from her chair. 'You need to rest . . .'

'No,' Sylvia said sharply, pushing back her chair, 'please don't . . .' In the sharp way she glanced at Geri, it was as if she had meant to say *don't touch me*.

This seemed to be what Phillip and Alice had been waiting for — an acknowledgment that, in crisis, the family would define itself strictly by blood.

Capitalizing on the moment, Alice leapt up and moved to Sylvia's side. 'This has been an awful shock, mother. Let Phillip stay down here and see what he can do to get some more information. It really would be best for you to lie down a while. I'll take you to your room. Come, mother. I'll stay with you . . .'

Given the prerogative to say 'mother', Alice was able to cut through Sylvia's shock in a way that Geri could not. Sylvia rose and left the room with her.

The atmosphere left between Phillip and Geri could have been no more explosive if the air was filled with gasoline fumes instead of merely unsaid thoughts. It was Geri who lit the match. 'I couldn't leave her now,' she said.

'We've done what you asked,' Phillip said. 'Now it's your turn.'

'But you *can't* expect me to leave now.'

'As much as ever,' Phillip insisted coolly. 'This is a time for a family to be together . . .'

'But I love Steve, too!' she cried out. 'I love Sylvia. Whatever happens, she'll need me.'

'She's our mother,' Phillip said. 'We'll take care of her. She won't need anyone else.'

Geri shook her head, in disbelief at his callousness.

Phillip took it as a gesture of refusal. 'Don't force our hand, "cousin",' he said, his lip curling back to emphasize the threat. 'Face the facts and go quietly.'

She turned from Phil and looked through the door that led upstairs. She had an urge to run to Sylvia, tell her the way she was being forced out. But would Sylvia do anything in her present state? With one of her children missing, perhaps lost, she was clinging to the others. Only to them. In the way Sylvia had rejected her just now, Geri realized, there had been something at work beyond an old woman's overwhelming shock.

It struck her now that she might have taken the bad news about Steve as the fulfillment of Phillip's prophecy — that as long as Geri was in the Balkin house, there would be more bad luck to come.

She turned back to Phillip, prepared to beg for time, a chance to find an alternative. But as she looked into his spiteful eyes, the urge died. She could no longer fight his hatred and Alice's — nor the fact that she owed Sylvia too much not to spare her the risks of sheltering her. What had happened to Steve in Mississippi would focus the attention of the news on him and his missing co-workers. The odds were that his true identity, his ties to Sylvia, would now be uncovered.

Even if Phillip and Alice hadn't threatened her, she would probably have had to go.

233

And, after all, hadn't Sylvia said any number of times that she was extending this largesse only as payment of a debt to Steve? If Steve was gone, then what reason would Sylvia have to go on paying? For all her generosity and kindness to Geri, she had never expressed any affection of her own.

The tears brimmed in her eyes, but Geri didn't blot them away as she lifted the fine damask napkin from her lap. She laid it at her place as she pushed back her chair. 'If you'll excuse me,' she said, trying to display the kind of bearing she had learned from watching Sylvia, 'there are things I have to do.'

She walked from the room with her back straight and her head held high.

She didn't plan to take away much more than she had brought with her. Certainly not the clothes and the gifts, and no more than enough money to get her to the next place — wherever that was to be. But the knowledge and the style would have to go with her. There was no way to give those back.

CHAPTER FIVE

The winners cheered, the losers groaned, and the huge crowd started to flow toward the exits. Geri let her ten-dollar win ticket on a horse in the final race flutter to the ground and headed for the refreshment stand where she had persuaded a counterman to hold on to her valise.

It had been late last night by the time she finished writing the letter of goodbye to Sylvia which she had left propped up on a vase in the entrance hall as she slipped out of the house. Carrying an overnight bag packed with only a few essentials, she had walked aimlessly until, by morning, she found herself standing in front of the bus terminal. Unconsciously she had been drawn back to her point of entry into the huge, lonely city.

For several hours more she had sat on a bench and pondered where to go. Again and again her small reservoir of courage would run dry, and she would think of returning to Sylvia. But each time she would realize there was too much danger for both of them. Whether or not Phillip and Alice gave her away, the publicity around Steve's disappearance might soon steer reporters to the Balkin house.

She thought briefly of Tony. But after what Sylvia had revealed about him, Geri couldn't imagine barging into Tony's private life.

And then the idea came. She wasn't sure exactly what had made her think of the racetrack. In some way, she guessed, it had to do with Steve — a reaction to the news about him and the way it had affected Sylvia. She needed a place to feel closer to him, to pray for him, find some distraction from fear and grief — and perhaps prove somehow she didn't contaminate the lives of others with bad luck. The track might provide it all.

Since she had begun reading the newspapers, she always took a few minutes to browse the sports pages and she knew the race meeting had moved to Belmont Park from Aqueduct. She also knew that Oakie Whitten might be found there — his name had been reported a few times as the trainer of a horse that won some feature event; there was a chance he would give her some help.

As if to confirm the inevitability of her choice, she had found a bus that went straight from the terminal to Belmont Park in Jamaica, Long Island.

The track, named for August Belmont, the rich racing enthusiast who had spearheaded its construction at the turn of the century, was bigger and more beautifully landscaped than Aqueduct, with surroundings of tree-shaded lawns and walkways, and a bigger lake on the infield. Arriving close to noon, Geri fell into a crowd that was funneling toward the grandstand, and soon found herself buying a ticket at the admission gate. The exhaustion from a night without sleep disappeared as she was swept up once again, as on that first occasion, in the excitement of a day at the races. This time she was able to fulfill her wish to be with the more voluble crowds. The day was sunny and not too hot, helping to instill a sense of well-being that, in turn, fed the idea that she was where she belonged. She would prove herself, she was sure, she would show that bad luck didn't cling to her.

Testing her ability, believing that sooner or later she would repeat the trick she had pulled off so easily before, she had held nothing back. A bet on every race, no less than ten dollars each time, always to win.

By the end of the afternoon there was nothing left of the one hundred dollars she had permitted herself to take last night — a small portion of what she had saved from pocket money

Sylvia had liberally dispensed. Not one of her bets had paid off. So much for her sixth sense about the horses. She hadn't a cent left to buy a meal, nor the money to pay for a room overnight.

'How d'ya make out, kid?' the paunchy middle-aged counterman asked as Geri stepped up to reclaim her valise.

'Not too good,' she admitted.

He wiped his hands on his white apron, lifted the suitcase and passed it across the counter. 'I thought maybe you brought this thing 'cause you figured you'd hit so big you'd need it to carry home your winnings.'

It brought a smile. 'Thanks for keeping it.' He winked an acknowledgement and Geri started to turn away, then stopped on an afterthought. 'You don't happen to need anyone to help you here, do the cleaning up . . .?

He shook his head. 'That bad, huh . . .?'

She nodded.

He explained that he was hired himself by a concession, and didn't earn that much. Then he put a hot dog and a soda on the counter. 'Compliments of the house,' he said.

'That's very kind.' Geri started to eat the hot dog slowly, to make it last.

The eyes of the counterman went from her face down to the suitcase on the ground, and came back to her face. 'You don't strike me as the usual railbird. A looker like you, don't you got some better place to be . . .?'

She didn't want to make a bid for sympathy. 'I didn't know there was a better place.'

'You're really hooked on the ponies, huh?' The counterman appraised her with the practiced eye of a man who had seen a lot of losers come and go — and only a few winners. 'Shame to see a nice girl like you gamble your life away . . .'

'I'm not hooked on that part. What I like about . . . "the ponies" is just watching them run.'

'But somehow that took your last dollar and left you lookin' for any bum job . . .'

'Yeah. I guess it did.' Now she hurried through what was left of the hot dog, anxious to escape from the counterman's grim candor.

'Try the backstretch,' he said suddenly.

She looked at him blankly. An odd moment to suggest exercises.

'The backstretch, kid. It costs nothing to get there, and there just might be a job. A place to sleep, too.'

'What is it?'

'You don't know . . .?' The counterman laughed heartily. 'You're here tapping out on the ponies, calling this home, and you don't even know . . .?'

She shook her head sheepishly.

'It's the other side of this crazy world, kid. The dreams die over here. The backstretch is where they're born.' He lifted his arm and pointed.

The backstretch of Belmont Park covered hundreds of acres. Past a guarded gate, a network of roads led to rows and rows of long barns — stabling for more than two thousand horses — as well as dormitories for track workers and clusters of houses, some of them small and ramshackle, others no less sizeable and well kept than the homes of any residential suburb. A number of clean white shingle cottages also housed offices for the Racing Association, the track veterinarian, or the track chaplain. And there were several 'kitchens', small shacks where meals were cooked and sold to the people who lived and worked around the track.

Geri had the feeling that she had entered a large bustling town where the inhabitants were equally divided between humans and horses. Along the roads traversing the backstretch many of the animals were being walked or trotted on their way back to stables after races or late workouts, the steam from their sweated hides rising into the cool afternoon air. Cars bearing trainers or stablehands to or from work drove slowly, stopping at intersections to give passing horses the right of way. Geri noticed that the names identifying each thoroughfare, posted on signs at the corners, all honored some champion racehorse of the past.

Surveying the scene for a minute from the corner of 'Citation Avenue' and 'Man O' War Road', she knew that she had arrived at last at the place where her destiny had always been waiting. Sylvia Balkin had provided a privileged haven, but she couldn't have been happy living that kind of life much longer. She had to work, discover her own worth — and from the day she had thrilled to the magic sight of horses roaming through blue grass, she had known instinctively that the horses would have to be part of that discovery.

Destiny or not, she almost hadn't been allowed in. The guard at the entrance had stopped her and said she couldn't enter without a pass. She had only managed to talk her way past him by dropping Oakie's name. 'Mr Whitten told me to come out here today. He's got a job for me . . .'

The guard had looked slightly dubious, but after she summoned up a little of her old mountain twang and said, 'Known him ever since back home in Kentucky,' his resistance had melted. He not only let her in, but referred to a directory, gave her the barn number where Oakie's horses were kept, and told her how to find it.

Now, as she turned into the long row of stable buildings to which she'd been directed, she was stricken by a fresh attack of doubt. Oakie had liked her, but she had met him at a time before her trouble with the law. What would the trainer think of her now? He would have known about her trial and disappearance — and he was a decent man, who might think it was his responsibility to call the police. On the other hand, he had been Steve's friend, too. For that reason more than any other she decided to trust him.

In an area outside the stables shaded by tall oaks, horses were being led in large circles by hot-walkers and being sponged down by grooms. Geri went up to one of the grooms, a young man about her own age in jeans and a sweatshirt, and asked which barn was number eighty-seven. He paused to give her an appreciative once-over, then pointed to the third barn in the row.

Stepping out of the golden light of late afternoon into the barn's cool shade, she saw more horses being given walking exercise along the hay-strewn aisles that went around the perimeter of the stalls. She stopped the first hot-walker who passed by to ask where she could find Oakie Whitten and he nodded to a door at the other end of the barn.

Through the door she found a small cubicle defined by walls of raw barnwood, furnished with several chairs and a desk heaped with papers. There was one man in the room, and it wasn't Oakie. He was about thirty, with crew-cut black hair and a wiry build that filled out an undersized tee-shirt. He was at the desk talking on a phone, but as soon as Geri came in he told the other person on the line to 'hold on', and turned to her inquiringly.

'I'm looking for Oakie Whitten. Isn't this his barn?'

'Yeah, Oakie keeps his string here, but he's not around now.' The man with the crew-cut was obviously impatient to continue his phone conversation.

'When's he coming back?'

'Could be a day or two, I'm not sure. He's got a horse running in Maryland today, so he went down there last night . . .'

A day or two. She could manage, of course. Yet, marooned in a strange place, it sounded like an eternity of waiting.

From the tone of his answers, she thought the man on the phone didn't work for Oakie, but on impulse she asked, 'You have any jobs I could do . . .'

'Not me, kid. Don't use girls. Did Oakie say he had something for you . . .?'

She was afraid to lie again, thinking it might backfire when Oakie returned. 'No. But I . . . used to know him, and I just thought there might be a chance . . .'

The wiry man shrugged. 'I doubt it, kid. Got a full barn crew. But if you're around tomorrow or the next day, stop in again.' He turned back to the phone and went on with his conversation.

She walked out into the sunshine and looked along the stable row. Everywhere she saw stablehands and grooms tending horses. Why wait for Oakie? There must be hundreds of other opportunities, and perhaps it would be better to work for a stranger, someone who knew nothing of her past.

She began to work her way along one row of barns after another, inquiring of the trainer in charge at each barn — and to every request she made for a chance to work, she got the same answer. 'No girls . . . don't hire girls.'

At first, she took the rejection philosophically. There had to be someone who wouldn't discriminate against her on such an idiotic basis. There was nothing required in any of the jobs that she couldn't do. And indeed, as she went in and out of the different barns she *had* seen one or two girls doling out grain to the animals, or sponging them off.

By evening, though, she had covered more than fifty barns without getting the slightest encouragement. There were many more to go — at least a hundred, she thought — but she began to realize there was no point in going on. There was very little activity around the barns now, with most of the horses already fed and cooled and locked into their stalls, many of the trainers gone home. 'Come back tomorrow,' she was told — wherever she wasn't told outright that there was no work.

For all the discouragement, however, she wasn't ready to give up completely. There were still a hundred barns she hadn't tried — and Oakie would be back tomorrow or the day after . . .

But when night came on, and she was left trekking alone through the dark, her optimism faded. Lamps shone in the windows of the dormitories, and a couple of the kitchens that had yet to close, but somehow they felt as distant from her as cabins on a vast prairie. Without a dime, without a friend, could she find a place to sleep unless she begged? The idea of begging for the barest essentials of life made her feel as if she had traveled back to her very beginnings — sunk even lower. She would never beg.

Except for the snorting and stamping of horses standing asleep in the stables, or the sound of 'Strawberry Fields', one of the hot new Beatle tunes, playing on a radio somewhere, the backstretch was quiet. Most of the stable buildings were dark, or lit only by a dim bulb. Several times, passing the wide entrances to the barns, Geri saw stableboys keeping a nightwatch, stretched out over a couple of chairs or napping in a pile of hay. Hunger had begun to gnaw at her stomach, but the need for a place to sleep was even greater. At last she could no longer fight off the drowsiness. Choosing a stable that was completely dark, she crept in through a side door, found a store of hay, arranged the bags she had been toting all day to provide a pillow, and lay down.

Tomorrow would be better, she thought. She had only just begun the race, there was plenty of time to come from behind.

CHAPTER SIX

She came awake to the sound of jingling bridles and horses being walked out of the barn across its hard cobbled floor. A light had gone on, but when Geri sat up to work the stiffness out of her body, she could see through a door that it was still dark outside. Nearby, other barns could also be heard stirring with activity, and saddled horses were clopping along pathways on their way to the training track, black silhouettes faintly visible against a sky tinting to purple. Mixed with the redolent smell of hay, Geri detected the faint aroma of brewed coffee and fried bacon. It wasn't yet dawn, but at the track the day was beginning.

Suddenly a stablehand dressed in denims and a checkered cap rounded a corner and saw her. The pitchfork he was holding looked menacing, and Geri made a move to get quickly to her feet.

'Hey, don' worry, *muchacha*,' the stablehand said, with a glance at Geri's bags and the makeshift hay bed. 'Nobody min' if you sleep here. Plenty people do the same thing every night. I take what I need and you go back to your siesta.' The stablehand speared the pitchfork into the hay.

Geri relaxed. It was difficult to see through the gloom broken only by a dim bulb some distance away, but the timbre of the Spanish-accented voice indicated the intruder was only a young boy. Then, as she studied the trim figure in denims, she broke into a smile. 'A girl,' Geri blurted out. 'You're a girl.'

The stablehand turned, holding the pitchfork with its load of hay. '*Si*. So . . .?'

'Well . . . I am, too.'

One of the most prominent features of the pretty copper-skinned face were the well-defined dark eyebrows over glittering brown eyes. They knit together in confusion at this declaration of the obvious.

'See, it's nice to know that I have a chance,' Geri explained. 'I've been trying to get a job like the one you've got.'

'I keep my job . . .'

'No, I don't want *yours*. Just the same thing.'

As the dark pretty girl nodded comprehension, a curl of long black hair fell across her forehead from beneath her checkered cap. She lowered the pitchfork, and leaned on the handle, studying Geri. 'Is no easy,' she said. 'No too many girls, an' my boss got no more job. But try, maybe you fin'.' She glanced through an opening at the lightening sky. 'Good time to look now. Be an early worm, eh?'

From somewhere in the recesses of the barn, a man's voice called loudly. 'Ramie! Where the hell's that hay . . .?'

The stable girl murmured to Geri. 'Tha's me he want.' She scooped up the pitchfork again, then nodded toward Geri's bags. 'You leave tha' stuff here, eh? I watch for you.' She darted away.

Geri smiled to herself as she left the barn . . . to be the early worm.

She headed straight to Oakie's barn, but still he wasn't there and no one could tell her when he would be. As she made her way across the backstretch the smells of food floating out of the kitchens stoked the fires of hunger. She'd had no supper last night, she hadn't the price of a breakfast, and as the day wore on she didn't see where she'd get the money for any other meal. Most of her new efforts were met simply with flat rejections. A couple of times she was asked about her experience, but before answering she realized that if she talked about Kentucky, or Skyevale, or working for a vet, the risk of someday being identified would be magnified. She dared to say only that she'd picked up a little 'here and there'. It wasn't enough to persuade anyone.

Her spirits sank even lower when she spotted a tabloid newspaper discarded near the barn with a front-page photograph of an abandoned car tilted over on the shoulder of a road and the headline FIVE MISS. RIGHTS WORKERS MISSING. She picked it up and scanned the article, but there was nothing beyond what Sylvia had been told.

At noon, with other opportunities dwindling, she decided to stop back at barn number eighty-seven. When she saw Oakie standing by a horse out front, his plaid wool hat tipped back on his head as he contemplated the hoof that another man — probably a vet — was holding up for inspection, she had to stop herself from joyfully shouting out. There was no guarantee of how he'd respond, she reminded herself. She ought to wait until she could catch him alone.

She stayed out of sight around the corner of the adjacent barn until the horse was led away by a groom, and the vet got back into his Jeep and drove away. Then, while Oakie remained standing under the shade of an oak as if mulling some diagnosis the vet had made, she hurried over. He looked up as she approached.

'Hell's bells,' he exclaimed, flicking his plaid hat even farther back on his head, 'fella told me there'd been a girl askin' for me. The description he gave — a hall of fame winner, he said, with maybe a little Kentucky music in her voice — it half crossed my mind it might be you . . .' Only now his brow furrowed and he glanced warily in each direction obviously reminded that being seen with her could bring trouble.

'Tell me to go, and I will, Oakie. I don't want to cause any problems.'

He beckoned her closer, and lowered his voice. 'Problems are mother's milk to any man who's spent his life in racing. Whatever they are, we can lick 'em.' He put an arm around her. 'Now, we got a little catchin' up to do, and it just occurred to me you might feel better doin' it somewhere there's a little less traffic.'

With the same intuitive ability that allowed him to divine the needs of animals who never spoke, he must have perceived that she was famished, because he proposed talking with her over a meal at one of the kitchens, and pointed her to his old Buick sedan so they could drive there.

'Clara's Kitchen' was one of the smallest. It had a counter with a few seats, and half a dozen square formica-topped tables. The walls of bare wooden siding were covered with yellowing vintage pictures of great horses, an official track photo of a famous three-horse dead-heat finish, and lists of dormitory rules and other notices that had been more recently tacked up. He bought her a steak and home-fried potatoes and blueberry pie à la mode, and smiled knowingly as she finished everything off in a few minutes. 'You hit the feedbag like you haven't eaten since the last time we met.'

She smiled. 'I was eating real well until yesterday.' She hesitated, not certain whether to reveal the way Steve had helped her. Perhaps she wouldn't have, but since he was missing she wanted it known how good he had been, wanted someone else to care that much more about finding him. So she told Oakie how Steve had helped her to escape an unjust punishment, and where he had sent her, and who his real family was, how she had adjusted to living with them — including her change of name — and the reasons she had finally left.

He listened sympathetically. He was aware of the news from Mississippi, and he felt it as deeply as she did. 'Steve's a hell of a guy, hon',' he said. 'I'm bettin' he'll turn up safe and sound. When he does, he'll want to know you're in good hands, too . . . so I'd say you ought to head back to his Mama —'

'No, Oakie. I can't go back now. This is where I want to be. I want to stay around the horses — and you. I want to learn all the things you said I would if I watched long enough.'

'Honey, this is a tough life. There's dozens of things you could aim for that would be better. Goodness, with a face like yours, and some money behind ya —'

'*This* is what I want,' she said fervently. 'Just give me a job.'

'Workin' for me ain't the answer. Too much of a chance you and the Mitchells'd bump up against each other sooner or later.'

She reared back in surprise. 'But you don't train for them anymore. I saw in the program —'

'I'm a freelancer now. I don't work exclusive for anyone, but there's still a couple of Skyevale horses in my string. Any day now I expect to be racing one of 'em, and the Mitchells could show up for the race. Chances are they wouldn't be around the barn much, but if they did spot you, I doubt they'd look the other way. It ain't fair, but they blamed you for draggin' their son into the kind of public mess proper folk try to avoid. Took it out on Steve, too. Stopped using him, and got him blacklisted with a lot of their friends.' He frowned. 'Tell you the truth, I don't care for 'em much. But if I had to weigh the nature of most folks ahead of the nature of their animals, there's too damn few people I could work for. I don't work for the Mitchells 'cause I like them. I like their horses.'

'I can't blame you,' she said. 'The same thing got me into trouble.' She shrugged disconsolately. 'Well, if you've got nothing for me, then maybe I'll have to move on somewhere else . . .'

'Now hold on, peach blossom. All I said was I don't want you to stumble comin' out of the gate. You can't stay too close around me . . . but if you work for another trainer, it'd be easier to stay outta the way of trouble. There's plenty others around who should be glad to take you on.'

'I've been everywhere.'

He chuckled. 'It might come out different if we try it again,' he said. 'Together.'

The trainers were the barons of the backstretch who shared among themselves the essential assets of its territory, the barns and stall space. Allotments were made by the Racing Association according to the importance of a trainer, the number of horses he had and their quality. It was in the interests of the sport to accommodate the best horses, and the men who controlled them were often given a whole barn to themselves. They might be trainers who served only one owner, so that every stall was filled with horses of one racing stable. Families who had owned and raced horses since Belmont was built, and even before, had whole barns to themselves — the Wideners, the Phippses, the Whitneys and Vanderbilts and duPonts — and there were some devoted only to more recently established but successful Kentucky-based stables like Claiborne Farm, Calumet Farm, and Kismet Farm belonging to Laurette Wilkey, the matriarch of blue-grass society. But in most of the barns the stalls were shared out among horses of several different owners; the single factor that unified them under one roof being that they were all in one 'string' — being trained by one man.

Oakie hadn't been freelancing for long, so his string was still small, and didn't occupy a whole barn. Yet the other trainers all regarded him as a shrewd, honest and able man who would eventually rise to the top.

Of course, all that was needed was for Oakie to bring Geri to a friendly trainer with his recommendation. Ten minutes after leaving Clara's Kitchen Geri had been hired as a hot-walker.

She was paid sixty dollars a week and given a place to sleep. The job required little beyond willingness and patience with the animals. After a horse had been run, it had to be walked around for a long time to let it cool slowly. There were horses too, that were not being rigorously trained for one reason or another, but still had to be given regular slow exercise. Whenever she wasn't walking a horse around the barn or in one of the outside rings, she might bring the animals feed, or clean their stalls, or oil their tack, ice their legs, or hold them while the vet gave a shot. Occasionally, at the end of a day, she might have time to ride one of the docile lead ponies used to accompany high-strung thoroughbreds and keep them calm on their way to and from the track.

The reluctance to hire girls, Geri learned, lay partly in the traditions of the past — and the superstitious idea that changing such traditions, having women around where they didn't belong, could bring bad luck. But there were some practical considerations that had made it harder to break down the old barriers, even though it was recognized that women were as capable as men of handling most of the necessary physical tasks. Tending thoroughbreds called for long days that started early, and more or less round-the-clock vigilance, so grooms and stablehands were quartered in nearby dormitories. Whenever a girl was hired — and there were half a dozen working in one capacity or another at one of Belmont's 170 barns — it required some special accommodation. In Geri's case, a separate space was found in a loft above the shack that housed the tack room.

Lenny Burkeholz, to whom Oakie had taken her, was a beefy middle-aged man who shouted a great deal, but enjoyed laughing and kidding around with the barn crew between his fits of temper. Geri liked him and took his excitability as the understandable result of his position. His string came from several owners, successful people dabbling in the sport by buying two or three horses. Some of their animals were good, some were mediocre, but all — especially since they had been purchased by eager, inexperienced amateurs — had cost a great deal of money. Lenny's responsibility for eighteen expensive horses, any of which might have its value reduced or wiped out by a moment of human error, was sufficient reason for his volatility.

To oblige a request Oakie had made, Lenny provided occasional opportunities for Geri to learn more about what went into conditioning the animals to race. Though horses were usually ridden from the barn to the training track by the exercise riders, Lenny sometimes told Geri to ride the horse over, then let her stay to watch the work-outs. Sometimes Oakie was there, and he would take a few minutes out to visit with her, and offer a few comments.

Tuning a thoroughbred to deliver its best was a largely mystical and unscientific process. Many horses with great bloodlines and a proven capability to run at winning speeds

249

were never able to produce their best on the racetrack. Sometimes this had to do with nothing more than their own temperament, a failing of competitive spirit to compare with any in the human personality. Yet there was always a chance that the animal had not been given the proper preparation and handling. A good trainer was expected not only to oversee the physical conditioning of his horses, but to understand their psychology, recognize their individual quirks, and devise ways of accommodating them so they didn't interfere with the inbred ability to run. There were some who were thrown off their stride by shadows on the track; they were given a 'shadow roll' that went across the bridge of the nose and prevented them from seeing the surface of the track. Horses who couldn't deliver their best because they got bored or tense in their stalls were a problem that required ingenuity to solve — putting a pet in the stall, or playing music on a radio (though there was a famous horse who only liked listening to the news). One trainer believed he had kept the will to win constantly fired in one of his champion stallions by constantly showing the horse movies of his past victories — a practice grounded simply in superstition, since all savvy horsemen knew the animals had good peripheral vision but could barely see images in front.

Of course, developing the physical potential exceeded all other priorities. This involved the over-all program of exercise and diet given the horse from birth, and a steady monitoring of health with a veterinarian. Finally, more than anything else, it depended on the regimen of workouts in which the speed of the horse was exposed and tested and improved to the maximum extent.

It was this vital process that unfolded every morning on the training track of the backstretch as 'exercise boys' would ride each horse to the specifications prescribed by the trainer. In building the strength needed to go all-out at an average speed of almost 40 m.p.h., a horse had to be galloped regularly over distances corresponding to the races it would run. The trick was to work the animal fast enough to build its stamina, but without running it so strenuously that its reserves were totally used up and — in the trainers' phrase — the horse 'left his race on the track'. A workout might start with a jog to limber up muscles, then an eighth or a quarter of a mile run at a slow gallop — the distance marked by poles around the circumference of the track — and more rigorous testing at the end.

'Jog him to the turn, breeze the next quarter,' a trainer would say, 'and, when you get to the stretch, ask him . . .'

Leaning on the rail of the training track on these balmy June mornings Geri would take it all in, studying the techniques and absorbing the special language of this world. *Ask him.* She liked that one especially, the cryptic directive to make an animal dig down and show its stuff.

She had been friends with Ramie Marquez since the evening she had returned to fetch her belongings and the pretty dark-eyed gamin had cheered her success in landing a job. Often as Geri watched the work-outs Ramie would be there beside her, leaning on the rail. From Ramie, too, Geri picked up pointers on how to ride the fast horses. Standing in the stirrups to keep the center of gravity forward, adjusting one's balance to synchronize with the driving movement of the horse. At the end of the day they would sometimes each take a hack to the training track, and run mock races against each other.

Ramona Marquez was twenty years old, a native of the Dominican Republic, born into a family of fourteen children. One of her brothers had been a jockey in South America until he was trampled to death after falling off his horse during a race. Despite this misfortune, Ramie herself had an ambition to be a jockey. Though the standard twenty-five dollars paid for each ride didn't add up to much for a rider who had too many losing mounts, one who rode enough winners could become rich since he also collected ten per cent of all purses won by his mounts. The potential to become rich had recently been attracting more and more poor young men from Ramie's country and other places in South America where opportunity was non-existent. The poverty and malnutrition that bred small, underweight

251

people could be turned to advantage in the sport of racing. Ramie had come to the U.S. two years ago thinking that the *macho* attitude against women riding racehorses might be more easily overcome outside of South America. Her size and weight and riding skills should have qualified her for a chance, but as long as there were men to do the job, no owner saw any reason to break with tradition. Ramie's rides were restricted to very rare occasions when a regular exercise boy failed to turn up for a work-out, and no one else was available. To be ready for these opportunities she hung around the training track as much as possible, and cultivated contacts with anyone who might help her, especially other jockeys. With many of them, she was a casual friend; and with several others, she was a casual lover.

As Geri grew closer to Ramie, and observed that the pretty Dominican girl stayed the night with three or four different men in the course of a single week, she was initially shocked — to the point that she questioned whether or not the friendship could continue. The suffering Geri had endured in the past because of conflicts over sex with her father and Bard, left her feeling somewhat puritanical on the subject herself. For the present, it was easier to lock sex out of her life than to think of facing new confusions or conflicts. But Ramie was so open in gossiping about her liaisons, that eventually Geri was forced to confront Ramie with her own feelings about it.

'Don't you think more of yourself,' she finally said, 'than to sleep with any man who asks . . .?'

Her accusatory tone had touched off Ramie's Latin temper. 'I sleep only with who *I* want!' Ramie replied hotly. 'But you tell me, *muchacha*, who think less of himself. Me — if I enjoy when a man wants me, and think I deserve to have some fun? Or you — who's afraid to be touched by anyone . . .?'

Ramie's perceptions turned the argument around. Whatever judgment she might make about Ramie's behavior, Geri realized, her own was no less extreme in its way. She needed someone, too, needed to be touched and loved, but she was afraid.

After their confrontation, Geri accepted Ramie un-
critically, and tried to absorb from their friendship some
encouragement to explore her own sexuality. She wished she
could be as free as Ramie . . . but nothing changed. She went
on avoiding all the young men who had even hinted at an
attraction to her, and continued to laugh off Ramie's
invitations to join her in a night off the backstretch. What
had happened with Pa, and Bard's unfeeling manipulations,
had made sex seem too charged and dangerous.

Geri remained a puzzle to Ramie. With her own clearly
defined ambition, Ramie knew what she was trying to
achieve here on the backstretch. But she couldn't understand
what drove Geri, who had no clear ambition to be a jockey
or anything else.

'Why you came to Belmont?' she asked once, after she had
talked about her own ambitions. They were leaning on the
rail watching a morning work-out.

'I like the horses,' Geri said.

'Sure. But you gotta have somethin' you wanna get from
them.'

'I want to win, Ramie.'

'But how you do tha' . . .'

'I'm not sure yet. Maybe I can get to be a trainer. I guess
I'd also like to have some horses of my own someday.'

'Where you gonna get so much money for this kind of
horse . . .?'

'I don't know . . .'

At times, Geri was puzzled by her own vagueness about her
goals. If she was going to stay here and achieve anything, she
knew, she ought to have a more definite plan. But for the
moment it was easier not to think too far ahead. She had
learned early that the future had a way of determining itself —
that innocent dreams and happy plans could be suddenly
washed away.

Living from day to day also made it easier to deal with her
lasting concern about Steve. For now there had been no
further developments; that wasn't good but at least there was
no confirmation of the worst. As weeks passed, attention to the

case of the five missing rights workers dwindled in the news. Sometimes Geri wondered about Sylvia Balkin; once or twice she considered contacting her. But she could only imagine that by now the Balkin family had closed ranks in response to their shared problems, and Sylvia had no great wish to see her. If she did, wouldn't she have sought her out? Geri had kept in touch with Tony Novello since securing her job at Belmont, and when he had asked Geri if she had any objection against telling Sylvia her whereabouts, she had said no. But Geri sensed that Sylvia would never come; she had felt the breaking of all bonds from that moment, on the night Steve disappeared, when the queen would no longer take her hand.

CHAPTER SEVEN

On a drizzling Thursday of the third week in June, Geri woke to an alarm set at 4.30 a.m. Lennie had told her yesterday that there was a 'daylighter' to be worked this morning.

Normally the work-outs began at 5.30 when the gate was opened by a guard. Training had to be started after dawn when the track was clearly visible, not only for the safety of the horse, but so its speed could be accurately timed by the clockers who worked for the track and the Racing Form and the owners. Work-out speeds gauged the condition of a horse for its trainers, and for the bettors.

'Daylighting' was the tongue-in-cheek term for bringing a horse out to work before the gates were opened. Galloping alone through the pre-dawn gloom, its true speed could then be concealed from all but a few. This allowed a promising young horse, or one that had been brought back to peak condition after an injury, to run at long odds although its chances of winning were excellent.

Geri went down and saddled a two-year-old named Jambalaya, and walked it quietly through the rain to the point where she had been told to meet an exercise boy who knew the way along a lane behind the Vanderbilt stable that led to a narrow gap in the fence. The boy took the horse from her, and she followed him. Once inside the training track, they discovered that theirs was not the only daylighter this morning. Agitated whisperings of another group of people, and the nervous stampings of a second horse broke through the darkness. While she and the exercise boy waited for Lennie — who would come with his assistant to clock their horse, signaling to each other with flashlights — Geri edged curiously nearer to the other group and listened. An argument was going on, the exercise boy apparently refusing to ride the horse a trainer had brought to be worked.

'I didn't know it was *this* son-of-a-bitch,' he was saying hotly. 'Get someone else.'

'There's no someone elses around at five-fucking-o'clock in the morning, and this horse is on the card tomorrow. I don't run him the day of the race, so I want it done now. Let me down on this one, chum, and you won't work for me again.'

'Another ride like the last one, and I might not be able to work for *anyone*. Forget it!'

Geri could hear boots stomping angrily away, and a stream of curses from whoever was left behind. She looked around, wishing Ramie would turn up; it was the kind of opportunity Ramie was always looking for. But it was rare enough for anyone to be here at this hour, let alone *two* daylighters at the same time.

Now Geri could hear the trainer talking to the groom who was holding the horse, asking him if he would like to try riding. The question was half-hearted and the answer was a mirthless laugh.

A sudden impulse moved her in the direction of the disembodied voices. 'I'll give it a try,' she called out.

'Who's that . . .?'

She came up to the shadowy figures standing with a horse — a bulky one in a raincoat, and a groom. 'I'm one of Burkeholz's walkers. I can breeze your horse for you.'

The trainer peered at her through the drizzle. 'Okay. Standard rate, though.' He asked for no credentials, assuming anyone would be crazy to claim they could ride a thoroughbred if they couldn't.

An exercise boy got three dollars a ride. Geri said she'd take it, and the groom held the horse for her while she mounted and the trainer gave instructions: jog for a mile, then a breeze. 'And on the last half, ask him.'

Ramie's coaching had improved Geri's riding ability, and the work-out went without a hitch. As she galloped past the last marking pole, the sun had just begun to rise, the rain had stopped. Geri saw that there were more people watching now than just the trainer and groom, and the people from Lennie's barn. There was no applause, but from the nods of the spectators she realized her performance was being approved along with the horse's.

As she dismounted and the groom came to take the reins, a man broke from the group at the rail and walked toward her. She thought for a second it must be the trainer coming to pay her — she had seen him before only as a murky figure in the dark — but then decided no trainer ever looked quite this polished. The man was tall with hair as lustrously silver and carefully cut as a fine old coin, and, for that matter, a face that projected the same nobility as the kings and emperors that had been stamped on old money. Even his clothes, loose and casual as they were, somehow suggested the trappings of a king. The lush suede of his jacket rippled like liquid gold under the rising sun, and was perfectly fitted to show off a body that appeared lean and strong. He was, Geri thought, the handsomest man she had ever seen.

'That was a well-controlled ride on a very headstrong animal,' he said as he reached her. 'My trainer tells me you were a last-minute substitute. Are you regularly employed here at the track?'

'His' trainer, he had said. So he was the owner. 'Yes, I work for Mr Burkeholz.' Geri pointed to Lennie.

'Would you consider changing employers? I need someone to exercise this horse. Or maybe I should say the horse needs you. If you'd work for me, I'd pay you three hundred dollars a week.'

Five times what she was earning now! She wasn't sure what held her back from accepting instantly. Mostly loyalty to Lennie, who had given her a job when so many others wouldn't. But there was also something about this polished older man that made her hesitate. He gave off an aura of power that simultaneously attracted and frightened her. 'Let me talk to Mr Burkeholz about it,' she stalled.

'If he wants, I'll pay him, too — to buy your contract, you might say.'

That sparked her ire. 'No one's going to buy or sell me. I'll make up my own mind.'

The tall silver-haired man gave Geri a long look, then smiled again. 'I think I see now why you and my headstrong horse get along so well. I'll wait and hope that this singular mind of yours reaches a decision quickly. Good morning.'

He walked away, erect, yet with a gliding grace. The gates had been opened now for the regular work-outs, and there were a lot more horses and people around, but she kept her eye on the silver-haired man as he walked through the clusters of other spectators. By the gate a large low-slung convertible had pulled up to wait for him, a sports model of a kind Geri had never seen before. Like everything else about the man, it was exquisite, highly polished and expensive-looking. So was the young blonde woman who slid away from the wheel to the passenger seat as the man climbed in to drive.

Lennie walked over. 'Wants you to exercise for him, huh?' Geri nodded.

'I'll bet he offered a good deal. I know he's had trouble — that horse throws all his boys. One of 'em broke an arm last week. Craziest thing. Put the horse in a race and he's smooth as silk.'

'Who is he?' The car had driven away. She could see little more to it now than a glint of sun from its polished chrome.

'Camerade. Maybe the top two-year-old. Already won —'

'No, Lennie, not the horse! The man!'

He looked at her wide-eyed. 'Didn't he say? That was Dolph Justinean.'

She had heard the name around the track, the rich owner of one of the biggest, and most successful, racing stables.

'Exercising for Justinean's stables would be a big step up,' Lennie was saying. 'What'd he offer you . . .?'

'Three hundred a week.'

Lennie raised his eyebrows. 'If you don't grab it,' he said, 'you're gonna be out of a job, anyway — because I don't want anyone dumb enough to turn that down working for me.' From the look she threw at him, he realized she had taken him too seriously. 'It's up to you, kid. I just want you to know, it's okay with me.'

'Thanks, Lennie.'

She spent the rest of the day mulling it over. The aura of power that surrounded Justinean suggested that he controlled everything within his orbit, for better or worse. Wasn't he already tempting her into danger with his offer? The horse he wanted her to ride was notably difficult to handle. Perhaps she wasn't up to the task; perhaps she'd just been lucky this morning.

Toward noon, when she finished her chores at Lennie's barn, she made her way across the backstretch, until she found the barn that was occupied by Justinean Stables. Visiting, she thought, might help her reach a decision. There was often a distinct atmosphere that came through around a racing barn, a mood determined by the trainer or the owner. Some ran things with military precision. They went by the book, and they tolerated no mistakes. Some worked on instinct; they experimented, and had fun, and when it went well their enjoyment of the sport embraced everyone around them. Oakie was like that. And Lennie. He shouted and blew up when he was worried or uncertain, but around Lennie there was also laughter. That would be one of the hardest things to give up. She's had so little of it in the past.

Approaching the barn, she saw that the beautiful convertible Justinean drove was not among the cars pulled up outside. If the trainer wasn't here, either, it was hardly the moment to get a feel for the atmosphere he created, but she ambled inside for a look.

A few boys were there, feeding horses, cleaning stalls and tack. One nodded to her, and she recognized him as the groom who'd been at the training track earlier.

'He's down that way,' the groom said, gesturing to an aisle of stalls. He had apparently assumed she'd come to look at the horse she was being hired to ride.

Well, that might help, too. She went down the aisle, which was lit by dim electric bulbs, looking at the name plaques outside the stalls that identified the horses. Far ahead, at the other end of the barn, she saw a child staring into one of the stalls. No, not a child, she realized as she advanced, but a man. Very short, thin, fine-boned — obviously a jockey. Closer, she saw that he had stationed himself in front of the stall where the plaque read 'Camerade'. The jockey didn't appear to notice Geri. He kept looking at the horse.

This morning, in the pre-dawn light and with the excitement of the ride, she hadn't really taken a close look at Camerade. But now, as she leaned on the stall gate beside the little jockey and looked in, she saw what an exquisite horse he was. In the barn's dim light, his glossy reddish coat picked up every beam, making reflections that glowed softly like coals in a fire.

'You riding him tomorrow?' Geri said to the jockey.

'Nope, just here wishin',' he answered. 'This one's got a shot at Horse of the Year, so he's all set with Shoemaker — nothing but the best. He wouldn't go to a bug boy like me.'

Since first hearing the term a few weeks ago, Geri had learned that a bug boy was an apprentice jockey, in his first year of racing at the big tracks. The term derived from the way in which apprentices were always identified in a racing program — by an asterisk which appeared next to their name, resembling a tiny bug squashed on the page.

The bug boy spent another moment gazing at the horse, and then turned. He had large brown eyes, short sandy hair, a slightly upturned nose, and a firm jaw that gave a suggestion of strength despite the thinness of his face and an expression of sweet guileless innocence that, along with his height, belonged more to a child than a man. When he tilted his head back to look at Geri, she was struck by how much smaller he was. She'd had her last medical check-up while living with Sylvia and had been measured at eight inches over five feet. The jockey was more than a head shorter.

Looking up, his eyes brightened as if in recognition. 'It's you,' he said, with a ring of astonished familiarity.

She supposed he'd seen her at the track this morning.

Before she could give an answer, he went on, his voice suddenly tremulous and his eyes avoiding hers. 'Last place I thought I'd see you. I mean, I been in lookin' at this horse dozens o' times and you were never here.' He forced his gaze back to her. 'Guess I just chose the wrong times to come around . . .'

He spoke with a drawl, not a mountain twang but something a bit like it. Was it possible he knew her from some encounter she had forgotten? Or had he simply mistaken her for someone else in the dim light?

'I'm not usually here,' she said. 'I just came by to have a look at the horse before I make up my mind.'

'About what?'

'Mr Justinean asked me to ride the work-outs.'

The jockey gave a quick low whistle. 'Hope you know what you're gettin' into. Camerade loves to race, and hates to work. He shakes more exercise boys than an oak drops acorns.'

It sounded as if he didn't know she'd already been on the horse. 'I rode him this morning,' she said.

'You must be good,' he said. In a quick burst he added, 'Figured you would be, whatever you did . . .'

She had to ask now. 'Do we . . . know each other?'

Looking suddenly embarrassed, he shook his head then thrust out his hand. 'Nicholas Tennyson. Around the track they call me Nickles.'

She shook his hand, and introduced herself as Geri Keyes. For a moment, he kept his hand clasped around hers and stared at her. Then he went back to gazing at the horse. There seemed to be nothing left between them, and Geri was about to say goodbye when he started talking again. 'Caught sight of you the first time a few weeks ago. I knew there'd never be anyone who looked better to me, but I didn't know what to do about it. Just kept comin' around, standin' somewhere you wouldn't notice. With all the guts it takes to ride, I just felt so damn afraid to come straight out and say somethin' to you. Maybe that's why I got into lookin' at the horse, too — 'cause at least that was somethin' I *could* have someday. Oh, I'm gonna ride all the best before too long, see if I don't. I never have any doubts on *that* score.' He took a breath and turned to her. 'I wouldn't have said anythin', Geri, except chance put us together now and if I let the chance go by, tomorrow I'll be back to peekin' at you from behind trees. And damn it to hell, I'm not ever gonna get any taller if that's gonna make a difference so I might as well get this out in the open now, and let it be over with . . .'

While she tried to find an answer for him they kept standing beside each other, still looking at the horse. It was odd to have a stranger expose such emotion, but recalling how much she had always wished her father could show his feelings, Geri was more appreciative than embarrassed. She turned to him at last.

'I'm glad we met, Nickles. I don't know what kind of sense it makes for you to like me so much before we get to know each other, but I don't have so many friends I can't use one more. It's not fair, though, to expect anymore than friendship — not before you have a chance to find out what there is to me beside what you can see. And,' she added, 'I imagine you'd want me to have the same chance.'

At the subtle reference to his height, he laughed lightly. Then he stepped jauntily away from the stall as if to give her a better look at him. 'You bet I do. Inside, Geri, I'm a giant.'

They left together. The races would begin soon and Nickles said he had horses to ride in the second and third events. Before rushing over to the track, he walked Geri part of the way back to the Burkeholz barn. On the way, he told her how he had become a jockey. He had been born on a farm in Texas, and his father had died young. Looking for money to help his widowed mother pay her debts, he had done his first jockeying when he was fourteen at state fairs in races between plow horses. From there he had moved on through the small regional tracks and now, at the age of nineteen, he was ready for the big time. A good agent had picked him up already — the big jocks all had agents who arranged their mounts — and he was beginning to get good horses, once or twice a couple of Justinean's. He couldn't help boasting he'd already won more than two hundred thousand dollars in purses this year, ten percent of it his.

When he asked Geri about her own past, she admitted only to being born in Eastern Kentucky, and steered him off any more questions by saying she wanted to hear whatever he knew that might help her decide about working for Justinean.

It wasn't much, Nickles admitted, nobody knew very much about Dolph Justinean beyond the obvious. He was rich — probably among the half-dozen richest owners — but of course he had to be, owning a stable of the size and quality he did. The details of how he had built his fortune weren't known, but his business empire now included a whole airline, a huge car-rental concern, several manufacturing businesses, hotels and lots of other real estate.

'I've heard he came to this country twenty years ago without a penny,' Nickles said. 'Don't know where from. There's all kinds of stories — that he was a young German spy who got away with some stolen gold at the end of the war, a Russian soldier who deserted, a guy who was in the black market somewhere. It's probably all bunk. He's just the kind of character people can't help talkin' about.'

'What's he like to work for?' Geri asked.

'When I rode, he wasn't around — they weren't big races. But, from other jocks, I've heard he's tough, a perfectionist. Mess up once, and you don't get another chance.'

Nickles glanced at his watch. 'I'd better go and get into my tack. I want to see you again, Geri. Okay?'

'Sure. But just remember —'

'Not to rush things. That's tough for a jock — rushing things is what the work is all about — but my schedule is going to keep me from even seeing you for a few days.' He told her that his agent had him booked to ride tomorrow in the feature at Monmouth in New Jersey, and the day after he might be going to Arlington in Chicago.

Geri knew jockeys had to travel where the best mounts were, and said she would be happy to see him again whenever he returned. As she hurried the rest of the way back to Lennie's barn, she felt her decision about the job with Justinean had crystallized. The fact that Justinean was a demanding

263

perfectionist didn't put her off. If anything, the opportunity to be tested against the most exacting standards attracted her more. And there was the money he had offered. Lennie was right; she'd be a fool to turn it down. If she was going to make something of herself, she had to start climbing the ladder.

Already rehearsing her explanation to Lennie, she turned the corner into the row where his barn was located and stopped dead at what she saw ahead. Pulled up by the barn entrance was Sylvia Balkin's burgundy-coloured Rolls-Royce. Through one of the rear windows, Geri could see Sylvia, calmly reading a newspaper through a pair of gold lorgnettes. Hinchingham sat at the wheel, stoically watching a horse being sponged off. It appeared that they had been there a while, waiting for her to return.

She wavered for a second between retreat and confrontation, then walked to the car and pulled open the rear door.

Sylvia looked up sharply, lowered the lorgnettes, and folded the paper, dropping it onto a pile of others at her feet. Hinchingham had gotten out of the car to stand at the door that was already open.

'You look well, my dear. The outdoor life seems to agree with you. Won't you get in?'

Geri hesitated. There was so much she wanted to say now that this woman who meant so much to her was finally here. She wanted to cry out that she was grateful for all Sylvia had done, tell her how much she respected her — and, yes, how much she had begun to love her.

But she wanted to rage against her, too, for having rejected her — letting her go so easily, waiting so long to come . . .

But, as always, Sylvia's perfect composure froze everything into the unshakeable mold of manners, where emotional confessions remained unsaid. Geri climbed into the back, and Hinchingham closed the door quietly behind her.

'Tony told you where to find me?' she said, looking off through the window.

'Yes. I've known for quite a while . . .' She nodded through the glass to Hinchingham, indicating that he should leave them alone. After the chauffeur had strolled away, Sylvia went on. 'When I learned you were here, I didn't come after you because I thought this was someplace you wanted to be, and I thought you needed a chance to explore this interest of yours. The first thing Steve ever told me about you was how important the horses were.' She paused. 'I thought it was best for me, too. For my family. I thought it would help . . . to restore our perspective.'

Geri turned to Sylvia. She spoke so obliquely about anything deeply personal that it was hard to be certain, yet it seemed Sylvia was confessing to have unfairly laid some blame upon Geri for what had happened to Steve.

'And has it done that?' Geri said.

Sylvia's glance fell to her lap. 'That night, my dear . . . when the news came, it was a very hard moment for me. I cannot deny that Steve is the child I always cherished the most — nor that, when I thought I might have lost him forever, nothing and no one else mattered. If that came through to you, I can imagine how it must have hurt.'

Behind her neutral tone, Geri couldn't tell if Sylvia was asking forgiveness in her own proud way, or indicating that she still harbored the same irrational negative attitude. Geri wanted to ask — wanted the chance to forgive — but before she could speak, Sylvia continued:

'I can quite understand the difficulty you would have in giving me your . . . trust again, and the truth is I may not deserve it. But, in any case, settling matters between us is not what finally forced me to come.' She looked back to Geri at last, and though no tears glistened now, some dark shadow in the depths of her eyes warned of what was coming. Geri's fingers dug into the soft upholstery of the seat, clinging to it with no less desperation than if she was trying to save herself from falling off a precipice.

'. . . Steve . . .? she whispered.

Sylvia's gaze fell to the papers at her feet and Geri realized the story was there, today's news. Her hand darted out to grab a paper, but Sylvia stopped her.

'I think it's better if I tell you,' Sylvia said. 'Some of it is so ugly. They were found after an anonymous call. The F.B.I.

went to a place where a new county water project was being built, and they found the bodies buried there — Steve, and the three other men, and the young woman. They still aren't sure who was responsible, but there are leads. They know, of course, it was some sort of white supremacy group that wanted to frighten off all the rights workers, kill the movement. If there's anything in which we can take comfort, it's the certainty that the opposite was achieved by creating these martyrs.'

'I can't take comfort in that,' Geri said, curtaining her face with her hands as she began to sob.

Sylvia made a tentative move to bestow a comforting touch, but then drew her hand back. 'There's something else,' she said. 'After the shooting incident at his house, Steve was more aware of the peril his beliefs exposed him to, and he left some letters in the care of his lawyers, along with a will and a set of instructions to be carried out in the event of his death. Last night, his lawyers contacted me and arranged to deliver a letter to my care.' She reached into her purse again and extracted a white sealed envelope. 'It's for you, my dear. He left some money to you, as well. I gather there are conditions attached to its use — that's all the lawyers would say. You'll learn what they are from this.' She handed the letter to Geri.

As she gripped the envelope, Geri recalled the day in Alice Balkin's apartment — the accusation Sylvia's daughter had made. 'I never knew about this,' she said defensively. 'Believe me, I never tried to get anything from Steve . . .'

Sylvia looked at her benignly. 'I never imagined that you did.' There was a silence.

Geri kept waiting for Sylvia to ask her to come back again. Whether or not she would accept, she needed to hear that she was not banished. But then Sylvia said, 'Now, my dear, I can imagine you want to be alone — to read that.'

No! she wanted to cry out, I don't want to be alone. I want you to care, to see me as more than . . . another philanthropy you took on as a favor to your son. But she couldn't break through the wall of manners that Sylvia had built. And, in the lasting silence, Geri finally realized what had not been said.

With Steve's death, Sylvia was clinging closer to her other children; she could not take Geri back if it meant another rift.

Geri reached for the door. Hinchingham, attentively watching for signs that the conference had ended, hurried over and opened it. As Geri stepped out the chauffeur said, 'Goodbye, Miss Keyes. I've missed seeing you.'

As she paused to smile at him, Sylvia called out from behind, 'Geri . . . Geri-Jo . . .?'

She stopped and looked back, hoping once more . . .

Sylvia hesitated, as though debating with herself. Then she added, 'I'm so sorry, my dear.' And she motioned Hinchingham to close the door.

Sorry. The word echoed painfully in Geri's thoughts as she walked away. Sorry for what? Being the one to bear the news? For failing her before? For not being able to feel more than she did?

Damn it, she needed more. But from this day on, she knew she could never expect anything more from Sylvia Balkin.

In a deserted section of the backstretch, where she could be alone, Geri opened the letter.

It started 'Dear Geri-Jo.' Seeing her name — a piece of herself she could no longer use — made her feel that she had, in a way, died and left only a vestige of herself behind — as Steve had left this letter.

It went on:

> If you read this, I know it will be under unhappy circumstances. So I must tell you first how much I regret being responsible for any sadness in your life, because knowing you has given me so much pleasure. Your courage has reminded me often of why I go on believing in the essential goodness and good sense of the human race, even when there is so much about people that also makes me despair.
>
> To show you my thanks, I have put aside $30,000 for you, on the provision that it will be applied to continuing your education. This amount will take you through college if you work to make ends meet. I want to

267

be sure you will keep working; I've seen what happens to people when they have too much money. Other than expecting you to use this gift for schooling, I have no conditions. It would be my hope, though, that you will try to enter a veterinary college. I'm sure your special feeling about horses could be the foundation of a productive career, and a good life.

If I had been able to talk to you personally, and persuade you to make this choice, I would have told you that I hope someday you will join my practice as a full partner. Now, if you do become a D.V.M., I shall be looking over your shoulder anyway — but from a little farther away than I would have liked.

All my love,

His signature was blurred when she finished, but not this time by his own careless writing or sweat from her palms.

The place she had chosen for solitude was along the back rail of the main track. With the letter clutched in her hand, she leaned on the rail and gazed across toward the grandstand which had begun to fill with spectators. From where she stood the finish line seemed very very far away, but as she looked toward it across the infield, she thought she could imagine the instinct that drove a thoroughbred to plunge toward that goal with all its strength, sparing itself nothing.

She looked up toward the clear blue sky that promised a fine day at the races. 'You made a good bet,' she said, waggling the letter as if it was a winning ticket. 'Just ask me.' Fresh tears dulled her vision of the sky, but still she kept looking up.

'Ask me,' she said again in a whisper. 'Ask me . . .'

BOOK IV: *ON THE RAIL*

Saratoga Springs — Summer, 1971

CHAPTER ONE

Geri pushed through the doors of the bus terminal, and walked briskly up the street, the heels of her new gray leather pumps clicking on the sidewalk in a solid steady rhythm that conveyed her purpose and optimism. Tilting her head back, she shook out the gleaming hair she had allowed to grow long, and gazed at the sky. Sun shining in cloudless blue — no sign the Devil would be beating his wife, she thought with a smile. How distant the hollow and all its ideas seemed to her now.

Pausing to get her bearings on a corner of the town's main street, Union Avenue, she recalled the time Sylvia Balkin had first told her about Saratoga. She had wondered then why a small out-of-the-way place had become a magnet for racing. From this angle, it certainly looked unimpressive. Several old-fashioned red-brick hotels of a few stories, many going to seed. Rows of unfashionable stores. No sign here of the grandeur of its past. But Geri knew that in the outskirts there were some grander resort establishments, and once there had been others even more magnificent — hotels that stretched a quarter of a mile in length, with verandas lined by a thousand wicker rocking chairs. It was a habit now to arm herself with as much knowledge as possible about anything that involved her, so as soon as she knew that her career as a veterinarian would be starting in Saratoga, she had researched the town and its history. The name, she had learned, derived from the Indians of the region — *Saraghoga*, they had called it, meaning 'place of swift water', a reference to the many springs that spouted up from the land and were said to have amazing curative properties. By the early 1800s, news of these medicinal benefits had spread and Saratoga Springs was established as a spa. A place for the affluent to rest and escape the summer heat of the growing cities in the cool breezes that wafted across the peaceful Adirondack valley. It was the Civil War, however, that turned the spa into a full-fledged resort, where ways of improving one's health went hand-in-hand with ways of ruining it. Flush with fortunes built out of war profiteering, a new and larger class of rich came looking for ways to enjoy their money. Before the last dead of Gettysburg had been buried there were thoroughbreds being raced across a local meadow known as Horse Haven, and casinos being built, and great hotels, and then a racetrack — the first one in the nation. Saratoga had become the birthplace of organized racing in America and, every year since, the descendants of the same profiteers who had founded it — their rough edges polished away by generations of piling up even greater wealth — returned every August.

Traditions. Here they were, Geri thought, as she strode along the street. She had more than a chance to learn them now. She was going to be part of them.

She had spent the past five years working to fulfill Steve's wish for her. The process had started with a phone call to Tony on the same afternoon that Sylvia had brought news of Steve's will.

'I want to go on studying with you,' she told Tony. 'I'll pay the same as Sylvia. Just get me ready to go to a vet school.'

'That's college level, Geri. Getting you ready for that will take time. And if my case doesn't go well, I may not be around that long.'

'I'll work hard. Whatever you dish out, I'll take. And,' she added, 'wherever you have to go, I'll go with you to keep working . . .' She had heard his laugh through the phone.

'Some places you might not be allowed — like if I get sent to jail. But let's make a start, anyway.'

The possibility of working for Justinean remained so tempting that she had been reluctant to leave Belmont. Tony had insisted, however, that if she was going to prepare for taking college entrance examinations, she couldn't stay at a rigorous job and also spend so much time travelling between the city and the track. Winning a place in the freshman class of any veterinary college, he warned — especially in the absence of any high-school graduation — would require her to do so well on the entrance exams that the admission committee waived all other concerns.

The next day, Geri had said goodbye to Ramie and moved to a small apartment Tony had found for her in a tenement in lower Manhattan, on the same street where he lived. The apartment was poorly heated and when she moved in the walls and ceilings were crumbling, but it cost only fifty-five dollars a month and she was able to brighten it up with a quick coat of paint.

While she lived on money doled out by the bank Steve had named as his executors, Geri's life throughout the summer and fall consisted only of moving between Tony's apartment and her own, being tutored and doing the assignments he gave her. In December, he said she might be ready, and Geri applied to a number of veterinary schools. Her heart was set on the College of Veterinary Medicine at Cornell because that was where Steve had gone, but she was ready to go wherever she was accepted. Even before she had made formal application to Cornell, however, she was contacted by the admissions office to arrange a meeting. Only after expressing her amazement to Tony did he admit that he had been keeping Sylvia informed of Geri-Jo's progress, and that she had written to the college on Geri's behalf. 'The Balkin name carries more than a little weight with the administration of several schools,' Tony explained. 'In the case of Cornell, they've contributed several million dollars.'

At first, Geri had regretted Sylvia's interference, and had sent no word of thanks. The feeling that Sylvia had dispossessed her still hurt. She had admired the older woman so much, had yearned so much to move closer to her, that she could not easily accept the use of power or money as a substitute for what she had most wanted — the gift of simple affection.

Later, after Cornell had officially accepted her, Geri had sent a short letter of thanks, a pebble tossed into the pond of silence to see what ripples came back. But there was no answer. Sylvia, it seemed, could still make a gesture of charity. But she could not reach out at the expense of angering her children.

Though her scores on the entrance exams were respectable, once in vet school Geri was constantly on the verge of flunking out. Having flourished under the special attention she got from a tutor devoted solely to her, she was unused to the dry lectures that went with textbook courses taught *en masse*. Her difficulties in the classroom were compounded by devoting too much of her time to lab work with living specimens. As her grades sank, Geri despaired of ever achieving the goal that she had set for herself — and that Steve had set for her. Learning to be a doctor to animals, she came to understand, was no less difficult or demanding than going through any ordinary medical school. Instead of learning merely the 'standardized' human anatomy taught to aspiring M.D.s, a veterinary student was required to know the body structures of many different species of animal. The list of ailments afflicting animals with four legs — or none — was no shorter, their symptoms and cures no less complicated, than those known to affect the two-legged variety. Learning the art of diagnosis and treatment was complicated, too, by having patients that couldn't talk to explain their symptoms.

Daunting as it was, though, Geri simply would not allow herself to fail. She wanted to be a vet, in part, because to justify Steve's faith in her and take up the same work he had done, seemed somehow a way of keeping his spirit alive. But she recognized, too, that it might be the best way for a woman without money to work her way up to a respectable niche in the world of racing. First and foremost, since the days she had worked alongside Steve caring for the horses, she had always found the work itself challenging and gratifying.

Geri had lasted through her freshman and sophomore years only by burning a lot of midnight oil, and doing extra summer make-up courses. Difficult as it was to keep up with her studies, however, she welcomed the excuse to retreat from the attention attracted from male classmates. After accepting a few dates, she found that almost all of them were devoted to preparing for careers of their own, and they sought relationships that made no demands. After her brutal experiences with sex in the past, Geri could not be so casual. Before a man touched her again, there would have to be real love, patient and gentle and enduring. Even with the two or three men who dropped references to marriage, she knew there was not enough. She always sensed their interest derived from a desire to have her as a valuable decoration to their own careers; to keep her available for this purpose, she was sure they would stop her from realizing her own ambitions. After a while, she had not even bothered to date. Every bit of her energy was spent on fulfilling Steve's expectations. Her sharpened commitment began to bring her better grades. Through the third and fourth year she climbed up the ladder of class standings until she was among the top students.

Arriving at the top of her class by the end of her senior year, she had been able to pick and choose from some of the best openings available through the college placement office — and there was nothing that she had wanted more than the job that had brought her now to Saratoga.

Passing a souvenir shop where a rack of postcards stood on the sidewalk, Geri stopped and bought a couple. Ever since she had been forced to leave Kentucky, the thought of her brother confined to the institution, deserted with no idea of what had become of his family (she sensed that Molly would have done nothing to help him), had been a constant heartache to Geri. She dreamed of the day when she could be secure and established enough to rescue Caybie from the institution. In the meantime, the most she could do was send reassurances that she existed and was thinking of him. This was made possible by a contact she maintained with Charlie Hoyt, whom she had risked calling soon after receiving Steve's money. As she had hoped, Charlie had been glad to hear from her — grieving himself since the confirmation of Steve's death — and he was pleased to help her by acting as a secret intermediary in transmitting messages to Caybie. He had set up a post office box where the cards where received in unmarked envelopes, and then he remailed them later from various places around Kentucky. Since then Geri had continued sending brief notes to her brother saying she thought about him and still loved him and would come someday to take him to live with her. It was all she could do.

The other postcard she'd bought would probably never be mailed. It would be added to all the others Geri could never bring herself to send Molly.

Past the souvenir shop, Geri turned off Union Avenue and began walking along one of the elm-shaded side streets looking for an inexpensive guest house where she could put on some fresh clothes for her appointment later this afternoon, and stay until she got more permanently settled.

When the taxi turned into a drive a few miles outside of town, she saw nothing but a house seated well back atop a gentle rise, a large greystone mansion of the kind that would have been built in colonial times for a gentleman farmer. She had missed a sign, if there was one, and for a moment Geri wondered if the driver had made a mistake. Then, as the taxi came over the rise, Geri saw a group of low buildings lying in a dip beyond the mansion, modern structures with sparkling surfaces of glass and stainless steel.

The taxi stopped in front of the largest. Geri sat for a minute and stared out, somewhat startled by the look of the place. Where were the weather-beaten barns?

'This is it,' the driver said, shaking her out of her reverie, 'the Graymar Equine Clinic.'

'Yes. Thank you.' She paid the driver, adding a very generous tip. For years, it had been necessary to be very careful with money; no taxi rides — no luxuries at all. As though Steve had calculated his bequest precisely to keep her from becoming spoiled and lazy, it had stretched just far enough to see her through school with less than three hundred dollars remaining. But with expectations of a good job, she no longer had to watch the pennies. The appointment with Thomas Graymar had been described as an interview, of course; one of the country's foremost equine veterinarians was not about to hire an assistant without a preliminary meeting. But even before she had left Cornell, one of her professors had told her that he knew no one more qualified for the kind of work being offered, and he would be rounding up some glowing recommendations that would surely guarantee her the position.

Pleased with his tip, the driver asked if she wanted him to wait.

'No, thanks, I'm not sure how long I'll be.' Probably she'd be given a tour, a chance to start getting the feel of the place.

Before going through the glass entrance doors, Geri paused to pull down the jacket of her suit. She had gone shopping for clothes especially for the interview, and had been fortunate to unearth a pale gray Trigere copy from under a heap at a resale shop in Ithaca. After all Geri had heard about Dr Thomas Graymar, founder of this establishment, she realized he was as much a businessman as a doctor, as much a public relations man as a healer, and she hoped to impress him by looking as well prepared to do business as to do a worming.

In the spacious air-conditioned lobby a woman wearing a modish white uniform with lavender piping sat at a reception desk.

'I have an appointment to see Dr Graymar at four.'

The receptionist directed her to one of several corridors radiating from the lobby. As she went down the long corridor toward Graymar's office, Geri looked through the open door of an unused operating room, and stole quick curious peeks inside doors marked 'Pathology' and 'Dispensary'. She could see that the clinic Thomas Graymar had built to provide therapy and cures for ailing thoroughbred horses was as comprehensively equipped as any modern city hospital. Though, of course, there were differences. The operating room had an operating table as big as a barn door; and the subject of the autopsy in progress in the large pathology lab was a horse. There were sterile stabling facilities for horses undergoing treatment, and a whole separate system of corridors ran through the core of the building, allowing the animals to be brought in and out of the necessary rooms without using the public hallways. Geri knew, too, that the clinic incorporated extensive facilities for research in equine medicine. Thomas Graymar had already contributed several important new techniques for extending the racing careers of champion horses that would previously have been retired — or destroyed.

At the end of the corridor, she came to a suite of carpeted offices.

'Name, please,' said the secretary who sat behind a desk in the outer office.

'Geri Keyes.'

'In there,' the secretary said. She made a note on a lined pad, and pointed to a spacious alcove where five other people were already seated.

Seeing her name added to the bottom of a list, Geri said quickly, 'I have an appointment for four o'clock.' It was nearly four now; she didn't want to be late because the secretary mistakenly shuffled her in with the wrong group.

'All the interviews begin at four o'clock,' the secretary said. 'The doctor will see you in order of arrival.'

It struck her suddenly that she had been too cocky in assuming the interview would be nothing more than a formality. If she had been skimmed from the cream of her own graduating class, that would be true of anyone else summoned to meet Graymar. Entering the waiting alcove, she saw that the others to be interviewed were all men. Her hopes sank still further. The traditions were beginning to change, but the trainers, jockeys, grooms and vets who worked with race-horses were still predominantly men.

The other applicants had been conversing, but when she entered they paused to look up. Two raised their eyebrows in open appreciation of her beauty, while the others turned away, working to appear nonchalant. Geri slid into a chair, and escaped from the lingering stares by grabbing up an issue of *The Blood Horse* from a pile of journals on a coffee table. Soon the men went back to companionably exchanging remarks about Graymar and the position being offered.

'Actually, I hear there are two openings,' said one young man, which relaxed Geri a little since it improved the odds.

Another chimed in, lowering his voice down so the secretary wouldn't hear: 'There's a big turnover because he pays shit . . .'

'And because he's supposed to be a world-class prick,' a third offered.

Geri had heard all the scuttlebutt about Graymar before coming. He was said to be a driven workaholic, a shrewd opportunist who had conceived this glossy installation because he foresaw the vast amounts of money rich thoroughbred owners would happily pay to preserve the value of horses which cost a small fortune to buy. With inflation festering because of the war in Vietnam, the market in thoroughbred horses had begun to boom and Graymar's fortunes were rising with it.

But whatever else was true of the man, he was also known as one of the world's best equine vets, an innovator whose ideas had erased the image of a horse doctor as nothing more than a man making 'barn calls'. The service offered by his clinic was complete even to an all-night emergency room, which provided crucial service to the thoroughbred owners and breeders with farms in the area. One of the job applicants in the alcove, obviously an eager beaver, had voluntarily sat in on emergency-room duty last night, and was telling the others now about the activity he had seen: a valuable mare brought in with internal bleeding, a colt with colic — potentially fatal in horses — that had been relieved with surgery.

For all Graymar's innovations and skills, what impressed the five men hoping to be hired as one of his assistants was the vet's shrewd business sense. As they shared rumors about Graymar's personal income, the estimates went from three quarters of a million dollars a year, to three or four times as much. So even if he paid small salaries, money was still the magnet that brought them. They would watch how Graymar ran his operation, make their contacts with owners, then go off to get rich themselves by opening clinics of their own around breeding and racing centers in Florida or California.

It wasn't the money that had brought Geri, however. It was the man. She was still learning, and she wanted to be taught by the best.

Graymar was obviously an exacting interviewer. The first three applicants called into his office each stayed for an hour, and emerged looking as if they'd been put through the wringer. By seven o'clock Geri's 'appointment' had still not been kept.

After the fourth man was called in, the secretary shut off the light at her desk, and brought her list of applicants into the inner office before going home. The lone young man left with Geri tossed down his magazine and checked his wristwatch.

'It'll be nearly midnight by the time he's done,' he said to Geri. 'Think you can hold out?'

Had she detected a subtle challenge in the question? She examined him for a moment. He had a narrow studious face set off by spectacles with black plastic frames and short, stiff black hair. 'I've managed so far,' she said.

'I hear it's this way all the time. He pushes everyone to the limit. Never stops, and expects everyone to keep up with him.'

'That's what separates the men from the boys,' Geri said, savoring the irony.

He smiled. 'Which one are you?' he said. The tone of challenge was unmistakeable this time.

'Should be obvious,' she said lightly. 'I'm in a class by myself.' As she glanced back to her reading, she saw him regarding her with a look that seemed to mix respect with suspicion.

Later, on his way out through the alcove after his hour-long interview, he murmured, 'You'll have to be.'

From the size of the reputation he had built, Geri had assumed Graymar must be a venerable character, in his late fifties at least. She was surprised to see that the man on a couch in a corner of the large inner office was trim, vigorous and youthful. Workaholic he might be, but he showed no signs of tension or exhaustion after his long day. His wavy brown hair looked freshly combed, his hazel eyes were clear, his skin was smooth and unlined, even the tweed jacket he was wearing still looked newly pressed. Geri guessed he was in his mid-forties. Perched on his crossed legs was a yellow pad on which he was briskly making notes. Without raising his eyes, he motioned her to a chair opposite the couch and went on filling a page with small precise writing. Finally he looked up.

He gave her a puzzled look before asking, 'Who are you?'

'You should have my name,' she replied. 'Geri Keyes . . .'

He rose and went to his desk where he scanned the list his secretary had left for him earlier. 'Ah, I see, there it is. I'd have saved you the trouble of waiting if I'd caught the mistake.'

Mistake? Had he expected her earlier, after all? 'I didn't mind waiting,' she said uncertainly.

'But there was really no need.' He came back to her, held out the appointment list his secretary had left for him, and pointed to the line where she had written *Jerry Keyes*. 'I just assumed it was a man's name. Sorry about the inconvenience. If I'd caught the mistake earlier, I could have spared you the trouble.'

'Trouble . . .?' she echoed, nonplussed.

'Of waiting. You see, I only hire men . . .' He gave her a curt smile as if the matter was concluded, and started to turn away.

No girls. The same demeaning rebuff that had locked her out of the first job she had ever tried for in the racing world. Damned if she'd take it lying down this time! She shot to her feet glaring at Graymar, and he stopped short.

For a second she sifted through her thoughts, fighting to

keep control of her temper. 'Listen, Doctor, I can't speak for you, but this was no waste of my time. Whatever you've suddenly seen walking out from behind a name, I know that given a chance I can do whatever you ask me to do as well as anybody else. Better, probably. Didn't you see my recommendations?'

'I don't read anything about applicants,' Graymar answered flatly, 'until after I've met them and made my own judgment.'

'Well then, make one now — a *real* judgment, based on evaluating my knowledge and ability, not a snap decision based on sex.'

He shook his head. 'Miss Keyes, please don't make this . . . a political issue. Restricting my staff to men is not a temperamental choice, but a sensible policy based on the real demands of this job. We work with very heavy animals. When we have to move a doped horse in the operating room, or autopsy a dead one, it requires strength. That calls for certain physical capacities as well as knowledge. I'm sorry, but I'm afraid you really have come for nothing. Can I call a taxi for you?'

His cool dismissal frayed at the restraints she had placed on her anger. Her eyes flicked around the room, as if searching for some ally to help her — or perhaps for something to throw at him in her impotent rage. But then her attention was caught by some of the photographs on the wall — horses, many in the winner's circle — no doubt given to him by grateful owners. Now her cunning asserted itself.

'They don't stack it against you like this at the track,' she observed mildly.

The shift in tone perplexed him. 'Pardon me . . .?'

'When they run the big stakes. If it's really meant to test the horses, let the best one win, they keep the field open. They don't lock out the fillies.'

He permitted himself a smile. 'We're not just running in circles here, Miss Keyes.'

'Whatever the game is here,' she said, 'it's fixed, no contest. If you really want the best, you've got to keep the field open.'

He paced a few steps away and stared down, mulling her proposition. 'So what kind of test should we make it,' he said at last, 'considering the demands of the job? Would it satisfy you if I just put a dead horse on the floor, and let you try to lift it?'

She had never met a man more infuriating. But she refused to let him see how rattled she was. 'Finding the best vet isn't about strength, any more than it's about speed. It's about knowing the animals. Just watch me alongside all your strong men and see who handles *that* best.'

Studying her, his eyes narrowed as if considering a diagnosis. But before he could respond, the phone rang. The reminder of an outer world, of people who were happy to pay him to do things *his* way, seemed to cancel any thought of yielding to her plea. 'No, I don't think so,' he said, as he moved to the desk and reached for the phone. 'Now, you'll have to excuse me. I have to get back to work.'

As if talking with her had been something *else* than work — an empty flirtation, a brief diversion. But her fury was burnt out. Graymar's position was utterly unfair, but it was a defeat she would have to accept. She started toward the door, his voice grating in her ears as he ignored her to converse with one of his clients:

'No, not a thing . . . yes, I know the workouts have been disappointing, but he's fit. Maybe he's just having a little trouble settling down after the move from Belmont. Mmm . . . I know, but some horses can take several days . . . I think you can enter him, Jock. Scalawag looks as sound to me as any horse I've seen . . .'

Geri stopped short at the threshold. Scalawag was a leading three-year-old, owned by 'Jock' Cotsworth, a famous member of the racing establishment. In almost every book she'd read about racing, she had seen the Cotsworth name mentioned; the family had been breeding and racing great horses for three generations. But now there was a problem — and Geri saw the tiniest glimmer of a chance to reverse her defeat.

She was still in the doorway when Graymar cradled the

phone. Seeing her, the vet moved quickly out from behind his desk, his voice hardening as he spoke. 'I've tried to be patient with you, Miss Keyes. But this has gone past the point where —'

'I'll bet on it,' she snapped.

'On what . . .?'

'That I can do what a man can't — what *you* can't.' She advanced on him again. 'Make it a horserace. Why not? It's the thing that makes our whole business go around — betting on which is the winner. If you're so damn sure you already know who's best, are you willing to back your judgment with a bet?'

He sighed with exasperation, but the hook had caught. 'What stakes are we talking about?' he asked. 'And what's the track?'

'I happened to overhear your conversation just now. There's a horse that isn't running true to form, but you can't find anything wrong. Suppose you let me take a look — and suppose I *can* find a problem. Then I win a job. Here.'

Graymar folded his arms. 'And if you find nothing?' he said tartly. 'What would I win? You can't give *me* a job . . .'

'I'll muck out all your barns for a month — free of charge.'

Graymar let out a short derisive laugh. 'Penny ante.'

'Three months.'

'I don't pay very much to have it done, anyway.'

'All right, then what *do* you want?'

He looked her up and down rather provocatively. Then, before she could stop him, he snatched up her hand and gently pressed it between both of his. 'All right,' he said. 'Here are the terms. I'll arrange for you to see Scalawag tomorrow. You can examine him alone for up to an hour in his stall. If you find anything wrong with him you get the job. But if you don't, if that horse is as fit as I say, then here's what I want. You'll come straight to me, and walk in here looking as beautiful as you do now, except not so angry, and in your sweetest, sexiest little girl voice, you'll say, "Tom, I'm sorry I was such a relentless pest, but now I'm gonna spend the rest of my days and nights making it up to you —"'

284

Insulted by the proposition, she had already snatched her hand back before she heard him go on:

' "— by getting on the first train out of Saratoga to somewhere I can find a nice permanent job in a dog-and-cat hospital, far away where I can never bug you again." '

When he finished, she couldn't help laughing with relief.

'Bet,' she said, spearing him in the chest with her finger. She turned and went out the door, smiling.

CHAPTER TWO

From a corner of the stall, she eyed the horse standing in front of her. Once more she dug into her memory of all the courses in animal virus diseases and intestinal parasites and even horse psychology that she had taken during the past four years. In a vain attempt to know everything there was to know about horse diseases, she had also fortified herself for today's test by unpacking her old textbooks and cramming until sunrise.

Geri glanced at her wristwatch. Since arriving at ten for the examination arranged by Tom Graymar, forty-two minutes had passed. She had made a lightning pass at all the essential parts of a basic check-up—taken the horse's temperature with the special thermometer as big as a rolling pin, looked for symptoms of equine flu, checked for hoof canker, searched for indications of parasites, pulled a sample of blood to do a quick analysis with chemicals she carried in her bag, and of course she had felt for swellings around the bones. Everything appeared normal. With growing despair, she had to admit that the horse certainly seemed fit. Her challenge to Graymar had been a futile longshot. The only consolation was that he had agreed to let her examine the horse alone. At least she didn't have to endure the humiliation of failing in front of him.

And yet . . . there were the workouts. In racing, time was as much of a symptom as aches or pains and there *had* been a decline in performance. Graymar's explanation — a problem of adjustment — was not unreasonable. Highstrung thoroughbreds could be thrown off by changes of atmosphere or climate. There were horses that always won in the rain — so-called 'mudders' — and faded to last place in the sunshine. Still, the diagnosis had sounded *ad hoc* to Geri, an egotist's excuse for the failure to find any other cause.

She turned to the young black groom who was leaning on the open Dutch door of the stall, watching her. 'His last two work-outs — what d'you say those times were?'

'Couple of days ago he sprinted a half in just over fifty. Yesterday it was fifty-one and heavy change.'

For a horse of Scalawag's calibre, a good time for a half mile run at a brisk pace would be around forty-eight seconds. An additional two or three seconds could seem a small difference, but in a race that might be enough to bring him in ten lengths behind a winner. There had to be a physical reason, she told herself again.

Yet she was prepared now to accept that the problem wasn't likely to be pinpointed in the hour Graymar had allotted her. The answer might come through X-rays, or more intensive blood tests, or even a biopsy — though cancer was extremely rare in horses — but it would take time to find.

Still . . . fifteen minutes were left. Geri probed once more through her bag for something else to try.

'What have you found?' a voice boomed out suddenly.

She spun around. A broad middle-aged man with a wide ruddy face shaded under a broad-brimmed Stetson had displaced the groom at the stable door. 'I'm Cotsworth,' he added. 'So tell me: what's the problem?'

'I don't know yet, Mr Cotsworth.'

'And when do you think the lights'll go on? I've got him entered in the big stakes Saturday . . .'

'I'd advise against running him. There's obviously something bothering your horse. It could get worse before it gets better.'

He raked her with dubious eyes. 'Who are you, young lady?'

The inspection made Geri acutely self-conscious. After studying all night, she had dressed this morning for speed and convenience in jeans and a gingham shirt, and she had tied her hair back in a ponytail with a rubber band. Suddenly she realized she must look like nothing more than a farmgirl. Cotsworth needed to see her in a white coat to believe she was a doctor.

'I'm Geri Keyes. Didn't Dr Graymar explain —?'

'Tom Graymar asked me to give you an hour to examine the horse, so I did. But Tom also says the horse is fit to run. It seems a little unethical for you to be going against the opinion of the man who sent you in here. Not to say unwise, considering he's the number one man in the country . . .' His expression was enough to add a silent comment on her own relative merits.

'A second opinion isn't a rubber stamp,' Geri observed.

'But you haven't found anything . . .'

'No.' She looked back to her bag. 'I'm not finished, though —'

'Never mind. I'm going to stick with Tom's advice. If all Scalawag needs is a chance to settle down, he isn't going to be helped by having you pester him any more.'

'Pester him?' Geri moved to the door. 'Mr Cotsworth, I want to help this animal. His times are long by —'

'A couple of seconds, give or take. I know. But he can knock that right off if his mood picks up. C'mon outta there, young woman. Right now.' He motioned to the groom. 'Give him his feed, Willie.' He tipped his Stetson to Geri and walked away.

That was it. Orders from the owner. She snapped her bag shut, wondering now where or when she'd ever get a chance to use all the special paraphernalia inside it. Anxious to arrive prepared, she had bought it all mail order weeks ago — almost a thousand dollars prematurely spent.

The groom brought a bucket of oats which he hung on a peg by the door, then he went away. Geri reluctantly started to move out. She noted that Scalawag had quickly dipped his head into the bucket and started greedily munching the oats. Nothing wrong with his appetite — chalk up one more thing in Graymar's favor.

He had won. She'd have to go to the bastard and eat crow . . . before moving on to get job somewhere tending pet parakeets.

'Shoot,' she hissed to herself as she picked up her bag to go.

The horse bobbed its head up suddenly. Though probably just startled by the noise, it looked like he was nodding, seconding her hopeless assessment. Another goddamn male chauvinist, Geri thought to herself. Then she noticed that the horse hadn't just pulled his head up, but was tossing it to one side, with his mouth slightly open. Setting her bag down, she moved back to the door and stood absolutely still, watching as the horse started to eat again.

Half a minute later the horse brought his head up sharply, and tossed it to one side. With his mouth slightly open. And after going back to his feed for a little while, he repeated the identical movement a third time.

Geri looked at her watch. Six minutes still to go before the hour was up.

Tom Graymar's black Jaguar sedan came to a skidding stop in the stable parking lot. He charged out of the car, waving the dust away as though beating off an attack of bees, and went to where Geri was leaning against a railing. 'All right, what've you found?'

What was it he had asked for — her sweetest sexiest little girl voice? She gave it to him now. 'Let's go and look, shall we, Doctor? I never like to talk behind a patient's back.' Before Graymar could reply, she walked off quickly toward the stables. She made sure to keep a few paces in front of him until they were in front of Scalawag's stall. During the ten minutes since she had made the phone call, she had left the horse's bucket of feed on the floor outside the stall door. Still hungry, Scalawag was standing at the open Dutch door, looking down at the oats. Geri lifted the bucket back onto the peg by the door.

'Never mind feeding him,' Graymar snapped. 'Tell me what in hell is wrong.'

The horse started to eat. 'Let's see if you can guess,' she said tauntingly.

'Look here, Miss Keyes, I'm through playing games. If you've got something to tell me —'

'He'll tell you,' Geri cut in sharply, 'if you just shut up and pay attention. He'll tell you just the way he told me.'

Graymar glared at her, but then followed the gaze she had trained on the stall door. Only a few seconds later, the horse stopped munching oats, lifted his head out of the bucket, and tossed it agitatedly to one side with his mouth slightly open. Graymar shot a sidelong glance at Geri, and went back to watching the horse.

They stood silently in front of the stall until the horse had repeated the distinctive movement four more times.

At last, quietly scolding himself for his oversight, Graymar said, 'They told me he was eating well . . . so I left it at that.'

Geri contemplated what measure of grace she could afford to show in victory. If she had seen the particular twitch that was a recognized symptom of toothache in a horse, it was not because she had gone looking for it. Few vets would have suspected the problem, since it was uncommon in horses and generally came to light only when they were eating. 'I'd given up,' she said. 'I was walking away and it happened to be feeding time.'

Graymar acknowledged her gesture with a nod, then went to the horse, pulled the mouth open and expertly examined teeth and jawbone.

'See anything?' Geri asked.

'Doesn't seem to be abscessed yet — though it must be bad enough to pull him down off his best performance.' He turned to her. 'Since I'm accepting your opinion, Doctor, perhaps you'd also like to prescribe treatment?'

She shook her head. 'I'm only fresh out of school. My advice would be to refer this to someone with more experience in this kind of problem. I imagine you have someone like that on your staff . . .' She smiled at him — sweetly. 'I mean on *our* staff.' She picked up her bag of instruments. 'I'll take the weekend to get organized and settled in. I can start any time after that.'

'Monday morning, eight sharp,' Graymar shot back. 'I'm going to need the weekend myself . . . just to get used to the idea of working with a woman.'

Grinning broadly, Geri strode away from the stables.

Behind her she heard the horse whinny, a gentleman cheering her on.

America's oldest racecourse sat among fulsome elm trees in a field off Union Avenue like a well-preserved old dowager resting in the shade. The structure was decorated here and there with ornate woodwork and lattices, and the roofline was accented by several cupolas. Red and white candy-cane stripes ran down the back of the grandstand and clubhouse, and the same colors were repeated in the cascades of geraniums and petunias that tumbled from pots lining the second-floor balconies. There was something of a carnival atmosphere in the setting, and as Geri mingled with the large Saturday crowd, she felt the same delight of a child on a midway. At moments she would wonder at the twists and turns of life that had brought her here, would remind herself that the world of thoroughbred racing was decried by many as purely frivolous, a pastime perpetuated mainly for the benefit of the rich. There were such times criticism had pushed her to examine her ambitions — never more than lately. Just four months ago a young lieutenant in the Army had been convicted of cold-bloodedly ordering the massacre of 22 Vietnamese civilians in a town called My Lai; only at the end of June newspapers had won the right to begin printing 'The Pentagon Papers' detailing information about the war in Vietnam that had been kept from the public by the warmakers. In a society that seemed to be falling apart at the seams, how could she justify her participation in this frivolous sport?

But self-conscious doubts about her involvement never lasted. If watching horses race relieved the tedium or the disappointments of anyone's hard life, then it served a purpose. For herself, she didn't even have to bet to enjoy the pleasures of the track. She loved seeing the fashionable clothes worn by the rich women, the wives and daughters and girlfriends of the owners. Loved the harmless suspense of those minutes when the horses battled each other for supremacy. Above all, she loved the feeling of having a place where she belonged.

Entertained by the spectacle, content to picnic alone under a tree between races on cheese and fruit she had brought with her, Geri made no bets, and didn't even bother to look through the racing program until after the first two races. When she did, she saw 'Nickles Tennyson' listed as one of the jockeys in the upcoming race. She wasn't surprised; she had kept up with turf news and knew that the former bug-boy had become one of the most successful jockeys in the country. But having him nearby brought back the sweet memory of that evening when he had confessed his adolescent crush on her. She smiled as she thought about it — until she remembered that it was also the last time she had seen him. Just after that, she had learned of Steve's bequest, and had set out to become a vet.

The program showed that Nickles was riding a 7—1 shot named Quietly in the next race. Geri drifted to the paddock, curious to see what would happen if she was standing at the rail as he went by. He had been shy and self-conscious when they met, but he was a celebrity athlete now, earning hundreds of thousands of dollars. Probably he wouldn't even remember her — or would choose not to, mistaking her sudden disappearance after their last brief meeting as a rejection.

The horses hadn't come out to the paddock yet, and Geri passed the time looking through the rest of the program, adding up Nickles' mounts. She came to the list of horses running in the day's main event — a handicap, in which the horses carried extra weights in their saddle according to how they were rated, with a prize of $50,000 to the winner — and saw that he was riding in that, too. Then something else caught her eye: Scalawag was entered in the race. Geri had imagined the horse would be scratched once the tooth problem was discovered. Apparently, however, Graymar had been able to have the problem quickly corrected, and Cotsworth expected the horse to be back on form.

The horses started filing into the paddock, jockeys perched on their backs. And there was Nickles, fourth in line, dressed in brown and yellow silks. Many of the spectators seemed to know him — there were bettors who backed the jockey more than the horse — and they called out: 'Do it, Nickles,' 'Bring him home, Nicks.' In the way he smiled and waved to acknowledge their support, Geri could see that he was no longer the shy bug boy she had once met.

He was still looking at the people along the rail when he came to the point where Geri was standing. He went past without a sign of recognition.

Slightly let down, uncertain now whether it would be pleasant or embarrassing to make herself known to him again, Geri pushed back from the rail preparing to go. But suddenly Nickles twisted in his saddle, and glanced in her direction. Amid the distractions, his thoughts about the race ahead, it had taken an extra moment to see what had been right in front of him. Their eyes met, and his face lit up. Soundlessly he mouthed her name, and she nodded.

He looked as though he might jump right off the horse. Standing in his stirrups, he sent frantic hand signals, too fast and too many, a stuttering mime. She laughed, and clung to the rail again, waiting for him to come around as the horses were making their second circuit of the paddock. Leaning over as he approached her, he said breathlessly, '. . . got to see you . . . end of the day . . .'

'I'll be here.'

He reined up long enough to lean down and whisper one more thing in his Texas twang before following the parade out of the paddock: 'Bet me big, Geri. Gonna win it all for you.'

No one could promise that, of course. But the sentiment was too good and strong not to be matched with a gesture of her own. Geri went to the betting windows and put a hundred dollars of the money she had left on a ticket to win.

She didn't feel bad when she saw the horse was seventh in a field of nine as it started into the final turn. She only hoped that he wouldn't be embarrassed by failing to bring it off. But at the very moment she gave up, Nickles began whipping the horse into a stretch drive that brought the entire crowd to its feet. His horse came across the finish line first by a neck.

As the jockey walked the horse back past the stands to acknowledge the cheers and applause, he pressed his hand to his lips and threw a kiss up at the crowd. He couldn't find her among all the faces she knew, but the kiss was for her.

He wasn't in the next race, then came the main feature. She kept away from the paddock this time rather than tempt Nickles into another bravado gesture. His mount this time, a filly named Hotchilada, had won a couple of minor stakes last month; but Scalawag would have a huge edge if he was in shape — and she didn't think Graymar would have allowed him to run if he wasn't. The crowd certainly agreed. Scalawag's poor workout times were printed in the racing form, but these were routinely affected by so many variables — the weight of the exercise rider, or the instructions given by a trainer — that they had been discounted by the handicappers. As expected, Scalawag was today's favorite, going off at even money.

When Nickles rode out on the track, he scanned the grandstand, and then gave a thumbs-up sign. Again, she knew, it was for her, and again she made a sentimental bet. This time, though, she was prudent and bought only a five-dollar ticket.

He did, as it turned out, ride a very different race. There was no stretch drive salvaging victory at the last moment. His horse broke in front from the gate, led all the way and finished six lengths in front. Geri cashed in her five-dollar ticket for twenty-six dollars and eighty cents. Scalawag ran out of the money.

In the last race of the day, Nickles again crossed the finish line first, but the runner-up jockey charged that his horse had been bumped in the stretch and asked for an inquiry. Though the victory was then awarded to Nickles anyway, Geri knew he might be kept for some additional questions by the stewards. She wrote a note and gave it to a clubhouse attendant to bring to the jockey's changing room so Nickles would know that, however long it took, she would be waiting.

It was early evening when he emerged, the air cooling under a luminous blue-green summer sky. As he came toward her, Geri nearly forgot that he was a small man. The look of a winner was all over him, in his bearing, the perfectly fitted expensive clothes, and the way he opened his arms to embrace her without any self-conscious hesitation. Then he moved back and held her at arm's length. 'Christ-almighty, woman, you are a heap of gorgeous.'

'You look pretty good yourself.'

'What there is of me,' he said.

But Geri detected no edge of self-deprecation. It sounded more like a practiced line he had developed to use with other women. He put his arm around her and ushered her toward the reserved parking enclosure while spouting a steady patter: 'Listen, sweetheart, I've got a party to go to, and you're invited. So don't tell me you've got other plans — and of all things don't tell me there's a guy waiting for you, because I'm still crazy hopeless in love with you, and I'd take the favorite, tie him into a racing saddle, and ride him fast and straight to the glue factory.'

There was none of the tremulous emotion that had underlined his first confession of infatuation. This was just part of his smooth line, she thought. 'You talked me into it,' she said, laughing. Then she looked down at her floral-print summer dress. 'But if we're going to a party, I ought to go home and freshen up . . .'

'Oh no, I'm not letting you out of my sight for a second. Last time I did, you stayed in the powder room for five years! Anyway, doll, you look just about perfect right now.'

With evident pride, he snatched open the door of his car, a yellow Ferrari with a California vanity plate inscribed with his nickname. She showed him a broad expression of approval, and when he beamed with pride, she gave him a brief, light kiss. Even if it was only the second time they had met, she didn't think she had a dearer friend in the world.

In the car, she kept him busy answering questions about Ramie and the development of his career in the past four years. Ramie had gone to California a couple of years ago, he said, and they had lost touch. His own career had started to take off not long after that summer at Belmont when they had met. His mounts were booked now by a top agent, and he rode the biggest stakes on both coasts. With the purses he expected to win by the end of the season, he boasted, his ten percent would probably earn him half a million dollars for the second year in a row.

How much he enjoyed his success and liked spending the

money became more obvious when they arrived at the Gideon Putnam, Saratoga's most luxurious hotel, named for the pioneer who had first attracted a resort clientele in 1802 by erecting a tavern on land adjacent to one of the biggest geysers of mineral water. The geyser was now known as Congress Spring, the land around it was Saratoga State Park, and the tavern had given way to an impressive structure of red brick with a grand facade of white pillars. For the rich who didn't keep homes in the resort to be used only during the twenty-four-day racing season, the Gideon Putnam was the place to stay.

The parking valet who took the car greeted him as 'Nickles', the maitre d'hotel who bowed him into the fancy dining room called him 'Mr Tennyson', and pushed aside a proffered tip, murmuring gratefully that he had booked twenty bucks on the nose in today's third. As Nickles was led to a corner table, he tossed hi-signs to a dozen scattered people who had waved or called out to him.

The table was adorned with a vase of blue parrot tulips, and a cooler with iced champagne stood nearby. As soon as Nickles was seated the maitre d' showed him the bottle for his approval.

'Nothing better?' Nickles said.

The head waiter's jaw dropped. 'Better than Dom Perignon '38? Mr Tennyson, you asked for the best and I assure you, in our cellar this is absolutely —'

Nickles held up his hand. 'No insult intended, Mario. I just wanted to be sure because this is a very important party I'm throwing . . . for a very beautiful party.'

The head waiter noted Nickles' glance at Geri, and smiled knowingly as he popped the cork.

When they were alone, they raised and clinked their glasses. Geri waited for his toast. All he said was, 'Thanks.'

'Hey, what for? You're throwing the party.'

'For coming back. There's been a hole in my life ever since you disappeared.'

It was clear now that his infatuation had never died; it had merely been held in suspended animation like a mammoth preserved in a glacier.

296

All through the rest of dinner she told him about the past few years, and why she had disappeared so suddenly after their meeting — the gift of money that had come to her, and had thrust her into a quest she could not wait even a few days to begin. Having earned her D.V.M., she concluded, she had come to Saratoga to work for Thomas Graymar.

'Too bad,' he sighed when she finished. 'For a moment there, I was dreaming you might have turned up looking for me . . .' Before she could say anything to soothe him, he went on brightly. 'But it calls for a celebration, anyway, and I couldn't think of a better way to celebrate than riding those three winners for you. Hope you bet me big.'

'Those were my orders, weren't they? I went straight from the paddock and put a hundred on the nose.'

He whistled, recalling the horse had paid off at good odds.

'It'll come in handy, too,' she said. 'I can use a car to get back and forth to the clinic. I was wondering how I'd be able to afford it.'

'No trouble now. Six thousand bucks'll get you a jazzy new convertible with plenty left over.

'Six thousand? Nickles, your horse was a seven-to-one shot. I won seven hundred.'

'But then I brought in a five-to-one shot, and a —' He read her expression. 'You didn't *parlay* it? But I said I'd win 'em all for you . . .' He looked extremely dismayed, almost insulted.

'Nickles, I needed that seven hundred, I was thrilled to have it. I wasn't going to turn around and put it all down —'

'I said I'd do it for you,' he repeated. 'Win 'em all.'

She shook her head apologetically. She knew what the gesture must mean to him — a wild improbable boast and he had brought it off.

'I'm sorry, Nicks. I was thrown off, I guess, because I knew something about the favorite you were riding against in the fifth.'

'Scalawag? He never had a chance. He's been way off form.'

'I know. I examined him a couple of days ago, found out he was being troubled by a sore tooth. I won my job, in fact, because Graymar had missed it. But once I'd pointed it out, I

297

didn't think he'd let the horse run unless it was cleared up.'

Nickles' narrow face creased with a forgiving smile, and he patted her hand. 'There's a lot you didn't learn in school, doll. A horse with a sore ankle might get pulled from a race because you don't want it to get worse. But running a horse with toothache won't really hurt him, and it can do a lot of good for a lot of people.'

'In what way?'

'How do you think it kicked all the odds around having Scalawag in the field? He was the sentimental favorite, he pulled a lot of money that could have gone down on other horses. Take him out of the race, and the odds on my five-to-one shot might have been cut in half . . .'

Geri stared at Nickles. 'Are you saying . . . there was some kind of fix?'

'No, Geri. The best horse won. But anyone who bet that horse collected twice as much than if Scalawag had been scratched. That could add up to a great deal of money to someone who knew that the real favorite was the horse I had under me.'

'Someone . . . meaning Graymar: it was his decision to let Scalawag run.'

Nickles shrugged. 'An innocent one, maybe. A matter of opinion. A gray area . . .'

Nickles' suggestion irritated Geri. It *was* an accusation no matter how he fudged it. 'There's a lot I don't like about Tom Graymar,' she said sharply, 'but I don't think he's a crook. He's a great vet, and I'm damn lucky to be working for him.'

Seeing she'd taken it personally, Nickles backed down. 'I'm lucky you are, too,' he said. 'I didn't mean to throw mud. But you're going to learn there's a lot more to this game than meets the eye. It's a great sport, a great life for the people behind it. But any time there's this much money involved in anything some people are going to be tempted to play the angles.'

Was he telling her something about himself she wondered — part of their getting acquainted? 'I suppose a jockey could do it, too. Not always make an all-out effort to win . . .'

'It happens,' he said, and anticipated her next question. 'I'm out there to win every time, and I don't personally know a jock who doesn't try. But it's an angle — and there's bound to be someone somewhere who'll play it.' It was amazing, he added, that professional riders had evolved into such an honest brotherhood. When Geri asked what he meant, he explained that the word jockey had derived from an English term that meant vagabond — and usually hinted also that the person was a cheat or a thief; in fact it had first been applied to race riders in England because they were believed to be so dishonest and open to bribery. The famous Marquess of Queensberry, Nickles reported, had once been so dismayed to learn that the rider of his horse had been bribed, that he threw the jockey off his horse, and rode the race himself. 'Compared with its origins,' he concluded, 'the sport today comes up smelling like roses. But don't romanticize it, kid. It may be the sport of kings, but even a king now and then has been known to cut somebody's throat.'

After that, the sparkling mood of reunion went flat. Nickles told more history, and funny racing anecdotes, but Geri was preoccupied with the doubts he'd raised. She wanted to believe in Graymar, and in the life she'd chosen. It hurt to think that perhaps nothing, no one, could be as simply good as she believed.

She had recovered, though, by the time he drove her back to her rooming house. Still seated in the car, he asked how soon he could see her again.

'Give me a few days. I start work day after tomorrow, and I have to give that my best shot.' He looked away, and she could tell he felt it was an excuse. 'Nickles, I'm glad we found each other again. But I've worked damn hard to earn this chance and I've got to give it everything. Do you understand?'

He nodded, and came around to help her out of the car. But at the door of the house, he said, 'It was hard enough to reach up for you when you were only beautiful. Now you're educated. Just when I thought I was getting taller . . . you've grown.'

She put her hand to his cheek. 'Give it a chance, Nickles.

299

We're taking up right where we left off; we still need time to get better acquainted.'

'Yeah, that's right,' he said, 'we hardly know each other. The only difference now . . . is that we're old friends.'

He went back down the path without trying to kiss her goodnight.

CHAPTER THREE

To have proven wrong a man with the conceit of Thomas Graymar, Geri soon realized, was an insult for which he was determined to extract vengeance. From the minute she went to work he tested her unremittingly. Her assignments to the operating room seemed calculated to remind her of the initial interview, in which he had tried to persuade her she was unsuited to a job that required physical strength. Each time he brought her into surgery, the room would be understaffed and there would be a sedated horse to maneuver on the table. Although there was a system of automatic lifts and pulleys to assist in shifting the dead weight, Graymar always insisted on having her do it manually, explaining that positioning by hand was preferable. He also gave her some of the most difficult cases to treat on her own. It was expected that assistants would help with the case load, but Geri often found herself dealing with situations that required a more experienced vet. When a breeder called for help with a mare having a hip-locked foal — one caught in the birth canal — and Graymar sent her out to wrestle with the problem, Geri sensed that he was pushing her off into deep waters with as much sadistic pleasure as a pirate making an orphan walk the plank.

And he kept her teetering on that plank sixteen, eighteen, sometimes twenty hours a day. At a salary of a hundred and ten dollars a week it was slave labor. As soon as she finished assisting in the operating room, he might order her to stay and help him log results from one of his research projects. The first time he had told her to go to his lab straight from the O/R, sheer exhaustion had prompted her to ask if the job couldn't wait until the morning. Immediately he had blown up. 'I thought you wanted to be a vet, Miss Keyes, to learn everything possible and be the best. If you want a job where you can leave early, why the hell don't you be a bank teller?'

Leave early! She had only begged a little time for herself when it was already past eleven o'clock at night. In her first two weeks she had gone from her room to the clinic, with never an afternoon free to see the races, and no more than an occasional hour to grab a late snack with Nickles at the Cafe Lena — which claimed to be the oldest coffee house in the nation — before catching up on her sleep. She longed to witness the excitement at one of the Saratoga summer sales, where millionaires from all over the world assembled to bid for yearlings sold by the famous horse auctioneers, Fasig-Tipton, but Graymar had made it impossible, keeping her busy all three days of the sale.

She reminded herself constantly, however, that her job was no more rigorous than the internship any regular M.D. went through. And she took delight in believing that, even while Graymar was throwing the work at her too hard and too fast, she was having her own revenge. Because she was standing up to every test, soaking in everything that could be learned . . . and, by God, before Thomas Graymar was through with her — or she with him — she was determined to be the best, or damn near it.

Whatever the drawbacks, Geri never doubted she was in the best place to study thoroughbred medicine and treatment. Tom Graymar had the flaw of conceit, which led on occasion to errors in judgment. But his margin of error was very low, and however hard he drove his staff, he was no less demanding of himself. Along with his regular casework, he was trying to develop vaccines for several equine diseases, and experimenting with procedures that might allow thoroughbreds with severe leg injuries to be saved. Until now there had been no alternative but to destroy them; surgery was ineffective because bones were hard to set in the large and high-spirited animals, and fractures could not heal because a horse had to be on its feet within forty-eight hours or its respiratory and digestive tracts began to fail. Graymar was working on some inventive solutions to these problems, and Geri was excited by the chance to help.

Other assistants, who resented their poor salaries even if they weren't being tested as hard as Geri, still griped and questioned whether any sense of purpose existed in Graymar beyond enriching himself. Most saw him as a greedy opportunist milking an area of veterinary medicine guaranteed to yield a fortune. He did, however, have one staunch supporter in Martin Shields, the cocky young vet who had been interviewed just before Geri, and hired that day. You didn't have to love the horses to give them the best treatment, Marty Shields said; more power to Graymar if he had been shrewd enough to see that any man who had a thoroughbred worth a million dollars wouldn't mind what a vet charged as long as the horse was kept on its feet.

'You could leave him, you know,' Nickles said. 'I could help you build a practice on your own, drop your name in the right places.'

They were sitting at a table in The Wishing Well, a popular roadhouse outside of town where the food was tasty and inexpensive, and the atmosphere bloomed from a grandmotherly old woman jubilantly banging out favorite old tunes on a tinkly spinet. On any evening after a day of racing, jockeys, trainers, assorted millionaires and busted railbirds, could be found gathered all together around the piano singing 'I Met a Million Dollar Baby', or 'Brother Can You Spare A Dime?'

It was the first evening out Geri had been able to give Nickles, and she had found him to be wonderful company, cheerful and expansive, proudly introducing her around to the other jockeys in the bar, Turcotte, Ycaza, Cordero and the others. He ate, too, with amazing gusto, and she wondered how a little man could pack away so much food and stay so thin.

Halfway through dinner, the lady at the piano in the paneled bar adjoining the dining room had launched into a medley of old Gershwin tunes. When she got to 'I've Got A Crush On You', Nickles had begun singing along. Looking directly across the table at Geri, he sang the old standard to her as if the words were new, coming straight from his heart.

She applauded him when the song ended, trying to make light of the moment, but it was clear that the torch he had started carrying years ago was burning hotter than ever. To dampen the flame a little, while saving his feelings, she had begun to talk about how Graymar was working her, how little time she had to herself for anything but work. That was when he had suggested she leave Graymar and start her own practice.

'I'm nowhere near ready for that,' she said.

His canny eyes inspected her from under a fringe of brown hair. The bug boy's crewcut had given way to stylish shaggy styling by a Beverly Hills barber. 'Or maybe,' he said, 'you just like having an excuse not to spend more time with me.'

'Nickles, I like being with you. You're the only person I see away from the job. Can't that be enough for now?'

He paused to take a sip of wine, as though fortifying himself. 'Geri, I'm a man. Whatever my size, I'm all here. It won't be enough for me . . . until I can make love to you.'

She gazed at him, not certain how to answer. The need had been building in her, too. To be loved, touched, held. She had been alone so long, her whole existence devoted to proving she deserved what Steve had given her. She was twenty-four now, and through the summer nights her body ached with the need for release. She had been holding out for a man who would fire her own passions. But where was he? Perhaps it was enough to have a good man who loved her.

She reached to touch Nickles, to ask him to be patient a little longer. But he perceived that her expression was one of consolation not consent, and pulled his hand away. 'What is it, Geri? What's wrong with me? There's plenty of women, I can tell ya, who've thought I was pretty special. So why can't I make it with you . . .?'

His tone, suddenly a bit surly, was taking the pleasure out of what had been a lovely evening. 'Nickles, please . . .'

He stopped only long enough to pour himself another glass of white wine from the cooler beside the table. 'It's the size thing, isn't it? Some people, you know, look at jockeys as if they're freaks . . .'

She hated to hear him run himself down, hated to think she was the cause. 'Don't, Nickles, please. It's not that . . .'

'Of course, we've got something in common with freaks.' He took a swig from his glass. 'We use what's abnormal about ourselves to make a living . . .'

'You're an athlete,' she said, her own tone betraying irritation because she sensed that he was manipulating her sympathies. 'You've picked a sport that can use what you *are* — the way a big man would play football.'

He stayed with his theme. 'No . . . I even work in a kind of circus. What else do you think the track is? That's where the word circus came from, you know? That's what the Romans called the place where they held their chariot races . . .'

'I never knew that,' she said quietly. Casting her gaze down into her own glass of wine, she recalled her father telling her once about the Romans, the place where they had watched men fight lions. When she looked back to Nickles, she was still filled with the sorrow of the past, a memory of yearning for love from someone who hadn't known how to show it. 'You know, Nicks, if it'll get you to stop this self-pitying forever, I just might go to bed with you tonight. But if you want me to do it for that reason — as therapy — it won't be the beginning of anything. It'll be the end. We might have a chance at something better, though, if we can wait . . .'

It was a moment before he shrugged. 'Well,' he said jauntily, 'I had to try. Works most of the time . . .'

She reared back. 'You mean that was all an act?' she asked sharply. 'You get other girls into bed with that number?'

He gave her a sheepish grin. 'Hey . . . the big guys don't need any tricks. The little guys have to play the angles.'

She was caught between being amused and affronted. But then he tipped the balance.

'To tell you the truth, Geri, I'd have probably been awful disappointed if you'd answered me any other way. I do want something better with you. And as long as there's a chance, I won't give up trying . . . or waiting. But there is one thing on which I won't take no for an answer. No excuses permitted, and if you tell me Graymar won't give you the day off when the time comes, I'll personally burn down his horse hospital.'

The sparkle was back in the evening. She smiled as she took the bait. 'And what's the occasion?'

On the last Saturday of the twenty-four-day Saratoga race meeting, he said, he would be riding in the Travers Stakes. The race, named for one of the founders of the Saratoga track, had been run for over a hundred years and was one of the great Grade I Stakes for three-year-olds, a mile-and-a-quarter paying — these days — $75,000 for the winner. His ride, a gelding named OhByGosh, wasn't the favorite, Nickles said, but he was a good horse with a solid chance.

'If you're there,' Nickles said, 'then I'd be unbeatable.'

'Your own horse could beat you, Nicks. You know that.'

'No way, Geri. You're my lucky charm. With you in the stands, I'll win the biggest race of the meet, and then we'll celebrate together. There's a big charity ball that night . . .'

'A ball? Nickles, I'll come to the race. I want to root you home. But I don't see myself at one of those fancy Saratoga balls.'

'Think we might look too silly waltzing together?'

'Hell, no. I'd take the greatest pleasure in curing you of that self-pitying stuff by dancing every goddamn dance with you and stepping all over your dainty little toes.'

He laughed. 'Well —'

'Cinderella had a lady with a wand to turn her rags into a gown. But, Nicks, I just can't afford that kind of get-up.'

'No problem. There's a lady I know who runs a shop in town, sells dresses to all the rich dames. I can borrow something for a night . . .' When she hesitated again, he put his hands together, playfully begging. 'Please, doll. It's gonna be my victory celebration and I want you there.'

'Jesus,' she muttered, 'a ball. Okay. But on one condition.'

'Name it.'

'For this race, you've got me handicapped with too much weight. You can't go in there thinking the outcome depends on me. I'm not a witch, Nickles, and I'm not a goddess. I just want you to remember that. I can't turn a loser into a winner.'

He nodded gravely. But as he pulled out his money to pay the bill, he gave her a twinkling glance. 'You could do it with me,' he said. 'But for that I wouldn't even need the horse.'

CHAPTER FOUR

At odds of four-to-one, OhByGosh was the third choice in a field of eleven for the Travers Stakes. The even-money favorite had won the Kentucky Derby, and the second favorite had recently won a major race in California.

Nickles had booked a small table on the clubhouse porch where Geri could have lunch while watching the races. As she arrived, Geri spotted Tom Graymar sitting with Jock Cotsworth at a larger table the Cotsworth family had probably held on subscription since the days when other regulars had included Jim Fisk and 'Bet-A-Million' Gates — the Wall Street speculator who had actually plunked down a million dollars in wagers at Saratoga one afternoon in 1902. The clubhouse crowd at Saratoga still conveyed much of the same color and dash as they had in the Gay Nineties. There were women in large picture hats, wearing their 'daytime' jewels, and men pulling out enormous wads of hundred-dollar bills, peeling them off in handfuls to the bet boys.

While Geri surveyed the scene over a glass of the champagne Nickles had ordered to be waiting at the table, Graymar spotted her, too, and they exchanged cordial nods. He had surprised her by quickly consenting when she asked for this day off. 'Take the whole weekend,' he had said. 'Does no harm to have you getting as chummy as possible with a top jock like Nickles Tennyson. He might be in a position to recommend the clinic to one of the owners he rides for . . .'

To appease Nickles' superstitious sentiment, Geri visited the paddock before the race. Later, as the jockey rode toward the starting gate, he threw a kiss exactly as he had on the day he'd ridden three winners for her, a ritual he seemed to think would guarantee victory.

But his hopes appeared to be dashed in the first seconds of the race. When the starting gate sprang open to the track announcer's unvarying cry of 'They're off!' OhByGosh stumbled and got away late. At the quarter pole he was still trailing in last place. As much as Geri wanted Nickles to win, she also felt a sense of relief. His belief that she was his lucky charm was a burden; she wanted to be loved, not worshipped.

But by the half pole his horse had already moved up into the thick of the pack, and with each furlong he gained ground. Coming around the last turn, OhByGosh was in a stretch duel with the leader.

They went under the finish line head-to-head.

The crowd milled restively during the pause while the judges studied the photos from the special finish-line camera. At last the official result was announced. OhByGosh had won, his neck reaching out to put the barest fraction of a nose in front.

At the day's end, Nickles dropped Geri off at her rooming house and said he would return with the gown in time for her to dress for the ball. A couple of hours later he arrived in a tuxedo carrying three boxes, one enormous, one small and flat, and a shoebox. Unfolding the gown from its large box, Geri gasped with delight. It was a *decolleté* emerald silk shot through with gold threads, a perfect compliment to her hair, touched since the summer with its own golden highlights. The dress was cut along narrow lines, so it would cling to her body. Having wistfully scanned *Vogue* on occasion, Geri realized the gown was a designer original that would probably sell for five or six thousand dollars.

Reaching for the shoebox, she said, 'I wouldn't be surprised if these were glass slippers . . .'

'Nah, glass'd break when you stepped on my toes.'

The shoes, covered in gold silk, had been made to match the gown. Nickles beamed proudly as he observed Geri's thrilled reaction to the ensemble.

'Comes straight from the stable of some hot French designer,' Nickles said. 'His name's Evening Saint, something like that . . .'

Geri laughed. 'You can't remember a name if it doesn't sound like a horse! Must be Yves St Laurent.'

'Yeah, that's it. Supposed to be a Grade I entry.'

At last, he opened the small box and, from a nest of tissue paper, pulled out an emerald necklace and lavalier earrings.

'These are yours to keep,' he said.

She was speechless for a second. 'Oh no, Nickles, I couldn't —'

'What are you talking about? They're only costume stuff. Not that I'd mind giving you the real thing — but I don't want to pressure you *too* much.'

She laughed then, and was overcome with an urge to kiss him. As she leaned down, inclining her head to place her lips on his, it felt awkward. But they were in her room, and as he put his arms around her, she sank down to the bed and then his height made no difference. The kiss lasted long, and it felt sweet to Geri. She wasn't excited by it, but she thought again that the love he felt for her might compensate for what she couldn't feel herself.

When their lips parted, Nickles glanced around and patted the bed. 'First time we've worked out on this surface,' he said. 'Why don't we go the full distance?'

She hesitated. Could she wait forever?

Not forever. But it was too soon to let go of the dream that a better love was waiting.

She tried to keep it light. 'Have a heart, Nicks. I may never get to wear a dress like that again. I'll be damned if I can wait a second to get into it.'

Nickles didn't insist. He knew he was being let down easy, but he was grateful for the kiss.

Saratoga had always been known for the opulence of the parties crammed into a short month by rich hosts vying to outdo each other. The luxury and excess to be found in any one of the grand houses had changed little since turn-of-the-century days when Diamond Jim Brady would arrive with twenty-seven Japanese houseboys and thirty sets of jewels — a different one for each day of the month — incorporating no less than 20,000 diamonds.

The high-powered social activity had been remote from Geri, so it had no reality for her other than as fabled history until Nickles turned up a long straight drive between an avenue of trees leading to a huge white limestone mansion. Approaching the circular roadway in front of the mansion, Geri could see the polished black surfaces of dozens of limousines already there. The music of a large orchestra floated on the night air. Standing out from the darkness in the soft illumination of yellow floodlights, the house itself seemed to have walls of solid gold.

Once intimidated by such grandeur, the period spent with Sylvia Balkin had made Geri more blasé. 'Quite a little shack,' she said. 'It must take acres of sheets just to cover the furniture when they're through using it for the month.'

'This place is probably a little more lived-in,' Nickles said. 'There's a big breeding operation attached to it. If it wasn't dark you'd see all the barns and pastures, miles of 'em. I doubt there's anything bigger or better equipped between here and Kentucky than Justinean Farms.'

'Justinean . . .' she echoed automatically. A memory of that day she had seen him at Belmont flashed through her mind.

'Couldn't be a better place for us to celebrate,' Nickles said. 'In a way, it's Dolph Justinean who brought us together.'

Geri kept a thoughtful silence. Her life had changed course so suddenly, that she had left without ever seeing Justinean again. Yet now she could vividly recall what he had looked like as he walked toward her through the early morning mist, could hear the sound of his voice as he offered her a job to ride for him. Odd what the memory retained.

A parking valet took Nickles' car, and Geri walked up the

steps with a mounting sense of excitement, a curious intuition that this would be a fateful evening.

As much as she had heard about it, without seeing it for herself Geri would have had difficulty in believing the kind of opulence that unfolded before her. For this single evening, a tropical theme had been chosen for the decor. Huge baskets of fresh orchids, birds of paradise, bougainvillea, and other jungle flowers evidently flown in for the occasion, had been placed everywhere. Some were even hanging from the bannister of a sweeping stairway, the planters cleverly disguised to make it seem that wild flowering vines had sprouted up in the middle of the grand entrance hall. In smaller, separate baskets there were arrangements of blooms evidently chosen for their fragrance. To accent the tropical theme, a number of large white bird aviaries had been placed around containing parrots, toucans, and macaws. The cawing of the birds was submerged in the babble of hundreds of guests.

Following Nickles deeper into the house after giving her coat to an attendant costumed in the plain silk smock of a Maharajah's servant, Geri passed among dozens of sleek men in white dinner jackets, and women all gowned in creations that had cost thousands, gems of every hue and size adorning their hair, necks, ears, wrists, fingers. If the jewels had fallen in a hail storm, it seemed to Geri, they would have been spread no less thickly throughout the huge rooms of the mansion.

Her eyes searched for Justinean as Nickles led her through the jam of people to a real ballroom, half the size of a football field. At one end of the room a fifteen-piece orchestra was playing on a platform, at the other there were tables and a buffet from which champagne and delicacies were being served.

'How about a dance?' Nickles said. 'Having you in my arms will be the best part of the winner's purse . . .'

Geri hesitated, staring at the many couples who filled the dance floor, a sea of sparkle and fashion. She had thought being exposed to the wealth of the Mitchells, the sophistication and style of Sylvia Balkin, had finally prepared her to accept being in this company. Yet as she confronted the dazzling spectacle of the rich, all gathered together, comfortable with each other and with their privilege, suddenly all she could think of was the contrast between this carefree scene and her origins. A wave of resentment rose within her as she remembered Pa that day up in the cemetery, ranting about the folks who ran the companies that kept down the poor — about the divide between the world of the rich and the people in the hollow.

A moment ago, Geri had worn the gown with pleasure; now, having taken just a few steps across the divide between rich and poor, she felt suddenly like a traitor in the uniform of an enemy army.

Nickles started to pull her onto the dance floor, but she was frozen, unable to join the enemy's dance.

'What's wrong . . .?'

She couldn't bring herself to ruin it for him, either. 'So many people. A touch of claustrophobia, I guess.'

'Don't I get my victory dance?'

'Sure. Just let me take a moment . . . to get a little air . . .'

Nickles peered at her dubiously, but she was saved from further alibis when some people came over to congratulate him on his winning ride. The group included the attractive willowy daughter of an owner Nickles had ridden for, and he quickly asked her to dance. He had been hurt by her retreat, Geri knew, but her own confusion was too complicated to attempt explanations.

She hunted for a place to think, to try and adjust to this milieu of wealth and privilege. It was aligned, after all, with the work she had chosen; the horses were a quintessential symbol of this world. How could she care about them, believe in their worth, if she angrily rejected what they represented? *Get used to it*, she told herself. *This is your world, now.*

But each time she turned a corner in the mansion there was more of it — rooms furnished with antiques bought at auction for tens of thousands of dollars, tapestries and rugs

313

that must have once graced castles and chateaux, a Rembrandt in a dining room, Gauguins and Van Goghs in a library. And amid all these priceless objects, all she could think about was her brothers and sisters — dying in the mud because they had been so desperate to save the mere hundred dollars' worth of crops that sustained them. Thinking of it, Geri felt as if she herself were suffocating, drowning . . . She pushed on blindly, trying to escape from the crowd.

Suddenly, she found herself passing through a door into a separate wing at the back of the house. Though the lights were all on, and she could hear the faint incessant rattle of some sort of electric machine, the wing was deserted. She leaned for a moment against the wall of a corridor, recovering her breath. Then curiosity pulled her along the corridor toward the chattering noise, which originated from a small room where a bank of telex units were receiving transmissions. She glanced over the long tongues of paper unrolling from the nearest machines and saw prices from world economic markets that were either opening or closing according to the time differentials, and messages from the executive offices of various businesses. It was from this wing, Geri realized, that Justinean must run his empire when he was in Saratoga.

Continuing along the corridor, she came to an office. Only two small lamps were burning, one affixed to the frame of a painting on a wall between bookcases, the other an old-fashioned accountant's lamp with a green glass shade that sat on a long antique refectory table cluttered with stacks of paper, a few telephones, and a couple of silver trophies. By the dim greenish light, Geri could see that the room had the cozy serious look of a library, with burled walnut paneling, and leather easy chairs.

If a man's office could be said to hint at his personality, then what she saw revealed a different man than the one she had seen years ago. She would have guessed Justinean was smooth surfaces, everything neat, stainless steel.

Looking for more clues, she moved into the room and slowly circled the perimeter. One wall was covered by a large

314

corkboard on which breeding charts had been tacked up. The bloodlines, sales history, racing record and breeding plans of every horse in Justinean's stable were recorded on the charts. His investment in thoroughbreds was shown to be in the tens of millions. Other walls were hung with half a dozen paintings depicting horses or racing scenes in a style similar to the one that was lit, a simple sideways study of a horse and his jockey.

Geri paused to admire it. The anatomy of the animal was perfectly captured, the detail of veins in the neck seeming almost to pulse with life, the highlights on the body flickering as though the hide rippled with movement. It was a homage to something she loved, too, and looking at it made her feel less of a traitor to herself and her ghosts. Then she noted the signature was that of George Stubbs. The Balkins had owned a Stubbs, and Geri knew that the racing portraits of the eighteenth-century painter were considered master-pieces, and one had sold lately for hundreds of thousands of dollars.

And how many were there in this room? Her eyes probed the shadowy walls. Nine.

Her fury at the injustice rose again. The proceeds from any one of these canvases would have meant salvation to a dozen families in that miserable place where she'd been born, would have educated their children through college. How had she become so corrupted, Geri wondered, that the work she had chosen was to care for pampered animals who raced for money that only went back into the pockets of those who didn't need it? If she had any guts, she thought, she would lift this painting right off the wall, and run to where it could be turned into money and then do something to relieve the terrible poverty that doomed all those who were born into it. From the mountain of wealth on which Justinean sat, the loss would be minuscule, unnoticeable. This crime, at least, was one for which she would have no regrets.

In the grip of the idea, she advanced toward the painting and her hands floated up from her sides, moving toward the frame, to grasp it — if only to vicariously test the sensation —

A switch by the door snapped, more lights went on, and her dark fantasy vanished along with the shadows.

'If you like that one,' said the voice she still remembered, 'you might enjoy having some light to see the others . . .'

She spun around as Dolph Justinean came toward her.

Tall, silver-haired, ageless. He looked no different from when she had last seen him. Her heart pounded, and her throat went dry. Was he aware of what she'd been contemplating?

'But I think this one is the best of them all . . .' He paused at her shoulder, and for a couple of minutes he went on speaking about the painting. He named the winning English horse that had been the model, and talked about his passion for Stubbs's work, and revealed his special pride in this canvas because he had bought it in London twenty-nine years ago for seven hundred dollars — 'when that was practically all the money I had in the world.'

Even that glimpse into a poorer background didn't quiet the storm in her nerves that was raging through Geri. He didn't sound the least bit suspicious of her, yet the ease with which he accepted the presence of a strange woman in his private office was also unlikely. It took the greatest control to listen and pretend to admire the painting while he stood at her shoulder and went on talking, the smooth fabric of his tuxedo rubbing sensuously against her bare arm. Then he gestured toward one of the other canvasses, as though to guide her all around the room.

'I ought to go,' she said, making an effort to keep her voice from quavering. 'I hadn't meant to come in here . . . I just took a wrong turn somewhere . . .'

She started to step toward the door, but he put his hand on her arm. A firm grip, the feeling of strength behind it absolute, yet it didn't hurt at all. 'Not yet, please,' he said. 'First I must know: how does a woman change so much . . .?' She turned and shook her head, uncomprehending. His hand slid away from her arm and he smiled slightly, enjoying his riddle. 'I was dancing,' he went on. 'In the middle of so many people, I must confess I am usually very lonely. But then I saw you standing at the entrance to the ballroom, and the sight of you delighted me. At that moment, I dedicated myself to discovering how such magic is done — how this child I once saw ride a horse at sunrise became a woman who turns my head tonight.'

He had recognized her — and followed! But how much had he seen after following? She summoned the composure to answer his question. 'There's nothing unusual to tell. Time changes everyone doesn't it?'

He gave a slow stoic smile as he studied her intently. 'I think it took more than time to make you what you are. I must know more about you.'

She couldn't break free of his magnetic field. She watched motionless as he went to open a bar concealed behind the walnut panels, and accepted the brandy he offered though she doubted she'd drink it. Her control was fragile enough without the weakening influence of alcohol.

He handed her the snifter, and motioned to a leather davenport. 'Come, sit. And explain this magic transformation.'

She sat down and tried to relax, though she was afraid of him. His aura was so powerful that she felt if he had quietly said 'fly' instead of 'sit', she would have tried. From his place at the opposite end of the couch, he stared at her, waiting for an answer.

'No magic about it,' she said. 'Simply an education. I went to veterinary college, earned a D.V.M., and that got me a job here with the Graymar Clinic.'

'Bravo. A great success.'

'A good beginning,' she corrected. 'There's much more to success, isn't there?' She skimmed a wry glance over their surroundings.

'It's the same as beauty,' he replied. 'Success exists mainly in the eyes of those who behold it. You look at what I have and think that defines it; but there are things I envy you.'

'What could you possibly . . .?'

'I never went to college.'

317

'Too bad. Tomorrow you could buy the best in the world, fill it with all the best professors and run it just for yourself.' She heard the edge of resentment in her own voice, and could see by his wary glance that he had detected it, too.

'Only those who are born very rich or very poor,' he said 'could sound so disgusted by money. Which was it in your case?'

She was safest if her history remained unknown, buried. Yet his sharp insight drilled into a simmering pool of cravings, and her resentment spouted out. 'In mine, if you want to know, it was poor. The worst goddamn low-down hellish grind-every-last-man-down-to-shit kinda poor, if you *really* want to know.' Her body coiled as she pulled herself to the edge of the couch. 'But I'm not disgusted by money. Just by the people who pile it up in mountains . . . and then stand so almighty high on those mountains they never look down to see how many people are drowning in the mud.' Her eyes flashed at him, all caution forgotten. 'Yes, it does make me sick to think of that — to think of all the people who'll never get out of it — while I can see how much you've got. Makes me hate myself for being here; in fact, made me want to take just the smallest portion of what you've got and . . .' She cut herself off, and stared at him for a moment, no longer scared of what he'd heard or seen, but hating him for all he represented, and for the way he sat listening to her, so cool and unaffected, his legs gracefully crossed to show the dark gray silk socks with his monogram on the ankle. And now she sensed within herself the strain that had come through from Pa, the irrational temper, the urge to violence. She could only keep herself from striking out by bolting up to go.

But his hand darted out and caught her wrist, tight enough this time to hurt. 'So where do you go now — away from this comfort you despise? To what?' He stood up beside her. 'All this guilt, this penance of yours, will that change anything, will that lift anyone out of their hell?' He paused, and gave her a long look. For the first time, she noticed the color of his eyes, a deep bluish gray like mist over a harbor at dusk.

'No,' he answered himself, 'that will change nothing. But I will tell you what *will*. Accept your luck. Go with it as far as it will take you, be as beautiful and smart — and as rich — as you can be. Then, maybe *then*, you can change the world.'

He went on gazing at her, and once again she felt herself immobilized by the aura that surrounded him like a magnetic field. She felt acutely conscious of his strong grip on her arm, a burning sensation where his fingers were clasped in a ring around her wrist, and she longed to free herself. Yet she stood staring back into his eyes, knowing some message was passing between them even as she was unable to consciously define exactly what it was.

He broke the silence. 'But if you do not believe me, then I will give you an alternative.' Only now he withdrew his hand, and gestured with it toward the painting under the light. 'Take it. Go ahead. I give it to you. If you really think it will make the difference, take it away.'

So he had seen her.

But she felt unashamed now. She believed in the rightness of the declaration she had made. There was no justice in any one man having so much while others starved.

Yet it was harder to take as a gift than if she had stolen it. To accept it as a rich man's whim somehow held less hope of making a difference than to seize it out of her own defiant act of will.

'No,' she said, her tone hard and steady. 'I'll try it the other way. I'm going to ride my luck to the limit, and see where it takes me.'

'With no guilt if you succeed?'

It seemed like a dare. 'Not a bit.'

'And no apologies to anyone . . .'

'No apologies.' In the moment of echoing his caveats, she felt as if she were accepting him not as her master but her mentor.

'Bravo,' he said.

For another moment they stared at each other. Then she broke away and left the room.

She didn't stop until she had returned to the ballroom. There she saw again the panoply of the privileged spinning before her. Nothing stopped her this time, however, from wading into the crowd, from joining in the dance when Nickles made his way to her side and asked her. Justinean had thrown down a gauntlet . . . and she had taken up the challenge.

In a few minutes, she saw him follow and find his own partner, a beautiful young blonde whom Geri recognized as the one she had seen in his car at Belmont that day several years ago.

For the rest of the night, she spun through the crowd, drinking champagne and dancing with Nickles and the dozen young heirs of the Saratoga rich who begged for dances.

She didn't see Justinean again, didn't even look for him. She was too busy having the time of her life.

CHAPTER FIVE

Only minutes after arriving at the clinic Monday morning Geri heard the paging system order her to report to Graymar's office. When she entered, he was at his desk writing notes. As usual he left her standing while he continued to write. She no longer took it personally; he was rude with everyone who worked for him.

He looked up at last, his hazel eyes glinting like cold tarnished brass. 'Quite the saleswoman, aren't you? There's a man I've been trying to get for a client ever since I opened this place. Never needed me — he's got two staff vets, and his own surgery — but half an hour ago he calls and says he met one of my assistants over the weekend and *she* persuaded him to try using some of my special facilities.'

Graymar's harsh tone perplexed Geri. If she had been responsible for landing this long-sought account, then why did he sound so displeased? But, equally puzzling, she couldn't recall giving anyone that kind of professional advice. Of course, she had drunk a lot of champagne on Saturday night; she couldn't be absolutely certain of everything she'd said to all the two or three dozen men with whom she'd accepted dances. Still, she had a pretty good handle on her memory. She could remember walking a fairly straight line out of the mansion, and pretending not to see Justinean off to one side of the foyer bidding other guests goodnight. And she remembered the way, at the door of her rooming house, Nickles had pleaded to sleep with her, and she had told him again there was no hope for romance unless he gave her more time.

'How much more . . .?' he had pressed her.

'I don't know,' she answered honestly.

'That sounds a little too much like forever,' he said. He told her then that he wouldn't be seeing her again for a while — early the next morning he would be gone to begin the fall racing season in New York — and he gave her a quick chaste kiss. She got the sense that he had given up chasing her, and all Sunday she had wondered if disappointing Nickles had cost her a friendship that might have someday evolved into something more. She was still brooding about it today . . .

Graymar's voice cut into her thoughts. 'Maybe I ought to be grateful you've brought us in a big new account. But the customer is laying down some special conditions. He'll agree to give us his business only as long as all his cases are supervised exclusively by our Miss Keyes.'

'Tom . . . who is this customer?'

He greeted her need to ask with a skeptical glance, but he answered, 'Dolph Justinean. Sound familiar . . .?'

Now she understood Graymar's pique. He suspected she was using the clinic merely as a base to start building a valuable clientele of her own. 'Tom, believe me, I didn't pitch Justinean. And I wouldn't have tried to grab him for my own —'

'Don't bother explaining. I want him any way it comes. I'll be collecting the fees, anyway, not you.'

'But I want you to know —'

'Forget it, Geri! To tell the truth, I was hoping that if you circulated with some of these rich romeos, it would turn into a good come-on for the clinic. Just remember, though: whoever Justinean wants to see in his stables, he's still *my* client not yours. Now get back to work.' He looked down at his notes.

She gave up. Ruled by ambitions himself, Graymar would never believe she hadn't been conniving only to sell herself. She was at the door when she heard his voice again:

'By the way, Geri, you might like to know that Justinean's

already got a gorgeous young wife — but she doesn't seem to slow him down much. He's still known for keeping as long and fast a string of ladies as of horses. So watch your step — and, for my sake, if all he really wants is your ass . . . think twice before you turn him down.'

Graymar was smiling when she darted a dark glance over her shoulder, but she knew he wasn't kidding.

The Saratoga racing season was over, but young horses were still kept and trained at the local track, and at the several breeding operations surrounding the town. The clinic remained constantly busy through the year treating racehorses with serious problems that were shipped from stud farms and racetracks all over the east coast.

Several times during the next few weeks, Geri was called out to Justinean's stables to treat an ailing animal. She had imagined that his motive for engaging her must be to maintain contact; it made little sense otherwise, since he had two staff vets. But whenever she went to his stud farm, an assistant trainer or stable foreman would give some perfectly reasonable explanation for calling her in — the other vets were away, or too busy with other animals — and she never saw Justinean.

In his absence, her curiosity about him grew, and the recollection of their last meeting became ever more vivid. The advice he had given her — to be unashamed of her ambition, and guiltless about her luck — had stayed with her; indeed, she regarded it as something of a turning point. She no longer questioned her dedication to a sport that served the interests of the rich. She saw the merit in the rationale he had given her: climb as far and as high as she could go, and maybe then she would have the power to change the injustices she despised.

Justinean Farms was an especially lavish installation, with landscaped pathways and fountains burbling in courtyards of inlaid stone outside each of the clean modern barns. Whenever she went there, Geri couldn't help reflecting on how far Justinean's own ambition had taken him, and she would wonder where his climb had begun. He had dropped a hint that his beginnings might be no less humble than her own. She began to gather whatever information about him she could — from his employees whenever she made a call at his stable, or from sportswriters and other knowledgeable racing buffs who passed through the clinic — learning enough to patch together an idea of his origins that was clearer than the rumors Nickles had once passed along.

He had been born the son of a farmer in a rural part of Yugoslavia. When the Nazis had occupied his native country in 1940, he had been in his teens and he had gone off into the hills to join the partisan guerillas led by Josip Tito. Hiding in the many caves by day, and by night ambushing convoys on the roads, he had remained free until the end of the war when he managed to make his way to America. Starting with a business that dealt in scrap metal, he had gradually expanded into used machinery, then into used auto parts, and from there into manufacturing new items. In thirty years he had built an empire that included an international airline, automobile rental and trucking firms in several countries, tire manufacturers and rubber plantations, and massive holdings in commercial real estate all over the world. Tending his empire might take him one week to Japan, another week to South America, then to Europe. To keep in touch with all his interests, he travelled on his own plane, and he maintained many homes around the world. He also had a second stud farm in California. Horseracing was his principal hobby; he tried to arrange his schedule so that he could always touch down where a major stakes was being run — whether it was the 'L'Arc de Triomphe' at Longchamps in Paris, or 'The Derby' at Epsom, the 'Jockey Club Gold Cup' at Belmont, or 'The Suntori Stakes' in Tokyo.

There was one other fact about him, told to Geri by a newsman, that changed her curiosity to fascination: Justinean was not his real name; like her, he had changed his identity. She could only admire the audacity of a man who adopted the name of an emperor — and then actually built an empire.

Despite Graymar's initial reaction to the circumstances

under which Justinean had become a client, he didn't harbor any lasting suspicion of Geri. Through the autumn and early winter he worked her harder than ever, but the nature of her duties changed. He began to rely on her more and more, turning over some of his own responsibiltiies to her. If he was summoned away for a few days to attend an important horse entered in a major race at some distant track — not necessarily a sick animal, but one the owner wanted to be sure was in prime racing condition — Graymar left instructions that any decisions on treatment of the animals at the clinic were to be cleared through Geri. This led to some friction between her and Marty Shields, who felt he was better qualified — and held the dubious seniority of having been hired a day earlier. But when Graymar announced to his staff that the success of the Saratoga clinic had finally persuaded him to build similar installations in the racing and breeding centers of Florida and California, Shields was placated; he assumed he would be put in charge of one of the other clinics as soon as they opened.

Christmas and New Year were marked by dreary parties given by different staff members at the clinic, a call from Nickles, and an engraved card from Sylvia Balkin. As always at holiday time, Geri-Jo was tempted to contact Caybie directly or to try finding out what had happened to Molly. But she couldn't bring herself to take the risks. Fortunately, work kept her too busy to get mired down in holiday blues. Tom Graymar had gone to Florida, to supervise the ground-breaking for his new clinic, Marty Shields had contrived to pay a Christmas visit to his family in Chicago, and the other assistants were on a rotating schedule. Left in charge, Geri worked to the point of exhaustion, and, to keep a closer eye on her responsibilities, she spent nights sleeping on a cot she had set up in a spare room off the pathology lab.

Several days into the new year, she returned from a late barn visit to find a message waiting: Mr. Justinean had been urgently trying to reach her. A number had been left for her to call. She recognized the 213 area code as being in California.

It was his voice that answered with a simple 'Hello'.

'Mr Justinean, this is Geri Keyes.'

'Ah! I'm glad you called back so soon . . .' Quickly, he explained that one of his best four-year-olds, entered in an important race at Santa Anita Park the day after tomorrow, had developed a slight soreness in his ankle. A couple of vets had already advised that the horse could run, but he still wasn't satisfied. 'The report I've gotten on the treatment you've given my horses is very favorable. I don't like to pull my other people away from their work at the stables, so I'd be obliged if you would also provide an opinion in this case.'

'I can't really do that without looking at the horse . . .'

He laughed. 'That's exactly what I had in mind.'

She was astonished. Santa Anita was near Los Angeles; there were hundreds of other vets he could have called in, and at much less expense — though, of course, that wouldn't be a consideration for Justinean.

In the pause, he asked, 'Is there any reason you can't?'

Was there? Tom was away, too, but he would probably want her to go. The clinic could levy thousands of dollars in fees for what amounted to a three-day consultation. Marty Shields had returned from his holiday and could handle things at the clinic.

'I can be there tomorrow,' she said. 'I'll let you know what time after I check the airline schedules.'

'No need for that. I've already dispatched my plane from here. It will land at Albany airport to pick you up two hours from now.'

Albany was a half hour's drive, giving her more than an hour to pack. She murmured assent, he said he would meet her at the track tomorrow, and they said their goodbyes.

If the plane was landing in two hours, Geri thought, it had left California five hours ago. Apparently, Justinean had been quite sure of what her answer would be.

She had never flown in a plane before, but Geri felt no apprehensions as the jets revved up and the plane zoomed down the runway. She sat back and reveled in the new sensation, all the more enjoyable in the luxury of Dolph Justinean's specially outfitted 727. Three stewards stood ready to serve her every whim. After sitting in the main lounge for a while, she felt hungry and asked one of the attendants if there was anything to eat. He ushered her forward to a dining compartment and seated her at an antique rosewood table where she was served a full dinner. Champagne was offered as accompaniment, but she declined this and the other wines. After being with Justinean last time, she'd had all too much to drink. When she saw him tomorrow, she wanted to be sharp as a tack.

Later, when she grew drowsy, a steward showed her to the bedroom suite at the back of the plane. Before getting into the large bed, she noticed the two sets of mirrored doors built along either side of the entrance to the bathroom. Curious, she opened one and found a closet hung with his clothes. On an impulse she reached out and ran her fingers over the rich fabrics. The sensation brought back the memory of his tuxedo rubbing against her bare shoulder that night as he had talked about the Stubbs. For a moment she felt oddly excited and her thoughts drifted into a fantasy. What if she had not fled from Justinean that night? In her mind's eye, she saw him embracing her, taking command, undressing her . . . Her skin tingled as if he was kissing her now. She felt he was the man who could release her imprisoned urge to love fully and without fear, and as the certainty grew she realized how deeply she had longed for him — and how stubbornly she had denied the longing — since that night in his library. Aching for his touch, she reached down and, as one hand still held onto the fabric of his sleeve, she ran the other along the inside of her thigh, touched herself and imagined him there, wanting her —

She opened her eyes to the reality of an empty jacket on a hanger, and instantly pulled her hand away from his clothes almost as if she had touched something scalding. She mustn't let herself be caught up in any fantasies, not with a man like Dolph Justinean. He was used to owning everything and everyone around him, and she had her own destiny to fulfill.

She closed the door and was turning away when she saw

the second closet. She moved to open it. As she had expected, it was full of a woman's clothes, all beautifully made and redolent of expensive perfume. In the past year, Geri-Jo had splurged a couple of times on good new clothes, and she had brought them along. But she saw that her best things were shoddy next to any of the items worn by Justinean's wife.

For a moment, she was seized with regret for making the trip, exposing herself to disappointment. And then she told herself that if she expected anything from Justinean it was all part of the fantasy that had to be put to rest.

It was only a professional relationship that was taking her across the country. Nothing else.

The limousine that met Geri the next morning at the Los Angeles airport drove north for an hour to the town of Arcadia. There, in the shadow of the San Gabriel mountains, Santa Anita Park had opened in 1935. Just as the movie business boomed in California all through the dark days of the depression, so too did racing. While the homeless and hungry lived in shantytowns and stood on breadlines, here in Santa Anita's blue and cream-colored Art Deco clubhouse, movie stars and other well-heeled sports fans gathered in the clubhouse boxes and waited on betting lines.

Justinean's driver started to take Geri to the backstretch but she asked to be dropped at the main building. She wanted to see famous Santa Anita, and she also thought the long walk to the stabling area through the grass and palm trees around the paddock would relax her. For all the assurances she had given herself, the prospect of seeing Justinean again still unnerved her.

Justinean had said he would meet her at the track, but when she got to the stable she was greeted by his trainer, Cesar Belize. A rotund man in his mid-seventies with a large mustache and an egg-smooth bald head, Belize had come from Panama when he was a boy and had been training winners for forty years, long before he was engaged by Justinean with a contract that reportedly paid a fee of a million dollars in addition to his percentages. He took her to his office at one end of the stable, served her a cup of the strongest coffee she had ever tasted, and handed her the reports of the other vets, along with the latest X-rays, taken a short while ago with the compact portable machine that many barns kept handy.

Geri saw nothing of concern in the X-rays, and nothing to criticize in the recommendations of the other vets. It wasn't unreasonable to allow a horse to race with a sore ankle. The stress of racing almost invariably created a degree of soreness in every horse, particularly in some part of their legs. The knee, and the bones and joints below it, took an especially hard pounding because a horse had no muscle in the leg below the knee. Since the horse with the sore ankle was a four-year-old, it was even more likely that the problem would not become more serious through being used. At four, a horse was fully grown and developed. With the younger horses, the two- and three-year-olds, more care had to be taken. Indeed, if no horse was run until the age of four, there would be fewer injuries. Unfortunately, the expense of racing did not allow for an owner to keep on feeding a horse for so long without trying to win back his expenses in purse money.

A routine treatment to alleviate problems of the lower leg was to 'ice' the horse — stand the legs in a bucket of ice for two or three hours — but Geri could see from the records that this had been done several times and the tenderness had persisted. There had also been some medication, but this had been discontinued to be sure the horse passed the drug tests that would be taken after the race.

Having reviewed the records, she asked for the horse to be taken out of its stall so she could include some observation of its movements in her examination. She spent nearly an hour with the animal, a handsome chestnut named Grandee, concluding with a very thorough application of the hoof-tester, a metal vice-like instrument which was used to check for tenderness in the hoof that might indicate an underlying abscess. At the end of her examination, she was able to endorse running Grandee in the big stakes the next day.

After hearing her opinion, Cesar Belize escorted her to where the limousine waited. Geri felt a growing confusion at Justinean's failure to appear. Of course she was here only on professional business — yet the task had been so basic and uncomplicated she couldn't believe he wouldn't have used another vet unless there was some ulterior motive. Had he simply been indulging a whim he could easily afford, demonstrating the reach of his money and power?

As Geri was chauffeured back toward Los Angeles, her confusion turned to anger. She didn't like being used as a pawn to salve a rich man's ego.

A buzzing noise broke into her thoughts. She didn't realize the source until the driver told her to pick up the telephone set into the armrest. No fancy apologies accepted, she thought to herself as she snatched up the receiver.

But it wasn't his voice she heard. 'Miss Keyes, this is Connie Fuller, Mr Justinean's personal secretary. He's sorry he had to be away when —'

'Away? He called me from Los Angeles last night.'

'Yes, but a take-over threat against one of his companies was brewing and he flew off early this morning to take care of it. He's been locked in a roomful of bankers since he landed in Chicago. He'll be back tomorrow, though, and he'd like you to stay on for the race, and have lunch with him at the track. As his guest, of course. He's arranged for a suite at the Beverly Hills Hotel . . .'

Geri hesitated. Justinean had treated her high-handedly, bringing her all this way and then failing to appear. She didn't care what his excuse was, takeovers be damned. Yet in spite of herself, she heard herself saying to the secretary, 'I'll stay.'

'Good,' said the secretary. 'Mr Justinean will be very pleased.' She added that a car would collect Geri at noon the next day for the ride to the track.

There had been several good reasons for the decision, she thought as the car drove on to the hotel. It was cold back in Saratoga, and she'd never had even a day's vacation. And it was something of a professional obligation to observe the

330

horse she had certified ready to race.

But she had to admit now that none of the good reasons had really made the difference. She was staying for the same reason she had agreed to come, because she was compelled to know more about Dolph Justinean. Because in some part of herself that operated on pure instinct, she felt they were kindred spirits. He had been born in rural poverty, had lived through catastrophe, had even changed his identity. And he had risen far beyond it all.

To know him, she thought, was to know how far her own dreams might take her.

CHAPTER SIX

The Turf Club at Santa Anita was one of the most lavishly appointed places Geri had ever seen at a racetrack. In the entrance lobby, decorated in a coral and gold motif, huge urns of carved wood held gigantic flower arrangements, their lush colors reflected in mirrored panels that rose from the floor to a ceiling twenty-feet above.

When Geri mounted the stairs leading to the dining room and asked for Justinean's table, she thought the headwaiter gave her an odd look. Then she dismissed it as her imagination, the result of self-consciousness about the meeting. She couldn't deny to herself that the purely professional aspects of their appointment had been cast to the wind. If there had been any lingering doubt on that score, it hadn't lasted beyond this morning — when she woke already looking forward to lunch, and worried about what she would wear to look her best for him. Deciding that nothing she'd brought was good enough, she had gone to a boutique in the lobby of the Beverly Hills Hotel and had splurged wildly, spending nearly eight hundred dollars — two months' salary — on a bold Ungaro print. After trying it on in the bungalow, sanity had returned and she had taken the dress back for a refund. She couldn't bring herself to spend so much money on a mere dress. If she was going to make herself attractive to Justinean, it wasn't going to be by gilding herself as if she was one of the rich women in his set. He'd have to take her as she was . . .

Yet, with or without expensive plumage, the crux of her thinking could no longer be disguised, even from herself. She did want to be taken. Dolph Justinean had awakened a part of her that she had been denying for as long as she had been a woman.

The boldly patterned black and turquoise shift she had worn instead of the Ungaro was only an eighty-five-dollar mark-down bought at a small dress store in Saratoga. But with a cut that perfectly accented her height and her lithe figure, a hem that showed off her slender legs, and a pattern that provided a spectacular contrast to her long hair, the dress caused all eyes to follow her as Geri walked behind the headwaiter.

The Santa Anita clubhouse faced out across the track toward a view of the San Gabriel mountains, a shimmering line of silvery purple beyond the smoggy haze. Captivated by the vista, Geri didn't realize that she had arrived at her table until she practically bumped into the chair the headwaiter was holding for her. Only as she turned to sit did she become aware of the woman already occupying another place at the large round table. She was very beautiful, with large blue eyes, a flawless milky complexion, and long pale blonde hair that tumbled in flamboyant curls around her shoulders and down her back. Her face wore an expression of childlike innocence that contrasted sharply with her sophisticated dress, and the air of sensuality she exuded. A gold and emerald clip sparkled from one lapel of her tailored suede suit, and a diamond ring of several dozen karats sparkled beside the plain gold band on the fourth finger of her left hand. She was the same young woman Geri had seen dancing with Justinean the night of the ball, and sitting in his car at Belmont five years earlier. His wife.

She smiled a bit dreamily, which broke the momentary paralysis afflicting Geri. Though she felt caught in a sticky situation, Geri sat down. It was, after all, her own expectations that had created the difficulty. Lunch in the presence of Justinean's wife would be a fair penance for the presumption that Justinean had wanted to see her alone.

'Can I bring you a drink, Miss . . .?' the headwaiter asked.

In somewhat the same way a duellist would accept the

identical weapon to an opponent's, Geri gestured to the ice bucket where champagne ordered by Justinean's wife was chilling. 'I'll have a glass of that.'

When they were alone, the other woman spoke first. 'I'm Diana Justinean.'

'Pleased to meet you. I'm —'

'I know who you are. Dolph told me you'd be here today — Geri Keyes, the fabulous lady vet.' She raised her champagne glass as though toasting her. 'Good gimmick. I used to have one, too.'

'Gimmick . . .?'

Diana drained off her champagne. 'I suppose you might be calling it something else,' she said as she grabbed the bottle and refilled her glass. 'Let's see . . . what would that be? A job, a career? That's what I used to call it . . . when I had one.'

Geri pretended to ignore the bitter tone. 'What did you do?'

'Photographer — fashion, travel, rock stars for the magazines. Pretty good at it, too. True, I had to fuck to get my chances, but I knew what to do once I had them. I was really going somewhere. Then I met Dolph. Went out to shoot him on an assignment — the great Mr Justinean and one of his goddamn horses. Bingo, that was it. No way to be anything but Mrs Dolph Justinean after that.' She took another sip of champagne and sighed loudly. 'So, looking back, it seems like the work couldn't't've been anything but a gimmick, a way to make myself look interesting to the right man.' She looked down into her glass, talking to herself more than Geri. 'Otherwise why the hell did I give it up so damn fast . . .?'

'You made a choice, that's all.' Geri tried to offer something neutral. A faint slurring of words in Diana's speech hinted that she wasn't on her first bottle of champagne, and Geri didn't want to light any fuses.

Diana finished another long sip. 'No, doc, that's not the way it works with Dolph. I didn't make any choices. He makes them all. Look at the way he got us here, squaring off against each other.'

'Is that what we're doing? I'm just waiting to have lunch and watch the races.'

Diana gave one of her sleepy smiles. 'And waiting for Dolph,' she said. 'But he's delayed again, didn't you hear? Still locked up in a vault or something. Won't be joining the party for a couple more hours, which leaves little old us sitting here staring at each other. And from what I see of Doc Keyes, I don't think that's a choice I would've made for myself . . .'

Geri had been uncomfortable from the moment she had seen Dolph's wife. Diana's antagonistic tone only made it worse. 'Look, maybe you'd rather I left . . .?' She started to rise.

Diana reached out. 'Oh no, Doc, don't think I'm being unfriendly. I was just sympathizing, that's all. I know what it's like, being put in a place you didn't want to be . . .' Her tone was suddenly plaintive, genuinely wounded.

'But I like being here,' Geri said, relieved that the level of bitchy tension was de-escalating. 'Horses are part of my "gimmick", after all. For me, anyway, coming here was an easy decision.'

Diana Justinean nodded knowingly. 'He's good at that, too, honey.'

'At what?'

'Making the decisions seem easy — at the beginning, anyway. Watch out, though, they get tougher later on.' She drained her glass again, and reached for the bottle. Finding it empty, she held it aloft and indicated to a waiter she wanted another.

The first race was run, and for a while they were diverted. Geri had thought of leaving, but she also felt sympathy for Diana Justinean — but not because she believed her talk against Dolph. She couldn't believe Justinean would have deliberately damaged anyone's self-esteem. After all, he had done the opposite for her. He could have demolished her when he'd found her in his office on the brink of theft. Instead he had been sensitive and perceptive, sent her away with a new sense of direction. Dolph Justinean might have the rich man's habit of wanting everything his own way, but he could only get it as long as others yielded. His wife's grievances must come out of her own flaws, the same weakness that drove her to become drunk in the middle of the day.

As the first race ended, two more guests arrived, a couple. The man was fortyish and paunchy, and wore gold-framed aviator spectacles; the woman was a good ten years younger, and probably beautiful though it was difficult to make out the face behind a pair of enormous sunglasses, and a tangle of long panther-black hair. Diana introduced them as Bernie Holtzman and Teri Raynes.

As the lunch progressed, Bernie revealed himself to be the producer of several television shows, one of which starred Teri as the sister of a murdered private detective who had taken up his work. Geri almost never watched television, but she could tell that the show was quite successful. Teri's conversation consisted mainly of repeating last week's Neilsen's audience shares, and boasting about a spread on her appearing in *People* next week. They were odd friends for Justinean to have, Geri thought, so much more flashy and rough-edged than the social set he mingled with in Saratoga. She asked Bernie how they had met.

'Right here at the track several years ago,' he said. 'I had a couple of horses myself then — just dog meat compared to Dolph's, of course, but we rubbed elbows a little, and when I needed backing for my new production company I asked him. Now we're partners.'

That brought a laugh from Diana. 'Just don't let *him* hear you say that, Bernie baby! Dolph doesn't have partners. He bought your soul in exchange for a little piece of the empire he's building. Right, Bernie? You're his ... his ... watchamacallit ...?'

Bernie shot a worried glance around the clubhouse. 'Keep it down, Diana. There are a lot of people here I have to do business with. It doesn't help if —'

'Lackey,' Diana blurted, 'that's the word. The sonofabitch does it to all of us. Turns us into slaves. Just a bunch of ... tacky lackies.' She laughed shrilly.

Bernie signalled to Teri.

'Diana,' Teri said, 'let's take a walk.'

But Diana was pointing at Geri. 'That's his latest right there. He snaps his fingers, she jumps. Doesn't know what kind of hoops he'll end up putting her through . . .'

Teri rose and went around the table. 'C'mon, Diana. Let's powder our noses and take a walk to the paddock.'

Diana went on gazing at Geri for a moment, but she was suddenly silent. She allowed Teri to pull her out of her chair and lead her away.

'Sad, sad lady,' Bernie said. 'She's never gotten over it.'

'Over what?'

'Having the moon. Got smashed on too much champagne at her wedding to Dolph, and hasn't stopped since. I hear she's gone on to bigger and better kicks, too.'

Geri turned to her program, shutting out the gossip and trying to forget the scene that had just been played. Again, she considered leaving, but now she felt there was a mystery to solve and the clues could be gathered only by remaining. Was Dolph Justinean a quietly masterful and sympathetic man who had married a young neurotic, or did he deserve to be charged with responsibility for what his wife had become?

Another race was run before Teri returned with Diana. Perhaps the air had helped, or a cup of coffee she'd grabbed somewhere, but Diana was no longer loud and hostile. Now she immersed herself in the races, pulling hundred-dollar bills out of her alligator purse, and betting them in handfuls on losing horses.

By the feature race, Justinean had yet to appear, and Geri had given up expecting him. But she stayed to see what happened to the horse she had certified ready to run. After Grandee had finished a respectable third, and paid $5.20 on a two-dollar bet, Geri said goodbye to everyone at the table.

'So long, doc,' Diana Justinean said. 'Hope we bump into each other again sometime.'

Geri felt that the wish was sincere, that Diana meant to apologize for her earlier behavior. But she couldn't see any reason they would meet. Whatever idea she'd had about herself and Justinean had obviously been a crazy, misguided pipe dream.

A minute after she called the hotel desk to have her bag picked up, there was a knock at the door of the bungalow. She was at the bathroom mirror, giving her hair a last-second brushing as she called out, 'Door's open, bag's next to the bed. Can you take it straight to a taxi. I've got a plane to catch . . .'

'Is it in your blood, too, like the horses — this need to run?'

She turned and saw Justinean in the doorway. If he had spent the day travelling and haggling with financiers there was no sign of it. He looked as fresh and strong as a knight in the flower of youth. Whatever iron she had in her will was only drawn to the magnet of his charm. But she was resolved now to fight against the attraction. She turned back to the mirror, but she could not escape his reflection and the hold of his gray-blue eyes.

'My work's done,' she said flatly. 'There's nothing to keep me now.' Wrenching her gaze from his, she tossed the brush into the kit, and snapped it shut.

'I'm terribly sorry I wasn't there. I hope my secretary explained —'

'Something about fighting a take-over. I understand . . .' She pushed past him, carrying her cosmetic kit into the bedroom where she put it beside her suitcase.

'But about Diana,' he said. '*That* you do not understand.' She faced him, surprised he had raised his wife's name so quickly and bluntly. 'I was told about the way she behaved,' he continued. 'I must admit I expected nothing different from her, but I hope you will forgive me for putting you in such an awkward position.'

Geri hadn't believed there was anything callously pre-meditated in confronting her with his wife. If the situation had been awkward, it was as much her own fault. But now she sensed there had been a purpose, after all. He'd expected nothing different, he said. As Diana had claimed, he had arranged to have them 'square off'.

'Why did you do it?' she asked.

'I wanted you to have a chance to judge me?'

'Judge you? How?'

'By hearing the testimony of the most hostile witness against me. My wife blames me for everything. If she's a hopeless alcoholic, a pathetically lost soul who can't be happy in spite of all her beauty and wealth, then I'm the culprit. Perhaps she's right. I offer no defenses; I'm not in a position to judge. I thought you would be.'

Geri shook her head. 'Why should you want me to . . .?'

He gave her a long look before gently putting a hand to her face. 'Dear Geri, were you not aware that night we met last summer that we were discovering a destiny? I felt then that whatever I had survived, whatever I had made of my life, it was all leading me to that moment I met you . . .'

As she listened she felt that he was only articulating her own thoughts. And yet something in her feared the words more than welcomed them. She wanted to believe her heart had a destiny, and that she had found it. But what if she believed too quickly and, as in the past, belief led only to disillusionment?

Sensing her retreat, Dolph moved closer. His hand slid down her cheek, and along her neck until he was grasping her shoulder. She shivered with pleasure at his touch, though her only response was to look more deeply into his eyes, searching for the truth as though looking through fathoms of water for a treasure.

'I want to love you, Geri,' he said. 'I've never wanted anything as much. But first, I thought you should see what happened to someone else I once loved. Before anything happens between us, I want you to be sure you're strong enough to survive . . .'

With all she had lived through already, she shouldn't have doubted that she was strong enough. But living through a flood didn't guarantee living through a hurricane; Dolph Justinean was a force of nature different from any she had ever faced before. How could she know for certain that she wouldn't be overawed by Dolph as his wife had been? Did he assume, because they had met in a playground of the rich, that she was as sophisticated as he? Had he even imagined how naive she was?

His hand still rested on her shoulder, lightly holding her as he waited for an answer. She inclined her head to rub her cheek along the back of his hand. 'I want you, too,' she said,

339

her voice barely above a whisper. 'But . . . I don't know if I'm ready for you.'

'What does that mean?'

She raised her eyes to his. 'There hasn't been . . . anyone else.'

He smiled slowly. 'Oh, my darling,' he said, 'what a miracle you are — as innocent as an old-fashioned bride.' He gave her a sidelong glance. 'Or is that the reason — you're waiting for the man you'll marry?'

'No. I've just been waiting for the man I can love.' She lifted her face and started to pull him nearer, when there was a knock at the door, then the voice of a bellboy saying that he'd come for the bags.

'Never mind,' she called back. 'I'm not going . . .'

In the next second, Dolph bent to kiss her. The first touch of his lips was as gentle as a warm summer breeze. For as long as that gentle wind blew, Geri believed, there would be no rain, nothing to threaten her. When his arms tightened around her, she clung to him and they kissed again, silently telling secrets with the play of tongues.

All at once he lifted her. His strength, the ease with which he moved her to the bed and laid her down, amazed her. And when he undressed her, it was so quick, so effortless, that it was almost as if he had dissolved her clothes in a spell. Suddenly she was naked, waiting for him, and she made an impatient reach to undress him, too. But he took a step back and disrobed himself slowly, in a way that made her ache for him even more. At last he was unveiled, his skin taut and tanned golden, but decorated across his chest and stomach and on his legs by hair of the same pure fine silver as on his head. The shiny metallic hair nested, too, at the root of the long stiff shaft pointing toward her. She moaned with anticipation as he climbed over her and kissed her again, and then began making a trail of kisses that started with her mouth and went down her neck and across her breasts, slowly, making her shudder with delight, until his mouth was sipping at the juices she felt flowing out of her. She started to tremble and cry with joy, and then he moved up to kiss her tears, and she opened herself wider, wrapped her legs around him as he drove down at last, a wave of thrills shooting through her as the warm smooth piston slid deeper, then up again, then plunging deeper still. Again and again, until she gave a sighing scream and a sweet shudder ran through her. The last fortress of her heart fell as he rammed one deep final thrust, and the long heat exploded in her core sending her flying up into the sun. He gave his own roar of ecstasy and his strong hands gripped her under the thighs and pulled her in, melding them together.

Famished after satisfying each other, but still wanting to remain in their private world, they ordered dinner from room service and then made love again. It seemed even better to her this time, and he was no less vigorous and giving. But afterward, he said apologetically that he wouldn't be able to stay the night.

She asked no questions; she guessed that he might feel some obligation to Diana, but didn't rule out that he might have business. Dolph was obviously capable of perpetual motion, which made her treasure all the more the moments he chose to spend alone with her. As he left, he said he would be back early in the morning and told her to dress 'for work'. He was going to take her to see his California breeding operation.

Early the next morning, he called for her. A limousine to the airport, next a small corporate jet — breakfast served aboard — then a helicopter. Within a couple of hours they were in a green valley he told her was somewhere near the Del Mar racetrack in lower California.

The farm here was even larger than the one in Saratoga, with more stables and more bloodstock. Though the East was the traditional center of racing, Dolph told Geri, he believed that the West Coast was going to become more important in the next ten years — while attendance at Eastern tracks would continue to dwindle — and he would have a greater chance for establishing supremacy here than bucking the old racing establishment rooted so long in the East.

She had known, of course, how much Justinean cared about excellence and achievement. But it wasn't until he spoke about establishing supremacy, dominating all of Western racing with his horses, that she understood the full scope of his desire to rule any territory he entered.

After spending the rest of the morning at his California farm, they lifted off in his helicopter, and soon touched down again on a beautiful beach, a sweeping curve of empty sand that stretched for miles along the Pacific Ocean. There were no houses or roads, no other visitors — though there were signs that someone had been there before them: on a fine carpet that had been laid over a raked patch of sand stood two chairs and a table set with crystal and fine china. A cold lunch of lobster salad, fruit, cheese and wine waited on the table.

It was romantic, and also somehow comical, like an image from a surreal painting or a silent film. Geri laughed at the extravagance. 'So much trouble,' she said. 'Why?'

'Just for this. To hear you ask . . . see you laugh.'

He sent the helicopter away, telling the pilot to return for them in a few hours.

Until now, she had hardly spoken to him at all about her youth. But as she sat with him over lunch in his private kingdom, she felt compelled at last to tell him about how far she had come to this moment of wonderfully absurd luxury, the trials of the journey she had made. It was only when she came to the point of explaining why her family had been forced to move from the hollow to the blue-grass country that she broke down. She would have skipped past it, but Dolph urged her to go on. He took her on a walk along the beach and she talked, letting herself relive it. The pain was all but unbearable. She wailed loudly across the vast empty crescent of sand as she described Lor' going under, and her mother and all the others being taken by the mountain. But when she finished and he stood holding her, the fresh salt air drying the tears he hadn't kissed away, she knew that she had wrenched something from within that had been embedded in her soul like a poisoned arrow. The fear that anyone she dared to love would suddenly disappear had been purged from her heart.

Yet she wasn't ready to confess everything. When Dolph asked what had happened to the three who had lived through the mudslide with her, she said, 'My brother still lives in

Kentucky. And my sister, too, I think. But . . . I've lost touch with her . . .'

'That's a shame,' Justinean said. 'The kind of tragedy you all lived through, I would have thought . . . it would bring you closer.'

She said nothing, though his comment stirred up the pool of regret that was always there. It was a shame, she thought; it was too late for her to reach out again to Molly . . .

'And your father?' Justinean said. 'You didn't mention him . . .'

'Oh, yes. He . . . died a few years ago.'

'He must have been quite a young man . . .'

'He had an accident in the garage where he worked.' She could not begin to open the door to all the truths surrounding her father's death.

Finally, the sun warming their bodies, they made love on the beach. She couldn't get enough of him now, nor give herself enough. At the end of the afternoon she lay in his arms drained and sleepy, weak from loving, and stronger than she had ever been. The tide had been coming in, and a finger of surf came up onto the carpet of sand and washed at her feet. She flinched and his arms tightened around her, guessing at the deep reflexes that had been stirred by the cold touch of the water.

'We should go,' he said at last.

'I don't want this day to end.'

'Because you're worried about tomorrow?'

'Because even Dolph Justinean can't improve on perfection.'

He laughed. 'That, my darling, is exactly the kind of challenge I can't resist.' The surf touched them again. 'But it will have to wait, I'm afraid. It's no different in my empire than it was in my namesake's. There are always borders to expand, new walls to build, always an uprising to put down in some far corner. There are many places I have to go — places I should have been yesterday . . .'

'I could go with you. I'll phone the clinic and tell —'

'No. I won't let what happened to Diana happen to you. You

343

have a life of your own. Don't give that up so quickly to move in my shadow.'

'I'll survive . . .' She wasn't worried anymore. She felt stronger than ever, and Dolph had made her so.

'After hearing what you've come through, I'd have to agree the odds are excellent.'

'But not a sure thing . . .?'

He paused reflectively, ran his hands over her shoulders, and lightly caressed her breasts. 'For a long time it's been too easy for me to own anything I wanted. No battles, no trade-offs. There is a price, however, beyond money. When I get what I want . . . often I don't appreciate it enough.'

'It's too late for me to play hard to get,' she said.

He smiled. 'You don't have to. For once I appreciate what I've got, I know how lucky I am. But I'm not sure how fragile that feeling is, and I want it to last. Forever, if possible.' His voice sank. 'Diana is a sick and vindictive woman. She won't make it easy for me to end the marriage — and, to be honest, I won't make it easy on myself. I know it will be easier to leave her if she can first be made stronger. That will take time. Can you spare me that time . . .?'

She thought about all he'd said, and she understood all he wanted. It was, in its way, a proposal. But in the meantime, they would go on with their lives, see each other at intervals. It would be the kind of romance categorized as an affair; and she would be his mistress. It didn't matter, though. If she could have no more than one day in a year with him, she would have accepted the terms.

She gave him her answer with a touch, and took him in once more.

CHAPTER SEVEN

Through the rest of winter and into the early spring, she saw
Dolph two or three times a month. On occasion he came to
Saratoga to check his breeding operation. The other times he
sent his plane to fly her out to a place one of his horses was
running. Her trips were always initiated with a request made
through the clinic for her veterinary services. Convenient as
this was to their relationship, it wasn't merely a ruse.
Justinean valued her opinion, and consulted her not only on
the health of his horses, but on purchases of new bloodstock.
All the same, centering their meetings around racing activities
minimized the chances of any conflict with Diana. The horses
bored her, Dolph explained; lately, if Diana didn't choose to
stay secluded in their New York apartment or the house in Bel
Air, she would be off shopping in Paris. Or else she would be
'drying out' somewhere, trying to pull herself together.

As the rhythm of their romance became established, Geri
realized how wise Dolph had been to insist she continue with
her career. Her love for him had deepened, but she wasn't
certain the intensity of her commitment could be maintained
if she was with him all the time. Dolph was too strong, too
overwhelming. A time would come for marriage, but she had
to grow first, make a foundation that wasn't built solely on a
man. The anchor was her work. She had virtually taken over
the day-to-day running of the clinic as Tom Graymar's own
absences expanded and multiplied. Tom was being taken away

not only to supervise the building of the new equine clinic in Florida, but he had recently entered the business of importing bloodstock from South America. Every six or seven weeks he went to Argentina or Uruguay and purchased thoroughbreds at prices that were low in comparison with the booming domestic market; the horses were shipped back to the States and resold at substantial profits. Graymar's credentials simplified the necessary health certifications, and his standing with owners made it easy for him to find buyers.

Lucrative as the business seemed to be, Geri thought it was a waste of Graymar's time and talent. He had so much going for him, so many plans related to his own field, why did he need anything more? She said nothing about it, however. Perhaps the business was really a form of recreation to which he was entitled. At the clinic, he still drove himself at a frenetic pace.

On a Wednesday in the middle of April, Dolph called and asked her to fly with him to Europe for ten days.

'I can't, darling. I don't even have a passport.'

'Get your picture taken, tell me where you were born, and I'll have your passport in twenty-four hours.'

He could do it, she knew. He had excellent connections in Washington and any number of employees he could send off to Kentucky to dig out a birth certificate and bring it back. But did she dare to let the records be searched?

Or was it time to tell him everything? Her secrets stood as a barrier to the total, ideal love she wanted.

But even if she were to tell, she thought, it couldn't be now. 'Tom may not let me leave for a whole week on such short notice,' she said.

'Even if it's a professional trip? One reason I'm going abroad, is to see next week's running of "The 2,000 Guineas".' The event was one of the great classics of European racing, he told her, named for the purse that had been offered when it was first run at Newmarket, England, in 1809 — an amount roughly equal to ten thousand dollars, huge for its time. The prize money had been raised since then, of course, and the event remained one of the richest in international racing. 'I'll have a horse running I just bought from an Irish stable. After the race, we could take a trip up to the Curragh — that's the Irish equivalent of blue-grass country. That would make it professional, and Tom could bill me for a lot of your time. Though not the part where I'd fly you over to Paris, buy you a heap of beautiful clothes, and then dine you on so much good food that none of them fit . . .'

It sounded like a dream trip, and Graymar probably wouldn't object as long as he could bill for a lot of her time. The chances were good, too, that a birth certificate could be obtained from a county records bureau without anyone tripping across an arrest warrant that was now seven years old.

Yet something else troubled her, too. 'What about Diana?' she asked quietly. 'What will she do if we're away for so long?'

'Diana's got her own vacation arranged,' he replied, 'another attempt to dry out. I have high hopes for this one, it's a new program run by some health and fitness guru in Colorado. She'll be there for a couple of months. They say he's gotten quite a few drunken movie stars and politician's wives back on their feet. If he can do it for Diana, then I'll feel free.'

She was silent, thinking about what his freedom would mean to hers.

'Come with me, Geri. We haven't had enough time together.'

'Let me speak to Tom.'

Tom Graymar's level of courtesy to Geri had been raised to be consistent with the degree of trust he put in her. When she entered his office he gestured her over to the sofa. Since it was near the end of the day he offered her a glass of wine or sherry from the bar in his office.

'Sherry, thanks.'

As Graymar went to the bar, Geri reflected on how tired he looked. Instead of meeting her as he usually did with his jacket on, in neatly pressed pants, he was in his shirtsleeves, his tie pulled loose and his pants as rumpled as if he had slept in them. Was the work finally catching up with him?

While he stood at the bar pouring glasses for both of them,

Geri said, 'Dolph Justinean has a horse running at Newmarket this weekend. He'd like me to stand by.'

'Sounds okay.'

'I'd also like to take the next week off . . .'

He brought her drink over and sat down. 'Is that all you want?'

'Sure, I'm not feeling overworked — no more than usual, anyway. But since this would be my first time in Europe, I thought I'd do some —'

'I wasn't talking about vacation time, Geri. I mean don't you want anything more than to be Justinean's concubine, his piece of ass on the side?'

She glared at him. Then she realized how foolish she'd been to think he wouldn't have guessed by now. 'It's not like that,' she said sharply.

'Then what is it like? A dream come true, a real Cinderella story? You love him, he loves you and it'll last for ever and —'

'Drop it, Tom. If you can't spare me for a week, say so. But my personal life is none of your damn business.'

'My business, Geri, is exactly what this is about. I've begun to depend on you. Suppose you call in one Monday morning to say "Sorry, Tom, I've just switched over to fucking my billionaire on a full-time basis".' She started to sputter a protest but he rode over her. 'You sold me damn hard on giving you this job, and I'm glad you did. You've got more horse-sense than any other young vet I've come across. Hang in here and you'll be a partner. But don't jerk me around. I don't want to count on you if you've got plans of your own to leave me high and dry.'

Staring at him, she noticed for the first time the streaks of gray in his hair and the lines around his hazel eyes. For all his abrasiveness, she felt a rush of sympathy for him — a dedicated man who had given too much to his work and found nothing to replace it.

'I don't plan to leave you,' she said.

'If you've really latched onto all these solid gold hearts-and-flowers, why on earth *would* you stay?'

'I want a life of my own, and this is a damn good one. There's still a tremendous amount I can learn from you.'

Graymar sat back and sipped at his sherry. He looked very pleased by what she had said. 'But you and Justinean, that's supposed to last, too . . .?' He had switched in a flash to an earnest paternal tone.

His mention of a future partnership made her feel warm toward Graymar, even if he had been gruff and crude. She confided to him that she and Dolph planned to marry eventually, and explained the difficulties involving Diana.

Tom sipped thoughtfully at his sherry for a moment. 'I had a favor to ask Justinean, but since you're so close to him, I thought you might do it. It's something for the business,' he added hastily.

She gave him a hard look, and wondered if the whole conversation had been part of a maneuver. 'What sort of favor?' she asked warily.

'I need a million dollars, quickly. Might be more later —'

'No, Tom,' she came back at once. 'You can't ask me to trade on my friendship.'

'Wait a second, Geri. All I want is a loan, a straight business arrangement.'

'Why not ask a bank?'

He went back to the bar and poured whiskey into his sherry glass. 'I've already used my full line of credit to finance the land and building down in Florida, and buy another site in California.'

'Then what's this money for?' she asked.

'There have been hitches in the Florida construction. The original budget's been eaten up. I'll have to stop unless I get more cash.'

'Would that be so bad, Tom? Maybe you've taken on too much, been driving yourself too hard.'

'Listen, when I built this place there were skeptics who said there wasn't a need for it. I went into hock to do it, but it paid off, and now I see a chance to do the same thing again. I just need help so I can move quickly. The longer building stops, the more money it'll take to start moving again.' He came back to her. 'You know a million dollars is pocket change to

349

Justinean.' He gave her an appealing glance. 'Do it for me, Geri. I'm in a deep hole.'

'You've done a lot for me, Tom,' she replied after a pause. 'Even if I had to shoot my way in here, I still owe you. I'd be glad to put a word in for you with Dolph. I'll do more: I'll arrange a meeting where you can state your case, show him the balance sheets, and ask for the money yourself. But if you're putting me out front, I'm guessing it's because you know it isn't a sound business proposition. I can't set Dolph up for that. I can't go knowing I'm just cashing in on what he feels for me.'

Tom Graymar gave her a sullen look, but then he shrugged. 'Okay, fair enough. Had to ask, though.'

'When do you want to sit down with him? Give me a date and I'll fix it up for you.'

He hesitated. 'I don't know. Maybe this isn't my best shot. Let me sleep on it.'

That sleep, Geri guessed, would last indefinitely. If he hadn't taken up the offer she had made, then apparently she had been right that the risks were too big to appeal to Justinean on a strict business basis.

She got up. 'What about my week off . . .?'

He walked to his desk. 'I'm expecting a shipment of those Uruguayan horses. It may get here on the weekend. I want you here to help check 'em out.'

She advanced on him angrily. 'Oh c'mon, Tom, what kind of petty crap is that? You're only keeping me —'

'Because I need you here,' he cut in.

In her fury, she was ready to take any risks connected to getting the passport. 'I'm going anyway,' she declared. 'Justinean's a client, too.' She started to walk out.

'Go if you want. But then you're leaving for good. I won't take you back.'

She stared at him, immobilized. The disagreement had blown up out of all proportion. 'Tom . . . try to understand. I can't use what I have with Justinean as —'

'I believe I saw you on the surgery roster for six o'clock. You ought to be scrubbing up.'

She glared at him, the words burning on her tongue. *I quit.* But if she did walk out, then what? To build a practice of her own would take time, and meanwhile she would have to fall back on Dolph, surrender her independence.

She clenched her teeth, swallowed her pride, and left Graymar's office without another word.

A shipment of imported horses did arrive on the weekend. There were two stallions and three fillies, all of which had raced in Uruguay. Geri had a brief look at them as they were unloaded from a horse van late Saturday, and judged one four-year-old stallion named Pelota to be a strong and well-formed specimen, a thoroughbred that compared favorably with domestic animals. Glancing over the records, she saw that he had taken victories in many of the richer stakes in the country of origin, and had been in training right up to the time of shipment. She estimated that Tom would be able to sell the horse for anything up to a hundred thousand dollars. The others were older, though, and of more dubious value. The fillies would probably never win a race but might do for broodmares. On this basis Graymar had already sold them to three local breeders at low prices that still netted him a 40 percent return on his investment. The fifth and oldest horse seemed unfit for any purpose. At a quick glance, it made a nice appearance, had a glossy coat and lines similar to Pelota's, but Geri saw marks on the legs — tell-tale patches where the hair had grown in white — indicating they had been 'fired' several times, a sign the bones were weak. The breeding record also showed that he was one of a set of twins. As a rule, twin colts never developed well. An operation Geri had performed several times at the request of a breeder was to 'pinch off' a twin, eliminate either of the two at the embryonic stage. In view of the animal's mediocrity, Geri thought, the name under which he'd been registered seemed fittingly prophetic: Chorizo — after a kind of Spanish sausage.

The arrival of the imports moderated Geri's anger at Tom Graymar. It had been true, at least, that there was real work for her to do; the animals had to be given thorough physicals and certified ready for sale. She was astonished, therefore, when she cut short a lazy Sunday morning to drive out to the clinic, and was met by Marty Shields who told her the task had already been done, and the necessary certificates prepared.

'You did it?'

'Tom and I.'

She shook her head dubiously. 'A total work-up? Blood tests and everything for five horses? You would've had to work half the night and come in early this morning . . .'

'Tom needed it. He's sending those fillies on to their new owners today.'

Matter-of-fact as Marty Shields tried to make it sound, it was unusual to be treating this kind of work on the same basis as an emergency. It seemed to her that Tom had rushed it through out of spite, cutting her out of a chance to make a useful contribution at the same time as he had forced her to stay. For all his talent, she thought, the point might be near where she could no longer excuse his behavior.

She felt so unforgiving that a few days later she had her own mean reaction to a tragic event. Arriving for work on Tuesday morning, she saw a tarpaulin-covered carcass being moved out of the holding barn into a truck operated by a local service that handled horse cremations. She went over to one of the two men supervising the loading.

'What happened?'

'Got cast in his box.'

Normally horses stayed on their feet even when they slept. If they did lie down or kneel down, either because they were ill, or perhaps to scratch a fly-bite by rolling over, then they needed a certain amount of room to get up again. But a horse that settled in the corner of his stall might not have the room — a situation known as being 'cast in his box'. In this position, a horse often panicked, and kicked out so violently at the constraining walls that it could sustain serious injuries.

'A leg . . .?' Geri asked.

'Two. They put him right to sleep.'

'Which horse."

The man referred to a removal order he was holding. 'Stallion named Pelota.'

352

The only decent animal in the Uruguayan consignment, she reflected. The screws on Tom would be even tighter now.

But whatever grudging satisfaction she felt was short-lived. Now that he had been hit by sudden unexpected disaster it was easier for her to feel sympathy for his predicament. And what he had said couldn't be denied: a couple of million dollars would be an easy loan for Dolph to make — no more than the amount of interest he collected every week on the rest of his fortune.

The next time she and Dolph were together, Geri decided, she would find an opportunity to make an appeal on Tom's behalf.

CHAPTER EIGHT

Without Geri for company, Dolph returned immediately from England where his entry in the 'Two Thousand Guineas' had placed second. The next big race in which his stable had an entry was the San Juan Capistrano Handicap at Santa Anita the following weekend, and he invited Geri to join him. He sent his plane to pick her up Friday night.

She said nothing to Tom Graymar about the trip beyond submitting a standard memo to report she'd be away on call to a client. He might have questioned her about it, but by the time the memo went in he had already been called away himself by a client with a horse running in the spring meeting at Aqueduct.

The annual 'San Juan Cap' was being run for the thirty-second time, and remained one of the most gruelling and exciting events in the racing calendar. Limited to horses of four years old or more, it was run on turf — a surface of grass rather than dirt — over a course of one-and-three-quarter miles, one of the longest distances of any major race. The stronger horses, rated according to their previous record, were liable to carry extra weight. The drama produced in such a test of strength and endurance generally exceeded that of shorter races because the outcome was even more unpredictable. Champions over the more common short haul of seven furlongs or a mile might disappear as contenders long before the finish. And horses that had never before been anywhere in the money might find the stamina to burst to the front just as others were failing.

At the stables a few hours before the race, Geri examined Dolph's entry, a large bay named Partisan. Another vet had already pronounced him sound, but it had become a ritual for Geri to add her seal of approval. The horse appeared in excellent condition, though she noticed that a couple of his standing bandages — the leg wrappings put on to help prevent accidental stall injuries — were frayed and pulled loose at the fringes.

'He's been ripping at those with his teeth,' she observed.

'You think it's a symptom?' Dolph asked.

'A good one. He's probably bored with standing around, and raring to go. But I wouldn't want them so torn up he's tripping on the ends.' She called a groom and told him to smear the bandages with red pepper to keep the horse from biting them anymore. Then she and Dolph went to lunch.

At the clubhouse restaurant they were given a table for two right above the finish line. In the past when they had appeared at the California tracks, Dolph had taken trouble to camouflage their relationship by including other guests from his circle of Hollywood business acquaintances. Pleased as she was to be alone with Dolph, Geri also felt apprehensive that their affair might now become fair game for public comment. There were bound to be journalists and gossip columnists lunching in the clubhouse.

Yet Dolph made no concessions. As he pulled a chair for Geri, he kissed the back of her neck. She was unable to suppress a visible shiver of pleasure. She had come to the track straight after the plane landed, and it had been weeks since they'd been together.

After he was seated, she said, 'When the news gets around that your present wife is suing for a divorce settlement of — well, what would you say? — twenty million dollars . . . and you've lost your head over an animal doctor less than half your age, will that send Wall Street up or down?'

'They will tremble and quake, and they will all sell short. But when I look at you, my love, I know there's only one

355

position I should take — and in fact I'm doing it right now.'

'And what would that be?'

'I'm going long.'

She burst out laughing. The sound, full of a lover's open delight, attracted glances from all the surrounding tables and she knew it was useless to hide anything. She let her hands link with Dolph's across the table.

'I missed having you with me last week,' he said.

'We'll have other chances.'

'Of course. But will we be able to use them? Why should you be dictated to by anyone? I've been thinking the time has come for us to stay together.'

'And Diana. Has the time come for her to let go . . .?'

He paused. 'Perhaps we should talk about her later. Today is so beautiful, I feel so good with you, I don't want anything to spoil it.'

Something had happened, Geri realized, so that Dolph no longer felt protective of Diana, was impatient to have her out of his life. And much as she longed to be with him, she felt unsettled by the sudden change in the balances.

Yet she went along with his desire to savor the pleasure of the moment and didn't press for explanations. They ordered lunch, and looked at their programs. There was always a playful competition between them in analyzing the horses, and picking the likely winners.

She had flipped ahead to study the entries for the third race, when one of the names jumped up at her: Chorizo. Could it be the same animal that Graymar had imported? That horse had left the clinic a week ago, she knew; Marty Shields had told her a personal friend of Graymar's had bought it as a saddle mount for his daughter. The Jockey Club registrations kept careful track of names to avoid duplication, nevertheless it seemed inconceivable that the horse running here could be the same one she had seen at the clinic. The third race was a fairly low-grade event — a claiming race, in which all the entries were eligible for purchase by any person willing to pay the price of $25,000 stated in the program — even so the likelihood of such a poor quality horse winning was extremely slim. Certainly not enough to justify the cost of flying it here from the east.

Yet the name was the same . . . and the official track handicappers had obviously studied Chorizo's record and his bloodlines, and had decided that his chances were virtually nil. The betting odds given for the morning listed in the program were 99—1.

As the time for the race approached, the crowd's judgment of the horse made it unanimous. Such a small percentage of total money wagered had been put down on win-tickets for Chorizo, that the odds had soared up to 144—1.

Preoccupied by the mystery of Chorizo, Geri had grown less responsive to Justinean's ebullient mood. Mistaking the cause of her silence, he said abruptly, 'I thought you'd be pleased by the prospect of spending more time together, hiding less . . .'

'I am, darling.'

'But you seem more concerned about Diana.'

She shifted her eyes from the track where the trumpeter had just blown the call to announce the post parade. The horse was forgotten for the moment. 'One of the things that's made it easiest for me to be with you is that I never felt I was stealing you away, forcing you to be unkind to her. When you said you didn't want to leave her until she was able to stand alone, I understood. If you've changed . . . I don't know whether to be glad. I want you, Dolph. But I don't want having you to cause anyone else pain.'

He shook his head slightly. 'What a wonder you are. How many women would ask a rich lover *not* to leave his wife.'

'I'm not asking that. I'm telling you I can be patient, wait for a time when Diana's less weak and vulnerable. Isn't that what you wanted, too?'

He nodded. 'I did. But I've given up believing that time will ever come.'

'Why? What's happened?'

He looked down bleakly and said in a quiet voice, 'Two nights ago she left that treatment center in Colorado, walked out without even packing her bags. Easy enough, the treatment is entirely voluntary. But she didn't come home. She walked down the road, went into a bar — a rough place, I

357

gather — and she proceeded to get drunk. In the course of things, one of the men at the bar approached her, and she went off with him into a back room. When the man came out, he sent another one in . . .' He shook his head and ran a hand across his brow. 'At some point — I don't recall the police report exactly — a few men decided to go together and —'

'Oh God,' Geri whispered, torn by pity.

'Diana screamed and fought them, and someone finally called for help . . .'

'Oh God, the poor woman . . .'

'Poor?' Dolph echoed ironically. 'With all she has, with all the help I can afford to give her, it means nothing. She only wants to sink lower into filth, destroy herself.' He reached across the table again, took Geri's hand in an intense grip. 'You and I are the same, dear Geri. We have risen from mud and ashes, and remade our lives, found greater strength. Perhaps Diana's greatest hope lies in being forced to dig herself out of the mud. But if she will never be strong enough, should we sacrifice our happiness?'

The answer should have been obvious. Yet Geri wasn't sure happiness could last where love was pursued at the cost of claiming a victim. Suddenly their attention was drawn to the track. The post parade had finished and now the track announcer was declaring that the horses were in the gate, under starter's orders. A moment later, the chutes opened and the animals charged ahead.

Not quite seventy seconds later, Chorizo galloped under the wire three lengths in front of the second horse. The cheers were thin. There had been no stretch duel to excite the crowd, and only a handful of bettors had taken a flyer on such a long-shot. Looking at the toteboard as the winning prices came up, Geri noticed that the horse was paying $220 for each two-dollar bet. The odds had apparently lowered yet again as more money was attracted to the horse in the closing phase of the betting.

As Chorizo trotted back past the grandstand to take the salute of the crowd, Geri picked up Dolph's binoculars. When she put them down again, she was thinking of some advice

Nickles had once given her about not romanticizing the sport.

At the end of the day Dolph wanted to get away from the track quickly. He was disgusted with the showing his own horse had made in the San Juan, coming in fifth, and eager to be in some romantic atmosphere conducive to resolving questions about the future that Geri had raised at lunch. From the track, he telephoned the pilot of his plane and told him to prepare for a flight to Hawaii.

But Geri insisted on going to the stables, using as an excuse that she wanted to check Dolph's horse to be certain his poor performance didn't reflect any problem. She kept to herself the suspicions aroused by the third race; without proof she didn't want to set any wheels in motion, especially not the kind of crushing juggernauts controlled by Dolph Justinean.

She examined Partisan briefly, then while Dolph talked to the trainer, she located the barn where Chorizo was being kept. The horse was outside being washed down by a groom. Inspecting the animal closely, Geri noticed that there were no spots on the legs to indicate that they had ever been fired.

She was certain now. A crime had been committed, and she couldn't help feeling partly to blame.

It still weighed on her as she got into Dolph's limousine. She paid no attention when he directed the chauffeur to take them to the airport.

'You've been miles away ever since I told you about Diana,' he said. 'Does it change things so much if I'm ready to marry you?'

'I wasn't thinking about that.'

'Then what is bothering you?' he asked, his tone mixing concern with impatience.

She was tempted to lean on him. But if she told Dolph what was troubling her, the matter would either be taken out of her hands — or she would have to plead with him to join her conspiracy of silence, making him liable to punishment. 'It's something I think I have to deal with myself,' she said.

'If it's a problem, I want to help.'

'I know, darling. And if I need help, you're the first one I'll come to . . .'

359

He gave her one more dubious glance, but then he dropped the subject. 'I've arranged for us to fly to Hawaii for a few days,' he said. 'We can relax — talk out your concern about Diana. And whatever else is on your mind, maybe that will seem less important when you're a thousand miles away on a beach —' She took his hand. 'It sounds heavenly. But . . . can it be for just a day? I have to be back at work on Monday.'

He was silent a moment. 'It's too far to go for so little time,' he said. 'Never mind the trip. We'll stay here, and you can go home tomorrow. To your work.'

He had obviously misunderstood her reticence to share what was on her mind. Once more she considered telling him. But she remembered that standing on her own, having her own life — with all its own problems — might be essential to keeping him.

Yet she noticed, too, that for the first time there had been a slightly bitter edge when he mentioned her work.

He arranged for the same bungalow at the Beverly Hills Hotel where they had spent their first night together. The misunderstanding between them remained unclarified, yet it didn't affect the physical need they felt for each other. They made love all the more savagely and insatiably, as if the heat generated by the friction of skin and muscle could burn off a fog in the mind. Even when she was drained, ready to stop, he wanted to go on and touched her until she was excited again. Soon she was eager to let him use her in the way that he wanted — even though it was something she'd never done before, hadn't thought she would allow. And even after that he wanted her again.

'No more,' she had to whisper at last.

She saw him smile faintly then, and she understood that he had made it a kind of test. He'd needed to show that he could outlast her — and that if she ever let him go, her heart would be the first to break.

CHAPTER NINE

For two days after she returned to Saratoga, Tom Graymar remained away. He was in Florida, his secretary said, busy supervising construction of the new clinic.

Geri had come back from California brimming with righteous anger at the horse scam, and impatient to confront Graymar. Having been the butt of his smug superiority right from the day she'd had to battle her way into a job, it would be sweet justice to lay before him her private knowledge that he had criminally twisted to his own ends the sport he served.

But in the two days that she waited for his return, the fire of anger burned itself out. Left behind was only a puzzled sadness that this talented man had been driven to perpetrate such a scheme. As she went through the routine of her work, Geri was constantly reminded that, whatever his faults, Graymar had more than paid his debt to her: he hadn't only taken her in, but he had given her the rigorous training which had made her so good at her work, and finally demonstrated full acceptance by sharing authority with her.

She owed Tom something in return — and wondered if she hadn't failed to recognize the debt early enough; helping him to obtain a loan from Justinean might have cancelled the need to seek money unlawfully. But how could she make it up to him now? She couldn't ignore what he had done without feeling that she had become an accomplice.

The dilemma kept her awake through all of two nights.

On Wednesday morning, she finally saw his black Jaguar in the parking lot. She headed for her rounds, no longer eager to see Graymar, but at last she realized that the matter couldn't be avoided indefinitely.

At a little after noon, she went to his office. He was at his desk, eating a sandwich as he reviewed the case files that had built up in his absence. She stood patiently silent until he looked up. Even then she couldn't muster her words.

'You all right?' he said. 'You don't look well . . .'

'I'm not. I'm kind of sick about something, Tom . . .'

He pushed the sandwich aside. This tone of personal confession was one that had never been used between them. In all the time she'd been with him, it had been important for her to show no weakness, no emotional frailty. He perceived at once that her confession signalled something extremely serious.

'Sit down, Geri,' he said, frowning with concern.

Another first, the show of avuncular kindness. It made her task all the harder — realizing that if only they could have departed long ago from the harder roles into which they had cast each other, their relationship might have been so much richer. But it was too late now.

She took a seat on the couch. With an effort, she made her eyes meet his. 'I was with Justinean over the weekend,' she began at last.

He looked perplexed for a moment, uncertain of how this piece of information could relate to her initial statement. Then he said, 'If you're feeling bad because you talked to your boyfriend on my behalf, after all, and he refused the loan, don't worry about it. I got my money, anyway. I'm out of the woods.'

She shook her head, and bit her lip to keep herself from crumbling. 'No, Tom. I don't think you are. You see, I happened to join Dolph at Santa Anita; he had a horse running in the San Juan . . .'

He kept looking at her steadily.

'But the big excitement,' she went on, 'was in another race. Do I have to tell you about it . . .?'

362

'Why not?' he said. 'I wasn't there.'

'A bad horse paid such a big price that someone who had any idea it would stomp all over the opposition could've made a killing. A thousand or two put down at the track in small bets — made through a friendly groom or two — a few more thousand laid off with bookies, off-track joints here or there. Not easy to arrange, but if somebody had the right connections . . . the winnings would add up to a million or more. Nice pay-off on a nag named Chorizo. Only that was Pelota, wasn't it, Tom? Chorizo's dead — but you put Pelota's name on the death certificate and made the switch . . .'

There was a long silence. Graymar sat absolutely still, staring at her. Then a rueful smile came very slowly to his lips. 'Of all the luck, huh? I sent the damn horse as far away as I could — and it had to be the same goddamn time you were there . . .'

She sat forward. 'Tom, I wish to God I hadn't been. I wish I didn't know. You've done so much for me. Damn it, I don't like being the one . . .' The words dried up.

'To turn me in — is that what you were going to say?'

'I don't know.' She bolted up and started pacing, all nerves, on the brink of escaping from the room, letting the whole matter get buried. 'I haven't told anyone. I'm not sure that I will . . .'

'Not even Justinean?'

She shook her head. 'I can't bring myself to ruin you, Tom. Especially because I keep thinking I might have done more to save you.'

He rose, came around the desk and stepped into her path. When she tried to move past him, he seized her by the arms, firmly but careful not to hurt. 'So what's this about, Geri? I think I know you pretty well — and I can't imagine you'd completely keep quiet about this. Of course,' he added, with a little smile, 'if I don't know you as well as I think, and you *would* forget it — in exchange for a nice cut . . .'

It was almost a joke, and she smiled sadly in return as she shook her head. And then, as he stood holding her, she looked closely into his face and saw, hidden behind the facade of the

363

man with time for nothing but work, the kindness and humanity that had always been linked somewhere within him to his care for the animals. Suddenly, all the positive feelings she had for him — gratitude and admiration and professional respect — collided with her disappointment and anger. 'Oh damn you, Tom,' she cried out, her voice breaking as she fought not to weep, 'goddamn you, why did you have to do this . . .?'

'You sound,' he said quietly, 'as if you're taking it personally.'

'I am. You were my teacher, my inspiration . . . and you spoiled my belief in you.'

He let go of her and moved away to stare out a window. 'Thanks. It's nice to be an inspiration. Just don't make me your model. I screwed it up, Geri. I tried to do too much, and it caught up with me. It was this or bankruptcy, losing everything . . .'

'I'm sorry, Tom.'

There was a pause, then he turned to her. 'So? What next? You know I can't just pay back the money. Could you go on with things as they were . . .?'

'No. Maybe it's stupid, to think the sport has to be kept honest, but it can only mean something to me if the winning is real. If it can't be, then I'll get out of it.'

His eyes narrowed. 'You haven't told anyone . . . and you said before you wouldn't be the one to ruin me. But you won't stay in racing and hide the lie. Sounds like you're asking me to turn myself in . . .'

'I guess I am.' She hadn't realized it herself until now.

'For Christ's sake, Geri! What do you expect me to say?'

'You've told me I have a gift for what I'm doing. Do you think it should be thrown away?'

'It doesn't have to be. It's only this bullshit nobility of yours that could make that happen. And if it did, would that be so bad? Hell, you've got Justinean. Marry him and you'll be one of the richest women in the world!'

'But I love *this*!' she shouted, pointing at the ground under her feet, the very place where once she had stood to beg for a job.

364

'And you want me to choose your ambitions over mine?'

'I didn't make your mistake, commit your crime. So don't make *me* pay for it. Tom, whatever caused you to misuse your knowledge, whatever you've ignored about the standards of the profession or the sport, one thing I know you haven't forgotten is what it means to love this work, to want to do it more than anything else. Don't take it away from me.'

He gazed at her another second, then turned back to the window and the view of a pasture beyond where some horses had been put out to graze.

'Give me a day,' he said, 'to make *your* choice . . .'

'Tom, I —'

He cut her off, his tone hard again. 'We've talked long enough, Ms Keyes. You'd better get back on the floor. There's a lot of work to do.'

He left the clinic early that day, and didn't come in the next. Was he simply avoiding her? Of course, she had been foolishly naive; she couldn't expect him to ruin himself to save her sense of honor. But she decided to wait one more day before giving up. If Tom hadn't come to her by then, she would go to Dolph. Tom was right. After all, being with Dolph, being his wife someday, was hardly a difficult fate. Not as much of a punishment as Tom would face if he accepted her terms.

But when she returned to her room that evening, Graymar's letter was waiting, delivered by a local florist along with a dozen yellow roses. 'It didn't take me long to decide,' he wrote. 'I only waited to let you know so this would reach you after I'm out of the country. You are good, Geri . . . and maybe it's time I took a long vacation, anyway. I always worked too hard.' Instead of turning himself in, he added, he was giving her his blessing to go to the racing commissioners and tell what she knew. It was probably inevitable they would learn, anyway, he said — revealing then that Marty Shields, who had participated in the scheme in return for a share of the winnings, was demanding an even larger amount than originally agreed in return for not informing the authorities. 'I'd rather see you get the glory,' Graymar concluded, 'than pay the greedy bastard blackmail.' A business card was enclosed with the name and address of a legal firm in New York, and Graymar had scribbled a short p.s. saying he had sent the firm all the documents necessary to transfer title to the clinic to Geri-Jo. It would be hers — as long as she could keep it from being seized to settle his debts.

The horse substitution scam made such a good story that, in many newspapers across the country, it broke from the confines of sports sections and was featured on front pages. Marty Shields was arrested, and an effort was launched to have Thomas Graymar extradited from the country to which he'd fled, Brazil.

Geri had not anticipated the attention that would focus on her personally from the time she contacted the California Horse Racing Board. While she agreed to fly out to the state capital and talk personally with the commissioners, she had asked for closed hearings, and expected she would be able to duck the press. However, a sports columnist with inside contacts had learned about her role, and soon she was besieged at her motel in Sacramento.

As quickly as she fled back to Saratoga, it made no difference. The news value in a beautiful young career woman exposing one of the biggest frauds in the history of horseracing was honey to the bees of the media. The story only got hotter when a Hollywood gossip columnist reported that Geri was romantically linked with Dolph Justinean.

She tried to dodge the cameras, fearful that as her picture was widely circulated it would inevitably be spotted by Kentucky authorities and connected to a fugitive girl being sought under the name of Lockely. But it became impossible to hide; she could only hope that the old arrest warrants had been consigned to some bureaucratic limbo — and that anyone still harboring a personal grudge would miss connecting the escaped mountain girl to the chic, accomplished young woman who appeared in newspaper photographs and television clips.

Still, there were moments when she wished that the story might find its way to her sister. Molly was over twenty-one now; perhaps she had undergone a transformation, would be glad to unite the family again.

In the first weeks after she was written about, Geri was deluged with letters and telegrams and calls. There were hundreds of contacts from thoroughbred owners who had read the laudatory profiles of her career as a vet, and wanted to become clients. There were telegrams of praise from Oakie and Nickles and Ramie and teachers she'd had in veterinary college. She opened each envelope hoping it might be from her sister, but it never was.

Though some odd calls started to come to the clinic, one every three or four weeks. She would pick up a call that had been switched through to her, and there would be a click as the line went dead. Of course, notoriety attracted all kinds of kooks. Did she dare to think it was Molly?

Once, told by her secretary that the young woman waiting on the line had been so impatient to speak to Geri she had refused to give her name, Geri snatched up the phone and began at once, 'Molly, if that's you, please don't hang up . . .'

But it had been the daughter of a small breeder in Canada, simply calling for advice.

Perhaps because her own life finally seemed set on a solid course, thoughts of Molly — of daring to seek reconciliation — began to haunt her persistently. At last, one night, she drove to a public telephone in town, obtained the Parkers' number from long-distance information, and placed a call. The voice that answered was Ed Parker's. Geri stood in the phone booth unable to speak until the voice on the line prodded insistently: 'Hello . . . hello . . .'

'I'm trying to reach Molly Lockely,' she said, adopting a hoarse voice unlike her normal tone.

'Who is this?' The question had a suspicious edge.

Geri fought the urge to hang up. 'Just . . . a friend.'

'A friend'd know that girl hasn't been welcome around here in years.' There was a silence, while Geri weighed how far to go, whether to ask what had happened, where Molly had gone.

Then a strange quality came into the silence — and Geri could feel that Parker had guessed even before he said, in an incredulous hush, 'Geri-Jo . . . that you . . .?'

Hearing the old name — the mountain girl she had escaped

367

from — gave her such an electric jolt that she slammed down the phone, and stood for a long time in the phone booth, somehow afraid to go out into the night.

There was one other after-effect of the publicity she received for exposing the horse scam. Dolph suddenly stopped calling, and when she tried to reach him, he was always unavailable.

As she thought back to their last weekend together, she realized that he had virtually proposed — and he could have easily construed her response as choosing her career over marriage. Being the man he was, he wouldn't have wanted to play second fiddle to her career — especially one that was now entering a boom phase. Probably, too, his gargantuan pride had been wounded by her failure to confide the very matter that had given her career such a boost. Whatever the cause, it seemed their affair was over.

She would have grieved for the end, but the satisfaction she was finding in sole responsibility for the clinic salved the wound. In fact, if it had come to choosing between standing on her own, or standing in Dolph's shadow, then she felt she had made the right choice.

As the surface glitter of sudden celebrity faded to the more lasting polish of a solid and growing professional reputation, Geri immersed herself in the demanding task of digging the clinic out of debt. There was no lack of work, but to take in enough fees she had to work as hard as Graymar ever had, harder. She kept all the technicians and clerks that had worked in the office and barns and labs, but she couldn't afford to hire any associate vets. It would be summer before she could draw from a new pool of graduates who might work for the same coolie wages that she had willingly accepted at the start.

Soon she had to acknowledge that the financial situation wasn't improving. There weren't enough hours in the day to produce the necessary income. She had stepped right into the same crisis that had led Tom Graymar to plead for her help.

It was even harder to do for herself what she had refused to do for him. Day after day went by, and she couldn't pick up the phone to call Dolph. Not for this.

She rented out the mansion where Graymar himself had

lived in splendor as office space for local professionals, and she made cutbacks. The secretary she had inherited from Tom was put on a part-time basis; she reduced the eight-man barn crew to three, easing her conscience by managing to get jobs at nearby breeding farms for all the men she let go. But it was no more than a stopgap.

On the last day of Spring, in the pile of mail she now opened herself each morning, she found a letter from Charlie Hoyt. It began with some light-hearted congratulations for her newfound celebrity, and went on to some assurances that, as far as he knew, there had been no new attention to her case. In fact, he said, he had been able to gain admittance to some of the old case files in connection with another matter, and a discreet check had indicated that her case material had been lost or misplaced — making it unlikely that she would ever be pursued or prosecuted.

Then he went on: 'But I have some less happy news for you, too. The last letter you sent me to forward to Caybie was returned last week to the post office box from which I sent it. The reason for the return, I'm sorry to say, was marked on the envelope — "addressee deceased". I called the institution, and they told me that Cabie Lockely died five weeks ago. The cause, they said, was pneumonia. He's buried there. Let me know if you'd like anything special to be done . . .'

She sat at the desk and cried, remembering the small efforts she had made to maintain the bonds. God! Such a stupid, old-fashioned way to die, she thought bitterly. Pneumonia! The word took her way back to the hollow, a place where an illness like that might often be fatal. But where there was modern medical care, antibiotics, why had he died . . .?

He must have given up, she thought. He had perished from a chill contracted in a hard cold rain almost fifteen years ago.

As if some telepathic distress signal had gone out, he came to her that very night.

He was there when she went home, sitting in shirtsleeves on the steps of her rooming house, his jacket hooked on one finger and slung across his shoulder. Except for the silver hair, he

369

could have been one of the college boys she remembered waiting outside the dormitories at Cornell on warm evenings. She saw no waiting limousine. He wouldn't leave in a rush, she thought, he hadn't come to deliver an ultimatum.

He stood as she turned up the path, and she couldn't stop herself from running to him. Kissing him, being held, for a minute she felt safe. When they sat down together on the steps, and held hands, and inhaled the scents of the June night, even the fear that he would dominate her began to ebb.

'Every day it got worse,' he said. 'I waited for you to call for me. It's been like that for so long, I was always the one people came to — the emperor — that I was sure it would happen. At last I knew it never would. I had to be the one to kneel.' He kissed her again. 'I want you, Geri. On any terms.'

She rested her head on his chest. 'I thought of you every day. Longed to talk to you, touch you . . .'

'Then why —'

'Because I needed you too much.' She looked up at him. 'And I was afraid I needed the wrong thing.'

'Not love?' He smiled. 'Then it must have been money?'

She said nothing.

'For what?' he coaxed.

'To keep the very thing I thought you were ready for me to lose.'

He nodded. 'I wanted more of you, it's true. But I was wrong to press you the way I did. I shouldn't try to take you away from the work you love — not for a day more than you're ready to give me. Go on working. We'll take every chance to be together . . . and take our time about planning the future.' He paused. 'How much do you need? Go on, tell me. You know it's easy for me. I'll write a check tomorrow.'

'No. I don't want you giving me a career as a gift — the way you'd buy a closet full of furs for Diana. I won't kid you: taking your money is the only hope I've got left to make this go. But it's got to be a straight business deal.'

'I never object to that. What's your proposition?'

'Take your pick. You can be a full partner, or I'll pay everything back with interest.'

'Very well,' he said. 'Business. In which case my choice is clear. I owe my success to one rule more than any other. No partners. So it will be a loan. Interest at the prime rate.'

They studied each other for a moment, and shook hands. Then he grasped her arms, and lifted her to her feet. Down the street a pair of headlights went on and the limousine pulled up. It had been there all along, waiting for his signal.

But Geri was content. She had her lover, and she had her career.

It bothered her only a little that Justinean, who hoped to marry her someday, hadn't chosen to be a partner.

BOOK V: *THE BACKSTRETCH*

Keeneland, Kentucky — Summer, 1978

CHAPTER ONE

Flying high over the terrain of thickly forested mountain ridges far below, Geri looked down and wondered if there might be some signpost to mark the place of her beginnings. The cemetery up on the mountain, perhaps — situated, she remembered Pa saying, so God wouldn't miss it. All she could see, however, was the dark green carpet of trees, torn in places by dusty roads. From up here, it was hard to believe anyone had ever lived in those hills.

She was flying alone from Saratoga to Lexington in Dolph's private Boeing 727. Dolph was in Washington trying to head off government interference in a planned merger of his airline, and expected to join her in a day or two. In the meantime, Geri would be a houseguest with Dolph's friend Laurette Wilkey, *grande dame* of the blue-grass racing establishment.

There had been a time when she thought it would be impossible ever to return to the place from which she had fled. Throughout the six years she'd been with Dolph, he had never stopped urging her to join him on a trip to Kentucky — to see the Derby, or go with him to the Keeneland yearling sales. But she had always managed to dredge up some acceptable excuse to stay away — not difficult now that all three clinics were operating successfully. In racing circles it was well known these days that her diagnosis and treatment had lengthened the careers of many valuable animals. Her reputation as a specialist in equine medicine brought requests for her services from all the breeding centers here and abroad. She had also taken up research, and produced innovations — the use of bullet-proof resins developed during the Vietnam war to restore cracked hooves, and progress toward the repair of broken bones that allowed some horses to be salvaged for their breeding value if not for racing — that had put her in demand as a consultant to businesses in the equine field. Her success had made it possible to repay, over the past six years, more than half the two million dollars Dolph had loaned her. Knowing how much in demand she was, Dolph had never been suspicious of Geri's motives for staying away from this part of the country.

Yet she knew her excuses could not go on indefinitely. In the world of thoroughbred racing, Kentucky was still the hub. The more involved she became with the business of racing, the more she felt that her exile from the very heartland of the sport was intolerable.

Even so, she might have gone on postponing a confrontation with the past. Her change of heart had begun with a letter she had received from Sylvia Balkin inviting her to come to New York for a visit. There was a tone of urgency in the letter that caught Geri's attention. Writing in the purple ink she always used on her pale gray monogrammed paper, Sylvia concluded her invitation: 'It has taken me too long to reach out to you, my dear. But if you can find it in your heart to forgive me, there is no one in the world I would rather see right now.'

Their contacts had been few since Sylvia had seemed to cast her out, yet any resentment on Geri's part was gone. She remembered only Sylvia's generosity, the things she had taught her. She wrote back that she would make the trip to New York the following weekend.

When Geri arrived at the huge townhouse, it was not as she remembered it. Margaret, the perky housekeeper was gone, replaced by a stolid, grim-faced practical nurse. The once immaculate decor had gone to seed, carpets and surfaces layered with dust, wilted flowers left standing in vases. Where fine art had once hung on the walls, there were only blank outlines against the faded paint and wallpaper. The art, Geri guessed, had been removed by Phillip and Alice Balkin to grace their own homes.

As the nurse guided her into the elevator, explaining that Sylvia was confined to her bedroom, Geri understood that Sylvia must be dying. Only in such circumstances would she have ceased to cling to the beauty that had always surrounded her. Her letter had evidently been sent out of the human need to close out her life with all accounts settled.

Upstairs, the once elegant bedroom had been converted into a sickroom, antique furniture shoved in a clutter against the walls to make room for oxygen tanks and electronic monitoring equipment. Sylvia lay propped on some pillows, drained of all the vitality that had made her so impressive in the days when Geri had lived with her — and had tried so hard to love her. Her face and neck above the lace-bordered covers were gaunt, the flesh ashen. The hair she had always kept so perfectly coiffed straggled across the satin pillowcase.

The nurse motioned Geri to a chair that had been placed beside the bed. Noting Sylvia's eyes were closed, Geri sat quietly.

'Mrs Balkin,' the nurse said, in a jarringly loud voice. 'You have a visitor.'

A visitor, Geri echoed in her mind. That was all she had ever been. A temporary guest in this woman's emotions.

Sylvia's eyes fluttered open. For a moment, she seemed to have trouble focussing. 'Oh, my dear,' she said at last, with a slight lilt of recognition. 'It's so very kind of you to respond. I know how busy you must be . . .'

The irony of their reversal suddenly struck Geri — that she should be the busy one, while this once powerful and influential woman expressed gratitude for a small gift of time. A lump rose in her throat, and it was a second or two before she could respond with the cool, unemotional tone that she knew Sylvia would appreciate. 'There's nothing more important on my schedule than seeing you.'

Sylvia smiled, like a ballet teacher approving the pirouette of a prize student. 'You look marvelous, my dear. I like that cut for your hair. Who does it for you . . ?'

Geri's hair was usually worn casually loose and long, neatly pinned back if she wanted it out of the way or preferred the more formal look, as now. When it needed cutting, she usually asked one of her assistants, a young woman who had come to the clinic after a stint of being a hairdresser, to do it in her spare time. But Sylvia's compliment reminded her of the time, right after arriving from Kentucky, that she had been given her first real make-over.

'Just a friend,' she said. 'I'm afraid I haven't been back to Arden's since the time you took me.'

'Ah well,' Sylvia said distractedly. 'I don't think I've been there myself for a while.'

There was a pause, the momentous silence of conversation waiting to be steered from weightless small talk into heavy substance. Looking at Sylvia's prostrate form, Geri was struck by the preciousness of each second being wasted.

'You . . . did so much for me,' she said abruptly. 'I don't think I ever had the chance just to say . . . thank you.'

Sylvia gave a very slight nod. 'I never *gave* you the chance, did I?' She sighed. 'Oh, my dear, I'm so ashamed . . .'

'For what?'

'Having once made that lofty pronouncement about the obligation to behave decently, I realize that I never failed so badly in that obligation as I did in the way I abandoned you.'

'Perhaps it was my fault, too,' Geri said. 'I should have been . . . braver, not let myself be chased away so easily. Oh Sylvia . . .' She trailed off. There were words to be said, but the barrier against saying them seemed insuperable.

But then she saw Sylvia's withered hand inch across the coverlet toward her. Geri reached for it, and as their hands clasped, all the feelings Geri had been forced to suppress in the past were suddenly revived. Impulsively, she pulled Sylvia's hand to her face and pressed it against her cheek.

'I love you,' she whispered.

She thought she felt the hand tighten slightly, and then Sylvia spoke, her voice displaying a little more of the old strength. 'Thank you so much, my dear. You can't imagine how much that means to me.'

Geri stayed for another hour, talking mostly about her work, filling in the details of what had happened since she had left.

Toward the end of their time together, Geri had also explored the truth of something that she had understood only vaguely long ago. She recalled that Phil and Alice Balkin had berated their mother for using her money and connections to protect Geri. Aside from sheltering her, Geri wanted to know, exactly what other steps had been taken?

'Why does this concern you now, my dear?' Sylvia asked. 'You haven't been hounded, have you?'

'No. But sooner or later I may want to go back where I came from, and I need to know how safe I'd be.'

Sylvia confessed then that not long after she had taken Geri into her home, she had paid three hundred thousand dollars in bribes to arrange for all papers and other evidence pertaining to 'The State of Kentucky vs. Geraldine-Josephine Lockely' to disappear from official files. Exactly how the money was disbursed to accomplish this, she never knew. All Sylvia's dealings had been with a powerful New York lawyer known to have shady political connections.

As evening came and the room darkened, Sylvia had drowsed off. Geri stood and leaned over to kiss her, then stopped herself, oddly inhibited by a feeling that it was taking advantage of Sylvia while she was helpless. She stood by the bed for another minute and, with a comb from her purse, arranged Sylvia's hair in the perfectly neat upsweep she had always worn.

Silently, Geri promised that she would return. But it was only three days later that she saw the obituary — published in the Saratoga paper because of Sylvia's onetime prominence as a stable-owner. Neither Phillip nor Alice contacted Geri about the funeral, and she didn't go. Her farewell to Sylvia had been all it could be.

Assured by Sylvia's confession of her role in suppressing the legal documents, Geri felt that a legal basis for any prosecution no longer existed, and she might return to Kentucky in relative safety.

And then she had been provided with a professional reason

that clinched her decision. Prior to the annual yearling auctions at Saratoga three years ago, she had been asked by a couple of clients at the clinic to examine the colts for sale and provide purchase recommendations. The horses she had recommended had gone on to perform well, one of them as the leading money-winner among the two-year-olds. Since then her advice had been in demand. While there were many bloodstock agents whose business was to assess young horses and bid on them for clients, Geri's veterinary knowledge made her judgment especially useful. In return for fees as large as ten thousand dollars, she was often engaged to render opinions for clients prior to auctions in Saratoga and Florida and California.

Keeneland, however, she continued to avoid.

But a month ago, she had been visited at the clinic by a man who introduced himself as an emissary from a sheik of one of the oil emirates, Abdul Ibn-Rashid al-Sadir. Having just decided to take up the gentlemanly sport of thoroughbred racing, the emissary explained, Sheik al-Sadir wished to offer Geri $50,000 to make an appraisal of all this year's Keeneland offerings and select the three most promising colts for his purchase.

Dolph's 727 taxied across 'Blue Grass Airport' and pulled into a space in a rank of twenty other private jets. Though the Arab oil embargo of '73 had produced an economic upheaval from which the rest of the country was still feeling aftershocks, here at Keeneland there was no sign of hardship. For these few hot July days, the Keeneland Select Summer Sale would bring together many of the wealthiest men in the world for the purpose of buying year-old, untested thoroughbreds at auction. Nor would the high-bidders be restricted merely to men. There were a number of women who ran successful stables and acquired new stock at Keeneland. Among those who had sometimes been active buyers — not always bidding for themselves, but through 'bloodstock agents' — were Elizabeth Arden and Queen Elizabeth II.

As Geri walked through the terminal building, she searched the faces of other travelers arriving and departing — thinking of Molly, wishing that some freak coincidence might bring them together again. If time had prepared Geri to forgive, wasn't it possible Molly also longed for reunion? It occurred to Geri that during this visit she might try to track down her sister.

Outside the terminal, beyond a line of limousines and liveried chauffeurs, Geri saw a black man holding up a piece of cardboard with hastily penciled lettering that read 'Dr Keyes'. The man was dressed in barn clothes, and he led her to a Ford station wagon so old the side paneling was made of real wood.

It was only a short ride from the airport before Geri saw a large group of barn buildings distinctively painted sky blue with red trim. How many times she had passed them when she lived here, the very symbol of all that had seemed unattainable.

Its fortunes had declined in recent years, but nothing could dim the record that Kismet Farms had once compiled as the most successful racing stable of them all. Two and three decades ago, Kismet horses had consistently garnered Horse of the Year awards and been led to the winner's circle in every top event. Its owner, Mrs Laurette Wilkey — 'The Queen of Kismet' — had worn the twin laurels of being the most influential woman in horseracing, and the unchallenged leader of Blue Grass society. Though it was her husband, a wealthy inventor of patent medicines, who had started the stable, it was only after his death in the early 'thirties when Laurette took over the enterprise that it had achieved its greatest days. In recent years, as other wealthy women had involved themselves in the sport, and as Kismet Farms had failed to produce so many astounding champions, Laurette Wilkey's influence on racing and breeding had slipped. But she had yet to lose one iota of her power to make the rules on the social track where wealthy and well-born challenged each other for acceptance and rank.

The main house of Kismet Farms was not a mansion, but a rambling white colonial with the homey look of a farmhouse that had been added onto by many successive generations. No starched servant opened the door. The man who had collected

Geri at the airport led her into the house himself, and pointed her toward a room at the end of a corridor. 'You might enjoy waiting in there,' he said, 'I'll get Missus Laurette.'

Moving along the hallway, Geri passed the open doors of an office, a living room, and a dining room. All conveyed an atmosphere of unpretentious coziness, with many pieces of simple wood furniture, comfortable padded chairs, and carpets that looked well worn. Being around Dolph, however, had taught Geri to recognize that the carpets were fine Turkish orientals worth up to a hundred thousand dollars each, and every item of furniture was an irreplaceable antique.

Turning into the room where she'd been told to wait, she saw floor to ceiling shelves crammed with gleaming trophies awarded in the winners' circles after every important race. Here, in multiple, were the golden cups presented at the Kentucky Derby, the Jockey Club Gold Cup, replicas of the famous Woodlawn Vase given to the winners of the Preakness, and of the Man O' War Cup for winners in the Travers, and innumerable gold and silver bowls and plates from lesser events. Geri noted sadly as she studied the race dates engraved on the trophies that none had been won more recently than twelve years ago.

She heard footsteps in the corridor, and turned as Laurette Wilkey came into the room. Though she had turned the corner of seventy, Laurette Wilkey was buoyant and moved so briskly that a bob of her curly white hair kept falling over her eyes, requiring her to flip it back. Short, plump and rosy-cheeked, she wore a plain green dress that looked rather frumpy, set off by an old-fashioned cameo brooch pinned over her breast.

'Dr Keyes — I'm so glad to meet you at last.' She smiled as she extended her hand in greeting. 'You know, I've been asking Dolph for years to wangle you into coming down here. A woman of your interests should have come to Lexington long ago.'

Responding instantly to her warmth, Geri took a risk. 'I did, actually. I spent several years here when I was being raised.'

'Is that a fact? And this is your first time back . . .?

'Yes. But I never forgot the sight of your red and blue barns.

382

I can't tell you how many times I rode past this place, and wished I could look inside.'

'Well, you should have walked right up to the door and knocked. You know, Geri — may I call you that? — all you'd have to do is say you're a horse-lover and you'd never be turned away from my doorstep.'

As she looked into the woman's twinkling blue eyes, Geri could tell she was sincere: Laurette Wilkey liked and trusted people, and didn't wish to be cut off.

For a little while they stood by the trophies and Geri prompted her hostess with questions about some of the famous horses and their racing careers. Obviously delighted by a young woman's reverent knowledge of the sport, Laurette Wilkey overflowed with stories of the past, and an affection for Geri blossomed quickly. Soon it was time for lunch, and they sat down at a table on an outside patio that overlooked the rolling pastures. Geri's avid interest in the running of the famous stable prompted her to ask Laurette if she had any help in making the many decisions. Laurette's reply was tinged with sadness. While she had advice from her farm manager and trainer, she said, there was no one else to take an interest in the stable. Of her two sons, one had gone to West Point, served as an officer in Vietnam, and by the end of the war had been promoted to an important desk job at the Pentagon. The other had died in an automobile accident when he was in his teens.

'He was the one who loved the horses,' Laurette said wistfully. 'I do wish there was someone who'd carry it on, bring in new energy. I've been asked often to sell — that's how I met Dolph, you know, he wanted to buy me out. But I can't let go of this — it's so much a part of me. And the traditions, you see, I hate to think of the traditions dying. Racing shouldn't be run simply as a business, the way so many people do these days . . .'

The sentiment touched Geri. But she knew, too, that Laurette Wilkey had paid a high price for her adherence to tradition. In sharp contrast to the majority of other big breeders Laurette had not followed the new trend toward syndicating winning horses, selling shares in them and their breeding rights, then using the income to purchase fresh bloodstock. It remained the custom at Kismet Farms to retain sole ownership of every horse, and develop the horses it raced entirely from its own stock. Though some of their yearlings were also sold at auction, Kismet did not bring new horses into the stable by buying at auction. The result was a weakening of strains, and the absence of winners in recent years.

After only an hour, Geri already felt tremendously fond of Laurette. While she was at the auctions, Geri thought, she might look out for some good yearlings beyond those she would recommend to the sheik.

In the living room that evening over a pre-dinner drink, Geri met the two married couples who were Laurette's other houseguests for Sale Week. A middle-aged man and his wife were introduced as Malcolm and Elaine Peabody, and a glossier young couple in their early thirties were Neil and Gillian Langham. Geri recognized the names of both men. Langham, a boyish blond Englishman who had made a fortune as an electronics entrepreneur, had invaded the thoroughbred market with a splash in the past two years, paying the top prices for yearlings that he then brought back to England. Malcolm Peabody was among the most successful contemporary painters of racehorses and racing scenes. Working in the same genre for which George Stubbs had become known two hundred years ago, Peabody had built a reputation that kept him busy traveling around the world, doing portraits of prized horses for thoroughbred owners on lucrative commissions. In fact, there were a number of his oils in Laurette's house. But in Geri's opinion, Peabody was merely a competent painter, without any of the unique verve that characterized the Stubbs' paintings that adorned Dolph's walls. She was put off, too, by his inflated ego and an affected flamboyance that seemed designed to advertise himself — the purple velvet suit he wore, and his long hair and Vandyke beard.

Sitting with these people left Geri wondering again if her own priorities had gotten skewed. She loved her work, but at times its linkage with so much wealth, with people who seemed to feel so little passion or responsibility for anything besides winning horse races or winning a name for themselves, repelled her. She had strived for and welcomed wealth and position and a degree of fame. But at times she felt her hunger for those things could have taken her off on a detour away from something that might be even better. What had she dreamed of finding so long ago when she had first passed through this landscape and had pleaded with Pa to stop the truck? It was something more, she felt, than what she had now.

But had it really been here? And, if it was, could she still find it?

CHAPTER TWO

Geri came out of a light, tense sleep, puzzled for a second by the lacey cloud that seemed to be hovering just above her. Then she realized it was the canopy of a four-poster bed in a guest bedroom at Kismet Farms. It was still hard to believe that she was in Kentucky. She got up and went to the window. It was dawn. Outside, mist swirled over the hills, clouding the horizon so the lines of white fencing looked like floating highways vanishing into a lavender sky.

Restless, she dressed and went out. Yesterday during an afternoon tour of the stables, Laurette had shown her the barn where the saddle horses were kept, and told her to feel free to use one any time she wanted. At the barn, one of the early-rising stablehands picked out a palomino pony and saddled it.

As she cantered across the rolling green hills into the sun, full and golden as it crested a low hill, Geri felt the tension slip away — replaced by impatience with herself for the discontent that had plagued her. Did she have a right to want more than life had already given her? It was wrong to come back thinking that everything left unfinished and imperfect could be done over, put right. That would never be possible. Roaming the pastures where the ghostly shapes of horses drifted in the haze, she was finally calmed, reconciled to past and present and less anxious about tomorrow. It was time, she thought, that she and Dolph married and began a family.

As she neared the corner of a pasture where two fences

converged and prepared to turn her horse, she suddenly noticed the figure of a man standing at an easel. His back was to her, and he was dabbing on paint with such concentration that he evidently hadn't heard the approach of her horse. He went on capturing the view in front of him, a mare and her young foal grazing in an adjoining pasture. The rising sun turned all the dew on the hillside into tiny lenses that magnified and refracted the blazing light. Trapped in the splintered rays, the silhouetted horses seemed to be translucent mythical creatures stranded in a sea of gold.

Reining her horse to a stop, Geri sat quietly in the saddle and watched the painter's hand laying down a whirlwind of abrupt strokes in a dozen colors to convey his impression of the dazzling moment. The image, as he interpreted it, was breathtaking. Evidently Malcolm Peabody, like her, had gone looking in the morning mist for a truer definition of himself and his aspirations. What a shame, Geri thought, that he had never exhibited these rougher but more original images, and went on instead grinding out the conventional commissions he had no fear of selling.

For the few minutes that the horses stood etched in a field of light, the painter worked feverishly to save the apparition. Then the angle of the sun changed, the scene in the pasture became real and commonplace. The artist's hand fell to his side, and his whole body sagged. Peabody appeared to have poured his mind and spirit fully into that burst of creation.

Geri had always enjoyed living with the art in Sylvia's home, and had appreciated Justinean's marvelous collection, yet she had never before had any desire to own art herself. This painting excited her, though, and she was eager to buy it. Yet she sensed that it would be wrong to speak now. The painter's act had been no less intensely private than if he had been making love, caught at the instant of orgasm. Yet how could she ride away without drawing his attention? He was no longer lost in concentration.

She was still debating what to do, when the painter raised his wet brush and abruptly took a couple of long diagonal swipes across the width of the canvas, crudely 'x'-ing it out. Shocked,

Geri stiffened in the saddle, and barely stifled a gasp.

Unsettled by her shift of weight, the horse snorted and took a couple of quick prancing steps forward. By reflex, Geri murmured a soothing, 'Whoa there, boy . . . settle down . . .'

The painter turned abruptly. 'What the hell are you doing there?' he demanded, savagely as a soldier finding an enemy within his perimeter.

Geri said nothing, stunned as she was to discover that the man glaring at her furiously was not Peabody, after all. He had no beard, and he was younger than Peabody by at least twenty years. A worker on the farm, perhaps, who painted as a hobby? Or merely a trespasser in search of a picturesque scene?

At last she summoned her voice. 'I'm sorry, I tried not to disturb you . . .'

Flinging his brushes down into a paint box, he went on, muttering half to himself. 'Christ, if I'd wanted an audience, I could stand in a goddamn store window and do this, couldn't I? Came out here to be alone — crack of dawn, for chrissakes —'

His rude scolding would have ordinarily provoked her own tough response. Yet she could sympathize with his fury; however unwittingly, she had violated his private act of creation.

He was ignoring her now as he folded up his portable easel. Even with his features clouded by anger, she could see he was attractive. Green eyes, curly brown hair worn a bit too long and shaggy — not a painter's affectation, she thought, just an absence of vanity — a strong jaw and a nose that wasn't quite straight, hinting at some rugged encounters in the past. His clothes were like a student's, faded tan corduroys, a shapeless navy cable stitch sweater, loafers worn without socks; but he seemed too old to be in school. Just over thirty, she guessed.

After another moment, Geri dismounted. She dropped the reins so the horse could graze, and walked over to the artist. 'Look, I don't blame you for being annoyed. But it wasn't deliberate, I wasn't . . . spying on you. I just happened to be out for a ride and I couldn't keep myself from watching.'

He went on tying easel and paint box together with a piece of twine. Now her irritation crept up. 'If it's so hard to bear being watched, maybe next time you're out at dawn you'll post a few detour signs in a big wide circle. Just in case any other insomniacs turn up while you're around.'

'Good idea,' he murmured without looking up.

She almost got back on the horse, then decided there was nothing to lose if she ended by saying what she had wanted to start with. 'By the way, I would have bought that painting . . .'

He gave her a smile as faint as the last remnant of morning mist, but said nothing. After putting a last knot in the twine, he lifted his bundle and walked away. Her curiosity was aroused now. She picked up the reins and led the horse behind her as she followed the artist. He was tall and had a long stride, and it stretched her to catch up with him.

'I wasn't kidding. I liked it very much.'

He walked on a moment. Then he said, 'I imagine you're in the gang of high-rollers that's here for the auctions . . .?'

'I wouldn't call myself a high-roller. But, yes, I'm involved with the horses . . .'

'You wouldn't expect any of those fancy breeders to send a colt to sale if it had only three legs. It may be just good enough to stand up, but not to do what it's been made for.' He stopped and looked at her squarely. 'Same with what I did there. I wouldn't have sold that painting, because I knew it hadn't been made right.'

'Isn't it enough if somebody else likes it?'

'Nope.' He started walking again. They were heading not toward the house, but the stables and outbuildings. He was one of the workers, apparently, a gifted amateur.

'Suppose you're wrong,' Geri said. 'I mean, maybe you're not the best judge of whether your work is good enough to sell.'

'Best I've got.'

'A little advice wouldn't hurt, a chance to learn. There's a very well-known painter who happens to be a guest of Mrs Wilkey's right now. I could arrange for you to meet him . . .'

He paused to study her curiously, then broke into loud laughter.

Flushed with annoyance at the way her offer of help had been mocked, Geri snapped, 'Okay, you're a genius and you can't learn a thing. Excuse me for trying to throw a monkeywrench into your paintbox, Mr Van Gogh.' She whirled away and prepared to mount the horse.

But he caught her arm. 'Hey, wait a second . . . I appreciate the thought. That's not why I laughed.' The sharp edge had gone from his voice. 'I guess I ought to introduce myself. I'm Bill Quinn . . . Mal Peabody's assistant . . .'

'Oh,' Geri said sheepishly. She replied with her own name as she shook his hand, and examined him more closely. His grip, she thought, felt strangely weak for a man of his build and energy.

They started walking again. 'I should apologize, too,' Quinn said, 'for being so touchy back there.'

Geri smiled acceptance. 'Artists have a right to be temperamental.'

'Maybe, but I can't use that excuse. I'm just an artist's assistant.'

It touched Geri that Quinn kept putting himself down. First destroying his painting, now downgrading his position. 'What does a painter's assistant do?' she asked.

'You name it. Prime his canvasses, clean his brushes, carry his suitcases. He's even asked me to trim his beard.' He gave a deprecating chuckle. 'And then, of course, there's the paintings . . .'

She gaped. '*You* paint his pictures?'

'No, it wouldn't be fair to say that. I'm just a modern example of a very old tradition. The great masters — Rubens, Rembrandt, those guys — they always had a few students around to help fill in the big unimportant areas around the fringes. Didn't you know . . .?' Geri shook her head. 'It was the first assembly line. The big cheese would do a sketch, then have his apprentices — his "school" as they called it — paint all the curtains, the hems of the dresses, maybe the faces of a background crowd. The master would save his own precious time for the central figures and faces — the Madonna, a king, whatever. Well, Peabody's the same. He does the horse, and a jockey if there is one, I paint the grass it's standing on, the trees, a crowd watching the race, all that junk. That way he can handle three or four times as many commissions as he could on his own.'

Geri detected an undertone of scorn. He had not used the work 'junk' as idle slang. 'Do you learn anything doing that?'

He hesitated. 'Not as much as I might've from Rembrandt.'

'Then why do it? Looks to me like you've got just as much talent as Peabody.' She looked at him steadily. 'More.'

'Talent is half the story,' he answered soberly. 'I'm still short on technique.'

'What I saw looked pretty good.'

'I can't settle for that,' he erupted, temperament flaring again. 'I've got to be as good as I know I can be, as good as I *was*.'

'What do you mean?' she said. 'As good as you were . . . when?'

He sighed. 'It's a long story.'

'Short stories are usually jokes.' Impulsively, she tugged at his arm, stopping him. 'Tell me . . .'

He gazed into her eyes as though gauging her sincerity. Then he started ambling again, telling it plainly, without any hint of self-pity. He'd shown a talent for drawing back when he was in high school in Pennsylvania, and had decided then he wanted to try making a living with art. It didn't make sense to his parents, not as work — his father labored in a steel mill — but since he kept winning scholarships, to college then to Carnegie Institute of Art, they didn't complain. At twenty-four, he was placing works in group shows and selling to a few collectors. Small sales, but he was launched. Then, eight years ago, his deferments had run out, and the draft had called him for Vietnam. Halfway through his tour of duty, his squad had been ambushed, and the shrapnel from an incoming mortar had torn his shoulder open — his right shoulder.

'The good part,' he said, 'was that there wasn't even enough muscle system left to pull a trigger. The bad part was I couldn't hold a brush, not even enough fine control of the arm left to do it the way Matisse did when the arthritis locked his fingers — with a brush strapped to the wrist.' He'd spent a couple of years doing therapy to restore his right arm to the degree of usefulness it had now. At first, he'd hoped it might recover completely. When he realized it would never be good for anything but carrying his paintbox, he almost gave up. Then one of his old teachers had gotten him the job with Peabody.

'It was a kind of an ass backwards inspiration,' he said.

He left the phrase unexplained, but Geri understood. Seeing Peabody get paid a fortune to paint ordinary pictures to order had goaded Quinn into trying again. Now, too, Geri realized why his handshake had seemed so feeble — and how he had solved his problem. 'So you've learned all over again,' she said, 'with your left hand.'

'No,' he said. 'I haven't learned — I'm learning.'

'Well, it looked to me like you're making terrific progress. It's a shame you destroyed this morning's work. Maybe you're expecting too much of yourself now — I mean, asking yourself to reproduce exactly the same technique you had before. While you work for that, you might be overlooking something just as valuable, or even better.'

'No,' he said flatly.

His stubbornness grated on her. Raised echoes of Pa. 'How can you be so sure? This might be a different style, not as fine, but it could be just as effective, perhaps even —'

He rounded on her. 'Look, what the hell do you know about it? You think what I did just now was pretty good — and that's enough for you. But you never saw what I could do before. So whatever you think doesn't matter a damn. I have to suit myself!'

He paused for a second, and she thought he might be considering another apology, but then he swallowed it. 'Excuse me,' he said quickly. 'I'd better get to the job. The boss has got a few acres of grass that need painting.' He stalked away toward one of the small houses where the stablehands lived.

She glared after him for a moment. What did she know about art? All right, Mr Quinn, not a blessed thing. But so what? Artists be damned!

She could hardly wait now to start her day's involvement with the things she *did* know about.

The Keeneland Select Summer Sale ran for four days. From morning until late afternoon, potential buyers wandered from one barn to the other on the backstretch of the Keeneland racetrack, deciding which horses to bid for at the nightly auctions. Draped above the doors of a number of barns were banners naming the occupying breeder: Claiborne Farms . . . Gainesway . . . Spendthrift . . . Bel Air . . . Tom Gentry . . . Jonabel, and any others with enough horses consigned to occupy a full barn. Scores of other breeders with consignments of only one or two horses shared barn space. Most had been in business for generations, some were newcomers, using new ideas to market horses as if they were merely cars — like videotapes of the yearlings shown on TV monitors set up under the trees.

In the tree-shaded lanes between the barns, horses were paraded for the inspection of men and women with millions to spend for any animals that caught their fancy. Japanese electronics tycoons, German munitions magnates, the heirs of old Jewish banking families from England and France, and the sons of Arab sheiks drowning in oil wealth made within the past decade, all mingled companionably, national and political differences forgotten as they exchanged views on the horse-flesh prancing around them.

The atmosphere might seem relaxed, but it was important to be well prepared and advised. For the most essential rule of this market was 'buyer beware'. No guarantees were given that even the most beautifully formed animal from the finest bloodlines would perform well or remain sound. Nor that the horse came to market without pre-existing problems. The burden was on the buyer to know what he was paying for. If a horse had slightly crooked legs, anyone fool enough not to detect it was fair game — and if the problem escaped notice because a breeder cleverly arranged for his 'prize' yearling to be led from the barn by a fat groom who walked so slowly alongside as to obstruct the view . . . well, that was also part of the fun.

Thus, the $50,000 Geri was being paid to survey the selections at Keeneland and advise Sheik al-Sadir was a small insurance against mistakes that could be far more expensive. Almost every millionaire buyer leaned on the judgment of at least one person who could effectively judge a yearling by scanning the lines, the muscling, the curve of a neck or a leg.

Before touring the barns, Geri bought the sale catalog and stopped in a tent set up as a cafe to sit down and make some notes. The catalog listed each animal to be sold, its consigning breeder, the barn where it was on view, its sire and dam, and at least three more generations of sires and dams on each side. As yet unnamed, most yearlings were also described in the most basic terms of color and sex — 'bay filly', or 'gray colt' — and identified by a 'hip number' (the term derived from the Greek word for horse, *hippos*, and not from the fact that when the horse appeared in the sales ring it wore the number sheet on its flank).

Having acquainted herself with the basic information, Geri began to tour the barns. Recognized by many other browsers, she was often hailed, slyly prodded to offer an opinion, and interrogated on her own business at Keeneland. In each case, she confessed only to being here 'to meet a friend', then quickly found a polite excuse to slip away without offering any judgment of the horses. It was a condition of her deal with the sheik that she would keep his sponsorship confidential; it was also understood that her choices would be kept secret so as not to create bidding opponents at the evening auctions.

Through the day, her trained eye studied one horse after another. Flat muscling, angular lines and well-balanced bone formation marked the durable long-distance runner; more prominent muscling, a short back, and well-developed hind end were characteristics of the 'sprinter', a speed horse good only for shorter races. To judge each animal adequately, it was best to cease seeing it as an entity, and perform a mental dissection, studying it part by part. And even these separate parts had to be sub-divided, their components studied. A leg couldn't be viewed on its own, but according to the formation of each bone or joint — stifle, forearm, gaskin, knee, hock, cannon, ankle, pastern, coronet. Every one, to some degree, could affect performance.

Of course, even the most experienced judges could think they spotted greatness, and be dead wrong. Record prices were paid for colts and fillies that not only proved to be duds on the track, but worthless in the breeding shed. Conversely, Kentucky Derby winners had been bought for less than $2,000. Still, the percentages were vastly improved by knowing the value of anatomical characteristics. The sheer beauty of a horse was important, but wise horsemen were even more concerned that it should — as they said — 'pick to pieces well'.

As much as she concentrated on the task at hand, each time Geri walked from one barn to the next, she found her thoughts wandering back to the unsatisfactory encounter with Bill Quinn. In retrospect, she felt more forgiving of his final explosion. After what Quinn had been through in Vietnam, didn't he have a right to be sensitive and scared about his new work? She could understand how mere compliments might have seemed irritating. A few nice words from a stranger who'd looked over his shoulder could hardly compensate him for the grief and sweat he'd poured into resurrecting a part of his soul he'd given up for dead. If only there were something she could do that would have more meaning than words, yet not offend his raw pride . . .

No idea came to her, however, and she didn't spend more than an occasional few seconds worrying about it. At the end of each thoughtful walk, she would be back in front of another barn, with another crop of yearlings to inspect.

And finding the answers here was more important.

CHAPTER THREE

When she returned to Kismet at the end of the day, Geri found Dolph having tea with Laurette in the living room. The last time she had been with him was in Saratoga two weeks ago, and as he stood up from the sofa her first urge was to run and embrace him. In Laurette's presence she hesitated . . . until Dolph moved toward her and opened his arms. Then all reticence flew out the window and she kissed him fervently, overtaken by a hunger for him that surprised her with its intensity — until she heard the clink of a teacup in its saucer, and propriety reasserted itself.

Still flushed, she eased away from Dolph, and cast an apologetic glance at Laurette, who was discreetly devoting herself to refilling the teacups with no less concentration than a burglar trying to crack a safe.

'Don't worry, my love,' Dolph said. 'We don't have to be shy in front of this lady. She knows all about us. In fact, I've just been telling her a few things about us that even *you* don't know . . .'

'That sounds intriguing,' Geri said. 'When do I get to hear my own private secrets?'

'All in good time.' He led her back to the sofa. 'First, tell us about your shopping expedition.'

'Yes, do,' Laurette seconded. 'Any horses catch your fancy?'

'A few,' Geri admitted. 'It depends on the prices, of course. I have a hunch that the crowd is ready to spend a lot more than

396

last year — and *that* was a record. There are more Japanese, more Arabs, more talk about cutting into the American monopoly on great bloodstock. The pursuit will be very hot, and then it becomes a question of whether these horses can give their own prices a good run for the money. There are still times I can't believe any of these animals can be worth what they cost.'

'Price is beside the point,' Dolph said. 'If you want the horse, you pay whatever it takes to get it. I'm sure your sheik would agree. A million dollars, two. It's nothing to him.'

Geri flashed a wry glance at Dolph: what was true for the sheik was true for him as well. There was, of course, a sensible side to the large sums of money invested in thoroughbreds. The government had made liberal tax rules governing the purchase of racehorses — allowing depreciations over the life of the horse, and for all the expenses of running the farms — so that owning and breeding them provided a desirable shelter. Still, at what point would the readiness of men like Dolph, chasing hungrily after whatever they wanted, throw the market out of kilter?

'I had a trainer,' Laurette remarked, 'who used to say that there wasn't a horse in the world worth more than fifty dollars . . . plus whatever the traffic would bear. That sums it up for me. As long as there are people with too much money, our business will get crazier and crazier. But I personally refuse to get swept up in the madness.'

There was a pause as both Dolph and Geri considered telling Laurette that she might be making a mistake to avoid the sales.

'There are always bargains, too,' Geri said. 'While all the big bidders are chasing after a few glamor horses, some good solid prospects are going to be sold cheap.'

'Well now,' Dolph said, leaning closer, 'that has the ring of reliable inside information. You've spotted some diamonds in the rough . . .?'

'There are no sure things,' Geri said evasively. She could feel that Dolph was on the verge of asking for details.

'You're not going to be coy with me, are you, my love? Tell me what you've seen.'

Laurette intervened. 'Dolph, don't be wicked. You know Geri-Jo's under obligation to advise this Arab fellow . . .'

'Only to give him her top three choices.' He looked intently at Geri. 'If you have more than that number, you could . . . toss me the crumbs.'

'I haven't sorted out my preferences yet,' Geri said, uncomfortable with Dolph's persistence. For the first time, their interests had come into conflict and she could feel his underlying determination not to be thwarted.

'But when you do . . .' he coaxed.

'Darling . . . I told you price might be a factor in my selection. I may have my eye on more than three horses, but I ought to reserve them for my client. He might want a choice according to how the sales go, and we won't begin to see the trend until the first auction tomorrow night.' Dolph looked displeased. Before he could protest, she hurried on. 'The final choice won't be up to me, in any case. Al-Sadir has got a bloodstock agent. I'll tell him the horses I like, and he'll handle the actual bidding. He ought to appreciate having one or two extras as a fall back.'

'You were paid to pick only three,' Dolph said pointedly.

Now he wasn't just pouting over her secrecy, she thought, but chiding her for a sloppy attitude about business — selling something for nothing. She felt he was unfairly turning her desire to operate independently into a false test of loyalty.

Laurette piped up diplomatically, 'Dolph, you've been an extremely clever buyer completely on your own. It doesn't matter whether you have anyone else's advice or not. You're not coming in here for the first time like sheik what's-his-name . . .'

Dolph's frown relaxed into a smile. He turned to Geri, and took her hand. 'It's dealing with all these idiots and madmen in Washington . . . after a couple of days with them, I lose the knack of thinking sensibly about anything. Of course, I shouldn't be prying. Forgive me, darling.'

The little crisis was over. They happily accepted Laurette's encouragement to go up to their room and spend some time alone before dinner.

They were hardly through the door when he seized her, and began kissing her neck and breasts as he unbuttoned the top of her white linen Chanel suit. Excited by his sudden need for her, untouched for weeks, she gave herself over to him. But even as she responded she was surprised by his ardor. It wasn't Dolph's way, usually, to explode in a frenzy of desire. He had a slower rhythm, liked to orchestrate a long steady crescendo of sensation through foreplay to orgasm. He could lie naked with her for hours, deftly applying a repertoire of touches and kisses over every part of her body, then give himself over to the same langorous caresses of her hands and mouth, before they would finally build to that need to join, to fully entwine inside each other, slick and tight and clinging as they climaxed together. He took shamelessly and hurriedly from the rest of the world to make an empire, but he was tirelessly patient and giving in bed.

But now he yanked her skirt down, kissing her body as he undressed himself and in a moment they were thrashing together, savagely diving and thrusting as if plundering each other for thrills. Geri had the odd feeling that she was in a contest with Dolph, a joust of desires, and as he lanced down hard into her, she arched up with all her strength, as if to show she could carry him, hold him as deeply as he wanted to go, deeper. She wrapped her arms and legs around him and pulled him in, desperate to show him she wanted even more. And he knew exactly what she was doing and feeling. He gave a throaty laugh as her nails dug into his back, daring her to scratch even harder, vice him more tightly between her thighs as he whispered hotly, 'Yes, my darling, yes . . .'

Even when they came, the strange undercurrent of rivalry was there, to give more, take more, sustain the pulsing flow longer than the other, be the last to fade.

She kept him inside her until he had grown hard again, and they came again, together, his mouth on hers so that she screamed into his throat.

At last, panting for breath, she lay back. She had never been so thoroughly satisfied. She glowed with the memory of her morning ride when she had decided she needed nothing more in her life, she was ready for marriage if only it would come. But in this quiet aftermath, she had a sudden insight into the reasons behind their violent detonation of lust. He had taken her refusal to share information — just that small show of independence — as a challenge. It titillated him, she realized, made him want to test her, test himself. Could her love for him survive if she felt she were always pitted against him in a test of strength?

He shifted himself to turn on the bedside lamp. As her eyes scanned Dolph's body, the patina of silver hair coating his golden skin, she could only think now of how lucky she was to be with him.

He picked up the slacks he had dropped beside the bed, pulled something from one of the pockets, then turned back to her. 'It's time to tell you our secret. Lie back and close your eyes . . .'

She did, and a second later, she felt something slide lightly along the side of her foot, then over her ankle, and up the inside of her leg, something about the size of a fingertip, but cool, not living. It tickled along her thigh, and then he dipped it into her before gliding across her stomach and up one arm and across her breasts and down the other arm and along one of her fingers.

'Look now,' he said, at the moment he slipped the ring on.

Geri stared at the diamond, as large as the tip of her thumb. She had accepted other expensive gifts from Dolph over the years, furs and cars, but never anything remotely approaching *this*. 'Good Lord!' she gasped.

'To paraphrase the great Mae West, the Lord had nothing to do with it.'

'Dolph . . . I . . .' Her mind was racing, too fast to collect words. He felt it was time, too, and would wait no longer. He would pursue his divorce, and then Geri would become his wife.

'A Swiss gem dealer called me about this stone,' Dolph said. 'He acquired it a few weeks ago in Bombay, from one of those has-been maharajahs in need of raising a little cash. I suppose the dealer might have heard on the grapevine that I was looking for something suitable to give a lady, but as he told it his reason for thinking of me was because of the name this jewel has carried since it was found a couple of hundred years ago — "The Stallion's Eye".' Dolph lowered himself to the bed and picked up the hand on which he'd placed the ring. He admired the diamond a moment, then looked at Geri. 'I took it as an omen.'

'It's incredible,' she said. 'But it's awfully hard for me to imagine myself wearing something like this . . .'

'Whether you wear it or not, it belongs to you.'

It was only another instant before she pulled him down into a kiss. How could she expect there wouldn't be some doubt or fears at the moment of decision? He was an awesome man, a phenomenon, and she would have to work hard to keep from being overwhelmed by him. But he was her savior, her lover, her friend, her teacher . . . her family. Of course, she wanted him, too, with all her heart and soul.

They made love once more, and this time he gave in his usual style, everything for her pleasure.

Afterwards, they dressed to join Laurette who had arranged a small formal dinner party to introduce Geri personally to a few of the most important breeders. Having gone over the list, Geri knew that the Mitchells had not qualified, and she would be able to enjoy the occasion.

Just before they went out the door, she had to ask the question that had remained unspoken as they lay in bed. 'What about Diana . . .?'

'She's shaken off all the drugs, and stayed with the A.A. meeting for nearly half a year. If I cut loose now, she'll be all right. Of course, I'll see she's well provided for.'

'But . . . has she pulled herself together to prepare for being alone . . . or for the sake of trying to keep you? Because then she might unravel as soon as —'

Dolph cut her off. 'Geri. She must learn what we did — to survive. I can't sacrifice myself to her anymore. I want you, I want to spend the rest of my life with you. And I want heirs who have the kind of strength and spirit that we have.'

He took her in his arms again. 'There's one other reason I

401

think now is the ideal time for our engagement. I can mark the occasion by buying you a gift I know you'll prize above anything else, even the diamond . . .'

'What could I —'

'A yearling, my love, a top thoroughbred of your very own, to name yourself and race under your own colors.' As her mouth parted in amazement, he put a finger to her lips. 'Don't even think of saying no,' he insisted. 'This is something I want to do!'

'Then I don't dare refuse, do I?' she said with a smile.

'Perhaps you'll bid for one of those horses you wouldn't tell me about . . .' Dolph held the door open.

'If it's a bargain,' she said, and he laughed.

As she swept past him, she lifted her hand to caress his cheek — the hand adorned by the glittering Stallion's Eye.

CHAPTER FOUR

In the morning, Dolph wanted to look over the yearlings at the sale ground. Having already made her own list of good prospects, Geri decided to spend the day visiting some of the many breeding farms in the Lexington area, particularly those with horses at the auction that interested her. Laurette offered the use of her car — a 1952 Cadillac convertible, still spotless as new — and Geri set out on her tour. By studying the place a horse was raised, making sure it was clean and well run, she gathered useful insights into the soundness of the animal.

Amid the restful beauty of the farms, Geri was reminded several times of Skyevale. At last she was prompted to ask one of the breeders who was showing her around what had become of the Mitchells' operation. She learned that following Eldon Mitchell's death of a heart attack several years ago, his wife had sold the property to a neighboring breeder who joined it to his own. There had been no point in hanging on, after all; the Mitchells' son had never had any interest in the horses. Bard Mitchell was said to be living somewhere in the West, after squandering his share of the sale money on bad investments.

Hearing about the dissolution of Skyevale and the Mitchell family, made Geri wonder again about her sister. Had fate been kind or cruel? While she had so much in her own life, how could she turn her back on Molly?

Late in the afternoon, rather than heading straight back to Kismet Farms, Geri drove out along the Versailles Pike.

Rounding a bend several miles from town, she slowed the car, and almost halted and turned around — timid, at the last second, about confronting this piece of her past. But then, even before she could stop, she realized it was right there in front of her, so changed that she might have driven past if she hadn't been looking for it.

No gas was being sold, the office hut was boarded up, weeds were pushing up through the concrete around the rusty pumps. She pulled over, turned off the engine, and sat gazing at the garage, remembering the night when her whole life had violently changed course. How strangely things had worked out. For all the horror of that ordeal, if none of it had happened — if Pa were still alive, if Molly had not betrayed her, if Steve had not saved her from the threat of prison — might she be working here right now, pumping gas . . .?

Abruptly Geri switched on the ignition, and headed the car back into Lexington. With all she had, how could she not forgive Molly?

Arriving at the corner where Parker Chevrolet had once thrived, she saw a new dealership selling only Japanese cars.

A salesman intercepted her the moment she stepped into the showroom: 'You're doing the right thing if you're here to trade in that gas-guzzler.' He glanced at the old Cadillac parked outside.

'I'm not shopping for a car,' Geri said. 'I was wondering what happened to Parker's . . .?'

'The Chevy dealer? Sold out to my boss a couple of years ago and moved away. I told you, nobody wants those Detroit dinosaurs since the A-rabs jacked up the price of —'

'Do you know where he moved to?' cut in Geri anxiously.

The salesman shrugged, and suggested if Geri had questions about anything other than trading-in her car, she ought to speak to his boss, Harry Travis, the man who had bought out Parker.

She found the balding overweight dealer in his small office, the same room where she had once sat to do filing. As soon as she stopped at the door, his eyes swept over her, appraising her expensive clothes with a salesman's practiced eye.

When Geri explained that she was looking for information about Ed Parker, Travis supplied it immediately. 'He's down in Sarasota. We're in contact all the time — he took back the mortgage.'

'Can you tell me where to write . . . or call?' She saw his eyes narrow, as if suspicious of the request. 'I'm . . . a relative. From up North. We'd drifted apart . . .'

He nodded, then consulted his Rolodex and jotted Parker's Florida address on a notepad to give to Geri. 'But before you get in touch, maybe it'll save Ed some embarrassment if I fill you in. His wife, Lettie, she's been dead some years. The newspaper obit said "natural causes", but everybody around here pretty much knows it was pills . . .'

Geri let out a long silent sigh. 'There's something else you might know about . . . The Parkers, when they lived in town, they took a girl in. She was alone and they sort of adopted —'

'Oh that one,' Travis broke in, then leaned across the desk, and spoke in a low voice. 'It's old news, and Ed never liked to talk about it himself . . . but it didn't take much to know about that girl. Made quite a name for herself, if you know what I mean. Broke Ed's heart — and Lettie's, of course . . .'

'How? What happened?'

'Well, like you say they took her in, gave her everything . . . and then one night she didn't come home, and a cop who knew Ed showed up here the next day to tell him the girl had been picked up for hooking. Lettie wouldn't take her back then. Don't know if she did time or what, but the girl moved on. Parkers never knew what became of her, either. The whole thing really kicked the stuffing out of Lettie. She held on for a while, but when she did herself in, everybody knew why. Couldn't hold her head up after that girl shamed her. Lettie had a sense of . . . well, "class" I guess you'd call it . . .'

Geri stood silently in the doorway, staring down.

'Anything else, ma'am?'

'No,' she said, after a moment. 'Thanks for your help.'

When the dealer noticed the pad on his desk, the address still there on the top sheet, he ran after her. But she was already gone.

That night she went with Dolph to the first of the four auctions. Seventy horses would be sold at each one. Geri was glad all the yearlings that interested her had been assigned hip numbers higher than seventy. It gave her an opportunity to enjoy the atmosphere without caring about the outcome of a bidding duel, and to 'take the temperature' of the buyers before keeping an appointment tomorrow morning with al-Sadir's bloodstock agent, the man who would be responsible for masking the actual bids when the animals she selected came to the sales ring.

The ring was not, in fact, a circular arena, but a fairly conventional auditorium. A few hundred seats upholstered in green baize raked back in semi-circular rows from a stage with a dirt floor about as big as a bandstand. On a high raised dais behind the stage sat the auctioneer and his 'spotter', dressed in tuxedos. Large electronically controlled boards at either side of the stage lit up with the number of each horse as it was led out and its pedigree announced.

'Hip number forty-two, a dark bay colt by Scintillation out of NoMansLand . . .'

Other spotters, also dressed in tuxedos, ranged up and down the aisles keeping a sharp eye on buyers with whom pre-arranged signals had been agreed earlier. If the auctioneer didn't catch a signal, the spotters did and relayed it to him or his assistant. The bids were recounted to the audience in the same rapid-fire drone that Geri remembered hearing once when she'd gone to a tobacco sale with Pa. The auctioneer's tongue-twisting babble of numbers was unintelligible to her, and no doubt to plenty of others filling the seats around her, but there was never any doubt about the price to be topped. The constantly changing electric boards displayed the highest bid in numbers a couple of feet high.

In the course of the evening, Dolph bought three colts and a filly. At one point, he went after a yearling sired by a leading stakes winner of several years ago, and got into a bidding war with Neil Langham. Rather than using silent signals, both were lodging their bids openly by raising their hands. For Dolph to bid in this way could be dangerous; it might encourage sellers — who knew that he always got what he wanted and had unlimited resources — to artificially drive up prices by using accomplices to bid against him. Or it could cut the other way: seeing Dolph as an opponent, other buyers might decide quickly that their own quest was futile and drop out. It appeared to work to his advantage on the first couple of horses, both of which he bought for under $30,000 — prices Geri thought very reasonable. When he came up against Langham, however, the contest heated up. The Englishman topped Dolph's bid of seventy-five thousand with a raise to eighty. As the price crested a hundred thousand all buyers but Justinean and Langham fell away.

At a hundred and forty thousand, the bid was Langham's. He paused a second, then nodded. The auctioneer looked from Langham to Dolph. Without any hesitation at all, Dolph shook his head, resigning.

A buzz of surprise rose from the audience. Even the auctioneer raised his eyebrows. When Dolph was in, they all knew, he was in all the way.

Looking at him, Geri saw the hint of a smile play over his lips. 'You didn't really want that one, did you? You just bid it up . . .'

'Of course I wanted it. But sometimes one must . . . let go.' He gave her a twinkling glance. 'A little disappointment now and then builds character, doesn't it?'

What it also did, Geri thought, was show Neil Langham that his crusade to take some of the good horses back to England was going to cost him a bundle. And it would make anyone who thought of taking advantage of Dolph Justinean think twice.

She had arranged to have breakfast the next morning with Alain Loutrelle, the bloodstock agent who had been engaged by Sheik al-Sadir to actually handle the bidding on the horses Geri selected. They met in the dining room of the Radisson Hotel in downtown Lexington.

Loutrelle, a small middle-aged man with graying red hair and an elfin face accented by a small mustache with waxed tips, came by his knowledge of horses through his father who

407

had been a general of the French Cavalry in a time before the chivalric notion of fighting war on horseback had died out. General Loutrelle's cavalry had been mowed down by a Panzer division in the first day of the French defense against the Nazi invasion. His son, Alain, was dedicated to keeping alive the glory of the horse in a different kind of combat. As a bloodstock agent, he had been engaged at various times over the past forty years in finding and buying racehorses for various leading owners — the movie mogul Louis B. Mayer in the years just after the war, and more recently a different sort of mogul, the young Aga Khan. Now he had been hired away by al-Sadir, though his connection to the sheik, like Geri's, had so far been kept confidential. In addition to bidding on the horses Geri had suggested, he would make selections of his own. He had already purchased a couple of yearlings for the sheik last night.

Across the table while they had breakfast, Geri supplied a list of the five hip numbers she had selected, written top to bottom in order of preference. Loutrelle scanned them, and gave Geri his reaction — without bothering to refer first to his sale catalog, where the hip numbers would be matched to a description of the horses; apparently, he had committed to memory the specifics of all two hundred and eighty horses being offered.

'*Bravo*, Mademoiselle Keyes, I congratulate you on your taste. Your first, third and fourth choices tally with my own. *C'est très bon*. We can be sure of doing well by our client if we secure the animals on which we are in accord.' He looked at the list again, and pursed his mouth as though his Gallic palate had been offered a spoon of flavorless soup. 'I must confess, though, to amazement at your second choice — *quatre vingt-dix-sept*. Perhaps my recall is incorrect, but if it is the horse I think — a plain brown colt — he came from a rather undistinguished mare and stallion, his muscling was underdeveloped, and I believe there were signs of dormant skin rash on the abdomen. All in all, a poor specimen, a horse that ought to go very cheaply, *avec raison*.'

Quietly, without offense at Loutrelle's belittling tone, Geri countered all his objections. Since the colt was younger than most other yearlings in the sale, its musculature had not yet developed to the same extent. From her study of the horse's physique, she thought it would develop tremendous power. The rash was curable, with time and the proper attention. And there had been some impressive horses in the pedigree if the lines were traced back several generations. 'The only thing you may be right about is the price. But that's one of the reasons I like him. A horse doesn't have to be expensive to be good.'

'*Bien sûr, chère mademoiselle*. You and I know that well. But not our client. He is a neophyte, and one for whom money is no object. At the price involved here, I would certainly not mind if we took a risk — all the more since it is not our money we are risking. But I am also concerned about my reputation, as you should be about yours. If we buy any horse too cheaply, this Arab will only assume it's worthless — that we have not done our job well. You see, he expects to buy the best, and he expects that to cost him dearly.'

'Monsieur Loutrelle,' Geri replied, 'I can't tailor my recommendations to suit my client's ignorance. Sheik al-Sadir paid me to make these choices, and he wants you to bid on them. If he's not happy, I'll take responsibility.'

'But I see you have provided alternatives . . .'

'In the event the bidding went too high.'

'And at what point do you think this' — the imaginary soup was no longer merely flavorless, but distinctly distasteful — 'second choice of yours would be *trop cher?*'

She paused. Perhaps it was not worth pushing Loutrelle. If she liked this plain colt, why not let it be the horse Dolph gave her?

No, she couldn't bend her professional ethics. She had taken an enormous fee to provide her best judgment, and this was it. 'Let's see how the bidding goes tonight,' she replied. 'My gut feeling is that this colt has terrific potential and al-Sadir will never be sorry he bought him.'

Loutrelle shrugged. '*Alors*, I will bid until you tell me to stop.' They rose from their breakfast. '*Mais disez-moi,*

Mademoiselle Keyes: this feeling in your gut, how can you be sure it's something about the horse, and not just indigestion?'

Geri smiled. 'I looked him in the eye,' she said.

During sales week, there were parties at many of the farms, lavish buffets set out on long tables under enormous tents, entertainers flown in at great expense from Las Vegas or Los Angeles. Parties given prior to the nights when the auctions began, would start late and continue into the wee hours. On a sale night, they started late in the afternoon and ended in time for everyone to get to the ring by 8:30.

On the evening preceding the second auction, there was a tent party at Kismet Farms, virtually an open house for everyone involved with the breeding business in Lexington and those visiting for the sales. When she had been a teenager living here, Geri remembered, she had heard about a party at Kismet at which Elvis Presley had been paid to sing. This evening, as people sat sipping cocktails, Bob Hope got up on a stage for half an hour and leveled some good-natured ribbing at the crowd.

A number of local television crews and correspondents of the national press were admitted, and many pointed their cameras at Justinean or sought him out for a comment. Even reporters ordinarily devoted solely to sports or society gossip realized that Justinean's business plans and political connections made him a possible source of solid news. His recent appearances at Senate committees to endorse the Carter administration's plans for airline deregulation, and his maneuvering to get new routes for his own company had already attracted front-page attention.

But for Geri, being surrounded by newspeople induced the sensation of being smothered and confined — a reaction to the times when she had been mobbed by voracious reporters at the time of her trial. After Hope's performance, she left the tent and went out to walk in the cool evening air.

Without any conscious decision, she found herself strolling past the barn which had been converted into a guesthouse — and where she knew Malcolm Peabody had set up his temporary studio. Only then she realized that she had been expecting to see Bill Quinn again at the big tent party, and had felt some disappointment at finding Peabody there but not his assistant. From time to time over the past couple of days, she had thought about the encounter with Quinn, and had been disturbed by its unsatisfactory ending. She wanted somehow to set things right. He deserved encouragement.

Lights were glowing in the windows of the barn and the door was open. Entering, Geri passed a small foyer and found herself on a platform a few steps above a living room with a cathedral ceiling. The rug had been rolled back, the furniture pushed into a corner, and an easel and paint table set up in front of the large double-height windows. Quinn was at the paint table, brushing a canvas with white primer.

'Hello,' she said, anxious to announce herself before she could be accused of spying, and self-conscious since she had obviously come looking for him.

Quinn turned and rested his eyes on her, then went back to what he was doing. 'Shouldn't you be at the big party?' he said over his shoulder.

'Shouldn't you . . .?' she echoed, as she went down the steps and crossed to the table. 'You know what they say about all work and no play.'

' "Makes Jack a dull boy",' he chimed in. 'Luckily, my name's Bill.'

'I remember,' she said.

He continued stroking the primer onto the canvas for a moment, the silence between them growing heavier. At last he put down the brush and turned to her.

'Why are you here?' he asked flatly.

The question made her think. She knew why: to help him — a wounded man who was making a valiant effort to recover something an unfair war had taken away. But could she say that? He was already so defensive, so determined to deserve whatever he got — even if nothing more than a bit of praise.

'I've been thinking,' she said at last, 'about arranging a commission . . .'

Quinn nodded, then picked up the brush again and dipped it into the pot of primer. 'Well, you'll have to come back. One of

411

the few things I don't do for the master is handle the business end,' Quinn said. 'That he does himself.'

'But I want to commission you . . .'

He turned again to her, absently letting the wet brush drip paint onto the floor.

Geri went on quickly. 'I wasn't just tossing empty compliments around yesterday. I'm ready to back up my opinion with something concrete. I want a horse painting. Not one of Peabody's, though. One of yours, along the lines of what you were doing yesterday.'

'Oh yes?' he said coolly. 'Of which horse?'

She hadn't really thought of any particular horse . . . but now it came to her. 'I'll be getting a yearling at the sales — as a gift . . .'

He took a step closer to her until he saw that the brush was still dripping, and might spot her shoes. Then he put it down before coming back to her. 'What's this really about? I didn't tell you my story to make you feel sorry for me.'

'Good God, Quinn,' she erupted furiously. 'Why do you have to twist this around. I'm not sorry for you! With your talent I don't think I have to be.' She took a breath, and looked down for a moment, regretting her loss of temper. She had hoped to repair some damage, instead she had only widened the gap. 'I don't know,' she resumed. 'Maybe I am wrong. Maybe you can't do a decent painting of a horse — especially the gift variety — because you'll spend all your damn time looking it in the mouth.' She raised her eyes to his. 'Why the hell can't you just accept some encouragement? Hell, if I hadn't been helped a couple of times when I was down, I wouldn't be here. I know what it means to get a hand up.'

They stared at each other intently for a long moment. She had connected, she thought. 'Okay,' he said at last. 'If your commission is the real thing, then I'd expect to be paid fairly. You want a genuine "Quinn", you pay the going rate.'

She smiled slightly. 'I didn't know there was a "going rate" for a Quinn.'

'There is for a Peabody.'

Her smile faded. 'Oh, hold on . . .'

412

'You said I was *more* talented. Or was that an empty compliment, after all.'

She nodded ruefully. He had her. But maybe it wasn't unfair. And she could afford to play with money now, to be a generous patron. Fifty thousand for a few days of her own work, a million-dollar diamond resting in Laurette's vault. 'All right. What does the boss get?'

'Up to seventy-five thousand per commission, and that's with *me* painting the corners . . .'

'I want to be fair,' she came back at once, 'but I won't be a fool. Considering that this is your first commission, I think . . . fifteen thousand dollars would be more than reasonable.'

She needed only the glimmer of his eyes to see that he was bowled over. But he gave no other sign. 'I accept,' he said evenly. 'When do I start?'

'When I have the horse.'

He gave her a sharp sidelong glance. 'Ah well,' he said, and turned abruptly to continue priming that canvas. 'I guess I'd better keep doing this for the meanwhile . . .' The implication was clear: until she actually followed through, the offer remained meaningless.

Hurt by his skepticism, Geri almost erupted again. But then she held back her angry words. Perhaps it was a wise policy to trust no one until a promise was kept. Perhaps it was something she should have learned herself by now.

'If you'd like,' she said, 'I'll give you a part of the money before you even start . . .'

He shook his head. 'When it happens,' he said. 'When I'm done.'

She couldn't think of what else to say. It felt suddenly as though an invisible wall had been raised between them. All her good intentions could not defeat Quinn's suspicious defensiveness.

'Goodnight,' she said, and left the studio.

'Goodnight,' he called in return, without turning from the blank canvas.

As she walked across the velvet lawns of Kismet Farms, the bitter feeling of rejection kept churning through her. It had

413

been a mistake to approach him, she told herself. If she wanted to use some of her affluence to do good, better to send it to charity than invest it where it wasn't wanted or appreciated.

But by the time she reached the tent, her anger had cooled. The war had hurt Bill Quinn badly, she reminded herself, and the returning veterans were still being treated more as pariahs than heroes. Quinn had a right to his moods.

CHAPTER FIVE

When Geri and Dolph arrived at the auction, the first two horses had already been sold. The auditorium was more crowded than last night, and the current of excitement tuned higher. Among the yearlings in tonight's lot were a couple of colts sired by the famous Northern Dancer whose breeding record included more recent stakes winners than any other stallion. Geri hadn't included either of these two yearlings on her list, but she knew there was a chance they would set sales records — which might have the effect of dragging up prices of other horses to higher levels. She was glad that the colt on which she and Loutrelle had disagreed would be sold early, before such a fever could develop.

At last it was announced: 'Hip number ninety-seven, a brown colt by Rum Runner out of Coal Harbor.' The yearling was led onto the platform. The dull brown of its coat did not gleam under the lights the way the darker horses did. He did not — Geri had to agree with Alain Loutrelle — have any instant appeal. But she still liked the lines, sensed potential.

Geri caught the glance Loutrelle threw at her from his seat across the auditorium. If she shook her head it would signal a change of intention, but she merely smiled. The Frenchman shrugged, and turned toward the front. As the auctioneer announced a starting price of $5,000, Geri saw the bloodstock agent twist the tip of his waxed mustache.

The bidding jumped at first by increments of three

415

thousand, then two, and finally one. As the price reached $25,000, Loutrelle hesitated and looked toward her again. This time she gave an assertive nod. Loutrelle flicked one tip of his mustache twice, and the auctioneer declared a new bid of $27,000.

There was a long lull, and it looked like the auctioneer was about to knock down the horse at that price, when suddenly he announced a topping bid of $35,000.

The sizeable jump, silently transmitted, was an aggressive bidding strategy, designed to tell anyone who would contest it that the battle could be expensive. Unfortunately for the anonymous challenger, the identity of his opponent was equally well-masked: an oil-rich Arab sheik who was not going to be put off at any price — at least not as long as Geri signalled her approval. She nodded again to Loutrelle.

The Frenchman showed his own muscle by jumping the bid another $10,000 — brushing his hand twice across the lapels of his jacket, as though he had just noticed some lint.

In a second, the jump was matched by the other silent bidder, raising the price to $55,000.

Murmurs of astonishment rippled through the crowd. The dull brown horse standing on the platform in front of them had been expected to draw only routine interest. Now other buyers took a second look. Was there some information that had been kept secret? Had the horse shown brilliance on an exercise track . . .?

Geri, too, could not suppress her surprise. She glanced around the auditorium, seeking a clue to the challenger.

While she scanned, Loutrelle had already lodged his next bid. Impatient to chase the competition, he had gone up $15,000.

The jump was matched, bringing the price to $90,000.

Loutrelle went to $100,000. But this time he made his bid openly, calling it out. Known as a past adviser to some of the richest men in the world, he might hope declaring his involvement would frighten off the competition.

The answer of the silent challenger was instantaneous — his signals evidently well worked out in advance. The auctioneer announced that the price had leapt to $125,000. Glancing around again, Geri caught Neil Langham whispering to his wife. Almost too deliberately nonchalant, she thought. Could Langham have known about her interest in the horse? She remembered now that her marked sale catalog had been left lying in her room while she was out this morning . . .

The atmosphere in the sales ring had begun to crackle. Other prominent owners, feeling they might have been wrong to discount the animal, began tossing in bids. Even as Loutrelle remained silent, the price climbed up to $185,000 before there was another lull.

The Frenchman looked to Geri for instructions.

With Dolph beside her, she thought of what he had said. Price was no object. If she was in this game — if she was going to be his wife — she had to learn to think that way. Had to learn *how* to be his wife, not just his mistress. She nodded to the bloodstock agent and turned away, letting him know he did not have to consult her again.

He jumped the bid to $200,000.

There was a chorus of gasps from the crowd, and a long pause from the auctioneers. It seemed Loutrelle had won the horse for al-Sadir. The auctioneer began to intone the final warning: 'Going once . . . going twice . . . going —' Suddenly he interrupted himself and huddled with his assistant, who was looking toward one of the spotters. It seemed there had been some confusion over a signal.

At last the auctioneer spoke into the microphone: 'The price is now two hundred and fifty thousand.'

Geri shot a look at Langham's seat. It was empty. She was confused now, her confidence fading. The horse had become too big a risk, she decided. She turned toward Loutrelle to signal him to retire.

But at the same moment the Frenchman called a bid of 'Two seventy-five!' He wasn't looking for her instructions anymore. He was ready to go as high as he had to. At this price, he no longer worried that the sheik would feel cheated.

Within seconds, the auctioneer announced the answering bid of $300,000. Now it was madness. Geri had to get to

417

Loutrelle and tell him to withdraw. She turned to Dolph, who was on the aisle, and rose slightly, indicating she wanted to leave her seat. But he didn't notice, he was concentrating his attention on Loutrelle — and there was a slight smile on his lips.

She eased back and watched him from the corner of her eye as Loutrelle came back with a raise to $325,000.

As if musing absently, Dolph tapped the tip of his nose a few times with the eraser of a pencil he had been using to notate his sales book.

A moment later the auctioneer took a bid from a spotter at the front of the auditorium, and announced it.

'We have four hundred thousand, ladies and gentlemen. Four hundred . . .'

Geri grabbed Dolph's arm. 'That was your bid, wasn't it?' she demanded.

Justinean didn't reply. All his attention was focussed on the auctioneer as he came back with Loutrelle's reply, lifting the price another fifty thousand.

'Damn you,' she hissed at Dolph. 'Don't you realize what you've done?' Without waiting for his reaction, she shoved out of her seat, ran up the aisle, across the back of the auditorium and down the far aisle to Loutrelle's seat. She had almost reached him when the auctioneer declaimed Justinean's next bid.

'Five-fifty!' A jump of $100,000.

Arriving breathless beside the Frenchman, she could only stammer a few words. 'No . . . Alain, stop . . .'

He looked up at her uncertainly.

'Drop out,' she said.

Loutrelle saw then that she wasn't looking at him, but glaring across the auditorium at Justinean.

'Going once . . twice . . .'

The Frenchman shook his head at the auctioneer. The gavel was rapped down. The audience let out a collective sigh, and then broke into applause.

Geri ran up the aisle, out of the ring.

She was on the path to the parking area when Dolph caught

up to her, and grabbed her arm. She tore away and kept walking.

'Where are you going?' he said. 'Answer me!'

The words came, dislodged by his angry roar. 'Home. Away from here. Away from you.'

'Because I bought something you wanted? Is that reason enough?'

She stopped and faced him, eyes flashing. 'Why *that* horse, Dolph? Why did you have to chase it so hard?'

'I liked it.'

'And because you liked it, you had to have it. But did you know I'd picked it, too? Even if you didn't know before, you couldn't have missed it once the sale started. Did you ever think then — for just one second — how it would compromise me to have you in the bidding?'

'Compromise you?' he echoed mildly. 'I was only backing your judgment to the hilt. If you had a special feeling about the horse, why shouldn't it be yours. This was the one I'd picked for your gift.'

She teetered on the brink of forgiveness, and realized that if she went over she might be falling too far. 'I didn't choose that horse for myself. It was for a client . . .'

'You don't have to put clients ahead of yourself, ahead of me —'

'But I do — when it's for my work. If you can't let me do it now, what will happen later? You'll want to rule me, the way you ruled Diana. You must know this damaged me professionally. Isn't that just the first step to taking away everything I have . . . everything but you?'

His answer wasn't a denial. 'And am I not enough?'

'No man will be enough if I can't first own myself.' There was a pause. She waited for him to yield, to apologize, to say he accepted her need for independence. She loved him still, the first man she had ever loved, and she couldn't bring herself to leave him. But then his arms came up and he reached for her. Wanting to take her, but without an apology.

Her resolve might melt at his touch — they both knew it — so she turned and ran.

At Kismet, the main house was quiet. Exhausted by her party, Laurette had gone to bed and left instructions with a maid that she shouldn't be disturbed. Geri packed quickly, wrote a long note thanking Laurette for her hospitality and asking her to return the ring in her vault to Dolph, and then called a taxi for the airport. She didn't know which flight she'd catch, anything heading North . . .

Agitated, unable to sit still while she waited for the ride, she brought her suitcase outside, and left it in front of the house while she went for a short walk. From far out in the dark pastureland behind the house came the soft snorting and whinnying of horses. The sounds and smells of the night pacified her, and she paused to lean on a fence like an ocean traveler by the rail of a ship, content to look at emptiness and enjoy the illusion of standing still, while all the time she was being borne forward on a journey.

But to where? Had she been too hasty in leaving Dolph? Just yesterday she had seen her future in terms of a deepening commitment: marriage, family. For a moment she imagined how it would be . . . all the things that his wealth could make possible not only for her, but their children. Perhaps she had been scared off somehow by the prospect of having that ideal life within her grasp.

No, in an ideal situation, a man would acknowledge her as an equal. And Dolph could never do that, she realized. She loved him, but not enough to surrender herself totally.

Startled suddenly by the sound of footsteps nearby, she turned and saw Bill Quinn walking toward the main house, heading for his room after a night of work. As she turned, he saw her, too, and changed direction to join her.

'Thought you'd be at the sales,' he said.

'I have to leave,' she replied. 'I'm just waiting for my taxi.'

He studied her silently, obviously reluctant to pry into the cause of her sudden departure. Geri was on the verge of remarking it was a lovely night when he continued. 'Before you go, I hope you'll accept my apology.'

She smiled. She was getting an apology tonight, after all, but not from the man she wanted.

'You were quite right,' Quinn went on. 'My behavior before was inexcusable. But your offer . . . a show of faith like that, well, it threw me right off balance. I don't suppose I deserve a second chance, but if you still want to go ahead I'll do my damndest to give you your money's worth . . .'

Good Lord! She didn't even want the horse Justinean had given her — nor did she feel like celebrating, with an expensive gift to herself. Especially not when she felt bound to return the fee she had been given by al-Sadir. Yet if she withdrew her offer now, what would it do to Quinn's already fragile confidence?

'Of course I want the painting, and I'll pay what I agreed,' she said. 'But there's a change. I'd like the one I saw you working on for yourself . . .'

A horn sounded from the driveway. Her taxi. She started walking.

Quinn stayed beside her. 'Look,' he said, 'you know damn well I can't sell you that one. I destroyed it.'

She paused to look back at him before stepping through the door the taxi driver was holding open. 'The horses are always here,' she said, 'and every day starts with a sunrise.'

CHAPTER SIX

The style of her affair with Dolph had called for so many separations over the years that Geri hoped to adjust quickly to their break. The reality was different. Before, knowing her time with him was rationed had made their loving more intense, and contentment with her work during the times apart had promoted a concentration that was a significant factor in her success. Now she had lost that focus and equilibrium. The more she tried distracting herself with work, the more tedious the demands of running the clinic seemed to become.

Afflicted by insomnia for the first time in her life, she filled the sleepless hours with anything to keep her mind free of Dolph. She wrote papers for journals of veterinary medicine; she showed up for shifts in the emergency room — startling the young assistants she paid to exhaust themselves with that work; she painted and redecorated some rooms in her house, the colonial mansion she had taken over from Tom Graymar.

But inevitably Dolph crept back into her thoughts. Over and over, she reviewed the choice she had made — ran through the evidence on which she'd acted as if she was on trial in her own mind. Always she came back to the same decision. She loved him still, admired his strength and power. But he was a man who needed to dominate, and she could not survive as his vassal.

Less than a month after the Keeneland select sale, the season in Saratoga was in high gear. Geri expected this to be a difficult time — with Dolph in town attending the races and parties, perhaps even instructing his trainer to send any animals with problems to her. But then she heard that he hadn't come for this year's race meeting; he was off in various corners of the world, devoting himself to business. Nevertheless, many of his horses were entered in the Saratoga races. When Geri made calls in the backstretch, she often ran into Dolph's trainer, Cesar Belize, who told her that Diana was also abroad — though whether she was travelling with Dolph the trainer did not know.

At a time when they could have spent days together at the track, evenings dancing together at parties and balls in the grand houses, his absence became even more poignant and unendurable. Among the rich and privileged who came for the season, there were many young and attractive men who made no attempt to hide an interest in her, and she made an effort to like them. But they lacked Dolph's magnetism and force.

To confirm the separation from him — reinforce her will — she refinanced the clinic and sent a check for the full amount still outstanding on his loan, almost $900,000, to his lawyers. But she slept less, and drove past his darkened house often in the middle of the night. She longed to be with him so much it was a physical ache.

On the morning after the last day of the season, when she awoke to the prospect of autumn and winter without him, her will collapsed. She was bonded to him by all the time they'd been together — and perhaps by his being her first and only lover. She wanted no one else.

The list of phone numbers — his office, his plane, the Glen Cove house — were all still engraved in her memory. Reluctant to call his home, she waited until a little before nine o'clock and then called his office. There was no answer. Wondering if Dolph might still be abroad, Geri now dialed the phone that rang on the desk of Dolph's private secretary, Connie Fuller. When this also went unanswered, she was surprised and a little alarmed. To keep up with Dolph, who was often at his desk by seven, Connie was in the habit of starting at eight.

After a minute debating whether to risk an exchange with Diana, Geri returned to the phone and dialed a number that rang only in the study of Dolph's Glen Cove mansion. The line was answered by a male voice. 'Yeah . . .?'

Hearing the gritty New York accent conveyed by even a single word, she knew it wasn't Dolph — nor any of the servants. 'Is Mr Justinean there?'

'Who wants to know?'

'A close friend,' Geri answered, only for the sake of getting past this unpleasant roadblock. 'My business is personal.'

'You'll have to do better, lady. Tell me your name and the reason you want to talk to him . . .'

Who was he? A bodyguard? 'What's going on there?' Geri said, a tinge of panic creeping in.

Only muffled shouting came through, as though a hand had been placed over the mouthpiece: '. . . a dame . . . won't say . . .'

Suddenly another man came on the line. The voice was smoother, his manner more accommodating. 'This is Detective Captain Luther Wade of Glen Cove Police Department. May I ask who's calling?'

Police? She fought to sound reasonable while her heart began to pound. 'I'll explain myself as soon as *I* get some information.'

There was a pause. 'Okay. No point arguing, you'll get it all soon enough in the news. But did you say you were a friend of Mrs Justinean . . . or of Mr Justinean?'

It struck her now that their stalling might be more than idle stubbornness. Didn't the police keep people talking so they could trace a call? With that realization, she could no longer restrain the growing terror. 'What's happened?' she cried, on the brink of hysteria. 'For God's sake tell me!'

The detective paused another second before responding to her pleas. 'There's been an accident — or so we've been told. Last night Mr Justinean shot his wife. She's dead. Now Miss —'

She heard the rest of it as if someone was shouting at her from the end of a long tunnel.

'— if you're really a friend, in the interest of helping Mr Justinean, maybe you'll be good enough to tell me exactly who you are, and anything else that might help him . . .'

It took only a fraction of a second to weigh the consequences of identifying herself, and another instant wondering whether they could have already done the trace. Then she lowered the receiver into the cradle.

She spent the day torn between a fevered desire to run to him, and a sensible resolve to stay away. It could do Dolph's defense no good, she realized, if it were known that his mistress had been trying to contact him just after he had shot his wife.

Too nervous to work, unable to sit still in her house, she went at last to one of the clinic barns and saddled up a pony. Being in the saddle always restored her confidence in being able to handle even the most fearsome new challenges — just as she had discovered the courage to ride the first time she had ever climbed on a horse.

On a long aimless ride through the fields and forests around the clinic, her thoughts finally fell into order. Their affair was bound to be uncovered soon; they had never hidden in the shadows. But the fact that it was a thing of the past — appeared, at least, to have ended nearly two months ago — would make it easier for Dolph to be given the benefit of the doubt. She had to stay away.

Somewhat less shaky by the time she finished the ride, Geri attended to some clinic business, then got in the car at the end of the afternoon and drove to Saratoga to see if there were any late editions of the newspapers carrying the story. Finding none, she went into a dim cocktail lounge off Union Avenue, and sipped at a beer until the six o'clock news came on the television screen over the bar.

Because Dolph had frequented Saratoga, the story was featured on the local broadcast. Newsfilm came on of Dolph being led from the door of his Glen Cove mansion to be placed in a police car, as the anchorman spun out the story:

'In New York, business tycoon and noted member of the Saratoga summer set, Adolphus Justinean, was taken into

425

police custody today after an incident at his house in which his wife died of a fatal gunshot wound.'

The image on the screen changed: a covered body on a gurney was wheeled along the tree-lined driveway and placed into an ambulance.

'The shooting occurred in the early morning at Justinean's palatial estate in Glen Cove, Long Island. According to first reports from the scene Mr Justinean admitted firing the gun in the belief that the house had been entered by a prowler. Mrs Justinean died instantly of a single bullet wound in the head. More on this story tonight at eleven . . .'

Geri paid for her drink and left.

A prowler? Could Dolph have really mistaken Diana for an unknown intruder? Yet if he had wanted to commit murder, he was too much in command of himself and his emotions to do it with such laughable clumsiness or in an unthinking fit of rage.

Behind the wheel of her car, she paused before choosing her direction. She wished she could go straight to him, tell him that she believed in him. She knew from her own experience how vitally important it could be to have the trust and faith of friends, the sustaining power of love. But love, she reminded herself, could also be taken as a motive for murder . . .

The phone rang only minutes after she had returned home. 'Geri . . .?'

She started to weep with relief when she heard his voice. 'Oh my darling . . . I've been going out of my mind, wanting so much to help, not knowing how —'

'I wish I could have reached you first — so you wouldn't hear it the wrong way . . .'

'That doesn't matter. I believe in you.'

There was a momentary pause before he said, very softly, 'That means everything to me, Geri. I don't care what anyone else thinks. But I want you to know that I'm absolutely —'

'I do know. You don't have to say it.'

'My dearest love, I've wanted you so much. But it didn't seem fair to ask you . . . because I couldn't say you were wrong about me, couldn't promise I'd ever be different . . .'

'That's something we'll have to work on . . . together. I've missed you, too. I was calling this morning to tell you — that's how I learned. The police asked for my name, but I hung up.'

'I know. Afterward they questioned me about it. I guessed it was you.'

'Then they know . . .?'

'No, I didn't tell them. Though maybe I should. Keeping secrets can only make me look guiltier.'

Knowing what it was like to be under suspicion, questioned by police and prosecutors, it all came back as if it was happening again to her. Whatever it took to free him, she vowed, she would dedicate herself to it. 'How bad does it look right now?' she asked.

'It looks like some lawyers are going to be getting a lot of my money.' He had not been detained, he continued; after answering questions for a couple of hours, he had been allowed to go home. But two police cars were in his driveway, keeping him under surveillance. His personal attorney, Lew Yancey, had already warned him that he would be charged sometime in the next day or two and ought to engage special criminal counsel.

'Geri,' he said then, 'I don't know if it's fair for me to ask this . . . but it would mean so much . . .' He stopped.

Until now she had never heard him be hesitant about anything. 'What is it, Dolph?' She would have spared him from having to ask if she could have been certain.

'Be with me through all this. I need your strength.'

'I'll be there in four hours.'

Caught arriving at the Glen Cove estate by the horde of reporters and TV camera crews who had begun camping at the gates, Geri's picture was broadcast on the evening news and printed on tabloid front pages across the country. OTHER WOMAN MOVES IN headlined the NEW YORK DAILY NEWS, while a story about her long affair with Dolph in one of the gossip columns snidely dubbed her the 'jet set's pet vet'. Some of the press ever so subtly angled stories and pictures toward a presumption of guilt. Yet with the meager facts that confronted them, it was a prejudice that only echoed public sentiment.

427

As Dolph Justinean told it to the police, he had awakened in darkness to the sound of someone moving around the dressing area that adjoined his bedroom. He could only assume it was a prowler because the wall safe containing his wife's jewelry was located in a wall of the dressing room, and she was supposed to be a thousand miles away, being treated for 'substance abuse' at an exclusive sanitarium in Minnesota.

Justinean had risen stealthily and gotten a gun from his closet, an old carbine used during his wartime partisan days, kept mainly for sentimental reasons. He had taken aim at a figure he could dimly see — outlined by the light of a half moon coming through a window — reaching to the open wall safe. At this point, Justinean had spoken out, warned the intruder he was being held at gunpoint. But the figure at the safe had tried instantly to run, and Justinean had pulled the trigger. Switching on the lights a moment later, he had found his wife dead on the floor, a bullet hole above one eye, and the pockets of a raincoat she was wearing filled with jewelry that had been removed from the safe.

Beyond doubt was the fact that Diana Justinean had died from a single 30 mm. cartridge in the brain, and that her raincoat pockets were stuffed with gem-studded bracelets, necklaces, pins, and rings with a total value of just under three million dollars. Everything else in Justinean's story remained open to question.

Lew Yancey, Dolph's lawyer, was furious. As Dolph and Geri sat together on the long sofa in the living room of the Glen Cove mansion, the morning after Geri's arrival from Saratoga, Yancey paced before them, berating them both.

'For godssakes, Dolph, you can't go around parading the fact that there's another woman in your life at the very moment you need people to believe Diana's death was accidental. And you, Geri, running down here like some oversexed schoolgirl . . .'

A sturdy man with iron gray hair, Yancey had the sort of face that belonged more on a selfless priest in some European village than on a corporate lawyer — rough features that gave him a look of being tough yet sincere. Hearing his protest,

428

Geri was inclined to agree — and to go back to Saratoga at once.

But Dolph countered equably. 'Listen, Lew, plenty of people will be out for my blood no matter what I do, and the facts about Geri and me were bound to come out sooner or later — this is no fly-by-night affair, after all. So she might as well be with me right at the start. I need her.' He took her hand.

Yancey turned to her. 'There's nothing personal in this, Geri. But if you left now, we could say that this visit was simply a show of friendly support — that you'd actually split with Dolph a couple of months ago. You might not be seen as a factor in what happened to Diana . . .'

'"Might not!" Lew, you know this was just a crazy accident!'

'What we know isn't at issue, Geri. It's what people *think*.' He sighed. 'You know, I've only been handling the legal side until I could turn the case over to a great defense specialist. I've already been in touch with a few . . .' He paused pointedly.

'And?' Dolph prompted.

'Pay enough, and there will certainly be someone to take the case. But so far the best aren't too eager. Lawyers make their reputations by winning, Dolph — and they don't like to take on the ones that look like they're already lost.'

Geri turned to Dolph. 'Maybe I should go . . .'

He was still holding her hand and the grip tightened. 'No. This is where you belong. I'm not worried about finding a good man to fight this case, Geri. They'll do it for the money, if for nothing else, and I don't care how much it costs.'

The meeting ended with Yancey listening quietly as Dolph instructed him to get back to the top defense lawyers on his list and offer them triple their usual fees to take the case.

While Dolph went to his study to make business calls, Geri took Yancey to the door. 'Don't worry, Lew, if I see I'm hurting Dolph too much by staying, I'll go. But right now, I think he needs some moral support.'

'And — a *genius* at defense . . .'

'I've got an idea on that, too.'

'A lawyer? Who is he?' Yancey asked.

'Edmund Grace Markham.'

Yancey nodded respectfully at the name. 'He's number one, all right. Markham was naturally the first man I tried. But he turned the case down flat. Being a genius at defense only means you're a lot faster at spotting the cases that'll make you look good — or bad.' He gave Geri a consoling smile and wished her good luck as he went out.

The name of Edmund Grace Markham ordinarily wouldn't have been in Geri's mind. The attorney was based in Washington, and she didn't make a habit of following the kind of news stories where he was often prominently mentioned as winning acquittals — for a millionaire businessman charged with involvement in drug smuggling, or for an heir to one of America's oldest fortunes accused of hiring a soldier of fortune to murder both the brother and sister who would share an inheritance.

As it happened, though, Markham owned a number of racehorses, and one had been sent to the clinic last year. After Geri had operated successfully to repair a torn tendon, the owner had sent a follow-up letter of thanks which included an invitation to visit him at his Virginia horse farm. Intrigued by the gracious tone of his letter, she had taken some trouble to find out more about the writer. She had learned then that Edmund Grace Markham was not only the dean of criminal lawyers, but the author of several best-selling books wittily recounting interesting cases he had won, and an unofficial adviser to the last few presidents. She had read one of his books, *Soldier At The Bar*, but she had never found time to accept his invitation.

Now it was time to call. She had an idea that might change Markham's mind about whether or not the case could be won.

CHAPTER SEVEN

She called Markham at his Washington office that afternoon, and he agreed to see her the next morning at eleven. It struck her only after hanging up that he hadn't bothered to ask what she wanted to discuss.

Word came toward evening that the local District Attorney would arraign Justinean tomorrow morning on a charge of homicide. Dolph assumed that Geri would appear with him at the county courthouse, but she persuaded him that Lew Yancey's argument had some merit. They mustn't flaunt their togetherness. In fact, staying away from the arraignment gave her the opportunity she needed to visit Markham. She felt there was a better chance to change his mind if she could reason with him, than if Dolph tried to use his wealth as a lever.

She took a shuttle flight to Washington and arrived ten minutes before her appointment at the offices of Markham, Paine & Hofstadtler, located in the shadow of Capitol Hill as befitted a Washington power-broker.

Markham came out to welcome her personally. Tall and gaunt, with a severe face marked by a prominent nose, high cheekbones, and bushy eyebrows, glossy and blue-black like his hair, Edmund Grace Markham was firmly in the category of men who deserved to be described as Lincolnesque. His aura of earnest diligence was accentuated by appearing before Geri in shirtsleeves, with black suspenders holding up the

431

pants of his dark gray Savile Row suit. Geri put his age at under fifty, but in view of his reputation and accomplishments, she guessed her judgment on this score was as faulty as ever.

He led her through the enormous suite of offices to a cosily furnished sitting room. 'If I don't get away from the phones,' he explained, 'we'll be interrupted every third word.'

A tray with separate pots of tea and coffee and a plate of blueberry muffins was already placed on a table between two easy chairs. 'Ah good, it's all ready for us.' He motioned Geri to a chair. 'Do you prefer tea or coffee . . .?'

'Tea . . . sugar and lemon,' she replied. It occurred to her suddenly that he might have misunderstood her call, taken it as a belated follow-up to his personal invitation. 'It's so nice of you to go to this trouble and see me right away. You do understand, I hope, that what I'm here to discuss involves you as an attorney . . .?'

He nodded, and she sat quietly as he poured, charmed by the novelty of being delicately served by this stern man in shirtsleeves.

'I assume,' he said finally, 'that you've come on behalf of Dolph Justinean . . .' He held out the plate of muffins. Geri declined. 'So you know all about our . . . friendship?'

'Through my interest in racing, Doctor Keyes, I have been in circles where that particular romantic liaison has long been a topic of conversation rivaled only by who's running the best horse in the Derby, and how much Jackie-O spends on clothes.'

Geri took a sip of her tea and set the cup down. 'If you anticipated the reason for this visit and agreed to it, does that mean you're still open to representing Dolph?'

'I didn't think I could deny you a hearing. I admit, however, that I was more motivated by personal curiosity, the same desire to meet you and talk about interests we have in common that prompted my invitation in the past. In your field, doctor, you're rated as highly as I am in mine.' He settled back. 'But we'll get to horses. Let's start with the problems of the human animal.'

Quietly she began to lay out every reason she believed that Dolph could not have committed murder. She told Markham how, years ago, Dolph had said he felt honor-bound not to leave Diana until she had recovered from her drug and alcohol dependence and could stand on her own. Would he have waited years only to kill her in the end? And why would he choose a violent solution, when he had the power and means to solve his problem another way? Certainly, he hadn't shot his wife to keep her from taking what belonged to her. He was a generous man, who always gave expensive gifts freely. Diana might have wanted to claim a small fortune in jewels, yet Geri knew that Dolph was prepared to give up a great deal more in a divorce settlement.

When she was done, Markham said, 'Not bad. I could ask some of those questions of a jury, and they'd scratch their heads a little. But the ones the prosecution asks will be a lot harder to answer. Can you really believe Diana Justinean broke into her own home in the middle of the night like a thief? And if she had to, then what does that say about the state of her marriage — and Mr Justinean's fabled generosity? And, finally, if she heard her husband warning her that a gun was pointed right at her, why wouldn't she call out, tell him who she was, instead of *acting* like a burglar and trying to run? Now if you had an answer for those questions, Doctor, we might be in business.'

'I think I do. Diana was a terribly self-destructive woman. Whatever happened to her was only what she allowed to happen, but she blamed Dolph for ruining her life, submerging her. I think it's possible that she was finally so lost and sick . . . that she planned this thing as her revenge. She set Dolph up to shoot her — knowing he'd also be destroying himself.'

Markham was silent for a long moment, then distractedly offered the muffins again, this time with the encouragement that they were the best in the world, made by his wife with berries from their Virginia farm. This time, Geri accepted a muffin, chagrined to realize that, until Markham's mention of his wife, she had thought there was something more to his past invitations than a pure friendly desire to discuss shared interests.

'Well now,' he said at last, 'that theory has some juice in it — a kind of inverted suicide. What do you know to persuade a jury?'

Geri described for Markham the encounter at Santa Anita when Diana had spoken bitterly of abandoning her promising career as a photographer. Told, too, about the occasion when she had absconded from a place where she had gone for treatment, and then provoked a gang rape that was virtually an attempt at sexual suicide.

'But how could she have counted on Dolph to act as he did,' Markham asked, 'to pick up a gun . . .?'

'Of course she couldn't — not a hundred percent. But she knew that Dolph had been a resistance fighter in his youth, that he kept a working gun in his bedroom and wasn't afraid to use it. And that he would have a particularly fierce reaction to anyone attempting to steal his property.'

'For what reason?'

'Because Dolph isn't just rich,' Geri said. 'He's self-made.'

Markham smiled, approving the observation. 'So . . . in all the years you knew her, nothing really changed for Diana. She felt she'd lost her husband, appeared to accept that, but she did nothing about reforming her own life . . .' Markham stood and began pacing, talking as he might in front of a jury box. 'Diana was given every chance, but she couldn't make it work. At last she faced the moment when her husband could wait no longer. He wanted to go on, to a new love, new happiness. But what alternatives confronted Diana Justinean? What life was left for a woman who'd already had everything and still couldn't be happy. . .?' Markham stopped pacing abruptly to peer contemplatively out of a window at a view of Capitol Hill. Geri realized that the seed of an idea she had planted with Markham was putting down roots. 'I can make it work,' he said abruptly, turning back to Geri. 'I couldn't help noticing that you ran to Justinean's side as soon as this happened . . .'

'Yes,' she said tentatively, expecting that Markham would now echo Lew Yancey's advice.

'Good,' he said. 'Be seen together as much as possible. We can't hide your involvement, so the perception has to be that you're comfortable together — happy in a way that might very well drive a sick and jealous woman to the most pathetically desperate scheme out of sheer resentment.'

He leaned forward, lowering his voice. 'But don't fool yourself, Geri. I can see you're gutsy, but this is going to be tougher than you can imagine. You're too young to remember how Ingrid Bergman was raked over the coals when she carried on with Rosselini — a woman with the face of a saint — even played saints and nuns in the movies — and they called her a whore. Taylor, Happy Rockefeller, they've all gone through it. That's how it'll be for you, too. It could get so bad that you're sorry you started . . . and you hate Dolph for dragging you into this.' He sat down again and looked at her intently. 'If that's going to happen, then give it up now because we can't win. Because the worse it gets, the more you can take, the better it will be in the end. That's the way we like to do it in our society. Go all out to burn the witches, then suddenly have an attack of guilt and canonize the people we were ready to destroy . . .'

They made arrangements for the next appointment, to which Geri would bring Dolph, and then Markham escorted her out.

'We'll talk horses some other time,' he said, just before leaving her at the elevators.

All the way back to New York, she thought about the warning Markham had given her. Could it get so bad, that she would ever hate Dolph?

At the arraignment, he had been granted release pending trial after posting bail at half a million dollars. Since making that court appearance, he hadn't wanted to do anything else without Geri.

When he had first said he expected to draw strength from her, Geri had taken it as sweet cajolery; he had never needed any moral or emotional support from anyone. But having committed a fatal blunder of such magnitude, he seemed to have lost some essential faith in himself. In front of his subordinates and for the sake of the cameras, he still maintained the image of being totally certain and in command. Alone with Geri, however, he clung to her as never before.

'Promise you'll never leave me again,' he had said to her — not once but several times. She could sense that he thought nothing bad would have ever befallen him if he had not let her go.

The novelty of feeling needed by him was gratifying — at first. But as the weeks passed she missed the independence she'd had, and vaguely regretted the role in which she had been cast by events. True to Ed Markham's predictions, the way in which she and Dolph were protrayed by the press stirred up some fierce public indignation against them. Angry graffiti was spray-painted onto the walls of the Glen Cove estate and, one weekend, when Geri went to have her hair cut at a beauty salon, in a local shopping center, she was recognized, refused a chair, and followed across the parking lot by local women who screamed insults at her. After escaping to the refuge of Dolph's Corniche convertible and driving a short distance down the road, she pulled over and sat for an hour, dry-eyed but trembling more violently than she had at any time since the slide.

The next day, she told Dolph that she couldn't afford to go on neglecting the clinic, and would have to spend at least a few days in Saratoga. It was true, of course, that her business needed attention. But she also needed some breathing space, a chance to sort out her priorities. The shock of Diana's death had thrown her and Dolph together again too quickly and too violently. She didn't like having him feel dependent on her anymore than she had accepted his desire for her to be dependent on him.

It was a cold week in the middle of November when Geri returned to Saratoga. She found business at the clinic worse than she had been led to believe by the reports of her staff. Rather than add to her worries, the associates she'd left in charge had not reported the truth: only one-tenth of the capacity was being utilized. Aware that Geri had been spending her time at Dolph's side, many customers had gone elsewhere. The Graymar-Keyes Clinic, once a unique facility, had now spawned enough imitators so that there were several places thoroughbred owners could ship their horses for the same treatment.

If things didn't take a turn for the better soon, Geri realized, the clinic could probably not be saved. She would not go back to Dolph and borrow again the money she had so proudly repaid.

She spent a few days making calls to owners she had helped in the past, confessing her need for their support. Most said they would gladly entrust their horses to Geri under the usual circumstances, but they knew she wasn't attending to treatment personally, and couldn't possibly give the kind of concentration to her work that she had in the past. There were enough risks on the racetrack without putting valuable animals into questionable care.

One evening, Geri called to her office four of the six interne vets she'd been training and reluctantly told them they had better begin looking for other positions. After they filed out, she sat wondering if she'd given up too much for the sake of her romance with Dolph. Career, her good name? She was tempted to stay right here and build again, not go back to him . . . Then she reminded herself of Ed Markham's prescient warnings. She might come to hate Dolph for dragging her down, he'd said. She had to fight against it.

It was dark when she left the main clinic building and walked up to her house. A cold November drizzle pricked at her skin. Even the prospect of a quiet night in her own home did little to cheer her. Soon after she had joined Dolph, the pleasant local woman who had kept house for her in the past had stopped showing up and Geri had not replaced her. The rooms had quickly grown dusty; where the redecorations were only half finished, they looked now like rooms half in decay.

As she approached the back door she heard the kitchen phone ringing. It would be Dolph, she thought. He called a few times each day. Thoughtful, yet there was that sense of dependency, too. Was she still his love, or only his talisman?

The phone stopped ringing before she got the door open, and then began again ten minutes later after she had made a fire and poured herself a glass of sherry. She almost didn't answer it. She liked being alone, away from the cares of being damned as the scarlet woman, accomplice to the cold-blooded wife-killer.

Markham's words came back to her again —

She grabbed up the phone, ashamed of that momentary defection of the heart. 'I'm here,' she said.

'Geri?'

Not Dolph. But she knew this voice, someone she couldn't place. 'Yes . . .?'

'It's Bill Quinn. The painter. We met in —'

'I remember . . .'

'I've been trying on and off for a few days, not knowing when you might be there. I hope I'm not calling at a bad time,' he added, apparently sensitive to the nuances of her despair.

'It's all right, Bill,' she replied honestly. 'Lately, they're all bad times.'

'I can imagine. I've been reading the newspapers.' He paused. 'I was wondering . . . if you're free tonight?'

'Tonight? Where are you calling from?'

'Right here in Saratoga. Washed my last brush for the great Peabody a couple of weeks ago and headed here. I figured you'd show up sooner or later, and I could use the time meanwhile to put some finishing touches to your painting and start some new oils . . .'

The commission! Oh God, could she have asked for anything more? She had promised to pay him fifteen thousand dollars for a painting, c.o.d. Now, here he was — and from the sound of it he had given up his job on the expectation of payment, while she wasn't sure she could write a check to cover all her bills let alone buy herself an expensive whim.

The least she could do was explain it in person. 'I'm very glad you called, Bill. I have no plans tonight.'

'Good. Let me take you out to a nice dinner.'

'No. Why don't you just come over —'

'Don't worry,' he said. 'I'll be buying with your money,

won't I? Suppose I pick you up in half an hour. Can't wait to show you what I've done. You're going to be knocked out.'

She spent ten whirlwind minutes after the call tidying the living room and setting up a bar trolley with ice, wine and whiskey. They might both need the anesthetic. The next ten minutes she gave to reviewing her salary obligations and other debts, and checking the statements of her bank accounts. The quick accounting confirmed her fears: even aside from her mortgages, she was substantially in the red. She couldn't possibly honor her commitment to Quinn.

When she ran upstairs finally, jumped in and out of a shower, grabbed an electric blue Valentino shift with a low back, dried and brushed out her hair and dabbed on some Diorissimo, it was all an afterthought. She wasn't sure what motive had sparked the sudden impulse to make an effort. Was it to compensate Quinn by giving him a full evening with a woman going all out to look her best? Or to compensate herself for the psychological punishment she had been taking over the past weeks by masquerading — for just this one night — as a woman who could still enjoy herself, flirt, explore options, act unashamed of being sexy and beautiful?

She vaguely sensed still a third possibility in the little rush of excitement she felt when the door bell finally rang. In the vision of her memory he had been attractive, yet there had been a weariness about him, hints of suspicion or self-doubt constantly dimming his gray-green eyes. The man she saw when the door swung open instantly projected a warmth and confidence she hadn't seen before. From his quick smile, the timbre of his voice when he said, 'Hello again,' Geri got the impression of someone who was now totally in charge of himself. Perhaps it was the effect of graduating from the 'school' of Peabody. He looked less ragged, too, his hair recently cut, wearing pale gray flannel slacks, a wine-red silk shirt and a charcoal double-breasted blazer.

While she appraised the change in him, he also studied her. The moment of rediscovery captured them both until he lifted up the large flat object he had propped beside him — the painting wrapped under big sheets of cardboard.

439

She led him straight to the living room. Get a drink into him, she thought, and the blow might be softened a little. But before she could offer anything, he produced a bottle of chilled Perrier-Jouet he'd been carrying concealed behind the large canvas. 'Hope you won't mind drinking this with me. I'm in a mood for celebration.'

'Why should I mind?' She took two champagne flutes from a cabinet and set them on the bar trolley.

'The way things have been going for you lately, I know celebrations aren't exactly the order of the day.' He popped the cork.

She couldn't break his bubble, not yet. 'This one is yours, not mine. I don't mind helping out.'

'And I'll do the same for you someday . . .' He poured and handed her a glass. 'Hey, I ought to show you what we're celebrating . . .' Leaving his own glass of champagne fizzing on the bar, he bounded to the canvas he'd left leaning against a wall, tore away the cardboard, then carried it to the center of the room and turned it around with a flourish.

Pale dawn light, the clean open space of a field, shadowy horses standing in the mist, all trapped in a hurricane of quick brushstrokes. It had some of the same elements of the painting he had destroyed, but it was not a re-creation; she understood now why he had been dissatisfied with the other one.

Living with Sylvia Balkin, then Dolph, Geri had become knowledgeable about painting. She knew the difference between the mild feeling of appreciation produced by looking at good, competent work — and the pure visceral thrill that came with being a witness to unique talent. The paintings of Van Gogh brought that thrill, and of Monet, and Matisse and others hallowed in museums . . .

But she could hardly believe this painting did it, too. It occurred to her she might simply be overtired, or too eager not to dash Quinn's celebratory mood. If she saw what she thought was brilliant and masterful, perhaps it was only a form of hallucination. She moved nearer. Up close, where the cohesive image dissolved into a detail of colors dabbed on in

440

myriad lines and patches, she was still awed by the technique and the amount of labor.

'You like it . . .?' Quinn asked at last.

'As much as anything I've ever seen. More. Because the subject means more to me.'

'I admit I was fishing for compliments,' he said, grinning, 'but I didn't want to catch something too big to swallow.'

'I mean it, though. It delivers all you said it would: I'm absolutely . . . knocked out.'

He picked up his champagne. 'Let's celebrate then.' He lifted his glass. 'To a satisfied customer.'

Her heart sank. She hadn't the guts to do anything but smile — and raise her own glass quickly to hide the strain.

He drove them to The Wishing Well. It was quieter in the off-season, without the racing crowd, but the atmosphere was kept cheery by the lady at the piano, banging out the old favorites. Geri was grateful for anything that might keep the mood upbeat after she broke her news.

While they finished off the champagne at the house, he had told her he believed the painting was a personal breakthrough — the first in which he had fulfilled his capabilities. Then he confessed his gratitude to Geri for giving him the incentive to make the breakthrough — and for the generous fee, which had allowed him the freedom to leave Peabody.

It was cowardly, but Geri kept postponing the moment of revelation. She loved the painting, didn't want to let go of it.

When they were settled in the restaurant, their orders taken, Quinn said, 'I should apologize for getting so carried away with myself, running off at the mouth about what I've done — ze gr-reat masterpiece!' He mocked its significance now, rolling out the phrase as if pronounced by some vaudeville notion of an art critic.

'You have a right to be proud.'

'Maybe. But it's a little thoughtless, talking about all the warm sunlight shining down on me while you're stuck under your private thundercloud.'

'Not so private at that,' she remarked, rather than

441

dismissing his concern. She was hungry for a chance to unburden herself and she couldn't confess to Dolph how deeply demoralized she was — not while he had cast her in the role of his mainstay.

Quinn took the cue. 'I can guess how tough it is. I'd be devastated if the critics gave me bad reviews as a painter. You're getting bad reviews every day as a person.' He leaned closer across the table. 'I hate to think of you being hurt by this, maybe losing everything.'

It was an opening for honesty, and she had to take it. 'I've lost a lot already, Quinn. I didn't know how to tell you before . . . but all this time I've spent with Dolph away from my own work, my business has suffered.' Her eyes had been roaming, retreating from his, but now she looked at him directly. 'The thing is . . . I don't see how I could —'

'Pay for the painting,' he supplied.

'Yes. I'm so sorry. I do think it's truly magnificent.' She looked down. Disappointing him made her feel so rotten that her eyes had begun to fill with tears.

He reached over and grabbed her hand. 'Hey, there's nothing to feel bad about. You gave me a reason to dig down and come up with my best. I'll always be grateful for that.'

She liked his touch, but it made her self-conscious. 'I'm sure the painting could sell easily,' she offered brightly as she retracted her hand, covering the move by using it to wipe dry the corner of her eyes. 'Show it to dealers, one can probably get you a good price.'

'Oh no. I'm not taking this anywhere. It's yours.'

'It was a commission. I can't accept without paying.'

'Then you'll owe me the money.'

'Maybe you don't understand: I can't ask Dolph to pay, either. It just isn't possible to —'

'Damn it,' he broke in, his eyes flashing, '*you* don't understand. It makes no sense for anyone else to have it. You gave me the inspiration. It was done out of . . .' He stopped, then finished differently. 'It *belongs* to you, that's all.'

There was a long pause, a moment of unspoken confessions, with silence to bless the pretense that it had not taken place. It was the wrong time for it, they both knew.

'Then of course,' she said, 'I accept. I will pay, though, whenever it's possible . . .'

Retreating from the minefield of live emotions, they spent the rest of the meal exchanging histories. What had led to her career as a vet? he wanted to know. How had the son of a steel-worker developed an interest in painting? she asked. The answers took them both back to their beginnings. Geri found she could talk to Quinn about the hollow without getting melodramatic. The company town where he'd been born had its own version of poverty, lightened by small pleasures — not the rustic deprivations of the hollow, but the grind of boring dangerous work in poor conditions and living in cramped houses with windows always darkened by soot from the blast furnaces.

She listened with complete empathy when he told about the day he had decided to be a painter. He had been eight years old, a child climbing one of the hills outside the steeltown after school, and he had come upon an old man doing an oil painting of the view.

'It was such a god-awful ugly place, that town,' Quinn said. 'Dark smoke pouring out of the big stacks at that gigantic mill day and night, smudging the air and sky, turning even the trees gray. I hated it. But then I saw this man painting it, shrinking it down to fit on his little canvas — a poor steelman from the nightshift, using his off-time to make a picture, not a very good one. But I remember thinking: if only I could do that, then I could change my life, I'd be in control. It was like a magic spell. I could make that huge, dominating, hideous place small . . . and it couldn't hold me anymore. So I kept climbing that hill and painting pictures . . .'

The rain had stopped by the time he drove her home. The air was fresh and cool, and she wanted to be with him through the night. When they reached the door and he pulled her around gently and kissed her, she yielded to it completely —

Until the moment right before she knew the last restraints would be melted. Then she broke from him and turned away. 'It can't be now,' she said, nearly a whisper.

443

'Because of love,' Quinn asked sharply, 'or just loyalty?'

'I don't know. And maybe I can't know until Dolph is cleared.'

He waited quietly while she took out her key and opened the door. From the threshold, she looked back at him. 'You're such a lovely man, Quinn. I'll cherish what you gave me tonight.' She smiled. 'The painting, too. It's a cinch you're going far . . .'

'I might,' he said. 'But never too far.' He backed away. 'Look for me when you've done your duty, and you can be sure of what you want.'

She closed the door as he blew her a kiss.

CHAPTER EIGHT

The trial convened in the second week of May.

While she waited for the ordeal to begin, Geri had come to terms with her commitment to stand by Dolph. Often, she thought back to her night with Quinn. Every sensation of their kiss came alive again, the feel of his lips on hers, the smell of his skin, just a faint lingering trace of the soap he'd used, not the more refined smell of fine cologne she had been accustomed to with Dolph.

But from each small escape into her memory, she returned with her sense of responsibility intact. She knew too well what it was like to be unfairly accused to consider deserting Dolph while he faced the same predicament. And didn't she love him? Dolph was the magical emperor who had lifted her up into a world that had once seemed as far above her as heaven itself. He was the one who had freed her passions, truly made her a woman.

She had been warned that the stress of the pre-trial period would raise doubts. But once they could put it behind them, wouldn't they recover the joy in each other they had known at the beginning?

If they could put it all behind them . . .

At least, true to Ed Markham's prediction, public sentiment had already begun to change. Throughout the process of jury selection, as prospective jurors were questioned about any prejudices that might have been shaped by pre-trial publicity, it became clear that Geri was no longer strictly regarded as a scheming woman who had shattered the sanctity of Justinean's marriage. There were many who saw her as a steadfast companion who had not only remained by her man in his darkest hour, but might have provided him with relief in years past from a deeply troubled and self-destructive young wife. The seven men and five women finally chosen seemed able to judge the case without letting moral preconceptions interfere in a fair verdict.

The county District Attorney set out to establish, first, a motive for murder: Dolph Justinean's desire to be free of his neurotic wife — and without paying a settlement that might run into many million dollars — so that he could marry his mistress. In the opening days, the prosecution presented a series of witnesses to attest to the intensity of the affair between Dolph and Geri, including many whose sentiments actually rested with the lovers — servants of Dolph, staff from his stables, co-workers of Geri's from her clinic.

Proof of a passionate, illicit affair would have been enough to tilt some juries toward a guilty verdict. But the openness that these lovers had already demonstrated neutralized much of the damage — and, indeed, raised questions that aided the defense. Having been able to conduct their romance happily and without interference for so long, why should murder be necessary?

The other thrust of the prosecution's case was to prove that Dolph Justinean must have known the identity of his victim when he pulled the trigger. With charts and photographs, the D.A. illustrated that the amount of light produced by a half moon penetrating the uncurtained bedroom windows on the clear night when the killing had occurred, would have been sufficient to make the person standing before Dolph Justinean recognizable as his wife. Having made the point with seeming effectiveness, the prosecutor rested his case and Edmund Grace Markham rose to begin his defense.

Since Geri had suggested that Diana Justinean might have contrived her own death as a suicidal form of revenge on her husband, Markham had decided that this theory would be the cornerstone of his strategy to win acquittal. He found no lack of witnesses to help paint the portrait of Diana Justinean as a desperate and self-destructive woman. Psychiatrists who had treated her, friends from the time when she'd worked as a photographer, people who were with her at expensive clinics where she had been in the fruitless search for a cure to her drinking and drug abuse, casual sex partners, were brought to the stand one after the other, all painting the portrait of Diana Justinean as obsessed with a paranoid belief that her husband had forced her to become nothing more than a decorative sex object, with all sense of dignity and purpose stolen from her.

There were, too, character witnesses for Dolph to counter any idea that he could have been so cruel and insensitive, and Geri was also brought to the stand. Her honest confession of the long untroubled affair with Dolph, followed by an account of the immense pleasure she took from her work that made her reluctant to rush into marriage, bolstered the idea that there could have been no pressure on her part that might have instigated Dolph to dispose of his wife. Markham also brought out that Geri had only a limited interest in the luxuries that Dolph's money could buy. If she was with Dolph Justinean, he made clear, it wasn't because of his money.

In the courthouse hallway, during the adjournment at the end of the day following completion of Geri's testimony, Markham caught her.

'You were great in there,' he said. 'It ought to be hard for anyone to believe Dolph could be a bad guy and hold onto a woman like you.'

'You made me look good, Ed. Thanks. What's next?'

'I'll put Dolph on the stand tomorrow. We'll reinforce that his marriage to Diana was really over before he took up with you, and that he willingly put off the divorce until he thought she could cope with the break . . .'

To make sure that Dolph was prepared for the next day's testimony, Markham went off to confer with him briefly.

As she waited to go home with Dolph, Geri was tapped on the shoulder by one of the bailiffs. 'Phone call for you, Miz

Keyes. You can take it in the court clerk's office . . .' He pointed to a door off the corridor.

It would be the clinic, she guessed; the number had been left with her associates so they could consult her if difficult problems came up.

But there was an odd silence the moment she lifted the phone and said 'Hello', a silence that brought a vague sense of recognition.

'Hello . . .?' Geri repeated.

The voice came back at her, lower-pitched and huskier than when she'd heard it last, but instantly recognizable all the same. 'Been seein' so much of you lately on the TV, Geri-Jo, that I just had to call and tell you how sweet and pretty you look in all those fine, expensive clothes. Wouldn't half mind getting some of your hand-me-downs *these* days.' There was a short, throaty laugh.

Geri was rocked instantly by a collision of opposing emotions. Molly was alive — not lost to her forever. That was cause for relief. Yet, at the same time, she remembered that the last time they had been together, Molly had nearly taken away her freedom, cost her all the years of her youth. What did she want to take now?

To steady herself, Geri leaned heavily against the unoccupied desk where she had taken the call, at the same time glancing toward a door open to the corridor, hoping no reporters had been around to see her reaction. Some of them might sniff out a story, and dog her steps until they got it. And this story, Geri knew beyond doubt, had the potential to reverse the outcome of the trial which presently seemed headed for acquittal.

'Where are you, Molly?'

'Over at a motel somewhere not too far from Kennedy Airport. Just flew in a little while ago. Of course, I didn't wait too long to get in touch with you . . .'

'I'll come now,' Geri said flatly. 'Wait there.'

'Don't want me comin' around to your front door, eh?' Molly gave a throaty laugh. 'Sure, I can understand that.'

Molly gave her the name of the motel, and said she'd be waiting in the cocktail lounge.

Just before hanging up, Geri added a quick warning. 'Don't talk to anyone 'til I get there, Mol'. Please. I mean, about knowing me or —'

'Now, you don't have to fuss about that, Geri-Jo,' Molly cut in. 'Because, you know, if I didn't understand how all-fired important it is to keep certain things real quiet, I wouldn't have come all this long way . . .'

The Silvercrest Motel, a two-story box with a large electric sign spelling out the overnight price of $25 in neon, stood among the many used car lots and diners that lined Queens Boulevard, half way to New York City from the airport. Geri told the taxi driver to go past it a couple of blocks before letting her out. She had left the courthouse through a back door after telling Dolph that she had received a call from a trainer at Belmont who wanted her there for a consultation. Still, the possibility existed that some avid reporter might have followed.

Satisfied that she was unobserved, Geri entered the motel. At the door of a gloomy cocktail lounge adjoining the small lobby, she paused to let her eyes adjust. Several of the booths along one wall were occupied, but there were couples in all but one. There, a woman sat alone, facing away from the door. Geri could see only her hair, still vivid red and worn very long, pulled back on one side by a bright blue plastic comb.

As she went toward her, Geri was overwhelmed by a wave of sadness. Thinking of the little she knew about her sister's life in the years since they had last seen each other, she yearned to be able to start over with her, sweep away all the meanness and hatred between them.

As soon as Molly looked up from her drink, the toll taken by the past fourteen years was apparent. Her face was still beautiful, yet it wasn't the fresh effortless beauty which, at the age of twenty eight, should not have been beyond her. A tautness around the eyes and mouth gave an impression that the face was being held together by a steady application of will. Tiny lines that had begun to etch the skin seemed to be hints of a much more complex network of straining threads that existed beneath, like the guy wires used to keep the facade of a damaged

449

building from collapsing. Her eyes were still the color of the sea, but not so clear and bright, as though those seas had been polluted by the traffic of too many sordid visions.

In other ways, Geri reflected, Molly did not look so bad. Her low-cut green silk dress was stylish, and she was wearing a gold bracelet watch, and a necklace of heavy gold chain with a large aquamarine pendant.

For a long moment after Geri slid onto the opposite bench, they stared at each other. Not a word passed between them before a waiter appeared beside the table, and Geri ordered a martini.

When the waiter left, Molly took a sip of the iced whiskey in front of her, and said, 'I was down in Houston. Not too bad a place to be. Oil men spread their money around pretty thick if you know how to make 'em feel good. Especially the old ones, they're so damn grateful if you can help 'em sink their little ol' drill one more time . . . bring in one more tiny gusher.' Molly let out a small tired laugh, as she fingered the gem dangling at her throat. 'You get the picture, Geri-Jo? You know what I've been doin' while you were turnin' yourself into a famous fancy horse doctor . . .?'

'I know,' Geri said.

Molly went right on, not bothering to ask where or how Geri had learned. At the place where she worked in Houston, she said, there was television to keep the girls amused in the off-hours. 'I was watchin' a couple of days ago, and the news came on with a story about this trial up here. You looked so fine, Geri-Jo, walkin' up those courthouse steps on the arm of a man this TV reporter was callin' one of the richest men in the world. I guess I hadn't realized quite how well you were doin' when I saw your picture in the papers, some years back — that time you made a big splash for exposin' some crooked deal . . .'

'You called me then, didn't you? You called my clinic . . . but you wouldn't speak.'

Molly shrugged. 'When it came right down to it, I guess, I couldn't think of what to say . . .'

'What did you have in mind when you placed the calls?' Geri asked, hoping she could draw out some acknowledgement of the emotional need, the primal connection of family.

'Can't rightly say. Felt like . . . once I found out where you were, I ought to do somethin' about it. So I did that much, but I . . I couldn't take it further.' She smiled crookedly. 'Maybe it's as well I waited, though. 'Cause now, seein' you all wrapped up in helpin' this zillionaire Romeo of yours get away with murder —'

'Dolph is innocent,' Geri cut in.

Molly sipped at her drink. 'Yeah, I know . . . that's what all the smart folks will come 'round to believe. 'Cause, for them, if anythin's too simple they don't trust it. But I can tell what's in a man's mind as well as anyone — and I say Mr Justinean knew exactly what he was doin' when he killed his wife. The big thing savin' him right now, Geri-Jo, is that, standin' alongside you, he picks up a shine that blinds everyone who looks at it.'

It was the same old jealousy and hatred coming out, Geri thought. Molly's verdict was simply a way of bringing Geri down, shaming her for complicity in saving a criminal. There could be no doubt any more about what had motivated Molly to come. Geri's hope that she could deal reasonably with her sister, build an emotional bridge, all but vanished.

'But you and I know,' Molly was saying, 'how fast that shine would disappear if your very own sister came forward and let it be known that murder wasn't such a strange idea to Geri-Jo Lockely . . . if not to this fine smooth-talkin' lady, *Doctor* Geri Keyes.'

Molly drew out the second name, mocking it. Then she dipped her mouth to her glass and sipped at the last of her whiskey, her eyes smiling at Geri all the time over the rim.

Hearing herself called Geri-Jo brought no nostalgic pang; the way Molly mocked the change seemed to undo in one stroke everything that Geri had fought to make of herself. And the threat Molly had now made specific revived all the bitterness Geri had felt the last time they had been together and Molly had betrayed her.

Choked with rage Geri was unable to speak for a moment. As if it was the only way to purge the will of a demon within

451

her, she grabbed the glass out of Molly's hands, and splashed the last of the whiskey and melted ice into her face.

The look of shock vanished from Molly's face in an instant, chased by a slow, satisfied smile. It was a victory for her to have made Geri lose her control, and she consolidated it by not reacting in kind. 'Goodness, I didn't know you well-bred women did things like that,' Molly said quietly, and called to the waiter to bring another as she dried her face with a cocktail napkin.

Geri was torn between running out, and staying, making the hopeless attempt to reason. 'Damn you, Molly!' she seethed, trying to keep her voice from rising. 'Why do you have to come at me like this? Making it always a war between us . . .'

'What else can it be?' Molly said simply.

'What else?' Geri echoed, incredulous. 'We're *sisters*.'

'I'm just one of a few, ain't I? The rest all got killed, and that was that — we left 'em, moved on. So what difference does it make if that part of you and me is dead, too? We don't have to feel anything for each other, Geri-Jo. We each just got to make our own way . . .'

Geri's anger was spent. And with Molly's reference to the slide, it suddenly occurred to her that their sisterhood was just another victim of that terrible day in their lives. Rather than face the pain of any more losses after one catastrophic tragedy, Molly had stripped herself of all ties. In some way, maybe it explained what had happened with Pa: the incest was really her way of denying she had a father. She didn't want to think of herself as anyone's daughter, anyone's sister. Perhaps Molly had suffered in her own way over every death, suffered so intensely that afterward she could only shut down every bit of feeling that was left. Indeed, it might be the same raw sensitivity that had made her always seem so oblivious to her surroundings. It was her mechanism for surviving the hardships of the hollow, and the life of heartbreak she had been trained to expect.

'Molly,' Geri appealed to her, 'we could help each other. I could help you now.' Seeing the smirk that met her attempt at an armistice, Geri's fury welled again. 'But instead of coming to me for help, you start by trying to blackmail me . . .'

'I don't want your damn help,' Molly said sharply. 'I don't want to feel I owe you my life or anythin' in it. Understand, Geri-Jo? All I want is what I think I got comin'. You got so damn much — you've joined with those folks who used to keep the rest of us down when we were in the hollow. Well, the only way it makes sense to me is to *take* it from you, to make you pay for bein' one of them . . .'

This reasoning was twisted, but Geri could hear the echo of Pa's voice, the same resentments. She had escaped their full effect, but she understood how they had taken root in Molly, poisoned her vision of the world.

'Listen, Mol',' she said, unwilling to surrender. 'If there's something you need, I'll try to help you get it. A different life, a job, whatever . . . But you're to give it a chance — give us a chance to work this out —'

'Forget it, Geri-Jo. The chance I needed was one I lost a long time ago. To be born in a different place, to different people. But with all that's been, nothin's gonna help me now.'

'Anybody can change, Mol'. I was born to all the same —'

'No!' Molly shouted her down. 'You were born special.' She looked hard at Geri, and for a moment the burning glare of hatred was softened by something else, a grudging admiration. Then, the waiter set a new drink in front of her, and as she sipped from it that hard shell settled over her again.

'And I was born to be what I am,' she said, lowering the drink again. 'It's never been different for me. Never.' She stared bleakly into her glass. 'Tell you the truth, there's been times I wish I'd walked out into the rain that day and got caught in the slide with the others. Hell, it seems like I got buried in the mud, anyway . . .' The hard glitter came into her eyes, and she smiled, the line between her lips as fine as the edge of a blade. 'But that was before I saw you sashayin' along on the arm of that murderer, Geri. Right then it all turned around. I got hope now to have all the things I want for me and my —'

Abruptly, she hoisted the whiskey and took a long swig, as though she had decided to swallow whatever she was on the

453

verge of saying. But Geri caught it — the hint of wanting something for someone else. Geri glanced questioningly at Molly, intrigued by this tiny proof of some unselfishness.

But Molly dodged an answer, leaning across the table to demand in a throaty growl, 'You're my hope, Geri-Jo. Because I'm gonna get everything I need from you — and your solid gold friend.'

How was it possible, Geri wondered, that despite all the threats, she still had the absurd wish to grab onto Molly and try to convince her that she would give money gladly — whatever she had — if only the request could be redefined as a gift, asked and given out of love? Out of no more than a *hope* of love.

But to be squeezed for blackmail . . .?

The last burst of warmth Geri had felt toward Molly was snuffed out. 'If I had to worry about the past, you think I would've come out in the open with Dolph? I'm safe from that. I knew it when I started. Tell your story . . . but if anybody goes looking for proof they won't find it. So what you're doing would just look like a shakedown by a whore that didn't work.'

Molly took the insult equably, leaning back in the booth, looking smug and content. 'There's one more thing I ought to mention: there was a time when I was workin' the hotels down in Lexington during Derby Week. Got busted by a vice cop . . . and the way things worked out, this fella took a likin' to me . . .' Molly paused, looking down, and Geri sensed she was remembering the man, that he had been important to her. 'Ended up livin' with Mike, made it for more'n a whole year together. But then he got into drugs and I . . .' She looked up again, sharply, as if embarrassed at being caught in a moment of reverie. 'Didn't work out, anyway. But while I was with that cop, I happened to learn about how your case got scrubbed — how a whole bunch of police files and court records disappeared after a lot of money changed hands. Fact is, Geri, there was a bunch of people who knew — and that's one of the reasons you've been safe so far: not just 'cause the proof is gone, but 'cause there's nobody on the inside who'd want to blow open a story that makes the police, and people in the courts and even the statehouse, look so bad. But I'd do it if I had nothin' to lose. Once folks know you'd been accused of murderin' Pa, and then you'd run, and then somebody done all that payin' off . . . how do you think they'll put it all together? Like you was innocent . . .?'

Of course, Molly's ability to prove that the old case against Geri had been deliberately eradicated might be no less damaging than exposing the records.

If she simply yielded, Geri thought, that might save her and Dolph. But her sister would be lost forever; Molly would take the money and disappear . . . at least until the time she wanted more. Even while she made sounds of surrender, Geri was wondering what she could do to end the war between them without allowing herself to be plundered. 'How much money did you want . . .?' she asked Molly at last.

Molly gave a gloating smile. 'I want to be a millionaire — like you.'

It took a second for the immensity of the demand to sink in. 'Mol', there's no way I can manage that. I'm not that rich . . .'

'You've got that man, and he's got plenty. Listen, I've read up on the trial now, and I see where that mouthpiece, Markham, is gettin' a million dollars to speak up for Justinean in court. So I figure if I keep the same client outta jail by keepin' my mouth shut, it shouldn't be worth a penny less.'

Geri studied her sister's expression, hard as granite. 'I've never told Dolph about that part of my life,' she said. 'If I spring it on him now, it could tear us apart — and if he cut loose right away, it might not affect the verdict. With all the records missing since before I knew him, he could convince people I'd never told him — that I was a schemer who'd led him on. There's just as much chance he'd gain sympathy as lose it.'

Geri was glad to see Molly nodding slowly, as though the improvised reasoning had been accepted. In fact, such an outcome wasn't impossible; but Geri thought it more likely, given her closeness to Justinean, that a jury learning of past charges against her would believe the lovers had conspired to commit murder.

'Seems to me,' Molly said sullenly, 'you still got a damn good reason to pay me off, even if Justinean doesn't. I don't care how you do it, but you'd better find a way.'

'I'll give you as much as I can . . . without having to go to Dolph or anyone else.'

'How much is that?'

Geri was familiar with the limits of her credit from the financial review she had made at the time Quinn brought her the painting. Though she had borrowed heavily against the clinic, business had improved lately, and she thought she could increase her loan. 'Fifty thousand dollars,' she said.

'Won't do, Geri-Jo. You've got your man with all his mountains of money. Well, I want my piece of the action, too.'

The ultimatum had been expected. For once Geri was prepared. Whatever she paid, she knew, it would be a way of buying time, time for Dolph's trial to be resolved — and maybe, if she was lucky, time to work on Molly and resurrect that part of her that needed to believe in love. With this in mind, Geri dangled the hook she had been carefully baiting. 'You've got to let me get my hands on Dolph's money . . . or I can't share it with you . . .'

Molly's eyes suddenly flared open with comprehension. She sat back, picked up a plastic swizzle stick and drummed it thoughtfully on the table. 'All right,' she drawled at last. 'Fifty thousand . . . to start with. That'll see you through to the other side of the trial. Then you'll be able to get married, won'tcha? And when that happens, you'll pay off. But for waitin', I'll want a bonus. You understand, sister? When you're the wife of one of the richest men in the world, you'll keep payin' me off for helpin' you get there. One million won't get rid of me then. I'll want . . . well, *five* sounds like a good number.' She smiled when Geri's head jolted up in shock. 'If I didn't get it, I think I could still talk to your brand new husband and make you sorry I did. Don't you think I could manage that . . .?'

'Yes, Molly,' Geri said coldly, 'I believe you could.' She stood up. 'I'll need a week or two to get your money.'

'My down payment,' Molly said.

'Where will you be?'

'Haven't put down any roots yet. I'll call you.'

They took another long silent look at each other, and then Geri walked away.

She had hardly stepped out of the motel when she covered her face with her hands and started to weep. Not for herself, but for the rest of her brothers and sisters, all those fate had chosen to carry away instead of Molly.

The ways of destiny had never seemed as unfathomable as they did tonight.

CHAPTER NINE

Dolph took the stand the next day, and for the remainder of the week Ed Markham kept him there, answering questions about his marriage to Diana, his affair with Geri, and finally about the circumstances of the shooting. Markham's examination was followed by the relentless cross-examination of the District Attorney. Through it all, Dolph remained polite and self-controlled. Day after day, as she watched the faces of the jury, Geri felt that he was winning, proving himself to be a man who had far too much to lose — and was too much in charge of his emotions — to commit a rash, ill-conceived murder.

In every moment she could get away from Dolph, Geri worked on the problem of raising some money to appease Molly, enough to stall off the threat until the trial was over and won. By arranging a second mortgage on the clinic with an upstate bank, she raised a hundred and twenty thousand dollars. She had always known that the limit of her borrowing power would provide her with twice what she had promised Molly — but she knew, too, that Molly might at any moment make new demands. It would be wise to have some cash in reserve.

As Dolph went into his fourth day on the stand, Geri was still waiting for a contact from Molly. At last it came, this time via a message that was left at the clinic giving a New York telephone number. When Geri called, an operator answered: 'Regency Hotel . . .'

So Molly wasn't waiting to have the money before spending it. The Regency, recently opened on Park Avenue, was one of the city's most expensive new hotels. Geri asked for 'Molly Lockely' and was put through to a room.

'Got my money?' Molly demanded as soon as she heard Geri's voice.

'Yes . . .'

'Bring it to me here, tonight.'

Arriving that evening for their meeting, Geri was alarmed to find Molly occupying a suite, accommodations that probably cost six or seven hundred dollars a day. Strewn around the rooms were many other indications that Molly had already been on a spending spree. Several dresses from expensive boutiques along Madison Avenue lay across a chair, as if Molly had just taken them out of their boxes. On the floor lay several pairs of shoes from the Bennis-Edwards shop near the hotel, each costing several hundred dollars. Spending at that rate, it wouldn't be long before Molly had run through all of the money Geri had brought.

'This has to last for a while,' Geri cautioned, handing over an attaché case in which the stacks of bills were packed. 'I don't know when I can get more.'

'Not before your honeymoon, I imagine,' said Molly, as she laid the case on the bed and snapped open the latches. 'But don't worry about it, honey. Everything in here is going straight into my piggy bank. I won't have to spend a dime. New York's a great town for a girl like me,' she added. 'I should've come here a long time ago . . .'

The realization that her sister had set up shop took away any incentive Geri might have had to try reasoning again with her.

But in any event, words would have been lost on Molly right now. She had opened the lid of the attaché case and was staring mesmerized at the bundles of money packed inside.

Geri went out the door, and Molly didn't even look up.

It was early Wednesday afternoon when Dolph completed his testimony. Summations were given by the two opposing sides, and the case was finally delivered into the hands of the jury.

When the jury remained sequestered at the end of its first day of deliberations, Ed Markham confessed to surprise. After the defense he had built, he anticipated it would be a simple job to decide that Dolph Justinean could not possibly be declared guilty — as the law expected — beyond any reasonable doubt.

But on the Thursday as well, the jury stayed out. The foreman sent in a request to re-examine some of the prosecution evidence — charts illustrating the amount of moonlight on the night of the murder, and the way the beams would have fallen through the bedroom windows.

As the period of waiting lengthened, Dolph was permitted to remain at his Glen Cove estate instead of sitting in court. He would be notified as soon as a verdict had been reached. Geri and Markham stayed with him. The tension ratcheted tighter with every hour, though Markham and Geri did most of the pacing while Dolph remained outwardly calm. He spent time conducting business on the phone, and also put out a call to Cesar Belize at his Belmont training barn to talk about a horse that was being geared to run in a big stakes on the weekend.

When the jury was still out on the evening of the second day, Markham remained to have dinner at the estate. Dolph was at his most relaxed and charming, mixing stories about other business buccaneers he had come to know, with racing anecdotes. Recalling the period before the trial when Dolph had leaned on her, Geri was glad to see him mustering such optimism at the most critical moment of the whole process that would determine his future. Yet it struck her as somewhat unnatural. It was as if he believed, whatever happened, he could not be touched by it; he was outside the rules that governed ordinary men.

It was late when Geri took Markham to the door while Dolph went to make more business calls to the Orient, an earlier time zone. 'He's amazing,' Markham said. 'Doesn't seem to consider the possibility that this thing could go against him.'

'You said it wouldn't,' Geri observed. 'Maybe he trusts his lawyer more than you do.'

'There are no guarantees, Geri. I took this case because I believed I could work with your theory about Diana. But if I'd gotten it across, it should have been a quick knock-out. When jurors are locked up this long, it means they're talking theories to death, and I'm afraid the first casualty may be the one I tried to sell them. They might decide it's easier to know what was in Dolph's mind, than what was in Diana's. After all, *she* didn't get to testify.'

Geri studied the frown on his lean face. 'Ed . . . you're more than worried, aren't you? You think it might be lost.'

'I think,' he answered slowly before going out, 'it might be better if Dolph left a little room for the possibility . . .'

When Geri went up to the bedroom, she saw that a few logs were blazing in the fireplace. Dolph liked to make love by firelight, and even on balmy summer evenings like this one he would often have a servant make a fire; the air conditioning kept the rooms cool. Geri took the fire as a signal to her, and she prepared herself accordingly, bathing herself, smoothing oil over her arms and legs, and dabbing perfume around her shoulders, breasts and thighs.

Yet even as she sat before a mirror in the dressing room, preparing herself to receive him, she was troubled by the feeling that it was more out of obligation than her own desire. It had not often been a problem with Dolph; he was such a superb lover that she usually became aroused at just the prospect of being touched by him. Tonight, however, as much as she wanted to be close to him, her desire was for something more than physical sensation. In all the years they had been together, she did not believe she had ever fully pierced the image to know the man at the core. During the months before the trial when he had clung to her dependently, she had thought he was revealing more of himself. But as she looked back now, she had the impression that he had only been performing a different role, binding her to him more closely as an ally for the battle ahead. And now that the battle was fought — even if it still remained for the victor to be declared — would he show himself again as the man who feared nothing from anyone?

461

When she emerged from the dressing room he was posed casually in a chair by the fire, gazing into the flames. He had bathed in his separate bathroom, and was wearing only a black velvet robe. Placed on a small table by the hearth was a tray with two brandy snifters propped on warmers, and a dusty bottle of Armagnac.

Geri sat on the floor by the table. She noticed that the bottle bore a faded label giving the vintage as 1942. Dolph took a snifter from the warmers, handed it to her, and lifted his own.

'What shall we drink to?' she said.

'The future, of course.'

The touch of one Baccarat crystal balloon against the other rang like the tolling of a bell. As the strong brandy passed down Geri's throat and settled in her belly it seemed to dissolve the knot of doubt. *Don't let him vanish from my life*, she prayed silently.

'I want you to know,' he said as he lowered his own glass, 'that, whatever happens to me, I have already given instructions to make sure you're provided for. You can live in this house, or any of my other homes, decisions about the horses will be left to you, and you'll receive a regular —'

'You know I don't care about that,' she cut in. 'And I don't want to think negatively.'

'Being realistic,' Dolph said, 'always has a positive side.'

Geri stared at him, amazed to learn that, despite the facade he was keeping up, Dolph had obviously given full consideration to the possibility of imprisonment. 'Ed Markham thought you didn't realize . . . it could go either way.'

He smiled. 'Juries are only made up of mortal men and women; mistakes can be made.'

'And still . . . you're so calm.'

Dolph took a slow sip from his snifter. He rolled the brandy around on his tongue, savoring it, before he spoke. 'My life might have easily ended in war, the same year that the grapes were picked that I taste on my tongue right now — almost thirty-six years later. Millions did die, but I've had all that extra time, much more luck than I had a right to expect. So how could I begrudge destiny for taking any of it back? This mistake was mine, no one else's: I fired the gun, I killed Diana — that can't be denied. If my time and luck have run out, then so be it. I'll pay for what I've done.'

He looked and sounded so noble, she thought. She loved him again with all the fervor she had felt the first time she had ever seen him. Setting her glass down, she pulled herself up to kneel before him, and pushed her hands up under his robe.

He lifted her face. 'But if it goes my way — *our* way — I want to marry you. Will you marry me, Geri?'

'Yes,' she whispered. 'Oh yes . . .' A split second later, she remembered that her marriage was already held for ransom by Molly, and she wished that she had not answered Dolph so quickly — wished, at least, that he had not chosen this moment to ask.

They bared their bodies to each other, and lay down before the fire. 'And, in case it goes against me,' he said, 'make this the night I will think about for all the time I must be alone.'

She began to cover his body with kisses.

'Will the defendant please rise?'

Dolph and Geri had been halfway through a late breakfast when Markham called to say the jury was coming in.

Dolph stood at the defense table. Geri, seated in the first row of spectators, bowed her head and closed her eyes. She had a vision of a wall of earth sweeping down, and Dolph disappearing beneath it.

'Your honor, we find the defendant, Adolphus Justinean . . .'

Her heart pounded, and her ears seemed filled by sounds like distant thunder, the heavy drumming of rain on a roof, so loud that she couldn't concentrate on what the foreman was saying —

Her eyes snapped open. The noise came from chairs being pushed back, the commotion of reporters running from the courtroom. A few feet away from her Dolph was shaking hands with Ed Markham.

*　　*　　*

They celebrated that evening in the city with Ed Markham and some of Dolph's staff from his businesses and the stable — Connie Fuller, Cesar Belize, Lew Yancey and their assistants. Afterwards they were driven to La Guardia Airport, where Dolph's plane was waiting. Now that the trial was behind him, it was Dolph's wish to spend some time in Saratoga.

They arrived at two in the morning, but Dolph didn't take Geri straight into the house. There was something he wanted to show her, he said.

He led her to the stables, where he guided her along the stalls until they reached one where the name plaque read 'HEARTBRAKES'. The horse inside was sleek and glossy, his eyes bright and lively. The look of eagles. At a glance, Geri could see he had been in training, his tuned muscles rippling under a hide without fat.

She understood the significance of the name. This was the horse he had bought for her in Keeneland — the cause of the separation that had ended with Diana's death. He had already won a couple of races, Dolph told her, and Belize predicted he would keep improving, might be a candidate for all the honors as a three-year-old.

'He was worth every penny,' Dolph said, 'but none of the pain.' He put his arms around her. 'Will you accept him now?'

Even after all they had been through together this was the true moment of reconciliation. The same gift she had dreamed of so long ago in Kentucky — and had been given by Bard Mitchell only to have it snatched away. A horse of her own. Now it was finally given for her to keep. She pressed herself into Dolph's arms. This was the man she loved. She couldn't deny she had felt powerfully drawn to Quinn in those past days when her whole relationship with Dolph was teetering on the brink, imperiled by forces beyond their control. But now Dolph was able to take command again, his strength restored. Now he was the man who had taken possession of her even as he introduced her to womanhood. Tonight, looking back, her brief flirtation with Quinn seemed as distant and as shallow as a schoolgirl crush.

As they walked out of the barn into the cool night, holding

hands, Dolph burst out: 'Let's do it now!'

'What?'

'Is there a better way to celebrate freedom than surrendering it to the one you love? We'll get married — right now, wake up a Justice of the Peace.'

Swept up in his juvenile spirit, she laughed as he began tugging her playfully toward where the cars were parked. But then she realized that no sooner than she became Dolph's wife, there would be a ransom to pay before their happiness could be released from captivity. She held him back. 'Dolph, we can't.'

'Why not? Why shouldn't we do anything we—'

'It's too soon after the trial . . .'

'I've been exonerated. And all the world knows we were lovers.'

'We've seen how quickly the public mood swings. Let's not do anything to raise new doubts. If we hurry into this, it might seem we were lying about the contentment we felt before — that we weren't happy enough the way things were, and so we . . . made this possible.'

He stopped and studied her under the moonlight. 'You do still *want* to marry me? I know, in the past few months, there were times it was hard to be sure . . .'

She put her arms around him. 'I'm sure now.'

He nodded. 'I'll wait one more year. Not a day longer.' It was more than just a proposal, she thought; it was also an ultimatum.

As they walked wordlessly back to his house through the moonlight, she could only wonder if a year would give her the time to solve her problem. Either to satisfy Molly's terms, or defuse her anger, win her over as a sister.

She would have to do one or the other, Geri knew. For there could be no happy future with Dolph unless she could save him from becoming a victim of her past.

465

BOOK VI: *THE FARN TURN*

Aqueduct — Spring, 1981

CHAPTER ONE

In the pre-dawn darkness, with the three-lane Long Island expressway empty of traffic, Geri pushed her silver Lamborghini up to a hundred and twenty-five miles per hour. Since Dolph had given her the car last Christmas, she had never driven it at such reckless speed, never even been tempted. Yet now she pressed her foot down even harder on the accelerator. The powerful car surged to 130 m.p.h. For a moment Geri contemplated going still faster . . .

Then her foot eased off. Only as she watched the speedometer needle falling, was she struck by the realization that this had been more than testing the limits: she had been tantalizing herself with the idea of total, final escape.

For the year since the trial had ended, she had been holding Molly at bay, occasionally paying out five or ten thousand dollars from the money she had borrowed against the clinic. But that money was exhausted now, and Molly was demanding more.

'Better make some goddamn weddin' plans,' she had said on the phone yesterday. ''Cause I'm not waitin' much longer before I spill what I know.'

It was an old threat, but this time Geri heard a new pitch of determination in Molly's voice. When she had asked to meet Molly tonight, Geri had known she would have to convince her that the full demand would soon be met.

But how could she do that? Geri wondered often why she

couldn't bring herself to ask Dolph's help. Was the determination to keep Molly's blackmail a secret really proof of her love for Dolph — or the evidence that the bond between them was weakening? Dolph was away so much these days, driven by his boundless ambition, that Geri couldn't help feeling they were drifting apart. Lately, the press referred to him as a 'billionaire', yet no matter how much wealth he amassed, the desire to expand his empire only seemed to grow. Three weeks out of every four he was in Europe, broadening international operations, adding hotels to the airline, moving into banking.

Now and then he still raised the subject of marriage. He was eager to start a family, he wanted heirs for his empire. She wanted children, too. She was thirty-three now, the time for waiting was over. But Geri would not marry while it meant making Dolph another of Molly's victims. She went on stalling, though she could feel that Dolph, like Molly, was near the limit of patience.

Ahead now she saw the freeway exit that would take her to Belmont Park. She felt the despair that had descended on her as she was speeding down the dark road begin to lift. Waiting just ahead might be the means to free herself from Molly — free herself to marry Dolph.

Arriving at the gate to the backstretch, she stopped to show her Racing Association pass to the Pinkerton guard. Even those who recognized her were more careful lately to observe the formality of checking credentials. A year ago the breeding rights of the two leading champions, Seattle Slew and Alleged, had been sold off to syndicates of investors for twelve and thirteen million dollars respectively. None of these animals had yet been taken for ransom, but the chance that it would happen someday couldn't be ruled out.

It was nearly six a.m. when Geri arrived at the barn where Justinean's horses were stabled. Several horses were already waiting under the trees, groomed and prepared with the minuscule racing saddle, about to be taken away for workouts by their exercise riders. The riders, a mixed group of boys and girls exchanging gossip by the barn, gave Geri friendly greetings when she got out of her car. They knew she had once occupied the same niche as they did, and that it was because of her that the Justinean stable had taken the lead in improving the wages paid to barnworkers and overcoming the old prejudice against employing female help.

Stepping inside the barn, Geri inhaled the distinctive aroma, a mingling of sweet hay and humid horsehide not quite overwhelmed by the stronger odor of the Absorbine liniment used to massage away the aches of tired animals. She went back along a row of stalls to the last one in a rear corner. As another security precaution, there were no longer name plaques outside the stalls to identify the horses within. Everyone who worked in the barn knew the location of each horse from memory.

Approaching the corner stall where Heartbrakes was kept, Geri saw Robert Stuart, a young vet who worked around the track, on his knees feeling the horse's left front ankle while Oakie Whitten looked on.

After Cesar Belize had decided to retire last autumn, Geri had persuaded Dolph to hire Oakie. When she had called to personally offer him the job as Dolph's trainer, he had accepted immediately. 'But I won't be thinkin' of it as workin' for him,' he told Geri. 'I'm takin' this job for one reason and one reason only, sweetheart — and that's because of you.'

Neither she nor Oakie had ever fully explored the depth of their emotional attachment in words, but except for Steve there was no one else Geri had ever trusted as much, no one else she could rely on who had known her for so long.

'Mornin', hon',' Oakie greeted her.

Geri could hardly acknowledge him before asking anxiously, 'What's the problem?'

'The ankle seemed a little swollen to me. I thought it ought to be checked, and I wasn't sure when you were coming . . .'

Rob Stuart stood up. Somewhat chubby, with rosy cheeks and curly fair hair, the vet was well aware of Geri's reputation in equine medicine, and the deferential attitude he took with her accentuated his schoolboy aspect.

'You should check for yourself, Dr Keyes, but it seems fine to me.'

Stuart was a fine young vet, Geri thought; she didn't want to undercut his confidence. 'I'll go along with you, Rob. I noticed a while ago that ankle has a tendency to go up and down a little.' Recent X-rays had shown no sign of anything wrong — though of course that didn't mean a problem hadn't begun to develop. The constant concussion every time a horse set its foot down in a race was bound to create injuries eventually. At a normal gallop, the bones of the leg were able to expand and contract to absorb shock. At faster racing speeds there was no time for such tiny adjustments to be made and the slightly spongy bone structure was pounded together infinitesimally until all ability to absorb shock was used up. After three or four thousand strides, the bones of any racehorse were prone to develop hairline cracks at the least — and, ultimately, to fractures. Microscopic bone chips could develop, too small to be seen by the X-Ray.

'We could skip today's workout,' Oakie said.

'Not necessary,' Geri said. 'I want to see him work. He's got to be ready for Saturday.'

Accustomed to Geri giving slower, more thoughtful reactions where welfare of the animals was concerned, Oakie was surprised, and glanced automatically to Rob Stuart as if seeking a second opinion.

Timid about contradicting Geri, the younger vet gave a small shrug. 'Shouldn't hurt,' Stuart said, and closed up his leather satchel of instruments.

Heartbrakes was saddled, and Oakie gave an exercise boy the day's orders. 'Jog him around once, then we'll go for a two-minute lick. Shake him up on the last eighth.' Part of the exercise rider's skill was to have an innate sense of timing that made it possible, without referring to a clock, to run the horse at the speed Oakie had ordered — just fast enough to do a mile in two minutes, with an all-out gallop only at the end.

The exercise boy rode the horse over to the main track while Oakie got into the Lamborghini for a short drive across the backstretch to watch the workout from the grandstand area. On the way, Geri was aware of Oakie studying her.

'Dolph still away?' Oakie asked finally.

She nodded.

'Will he make it back for the race?'

'Depends on business.'

Oakie kept looking at her, trying to read her as well as he might read any skittish filly. 'What is it, hon?' he said at last. 'Anything wrong between you and Mr J.?'

She felt a momentary urge to unburden herself about the pressure from Molly. But she said simply, 'Nothing that can't be fixed. What do you think the chances are on Saturday . . .?'

'We both know the horse has what it takes,' Oakie replied. 'He's lookin' good, and there are still five days before he goes to the post. He'll be somewhere in the money.'

They had arrived at a parking area right beside the concrete flats in front of the grandstand. Geri pulled up. 'It's got to be top money, Oakie,' she said fervently. 'He's got to win.'

As she got out of the car, Oakie followed her with a penetrating gaze. It was obvious to him that she was counting heavily on Saturday's race — the 'Wood Memorial Stakes'. The Wood was an important event in the schedule — one of the warm-ups for the Kentucky Derby a few weeks away, with a prize of $75,000 to the winner. Yet Oakie couldn't imagine that the money would be important to Geri, not these days. Always before, she had shown a joy of being involved simply for the sport.

He joined her as she leaned on the rail, watching the horses breeze by on their morning exercise. 'You know the game, darlin'. I *want* it to come out the same way as you — I want us to win. But only God or a fool would make it a promise.'

Yes, she knew the game. But as Oakie's words sank in, she realized that her chances of appeasing Molly tonight were far slimmer than she wanted to believe.

The new address Molly had provided was on West 83rd Street, a block off the river. It was a neighborhood that had improved rapidly during the New York real-estate boom following the city's near bankruptcy in 1975. Many dilapidated rooming houses had been purchased for renovation as small co-ops or single-family homes, but the transition was far from complete. Aware of this, Geri hadn't known what to expect when Molly had directed her here. Did it mean Molly was stepping up . . . or drifting down? Even with all the money Geri had given her during the past year, nothing was certain. The last time they had been together Molly had flaunted her use of cocaine, taking a large vial from her purse and snorting up the lines she laid out on the mirror of her compact. If Molly's addiction was heavy enough, she could have run quickly through every penny she'd received so far; it might also explain her growing impatience for the rest of the money.

Arriving at a brownstone building, Geri noticed several limousines double-parked in the street in front, and heard the sound of someone playing lively jazz piano behind the closed shutters of a first-floor window. Geri mounted the stoop, and pressed the illuminated bell-button that glowed beside the entranceway at the top. The door was opened by a stunning young oriental woman clothed in a black dress, adorned with white apron, collar and cuffs. It would have looked like a standard maid's uniform — except that the skirt was cut high across the thigh, and the bodice swooped so low that the aureoles of her breasts were partly revealed.

'Good evening, come in, welcome,' the sexy maid said in a rapid sing-song that suggested she might have memorized the words without understanding them.

Inside, the old brownstone had been thoroughly modernized. Recessed lighting twinkled from the ceiling, a modern floating stairway led to the upper floors. In a large front parlor beyond a portal, two or three dozen men and women were mingling in dim light. The women were young, slim and beautiful, wearing provocatively sheer, slinky dresses. The men were older, graying affluent types still in the suits they had worn to work that day. Some stood having drinks, others sprawled on long low sofas. Seated at a concert grand piano in a corner was a handsome black man wearing a

474

white tuxedo. He finished his jazz piece, and switched into a cocktail-lounge rendition of an old favorite. 'I get no kick from cocaine . . .' he crooned the words. At which one of the women, sitting on a sofa in a man's lap, shouted out, 'Bullshit!'

As Geri's eyes ajdusted to the light, she recognized one of the men in the room as the chief executive officer of a major bank whom she had met through Dolph, another as a congressman who appeared often on television. For all the sophistication she had acquired, Geri couldn't help staring as it dawned on her that Molly had steered her to a brothel.

'Not go in?' the maid asked as Geri turned away from the portal, anxious not to be spotted by the men who knew Dolph.

'I'm here to see Molly Lockely,' Geri said.

'She busy. You here about job?' She appraised Geri with a glance. 'You do good, I think.'

The moment of shock gave way to a smile. 'No, it's . . . personal. Would you please tell her I'm waiting?'

The oriental girl cast a telltale glance toward the stairs. Only then, Geri guessed what must have been meant by 'busy'.

The maid motioned Geri to follow and went up the stairs. On the next landing, she pointed through an open door and told Geri to wait, then continued up to the floor above. Geri entered a sitting room furnished with good reproduction French chairs upholstered in silk, beige flocked wallpaper, a smoked mirror, and heavy damask drapes drawn across the windows. When Molly strode in a minute later, Geri realized instantly that all her assumptions must have been wrong. Molly looked fresher and healthier than at any of their previous meetings. The exquisite long gown she wore, an opulent flow of black and white silk, looked like a Scaasi original costing many thousands. Her red hair was neatly swept up, and her blue eyes and pale skin were perfectly set off with just the right amount of make-up, a trace of silvery eye shadow and a hint of blush on her cheeks. If Molly was hungry for more money it didn't come from being broke — and she looked much too well put together to have come straight from tussling in bed with a customer.

Basking in the approval she could read in Geri's expression, Molly smiled. 'Money makes a heap of difference, don't it? Put a fucked-out whore in clothes like these, and whadya ya know? A queen is born.' She pointed Geri to the brocade-covered sofa. 'Try out the furniture. Cost me a fortune, too . . .'

'Cost *you?*' Geri echoed in astonishment as she sat down. 'All this is . . . yours?'

'Did you think I'd just piss away everything you gave me? Oh no, Geri. Told you I had ambitions. Got sort of a clinic of my own, see. Only at mine, it's not horseflesh we're tending to.'

Geri noticed, too, that she wasn't dropping her 'g's' or saying 'ain't'. She really must be working hard at her own program of self-improvement, though it still seemed hard to believe that Molly could be 'madam' of this house. Over the past year Geri had paid over almost a hundred thousand dollars, but setting up a place like this had surely required more.

'Looks to me,' Geri said wryly, 'like your business is doing better than mine.'

Molly gave the room a prideful glance. 'No complaints. Maybe all I ever needed was a couple of good breaks. Coming here was one of them. This town was made for a girl like me. I got these cute little mountain ways, and that makes me special . . .' Molly started to sit, then paused to carefully arrange the fabric of her dress so it wouldn't be crushed and wrinkled beneath her. There was something touching in the moment, Geri thought. Molly could have been a dewy-eyed deb practicing lessons she'd learned at a charm school.

'If you're capable of putting this together,' Geri said, 'there are probably a lot of other things you could do . . .'

'Don't start preaching,' Molly snapped. 'I'm happy with this, my partners are happy, so —'

'Partners?' Geri repeated quickly. Her sister's proprietorship began to make more sense.

Molly looked chagrined by the slip, an admission that she had not managed completely on her own. 'Enough talk about careers,' she said sharply. 'All I want to hear is what you're gonna do about paying your overdue bills.'

'I've brought another five thousand with me —'

'No more nickels and dimes, Geri. I want every penny you said I'd get, or I'm not keeping my part of the bargain.'

'Molly, for God's sake. The money you want . . . it's so much. I need time to work out how —'

'No! I'm not gonna let you jerk me around anymore,' Molly lashed out, straining forward in her chair. 'Whatever I'm asking, it won't be no hardship for Mr Justinean to pay. Shit, he'll go to one of those horse auctions he loves so much, buy some dumb animal for a million bucks and write a check. So you just better tell him to write one for me . . . or I'll see you and that murdering bastard in jail.'

'Don't count on it,' Geri snapped back. 'When you started these threats Dolph was still on trial. But he's been acquitted now. Do you know what double jeopardy is, Mol'? It means he can't be tried again for the same crime.'

'But *you* can . . .' Molly's voice fell to a gloating purr. 'Think it'll count for nothin' once it's known you would've been nailed for murdering your own father if you hadn't run away and stayed underground until a lot of bribes were spread around was paid to make your past look clean?'

Geri glared at her sister. It was as if no time had passed since that awful day when Molly had stood with Lettie Parker, ready to tell the lies that would have meant unjust conviction and imprisonment. 'My God, Molly,' Geri gasped, 'why are you doing this?' She gestured around at the fancy room. 'You don't even need the money now.'

Molly stood and glared back. 'Do I have to need it to want it, Geri-Jo? Is that how folks like Mr Justinean get so rich? I learned something from Pa. I got as much right to be rich as you or your boyfriend or anyone else. And I want everything I can get. There's folks who got hundreds of millions — like you will when you marry. Well, five million seems like only my share, damn it. I won't ever be poor again, or let anyone I care about be poor . . .' Molly pressed her lips together and an odd look of embarrassment came suddenly over her face. It

477

wouldn't be at her admission of greed, Geri thought. No, it was something else — the admission that she could want the money for someone beside herself. 'Well, I'm not backing off anymore,' Molly resumed. 'All I'm giving you is one more week.' She turned and started for the door.

Geri had hoped to avoid total surrender, but now she knew there was no choice. She forced the words out. 'Wait, Molly. I've got a proposition . . . a way you'd end up getting paid even more . . .'

Molly stopped and turned, wide-eyed. 'More?'

It took Geri another ten seconds to decide it was better than going to Dolph. 'A couple of years ago I was given a horse. He's a three-year-old now, eligible to run in the big spring classics — the Kentucky Derby, the Preakness. This weekend he'll be racing at Belmont in a warm-up for the others. He's got a good chance to win, and then go —'

Molly cut in sharply. 'You think I'm going to wait to see if your horse wins enough money to pay what I want? I know the horse-race game better than that . . .'

Geri crossed the room to Molly. 'No, the winnings are beside the point. Just listen. If my horse comes out in front of the competition now, he'll be a favorite for the later races, too. And if he wins one or two of those, then . . . do you know what a breeding syndication is?'

'Breeding's not my business,' Molly said acidly. 'Just plain fucking.'

Geri ignored the vulgarity. 'Owners buy the right to breed their mares to a top stallion and keep the foal. In the last year, those rights have been going for more and more money. If Heartbrakes — my horse — proves himself a champion, I can put together a syndicate that'll bring in fourteen or fifteen million dollars, maybe even more. I could have the money by summer.'

Molly's eyes narrowed as she tried to work out what Geri was offering.

'Half,' Geri said. 'I'll give you a half share in the horse. In whatever he's worth. The winnings, the syndication — you'd be a full partner. From tonight — if you'll settle for that.'

Molly let a thoughtful silence pass before she asked shrewdly, 'This nag ever win before?'

Geri nodded. 'His maiden . . . first time out. Came in five lengths ahead of the field, just two-tenths of a second off the track record for the distance.'

Molly paced in a small circle, looking at the floor, smiling to herself. She was apparently taken by the idea.

Geri stood by, silent now, careful not to *over*sell. She didn't want to provoke any more questions. Though the possibility of a rich syndication was real, it was actually a long-shot. Her faith in the potential of the horse was sincere; it had certainly shown speed in winning its first race, a six-furlong stake at Aqueduct a month ago. What she hadn't mentioned to Molly was that in his second race two weeks later, Heartbrakes had finished seventh, trailing several lengths behind. Afterward, Geri could find no serious physical problem. It might have had something to do with the finicky ankle — or it could have been an off day. Oakie had since changed the training regimen, and the horse had shown brilliant speed lately in its workouts. Running today's mile, it had done 'elevens' — covered its last couple of furlongs in eleven seconds each, a time that was good enough to set a track record if maintained over distance. Yet its poor showing in the last race could not be overlooked; among breeders nothing could be as damaging to a horse's reputation as inconsistency.

Even so, Geri didn't think of her proposition to Molly as a cheap way out. If there had been any other choice, she would have preferred not to give away half of her horse. She had sensed right from the first time she had seen Heartbrakes that he was something special. She had seen the look of eagles.

Molly stopped pacing. 'God damn,' she said with a little laugh. 'You know, Geri, there is something that positively tickles me silly about the idea of being your partner. I reckon I'm gonna take your deal.'

Geri could say nothing. She gazed at Molly, once more trying to fathom how they could have sprung from the same origins. Then she walked quickly out of the room and down the stairs. Slamming the front door behind her, she stood in the cool night air for a minute collecting herself.

She had gotten exactly the terms she wanted, yet it felt more like a defeat than a victory.

CHAPTER TWO

In the middle of the week, Geri drove to Saratoga. With new money pouring into horseracing as the rich increasingly sought tax shelters, the clinic had become active again. The practice of equine medicine was also attracting more high-caliber students — among them many more women than when Geri had started — and she had filled all positions at the clinic with bright associates. This allowed her to be away more, consulting by phone, but she still spent a couple of days a week at the clinic handling the most difficult cases personally.

When she returned to the Glen Cove house Thursday evening, a maid met her at the door and told her Oakie was in the solarium. 'He called an hour ago,' the maid said. 'I told him you were expected back soon, and he insisted on coming over to wait.'

A knot of panic tightened in Geri's stomach. If Oakie had rushed over, she could only assume he had news so bad it required personal delivery. The horse! Even in a workout it might have broken down, had to be destroyed . . .

In the poolside solarium, Oakie sat with a drink in his hand, turning the pages of a magazine.

'How bad was it?' Geri asked, hurrying across to him. He rose and squinted at her in way that made Geri think he was gauging her strength. 'Don't hold back, Oakie. I know it's bad or you wouldn't be here. Could you save him . . .?'

The puzzled expression faded from the trainer's weathered

481

face. 'Heartbrakes — that what you're talking about? Honey, there's no cause to bother about him. He looked so good in today's workouts I'm startin' to get the fool idea I could make you a promise.'

'Then . . . what's wrong?' She subsided into a chair.

Oakie took the chair opposite, but before he could answer the maid entered to inquire if Geri wanted a drink, and offer Oakie a refill of his bourbon. Still edgy, Geri asked for a small whiskey.

After the maid left, Oakie still hesitated, obviously having difficulty with his revelation.

'Listen, Oak'. Whatever this is about, if you think it'll make a difference in the race, I'm not going to give you an argument.'

Oakie gave her a skeptical glance before he went on. 'It's Nickles . . .'

'Oh no. Another spill . . .?'

'No, not an injury, kiddo. Something else. We've got to dump him.'

The assurance she'd given Oakie only a moment ago not to argue was suddenly meaningless.

Geri stood up and walked to the glass wall that overlooked the pool, marshaling her thoughts. She thought she knew why Oakie wanted to fire Nickles — and, if she was right, then going against her trainer might make him decide she had lost faith in his judgment, and he would have no choice but to walk out. Either way, she lost one of the people she cared most about, and needed with her.

Months ago, as soon as Oakie had started preparing Heartbrakes to be campaigned as a three-year-old, one of Geri's first discussions with him had naturally concerned the choice of jockey. She had suggested Nickles at once. Sentiment played a role, but there were practical reasons as well. Different jockeys were known for bringing different qualities to their handling of particular types of horses. Some were prized for their physical strength, power and stamina that might give them an edge with controlling brutish, headstrong animals. Others were appreciated for their ability to conceive a strategy for the race as it unfolded, to mentally compute speeds and shifting patterns on the track, so they could avoid being boxed in on the rail at a crucial moment. Almost all jockeys were skillful and daring. Knowing that a hard bump into the rail at high speed might deliver roughly the same impact as an automobile traveling at forty m.p.h., or that a spill into the windmilling hooves of a dozen charging horses could be fatal, it always took guts to ride. But in a contest where a fraction of a second often separated victory from defeat, even an infinitesimal edge in brains or nerve or strength was highly prized.

Nickles Tennyson's reputation rested on finesse more than strength, an ability to use his delicate hands on the reins, and other almost mysterious means, to communicate with temperamental animals and coax out their best performances. It was this quality that seemed to be called for as the personality of Heartbrakes emerged in training. The animal was quixotic, unpredictable. Sometimes docile and sweet-tempered, the horse could also turn around and be unshakeably stubborn, resisting all efforts to bring him out of his stall with vicious kicks and bites. If forcibly led to the track, he might perform with contrary sluggishness.

In their first dicussions about a jockey, Oakie had agreed with Geri that Nickles' style of riding could be a good match for Heartbrakes. Yet the trainer had gone on to name half a dozen other riders he preferred. Nickles, said Oakie, did most of his riding these days on the West Coast. While he could fly East to ride Heartbrakes — jocks often flew between coasts in search of the best mounts — the traveling might further reduce sharpness, and dull the familiarity with each track and its surface peculiarities acquired by jockeys who rode there more often. Furthermore, said Oakie, Nickles had lost his competitive edge.

Geri couldn't deny that in recent years Nickles had not sustained the level of winning that marked the beginning of his career. His decline dated back to a spill he had taken two years ago in a race at Belmont. In second place, trying to catch the lead horse in a stretch run, his mount had stumbled and

Nickles had been pitched to the ground just as the twelve horses behind him came thundering along. Jockeys had been killed in such accidents, but Nickles was fortunate, his injuries limited to a broken collarbone and the tip of one finger amputated by the impact of a metal-clad hoof. In six weeks he was riding again.

But winning less. Not even half as many races. It could have been a dry spell, a matter of chance. But track scuttlebutt said that Nickles had never shaken off the effects of the spill, there was a level of necessary risk he would no longer take.

To change his luck — or to avoid the Eastern circuit where he would have to ride at the scene of his accident — Nickles had started taking mounts only on the West Coast. His record had improved, though it remained far below former levels. For Geri, however, this was only more reason to stick with Nickles. She had a natural sympathy for anyone who got up to try again after being knocked down. With the right encouragement, she believed Nickles would eventually climb back to the top.

Exercising her owner's prerogative, she had overruled Oakie and phoned California. She approached making contact again with some trepidation, remembering that Nickles had felt hurt by her years go. But Geri had worried for nothing. Thrilled to hear from her, Nickles had instantly accepted the offer to ride Heartbrakes in his maiden race — and he had brought the horse romping home with a five-length lead.

Then, in the second race, the horse had made a poor showing. Oakie had said nothing at the time, but Geri knew he had blamed Nickles. Now her suspicions were confirmed. Though why had he waited until only two days before the race to act?

She turned from the solarium window. 'You know what it'll mean if we give up on him now. Heartbrakes is his best mount in years. Doing well would impress other owners, put his career back in gear. Fire him, and we send a mesage that he doesn't have it — and leave him worse off than when he came to us. I can't do that to Nickles, Oak'. Not after he got us a win.'

'First time out,' Oakie said. 'But what about the next time?'

Geri's temper flared. 'You know as well as anyone even the best jock can ride a bad race. It takes more than one mistake for me to lose faith in anybody. Christ, Oakie, I've got to believe in second chances. My whole life has been built on them . . .'

Oakie looked down at the floor. 'I know, hon',' the trainer said gently. 'And I knew you'd go to the wall to be fair.' He brought his eyes up again. 'But it don't make sense if the people you trust aren't giving you the same shake.'

The maid returned with their drinks. Oakie stood up to take his from the tray and then walked over to Geri. He clinked his glass to hers as they hoisted them together, both silently toasting the hope of victory.

'What did you mean?' Geri demanded as soon as the maid walked out.

Oakie took a few paces away, not looking at her. 'There's been some talk that Nickles has tanked a few races.'

'What does that mean — "talk"?' Geri asked sharply. 'Rumors? If you're going to pass along the kind of crap that might ruin a man, least call it what it is!'

'Listen, I don't take any joy in this. But you have to hear it.' Oakie had raised his voice, very rare for him.

Geri nodded apologetically, then listened as Oakie made his report. Disappointed by Heartbrakes' loss in the second race, he had phoned a few trainers he knew in California and questioned them more closely about Nickles' recent performance out there.

'I wasn't lookin' for dirt, hon'. Just doin' my job, gettin' the background. I wanted to know how they felt about the grapevine buzz that said Nicks had lost his nerve. Most had nothing too bad to say, but they were all pretty clear that they wouldn't use Nickles on their own horses. I tried to get 'em to explain their objections, but they all kept it kinda vague. Finally, though, one guy said he knew I had too much at stake this Saturday to keep me in the dark — and he told me there'd been some whispers around the western tracks that Nicks had played along more than once to rig a race.'

'No,' Geri erupted automatically, 'Nickles wouldn't do

that.' Visions rose in her mind of the boy who had spoken to her so shyly and adoringly as they stood in a shadowy barn on a cool spring day . . . and then the brash, but still adoring young man who had bought her champagne on a summer's evening, and told her there were angles to be played, though he didn't play them. Could he have grown into an older man who would betray his own belief in the sport?

'No,' she said again, more quietly.

Oakie had moved up behind her. 'There isn't anything certain,' he said quietly, as though to offer hope. 'But some other jocks who've ridden against him lately — races Nickles lost with good horses — have been saying that, in the same circumstances, they could have won.'

Geri just shook her head, refusing to accept such murmurs as meaningful. Then she felt Oakie's hand on her shoulder.

'Darlin' . . . when it comes to this kind of thing, no one ever wants to blow the whistle, because it drags down the whole sport. And it's tough to get evidence because the heart of the deal is made between a man who won't talk . . . and an animal who *can't*. So, yes, you're left with nothing but rumors. But when they start, Geri-Jo, it can be the way the other jocks have of cleaning up the mess.'

'Can be,' she echoed, turning on Oakie. 'But what if it isn't? How do you steal a man's honor from him without having proof — without knowing who started the rumors, and whether it's someone who lost a girlfriend to Nicks, or has some other reason to kick him when he's down?'

Oakie reached out to her, imploring. 'Honey, even if there was proof to be had, we've got one free day before the race; we can't dig deep enough in that time.'

'I can talk to Nickles,' Geri said.

The restraint on Oakie's temper broke. 'And what in tarnation d'you expect him to tell ya?'

Yes, she thought, asking Nickles directly was foolish. But not only because if he had been corrupt enough to rig a race, he couldn't be relied upon for the truth. If the charges were unfair, confronting him might only topple his already shaky confidence at the worst possible moment. If she were going to stay with Nickles, Geri realized, she had to do it on faith. Or she had to abandon him right here and now, on Oakie's advice. 'He wouldn't do this to me,' she said, debating with herself. 'I can't see why —'

''Brakes went off the favorite second time out. Suppose somebody bet heavy on the second choice at better odds, and then paid some insurance . . .'

She barely heard Oakie. She was thinking again of her history with Nickles. The adoration she'd rejected. Could she be certain he still held his friendship with her sacrosanct? Was it certain that he had forgiven her for loving someone else? Or was he taking some revenge?

Dusk had fallen over the garden outside. Looking into the purple air, Geri strained to see the clear outline of anything solid and real. 'Rumors aren't enough,' she said at last.

'You're gonna stick with him?'

She nodded without turning around. There was a long pause, but she had nothing to add. She had hurt Nickles enough in the past without adding this wound.

Finally, she heard Oakie's footsteps retreating from the room.

CHAPTER THREE

Saturday was an April special, crisp and sunny. As soon as she arrived at the track Geri felt her spirits lift. All yesterday, brooding over her confrontation with Oakie, she had stayed away from the horse, and Oakie had not called her. Nor had she yet spoken to Nickles, who was scheduled to arrive this morning on a red-eye flight from the West Coast.

Last night's call from Dolph, who was in Paris, had done nothing, at first, to help her mood. It would be impossible, he said, to get back in time for the Wood.

'How does Oakie rate the chances?' he had asked then.

'No promises,' she replied. 'But he thinks we can win it.'

'Does he? Well, it's always more fun to have something at stake. How about making a bet — a big one.'

She couldn't tell him how much she already had at stake. 'I enjoy it enough without that. But if you want me to lay some money down for you —'

'I wasn't talking about money,' Dolph said. 'And this would be a bet for both of us.'

'Then I ought to put up my half. What is it?'

'Yourself, my darling — your half of *us*. I want to marry you, and you've kept holding me off. But it can't go on. I need a wife, children . . .'

If only, she thought, he could say he needed *her* instead of making it sound like an expanded family was all part of planning his empire. Or did she have a right to protest? It was true that she had refused to commit herself, no matter how and when he made his proposals.

'It occurred to me,' Dolph went on, 'that since you're having so much difficulty making up your mind, we might put the decision into other hands.'

'Who can decide this but us?' Geri said.

'The horses.'

Dolph's whimsical answer dissolved her pique. She couldn't help laughing as she echoed, 'The horses? How?'

'You have Heartbrakes entered in two warm-ups before the Derby — tomorrow's race, then the Blue Grass Stakes. So here's my proposition. If the horse wins both races . . . then you'll stop dawdling and marry me. We'll take it as a sign from the gods. What do you say?'

As playfully as Dolph had framed his proposition, Geri knew it was an ultimatum, the signal that his patience was exhausted. Part of building an empire was to create a dynasty.

A sign from the gods. If they let her win, then they would smile on the marriage, too. She said yes to Dolph's 'bet'. And when she lay awake later thinking about it, she decided it was a fine solution. If Heartbrakes won both these upcoming races, then his chances for the Derby itself would seem excellent — and he would be on the way to the lucrative syndication that would satisfy Molly.

And if the horse lost . . . well, that would probably mean the end of the road for her and Dolph, anyway.

Before every race, it was customary for owner, trainer and jockey to meet and discuss strategy. Some horses were stretch runners; they performed best when held back at first, before being let loose to try catching the leaders near the finish. Others had to be given their head right from the start. The choices had to be weighed each time in the light of the particular factors on the day of the race — the horse's condition, the weight it was carrying, its starting-post position as determined by a draw. A horse drawing an advantageous position, near the rail, might run a different race than from an outside slot.

Half an hour before post-time, Geri went to the saddling

enclosure where she and Oakie always met to give orders to the jockey. Oakie was already there, standing amid other gatherings of trainers and owners.

'Good to see ya, peach blossom,' he greeted her. The lilt in his somewhat gravelly voice told her there was no lingering resentment because she'd overruled him. 'Got the butterflies, too?' he added, and rubbed his stomach. 'The things I've got flyin' around inside me feel like dive-bombers.'

Oakie dropped his arm around her shoulder and squeezed. Their reconciliation seemed complete.

'How's Nickles?' Geri glanced toward the door from the jockeys' changing room.

'I haven't seen him yet. Didn't want to talk to him without you bein' there.'

The answer troubled Geri. Was Oakie signaling that he felt his authority had been gutted. Before she could say anything to reassure him, Nickles emerged from the door of the jockeys' room wearing the sapphire-blue and pink silks that Geri had designated to represent her. She had chosen the colors for no other reason than that they were the dominant shades in the only dress she could remember her mother wearing.

Despite his cross-country flight, Nickles looked and sounded fresh. He gave Geri a quick peck on the cheek, rubbed his hands together and said 'Great day for the races, huh?'

'Just don't be too fired up,' Oakie said, leaving aside any greetings or small talk. 'Because I want you to start out slow, hold him back for the first half.'

Nickles nodded. But Geri shot a surprised glance at Oakie. The one time Heartbrakes had won, he had led 'going away' — right from the gate to the wire. In his second race, they had decided to try pacing him a bit more, and he had fallen steadily behind. They had yet to see any proof that the horse was a stretch runner.

Oakie caught her look. 'I know what you're thinking, hon'. But when he won going away that was over just six furlongs, and it looked to me like he was burning himself out at the end. We've got a mile-and-an-eighth today, and the competition's better. In the latest workouts, 'Brakes has gotten rolling more toward the end. So we'll let the rabbits set the early pace,' he concluded, referring to the horses that always sprinted to the front and were prone to tire quickly.

Geri still didn't agree. But she had already overruled Oakie's advice on another crucial decision. Questioning him now might leave him no choice but to resign as her trainer.

Nickels deferred to her, however. 'Okay, princess? I'm out there for you, after all — and I don't want to be anywhere but first.'

She searched for the faintest flicker of a lie in the eyes. 'Oakie's my trainer,' she said. 'Ride it his way.'

A groom had led the horse into the enclosure. Oakie and his assistant, Pat McKay, put on the pads and saddle and made certain it was properly cinched and adjusted. Then they checked the horse's feet, to be sure the shoes were firmly attached, and that no stray object like a pebble or a nail had accidentally lodged in the sensitive pads under the hoof.

The voice of the paddock announcer came through a loudspeaker: 'Jockeys, please be mounted.'

While Oakie went off to circulate with his cronies, Geri walked to the paddock to watch the jockeys parade their horses. It had become a superstitious ritual for her and Nickles to go through the same motions of that day in Saratoga when he had presented her with three winners. Geri would watch him circle the paddock, he would throw her a kiss, and then she would show him a thumbs-up sign before he rode onto the track.

But as she entered the crowded paddock area today, she didn't move straight to the rail. She stood back and anxiously scanned the throng of spectators, expecting to spot her sister's wild mane of vivid red hair. She was certain Molly would be here — not to share in the sporting experience, but to gloat over having stolen a share of any victory.

Yet she hadn't seen Molly in the clubhouse earlier. And she was nowhere in the paddock. Had she stayed away, after all, forgotten the horse was running?

Geri moved up through the crowd to perform her ritual with

Nickles. As the horse circled toward her, Nickles spotted her and smiled. He always waited until he was just passing her to blow a kiss. Geri's glance swept over Heartbrakes as he approached. The horse was prancing very slightly, looking proud and eager — ready to win. Geri's glance shifted back to Nickles. His smile broadened as he came nearer. Even if he would be willing to undermine the sport, was it conceivable that he could betray her?

Suddenly someone pushed up behind her, and gave her a firm tap on the shoulder. *Molly*. Geri was already glaring as she whirled around —

And found herself looking at Bill Quinn as he removed the sunglasses that had been shielding his smokey green eyes. 'Sorry to startle you, Geri. But soon as I saw you, I had to come straight over . . .'

He looked glorious, she thought, even more confident and prosperous than the last time. Perhaps his beige Italian sportcoat was simply a better cut than he'd worn before, but he looked stronger, filled out. He was slightly tanned and his brown curls had been sunbleached at the tips, the evidence of having spent some part of the winter in sunny places. She noticed he had an open sketch pad under one arm. 'Nice to see you again, Quinn,' she said, making an effort to sound casual.

'Except you reacted as if you thought your pocket was being picked.'

'Don't think that doesn't happen around here . . . but I . . . I was expecting someone else.'

There was a silence, though silent voices went on speaking; the same memory was blazing in both.

She had not seen him since the night he had given her the painting. He had departed from Saratoga and left no forwarding address. As the clinic recovered, she had begun putting money aside to pay for the painting whenever she learned his whereabouts. Yet months had gone by without a word. At the time the trial ended, a phone call had come to the clinic on a day when she wasn't there. The switchboard operator had taken down a message — a few congratulatory words and a post office box in Middleburg, Virginia, where he could be reached if she wanted to contact him. She had sent a note, thanking him for his thoughts of her, along with a check for fifteen thousand dollars. No acknowledgement of its receipt ever came back, and she was surprised to discover as time passed that the check had gone uncashed.

She was going to remark on it now, when she heard the track bugler blowing the traditional fanfare that announced the entrance of the horses for the race. She turned and saw the last of the parade departing from the paddock. Heartbrakes had gone out near the head of the line.

'Oh no . . .' she murmured in disappointment.

'What's wrong?' Quinn said.

'I missed Nickles riding out, and . . . well, it's just a little thing that we do before every race.'

'Some superstitious mumbo-jumbo . . .?'

She smiled sheepishly. 'I'm not usually superstitious,' she said as they started ambling toward the clubhouse. 'But at the track, all these little rituals somehow take over. The shoes and dress I'm wearing are the same I had on the day Heartbrakes won his first race. I didn't think about what I wore for his second, dressed differently . . . and he lost.'

Quinn chuckled. 'And I'll bet you're not the only owner who's brought his magic charms along. Which means all the training, and the money that's spent at the auctions comes down to whose clothes have the strongest magic!'

She smiled. 'I know it's silly. But today . . . I just want everything working for me . . .' The intensity of her wish drew a concerned glance from Quinn. To head off any questions about it, she said quickly, 'Why didn't you ever cash my check?'

'Because I liked to think of that painting as a gift.'

'Quite an expensive gesture.'

'Not only rich people know how to make them,' he said a bit crossly.

'I'm sorry, Bill. Of course I'm touched. But there's no need for you not to take what you've got coming —'

'I don't need it now,' he cut in. 'And that's because of you, too, Geri. So you've paid me many times over.'

493

They had reached the clubhouse. She asked him to join her in Dolph's season box, and was pleased by his quick acceptance, an indication that he was on his own.

They had the box to themselves. She had invited no one else today, fearing that Molly might show up, and Oakie usually preferred to watch the race with the members of his training team — his assistant, the exercise boys and head groom — so they could analyze the race if it went badly and thought a change of strategy was needed.

'What did you mean when you said I'd already paid you?' she asked when they were seated.

'By getting me a lot of work.' He showed her the pencil sketch on the top sheet of the pad he'd been carrying. 'My job today, for one. Owner of another horse in the Wood wanted me to be on hand and see his horse in the winner's circle.'

'If he gets there,' Geri put in tartly, as she glanced at the rendering of a horse in the paddock, done in Quinn's distinctive whirlwind style. He had caught the lines so well that she recognized the animal. 'That's Rondalario, isn't it?'

'Right. He's owned by a Texas oilman named Harve Keller.'

'I know Keller. He's brought horses to me for treatment.'

'Yup. That's how he saw my painting . . .'

Now she remembered. The Texan had admired the painting which she had hung in the entrance hall of the clinic, and he had asked for the name of the artist.

'I've done quite a lot of work for Harve. Of course I'm not in Peabody's class yet.' Quinn paused for a tongue-in-cheek smile. 'When I paint one of his horses, Harve only pays me forty thousand . . .'

'Billy! That's fantastic.'

'And since I've worked for Harve, his friends have liked what they saw and . . . well, it's sort of like breeding, Geri: one painting gave birth to another. All because you hung my work where the right people would see it.'

'You're telling me I was the dam for all your horses?'

Quinn laughed. 'I wouldn't have put it exactly that way.'

'I don't take any of the credit. You did it for yourself. The work did it.'

Geri looked back to the track. As they talked the horses had been circling around to the gate, and she didn't want to miss the start. Grabbing a small pair of powerful Zeiss binoculars from her shoulder bag, she aimed them at the fourth position away from the inside rail and held her breath as she watched the loaders pull Heartbrakes into the gate. He went in smoothly, a good sign. A race could be lost in the gate if the horse was loaded badly, or reared and hurt himself. Lowering the binoculars, she became aware of Billy staring at her.

'You,' he said as she turned to him, his voice just above a whisper, 'you were the inspiration for what I did, Geri. Do you understand . . .?' His green eyes were focussed intently on her, his face set in a tender expression that conveyed all his longing, and all his desire to give and protect. She started to reach out —

But the voice of the track announcer boomed suddenly over the P.A. system giving the customary last-second alert: 'The horses are under starter's orders.'

Geri's total concentration whipped back to the track. A split second later came the traditional cry, no less thrilling for all the million times it had been repeated.

And they're off!

Knowing Heartbrakes was being ridden according to Oakie's plan didn't make it any easier to see the horse trailing way back in tenth place as it reached the first turn. Only four other horses were slower. And by the time the charging field of animals was heading down the backstretch, Heartbrakes had only moved up to eighth. The horse leading the field, two lengths in front, was the big bay colt, Rondalario. And he was widening his lead.

But on the far turn, the second and third horses began to pull even. Heartbrakes had continued to pass others in the field, though coming into the quarter-mile straightaway leading to the finish line he was only edging into fourth place. And there, clinging tightly to the rail, he seemed to stall, blocked from further advance by the tight phalanx of three horses running neck and neck in the lead. To pass them, Geri saw, Nickles would have no choice but to swing wider — which would cost precious distance.

The excitement of a three-way battle brought the crowd to its feet, the backers of each of the three leaders joined in a cacophonic chorus of shouts to root home their separate favorites. For one or two eternal seconds, the positions remained the same, Heartbrakes holding his place but not pressing forward. The distance left to the finish grew shorter. Was Nickles ready to accept defeat, Geri wondered, or was he balancing the choices — move out wide, or else wait for one of the horses in front to falter and leave an opening?

With only little more than an eighth of a mile left to run, Rondalario finally broke away from the trio bunched up across the front. The instant he pulled ahead, Nickles gave Heartbrakes the whip, urging his horse to slip through the gap left in front. Heartbrakes responded instantly, pulling into a triple tie for second. As the remaining track was gobbled up by the charging pack of animals, Geri could only resign herself to what she saw: there simply wasn't enough room left now for her horse to catch the leader. Rondalario was one length in front.

But then Heartbrakes surged forward, a quickening of pace so astonishing that it looked almost as if he had taken a leap. Suddenly he was only a head behind Rondalario . . . and only a fraction of a second later they were running neck-and-neck. They stayed that way as they closed on the wire, matching each other stride for stride.

The stands were roaring and shaking, everyone propelled to his feet by the spectacle, thousands of voices raised, not only to selfishly root home winning bets, but in tribute to the courage and spirit of the duelling animals. Still neck-and-neck the horses came on, the finish line only just ahead.

Only at the last second, Heartbrakes dug into himself somehow to produce an explosive burst of speed that brought his head clearly out in front at the very instant the horses shot under the wire.

Unable to contain her joy, Geri let out the kind of wild whoop she hadn't made since she'd stood atop the hills of Appalachia, a child making echoes. Beside her, Quinn laughed. Conscious again of his presence, Geri spent more of the emotion bubbling through her, throwing her arms around Quinn and impulsely planting a celebration kiss on his lips.

'He did it!' she cried. 'He won!'

Quinn kept his arms around her. 'I'd like to be with you every time it happens . . .'

The voice of the track announcer came over the loudspeakers with the result, now certified by the judges. 'The winner, in one of the most thrilling finishes ever seen at this track, Heartbrakes!'

'I've got to get down to the winner's circle,' Geri said breathlessly, gathering up her bag and binocular case. Then she became aware of him idly watching. 'Come with me . . .'

'No. I ought to look for Keller and sympathize a little. But I don't want to lose touch again, Geri.'

'Where can I call you?' she asked, with a quickness that made it obvious she preferred not to be called by him.

He brought out a wallet, and extracted a card. 'You can reach me through that number. They'll always know where I am.'

A track official, knowing where her box was located, was already waiting in the aisle to escort her to the winner's circle. Geri took Quinn's card just as she was hastily jamming the binoculars back into their case and dropped it in with them. 'I'll call,' she said as she left him, 'I promise.'

She was guided downstairs and across the track to the infield. Looking ahead to the winner's circle, Geri suddenly pulled up short. Among the usual crowd of well-wishers and dignitaries milling within, there was Molly. She looked respectable enough, dressed in a dark blue fitted suit, her face shaded under a broad-brimmed straw picture hat. Still, when their eyes met, a gloating smile broke across Molly's face, and it took all Geri's will to force down the impulse to retreat. To her relief, Molly did not come forward and greet her. She kept her place at the fringes, her arm linked through that of a heavy-set man with thick black hair, his face masked by large sunglasses.

Flanked by Oakie and Nickles, Geri was presented with the

trophy. Each time she looked at Oakie, he lifted his eyebrows and pulled his mouth into an apologetic frown, acknowledging that she had been right to choose loyalty over rumor. For all the joy she should have felt in triumph, however, throughout the brief ceremony, Geri was disconcerted. How had Molly gained admittance to the winner's circle if not by claiming some involvement with Heartbrakes or a kinship with Geri? And why had she been content to stay in the background?

At the end of the presentation, after Geri had said a few gracious words of acceptance into a microphone and the circle had begun to empty out, a few sports reporters began to cluster around her. As she began answering their questions, Geri looked past them, anxiously searching the group lingering in the winner's circle. If Molly intruded now, her share of ownership might even find its way into the news. No doubt, she would relish the notoriety.

Amazingly, though, there was no sign of Molly. Along with her unknown escort, she had quietly disappeared.

Glad as she was that she had not been subjected to any public embarrassment, Geri sensed that something ominous lay behind Molly's uncharacteristic behavior.

CHAPTER FOUR

In two weeks Heartbrakes would run in the Blue Grass Stakes, the week after that in the Derby. Geri had planned to stay in New York to attend to the training program, but on Wednesday morning one of the clinic internes called to report that a stallion named Disco King, admitted with an intestinal infection, had suffered a severe reaction to the medication Geri had prescribed by telephone. Geri rattled off a list of procedures that might stabilize the horse's condition, and said she would return to the clinic immediately. Within fifteen minutes a helicopter landed on the lawn of the Glen Cove house to fly her to Saratoga.

As a past stakes winner and sire of several other successful horses since his retirement, Disco King was worth five million dollars in the booming thoroughbred market. But there was another reason Geri felt it imperative to save the horse: the stallion was owned by Jock Cotsworth. During Dolph's trial, Cotsworth had been among the first to withdraw business from the clinic — and as a blue-chip member of the racing establishment, his decision had held sway over many other owners. Lately, she had won back his business, but if his valuable stallion died, Geri guessed the influential horseman would be quick to accuse her of malpractice.

Arriving at the clinic, she learned that Disco King had died twenty minutes earlier. She went straight to her office and called Cotsworth to report the news and express regrets.

'You can save all your goddamn apologies,' he railed. 'This could have been prevented, Miss Keyes . . .'

She ignored his pointed neglect of her proper title. 'Mr Cotsworth, every conceivable effort was made —'

'You should've been there instead of running things by remote control!' he shouted back. 'Before the day is out you'll hear from my lawyers!' He slammed down the phone.

Two hours later, a telegram arrived from a large New York law firm to say a suit was being filed. The figure sought in damages was put at twelve million dollars.

Whether or not she won in the end, Geri knew, the clinic would be driven under. Her credit was already extended to the limit. Fighting the suit would commit her to crippling legal costs even before the case was tried. She would be put into bankruptcy.

Could she turn to Dolph? The specter of Diana — of what she had become while living in Dolph's shadow — still haunted her.

Now, in every way, all her prospects for the future rested entirely on the performance of Heartbrakes.

To stay on top of other difficult cases, Geri remained at the clinic for the weekend and left Oakie to handle all training decisions. On Monday she returned to New York for appointments with a law firm recommended by Ed Markham, and with a couple of other highly regarded vets who might lend her professional support. To facilitate the round of meetings, Geri stayed over in the city at Justinean's duplex in the Olympic Towers. As she returned there late Tuesday afternoon, one of the maids who permanently staffed the appartment gave her a message to call Dolph in Paris.

'I'm sorry, my darling. I've been detained again . . .' Originally he had been scheduled to return from Europe in time to fly down to Kentucky with her for the Blue Grass next weekend.

Her mood sank even further. 'I never thought you'd miss this race — not with the kind of bet you've got riding on it.'

'I won't, I promise. We can't travel down together, but I'll be there on Saturday — when I win my bride!'

500

For a long time after lowering the phone, she stood by the bedroom's floor-to-ceiling window. The city sparkled in the amethyst light of dusk and she felt as if she were flying above it. How very far she had come, how very high she had risen. And yet what did she have of her own, what anchor to keep her from floating away into the night? Did she truly love someone to whom she found it impossible to confess her need? Or was Dolph just a symbol of her own attainment, one she could no longer relinquish? Where was there someone she could lean on without feeling that she was losing her treasured independence?

A phrase rose into her consciousness — words she had not heard well enough when they had been said. *You gave me the lift I needed.* Bill. Could he return the favor . . .?

The card he had given her at the track, a place to contact him — what had she done with it? She rummaged unsuccessfully in her purse, and then recalled the binocular case. She was already on her way to a phone as she glanced at the engraved printing and discovered that the name and phone number were for the 'Wagonner Galleries' at an address on East 57th Street. She recognized the name, one of the more successful and expensive dealers specializing in sporting paintings.

The small Cartier clock by the bed showed a few minutes past six o'clock. Would the gallery still be open? She punched the numbers into the phone quickly. The call was answered by a silky feminine voice.

'I'm trying to reach Bill Quinn,' Geri said. 'He gave me this number . . .'

'He's not here right now,' the woman on the line said.

'I'm a friend. Do you know another number where he can be reached?'

'If it can wait an hour, he'll be here for the show.'

'Show . . .?' Geri blurted out.

'His exhibition.' An edge of suspicion came into the voice. 'But don't you have the invitation? If you're a friend . . .'

She was momentarily struck dumb. If Quinn had been sincere in acknowledging her contribution to his success, how could he fail to mention this exhibition — a milestone in his career? It couldn't have been accidental. She was deeply hurt by the snub. After all she'd done for him, didn't she have a *right* to be there?

'I . . . I misplaced mine,' she said at last. 'That's why I was calling. To make sure of the time and date.'

'Tonight at seven.'

Geri said, 'Thank you,' and lowered the phone.

Invitation or no, she had to go. Moving to her closet, she contemplated the array of clothes. She had never before wanted so badly to be the most dazzling woman in a room, to make an entrance that would catch every man's eye — and make one man regret his insult. It was rare for her to think of using her beauty as a weapon. But tonight it felt oddly invigorating. Tonight she knew what it meant to dress with a vengeance.

'I forgot it, I'm afraid . . .' She shrugged ingenuously at the security guard who stood by the street door of the Wagonner Gallery carefully checking invitations, screening out anyone who might be attracted less by the art than by the jewels and furs adorning the partrons.

The guard studied her a moment. Geri was a bad liar, having rarely practiced the art, yet after appraising the Stallion's Eye glittering on one finger, the silk evening coat with its rich embroidery and, where the coat hung open, the Geoffrey Beene cocktail dress ornamented with sprays of gold sequins and the gold and ruby necklace at her throat, the guard passed Geri through with a quick nod.

Inside, a butler took her coat, then she paused before the placard on an easel — SPORTING PAINTINGS BY WILLIAM DANE QUINN — revelling in the awareness that she was drawing glances. She looked spectacular, but she guessed onlookers would also be commenting on her rare appearance alone since she had never gone to these things without Dolph. Men and women she knew from the racing world waved to her, and she smiled back. But after taking a glass of champagne from a passing waiter, she drifted off on her own. She wanted to look at the paintings

— and look for Quinn without being obvious about it.

Spaced along the walls were two dozen oils of well-known horses crossing finish lines at full stretch, posed in winners' circles, or caught in casual scenes around the stables. They were 'crowd-pleasers', done in the same plain representational style on which Malcolm Peabody had built his successful career. Nearly half the paintings already had small gold disks stuck to the frames signifying a sale, but Geri could only feel terribly disappointed for Quinn. Perhaps she had no right to take his professional choices personally, yet she felt her belief in him — and all his declarations of its importance — cheapened by his clear retreat from originality.

As she turned from the last picture, she found herself looking at him. He was standing in the midst of a group of apparent admirers, including Harve Keller and some other boisterous Texans, his gaze trained on her as though waiting to catch her eye. She stared at him a second, then headed toward the racks where she had checked her coat.

Quinn rushed across the floor. 'Geri. Wait, please . . .'

She stopped without turning, and he came around to face her. His eyes went up and down once, appreciating her, before he said, 'I know . . . I should have mentioned it. But there were reasons that I —'

'It's all right,' she said rigidly, more pained than soothed by his excuses, and started to move away.

He put out his hand to stop her. 'Listen, Geri. Can you believe I didn't want you here . . . only because you're so damn important to me . . .?'

He had to break off as an elderly couple on their way out stopped to compliment him on the show. As soon as he had bid them a gracious good night, he hooked his hand around Geri's arm and tugged her off to the side.

'I'm sorry you were hurt. Of course, I wanted you here. But I backed off because . . . it upsets too many balances. I can't get near you without wishing so many things were different, things that seem impossible to change.' His eyes glistened as he gripped her, gently yet with a shivering intensity. In the middle of the crowded gallery, they seemed to be alone, enclosed in their own world of fragile emotions, drifting aloft in a shimmering bubble. A wave of longing rose within Geri, and she leaned toward him, lifting her face . . .

'So here you are . . .!' The bubble popped and they crashed back to earth in the middle of the noise and smoke.

Geri turned to the woman who had come up beside them. She was slim and stunning, in her mid-to-late twenties, wearing an exquisite low-cut dress of burgundy silk chiffon. She had a narrow sculptured face, extremely pale blue eyes, and a fountain of lustrous coal-black hair that swirled up and away from a distinct widow's peak. Her striking face, and the smooth skin of her neck and bare shoulders were bronzed by some recent exposure to the sun. She flashed a brilliant smile at Geri as she slipped a proprietary arm through Quinn's.

'Pardon me for intruding,' she said to Geri, 'I'm Melinda Wagonner.'

Geri recognized the silky voice as the same that had answered the phone earlier. Before she could introduce herself, Quinn took over, presenting her as 'Dr Keyes, an old friend . . .'

Melinda Wagonner's eyes widened with recognition, before she turned quickly back to Quinn. 'Darling, I hate to break up anything . . . but we've gone all out to get you properly launched, and there are buyers here who feel cheated if they don't get their bit of personal attention —'

'I thought for just five minutes,' Quinn said, 'I might let my art speak for itself.'

'Darling, when your art speaks, it whinnies. Nothing can sell it the way you do.' The woman looked to Geri. 'Forgive me for taking him away, but this is part of the job. You understand . . .'

Geri nodded.

'Darling!' Melinda whispered urgently to Quinn. 'Do you see who's just come in! I must introduce you right away . . .'

'Wait,' Quinn mouthed to Geri before he went off.

Not until she watched them walk away, did Geri realize that the golden patina on Melinda Wagonner's skin and the blond highlights in Quinn's brown hair had probably been put there by the same tropical sun.

She waited until they greeted a well-known Greek shipowner and started strolling with him around the gallery. Then she collected her coat.

It was after eleven o'clock, and Geri was drafting a letter to the lawyer handling the malpractice suit, when the night concierge of the Olympic Towers rang on the housephone: Mister Quinn was in the lobby asking to see her. She weighed the alternatives of inviting him up or sending him away.

'Tell him to wait. I'll be down in a few minutes.' If she didn't see him, she thought, the agitation she had felt since leaving the gallery would keep her awake all night. A month of nights.

She didn't bother to change out of the jeans and handknit sweater she had put on after coming home. Pausing only to splash cold water on her face, and brush out her hair, she headed out the door, grabbing the first thing her hand connected with when she reached into the coat closet — a sable jacket Dolph had given her.

Quinn gave her a grateful smile as she got out of the elevator. They fell into step and had walked out of the building onto Fifth Avenue before Quinn said, 'Would you like a drink or something?'

'No. I'd like to walk.'

It was one of those fresh, promising nights that brought to mind all the romantic songs about New York that had ever been written. The windows of the Fifth Avenue stores were still lit. A mounted policeman went riding by like a knight of the city. They turned uptown and strolled a block, content with silence.

At last Quinn said, 'Didn't like the show, did you?'

'You're better than what I saw. We both know that.'

'I guess I didn't care to be reminded.'

'And that's why you didn't want me to see it,' Geri said. 'I never figured you for someone who'd settle for less than the best, Quinn — not from that morning I saw you junk a good painting because it didn't come up to your standards.'

'Succeeding at what I do takes more than talent, Geri. You

505

need connections — someone who knows how to hype your stuff.'

'Is that Melinda Wagonner's lesson in getting to the top?'

He gave her a rueful smile. 'Mel isn't behind the gallery. Her father owns it. He came to me after seeing my work at Keller's house. It was an opportunity I had to take. No one knows how to market art better than Griffin Wagonner.'

'Good art shouldn't have to be "marketed" like soap.'

'Unfortunately, that's not the way it works. You know the show sold out tonight? Griff was even right about my name . . .'

'In what way?'

'He said if I signed my pictures plain "William Quinn", I'd never build a reputation as fast as if I used "William Dane Quinn". More distinctive, more memorable.'

'I suppose it is.'

'But, you see, that's marketing. Because where I was born, giving middle names was a fancy touch a lot of people didn't go for. My parents didn't, anyway. Wagonner told me to put in the "Dane".'

'Oh, Billy,' Geri sighed, 'you're good enough to make it without all the hype and horseshit. Why don't you believe that?'

He took her by both arms, holding her so she had to face him. 'So I shouldn't settle for less than the best,' he said intensely. 'Is that what you think? Well, let me tell you when my starry-eyed principles began to slip. Right there on that morning you first saw me being so strict with myself. Because a moment later when I turned and saw you, Geri . . . I swear something in me said, "There it is, Billy — there's the best, the very best you'll ever see." And right then I didn't see how I could do anything but settle for less. Justinean's girl, a duchess of the horsey set, that's who you were. And what was I?' His hands slipped away from her arms.

She might have thought less of him for his self-pity if she hadn't once known the torments of being a beggar at the tables of the rich, known all the corrosive doubts that came with being poor or uneducated in the midst of beauty and wealth and confidence. But she did remember, and she could not blame him. She took one of his hands and pulled him nearer, as though by closing that small gap of sidewalk between them, she had taken him across the threshold into a mansion.

'Don't settle for less,' she whispered.

Slowly, he brought his lips lightly down onto hers. His mouth was warm and sweet, and she wanted more of him.

'Take me home,' she whispered.

He paused, chagrined. 'I don't have one. I've been a houseguest at Wagonners.'

She hesitated. More than anything, she realized, she wanted to be with him. 'Come with me,' she said.

Waking at dawn, Geri wondered how much longer to let Quinn doze beside her. The apartment had been quiet when she brought him home, the servants retired for the night, but if she let Quinn stay there was a risk that he would be seen, a report given to Dolph.

Though perhaps Dolph deserved to be told — perhaps she would tell him herself. Right now she wasn't sure what the aftermath of tonight would — or should — be. She wasn't married to Dolph, yet after all the time they had been together, she couldn't help feeling that vows between them had been broken as much as if she had committed adultery. She felt guilty of a betrayal, and yet she could not bring herself to feel regret.

She looked down at Quinn's body, the sheet turned back to reveal his muscular arms and chest, and a shudder of pleasure went through her as she thought about their lovemaking last night. Was it possible he was only the third lover she'd ever had? Over the past couple of years, Dolph had changed so much as different pressures affected him, that it seemed sometimes he was not one man, but many. In bed, too, there was something elusive about Dolph. He was so skilled at his technique, knew so well how to vary his touch and his tastes, that from one time to another with Dolph she'd had the odd sensation of getting into bed with very different men. It could be exciting, yes. But sometimes, too — when she got the sense that she didn't know all the many men he was, and never would — it was unsettling, even frightening.

With Quinn, though, there was a different kind of thrill, a discovery of mutual willingness and tenderness that went along with all the physical delights. Thinking of it now, she felt the desire to touch him again. Slowly she pushed the sheet down, baring his stomach, then moved down and kissed him, laying a trail of kisses over his skin. He moaned softly and she lifted her head to see if his eyes were open. She wanted to wake him this way — but slowly, to have him think first that it was a dream . . .

She saw that he was still asleep and started to lower her head. But then she saw again the patch of shiny tissue that radiated across his left arm and shoulder, a scar shaped almost like a flower where a piece of shrapnel had torn into his flesh. A few inches to the right, she realized, and it would have pierced his heart; she would never have known him. Conscious of the impermanence of life, she felt a strange urgency about having more of him, an intuition that this chance would never come again. She bent to kiss the scar, moved her tongue along the inside of his arm, tasted his faintly salty skin, and brushed her lips over the downy hair on his hard stomach. She felt him growing stiff and erect, pushing against her bosom, and she moved down to kiss him there, and warm him with her lips and tongue. He moaned again, and in a minute she felt his fingers entwining in her hair, coming awake. His hands caressed her shoulders and slipped into the moist vault under her arms and he pulled her up, lifting her above him so that he could kiss her breasts. Then he slid his hands down to her hips and raised her body above his until she felt the sweet thrust of his long warmth entering her, driving all the way to her core. They rocked together in a quickening tempo and with each stroke waves of heat went through her, rising and surging, carrying her to higher and higher crests of pleasure, until she came, clinging to him as if it would keep her from being washed away and lost in that dark bottomless sea of ecstacy.

She lay with him, drained and satisfied, as the sun rose high enough for the first golden beams to spill along the canyons of the city and flood over the sills of skyscraper windows.

'Good morning,' he said.

She smiled, and kissed his chest where her head was resting. After a minute she said softly, 'You should go . . .'

She could feel the tension enter his body even before he swung off the bed and started to dress.

Geri sat up, pulling the sheet around her. 'Billy, being with you was wonderful. I wish it could last. But . . .' She didn't have the words to finish.

'But it doesn't change anything,' he supplied.

'That isn't what I would have said.'

He stopped at the foot of the bed after putting on his trousers. 'Oh? Then tell me, Geri. What happens to us after I tip-toe away this morning? If it's just our little secret, will it ever be anything else?'

'I . . . I can't say. Not now, Billy. My life is very complicated now. It can't all be changed or settled by one night. Can yours?'

'It has been already. I'm never going to want anyone but you.'

'What about Melinda Wagonner?'

He grabbed up his shirt and looked away as he swirled himself into it. 'That was when I believed you belonged body and soul to Dolph Justinean, that I'd never have a chance.' He turned back to her. 'But I know different now. We both do.'

Geri didn't like hearing him talk about her relationship with Dolph as if it had been permanently spoiled. Whatever had happened last night, she was a long way from deciding she was ready to leave Dolph. But her feelings were too confused to argue it with Billy. She took a different tack. 'Melinda's very beautiful,' she observed. 'Has all the right connections to help your career, and you've told me how important that is. Are you really ready to give her up?'

'I don't have a choice,' Quinn said. 'Because I love you.' He went on staring at her a moment, waiting for the sentiment to bounce back at her. When it didn't, he resumed dressing.

'What is it, Geri?' he asked quietly. 'Is it because Justinean's so damn rich? I never picked you for caring that much about money. So why aren't you walking out of here with me?'

'He's been a big part of my life,' she said. 'One night can't be balanced against that — not even one night as beautiful as this one.'

'So,' he said, 'it comes down to loyalty.'

'It's not as simple as that,' she said, and stalled. She was happy with Billy, happier than she had been for a long time. Why didn't she let her feelings for Billy sweep her away? Could it be that Dolph's money and power did have some hold on her? Were they the guarantee of safety she needed after coming from the hollow, where a whole family — all she knew of love — could be lost in the blink of an eye?

Quinn sat down and slipped into his shoes. He said nothing to her, but Geri saw him shaking his head, heard him faintly mutter to himself, 'Jesus . . .'

She told him then that she would be leaving for Kentucky in a couple of days, and the significance of the trip, including the 'bet' with Justinean.

When she finished, Billy was staring at her, perplexed. 'I don't get it, Geri. After what's happened between us, can you really be content to let that decide your future — what happens in a horse race?'

'No, I'm not going to marry Dolph if I think it won't work. But until things have run their course, until some choices are made — or I'm forced to make them — I don't believe I can really know what I want.'

Quinn nodded slowly. Then he came over to the bed, and sat down beside her. 'I guess there's nothing I can do but wait for the results of the race,' he said.

She put her arms around him, and kissed him once more.

'I know the way out,' he said, and let go of her. 'I'll be very quiet.'

As the door closed, she almost called him back. But if she did, she knew it could not be for one more embrace, or even another hour together. She would be calling him back forever. And, still, she was not ready — not able to believe that love

510

alone could save her from the threat of losing everything she had.

Lying back, she strained to hear the faint sound of another door closing in the far reaches of the huge apartment. It was too faint, though, too distant. She knew he was gone only by the soundless closing of a gateway in her heart.

CHAPTER FIVE

Dolph and Geri were invited to stay with Laurette Wilkey while in Lexington for the running of the 'Blue Grass Stakes'. Though Dolph wouldn't fly in from Europe until early Saturday, Geri came a day earlier. After visiting with Laurette in the morning, she went over to the Keeneland backstretch to check her horse's condition.

As she entered the barn where Heartbrakes was stabled, Oakie intercepted her and led her outside under some trees, away from where the stablehands would hear.

'My California friend called me again about Nickles . . .'

'Oh no, Oakie, not more "talk". Nickles rode a great race last time! What more can we ask?'

'We have to be sure things are straight — or else people are going to question what happened with our horse, win or lose. The latest word is that a couple of other jocks are getting ready to go to the racing commission — and not just because they think Nickles held back his own mounts. They're saying he approached them about doing the same . . .

Geri was silent. Oakie was right: the case against Nickles was getting stronger. She thought again of the jockey as he had been when they met, the idealistic young man, committed to the rules of the sport. If it was true that an accident had changed him, how much sympathy did he deserve?

'I've made some calls,' Oakie added quietly. 'The good Eastern riders are already booked. To get a sub in from the

Coast for tomorrow, we'd have to make the move right now.'
He dug a piece of paper from a pocket and handed it over.

Geri's eyes went down the list of available jockeys. Familiar
names, good riders, but unremarkable. Could any one give her
the race that Nickles had two weeks ago?

But then, at the bottom of the list, she saw a name that had a
special meaning for her. 'Oakay, let's bring in a standby,' she
said. 'But I'm not going to bounce Nickles without giving him
a chance to answer the charges. If he can't make a defense that
convinces me, then we'll be ready for the switch.'

'You'll have to pay, even if you don't use the other jock.'
Geri nodded.

'Who do you want for the sub?' Oakie asked.

Geri turned the paper so he could read it as she tapped her
finger over the last name on the list.

'Hold on, hon'. That stuff's okay in California — they like
offbeat things out there. But I only threw in that choice as a
last resort . . .'

'Set it up, Oakie,' Geri commanded, spearing her finger
down once more on the name of Ramie Marquez. 'I want her.'

A suite had been booked for Nickles at the Radisson Plaza
Hotel. When he arrived on Friday evening, Geri was sitting in
the living room.

'Hey, babe!' he exclaimed as he came through the door.
'Now this is the V.I.P. treatment!' He was followed by the
bellboy, and a tall full-figured brunette in a mini skirt and knee-
length boots who looked young enough to be in high school.

The jockey moved to embrace Geri as she stood, but she
stepped back. 'I'm afraid I'm not here as a welcoming
committee, Nicks.'

He gave her a wary glance. Then he took a wad of money
from his pocket, peeled off a five-dollar bill as a tip for the
bellboy, and a few more bills which he thrust at the brunette.
'Go buy yourself a new dress or something, dollface.'

Without any change in her expression, the brunette took the
money, gave Nickles a quick kiss on the cheek, and left.

'How long have you been with her?' Geri asked as Nickles
closed the door.

'About ninety-six hours. That seems to be my limit in a relationship these days . . .'

'Life in the fast lane,' Geri remarked, sitting again on the sofa. 'What else is happening there, Nicks . . .?'

'Since when are you worried about my life style? The girls are nothing new.' His voice sank. 'I only ever met one worth trying to keep.' He went to a stocked bar and fixed himself a neat scotch.

Geri was quiet until he had gulped the drink. 'You know why I'm here, don't you, Nicks?'

She saw his shoulders sag a little as he kept facing away. 'You believe all that shit, Princess? You really think I'd ever pull the reins on you?'

'Those are two different questions, aren't they? What's true . . . and what you'd do to me?'

He turned back to her and came across the room. 'I can't deny there have been times I didn't go all out to push a horse. But that's a judgment call. Every jock has to make it sometimes. You're out there riding some piece of trash, and you know it doesn't matter how much stick you lay on his ass, he's not gonna pass one other number in the field. So you ease off, save the animal for another day. The owner grouses, of course. He thinks his horse could've won — hell, they *all* do, or they wouldn't enter them in the goddamn race; so they say you blew it . . . or worse. But it's part of the job, that's all. You can't win every time, and you can't run an animal into the ground for no goddamn reason.'

'Good answer, Nicks. That might explain a few slow rides. But you've got other jocks saying you asked them to save their horses, too. And not on a judgment call — not when you were asking before the race started.'

Nickles took a seat beside her. 'Jesus, Geri, you know what it's like in the jockeys' room before a race. There's all kinds of bullshit flying around — wisecracks about who's stuck with a plug, rapping about who's got a chance and who doesn't. I probably made a joke and somebody misunderstood, that's all . . .' He forced a shrug.

His voice had grown high and thin, taking on a begging

quality. The defense wasn't good enough, Geri thought.

'Clear it up, Nickles. If it's a bad rap, go to the commission and get the guys who are knocking you called off. Because I can't let you ride while there are any doubts.'

'But you *can't* have any doubts about me, Geri?' His voice cracked pathetically, as he clutched at her hands. 'Christ, baby, don't you know that whatever I did somewhere else, I'd never do anything but give *you* my best.'

She took it as a confession. 'It can't work that way, damn it!' She bolted up. 'I don't want you, unless I know you're playing straight right down the line — that whatever you do for me, you'd do for anyone.'

Nickles smiled sadly. 'Never has been that way, babe . . .'

'I'm sorry, Nicks. You're out.'

The small man stared at her, his narrow face etched with a pained disbelief that made him seem all the more childlike. As Geri looked around for her handbag, he got up and followed behind her. 'Look, kid,' he stammered. 'Heartbrakes is the best thing I've got right now. Toss me off — especially after I won with him — nobody's gonna wonder why. I'd be finished. So I'm not gonna mess this up. Because this is my chance to get clear, see, straighten things out so I don't have to . . .' His voice died.

She turned on him. 'Have to what?'

He looked away, and stood silently for a long moment. 'It goes back,' he muttered at last. 'After that spill I had a while ago, I was always scared. I went on riding, but I kept looking for the way out — to make a quick killing and retire. Started betting and . . . I got behind. They owned me then — the men who controlled the gambling here in the East. I went out West to cut loose, but they've got a long reach . . . and I still had debts to settle.'

Geri moved up and put a consoling hand on his shoulder. He spun around to face her.

'This time, though, they couldn't get to me. Believe me, doll: no matter how hard anybody pushes, you'll always get a straight ride.'

'I believe you, Nicks,' she said.

515

He brightened. 'Well, okay . . .'

'I'm sorry, Nicks. I still can't let you on my horse. Now that I've heard this, I can't let you get on *any* horse. It's not just one race at stake. It's the whole sport . . .'

The disbelief was gone from his face now, but not the pain. It hurt Geri to look at him — hurt even more to realize that she had no choice but to make the break quick and clean. He had admitted to race-fixing; the more time she spent with him now, the more she jeopardized her own standing. She headed for a small table by the entranceway and picked up her bag.

'I wish I didn't have to do this,' she said. 'I've never wished anything so much . . .'

'Then don't. Please, Geri . . .'

She hurried to leave before she broke down.

'All right, princess, if that's the way it is, then don't think you're gonna turn me in without getting hurt yourself . . .!'

It wasn't a pleading tone she heard now, but a harsh threatening rasp. She looked around, shocked by this vicious turn. His mouth was arched down in a mean scowl.

'There wasn't much I could do when you broke my heart because you didn't think I was man enough for you. But this time, damn it —'

'Nickles. That was never the reason we didn't —'

'Shut up!' he shouted savagely. 'That's ancient history, nothin' can change it. But I won't stand still for all this high-and-mighty bullshit about cleaning up the sport coming from *you*? Your connections aren't so different from mine. We're dealin' at a different level, maybe, with different branches. But they all work together . . .'

This wasn't about her past, she perceived suddenly: this was something else. She moved slowly back into the room. 'What are you talking about, Nickles . . .?'

'I saw Mr Caramati there in the winner's circle after The Wood. At the time I thought he was there to lean on me. But then he disappeared without a word. It didn't make sense, so I put out a few calls to people who know Caramati . . .'

Caramati? She'd never heard the name before. 'And what

516

did they tell you?' she asked, fishing for a clue to explain Nickles' accusations.

'About his piece of your horse. The cut he's getting from your sister . . .'

Now the puzzle pieces came together. The man with her sister in the winner's circle. Molly's mention of 'partners'. And Nickles' talk of connections, different branches of some organization that would be mixed up not only with gambling and fixed races, but prostitution.

Shame and horror seized Geri as she realized what Caramati represented, and what it would mean to have him involved in any way with Heartbrakes.

'Now look ahead and see what it'll mean if I blow the whistle,' Nickles said. 'For the present, Caramati can get away with mingling in the circle. He puts up his front as a guy who made his money in real estate, and nobody questions it as long as he keeps a low profile. But if I put the spotlight on him and his ties to a winning horse — at the same time as you're nailing me for riding some crooked races — well, Geri, you'd only be screwing yourself.'

Everything fit now. She understood why Molly and her 'partner' had shown themselves in the winner's circle — subtly staking their claim — and also why they had left quickly and quietly. She foresaw, too, that if a share in owning Heartbrakes was ever linked to them, the horse would be barred forever from running — and her own right ever to race another horse would be permanently cancelled.

Yet if she let Nickles ride, the future looked no better. He was going to be publicly denounced sooner or later by other jockeys; he would be stripped of his victories, and her horse would lose its value.

'Guess I'll have to do some gambling, too,' she said after thinking it through.

Nickles squinted at her dubiously. 'On what?'

'You.'

The jockey smiled. 'Attagirl, Geri. Best bet you could've made.'

She headed back to the door and paused before opening it.

'No Nicks, I'm not giving you the ride. I'm betting it the other way — that you won't talk about Caramati. Because if what you say about him is true, blowing the whistle would be more dangerous than taking another spill. And even if you did, by the way, you'd have a hell of a case to make . . . because you won't find ownership papers at the Jockey Club showing any name but mine. So I'm going to bet you don't want to cause yourself any more pain than you already have.' She took a step closer, as though to see past the man he had become to the young man he had once been. 'And I'm going to believe that you still don't want to hurt me . . .' She headed out.

'I won't let you run that horse with a new boy!' he shouted after her.

With all the tension, she still couldn't stop the smile as she said over her shoulder, 'I planned for that, too.'

She left him standing quietly in the middle of the room, looking like a child again, lost and puzzled.

The chartered Lear Jet bringing Ramie Marquez from California was silhouetted against a rising pink sun as it banked over Blue Grass Airport at a few minutes after six a.m. As she sat in Laurette's convertible watching the plane float down to a landing, Geri wondered if choosing Ramie had been dictated too much by sentiment, sensible judgments overruled by the desire to repay an old debt and pick up the slim thread of a lost friendship.

Since Geri had departed from the Belmont backstretch to go off to vet school, she had seen Ramie only once. Early in the affair with Justinean, she had gone to see a couple of his California-bred horses run at Del Mar. They had been visiting the backstretch when Geri had run into Ramie, still working as a stablehand while trying to break in as a jockey. The reunion had been joyous at first, but Ramie's ebullience had soon faded. Geri's professional achievement and romantic attachment to a man of immense wealth had obviously made Ramie painfully aware of the failue to fulfill her own ambitions. When they said goodbye, there were no eager promises to see each other again. Geri had suggested later to

Dolph that he might give a female jockey a chance to ride for him. But when she attempted to contact her old friend, Geri learned that Ramie had moved on, leaving no forwarding address.

The articles about Ramie that appeared so often these days revealed that the beautiful Dominican girl had spent the next few years scraping for mounts on the rough-and-tumble country fair circuit, then at small tracks in Mexico. When she surfaced again at the large California tracks she had compiled enough of a winning record to persuade a few trainers to use her, especially since one or two other young women had already infiltrated the all-male fraternity of jockeys. When she began to take seconds and thirds in races, that brought better mounts and led to some wins in low-grade claiming races. Eventually, she added victories in some big stakes to her record. She was acknowledged finally to have as much skill and guts as any other rider. Yet she could never be one of the leading money winners — because she never got as many mounts as the men, and was never given horses of first quality. Whenever Ramie Marquez won a big purse, it was always on a long-shot, always coming from behind.

But that only added luster to her story. Lately she had been written about as the most successful of the few women jockeys. She was photographed off the track as much as on, frequently as a companion to some movie or television hunk. Most recently she had been reported as seriously involved with Glenn Joye — a remarkable change of pace in her romantic life. Joye, the famous singer who had been a top box-office draw in the days when Hollywood was still turning out movie musicals, was very much older, still gifted with a charming smile, but no longer the slim matinée idol he had been when he had made pictures with Garland, and Alice Faye. The match with Ramie was further surprising because of the difference in their personalities. Ramie was notorious for being tempestuous and unpredictable, the singer was known as a quiet family man, a wealthy pillar of the Hollywood community who had been widowed after a marriage of thirty years.

Reflecting on this romantic involvement, Geri wondered if

it could mean that Ramie was settling down, losing some of her fire — and perhaps her competitive edge. Much as she wanted to believe that a woman jockey would deliver no less than a man, Geri realized that Ramie had probably never been tested at quite the level she would face today.

A moment after the door of the plane opened, Ramie came bounding down the built-in ramp, dressed as if she had just stepped out of a store window on Rodeo Drive — cowboy hat and boots, skin-tight jeans with belt, cuffs and pockets of alligator skin, and an ermine bolero blouse. Her black hair was still a mass of tangled curls, her mocha skin and gleaming onyx eyes set off by tangerine lipstick and silver eyeshadow. As soon as she saw Geri parked nearby on the runway, she started exaggeratedly blowing kisses, and then stopped to do a little excited shimmying cha-cha step before running to the car.

'Gerencia!' she announced as she pulled open the car door. 'You have give me the chance of a lifetime, and in return I make you the big win!' She plopped into the front seat, and gave Geri only a quick hug before she added, 'Well, *muchacha*, what you sit there for? *Vaya!* Take me to the horse.'

'Don't you want to rest?'

'Later. Right now, is more importan' the horse is meet with me. You know, I got only a few hours before the race to teach him Spanish . . .'

Geri laughed, and turned the car around for the short trip to the track, across the road from the airport. The question of whether Ramie had lost any of her Latin fire seemed answered.

The Keeneland Race Course has been called 'the Vatican of Thoroughbred Racing', a shrine dedicated to preserving the Blue Grass traditions from the carnival atmosphere that has invaded most modern tracks. Keeneland is still the only track in the country where no announcer's voice booms through a public address system calling the position of the horses during the race. Spectators must see it all for themselves, roused only by the sounds of the cheering bettors, and the throbbing beat of the hooves.

Normally, Geri enjoyed roaming the grounds, set amid

tranquil pastures, and picnicking with Dolph on the fried oysters and the traditional Kentucky dish called 'burgoo' — a thick meat and vegetable soup — served at the refreshment stands. But as the racing program began today, she had no appetite for the food or the old-fashioned atmosphere. She ought to be feeling relieved and optimistic, she told herself. Nickles had sought no revenge — not so far, anyway; he had checked out of the hotel this morning, bound for the airport. Also, after spending the morning with Ramie, watching her with the horse and hearing the way she took instructions from Oakie and asked questions about past performance, Geri believed she could have made no better choice for a replacement.

Yet she remained glum as she sat at Laurette's table in the gray stone clubhouse, a privileged sanctum restricted to members only, almost all of whom were drawn from the aristocracy of American racing and Blue Grass society. It was as Laurette Wilkey's guest that Geri had been granted entry, and after the first few races Laurette was still the only other person at the table which was set for three.

'Now, darling,' Laurette said after the fifth race, 'don't let this ruin the whole day. If Dolph couldn't get here, there must be a good reason . . .'

'He didn't even call,' Geri said.

'If I know Dolph he's en route, and nothing will stop him'

Laurette had stated the same cheery assurance several times earlier, and Geri could still find no comfort in it. She knew the force of Dolph's determination, too; nothing could have stopped him from being here *last night* if he'd wanted. She decided now that Dolph must have learned about her night with Quinn — one of the servants had seen him at the apartment, relayed the information — and this was his response: to cut the ties without a word.

The depth of sadness she felt at the thought of losing him surprised and confused her. Was this the measure of his importance to her? Or was she simply stricken with remorse for having brought about the end in the way she had, by a betrayal of trust?

After two more races were run, and only a half hour

521

remained before the running of the Blue Grass Stakes, even the knowledge that her horse stood a good chance of winning did nothing to keep Geri-Jo's gloom from deepening. She kept gazing toward the door of the Turf Club, praying Dolph would materialize.

Oakie hurried up to the table. Tipping his battered tweed hat to Laurette, he slid into the third chair. 'I was lookin' for you at the paddock, Geri. Must be the first time you didn't bother coming down to see your own horse . . .'

She would have explained her preoccupation, but Oakie rattled on excitedly.

'Honey, I hope you got deep pockets today. Because the odds on our boy make this a once-in-a-lifetime opportunity.'

Preoccupied with her vigil for Dolph, Geri hadn't even checked the tote board. Now she saw that Heartbrakes was listed as 16—1. Obviously the bettors — some of whom followed jockeys almost as much as horses — had taken the change of riders as an ill omen. Nickles had steered Heartbrakes to a brilliant win the last time out, so the change couldn't be read as desirable for the owner — not as long as his troubles in California weren't general knowledge. It would seem, rather, that something had made Nickles defect from the horse — a change in the animal's condition that threatened to affect its performance so badly that the jockey was afraid of being embarrassed. His replacement by Ramie might reinforce this theory, since the choice of a woman would seem a last resort after all the good available male jocks had passed.

'We ain't never again gonna get such good numbers on this horse,' Oakie said. 'He's ready, Geri, I'm tellin' ya. Gonna put down two or three thousand myself. What about you?'

'Nothing for me, thanks, Oakie.'

Oakie blinked at her. 'Honey, this is your horse. You've got to back him. For the sake of luck, if nothing else.'

When Geri didn't respond, Laurette piped up.

'Well, I owe it to the horse if not myself.' She dug into her purse for two hundred dollars which she handed to Oakie to bet for her. He turned back to Geri, who shook her head again.

'Darn it, girl. What's wrong with ya . . .'

'Dolph hasn't come,' Laurette explained softly.

'Still no reason to go lookin' for more bad luck,' Oakie said with open annoyance. In his catalog of superstitions, if you didn't show belief in the things you cared about, then you didn't deserve to win and you wouldn't. Oakie stood frowning at Geri for another moment, but when she didn't change her mind he walked away.

There was less than fifteen minutes left to post-time when Geri noticed a jet plane flying high above the track, etching the sky with the white vapor trail of its engines. Planes often passed over on their approach to the nearby airport, but this one circled a couple of times. Geri-Jo squinted up at it, then stood and raised the binoculars dangling from her neck. As the jet banked out of its circle and aimed for a landing path to the airport, Geri could see the blue and gold lines along the fuselage and the bold 'J' painted on the tail.

A surge of relief and joy went through her. He was *here*, he cared. She had not lost him — had lost *nothing* yet. And suddenly she cared about winning it all. Lowering the binoculars, she saw Laurette, who had been watching her track the plane through the binoculars.

'Didn't I tell you?' Laurette crowed.

Geri called to one of the clubhouse 'bet-boys', then turned out her purse, scraping together every last dollar she could find.

'Heartbrakes,' she instructed the bet-boy, handing over the fistful of money without even bothering to make an accurate count, 'on the nose.'

For the next ten minutes she hardly took her eye off the entrance to the club. The last couple of horses were just being loaded into the gate when Dolph came running through.

'Forgive me, darling,' he said as he reached her. 'There was bad weather for flying last night and it only broke —'

'It doesn't matter,' she said, her arms going around him.

Their lips barely touched as a roar went up from the crowd — in the absence of an announcer, the best indication that the horses had come bursting out of the gate. By the time they looked, Heartbrakes had already jumped out to a half-length

523

lead. And stride by stride, over the course of a mile and an eighth, the gap grew larger. When the horse dashed under the wire, it was a startling twelve lengths in front — though Ramie Marquez had never once used the whip.

The huge margin of victory seemed by itself to be an omen to Geri. She belonged with Justinean, the bet had settled it. Her night with Quinn was a moment of weakness — one she must pray that Dolph never learned about.

CHAPTER SIX

In the wake of his overpowering victory in the Blue Grass Stakes, Heartbrakes became everybody's favorite to win the Derby. There could be no doubts because of the jockey; Ramie Marquez had proven her mettle — and, at the moment, was receiving more media attention than any other athlete in the country. Heartbrakes was already being touted as a sure winner of the Eclipse Award for Horse of the Year. On the Monday following the Blue Grass, Geri received an offer of eight million dollars to sell to a syndicate of breeders. It was an excellent price, but she never doubted she could do better. And the very next day there were two more offers — one of twelve million dollars and, later, another for fourteen. The record price paid for last year's Derby winner, Affirmed, had been only a few hundred thousand dollars more — paid only *after* the horse won the race. Geri was dealing now with amounts that surpassed the highest expectations she'd had when she had rashly placated Molly with a half-interest in the horse. But even after that obligation had been settled, she would be rich in her own right — a financial freedom she counted on to protect her from the erosive dependency on Dolph that had destroyed Diana.

Still, she resisted the temptation of a quick sale. She trusted Ramie and the horse to triumph again. Waiting just a few more days might bring the price up another five million dollars. Perhaps even ten . . .

On the Monday before the Derby, Geri supervised moving Heartbrakes from training quarters at Keeneland to Churchill Downs. She and Dolph then stayed in Louisville to join in the fun of 'Derby Week', the days of revelry and partygoing that led up to the race. There were races of hot-air balloons, and the Pegasus Parade with elaborate floats and cars filled with celebrities, and the Great Steamboat Race down the Ohio River — pitting the two old stern-wheelers, the Belle of Louisville and the Delta Queen, against each other — and picnics on the sprawling lawns of old Kentucky families, and charity galas at night topped off by the ball given by Kentucky's Governor. They took it all in, riding on the crest because Geri was known to be the owner of the probable Derby winner.

Swept up in the whirl of events, Geri all but forgot the concerns that had been weighing on her so heavily only a week earlier. At moments, not least because there were many high-priced call girls in evidence during Derby Week, she was reminded of Molly, and then a tinge of fear would strike that Molly might show up here with Caramati. But even this worry dissipated as the week went on and there was no sign of Molly.

Together with Dolph every day and every night — more time than they had spent together at a stretch in a year — Geri found again that he was humorous and attentive and still able to charm her with the extravagant romantic gesture. On the day of the balloon race, he hired a hot-air balloon to take him and Geri aloft. There, soaring above Louisville, alone together, they had a picnic lunch while they watched the other brightly colored balloons drifting around them.

The nights, too, were magic. Dolph had taken the Presidential suite at the elegant Seelbach Hotel, and each time when they returned from a gala, there was champagne waiting in a silver bucket — and a beautifully wrapped gift. His wedding presents to her, he called them. A jeweled bracelet from Cartier one night, a rare, beautifully illustrated antique book on horses another . . . and, toward the end of the week, a painting: the Stubbs she had been attracted to that first night they had talked in his study.

She blushed at the memory. 'You do know,' she said, 'I came very close to stealing this once. You were very gallant about it . . .'

'I had no choice,' Dolph said. 'Because you'd already stolen my heart . . .'

They made love, as they had every night after she opened her gifts, and Geri felt that the true gift — one she had come so foolishly close to throwing away — was the irreplaceable union she had found with Dolph. Whatever frivolous method they had used to decide on their marriage, the decision was right.

As soon as Heartbrakes' last victory had settled their 'bet', Dolph had proposed arranging a big wedding as a climax to Derby Week. Laurette had offered full cooperation to make it a social highlight. But Geri had known this would mean having hundreds of strangers along with her friends, the many business associates Dolph wouldn't want to exclude, as well as celebrities in town for the Derby. There was also the chance that Molly might find her way to a large event. Geri wished she could have befriended her sister so that Molly could share this moment with her; no one else in her family would be at the wedding. But Molly's raging jealousy couldn't be trusted not to disrupt the marriage vows.

It was best, Geri decided, to have an intimate ceremony attended only by their friends.

'Still a simple girl with simple tastes,' Dolph remarked when she told him her preference.

'Am I what you want?' she asked.

His embrace was answer enough.

So on Thursday they returned to Lexington and, in the lushly blooming rose garden of Laurette's house, a Justice of the Kentucky Supreme Court performed the ceremony. Geri wore a white St Laurent suit as Oakie gave her away, and Ed Markham stood up as Dolph's best man. Ramie came as matron of honor, and brought Glenn Joye, who had flown from California to be with her for the running of the Derby. After the ceremony, Joye sang a Cole Porter ballad he'd performed in one of his last musical films, made in the late

527

1950s. From first to last, the atmosphere in the rose garden was as golden and effervescent as the champagne poured for Laurette Wilkey's nuptial toast.

Late in the afternoon, the wedding party boarded helicopters chartered to take them back to Louisville for the rest of the Derby Week festivities.

When they returned to their suite at the Seelbach Hotel Geri was astonished to see the living room heaped everywhere with gift boxes large and small. Putting her arms around Dolph, she thanked him and then added, 'I'm yours forever now, darling — signed and sealed. Maybe it's time you believed you don't have to buy me anymore with things and more things. I have everything I want.'

'I don't know how I can enjoy my money more than by giving you a few luxuries now and then. Dear girl, you're just going to have to get over all your guilt about being incredibly rich.' He surveyed the mounds of packages. 'Though I can't take full responsibility for all this. They're from all our guests tonight.'

'What guests . . .?'

'Darling, we have to celebrate our wedding somehow.' He motioned her toward one of the bedrooms off the living room. 'I bought you something for the celebration, too. Have a look . . .'

Geri moved slowly into the room, both apprehensive and intrigued. Inside, by a wall of mirrored closets, three mannequins stood, each clothed in one of the most beautiful ball gowns Geri had ever seen. One of pale yellow silk appliquéd with huge white lace butterfly wings, another of lustrous blue-black velvet, and a third of champagne-colored lace with seed pearls sewn on the bodice. Dolph explained that he had called several designers who knew her measurements from past fittings.

'To suit any mood you have for the ball tonight,' he said.

'Oh, Dolph . . .' she sighed, touched by his romantic gesture yet unable to suppress the old worry that Molly might appear to ruin it.

Yet her worries were swept away as Dolph went on

528

excitedly, explaining that he had been planning the ball for weeks — sure that they would marry in Kentucky during Derby Week. It was to be in the Grand Ballroom of the Seelback, and everybody who was anybody would be there. 'Keeping the surprise, I don't mind telling you, was quite a job. Invitations to our party have become the hottest ticket in town.'

He moved to the dresser and picked up an ornate wooden box. 'And now, my love . . . for my wedding present.' He opened the box, lifted out a magnificent emerald necklace, and held it up. She went to him and turned so he could drape the necklace around her. He was right, she realized; she still hadn't given herself over to the pleasures of having limitless wealth. He had more than they could ever spend, no matter what they bought.

After closing the clasp, Dolph leaned over and kissed her neck. 'There are still things *I* want,' he said, turning her to face him. 'Things that money can't buy. Will you give them to me?'

'If I can . . .'

He said nothing to explain before he undid the zipper on the back of her dress. But as she was eased back onto the bed, naked except for the emeralds at her throat, his meaning became clear. She wished that he could have waited to mention children. Of course she wanted a family. But the way he had raised it now, at the moment he was lavishing gems upon her, made her feel as if offspring were part of a bargain she was making, a biological gift bartered for all the material wealth he could give her.

The marble and gilt grand ballroom of the Seelbach had been transformed into a fantasyland. Hundreds of yards of deep blue chiffon had been draped across the ceiling, with thousands of tiny lights embedded in the folds so it seemed that a piece of starlit sky had actually been transported indoors. At ground level the room was a garden, with blooming dogwood trees in tubs spaced around the walls, and enormous bouquets of blue delphinium, white lilac, maroon orchids, and pink rhubrum lilies spilling from vases on every table. Peter

Duchin's orchestra played as hundreds of guests danced or mingled at buffet tables laden with all the most expensive delicacies — ten-pound tins of Russian and Iranian caviar, sliced Scotch salmon, Louisiana Gulf shrimp as big as a fist, and hot dishes prepared by Paul Bocuse and the Troisgros brothers — chefs from two of France's three-star restaurants — each paid $40,000 by Dolph to fly in from Paris for the weekend.

More than half the guests were known to Dolph from business or to Geri through her work, the rest represented the cream of the celebrity crop without whom no event of Derby Week would be complete. Elizabeth Taylor and Henry Kissinger and Joan Collins and Gerry and Betty Ford and the owners of all the biggest thoroughbred stables, and a throng of best-selling authors, other television stars, and movers and shakers in business and politics had all stood on receiving lines to meet Dolph and Geri as if being presented to royalty.

Geri had chosen to wear the champagne lace. Adorned by the priceless necklace, her flawless skin set off by the color of the gown and her long hair gathered on her head in a Victorian style, she looked no less than regal. Receiving the social homage of friends and strangers alike, she had a new awareness of what it meant to be Dolph's wife, to have her legitimacy established on a level far above that of mistress. It might have gone to her head if she didn't have Oakie and Ramie around to remind her of her origins. She was glad, too, that she had been able to locate Charlie Hoyt in time to invite him. The one-time public defender was now a prosperous lawyer in Frankfurt; he had been invited to become a partner in Sid Ross's law firm, and had taken it over when Frankin died of a heart attack two years ago. Charlie's presence at the wedding was a reminder of the darkest times in Geri's past, but it felt good for her to face those memories without trepidation.

'Sure went the long way round to get home again, didn't you, Geri-Jo?' Charlie whispered as he leaned over her in the receiving line.

She hugged him tightly as she whispered back, 'Couldn't

530

have made the trip without you, Charlie. Thanks . . .'

'Don't forget Steve.'

'I *never* forget Steve,' she said.

They smiled at each other and Charlie moved away. Geri felt safe from the past at last. Molly would be paid off, she and Dolph would be able to raise a family in peace.

By the time the newlyweds led off the dancing with a solo waltz, Geri's mind was fizzing happily on several glasses of Roederer Kristal. Then she caught sight of a late arrival standing at the entrance. It took a moment to recognize the darkly handsome man, since he was in a tuxedo, not the flowing gold-trimmed desert robes in which Geri was accustomed to seeing him. She directed Dolph's attention to the doorway, and they went over immediately.

'Mrs Justinean,' said Sheik Ibn-Rashid Al-Sadir, bowing to Geri. 'What a magnificent bride you are.'

'I'm pleased and honored that you accepted our invitation, Sheik Al-Sadir. I represented you so badly at the auctions a couple of years ago, I would understand if you'd never forgiven me.'

'The tradition of my people,' he said, 'teaches us to accept with grace what we cannot change. In the desert when the sun blazes down at its hottest or winds whip the sand into a blinding storm, we simply retreat to our tents . . .'

If he bore no grudges for losing Heartbrakes, Geri thought, it wasn't only because of his desert wisdom. The sheik had also been able to console himself by buying many other valuable thoroughbreds at prices that always set new records. It was widely known that in the past two years al-Sadir had invested over a hundred million dollars in stud properties and bloodstock in England, Ireland, and America.

Dolph welcomed the sheik warmly, too. 'Your presence tonight, Rashid,' he said, 'is one of our greatest gifts.'

'Do not say that yet.' Al-Sadir raised a finger in a cautionary gesture. With a glance over his shoulder toward the lobby, he clapped his hands twice. Immediately two brawny henchmen dressed in plain white *dishdashahs* entered the ballroom. Cradled in the arms of one was a long velvet-

531

covered box; the second hefted a huge, bulky object draped over with black silk. Other guests congregated to watch as the sheik presented his spectacular wedding gifts.

From the box, he removed an exquisitely crafted shotgun, with an ivory-inlaid ebony stock, a gold trigger and other gold metalwork finely engraved with hunting scenes. As he laid the gun in Dolph's hands, the onlookers gasped — not only in appreciation of the rare workmanship, but astonished by the choice of gift in view of Dolph's recent past. Dolph accepted with genuine gratitude, however. He was not unfamiliar with the sharp gallows humor common to the Arabs, and he recognized the sincerity of the sheik's gesture. The weapon, produced by the finest English gunmaker, Purdy, could have cost no less than a hundred thousand dollars.

Next, tossing aside the silk draped over the bulky second gift, the sheik unveiled a treasure surpassing the first — a saddle, heavily ornamented with hammered gold, and encrusted with jewels. He turned to Geri. 'This is one of a few saddles that belonged to my father, a prince of the desert. To a woman I admire and esteem as a ruler in her own world, I give it humbly.' Al-Sadir made the customary Arab bow, putting his hands together and touching them to his lips.

Geri had some knowledge of the Arabian customs in regard to horses, and she knew that giving any saddle to a woman was a compliment of the highest order, an acknowledgement that she could be as skilled with horses as a man. To have given her one of his *father*'s saddles made the tribute even rarer. 'I am not only deeply grateful,' she said to the sheik, 'I am also greatly honored.'

Al-Sadir mysteriously rattled off a few words of Arabic. Then he explained: 'Another saying of my people: praise me not by pouring honeyed words in my ear, I'd rather you simply lead me to water . . .'

'Water isn't quite so valuable here. Will champagne do?'

'My religion forbids alcoholic drink. But as a substitute for the oasis, I should be happy if you would lead me to the dance floor.'

Geri glanced at Dolph, who nodded permission.

After only a few turns around the floor, she said sincerely, 'You're the best dancing partner I've ever had.' The sheik's prowess didn't surprise her; she knew he was thoroughly westernized, having attended college in England, then filled various diplomatic posts in Europe.

'Unfortunately, I can only do this two or three times a year,' he said. 'The rest of the time I'd be tripping over those long robes. It's hard enough to walk in the damn things.'

She laughed, and they danced without speaking for a minute. Then the sheik said, 'Your judgment is impeccable about more than dance partners, Doctor Keyes. I regret that past circumstances prevented me from taking full advantage of such wise opinion.'

She understood at once he was talking about the horse. 'I regret it, too. Perhaps, you'd allow me to represent you at another auction . . .'

'That would be one solution. Or there may be another way. I am informed that you have already received some very generous offers from breeders' syndicates — and that you have turned them down. You're gambling, I expect, that your horse will win the Derby . . .'

'He's the favorite. If he wins —'

'Yes, you hope to get paid more. But why take risks . . . if you can have a sure thing?'

'It's beginning to sound like you're through sitting out the storm in your tent,' she said.

He smiled. 'Very well, cards on the table. Twenty-five million dollars. I am ready to agree to buy your horse for that amount.'

'And if he loses . . .?'

'You misunderstand, Mrs Justinean. I am offering to contract a purchase, at that price, tonight. Whatever happens on Saturday — win or lose — I would be the owner. And you would have your money.' To punctuate the offer he swept Geri into a few graceful spins.

The words were more dizzying than the dance. *Twenty-five million.* Even if the horse won the Derby, she could hardly expect to receive more — while a loss would reduce the offers she had received previously by at least half. To put off al-Sadir was to risk a loss of approximately twenty million dollars.

The sheik stopped whirling her. 'What is your answer?'

'It's a very . . . attractive proposition.'

'Is that all? From an Englishwoman I might expect such understatement. But from an American . . .?'

'All right,' she admitted, 'it's a fabulous offer.' But tempted as she was, she tried not to repeat the rashness that had indebted her to Molly. 'But the American also wants to know what the catch is . . .'

The sheik pulled his head back, as though affronted. 'There is none. The price would be high . . . if I wasn't buying more than just a horse. When I seek this prize, I am also reclaiming a heritage. All great thoroughbreds descend from the Arabian lines. Trace the pedigrees back far enough, and you will find that there were horses taken to England, and later brought here, that once roamed our lands. Nothing was left — none of the best. The time has come to reverse the tide. Whenever we see the best, we will take them back.' He fixed his black eyes on Geri. 'I almost had this horse once. Don't you think you owe it to me to sell him to no one else?'

She was ready to agree. Yet, as a gesture to consolidate her marriage, she couldn't accept here and now. 'I can't answer until I've spoken to my husband about it,' she said.

Al-Sadir seemed to detect that he had persuaded her. 'Of course,' he said in a bemused tone, 'the American marriage requires all this — what do you call it? — togetherness. Very well, I will give you until noon on the day of the race.' Adding that he would have papers drawn ready for her to sign, he handed her a card from his pocket on which he had already written the number of a special phone line in his hotel suite.

The dance ended and the sheik escorted her to the sidelines. 'We must do this again sometime.'

'And the next one,' she replied, 'will be free of charge.'

He said goodnight and headed out of the ballroom. At once, the excitement Geri had been suppressing bubbled to the surface. She scanned the room until she saw Dolph — and froze in shock. The band was playing again, and he was on the

534

floor, dancing — with Diana's ghost. The same lithe build, feline face, tumbling blonde hair . . .

The apparition lasted only an instant. Then Geri recognized the woman in Dolph's arms as Sabine Delvaux, the French movie star who appeared sometimes in American television commercials for cars and perfume. Advertisers were known to pay her million-dollar fees, believing that Delvaux's chic beauty and purring French accent automatically associated their products with the ultimate in high-fashion and sexy desirability. Her presence at Derby Week was part of a publicity tie-in paid for by a cosmetic company.

As Sabine Delvaux tossed her head, laughing at something Dolph had said, she seemed so comfortable with her own elegance and beauty, that for a moment more Geri had the rare experience of jealousy, sparking an urge to interrupt Dolph's dance. But she realized then that if she ever surrendered to such doubts, she would only be consumed by them. A man like Dolph would always be sought by other women — as she herself had wanted him when he was married to Diana. Their marriage could last only by having faith that it would.

Let him dance with whomever he wished. She could wait to tell him about the sheik's offer.

Even after every guest had gone, Dolph paid the orchestra to stay on so he could dance alone with Geri. He was at his gentlest, and most romantic — all the lights turned off at his request so that only hundreds of candles sprinkled the dark. As they swayed together in the middle of the floor, Geri told him at last about the offer al-Sadir had made. 'He wanted an answer right away, of course, but the offer stands until noon on Saturday.'

'No need to wait,' Dolph said. 'You could have told him tonight.'

'I'm a married lady now. I thought it would be nicer to tell you about it before I made the deal final.'

'Made the deal?' Dolph repeated. Abruptly, he stopped dancing. 'You wouldn't be foolish enough to accept . . .?'

Geri was stung by Dolph's patronizing tone. Her hold on him loosened. 'I'm intending to take it, yes.'

'For God's sake, why? This horse might be one of the greatest thoroughbreds of the last ten years. It's only the beginning for him. Why let that Arab grab all the glory?'

It was Dolph's sheer competitive drive that was talking now, she thought. 'Maybe because the horse should have been his, anyway,' she answered. 'And because he's ready to pay me magnificently.'

None of the romantic mood was left. As soon as they had stopped dancing, some of the lights went on and waiters started stacking chairs. The band music tailed off, and the musicians began putting away their instruments. Geri walked off the floor.

Dolph strode along at her side. 'I don't understand you. What difference does it make how much he pays. Money should be meaningless to you now.'

She rounded on him. 'Not to me,' she said harshly, 'never to me. And I don't see how it could be to you. My God, Dolph, remember where you came from. If money means nothing to you now because you have so damn much, then do something with it besides pile it up. Give it away. Help people who need it. I'll tell you where to send it . . .'

'Is that why you're so eager to have your own millions?' he said. 'To be a goddamn philanthropist?'

'No, I need this money to . . .' She hesitated, unable to explain the truth. 'To have something of my own, that's all.'

As they kept walking toward the elevators, Geri felt dreadful. A night that should have been the best of her life had been spoiled by this needless argument. It would never have happened if only Dolph understood the tensions that had been tearing at her since Molly had invaded her life.

A whole new phase of her future was supposed to have started today. Now she saw that it would be a future without hope unless she told Dolph everything. She was wrong to have kept the secrets.

But when they were in the elevator, he spoke first. 'I can't let you do it,' he said.

'Let me? I wasn't asking your permission. The horse is mine — to do with as I please. You gave him to me . . .'

'I wanted you to have him, yes. And as long as *we* kept him, I was content to have you consider him yours. But the papers have always remained in my name. Legally, Heartbrakes is still *my* property . . .'

She stared back silently, shattered by this new reality. Of course she had always known Justinean was strong, that he insisted on control in all his business dealings. But in marriage she had assumed it would be different. She had his respect, she thought, and he would treat her as an equal.

The elevator door opened at their floor. Dolph stood back, waiting for her to exit first. His attention to small amenities at this moment offended her as hypocritical, but after a moment she preceded him out.

In the room, he went straight to the phone. With several calls, indiscriminately waking people, he obtained the phone number at which the sheik could be reached. He never asked Geri. Nor did he think of waiting until the morning to settle the matter.

When he was placing the final call, Geri said quietly, 'Don't do this, Dolph. Don't do it to me — or to yourself. You don't realize everything that's at stake.'

'You're angry now, I can see that. I'm sure you'll remain angry for a day or two. But when that horse wins, when you have the satisfaction of that moment and all the rewards that come after — far greater than this Arab offered you — then you'll admit I was right.'

The connection was made. A servant of the sheik's had answered the phone and could not be badgered into waking him, so Dolph contented himself with leaving a message: Heartbrakes was not for sale — at any price.

As he lowered the phone, Geri walked into the second of the suite's two bedrooms, closing the door behind her. She didn't care anymore to warn Dolph of the dominoes that would fall if Heartbrakes lost. She hoped, too, that in time it would be possible to forgive him. But as much as she liked to play the longshots, the odds on this one seemed much too high to be worth a bet.

537

CHAPTER SEVEN

Geri rose at five a.m. to go and watch Ramie put Heartbrakes through a final workout at Churchill Downs. Most horses rested on the day immediately preceding a race, but Oakie believed Heartbrakes performed best on uninterrupted exercise, provided he wasn't run too fast and too far. The trainer told Ramie to jog once around the track, then breeze for a half mile, 'and ask him when you get to the last eighth.'

A thin mist not yet burned off by the sun hovered over the turf, and as Heartbrakes circled the track he seemed to be the mythical winged horse flying effortlessly over clouds. Geri felt her bitterness toward Dolph slip away. She could never excuse the high-handed way he had pre-empted her decision, yet she had to acknowledge that he might have prevented her from making a mistake. Once this animal was sold, she would probably never have another like it. If only Dolph could have reasoned with her, respected her right to decide . . .

Oakie clicked his stopwatch as Ramie let the horse stretch out to run the last eighth at a full gallop. A fraction of a minute later he clicked it again, and let out a soft whistle. 'We've got a steamroller there,' he said. 'Give him half a day's rest in the shade, and he'll flatten them all tomorrow.'

And maybe then, she thought, her longshot on Dolph would also come in.

A young stablehand was standing by to lead Heartbrakes back to the barn, but Geri had an urge to tend the horse herself. There was something curiously reassuring about performing the same simple tasks she had done long ago when she was a stablehand herself. While she removed the saddle and bridle, and slipped the simple rope halter over the horse's neck, Oakie and Ramie stood by, kidding her good-naturedly.

'So there,' she answered their heckling as she took the lead rope and started pulling the horse behind her toward the barns. 'I ain't forgotten how.'

It was more than a joke to her. It was an affirmation that what had been true in the past could be true again; she could survive by herself.

She had only gone a few yards when she felt an abrupt heavy strain on the rope. In the first second, she thought the animal had simply stopped mulishly in his tracks. But then Ramie cried out, and when Geri spun around she saw the horse rolling onto his side, keeling over slowly but with the same inexorable momentum as a tree being felled. As his head flopped onto the ground the sickening realization struck. Geri crouched quickly but even before she laid her hand on the horse's neck, she guessed there would be no pulse. In the startling totality of the collapse, the complete loss of any muscle control, she recognized the symptoms of sudden death.

As the news spread quickly around the backstretch, the large corps of national sports reporters covering the Derby gathered to press Geri for a statement. She admitted to being shocked and grieved, but she refused to speculate on what had happened pending the autopsy she planned to perform herself. At his first opportunity, however, Oakie pulled her aside and suggested any post-mortem ought to include some other respected veterinarians. Whatever Geri found, the trainer warned, would be subject to intense scrutiny. It was essential that the autopsy findings should not be clouded by her heavy emotional and financial stake in the horse.

Immediately, Geri placed a call to Dr Sybil Cheyney, a woman veterinarian attached to the new Bolton Center school of veterinary medicine near Philadelphia. Informed of the circumstances, Sybil Cheyney agreed to fly down immediately on a jet chartered by Geri.

Though Sybil Cheyney had been a class ahead of her when they were both attending Cornell vet college, they had encountered each other occasionally in the labs, and Geri had observed then that Syb Cheyney was a dedicated professional with particular talents in certain areas of animal medicine. Those special skills had since made her one of the top authorities in the field of 'large animal pathology'.

No less than in humans, the occurrence of sudden death from natural physiological causes was hardly a phenomenon unknown among horses. And within that species, certainly the group at highest risk was the thoroughbreds. With their systems often stressed by hard exercise and feed supplemented with special electrolytes and vitamins — as well as by those two frenzied minutes when they must pour every ounce of energy into a race — sometimes their hearts simply gave out. A blood vessel could rupture, a fatal clot form, some inbred genetic weakness might wreak physiological havoc. Horses could drop in mid-stride on a dauntless stretch run . . . or while grazing in a quiet field. It happened often enough; no one knew that better than Geri.

Yet she could not imagine this death to be anything so innocent. There were too many people who would have wanted the animal dead, and who had the motive and temperament to act. Had al-Sadir ever forgiven having a champion snatched away from him! With all hope gone of recovering it legally, perhaps he had paid someone to extract his idea of justice according to the rough customs of the desert. Nickles was another suspect. Or the culprit might be someone from the underworld sphere of John Caramati, an enemy who knew about his secret share of the horse and wanted to deprive him of it.

Along with security officers at Churchill Downs and detectives from the Louisville Police, Geri spent the hours before Sybil Cheyney arrived questioning stablehands, looking for any clue that Heartbrakes' feed or water had been poisoned, or some toxic substance administered by any other means. Nothing turned up. There had been no unauthorized visitors. The feed and water given to Heartbrakes had been

540

taken from common sources shared by animals who showed absolutely no ill effects.

Six hours after the horse's death, in the veterinary facilities at Churchill Downs, the autopsy was finally performed by Dr Sybil Cheyney with Geri assisting. During the three-hour procedure, they found no evidence of any fatal physical problem. No lesions in the heart or ruptured vessels that would have indicated a coronary attack. No hemorrhaging around other organs.

The two veterinarians emerged at last to face a press corps four times larger than when they had entered. As agreed before they stepped out of the autopsy room, Sybil Cheyney presented the results. A tall, broad woman, with a face and voice reminiscent of Eleanor Roosevelt, her understated delivery defused the atmosphere of sensationalism pumped up by the media. Even though she announced that the cause of death remained 'mysterious', and no absolute judgment could be made until a battery of toxological tests was completed, she convincingly discouraged speculations about foul play.

'From what I've seen so far,' she said, 'it seems far-fetched to assume there was any criminal tampering with this colt. Horses do break down, sometimes totally and disastrously. It's tragic that it happened to this one, and in circumstances where it was bound to attract attention and raise so many doubts. But at any other time and place, we would accept this as nothing more than one of the mysteries of nature.'

When she left the building after changing out of her lab coat and thanking Sybil Cheyney, Geri found Dolph waiting outside, standing casually by a hired limousine as he sparred with reporters. Lessons learned at the time of the trial had left a permanent mark on his manner with the press. He was always amiable, cognizant that a strategy might be devised to turn their attention to advantage.

Shocked as she had been this morning, Geri had not felt any desire to lean on Dolph. She had put out no call to him, and he had not appeared until now — wisely allowing her a chance to work off the resentments that would be all the more intense in the wake of losing the horse.

The reporters started to engulf Geri again, and Dolph opened the door of the limousine. 'My wife and I have both cooperated with you today,' he appealed to the reporters. 'We'll be available again later, but right now we'd appreciate a chance to be alone.'

In need of the quiet isolation offered by the car, Geri stepped in.

'We can find another like him,' Dolph said after directing the driver to take them back to the hotel. 'I don't care how much it costs. It's a loss, I know, but not something that can't be replaced.'

'The chance to forgive you,' she replied quietly, 'that's what I've lost. If there could have been a tomorrow, if he'd won —'

He took hold of her by the arms. 'It's a horse, damn it. Only a horse!'

'Wasn't there once a king, who offered to trade his kingdom for nothing more?'

'He was on a battlefield. And his horse was the difference between victory and defeat. Is that where we are?'

She gave him a bleak look. 'Maybe . . .'

He gazed back steadily. 'I warned you a long time ago that could be a danger with me. But I wanted you because I knew you were strong like me — a survivor, because I believed you wouldn't give up as Diana did. If you need more room, more freedom, then keep fighting for it.'

'I don't want to fight you, Dolph. I can't live that way. You have to be ready to stop trying to control everything.'

She waited for him to say something more, to make a pledge, but he sat back and they rode the rest of the way to the hotel in silence.

As soon as they were in the room he became solicitous. 'It's been hard for you. Rest a few hours. Then we'll have some fun . . . forget.' The ball given annually by the Governor of Kentucky was tonight, he reminded her. And tomorrow there was still the race.

'There's no point in my going,' she said. 'It can't be the race I needed to see.'

'Needed . . .?'

'To make my peace with you.' She was leaving today, she added, going back to New York. There would be problems that required attention, especially now that she had lost the horse.

He didn't ask what the problems were. He told her the car would be waiting to take her to the airport when she was ready. Then he went out.

As the door closed between them, she reflected on the irony that they had been married only a day. Could it still be saved? Once she got away, perhaps she could recover a perspective that allowed the rift to heal.

Or would she decide it made no sense to try?

BOOK VII: *THE HOMESTRETCH*

Glen Cove — June, 1985

CHAPTER ONE

Geri stared at the face of the baby in her arms, uncertain who it resembled most. Lorene, perhaps, as she had looked that last time, when she had turned back before climbing upward toward the deluge. But then, in the next second, the infant appeared to be incongruously old, its eyes burning with a fierce bitterness no newborn could possibly know. It was *Pa* looking back at her!

Groping for something to block out the apparition, her hand found the shirt of a jockey's silks, gold with diagonal silver-gray stripes, Dolph's colors. She draped it over the baby, but just then cold water surged up suddenly over her hips, and a moment later the baby was swept out of her arms. She tried to chase after it, but she could see it riding away on the torrent, becoming smaller and smaller until it was hardly a speck.

Then the speck exploded in a blue-white flash —

Waking suddenly, Geri heard the echo from the last clap of thunder rolling away. She bolted upright in bed and glanced around, desperately taking an inventory of sights to help fix herself in the real world. Through the window of the darkened bedroom, she saw sheets of rain slashing down, then a flash of lightning revealed the expanse of lawn, leading across to the stretch of sandy beachfront and, beyond, the shimmering water of Long Island Sound. She knew at last where she was.

Still, after the hideous dream, all the reminders of horror and loss, the terror would not leave her. God, how she wished there was someone here now to comfort her, hold her, *love* her.

She turned on a lamp, and swung her feet onto the floor. The Cartier clock on the night-table gave the time as a few minutes after three. Automatically, she added five hours, calculating the time it would be where Dolph was. Eight o'clock. Probably just getting up, about to have one of those enormous English breakfasts. It ought to be a good time to reach him.

Only yesterday evening he had called again, asked her to come and join him at Epsom to see the running of the English racing classic — 'the *Dar*by', as he had pronounced it in the traditional English style. It wasn't just an invitation to the races, she understood, but an expression of his desire to try once more to heal the breach. Last night she had refused, unable to summon the will to believe in one more new beginning. But in the wake of the dream, her resolve weakened. It was always hardest to be alone when it rained.

She went downstairs, into the library. Dolph was staying as a guest at the ancestral country home of his friend — and a lobbyist for Dolph's interests in Britain — the Duke of Colchester. The Duke had an unlisted telephone, but Geri knew the number would be in the notebook Dolph kept in the library desk.

She switched on the library lights and headed for the desk. But then her gaze was caught by the spotlit oil painting over the mantle — the one Quinn had sent years ago as a wedding present: Heartbrakes, with Nickles in the saddle, as they had looked in the winner's circle after the running of 'The Wood'. It was a traditional static pose, the horse in profile, but it had pleased Dolph enormously. 'This fellow Quinn,' he said, 'may be the only one who can hold a candle to Stubbs.' He knew that Geri had been instrumental in helping Quinn since they had met at Laurette Wilkey's, but seemed unaware of any involvement beyond friendship.

As Geri stood in front of the painting, recollections of the horse flooded through her, only to be overwhelmed by memories of Quinn. Yearning again for someone to hold her, she thought of that night she had once spent with him, imagined his touch . . .

Perhaps it wasn't Dolph she should call. Where was Quinn, though? He travelled widely now, taking commissions from thoroughbred owners all over the world. How could she reach him? In the first years of her marriage, there had been occasional contacts between them — the personal phone call she had made to thank him for the gift painting, a couple of meetings in passing at some racing event. Each time they met, she would wonder again what might have been. But always, before the ache of yearning could really take hold, she would fight it down. In the past year they had lost touch completely.

A clap of thunder hammered the air outside, and Geri began to shiver. Suddenly she felt the chilling loneliness of a survivor, swept up onto a small reef from a ship wrecked in stormy seas. To calm herself, she went to the bar in the corner of the library, and poured a couple of fingers of scotch into a crystal tumbler. As she touched it to her lips, however, she was reminded of Diana, could almost feel the ghost of her presence in the house. She set the glass down without drinking and went quickly to the desk.

With Dolph's book of private phone numbers in front of her, she hesitated again. Staring out at the rain, she knew she needed saving. But she couldn't quell the fear that whichever savior she chose would be the wrong one.

She had stopped trusting her decisions after the death of the horse. Foolish to blame herself, of course; it had been a freakish event. Yet she often thought that if she had not made an issue of disagreeing with Dolph, if she had taken *no* stand, then the consequences that had flowed out of losing the animal might have been less damaging. First, coming on the heels of her feud with Dolph, it had prevented them from ever properly resolving the argument. The marriage had gone on — it had been too new then to do anything else — but she and Dolph had co-existed in a strained and uncertain state. Their inability to reappraise the situation, as they might have done if Heartbrakes had been alive, set the stage for other grievances and resentments.

Without her share of the horse to bank on, Molly had immediately renewed her blackmail demands. This time, though, she hadn't gone through the discreet formality of private meetings with Geri. Three weeks after the wedding, she had marched into Justinean's offices and demanded to see Dolph, announcing that she was 'Mrs Justinean's sister.' After the reaction of the outer-lobby receptionist had been to treat her as a crackpot and have her escorted to an elevator, Molly had spent the next morning camped outside the office building. At noon, as he was on his way to a luncheon of business leaders, she had grabbed Dolph on the sidewalk. 'I'm your fuckin' wife's sister,' she cried out, 'and if you know what's good for your own goddamn hide, you'll give me the time of day!'

Whether he had been persuaded by the fire of vengeance in her eyes, or the vestige of a family resemblance, Justinean had commanded Molly to get into the limousine and, as she rode with him to his luncheon, he had listened to her demands, and read the dog-eared copies of a few court records that the Kentucky state policeman who'd once lived with her had managed to obtain.

Shocked as he was by the revelations about Geri, Justinean did not wilt before them, but coolly countered Molly's threats with warnings that he possessed the means to make her life hell if she didn't back off. In the end, he had managed to strike a bargain he could live with. To buy Molly's silence, and all the compromising records, he would pay two million dollars.

It had been done so easily, the deal struck by the time the car pulled up in front of '21', that Molly couldn't believe he was sincere. 'No tricks,' she cautioned sharply, as she got out of the car.

'Why should I trick you?' Justinean said.

'To save yourself a shitload of money.'

Justinean laughed. 'Two million? I'll make that back in a week. Come to my reception desk this afternoon at five, there'll be a cashier's check for the full amount waiting in an envelope with your name on it.' Molly had almost skipped away before Justinean called back to ask: 'By the way — what *is* your name?'

That night Geri had gone with Justinean to a charity ball in the city. Amid echoes of that evening when they had first talked together as man and woman at his house in Saratoga, when he had taken her onto a dance floor for the first time, she remembered why she had loved him, and willed herself to try again. But then, while he whirled her around the floor, Justinean said casually, 'I met a member of your family today . . .'

Geri froze until Justinean pulled her back into the dance step and reported his encounter with Molly. 'You should have brought her to me right at the start,' he said angrily. 'If she had dragged up your past, you know, Diana's case would have been reopened. As a price for your freedom or mine, the money she wanted was little enough.'

In retrospect, of course, her reasons for the secret seemed absurd. She had done it because she wanted to spare him being blackmailed, because she was afraid of losing him, because she could not learn to regard so much money as being inconsequential. And, in the curious sense of loss that came after hearing Molly's threat had been ended, Geri recognized one more motive. She had kept stringing Molly along because it was the only connection they had. As long as she could see Molly, there had always been some hope, however small, that a kinder bond between them could be reawakened.

There had been a time when Geri would have explained all this to Dolph. But now he didn't really care to know. He asked no questions — did not even ask if she was guilty of the crimes charged against her so long ago.

In the months following, Geri came to wonder if Dolph hadn't paid off Molly not so much out of a desire to end the threat of blackmail as to gain a bargaining chip in their marriage. Eventually, though, rather than nurse resentments or quit a marriage that was still so new, she had yielded to Dolph's desire for reconciliation. He desperately wanted children — wanted them only with her, he said — and she was also longing for a family.

Her career would no longer be as much of a hindrance. The clinic was burdened with debts incurred while holding off Molly, and Geri was adamantly opposed to leting Dolph pay them off — not after he had already made such a huge blackmail payment. A settlement of Jack Cotsworth's malpractice suit was the final nail in the coffin. Geri had to sell the clinic. Her enthusiasm for the sport of racing had been dampened, anyway — first by Heartbrakes' death, and by what had happened to Nickles. Almost a year after she had dismissed him, he had been brought at last before a grand jury in California. The local prosecutors hadn't sufficient evidence to form the basis of a criminal case, but the clear indications of 'unethical conduct' were enough for Nickles to have his jockey's license suspended for three years. The punishment effectively ended his career, since it would be hard to find any owner ready to trust him again once the suspension was lifted.

Then Oakie had drifted away. Without Geri's involvement in Justinean's stables, the trainer found it difficult to continue there. Other owners had been trying for years to lure him away, and at last he accepted a lucrative offer from the Chapman brothers, Boston real estate developers who had gone heavily into racing a few years ago. Since Oakie's departure, Dolph's horses hadn't won nearly as many races as before. Though he kept his breeding operations in Saratoga and California, he rarely visited them. His interest in maintaining thoroughbreds had waned as he poured himself into building his business empire.

Fifteen months ago, Geri had become pregnant. She had known for a week before she could bring herself to tell Dolph. He had wanted children so much, she feared he might focus so completely on the baby that it would end, once and for all, any hope of reviving the romance they'd had. But in fact, when she did share the news, it had marked the beginning of a 'honeymoon' period. Dolph had behaved toward her with a tenderness that had been missing since their earliest days together. He thought of new ways to delight her, taking her on trips with him again — to Egypt, to see the Pyramids; to Africa, on a photo safari. Sex with him recovered its spontaneity and joy.

Until, just two months later, she miscarried. Overnight the honeymoon mood was gone. As she mourned the loss of the

552

baby, Dolph said all the right things: 'we have each other . . . we'll try again . . . plenty of time . . .' But an inner light had gone out. He pulled away from her again.

Wounded as she was by his quick retreat, she tried not to judge him too harshly. Because he was active and powerful, kept himself in good condition, she tended to forget that he was almost thirty years older. But his age, she told herself, could be a reasonable factor in creating special anxieties about having a child.

There was a new round of business trips, long absences, the arrival of expensive gifts delivered by couriers and store messengers — compensations scattered by an incalculably rich man with no more emotional investment than if they were crumbs tossed to a bird. Finally he returned to tell her he was ready to try again.

Ready. The very way he presented himself to her, expecting her to be waiting, made her feel once more as if there was nothing more to the process than breeding. He expected his 'season' with her to produce the kind of champion that could someday take over his crown. She couldn't be ready when he was. For all the months since, she had held herself apart, suspecting that they must inevitably end the marriage — yet afraid while even the faintest spark still glowed to rekindle the passion they'd once shared. But he had taken a step backward, too, practically living aboard his plane as he flew from one deal to the next. The past couple of months had amounted to an unofficial separation. She expected that the next time he came home, they would discuss making it legal.

But last night there had been his call from London. 'I don't know why it went wrong, Geri. No one means as much to me as you. No one ever could. Stay . . .'

Experience had shown that Dolph would always have to dominate the woman in his life. But she still wanted to believe he could change. Didn't he deserve one more chance?

Across the room, Quinn's painting shone under the light. A longing surged through her — to go back, to live again that night with Billy, open the path to a world of different choices.

But going back was impossible — and anyway, the race was

won by going forward. She could try once more with Dolph, she thought, she could stay with him — if only she could be sure he wouldn't try to control her, would value her as a partner with something of her own to contribute to their marriage, not just as another of his possessions.

And then, as she stared at the painting, she realized what she must ask from him as proof of his respect. She picked up the phone and punched a single button. An operator came on the line. For one long moment, Geri gazed at the painting.

'International, please . . .'

CHAPTER TWO

'And remember,' said the Duchess of Colchester, 'if you converse with her, the preferred form of address is "Ma'am" — *not* "Your Highness".'

Geri gave a studious nod, and Dolph flicked a sympathetic glance from under the brim of his pearl-gray top hat that, along with a gray cutaway, comprised the compulsory gentleman's dress for Derby Day. They were on the grounds at Epsom, walking toward the Royal enclosure where the Queen customarily received visitors. The next race was to be the Derby, and the Duke and Duchess of Colchester and their guests had been invited to view it along with the Queen and the royal family. In preparation for being presented to England's monarch, Geri had been receiving non-stop coaching in comportment from the Duchess. An image of propriety, with her lacquered blue hair, her square body encased in a suit the color and thickness of tank armor, the Duchess gave instructions so detailed and restrictive — 'one must laugh softly, without opening the mouth too wide or showing the teeth' — that Geri would have happily passed up the chance to meet Elizabeth II, except that she didn't want to miss a minute of Dolph's company.

With that amazing talent he had to re-create himself, he had entranced her anew in the two days since she had arrived from New York. A gypsy violinist and an accordionist had been waiting at the arrival gate when her flight landed, and after she had been handed an armful of roses, they had played for her during the long wait to clear customs and collect her baggage. Embarrassed as she was by the curious stares from other passengers, she had relished every minute of it. That evening there were tickets to hear Domingo sing at Covent Garden, and the next morning Dolph had driven her to Hampton Court in a vintage two-seater MG he had rented. In the afternoon, they had gone farther into the country along narrow roads bordered by hedgerows, getting happily lost until they stopped at a picturesque country pub where they held hands across the table, lovers again. Once or twice she had thought of the request she wanted to make of Dolph — her test that he would accept her as an equal — but she deferred it, not wanting to dilute the romantic mood with the 'business' of marriage.

'You know, my dear, if it wasn't for what happened here, you wouldn't have had a Kentucky Derby in America?'

The Duke was addressing Geri. He was a large man with a bushy gray moustache, and a face burnished pink by sitting at many firesides in Scottish castles and the men's clubs of Pall Mall. She turned to him. 'I know, Sir Herbert, this was the original Derby.'

'Ran the first one in 1780,' Dolph put in.

'That's right, just four years after you colonial upstarts declared independence. Bunch of good fellows got together and put up a stake for three-year-olds to run a mile and a half. But it almost wasn't a Derby. Rather, it came very close to being a Bunbury — and that would have changed the history of racing everywhere. Imagine you colonials getting together every year to watch the Kentucky Bunbury.'

Geri laughed. 'I don't think it would've caught on,' she said. 'Good thing they decided against calling it that.'

'No one actually decided, old girl. You see, among the chaps who organized the race were the Earl of Derby, and a chap called Bunbury. Seems they were both rather keen to nab a bit of posterity, so they argued about who would give his name to the occasion. To settle it, they finally tossed a coin. The way it fell, they didn't have a "Bunbury" that day . . . they had a

556

"Derby". And so it's been ever since, here and everywhere.'

They had reached the royal enclosure, a grassy area at the trackside with its own pavillion, separated by a fence from the general viewing field. A bobby and a Queen's equerry were at the gate, admitting only those with proper credentials.

'Good afternoon, your Grace, Lady Colchester,' the equerry greeted the Duke and his wife.

After the Duke identified Justinean and Geri they were all passed through. Within the enclosure, the atmosphere resembled a large garden party. A sea of men in gray cutaways and women in model dresses and hats mingled, waiting to be greeted by the Queen. Geri exchanged an occasional smile with other visitors she recognized as Americans, past clients of hers. As one of the world's most knowledgeable and enthusiastic racehorse owners, Queen Elizabeth had many acquaintances from the American racing community. Horses from her stable had won the English Derby in the past, and she had a couple entered today.

'Get ready now,' the Duke said, after they had been in the enclosure only a minute, 'the Queen is coming our way.' Geri turned. The Queen, along with other members of the royal family, was just moving along the line already formed by Dolph and Lord and Lady Colchester. Geri drew in her breath, caught by the thrill that still overtook her in the presence of people who seemed somehow almost legendary. There was Prince Philip, his hand poised debonairly in the cut of his pocket, and behind him Prince Charles with his exquisite young Princess, Diana. While Philip, Charles and Diana stopped farther down the line talking to others, the Queen advanced ahead of them and paused in front of Dolph.

'Your Majesty,' said the Duke, 'may I present Mr and Mrs Adolphus Justinean . . .?'

'Mr. Justinean,' she began, 'a pleasure to see you again. Newmarket last time, wasn't it?'

'That's correct, Ma'am, eight years ago. Your memory is astonishing.'

'In this case I wish a little less so. I also recall we were there for the 2,000 Guineas — and a horse of yours beat one of mine.'

557

Geri had expected the Queen to be surrounded by a suffocating aura of pomp and tradition. But Elizabeth was friendly, almost homespun. Perhaps, by way of acknowledging the importance of Dolph's business activities to her country, she didn't limit herself to the usual perfunctory amenities. She asked several questions about his stable, showing an up-to-date knowledge of its recent record.

'I'm sorry to see,' she said, 'you have no entry in the Derby.'

'This year, Ma'am,' Dolph replied, 'I thought I'd give one of your horses a chance.'

The Queen laughed. 'I hope they will appreciate the gift as much as I do.'

At last she moved along to Geri. As the Duchess had demonstrated earlier, Geri dipped at the knee and inclined her head for a moment. When she looked up, an equerry at the Queen's shoulder was murmuring something into her ear.

'Mrs Justinean,' she said, 'how nice to meet you.'

'The honor is mine, Ma'am.'

'Or perhaps I should call you "Doctor". I've just been told you're a prominent practitioner of equine medicine.'

For a split second Geri pondered her reply. 'I was, Ma'am. I haven't really practiced since my marriage.'

'It's a field I should have been happy in myself. I subscribe to a number of the American journals on the subject, excellent publications. Would I have seen any contributions of yours in the past?'

'Perhaps, Ma'am. I did some writing for the journals.'

'Under what name?'

Geri was puzzled by the question, until she realized she had mentioned practicing only before her marriage. 'My name was Keyes.'

The Queen's eyes widened. 'Doctor G. Keyes? Would that be you?'

'Yes, Ma'am.'

'How extraordinary! And how surprising that you've given it up. As I recall, you were responsible for quite a number of innovative therapies.' Elizabeth was no longer simply chatty, she was relating to Geri in a way that seemed very personal.

'That idea of treating a broken leg with the horse floating in water — to keep the weight off, I thought that was remarkable. Did you make any progress there . . .?

'Some, Ma'am, and others carried on from there. I didn't have a chance to complete my own work.'

There was a pause. The Queen regarded Geri shrewdly, and then the mask formed by her responsibilities fell again. 'Well, I'm sure there was good reason. I hope you'll get back to it in the future.'

She said goodbye, offering her hand, and then moved on to another waiting group.

'I say!' the Duke burst out, eyeing Geri with fresh appreciation. 'This woman of yours, Dolph, why didn't you tell us she was famous?'

Dolph smiled and said nothing, as though assuming the question was rhetorical. Geri waited, wishing he could show some response to the recognition she had received, but for the rest of the afternoon he said nothing about it.

At their house in Eaton Square that night, the Duke and Duchess of Colchester entertained, a large gathering designed to give Dolph an opportunity to cement certain business ties and befriend members of the government who could cut through red tape. Among the wealthy and influential men, there were many racing enthusiasts who had been at Epsom in the afternoon, and had heard the story of Geri's encounter with the Queen. Their eagerness to have her comments on the thoroughbred market, and on ways of judging and treating horses, made her the center of attention.

Aware that Dolph's business purposes were getting sidelined, Geri would have ordinarily played a wifely role, brought the conversation back to his interests. But tonight she soaked up the attention, not out of vanity but because it restored faith in her potential. She had let the fire of will that had once carried her so far nearly flicker out. Now, through the grace of a queen's recognition, her belief in herself was once more blazingly alive.

'You're the only one . . .' she said to Dolph as they entered their bedroom after the party was over.

He glanced at her quizzically. 'Those would be words of passion in some circumstances — though your tone tells me that's not how you meant them.' He turned to a dresser and began removing his cufflinks.

'The only one,' she explained, 'who had nothing to say about what happened today.'

He exchanged looks with her in the mirror of the dresser. 'What would you expect me to say?'

'That you were impressed, perhaps . . . that you felt some pride in me. You heard how all the others went on about it.'

He smiled. 'But they're English! She's their Queen. You can't expect me to react that way to her.'

'To *me*, Dolph. Can't I expect you to notice that I'm someone special?'

'But of course you are, darling.' He came across the room to her. 'If I hadn't noticed that, would you be here now?' He started to embrace her, but she shrugged him off.

'It's not just deserving to be your wife,' she said with a cutting edge, 'that makes me special. I'd begun to forget that myself. Loving you, I started to let everything else come second. But I can't go on living that way.'

He moved toward her again. 'I didn't think you were still unhappy. After these last couple of days —'

'They've been wonderful,' she jumped in. 'But they're a dream. We can't live this way all the time.'

'There's no reason we can't. I can give you everything —'

'What I need . . . is only what I can give myself: something that uses my abilities, something I can take pride in . . .'

Dolph nodded thoughtfully. 'You want to open a new clinic? I can arrange that.'

'No. That would be just another expensive gift.' She went close to him again. There was no reason to put off her request any longer. 'I was afraid when I answered your call this time that I was hoping for the impossible. But you've made me feel we have a chance. If it's going to work, though, I have to achieve something on my own. I'd like to try something that wouldn't take me away from you so much — that might even bring us closer. And you wouldn't have to buy this for me, Dolph. You already have it.'

'What?'

He never liked to surrender control of anything, she reminded herself, she had to be ready for disappointment. 'The stable,' she said finally. 'You've ignored it the past couple of years. The horses haven't had the kind of attention they need. But we have good bloodstock, good prospects. Our horses could be showing terrific results —'

'You mean, if you took it over,' Dolph broke in sharply. 'If you were able to run it your way . . .'

'I have a talent for it, Dolph. Why waste it?' She put her arms around him. 'It doesn't have to be my way, though. *Our* way would be good enough. I'd be able to give it my time, stay on top of things. But we could do it together.'

He pulled her close. 'More than anything, I want you to be happy with me. But I'm sorry, Geri, I've never been able to run things by committee — even a committee of two. I believe efffective decisions have to be made by one person alone . . .'

Geri began to pull away from him, crushed. The last hope was gone.

But Dolph held on to her tightly. 'So there's only one way I'll agree to this. You'll take over the stable — and run it your way. No interference from me.'

Excitement surged through her. She hugged him, her eyes misting with gratitude. She had a life again, a calling of her own.

After a moment, Dolph said, 'As the outgoing head of Justinean Farms, I would like to make a couple of suggestions, if the new boss doesn't mind . . .'

'My door is always open.'

He revealed now that he'd been planning to take her up to Ireland for a few days to tour some of the great stud farms located in the flat green country around Dublin known as The Curragh. Ireland was a good place to buy new breeding stock. 'It would get the new management off to a good start,' he said.

'Recommendation accepted.'

Dolph wrapped his arms around her. 'And, of course,' he said, 'it'll give us a chance for a second honeymoon.'

Geri kissed him again, deeper and longer. 'We don't have to go to Ireland for that,' she said, as she pulled him toward the bed. 'That we can start right here . . .'

To take advantage of the plains of lush grass that formed The Curragh — as well as Ireland's cheap labor and low tax rates — American and European tycoons, Arab sheiks, and oriental potentates had all found it advantageous to maintain breeding operations in Ireland. These men, who had lately been driving the thoroughbred market to new highs — an untested yearling had been purchased for more than thirteen million dollars at the latest Keeneland auction — often shipped the prize horses they purchased in Kentucky straight back to their Irish farms. Sometimes the yearlings were not even bought to be raced; at maturity they were put straight to stud, their pedigree expected to refine the quality of other breeding lines.

On their visit to Ireland, Dolph and Geri were welcomed at all the great stud farms. There was usually excess bloodstock to be sold, and Dolph was well known as a big buyer. Basing themselves in a penthouse suite at the Royal Hibernian Hotel in Dublin, he and Geri went each day to tour a different place — Coolmore, owned by Robert Sangster, who'd made his fortune originally from the British soccer betting pools; Aston-Upthorpe Stud, which belonged to the oil-rich Defense Minister of Dubai, Sheik Muhammed al-Maktoum; and Ballymanny Farms, the property of the Aga Khan. The owners were rarely in residence, and it was always a farm manager who showed the Justineans around.

One morning Dolph called to request a tour of Derry Manor Farm, which had been taken over a few years ago by Sheik ibn-Rashid al-Sadir. The sheik had just arrived for a few days, having personally accompanied a horse he was shipping from England — Desert Star, the winner of the last week's Derby. Taking Dolph's call himself, al-Sadir expressed delight at the prospect of a visit, and insisted that the Justineans stay over at Derry Manor for as long as they liked.

Like all the other stud operations they had visited, Derry

Manor was breathtakingly beautiful, hundreds of acres of emerald pasture spreading out from a gracious old red-brick Georgian mansion perched on a knoll and surrounded by gardens. Dolph and Geri were admitted by a butler and shown into a sitting room furnished with English antiques and oriental carpets. Al-Sadir, dressed in jeans and a western shirt with pearl buttons, appeared in a minute to greet them warmly.

'My dear Mr and Mrs Justinean, what a felicitous surprise. How fortunate I could be here.'

Geri had not seen him since the night they had danced together. Impressed again with his charm, she thought back to the proposition he had made that night, and wondered if she had been tempted to accept it merely on practical grounds, or if she had been captured in the web of his personality. 'It's kind of you to open your house to us,' she said.

'The desert tradition is to make wayfarers welcome. I observe it whether in a tent, or a palace. Indeed, I am expecting other guests to arrive shortly. So we will have a house party, eh? Now, tell me what brings you to Ireland?'

As tea was served, Dolph replied that the trip was intended to expose Geri to the big Irish breeding operations to prepare her for her new role as head of Justinean Farms.

The sheik gave Geri a baffled look. 'I shouldn't think you need very much instruction.'

'I've spent my time taking care of sick horses, not breeding healthy ones.'

'I shall tell you, then, the basic secret I learned myself from the man who runs this farm for me: to produce great racehorses, there are only two essential ingredients — money and magic. I had the one and he had the other.' He looked at Dolph, and then back to Geri. 'You, too, are well equipped. Your husband has the money . . . and you have enough magic to outlast several fortunes. Now, change into something comfortable like this' — he preened in his cowboy clothes — 'and then I will introduce you to my magician.'

Willis O'Donnell was the stick-thin Irishman who made all

important breeding decisions at Derry Manor Farm. In his seventies, with a sharp dour face and limbs as knobby as a shillelagh, O'Donnell had been working around horses since he was old enough to carry a pail of water without spilling more than half of it. He gave Dolph and Geri a comprehensive tour of the farm, starting — at the sheik's direction — with the extensive computer installations in one of the converted barns. These were used, he explained, to keep track of the bloodlines of horses all over the world, to trace back the pedigree of each animal in the farm's inventory, and to compare this data along with physical conformations, health history and past racing records — all with the goal of scientifically pre-selecting the best pairings to produce the fastest and soundest progeny.

The use of computers was hardly new to Dolph or Geri. But recently breeding experts had designed programs which could supposedly predict the quality of the horse likely to result from a particular match of stallion and mare, and Dolph had neglected to keep up to date with these developments. Impressed by what he saw, he told Geri it would be worthwhile upgrading the computer installations at Justinean Farms.

Having done his duty by exhibiting the new methodology, O'Donnell offered his own opinion. 'It's all malarkey,' he expounded in his thick brogue. 'The sheik goes head over heels for all this new-fangled rigmarole. Can't believe he's doing a thing right unless he's spent enough bloody money to sink a fleet of cargo ships. But this junk isn't worth a tinker's damn if you put two horses together when the moon is hangin' in the wrong corner of the sky.'

At first, Geri thought O'Donnell was amusing himself, playing the expected role of the old Irish horseman full of quaint ideas. But as they went on it became more clear that he was sincerely guided by traditional practices. Leading Dolph and Geri from one barn to the next, displaying some of the most promising colts and fillies recently bred at Derry Manor, he said again and again that he had gone against the computer to make the match that had produced the foal, choosing certain phases of the moon ahead of the prescriptions of print-outs. Of course, he said, pedigree mattered. But it was also a known fact that all great horses stemmed from no more than a hundred and twenty past sires. If the blood of these horses was somewhere in the pedigree, in the right combinations — as known to O'Donnell — success would result.

As knowledgeable as Geri was about the veterinary aspects of horse breeding, spending an afternoon with Willis O'Donnell gave new insight into the sorcery that continued to influence the methodology of producing fine racehorses. She knew one of the leading American breeders' journals continued to publish the phases of the moon and astrological charts, regarding them as information some subscribers depended on, but she had naturally discounted the custom as a hangover of useless tradition. She was also aware of the 'dosage system' — which called for the best bloodlines to go back to a combination of those hundred-odd horses O'Donnell had cited — but she had not been ready to consider such formulae as the basis for the modern breeding operation she intended to run.

She was affected, though, by meeting O'Donnell. His reverence for what he called 'the art of breeding' — not 'the science' — struck a chord in her. She was surprised, at first, that she should feel comfortable with ideas that went against all the training she'd had as a doctor. Then she realized why. Similar superstitions had colored the habits and choices of people in the hollow. It was all part of a culture she had once rejected, as eager to clean it out of her mind as she had been to improve her way of speaking. Now she felt some nostalgia for the heritage she had sprung from.

Exasperated by Geri's obvious respect for the Irishman's outlandish theories, but resolved not to interfere, Dolph finally excused himself to make some business calls. Geri went on to spend several more hours with O'Donnell. If nothing else, she thought, it would be fun to try some of the magic as part of her approach to running a stable.

A couple of cars she hadn't seen before were in the drive when she returned to the manor. Inside, she found the company gathered around a fire in one of the sitting rooms, having drinks — Dolph, the sheik, two other men and a woman. Only as she walked over to be introduced to the new arrivals, did she realize that one of the men facing her was Quinn.

There was a tiny hitch in her step, but she urged herself forward, hoping the storm of emotions loosed within her wouldn't show on the surface. Seeing him brought back every sensation of their one night together as if it was happening now.

Al-Sadir introduced the other guests first, a sleek British couple named Alan and Pamela Cunningham. 'Alan's the broker from Lloyds who writes all the policies on my horses. And do you know the painter, Willian Dane Quinn? He's accepted a commission to paint Desert Star . . .'

Geri had avoided looking his way until now, almost afraid to see him too closely by the firelight. 'Yes,' she said. 'We're already acquainted.'

'Hello, Geri.'

He had never looked better, she thought, as though it had taken all this time to complete his recovery from the effects of war. Lately she had not kept close tabs on his career, but it was obvious if he had been selected to immortalize the latest Derby winner that Quinn had reached the peak of his specialized field.

Over drinks, Geri kept up the facade of full participation in the small talk, discussing insurance with Alan Cunningham, answering Pamela Cunningham about what it was like to be the wife of a business whirlwind like Dolph Justinean. Quinn engaged meanwhile in conversation with Dolph and the sheik. But he kept glancing in Geri-Jo's direction, and each time she could feel a mantle of tingling warmth steal over her skin. Thrilled by his effect, at the same time terrified that it might be exposed, Geri was quick to follow when al-Sadir said he was changing for dinner, and suggested others do the same.

As she dressed and chose jewelry and perfume, Geri couldn't escape the realization that she was doing it for *him*. Feeling as guilty of an infidelity as if she and Quinn had just spent the past hour naked in each other's arms, she kept reminding herself that her choice had been made long ago and that she had just rededicated herself to it.

On their way downstairs again, Dolph stopped her and pulled her into his arms. 'He's right, you know . . .'

'Who?' she said, her voice catching. 'About what?'

'Al-Sadir — about your magic. You get more beautiful every day.' He caressed her face with his eyes. 'I'd be jealous of his attention if I didn't feel you'd come back to me this past week.'

'Let's go home,' she said abruptly. 'Tomorrow, as soon as we can. I want to begin our new life.'

He studied her a moment, then lowered his mouth to hers.

Accepting the kiss, she felt shamed by the secret betrayal in her heart, resolved to kill the longings that had risen again.

But at dinner she was seated next to Quinn. Afflicted by the divine agony of excitement meshed with fear, she joined in the social banter around the table, but heard herself almost as though eavesdropping on someone else speaking in a distant room. She ate, but she couldn't taste the food. Only her sense of touch seemed to be acute. She was aware of every subtle shift in his movements beside her, of the electric field around him that sensitized every cell of her skin. Had she been foolish to let him go that night? Was she crazy now to let herself be taken over by vain desire? She and Dolph would be gone from here tomorrow; she had a new project to occupy her, and soon there might be children . . .

From across the table, Dolph smiled at her. Did he sense nothing? Or was he simply giving her a chance to move through it?

After dinner, the company moved to the drawing room for coffee and brandy. The sheik, who enjoyed entertaining in a thoroughly British manner, invited the men to his billiard room.

'I'd better pass,' Quinn said. 'I'm really not . . . equipped for it.'

Even before the sheik nodded, Geri understood. With one weak arm, Quinn couldn't manipulate the cue.

The other men departed, leaving him with the two women. Geri knew she ought to remove herself from temptation, but she sat rooted to her chair, praying that she and Quinn could be alone. For a while Pamela Cunningham questioned him about the special demands of his work, and he replied patiently. But perhaps the tension of unspoken wishes being generated in the room reached her at last, for she excused herself to go to bed.

For a long time after she'd gone, they sat in silence, gazing at each other from twin couches on either side of the fireplace. A maid came to ask if they wished anything, then puttered at the edges of the room emptying ashtrays before she disappeared again.

'Do you know how difficult this is for me?' he said then. 'To remember, and not be able to reach out and —'

'I know,' she interrupted, inflamed by the words, afraid that she might be swept away herself.

'If I'd known you were going to be here, I wouldn't have come.'

'It wasn't planned,' she said.

'Not by us,' he said. 'But I couldn't swear there isn't a plan somewhere that says we should be together. Or else why have I loved you from the minute I saw you, and why can't I stop? I read about your marriage . . . and I prayed that I'd forget, find another woman who could mean as much to me — more. But nothing's changed. And right at this minute, I'm glad —'

'Stop,' she whispered, as she lowered her head, unable to look at him anymore, to see the passion shining in his eyes. She ought to walk out, she knew, flee from the lure of his love. But she stayed.

'It's the same for you, isn't it?' he asked. 'You haven't forgotten what it was like, have you, to be together? Tell me . . .'

'No, I haven't forgotten a minute of it.' Abruptly, he started to rise, move toward her.

She held her hand up. 'No! Stay there. Please . . .'

Slowly, he sat back. For a long time they listened to the crackling of logs in the fireplace, a perfect accompaniment to hearts slowly breaking.

'The hell of it is,' he said finally, 'that you never did explain.

It isn't his money, you told me. It isn't just loyalty. And if it was love . . . you would have walked away from me already. So what is it, Geri? I want to make you happy. I know I can . . . and I don't think you are now. So why can't you cut loose, take something that might be better?'

When he'd asked that night, she remembered, she hadn't been able to answer. But now she felt an obligation to find the reason. Not only for him, but for herself, too.

'I want you, Billy — right at this moment, I do. As I did that night we spent together. But it isn't enough to live for a moment. If I left Dolph now — and I couldn't do anything but leave him if I was going to spend another day with you — I wouldn't feel I was running toward my happiness as much as I'd feel I was running away from a responsibility —'

He opened his mouth to speak, and she raced on, guessing what he might say. 'To try my best,' she said. 'That's the responsibility. Dolph wanted me, and I married him. We've been through a lot together. I just can't turn my back on that. It comes down to . . . to breeding, I suppose. To something like the will and the drive that makes a thoroughbred run for the finish line, determined to be first. Something in me can't let go of anything that has a chance of being saved, like my marriage. I have to try and win this one — to do my absolute best with what I have, simply because it's the track I'm running on. Does that make any sense to you?'

It was a long moment before he nodded.

Faintly, from the billiard room, came an explosion of voices praising a good shot.

'I ought to get to bed,' Geri said as she stood, though she knew there wasn't a chance of sleep. 'I think we'll be leaving quite early tomorrow. I won't see you again . . .'

Quinn rose, too, but let the gap remain between them.

'Good night, Billy,' she said.

'Good night, my only love.'

She ran then, knowing she had to escape from his magnetic sphere or she would be pulled off balance and the rest of her world would shatter.

CHAPTER THREE

As soon as she took over the Justinean stable, Geri felt a contentment unmatched even in her work at the clinic. Because her whole career in veterinary medicine had evolved out of being forced to prove herself, Geri had always felt that she was functioning under pressure. There had been all the tedious demands of overseeing a business, too; covering overheads, training staff, placating clients.

She had persuaded Dolph to use the Saratoga house as their primary residence, so that she could be closely involved in the farm rather than operating as an absentee owner. Rising early each morning, she joined in feeding the horses, then watched workouts of animals in training. A few hours in her office followed, reviewing agents' recommendations of horses available in upcoming auctions, considering which of the Farm's foals to offer for sale, taking calls from other owners to arrange a 'cover' by one of their stallions with one of her mares. In the afternoon, she often climbed on a tractor to mow hay or prepare new pasture, or pitched in with a stablehand on the repair of a barn. When a horse was sick or injured she provided veterinary treatment herself, and she delivered the new foals. With sixty mares and two dozen stallions, there were always horses requiring attention.

The racing record of the stable remained poor, reflecting Dolph's recent neglect, but Geri believed it would turn around when she could begin to run some of the horses she was breeding, and improve their training. Since Oakie had left, there had been a succession of other trainers, none as experienced or naturally savvy. She hoped he might come back when she was ready with her own crop of two-year-olds.

Dolph gave her unlimited backing, and never asked for anything on the balance sheet to be justified. His philosophy about owning a thoroughbred stable, he said, was the same as J.P. Morgan's about having a yacht: if you had to think about how much it cost, then you couldn't afford it. In fact, for all the many millions of dollars he put into the stable each year, the amount was becoming steadily less significant to him. As fast as his empire had grown in the past decade, it ballooned even faster with the increasingly freewheeling economic atmosphere under the new Republican administration. He took over a chain of television stations in a move that required a billion and a half dollars in financing. He bought into lumber land in Scandinavia, mines in Australia, traded in commodities, and engineered company take-overs by his manipulations in the stock market. His fever to continually acquire new businesses kept him traveling, but his absences became easier for Geri as she settled into her own routine. When he was home, they enjoyed each other's company; when they were apart, they were invigorated by their separate work. Dolph still spoke hopefully of having children, and they kept trying, but he didn't pressure her when almost two years went by without another pregnancy.

There were times she thought about Quinn, evenings alone with Dolph away somewhere on the other side of the world. The memories were poignant, but the mood was never tragic. She was content now, even if there was no passion in the equation.

Though when summer came, it was always a little harder. With all the great houses of Saratoga occupied and the racing season in full swing, she knew it was likely that a commission would bring Quinn to town. She walked every street with the wary eyes of a soldier on patrol, on guard against being ambushed by her own emotions. But she never saw him, and she learned eventually that for the past couple of years

William Dane Quinn had refused any commissions that required him to come East. He had a home in California's Carmel Valley, and he spent his time there or in Europe. He had enough work so that he could take only the jobs he wanted.

As the weather turned cold again, Geri often ended each day by touring the barns, making sure that heating systems were properly adjusted, the horses all comfortably settled in their stalls. Late on a freezing night in February, after completing one of her inspections, she was walking up a snow-dusted hill toward the mansion when she saw a figure flit across a swathe of light streaming from one of the ground-floor windows. It was as if she had seen a ghost; the figure appeared to be wearing a sheer material that billowed in the wind, and it was hard to imagine anyone enduring this cold night so flimsily dressed. Advancing another few yards, Geri saw a silhouette pass through the light from a second window — a woman wearing only a dress. And then the light fell so that Geri could see that the woman's hair was red.

She broke into a run, but the figure receded into the darkness, and when Geri came nearer to the house, she didn't see anyone else around. 'Mol' . . . Molly?' she called.

No answer. The vision of her sister had come and gone so quickly that she wondered if it hadn't been an illusion, a trick of the light born out of some subconscious wish.

'Molly!' Geri cried into the wind. 'Is that you . . .?'

She toured the entire perimeter of the mansion, and saw nothing. But as she came around to the rear and scanned the lighted area once more, Molly stepped into view from behind a high hedge separating the mansion from a swimming pool area and a couple of guest bungalows. She wore only the low-cut dress of white silk chiffon and glittering silver shoes with stiletto heels. Shocked, Geri stared as Molly staggered forward, hugging herself for warmth. As her sister moved closer into the light Geri saw the bruises on her face, and the streaks of blood caked along her arms and legs.

She darted forward as Molly stumbled the last step into her arms and stared back at her for a moment, still wordless. Then her eyes rolled up, and her body started to sag. A second later,

Geri was struggling to support her dead weight.

A cry for help rose into Geri's throat, but instantly she stifled it. There were only the servants to respond: could they be relied upon to cooperate if Molly needed to be hidden? Obviously she was in some terrible trouble; she wouldn't come here unless this was the last place of refuge.

Slinging one of Molly's arms over her shoulders, Geri pulled her to one of the bungalows beyond the pool. Consisting of living room, bedroom, and kitchen, kept warm by year-round heating, the bungalow would be an ideal place to recuperate. Geri got her into bed, then brought a bowl of warm water and some towels to bathe her. Examining the injuries more closely, she saw that Molly's limbs were covered with scratches and scrapes, probably the result of running and stumbling over rocks or through bushes; her face and body bore many ugly bruises, indicating she'd been restrained and beaten.

A few times while Geri cleaned and dressed the wounds, Molly's eyes fluttered open. Once she started to murmur something.

'Rest now, Mol',' Geri said. 'We'll talk in the morning.'

Finally, Molly drifted into a lasting sleep. Geri pulled an easy chair up beside the bed and watched her sister until she could no longer keep her own eyes open.

When Geri came awake, the bed was empty. She bolted up, then saw the dress and shoes tossed on the floor and heard the shower running in the bathroom. She went to the kitchen and started to assemble breakfast. The guest lodges were always kept stocked with juice, coffee, and muffins in the cupboard or freezer. In a few minutes Molly came out, one towel wrapped around her body, another around her head. She watched as Geri ran water from the tap into a percolator.

'Feeling better?' Geri said to break the awkward silence.

'Feel like shit. Clean though . . . and alive — which is a lot more than I was planning on.'

Geri put the percolator on the stove and turned on the flame. 'What happened, Mol'? Who hurt you?'

'You don't have to play sister-confessor, Geri-Jo. I didn't

come to cry on your shoulder. What I need is clothes and money, and I came because this was a place I knew I could get 'em fast.'

'Money . . .?' Geri murmured incredulously. Could she have nothing left of the fortune extorted from Dolph?

'Enough to get out of the country,' Molly said quickly. 'Twenty thousand dollars. Pocket change to you. And some clothes, just something to keep me warm until —'

'I want to help you,' Geri broke in. 'I've always wanted to help. But I can't let you take from me and then disappear again.' She moved to Molly. 'I want to help in a way that lasts. You said you were surprised to be alive. Well, damn it, let me help *keep* you alive.'

Molly looked away. 'Why should you care — with all I've done against you?'

The answer was so simple — the only answer there had ever been — that Geri couldn't hope it would change Molly's mind. But there was nothing else to say. 'Because you're my sister, Mol'. Because no one else is left.'

Molly took a step nearer. It seemed she was about to break down. Geri reached out.

But Molly turned aside and moved away. A moment later she began to speak, quietly recounting the events that had led up to last night.

She had dreamed at first of using the money to establish respectability, maybe find a rich husband. But then she had continued to postpone cutting loose from the life she knew. Running a fancy brothel in New York City represented a kind of achievement. What was the point of changing? She spent her time with rich and distinguished men, anyway, had them in bed. If she ever married one, she would know that her husband would be out many nights with expensive whores. So she had stayed on. And the money? She had blown much of it on luxuries and drugs; the rest she had given to John Caramati to finance wholesale drug purchases from which, he told her, she would profit.

Then a week ago, federal agents had intercepted a Colombian cocaine shipment meant for Caramati. He had been careful to cover evidence of his own involvement, but Molly feared that payments made to drug smugglers with her money would be traced to her. Expecting she was about to be arrested, she had been preparing to escape last night when Caramati had sent some men to intercept her. They had driven her out of the city to a deserted stretch of country road, forced her out of the car, and started to beat her, demanding an admission that she was the informer who'd told narcotics agents about the drug shipment.

'I couldn't tell 'em what they wanted to hear,' Molly told Geri, ''cause I didn't do it. But they were going to kill me, anyway. I guess John figured even if I didn't really deserve to be killed, it was better to shut me up before I could be pulled in by the feds.'

Molly had gone through the whole story in a droning emotionless monotone, without a hint of recalled terror or self-pity, as though she saw nothing wrong in what had been done to her. Now she emitted a small laugh. 'I got away, though. How about that? Those stupid assholes thought I'd been knocked silly, so they let their guard down for a second as they got their guns out. And that was when I did it.' She laughed again. 'Kicked one in the balls, and when the other grabbed me, I left him holding my coat while I took off into the dark like a bitch outta hell and kept going until I hit another road, and got a hitch, and never stopped for nothin' . . .'

The flow was broken by another low sound from her throat, and Geri saw Molly's shoulders shaking. More laughter, she thought, appreciating the joke of survival. But suddenly the sound became a howl, and Molly sank slowly to her knees. Rushing to her, Geri saw the tears streaming down Molly's face as she fought for breath through wracking sobs. Never, never in their lives, had she seen Molly cry, not even when the mountain had come down or Ma had been buried. Geri knelt in front of her, pulled her close.

'I was good as dead, Geri,' Molly stammered softly. 'Good as dead. Just a stupid whore who never amounted to shit, don't know why I even care to live. Forgive me for comin' . . . but I didn't know where else to go.'

'There's nothing to forgive,' Geri answered as her voice broke, 'you came to the right place.'

For a long time they rocked together, crying in each other's arms.

By the end of the day, they were talking without argument, without threats. But it hadn't been all sweet reunion, miraculous rediscovery of sisterhood. When the first rush of emotion was over, Molly had reverted to sullen cynicism, suspicious of Geri's desire to help. She had demanded money, threatened the old blackmail ploy again. But Geri kept coaxing her back to acceptance of shelter, food, and caring. And each time there were intervals when they talked, and Molly's confessions of the fierce jealousy of Geri she had nursed all her life became quieter. Now Molly seemed to believe that Geri truly wanted to take care of her. Then she reciprocated that gentle concern by admitting it wouldn't be fair to stay. 'The people who want to kill me, Geri, they won't stop tracking me wherever I go. Won't be good for you, if they find me here.'

'Dolph can swing some weight of his own. Mr Caramati's smart enough to know that. As long as you stay here — while you show you're not running straight to the law to tell everything you know — his mood may change.'

'If you keep me while I'm wanted, then you'll get in trouble.'

'We'll work it out. Dolph has lawyers, dozens of them — all the best that money can buy.'

'But he won't help. He must hate me!'

'I don't think so,' Geri said thoughtfully. 'Dolph understands survivors. That's what we are, Mol'. We did whatever we could to hold on, and we did it differently — but all of it was in the name of survival. Dolph will understand that. He never minded much about the money he gave you . . .'

Rather than pretend the guest house was empty and have to keep sneaking Molly food, Geri informed the servants that a woman writing an article for one of the racing magazines had arrived late one evening and had been invited to stay. To enhance the story she agreed on a fictitious name with Molly, and they drove over to the discount store in Cohoes and Geri

576

bought her sister a wardrobe of good clothes and some luggage.

For three days they spent every waking hour together, eating their meals alone in the bungalow, seated by a fireplace in the living room talking late into the night, or walking the farm. As Geri went through her daily routine, Molly began to pitch in. Tired and frightened, she let down the defenses that had separated her from Geri since they were children, and she listened when Geri talked about how her life could be changed. No matter how much money was required — for legal help, for psychotherapy to make peace within herself, for school if she wanted to go back — it was all there, as long as Molly wanted it to rebuild constructively.

'You just have to want something good for yourself, Mol',' Geri promised, 'and I'll do anything to help you get it.'

On the evening of Molly's fourth day at the farm, Geri was summoned to one of the barns by a stablehand: a mare in foal was about to deliver. When Geri went to attend the mare, Molly accompanied her and assisted at the birth.

Leaving the barn after working through midnight, Molly was especially quiet and introspective, keeping a few steps ahead of Geri as they headed back to the bungalow. Suddenly she stopped and waited for Geri to catch up.

'There's somethin' else . . .' she burst out in an anguished tone, as though tearing the words from herself. 'Somethin' I've been keepin' from you . . .'

Only a faint light coming from the barn complex illuminated Molly's face, but Geri could see the look in her eyes — pleading forgiveness even before the confession had been made.

'Whatever it is,' Geri said, 'we'll work it out.'

'It's not something I did to you,' Molly said. 'It's worse than that . . .' Her voice cracked slightly, and she turned away as though ashamed before she went on. 'I told you about that cop I lived with a while. I really loved him, Geri-Jo, and . . . well, I started thinkin' we were gonna make it . . . that we could be like normal people. So . . . I let him . . . I mean, I let myself . . .' She turned back and rushed to Geri, hugging her like a child seeking comfort as she began to sob. 'I had his baby, Geri. A little girl . . . Tammy . . . my Tammy . . .'

She gave in to the sobbing then, her body overtaken by such terrible heaves that she was unable to speak for a few minutes.

Geri held on to Molly tightly, trying to soothe her though she was gripped herself by a terrible anxiety. Molly's earlier remark that she had done something worse than anything Geri already knew about made it clear that the revelations were far from complete. And since there had been no sign of the baby, anything was possible. Not an abortion: Molly had said she'd had the baby. But then what? Had she let it live?

'What happened to the baby?' Geri asked when Molly's crying finally subsided. 'Where's Tammy?'

Molly broke from Geri's embrace, and for a second Geri was prepared to chase her. But Molly only took a step away before giving the answer. 'I don't know, Geri-Jo. That's the hell of it. I keep tryin' to find out, but I still don't know.'

She had been only three months pregnant, she explained, when the policeman she'd been living with had gotten arrested for accepting bribes from drug dealers. He was already in jail on a long sentence by the time Molly had given birth. For a couple of weeks, she had kept the baby, then a need for money had made her turn to the easiest way of earning it she knew. Once she was back in prostitution, she had decided that keeping the baby was impossible.

'She was so perfect, Geri-Jo, so beautiful. She didn't deserve just a cheap whore for a mother . . .'

Why didn't you come to me? Geri wanted to cry out. But she knew why. Already torn by so much jealousy, how could Molly have turned the baby over to her? Geri listened quietly to the rest of the story. On a visit to the prison where the father was serving his sentence, Molly had been persuaded to give the baby to his brother, a truckdriver. The brother lived in Tennessee with his wife of three years, and they wanted children but hadn't conceived yet. He had driven alone to Kentucky to take the baby, so Molly had no chance to meet the foster mother. A promise had been given that the child could be reclaimed if ever Molly wanted, but she had never really believed she would be able to shelter the baby . . . not until she had seen a chance to get a lot of money through blackmail.

'Do you see now why I did it, Geri-Jo? Once I had money in my pocket, it seemed like I could give Tammy everything she needed. Oh, I had such dreams. Tammy would've only been two years old then. I thought I'd bring her to New York, and send her to good schools, and dress her up like . . .' She started to break down again, but bit her lip and pulled out of it. 'But then I couldn't find her. I tried, God I tried. But Mike's brother had been in a bad accident with his truck, gotten put in a wheelchair, and his wife just went off and left him, takin' the baby with her. I heard stories then about how that woman had been a hellion, being so bad to Mike's brother after his accident — beating up on the child, too — so I was even crazier to get Tammy back. But nobody knew where that woman had gone. A lot of my money went on investigators, trying to track her down. And when I came up empty, it just made me feel life was more useless. So I spent more on coke, and threw away every last penny I'd gotten from you and Dolph . . . everything I'd wanted to make Tammy's life better than mine . . .'

Geri recalled the hint Molly had given once that there was someone else she wanted the money for. She went to Molly.

'We'll keep trying,' she said. 'I'll help you, Mol'. Together we'll find your daughter . . .'

'Oh, Geri. I need her now more than ever . . . need to know she's all right. Feels somehow like . . . like she's my only chance to be something . . .'

Geri gave a compassionate nod, and put her arm around Molly as they continued walking.

'Do you think, maybe, I could stay on here a while?' Molly asked tentatively as they neared the bungalow. 'You think that could work, Geri-Jo? While you're helping me, could I help you, too?'

'I'm ready to try.'

It was a clear cold night, and before heading through the door Molly lifted her head and stared at the bowl of sky surrounding them, blue-black with its sugar frosting of stars.

'Glory . . .' she gasped. 'I don't ever remember seeing so many stars since we were in the hollow.'

'They've always been there,' Geri said.

Molly nodded and her arm closed tighter around her sister. 'I guess,' she said, 'it's just been so goddamn long since I looked up.'

When Geri went downstairs the next morning a row of valises was standing in the entrance hall beside a couple of wrapped paintings picked up at some European auction house — signs that Dolph had returned. She found him in his office, already at his desk, on the phone to a banker about financing the purchase of a European company. He blew her a kiss when she walked in, and cut his conversation short, telling the banker to round up some co-financing and get back to him later. He got up from his desk and they embraced.

'Good trip?' she asked.

'No complaints. Everything okay on the home front?'

'Fine.' Her mind raced, wondering how to best tell him about Molly. He would already have heard that there was a guest in one of the bungalows. The servants always gave him a full report the minute he returned from a trip.

'Heard we got a new foal last night,' he said. 'How's it look?'

'Lovely. A bay colt.'

'And someone's here doing an article. What's that about?'

She hesitated, then took his hand, and asked him to sit down with her.

He listened without interrupting as Geri spoke, the expression on his smooth handsome face unchangingly neutral. Geri told the story of how and why Molly had come, but said nothing about the child, sensing it might set Dolph more against Molly, rather than making him more sympathetic.

'So even after all she's done to hurt you,' he said when she finished, 'you're still ready to take her in?'

'She can change, Dolph. She's started already.'

'Or she's put on a good act. Goes with her territory, doesn't it — playing the part of an angel to turn on the customers?'

'We have so much,' Geri said, disappointed with Dolph's

580

reaction. 'Forgiving her would cost so little . . .'

He hesitated. 'All right. I suppose I'd better give Ed Markham a call. If we're going to help, we'd better do it right.'

When she heard the words of acquiescence, she spun around and hugged him.

'Go ahead,' he said, as he went to his desk. 'Give Molly the news. But tell her she'll have to play by the rules. We can't just hide her, or we'll get charged with aiding and abetting . . .'

Molly was still asleep. Before waking her, Geri set up coffee in the kitchen, got a fire going in the living-room fireplace, and washed some dishes that Molly had dumped into the sink. One of the saucers, she noticed, was heaped with used matches. Then she saw a spoon blackened on the bottom by carbon, a white crust in its bowl, and the realization hit. She felt naive not to have suspected earlier, to have realized that Molly's habit couldn't be mastered as easily as her feelings had been reformed. But she wasn't shocked or alarmed. It was just one more problem they'd have to solve. Together.

She finished neatening the kitchen and started toward the bedroom when a high-pitched wailing sound rose in her ears, very faint but rapidly rising. She thought it might be Molly crying at first — except it was coming from somewhere outside the house.

And then suddenly she knew. She froze, torn between two hopeless plans — to hide Molly, or else to stop those who were coming to take her. But the sirens were very close now, screaming up the drive. Geri walked to the door of the cabin and opened it just as two State Police cars skidded to a stop on the gravel in front of the guest cabin.

And beyond them, on the rear terrace of the mansion, she saw Dolph standing by the balustrade, coolly watching, his hands in his pockets.

CHAPTER FOUR

It wasn't turning Molly over to the police that Geri found unforgiveably cruel, so much as the *way* Dolph had done it. The police had barged in, and hauled Molly out to a patrol car, kicking and screaming furiously. 'Got even now, didn't you, Geri-Jo? Waited long enough — but you got me good!' There had been no chance for Geri to explain she hadn't been the cause.

Watching the mirrored replay of that moment years ago when she herself had been taken into custody as Molly stood by, Geri despaired of ever convincing her sister that the fragile trust they'd built in the past few days wasn't part of a malicious scheme to wreak revenge.

Dolph was impervious to Geri's fury. He had brought in the police on Markham's advice, he said. 'Your sister's wanted on federal charges, so concealing her would be an obstruction of justice. Ed said she had to be turned in, the sooner the better.'

Perhaps there had been no choice, but Geri still suspected his motives. Was he abiding by the law, or had he meant to administer his own punishment to Molly?

Geri spent the rest of the day trying to arrange Molly's release on bail, but the State Police would do nothing until federal prosecutors arrived. When she returned at last to the farm, her first impulse was to pack a bag, leave Dolph. But then she saw the futility of such a move. Keeping access to his money and connections, would put her in a far better position to help Molly.

She phoned Ed Markham, who confirmed that he had suggested cooperating with the authorities, but expressed surprise at the way Dolph had followed through. 'My advice,' he said, 'was to get Molly to turn herself in.'

Yet the lawyer also urged Geri not to be too hard on Dolph. 'He probably did your sister a favor. From what I hear, she wouldn't have gone to the police on her own, but she's a lot safer with them than anywhere else. Those people she's tied in with won't stop trying to kill her just because they botched it the first time.'

Though Markham was too busy to take on Molly's defense personally, he recommended a couple of other lawyers who specialized in drug cases and promised he would be available for consultation. After talking with him, Geri felt more hopeful.

That evening, as a signal that she was ready for a truce, she dressed formally and ate dinner alone with Dolph in the mansion's large formal dining room, their customary ritual when he returned from a trip. 'But don't expect me to give up on Molly,' she announced. 'Anything she needs to be free and safe, I'll see she gets it.'

'Your sister,' he responded, 'is a worthless blackmailing tramp; she put you through hell and squeezed a small fortune from me. So I'll admit I can't sympathize with the notion of helping her. But if that's what amuses you, go ahead.'

Over the next few weeks, Geri made good on her pledge. While in jail, Molly exercised her right to refuse visits from anyone she didn't wish to see, and continued to deny Geri's requests. Nevertheless, Geri hired a lawyer in New York, where Molly was in the Federal house of detention, and when the court was finally persuaded to grant bail, it was Geri who posted the required sum of $250,000. She also sublet a comfortable apartment in New York for Molly, and arranged for her to receive a sizeable monthly allowance.

Rather than provoke an outburst from Molly that might jeopardize her release, Geri had stayed away from court the day bail was granted. Yet in spite of all she had done, Molly refused to meet with her for the next two weeks, and hung up whenever Geri telephoned at her sublet. At last, through the lawyer on the case, it was arranged for the sisters to talk in a conference room at his firm's offices.

Molly looked pale and thin when she came in, but Geri saw that she had already spent some of her allowance on good clothes and a new coyote coat. 'How's the apartment?' Geri said to break the ice.

'Gorgeous. Such a perfect place to bring tricks, I just might go back into business.'

Geri sighed, saddened by the return of Molly's harsh cynical tone. Then she tried to explain what had happened with Dolph, how she had felt betrayed herself, devastated by the setback to the reconciliation she and Molly had begun. 'I've backed you every step of the way, haven't I, Mol'?'

'Sure,' Molly said in a sarcastic tone. 'Putting me in that swell apartment could make it that much harder when I have to go back to a prison cell.'

'Oh God, what'll it take so you can trust me again? I've even hired a couple of good people to start looking for Tammy . . .'

The hard look in Molly's pale blue eyes softened slightly, a faint thaw in the ice. 'I'd like to trust you,' she said, abandoning sarcasm for once. 'Maybe it's hard because I couldn't blame you for hating me.' Then she toughened again. 'But even if I could trust you, there's your prick of a husband. It's his money paying for everything, isn't it? He could pull the rug out anytime . . .'

'I won't let it happen,' Geri vowed solemnly.

She kept to herself that she was already taking steps to assure Molly's legal and living expenses, by transferring funds from the large bank accounts she controlled in the name of Justinean Farms into a separate account she'd opened at a New York bank. She knew the practice was not without serious risks; the racing stable was a regular business — still, in fact, owned totally by Dolph — and so diverting money to her personal control was technically embezzlement. If Dolph ever did scrutinize the flow of finances, he might be outraged. But Geri had seen no other way to guarantee her sister's support. Charged as an accessory to smuggling large amounts of cocaine, Molly would stand no chance of ultimate acquittal unless she was given a legal defense that might by itself cost a million dollars or more. At any point Dolph might refuse to pay, dashing her hopes once more — this time beyond repair.

A silence passed between the sisters. Molly smirked at Geri as though dubious that she would keep her pledge, and rose abruptly to leave the conference room.

'Molly,' Geri said quickly. 'Even if you give up on me . . . don't give up on yourself. Get off drugs. Get straight so if we find your —'

'You want to help?' Molly cut in sharply, stopping by the door. 'Fine. Just keep the money coming. I'll decide how to spend it.' She strode out of the room.

Geri kept thinking about that night Molly had seen the stars. It would happen again, she thought; Molly would have to look up again someday.

Before leaving the lawyer's office, she wrote out checks for several thousand dollars to cover his bill for the bail hearing, and Molly's monthly allowance.

Through the next several weeks, Geri concentrated on the stable. The first crop of foals she had bred personally two years ago were training for maiden races in March and April. A couple looked particularly promising, and she contacted Oakie to ask him to come back to work for her.

'Much as I love ya, darlin',' he answered, 'I've got to turn you down.' The owners he was now working for had been good to him, he explained; it wouldn't be fair to leave.

The heavy emotion in his voice hinted at how difficult it was for him to refuse. Geri thought that if it had been a question of working for her alone, he might have said yes. When he had been Dolph's trainer before, there had always been friction between the two men. Outwardly it was always because Dolph seemed to overrule Oakie and question his judgment. But Geri thought it was also because Oakie felt protective of her and thought Dolph wasn't treating her well.

Although Dolph wasn't making any vocal objection to Geri's support of Molly, he expressed tacit opposition by staying away even more than before. Yet, at times, Geri blamed herself for driving Dolph away by choosing to defend her sister. Didn't he have a right to reject a woman who had blackmailed him mercilessly?

Anguished by a sense that her marriage was drifting to its end, she concentrated all the more on achieving success with the stable. When one of her two most promising two-year-olds was sidelined by a hairline crack in the sesamoid bone, she focussed all her hopes on the other, a jet-black colt she had named Redeemer. The horse was extremely fast and sturdy, but Geri knew his racing career might be limited by the fact that he was a 'bleeder'. It was not unusual for the effort of an all-out gallop to cause tiny hemorrhages in a horse's lungs or respiratory tract. After any hard race, trickles of blood might be seen coming from the nostrils of some animals. In most it wasn't a chronic problem, but in some the condition could be more serious, affecting their breathing or causing pain. Redeemer showed a tendency to bleed more than normal.

Geri was generally reluctant to run bleeders. She was eager to produce a winner for the stable, however, all the more because the money it might bring from purses and subsequent breeding fees would redress the shortfall from funds drained off to help her sister. Redeemer, Geri decided, would be raced — though not in the East. At most eastern tracks, the use of drugs that could control bleeding in racehorses was barred. In California horses were allowed to race while medicated with the anti-bleeding drug, Lasix, which often radically improved performance. Geri arranged to have Redeemer flown to the coast to run in the spring stakes at Hollywood Park.

On the evening before the day set for the horse's transfer to the airport, Geri went to sleep early. A van would come in the pre-dawn hours and she wanted to supervise the loading personally. When the phone rang after midnight, she answered by reflex, without coming fully awake. A voice uttered her name.

'Quinn . . .?' she murmured. 'That you?' Or was it a dream?

'The one and only.'

'Oh, Billy. How wonderful . . .' In the dark, she could imagine he was there beside her.

'You don't mind, then? I had to think twice —'

'Thank God twice was enough.'

'Hey . . . if I'd known I'd get a reception like this I would've called a lot sooner.'

'I wish you had.'

There was a pause as both of them were overwhelmed by the strength of feelings that had been covered over for so long. All drowsiness gone now, Geri felt somehow more acutely conscious than usual, attuned to his thoughts. He was in trouble, she felt.

'What is it, Billy?' she said. 'Those phone commercials get to you? You just thought it was time to reach out and touch someone?'

He laughed softly. 'This is more like touching the moon. But you're right: it wasn't just a whim. Have you ever heard,' he asked abruptly, 'of someone named Bradley Baird White?'

She recognized the name at once — only because being around Dolph made her aware of happenings in the financial world. Three years ago White had started up an investment firm in San Francisco specializing in gold and commodities trading. Not long after, he had come to Dolph's attention through rich associates who had put money into White's firm; the man was a phenomenon, they all crowed, producing annual returns for his investors of thirty and forty percent. Dolph had been urged to climb on the gravy train, but he had politely declined. 'A tower of gold that goes up too fast,' he had said, 'won't stand for long, and I don't want to be in the crowd that gets crushed when it falls.' Sure enough, eighteen months later White had been pictured on national television in handcuffs. It had been discovered that the phenomenal dividends he paid were coming not from wise investments, but from a rapid influx of new money poured in by other careless and gullible miracle-seekers. The scheme had collapsed, and an army of wealthy investors had lost a total of nearly two hundred million dollars.

Once Geri acknowledged that she was familiar with White's story, Quinn told his own. 'I fell for the pitch, too, Geri. A lot of the people I was doing commissions for — smart, rich people — they were putting their money with this guy, and it started to sound good to me. It happens that White owned a big ranch where he spent weekends here in the Carmel Valley, where my home is, and I was taken to meet him. I'd saved quite a bit over the years, and he hooked me on the idea of living off the interest. Because, you know, I wanted to stop working. Oh, I don't mean stop *painting*. But I wanted to get back to the kind of stuff you always told me I ought to be doing — paintings signed plain old "Bill Quinn".'

'Oh, Bill,' Geri gasped sympathetically, 'what a shame. How much did you give White?'

'Everything.' And not just his savings, Quinn added. While the swindler had been riding high, he'd poured his investors' money into homes, boats, cars — and everything else that was part of living in a grand style, including owning racehorses and collecting art. Quinn had thought he was building his equity when he'd sold most of his paintings to White and accepted payment in the form of increased holdings at the brokerage firm.

'After things collapsed,' he said, 'I would've been happy just to get my paintings back. But when White started going down, he'd sold them all off to raise quick cash for patching the holes . . .'

As she listened, Geri sat up and turned on the bedside lamp. The full dimension of Billy's problem had dawned on her, the reason he was calling. He had nothing, not even his work — and he had evidently endured the situation since White's firm had collapsed, many months ago. Perhaps he could have raised money by accepting new commissions, but having resolved to go back to the work he loved, it must have seemed like too much of a defeat.

'I don't care how much it is, Billy,' Geri said as soon as he left a silence on the line, 'any amount you need, count on me. You should have called earlier.' It would mean diverting more funds from the stable, she realized, but having already started down that path for Molly, she thought nothing of going even further for Quinn.

But quietly he replied, 'I don't want money from you, Geri. That's not why I called.'

'Then . . . why?'

'I want you to come out here.'

She was stunned. Did he mean for her to leave Dolph? Did he know her marriage was failing? Had he seized suddenly on the idea that he could rebuild only with her? 'Billy, I'm on your side. But I can't just —'

'I know you must be busy,' he rode over her, 'but you wouldn't have to be here very long. A day or two would be enough.'

'For what?' she said, not sure whether to be glad or sorry her romantic fantasy had been deflated.

Quinn explained that he had a chance to salvage something of value from the financial wreckage. White's remaining assets were being liquidated to pay creditors, and among these were two dozen thoroughbred horses. An option Quinn had been offered in settlement of his claim was to choose one of these animals.

'I'd prefer anything else, frankly — but there are hundreds of other creditors waiting in line, and none eager for the kind of asset that will gobble up even more cash without much chance of yielding a return. Everyone's holding out for something more solid than a horse, and there won't be much to go around. This, at least, is something the liquidators are ready to give me now.' He chuckled ruefully. 'I guess they figure even if I didn't race it, I could use it for a model.'

Geri laughed, heartened to hear that hard times hadn't dulled his sense of humor.

'But I need advice,' he went on. 'That's why I'm asking you to come out here where the horses are. I'd like you to appraise the opportunity, and — if you think the deal's fair — pick out a horse I should take.'

She ached to see him, to explore how much was left of the passion she had been forced to lock away. Yet she feared the complications that were bound to result. If he would want her to stay — and she didn't have the strength to leave — could she sacrifice all the things that Dolph had made possible? Then what would happen to Molly?

It was better not to take the risks now, she decided. 'You

don't need me for that. There are lots of people who've got the ability to give you a reliable —'

'I don't want anyone else, Geri.'

'Billy . . .' she murmured, and her eyes filled with tears. 'I want to see you so much. But it's not . . . the right time.'

'There is no other time. I have this opportunity now.'

'And is that the only reason you want me to come?'

There was a pause. 'No. I've never stopped wanting you with me. But this can give us both a reason.'

'It isn't —'

'Don't tell me it's not reason enough!' he shouted from across the far horizon. 'Right now my whole life could depend on making the right choice. You gave me a future once, and maybe I blew it. But if I'm going to start over, I don't want to put my future in any hands but yours.'

The tears were coursing down her cheeks now. 'I'll be there,' she whispered at last.

CHAPTER FIVE

The chartered two-engine Cessna banked over the surf-battered rocks of the Monterey coast. In the seat beside the pilot, Geri scanned impatiently for the airport. The sun flashing off the Pacific glared back at her, and she dug the sunglasses from her shoulder bag and put them on. The only figures distinguishable below were the seals clustered on the silvery wet rocks.

They had not spoken since he had phoned again, the morning after the first call, and she had agreed to come ten days later. By then Redeemer would be running in its maiden race at Hollywood Park. Dolph was not expected back from a European trip, but if he were to ask at any time in the future why she had gone to California, Geri-Jo preferred to have an excuse that would not reveal her personal business with Quinn.

Earlier today in Los Angeles she had seen Redeemer race. Medicated with Lasix, the two-year-old had come in a respectable second, earning a purse of several thousand dollars. Geri had left the track immediately after to take the flight up the coast.

The plane thumped down onto the runway of the small airport in Carmel. Outside, after the pilot had given her the overnight bag from the luggage compartment, she saw no man standing alone by the terminal, heard no one shouting to her. The way she'd imagined it, they would see each other from afar, their emotions would take over and they would be propelled into each other's arms.

So much for the dream.

She was about to go into the terminal and phone the number Quinn had supplied for his home, when she saw the open red Jeep speeding toward her, his face beaming at her over the wheel. He pulled up at the curb, and spouted an apology for being late. Before he could get out, she shoved her luggage into the back and hopped into the passenger seat. No chance for a plunging embrace in the separate bucket seats. She wasn't allowing her emotions to take over, after all.

They looked at each other, registering the changes of almost two years. When he reached out and lifted the sunglasses away from her aquamarine eyes, the gesture carried as much intimacy as if he had unbuttoned her blouse. 'You're as beautiful as ever,' he said.

'And you need a shave,' she replied lightly. It was part of the casual appearance that went with his life these days — faded jeans and an old plaid workshirt, face deeply tanned with lines beginning to show around the green eyes, curly brown hair tending toward shaggy, and a day's growth of stubble. He looked beautiful, too, she thought; she liked him better this way than in the smooth Italian clothes he'd adopted for the trendy New York art scene.

He smiled and rubbed a hand down his face. 'We may be doing some negotiating. I didn't think it would hurt to look poor.'

As jauntily as he'd said it, Geri had to wonder exactly how badly Quinn did need money.

The town of Carmel-by-the-Sea looked like the perfect place for a romantic reunion, its clean neat streets running along hills that overlooked the sparkling Pacific, all lined with inviting shops, little cafes designed to emulate those of French villages, or tea rooms in the English manner. As they drove through it, Geri longed to tell Quinn to stop, to take her into one of the cafes so they could simply talk . . . and look at each other. But he drove on, explaining they had to rush to make their appointment with an auditor from the firm handling the

White liquidation who was to meet them at the ranch where the bankrupt financier had kept his racehorses.

With the wind whipping around in the open Jeep on the thirty-minute drive from the airport to the Carmel Valley, conversation was difficult. After attempting a little small talk, they subsided into silence, and Geri occupied herself looking out at the great rippling stretches of brownish green grass, a less genteel landscape than the Kentucky horse country.

Bradley White's ranch consisted of a huge modern house and pool, and a barn complex surrounded by four hundred acres. As they went up the dirt road leading to the house, Geri saw numerous printed notices plastered onto the open gate and the trunks of trees announcing that the property had been seized by a sheriff's action for payment of debts. A bland young man dressed in a plain dark blue suit and patterned blue tie was leaning against a Mercedes coupe parked outside the house. He waved away the dust raised by the quick stop of Quinn's Jeep and came over to introduce himself as Carl Strump, from the firm of Dickey, Lane and Durfee.

There were a total of twenty-seven thoroughbreds accommodated in two separate barns. At a glance, Geri could see that the quality of the animals in the stalls was very uneven, with a majority that looked sluggish and poorly conformed. Bradley Baird White had obviously been in a hurry to acquire all the appropriate status symbols; assembling his racing stable too quickly, he had made himself as much a victim of hustlers with bad advice as his own customers had been in relying on him. There were a couple of horses that looked like they had real potential, but their condition had been allowed to deteriorate. Their coats were dull and matted as though they hadn't been groomed for days.

'Who's been handling the training?' Geri-Jo asked Carl Strump as they finished touring the first barn and headed across a tree-shaded alley to the second.

'Training?' the young auditor responded. 'Mrs Justinean, everything here is under a lien. There are debts of tens of millions of dollars. It's all we can do to pay a caretaker to keep this place from falling apart. He also feeds the animals, and there are a couple of local kids who come over twice a week to clean the stables.'

'So these horses are left in their stalls?'

The auditor shrugged. 'Shouldn't be for much longer, though. As I've told Mr Quinn, this entire property will be auctioned at the end of the month — minus any horses that creditors might agree to accept in advance as a full settlement.' He gave Quinn a sheepish glance. 'So far he's the only taker.'

'I can see why,' Geri said as they entered the second barn. Again the stalls were filled with animals that stood with drooping heads, their spirit dulled by months of poor care. She ambled past them, stroking their soft noses, pausing once or twice to enter a stall and feel the legs or study the musculature. One animal after another inspired only pity.

Until, approaching the last stall, Geri saw the head of its occupant extended over the low door, neck arched back proudly, eyes glinting through the murky air of the barn. The horse had a coat of rich chestnut, reddish highlights shining even in the subdued light of the barn. A blaze of white marked the forehead and there were streaks of white in the mane. Something within Geri responded instantly. As she went closer, her skin prickled as though there were a charged field surrounding the animal. Stepping up to the edge of the door, she saw that the horse was a filly.

'What's this one's name?' she asked Strump.

The auditor carried a sheaf of records on a clipboard listing the purchase prices of all the horses and other particulars. He flipped through it, obviously confused. Geri asked to look and immediately found the documents describing a chestnut female. No name was given, and the records explained the reason: the horse had never been registered with the Jockey Club, the clearing organization for all names.

'Why isn't there a Jockey Club registration?' she asked Strump.

'This was the last big purchase White made before his business collapsed. After that there was no money for extraneous expenses.'

Geri was relieved. Failure to register could have meant that

594

some early physical problem ruled out any hope of a racing career. While she had the documents in her hand, she looked at the horse's pedigree. There were some names in earlier generations that she recognized as past winners. 'I'd like to take the horse outside for a better look,' she said to the auditor.

'Okay by me.'

She reached to unhitch the stall door. Suddenly the horse's head darted down, and Geri felt a fierce pain knife through her shoulder. 'Ouch!' she yowled, and darted backward, out of reach of the horse. The filly's nipping teeth had not only torn straight through her silk blouse, but blood was seeping from a couple of places where the skin had been punctured.

Quinn threw a protective arm around her, and started to pull her back further. 'Hey, we better put something on that.'

Geri shook her head. 'Later. Right now, I'm going to show this nasty lady just who's boss.'

Geri moved up to the stall again, and maneuvered deftly to avoid the horse's mouth. But this time as she reached for the door, the animal shied and kicked out with one of its hind legs. A sound like a gunshot exploded as the hoof banged against the stall siding.

'Give up on that one, Geri,' Quinn said. 'She's no lady, nasty or otherwise. She's a vicious witch.'

Geri said nothing. She was darting glances around the barn, as if searching for some weapon for defense. Her eyes fell on the auditor. 'Mr Strump, would you be kind enough to lend me your necktie for a few minutes?'

His hand went to the tie. 'This?'

Geri nodded. Reluctantly, Strump undid it and handed it over. She fashioned one end into a small loop with a slip knot, and turned to the horse. Slowly she moved toward it, murmuring softly. 'Easy now, girl . . . be good . . .' With a sudden, deft forward move, she threw one arm around the animal's head, and maneuvered her other hand to grab the center of the horse's upper lip while slipping the looped section of necktie around it. Then she jerked one end of the tie to tighten the slip knot.

Because of sensitive nerves in the lip, she explained to

595

Quinn and the wide-eyed auditor, while the looped device known as a twitch was held there tightly, the horse would remain docile.

As she led the animal outside, Geri was thinking of the first time she had seen the twitch used — by Steve Kimball in the breeding shed at Skyevale. How long ago that seemed . . .

When they were outside in the bright sunlight, she handed the twitch to Strump with instructions to keep it taut, then circled around the filly, studying her from all angles. Although out of condition, flabby from lack of exercise, the horse picked to pieces nicely. Well-developed muscles bulged across the shoulders and hindquarters, and the shape of the chest indicated good wind capacity. Lifting up the legs, Geri felt the bones, thick and solid. She was impressed by the eyes, too, still flashing with spirit despite the pacifying twitch.

But there was another characteristic that sent a chill through her when she spotted it. There was one white 'sock' — a band of relief from the chestnut coloring starting just above the hoof of the front right leg. For the second time Skyevale sprang to mind. Absently, she muttered some words she remembered an old man reciting for her.

Quinn moved up beside her. 'What'd you say?'

'A line from a poem I heard once . . .'

Quinn studied the intensity in her eyes as she stared at the white foot. He seemed to guess there was something painful about her memory, for he took her hand before asking, 'Tell it to me.'

Even now she could see old Henry before her. ' "One white foot",' she intoned, ' "keep him not a day. Two white feet, give him soon away. Three white feet, sell him to a friend. Four white feet, ride him to the end." It's an old horseman's saying.'

'Putting aside the wisdom of old horsemen,' Quinn asked, 'what do you think of the horse? Could you make anything out of her?'

'That's always risky,' she said honestly.

'But what do you *feel* about her, Geri? I trust that.'

'She's got the most god-awful disposition . . .'

'You still haven't answered my question.'

'She's the best one here, that's for sure. And . . . with the right training, she might win a few and be sold as a broodmare for a reasonable profit. No promises, of course.'

Quinn turned to Strump. 'I think we might do some business.'

'Could I put the horse away first?' the auditor said. He was holding the improvised twitch as though it was the lighted fuse attached to a stick of dynamite.

'I'll do it,' Geri offered. 'You settle accounts.'

She led the horse back to its stall, and untied the twitch. As soon as the restraint was removed, the filly began stamping the ground, and darting her head forward, trying for another nip.

'You're not at all ladylike, are you?' Geri mused aloud. In fact, this was one of the worst-tempered horses she'd ever seen. Yet after the poor conditions the animal had endured for months, wasn't some rebellion only reasonable? 'Maybe,' Geri added before leaving the barn, 'I could learn a thing or two from you.'

Outside, Quinn and Carl Strump were talking in raised, angry voices. Quinn motioned her over. 'This clown won't let me have the horse,' he complained to her. 'I bring you all this way, and —'

The auditor also played to Geri. 'It's a matter of dollars and cents. The price of this horse exceeds Mr Quinn's losses.'

'Exceeds?' Quinn bellowed. 'The paintings I sold that crooked client of yours —'

'He's not our client!' Strump yelled back. 'We're assigned by the court.'

Geri interceded, and got Quinn calmed down so the problem could be explained. The filly had been among the most extravagant of Bradley White's excesses, purchased for $680,000 at a California yearling sale right before his firm started going under. Charged with liquidating assets, the auditors hoped to realize no less than half that amount from disposing of the horse. At that price, Quinn wouldn't qualify for this settlement, because his lost cash totalled only $175,000. Since the paintings he had also given White had been sold off for $15,000 when the swindler was raising cash, only that amount could be added to Quinn's claim.

'Those are fire-sale prices,' Quinn complained. 'I used to get four and five times that — for each canvas!'

'If you think you're getting a bad deal,' the auditor said mildly, 'you can sue. But I thought the idea was to keep you from waiting on a long line of other creditors.' He looked at his clipboard again. 'Some of these other horses have lower price tags.'

'They should,' Geri said. 'The rest are worthless. Even the one we like could never fetch anything like three hundred thousand.

'All I know,' Strump said mulishly, 'is what I've been told to do. Guess this just didn't work out.' He nodded goodbye to Quinn and Geri, and started walking toward his car. Quinn stared at the ground. Geri could see he was terribly disappointed.

'It's not that bad, Billy. Remember, it was a long-shot.'

He looked up. 'You liked her, though.'

'Except for that "one white foot" . . .'

He smiled. 'That didn't worry me. Somewhere I heard an old poem about that, too.' He gazed off toward the horizon, recollecting. ' "One white foot, ride him for your life. Two white feet, give him to your wife. Three white feet, give him to your man. Four white feet, sell him — if you can!" '

Geri laughed. 'One more thing I've had backwards for too long.'

'Stay around me and we could get everything right.' He paused. 'I can't deny it's one of the reasons I wanted the horse. I would've had an excuse to call you all the time for advice.'

Her eyes rested for one more moment on his face. Then she whirled toward the auditor who had almost reached his car. 'Mr Strump . . . wait!'

As she hurried to catch the auditor, Quinn strode alongside. 'What are you going to do?'

'Pay the difference to get that horse. The auditors should be glad to get some cash to meet other claims.'

Quinn grabbed her and pulled her up short. 'No, Geri. I won't take money from you . . .'

'You're not *taking* a damn thing. I run a racing stable, remember: this is going to be a business deal, plain and simple. I'm buying a half interest in that horse — and I expect to make a profit.'

Quinn hesitated another second, then put out his hand. 'Partners,' he said.

She took his hand. 'Partners.'

As they continued toward the auditor, their hands were still clasped.

For the rest of the afternoon, they were kept busy with the horse deal. They went into the town of Carmel and Geri arranged for money to be cabled from the East and paid over to Strump's firm, while Quinn asked his local lawyer to draw up a document making the partnership official. Geri also located a well-run boarding stable nearby and contracted to have the filly moved there until training plans could be made.

It was evening by the time they were ready to leave the office of Quinn's lawyer, from which they had made all their calls. Geri had also taken the opportunity to clean the slight laceration left by the horse's teeth, apply some antiseptic, freshen her makeup and perfume and change from her skirt and torn blouse into one of Ungaro's colorful print dresses. Quinn's eyes registered approval when he saw the transformation, but he remained circumspect.

Emerging into one of Carmel's picturesque seaside streets, he said, 'I reserved a room for you tonight at a nice inn out in the Valley. Sound okay?'

'Fine.' An evening wind was blowing in off the ocean and she felt chilled. She wished that he would warm her, as she had wished he might bring her home. But she appreciated, too, that he was moving slowly, demonstrating reluctance to pull her into adultery — obeying all the past signals she had given him to keep his distance. Should she make the first move? Since the moment she had seen him, she had ached to touch him. Yet she remembered, too, that in the aftermath of their past passion she had rejected the chance to stay with him.

Remembered that she had said it wasn't enough to live for the moment. As much as she wanted him now, she didn't trust herself not to mislead him. So she waited, hoping something would happen to take the choice out of her hands.

He suggested dinner, and they drove a few miles down the coast to a small restaurant that overlooked the ocean. They filled the time with talk about the horse, Quinn eager to know what steps they would take next, Geri educating him about the process of training, laying out a schedule by which they might begin racing in a few months. The exchanges were animated, yet both were aware that everything being said was only camouflage for the conversation they were avoiding. She could have asked about his life, the other women he knew, whether he was lonely. She could have told him about her marriage, the countless times she had thought about him. But over dinner they were all business, partners making plans.

They had almost finished the meal when Quinn asked: 'How will you explain this to Dolph — sharing ownership with me?'

She shook her head. 'I have to keep this a secret, Billy.'

'How can you? Won't Dolph ask where the money went?'

Geri took a last sip of wine. She was reluctant to damage Billy's respect for her, yet she didn't want to lie to him either. Finally she revealed that, under the umbrella of huge expenses involved in running the stable, she had siphoned off funds for personal use in ways that would circumvent the scrutiny of Dolph or his accountants.

Quinn looked worried. 'Geri, that doesn't sound entirely legal.'

She told Quinn now about Molly's situation and the large amount of money required to deal with it. She even shared with him the story of Molly's baby which she had kept from Dolph.

'When I started diverting funds,' she explained, 'I didn't feel I had a choice. Sooner or later Dolph may object to the cost of helping Molly, and I can't put my sister in a position where she gets cut off. It would be the end of her. Literally. I think she'd kill herself. I'll do anything to give her a chance.'

'Can money alone do it?'

'It makes everything else possible. I've finally gotten her to begin seeing a psychiatrist. Many women who drift into prostitution have had incestuous experiences in their background — as Molly did. Giving her perspective on that is just one way she can be helped. But the treatment's expensive. There are the lawyers, too — and, if she wins acquittal, the cost of setting her up in some business of her own. And then there's the baby. I've got half a dozen private investigators working on that.'

'Any progress . . .?'

'No. Vanished into thin air. America's a hell of a big place . . .'

Quinn nodded sympathetically. 'It's all worth doing, of course. But don't go farther out on a limb for me. I'll manage. My cause isn't in the same league as your sister's.'

'Oh yes it is, Billy.' She could no longer stop herself from reaching out. She put her hand across the table and took his. 'And I'm not just saving you. I'm saving myself.'

He didn't have to ask what she meant. 'Come home with me,' he said.

When he made love to her, it seemed as if no time at all had passed since that night so long ago. She wrapped herself around him and melted into him, pulled him in deeper, felt herself unbound from all self-consciousness. She couldn't have enough of him, making up for all the times — she felt now — that they should have been together, and hadn't been. Each in turn, they covered each other with kisses, and in the first arousal plunged into each other quickly, unable to wait, but so primed by memory as well as the need of the present, that they came together.

Only minutes later, they were ready again. They took it more slowly this time, and he insisted on giving to her first, lifting her up onto him and pulling her forward so that she was poised above him as he licked at her, drinking her in. When she came this time, she cried with joy, and as the shuddering delight kept rippling through her, she hurried to take him inside her, clinging with the prayer that she would find the strength and the will this time to stay with him.

She couldn't tell how many times they lay back after release only to reach out again, until once more the urge was rising and they were clinging and connected and whispering gentle demands, and then she was coming again, over and over, flooded with the sensation of relief and fulfillment. Dolph knew how to touch a woman, Geri reflected, knew perfectly. But with Dolph, she had long ago realized it was a knowing that could be used with all women. Billy Quinn, she thought just before she surrendered to sleep in his arms, had a different gift. He knew beyond compare how to touch her — her alone.

They had a long slow waking, still in an embrace, making love again before they rose and showered together. Then he made breakfast while she dressed.

'Out here!' he called from a patio as soon as she came out of the bedroom.

She hadn't been very aware of her surroundings last night. They had walked in and headed straight for bed. Now she saw that the rest of the small house consisted of a large area that was essentially an artist's studio, with a kitchen along one wall and a sofa and chairs around a corner fireplace, offering the essence of a living room. There was a glass ceiling overhead and a wall of glass sliders that opened to the patio with a view beyond of meadow bisected by a meandering stream. It was an idyllic setting, and a perfect house for a bachelor artist. Yet Geri thought it rather modest for someone who had made as much money as Quinn had in past years. Perhaps he was renting, a result of the decline in his finances due to his big losses.

A table on the patio was set with colourful Provençal dishes and cups, and a vase of daisies and buttercups that had apparently just been harvested from the meadow. Pitchers of orange juice and coffee, and a basket of croissants completed the arrangement.

'Not bad for last-minute planning,' she remarked.

'To say the least,' he replied, and pointed to the croissants. 'Baked those myself this morning, just to impress you. In case

602

the day came when we had breakfast together, I started *learning* to bake two years ago.' He pulled out a canvas-back director's chair for her before seating himself, and then poured her juice and coffee.

From the patio, Geri could see a wider vista, taking in a long slope at one side. Hundreds of yards away, cresting the slope, was a spectacular house constructed of redwood and glass. 'Who lives up there?' she asked.

'Currently, it's a weekend getaway for some Silicon Valley electronics millionaire.'

'Your landlord?'

Quinn smiled. 'No. Actually I'm his.' He owned the house and ninety surrounding acres, he explained, but after his bad dealings with Bradley White the only way he could meet his large mortgage payments was to earn some income from the property. 'This used to be my studio. It's a nice place to live, though. I never really needed the big place. It went with all the bullshit of being William "Dane" Quinn — a good place to invite rich clients for a weekend.'

'And who else did you invite?' She took a sip of coffee, trying to make the question seem casual. He wasn't fooled.

'I haven't lived like a monk,' he said. 'There have been a couple of very nice women who stayed a while. But not being alone isn't the same as not being lonely.' He put his hand across the table and stroked her arm. 'I've always missed you.'

Was it the sun or the light of truth that made his emerald eyes glow so brightly it was almost painful to look at him? She dropped her gaze again and drank from her cup.

'We have to talk about it,' he said. 'It can't be like last time, Geri. You can't just pick up the loose ends you've left dangling somewhere else and block this out, try to pretend it never happened.'

'It wasn't like that last time,' she said in a quick burst. 'Never for one second did I forget you.'

'Then how much worse it must have been. I won't let you live that way again. I couldn't endure it myself. We have to be together. We're meant to be.' His grip tightened on her arm.

She sprang up from the table to gaze across the meadow,

facing away from him. With the passion of last night behind her, she was surprised — and ashamed — to find herself feeling less bound by the oath she had made to seek her happiness with him.

'Isn't that what you want?' he said.

'Oh, Billy, of course it is . . .'

'Then, damn it. Why don't you take it?'

'Simply because it's what I want — what we both want — doesn't mean it's what we can have. You talk about what's "meant to be", as if there's really a Cupid — some generous spirit who cares about lovers and insists that everyone should be happy. But I learned long ago that's not the way it is. In real life, people who love each other are separated time and again, men and women, children and mothers, brothers and sisters. Hearts full of love are broken every day . . .' She was fighting to hold back tears, keep her voice steady. 'Want you? God, yes, I wanted you long before this. But I couldn't let myself know it then, and I really can't believe it's an answer now. Because if I take you . . . if I try to take that happiness for myself, it can't last. Don't you understand? So many other things might come tumbling down. I need Dolph's money now for Molly, and to cover what I've been taking from the stable, and even to help you. He won't let me go without making me pay a price, and there's nothing to pay with except our happiness. If we tried to be together, whatever we have could be gone overnight. Can't you understand?'

The voice that responded to her last words came from close behind. He pulled her around to enfold her in his arms. 'Sure I understand. You're afraid to think anything good can last, because you never got over seeing everyone and everything you once cared for taken away from you in a few terrible seconds. You've been content to stay in a bad situation because there was no risk, no way to be hurt if it did all get swept away. You've probably built the rest of your life around a sport that's built on risks, because you refused to take them any other way.' He held her away slightly, and trained his eyes on hers. 'But you've got to bet on yourself now, Geri. On us. You've got to take the biggest chance you've ever taken — that happiness can

604

last. Is that too much of a longshot to take with me?'

She moved against him, her head on his shoulder. 'I want to, Billy. Oh God, I want to take the chance . . .'

'Then do it, love. Place your bet.'

'If only I knew . . .' she murmured. The phrase trailed off, but he didn't ask her to finish it. He seemed to know every doubt she could have.

'There aren't any sure things,' he said. 'But there's a lot you can do to cut the odds.'

For a long time she held on to him, her mind full of the problem. How could she train herself for the big event, a chance to win the dream?

CHAPTER SIX

After spending another day with Quinn in California, Geri
returned to Saratoga. She came with a resolve to end her
marriage. Quinn had urged her to believe that, by discussing
the matter candidly with Dolph, she would certainly obtain a
generous settlement that would allow her to safeguard Molly's
future and go on living comfortably.

Through the following weekend she waited, expecting
Dolph to return from his business trip. But then he called
from Paris to tell her a new business opportunity had come up;
he was going to wrap up the deal, then stay for the opening on
Saturday of the racing season at Longchamps before flying
home.

Waiting for his return began to unnerve her. The courage
she had found with Quinn was waning. When Friday night
came, Geri knew she could wait no longer.

'Madame Justinean. *Bienvenu!*'

She had barely stepped out of the sunshine into the bustling
lobby of the Hotel du George Cinq when she was stopped by a
trim mustached man who greeted her effusively and
introduced himself as Claude Orfay, one of the assistant
managers. It amazed her to be recognized by a man she had
never met on any of her previous trips to Paris with Dolph —
though he always stayed in this hotel. Such personalized
greetings must be part of the fabled hospitality of the 'George

V'. There was probably a file somewhere with pictures of the wives of billionaires for ambitious sub-managers to memorize.

'Monsieur Justinean is not here at the moment,' Orfay said as he escorted Geri to the desk and gave her a registration card.

'He wasn't expecting me,' Geri said flatly. The Concorde she had taken from New York late last night had reached Paris at mid-morning. She had assumed Dolph would already be out. Even on Saturdays, he often went to the offices of his international subsidiaries, or had breakfast meetings with bankers and other corporate heads. She didn't doubt she could locate him, however. He never left himself to be completely incommunicado. Even if he wasn't at his office, there would be someone with instructions to refer important calls.

'If you like,' the manager said, 'we can put your luggage in the suite, I'll call a car for you, and you can go straight out. It's April in Paris, *n'est-ce-pas*? Not a time to waste a moment indoors.'

'Thank you, but I'll go to the room first . . .'

The maid had already been in to make the bed in the large suite; the only residue of disorder was a pile of papers on a desk in the sitting room. A brief glance at the top pages told Geri that they were related to Dolph's interest in acquiring a share in a large French tire manufacturer.

Geri sat down and phoned the office of Dolph's French holding company. As she had anticipated the office was open and there was a multi-lingual secretary taking calls. But even after Geri identified herself as Dolph's wife, the secretary professed ignorance of his whereabouts.

'I'm sorry, Mrs Justinean. Didn't he leave any message for you at the hotel?'

Geri couldn't bother to explain that she had sprung a surprise visit to ask for a divorce. After hanging up, she wondered if the secretary could have been stonewalling her. Dolph never liked to be completely out of touch.

She didn't think too much about it, though. Whether or not she made contact with Dolph in the next hour or two, she knew that by lunchtime she could find him attending the first races of the season at Longchamps. Meanwhile, she might enjoy Paris a little. Reminded of the manager's offer to arrange a car, she called the desk and told the concierge to have a chauffeured limousine come for her as soon as possible.

She had brought with her a small valise containing only enough clothes to last a day or two. She picked out a light Chanel suit appropriate for the April weather and that would, by itself, be a ticket of entry if she chose to visit the haute couture salons. Then she went to hang her other skirt and jacket in the clothes closet.

The moment the door swung open, she stopped and stared. Only a single other article was hanging there — a freshly pressed suit of Dolph's, evidently delivered by the hotel valet. But she knew Dolph always traveled with many changes of clothes. All at once, Geri realized the truth: even though Dolph was registered at the hotel, he wasn't really staying here. Checking the dresser drawers confirmed her suspicion. They were empty.

Her mind went back over the many absences of recent years, and the call of the other night when he had postponed returning home.

It had taken so long to muster the courage to think of leaving Dolph; now that she had boldly flown thousands of miles to seize the initiative, he was evidently off somewhere in another woman's bed. She felt no shock, no betrayal. She minded nothing but the time she had lost with Quinn.

She dressed and went to the lobby where she found Orfay.

'I would appreciate it, Monsieur, if you could tell me where I might reach my husband.'

The assistant manager responded with Gallic sang-froid. '*Je regrette, Madame*, I have no way of knowing. Have you tried his offices here in the city?'

'I have. They weren't helpful. I expect better service from you.'

Orfay shrugged uncomfortably. 'I'm sorry, Madame . . .'

Of course, Geri knew discretion would be a key element in the hotel's excellent service. But the obstacle could be surmounted. She might as well enjoy the power that went with being Mrs Justinean for one day.

'Monsieur Orfay,' she said reasonably. 'It's very important I talk to my husband about a personal matter, and, frankly, I don't think it would be wise for you to interfere with that need. I'm sure Mr Justinean wouldn't register here without making sure important business could be referred to him. I suggest you check your records and see if you can help me. Otherwise, your further career at this establishment, and any other decent hotel in the civilized world, may end here and now.'

Except for the telltale twitch of his mustache, the hotelier would have appeared imperturbable. He stepped away to confer with an operator at the main switchboard, and returned with a slip of paper on which a phone number had been inked.

Back in her room, Geri went instantly to the phone in the sitting room and called the number.

''Allo,' said the answering voice, '*chez Madamoiselle Delvaux.*'

Geri was instantly struck dumb, her mind racing back over the years, remembering the exquisite French actress with whom he had danced at their wedding ball. Had that been the beginning? Had Dolph snared another mistress on the very night she had given up that role herself to become his wife?

The maid broke the silence. '*Qui est là?*'

Geri set the receiver in its cradle, breaking the connection. The idea of Dolph spending a night with some anonymous woman had not disturbed her very much. After all, she had been unfaithful herself. But now the woman had a name and Geri faced the possibility that the infidelity had gone on through all the years of her marriage, all her effort of years to make it work.

For a long time she sat in the room half dazed. Tears stung her eyes, not formed from any sorrow but out of rage and frustration. She wanted the time back, all the wasted effort and trust that she had given to him.

When at last she was ready to act, she looked at the clock and saw it was past noon. It was time, she thought, to confront Dolph. Time to go to the races. The track was her territory, the place where she had first discovered independence, the place that had sustained her with a career

— and also where she had first seen him. There could be nowhere more apt, she thought, for finally cutting the ties.

Arriving at lunch time, she expected Dolph might be dining in the glass-enclosed *Restaurant Panoramique* atop the stands. She had barely turned out of the elevator when she spotted them at a table by a window, holding hands and laughing. A frieze of beautiful people in love that duplicated exactly her memory of being with Dolph in the days when he was still married to Diana. Looking across the room at Sabine Delvaux, Geri was gripped by a primitive feeling that this other woman had not only stolen her place but her soul. Yes, she was ready to let Dolph go, she had another love of her own. But for a moment Geri couldn't help wondering how different things might have been if only Dolph had remained faithful as she had tried to do.

Impelled by her rage to denounce Dolph publicly, Geri took a step forward. *No*, she thought then, *not here*. She was out of control now, nothing constructive could be accomplished, she would only make a scene. The ghost of Diana hovered around her. Geri didn't want to repeat the same pitiful role that Dolph's former wife had played with her years ago.

But even as she hurried away, the vision of her husband laughing with the exquisite actress stayed with her as though it had been burned onto her retina by an explosion of light.

It took only a few minutes to pack her few belongings. She was intending to head straight to the airport. But each time she was tempted to leave, she reminded herself that eventually they would have to talk. Better to do it now. Free herself for a new life.

She waited till the end of the afternoon, when she knew the races would be over, then sought out Monsieur Orfay once more. No pressure was necessary this time to obtain the address that went with the telephone number.

The long Mercedes limousine that had taken her to and from the races was waiting to bring her to the airport. She gave the chauffeur Delvaux's address instead. She was driven across a bridge leading to the Ile St Louis and turned into a street of renovated sixteenth-century buildings that backed onto the Seine. The Mercedes stopped in front of a house that had a gray masonry front and a lacquered door with an old lion's-head brass knocker. Geri saw colorful madras drapes hanging in the lower front windows, and she noticed a window on the upper floor covered by a shade with a playful design of rainbows and clouds. Taking it in, she sensed a different air about this house to the places Dolph had chosen to live himself. It was elegant, and yet less formal, less grandiose than Dolph's mansions and estates. More of a *home*, perhaps that was it.

The young maid who opened the door looked at Geri with the cold wariness practiced by people accustomed to guarding the privacy of celebrities. 'Oui, Madame . . .?'

'Is Mr Justinean here?'

The maid hesitated. Merely an evasion, or couldn't she speak English? To cut through either obstacle, Geri added, '*Je suis Madame Justinean.*'

Without any marked reaction, the maid stepped back to admit Geri, then she led her along a hallway to the back of the house where they entered a large room with a bank of French doors that looked out on the river. A beautifully landscaped garden ran from just behind the house to the edge of the *quai*.

Yet it was not the picture-postcard view that took Geri's breath away. It was something more mundane. In a corner of the garden a woman was engaged in a playful game of tag with a small towheaded boy, a toddler no more than two years old. Through one of the open French doors came a counterpoint of the scampering child's giggles, with the woman's loving taunts and delighted laughter. Sabine Delvaux, still dressed in the sportclothes she had worn to the racetrack, looked sublimely beautiful as she played with her little son. She epitomized, thought Geri, an image of glamor combined with motherhood.

Hearing a sound behind her, Geri turned. Dolph had come into the room. Unlike Delvaux, he had changed since the track, donning more casual clothes, loose slacks, a cashmere sweater worn without a shirt, and loafers without socks. His silver hair was wet, adding to the impression that he had just been summoned out of a shower, and that he was completely at home.

'So here you are,' he said easily. 'I wondered if you'd drop in for a visit, or just fly away.'

'You knew I was in Paris . . .?'

'I call the hotel regularly to get messages. They told me my wife had arrived.'

'And you did nothing about it. You might have kept me from ever knowing about this.' She swept a glance around her.

He shrugged. 'Since you'd flown an ocean to look for me, I didn't see any point in hiding the truth.'

They gazed at each other in silence as though the truth, once mentioned, became a solid barrier between them and its dimensions had to be studied before it could be surmounted.

At last Geri looked back toward the garden. 'And what about *her*? You didn't care about keeping us apart, keeping this double life of yours running smoothly . . .?'

Dolph glanced through the French windows. 'Sabine has always accepted the situation exactly as it is . . .'

As I did, Geri thought. Again, as she looked toward the garden, Geri had the odd sensation of having changed places with a dead woman. She recalled the moment many years ago when she had first met Dolph's previous wife — and the bitter remarks Diana had made about the way Dolph engineered their confrontation.

Geri vowed not to play his games, though, not to surrender her dignity.

'Won't you sit down?' he said. 'Can I offer you a drink?'

'No, I don't want your hospitality. All I want is to get this settled, and get out of here.'

He took a step toward her. 'Settled? And what does that mean?'

'We have to come to some kind of agreement . . .'

'Ah, yes. But must we stand like two prizefighters in a ring to do it?' He motioned her again to a chair. 'Please . . .'

She relented and sat down. Almost at once she was sorry, already feeling disarmed. 'Listen, Dolph,' she said quickly. 'There's no reason for me to keep you from having the life you want with another woman. There are other things I want, too. I'm only sorry we couldn't be honest with each other sooner.

Maybe I should blame myself for that as much as you because I wasn't honest with myself. Now that I know what I want — what we both want — it's easy for us to have it.'

She was encouraged to see him nodding as he took a chair opposite. But he made no reply, as though waiting to hear her proposition.

'All I want is enough to guarantee that I'll be able to take care of Molly — and go on with the work that I enjoy.'

'You have it,' he said.

'Then I'll need nothing else — except my freedom.'

His expression clouded. 'Freedom?' he echoed curiously.

What else were they talking about? His tone puzzled and alarmed her. 'A divorce,' she said emphatically, 'as soon as possible. I want to be free to find my own happiness, as you've found yours.'

Slowly he shook his head. 'But you are part of my happiness. I have no desire, and no intention, of letting you go.'

She stared at him incredulously. 'Whether or not you *let* me, Dolph, I'm leaving you. But I can't conceive of why you'd even try to stop me. You have what you want —'

'I want what I have,' Dolph amended quietly. 'All of it.'

She bolted up. 'Not me. You can't have me.'

He rose, too, and moved across the gap between them. 'I already do. You are my wife.'

She shook her head, disbelieving, then darted a look past him to the garden, wondering what Delvaux might think of Dolph's refusal to free himself for a new marriage, tempted to call out to her. But the woman and child were gone, as if they had been instructed to disappear.

Her eyes shifted back to Dolph. Disdainfully, she asked, 'How can you think I'd stay with you another day . . .?'

He smiled confidently. 'You'll stay . . . because it's the only freedom you can have.' He took her by the arms and held on tightly when she struggled to free herself. 'My dear Geri, do you think I'm not aware of the liberties you've been taking with my money to help your sister? I looked the other way as long as it suited me. But I wouldn't have the incentive if you walked out on me. And the very act of leaving would only make you seem all the more guilty of defrauding me.'

Stunned by the irrationality of his desire and the intensity of his malice, she remained speechless in his grip as he went on. 'And with all this closeness you've shown your sister lately, I doubt there'd be much difficulty getting anyone to believe that you and she could have been involved together in extortion. These are crimes punishable by imprisonment, you know. *Loss* of freedom,' he added sardonically.

She wrestled herself free at last. 'You bastard! You have a child now with Sabine, you'll have more. What can you want from me?'

'The same thing: I want a child from you.'

She tossed her head back, wishing she could force out a laugh, but instead all that emerged was a gasp of despair. How could she deal with his ego? '*From* me, you say, not even *with* me. My God, you make it sound as though you want nothing more than to breed — to re-create an image of yourself. And after what I've heard, I know that would only mean creating a monster.' She whirled away, unable to face him anymore, to stay in the same room. Whatever the risks of walking out, she would take them.

But before she had gone a couple of steps he grabbed her and whipped her around.

'You've spent half your lifetime working in a world that thinks about nothing but how to create winners from putting the right biological components together. Are we really so different, Geri, from the animals we breed? Are we not flesh and blood, all formed out of cells that contain whole universes — each coded with millions of special characteristics. Don't you see? It isn't simply children I want. As you said, I can have that with Sabine, with anyone else. But with you I can have something more — heirs who will take whatever I leave and build on it, go beyond it. That's why I gave you my name. Because you're beautiful, yes, and smart . . . but you've also got that mysterious extra something — maybe it comes from that rugged mountain pioneer spirit — that makes winners. I knew it when we met. Together we can create unique beings, sons and daughters who will —'

She couldn't listen to it anymore. 'No!' she cried out. 'We're not animals, Dolph — not just breeding to create beings who will have more power, take more. Those are the kind of mad ideas that once pushed this whole continent into a war. A man and a woman should have children as an expression of love.' She stepped back, retreating from him as she might slowly withdraw from an animal poised to spring. 'I don't want children with you. I don't want anything of yours, and I'll be damned if I'll let you rule me. Threaten me all you want, I'll fight you — I'll fight right down to the wire. And I'll win.'

She glared at him, until she saw the smile start to creep across his lips, her challenge answered by his contempt. Then, in a fury, she turned and started out.

Behind her, she heard him say quietly, 'Diana thought so, too. She had the wild idea that she could leave on her terms. I warned her against it many times.' The tinge of quiet menace in his voice was as subtle as the sound of thunder from the far side of a distant mountain.

Geri stopped dead. In the past, Dolph had always claimed that Diana was a clinging, vindictive woman, unable to give him up. But the different truth he had just spoken — that Diana had been ready to leave if she received some settlement — carried with it another, darker revelation. Suddenly Geri realized that she had just heard Dolph utter a confession . . . and a threat.

She turned back, half prepared to find him already aiming a gun at her. He was standing with his hands in his pockets, the contemptuous smile still on his lips.

'You were guilty,' she said in a hush, aghast not only at his crime but at all she had done to help him pervert justice. 'You wouldn't let her go, so she tried to take the jewelry and you just shot her where she stood.'

'I shot a thief,' he said coldly.

Geri nodded grimly at the irony of his reply. 'And now I'm the thief. You'd condemn me to death for trying to steal back my own happiness. Well, it won't work. You'll only hang yourself.' She backed away from him. He hadn't moved, but as he remained standing with his hands in his pockets and a slight

615

smile on his face, she could feel the emanations of danger extending across the room.

He spoke in the same level tone as before, yet each time the pitch of his gargantuan egotism came through more clearly. 'I've been tried and found innocent. Whatever you might say to the authorities, I'd escape prosecution on legal technicalities. For you, I'm afraid, it wouldn't be so easy — not once I produced some of the many old police and court files I got from your sister. Anyone reopening the case might even be persuaded to believe that you had instigated Diana's murder.'

She had entered the room with a residue of respect and even affection for Dolph — memories, however faint, of the love she had once felt. But it was all gone now, supplanted by consuming hatred. She had never perceived how evil he was, how singularly determined to subjugate everyone and everything within his sphere. Nor, she imagined, would Sabine Delvaux perceive it, until the time when positions were exchanged again, and the mistress became the wife and found herself in the place where Geri stood now.

She turned away.

'I warn you, Geri —'

'I'm not afraid of anything you can do to me. Because staying would just be another kind of death.' She turned on her heel and hurried from the room.

His last words reached her as she was pulling open the door to the street. 'Then be afraid,' he called out, 'of what you might do to yourself.'

The words echoed again and again through her mind as she rode from Delvaux's house to Charles de Gaulle airport. Away from Dolph she could not keep up the courageous front. She had been in jail once, wrongly accused of a crime. It could happen again. She was trembling so badly when the chauffeur helped her from the car at the terminal, that he asked if she felt well enough to fly.

As soon as she was in the terminal, she ran to a phone booth.

'Geri?' Quinn said when the connection was made. 'Where the hell are you? I tried the farm all day and —'

'I'm in Paris, Billy.' It touched her that he had been trying to reach her at the very moment she needed him most.

'Paris?'

'I came to see Dolph. Oh, Billy . . . he . . .' Her throat closed as she fought to keep from breaking down.

He filled the silence. 'So that's where you go for a shoulder to cry on? And I thought you'd need me —'

'What are you talking bout — a shoulder to cry on? I came only to tell Dolph I was leaving him.'

There was a pause. She thought the connection had been lost, then his voice came on again. 'How long have you been there, Geri?'

She was surprised he didn't first express some appreciation of her mission. 'I took the Concorde over last night,' she answered.

There was another brief pause. 'Are you coming to me, Geri?' he asked then.

'I want to. But Dolph has threatened —'

'Come to me,' he broke in. 'Come now.'

'He'll make it very hard. For both of us. And Molly, too. I could take it, but with Molly needing so much help —'

'Geri,' he cut her off again, 'there's something you don't know yet — it only happened very late last night. Molly's lawyer went to her apartment. He'd been trying to get her on the phone for days to let her know about a court appearance, and there was no answer, so he had the building superintendent open the door. He thought maybe she'd skipped bail . . .' Billy paused once more, and Geri felt the onrush of inner pain as intuition forewarned her what she was about to hear. 'They found her in the bedroom, Geri. She'd been shot a couple of times. It might have been someone she brought in, just a nut. But the police think . . . it was a kind of execution. It's been on the news. I thought maybe you'd heard and gone to Dolph . . .'

She had begun sobbing soundlessly. Molly was dead. A victim of underworld retribution, the reports would say. But she knew better. Molly, like all the others, was just another victim of the slide.

As she herself might be, too, if she made the wrong choice.

'I'm coming to you, Billy,' she said. 'If you really want me, I'm coming.'

'It's all I've wanted for years. If I thought the odds were even one in a billion, you'd change your mind, I'd come after you right now and —'

'Don't worry, darling. This is no long shot.' Even while she had not yet finished crying for Molly, she found exultant laughter rising up with her words. 'If anything, it's the only sure thing I ever bet on in my life'

BOOK VIII: *THE WIRE*

CHAPTER ONE

In the blue-gray dawn light, the featureless figures of men and horses moving through the mist hovering over the ground looked no more substantial than shadows.

As Geri drove slowly along one of the roads of the Belmont backstretch, she had a sudden fantasy of being transported in a magic machine through a limbo where all the ghosts of her life paraded before her. What would happen only hours from now might determine whether she could cut loose once and for all from the threatening spell of the past and fulfill the carefree future she had wanted so badly when she had left Dolph.

Arriving at Oakie's barn, she found him outside instructing one of his assistants on the day's workouts. Two years ago, he had given up contract work for a single stable to become an independent trainer, accepting horses from various owners. He had thought of the change originally as a form of semi-retirement, but the fine reputation he'd built over the years brought him many of the most promising horses, and soon he was twice as busy as ever. In his second season as an independent, Oakie's string had won enough stakes to rate him one of the top five trainers in the country in terms of total purses won.

He greeted Geri with a hug. 'You're here awful early.'

'Couldn't sleep.'

'Nothing else to keep you indoors?' he asked lightly.

'Not last night.' Quinn had been away, as Oakie knew. 'How's our girl?'

'See for yourself.' Oakie gestured to the barn.

At the entrance, one of the armed security guards hired by Geri was seated in a chair, positioned to give him a view along the whole row of stalls. She greeted him and made her way toward a rear stall, Oakie trailing behind her.

The chestnut filly was standing with its head extended over the half-door, neck arched proudly as always, the large black eyes glittering with malice. Geri paused a short distance away and purred some gentling words before she entered the stall, moving slowly and gingerly. She had made an uneasy peace with the animal in the time since she and Quinn had acquired it, but she never felt a hundred percent safe. The horse's disposition was as mean as ever. If Geri had learned to handle her, it was only by the application of skill and caution, not because familiarity had made them friends. The name she and Quinn had given the horse was an ironic comment on her unfailingly bad temper: Ladylike.

'Looks ready to go, don't she?' Oakie said.

'I just wish she knew how much this one means to me.'

'Don't expect she'd give a damn anyway. Lady runs for herself — got a fever to show all the men she's more than a match for 'em.'

Geri smiled. 'I can sympathize with that.'

'Heard the morning line,' Oakie said, referring to the odds assigned by the official handicappers. 'Not so much sympathy there. Pretty long odds, considerin' . . .'

'No surprise,' Geri said. She didn't have to be told, either, which horse had been chosen as the favorite. Carefully, she reached out and stroked her hand along the blaze of white on Ladylike's nose. 'Do it for both of us,' she said.

The horse twitched its head up irritably, attempting a nip. Always alert, Geri had already pulled her hand away.

'C'mon, darlin',' Oakie said, slipping his arm through Geri's. 'Let's give the Lady her thinkin' time. Haven't bought you a meal over at Clara's Kitchen since — gee, how long is it? — twenty years. How about an anniversary breakfast?'

They walked out of the barn. The sun was climbing, no more faceless specters floated through a murky haze. Yet images of the past still occupied her mind.

'I heard a weather report on the way here,' she said. 'They're talking about a chance of rain . . .'

'Wouldn't matter,' Oakie said. 'Ladylike's handled the mud before. But look at that big old sun shinin', Geri. No reason to fret about rain, or anythin' else. We're gonna win it today, don't you worry. We're gonna make some history.'

As they walked, her eyes kept scanning the sky. She could never forget there were times when the sun and rain could come together — times when folks would say 'the Devil's beating his wife.'

'Something wrong . . .?' Oakie asked.

She smiled at him, and shrugged off the fear. 'Nothing wrong,' she said. 'I was just thinking it's about time the Devil's wife fought back.'

In the two years since she had left Dolph, Geri had come to regard him as virtually personifying the Devil. At the time she discovered he had knowingly committed murder — and used her no less cold-bloodedly to gain the sympathy that helped win his acquittal — she believed she had confronted the full extent of his evil. But she had learned since that there were no bounds to his cruelty and egotism. His meanest act had been to keep her legally tied to him as his wife.

For the first months after joining Quinn in California, her existence had been an incredible combination of bliss and torture. She and Billy gave to each other every day — gifts of pleasure, and strength, and love. He had helped her to work through her grief for Molly in a way that Dolph never would have, understanding that even if Geri had barely known her sister, the loss of any opportunity ever to know her was no less something to be bitterly mourned. He had been the first to suggest that they ought to redouble efforts to find Molly's missing daughter and make sure her future was secure. He and Geri had supported each other, too, as they made plans to rebuild both their individual careers. Quinn started to paint

623

again — the kind of boldly original work she had always hoped he would do; and she concentrated her efforts on realizing some profit from the only worthwhile asset she still felt truly entitled to call her own — the horse she and Quinn had bought. She put the filly in the care of a young trainer in California, not hoping for any miracles, simply aware that it was time to begin the process of conditioning the animal after a long period of neglect.

Yet through every moment she and Billy were trying to build a life together, they were kept busy fighting Dolph's efforts to destroy them. First, he had made good his threat to accuse Geri of embezzling money from Justinean Farms. Only two days after she left Dolph in Paris and arrived at Quinn's home in Carmel Valley, a phone call had come from Lew Yancey.

'It's obviously a grotesque misunderstanding,' he said, after explaining that Dolph had instructed him to proceed with building a case against her for criminal embezzlement. 'But until it blows over, Geri, I have to warn you that Dolph has told me to press charges. I'm sorry, I really don't —'

'Don't bother apologizing, Lew. Without Dolph you don't have a law practice, I know that . . .'

'Have you thought about going back to him? That might be a solution. Can I tell him it's a possibility?'

'Tell him . . . at long last I'm right where I belong.'

'Then you realize what I have to do.'

For only a moment Geri mulled the wisdom of revealing that Dolph had admitted to deliberately shooting Diana. But if she reopened the case there was nothing to be gained for herself — only more to be lost.

In the ensuing days and weeks Dolph had broadened his charges against her to include conspiring with Molly to extort money from him. He succeeded in having warrants issued so the California police were called upon to consider extraditing her to New York. As the pressure built, Geri began to sense a more demonic purpose than merely trying to dislodge her from Quinn's side. He was taunting her, daring her to defend herself by exposing his act of murder. He welcomed a contest, a chance to measure his ability to survive against hers.

If she managed to withstand the savage legal offensive, it was not purely because of her fighting spirit or Quinn's moral support. The difference had been Ed Markham. As soon as Justinean's press representatives had planted news stories about Geri's 'embezzlement', the Washington lawyer had called to offer his help.

At first she declined. 'I know the fees you command, Ed, and I can't pay. Dolph's frozen every one of my accounts. Left all the jewelry, too — and I've got too much to live for to think of going back for it. It was insured as his property, anyway.'

'I didn't call to drum up business, Geri. I'm your friend. No one will ever convince me you didn't have a good reason for anything you did. And I like to see justice done.'

Geri returned to New York voluntarily and Ed Markham stood with her at hearings on the embezzlement and extortion charges, pleading successfully against an indictment so that she remained free pending further investigation and was permitted to fly back to Quinn in California. Markham failed however to advance divorce proceedings or secure money for maintenance. As long as Dolph's lawyers could claim Geri had already helped herself to vast sums, the question of whether she was entitled to a divorce settlement remained clouded. Markham offered to lend Geri money, but she refused. 'You've already done more than enough,' she told him as they emerged one day from a court hearing, 'and I'm not feeling deprived because I can't live the way I did with Dolph. I'm much happier the way things are now.'

Perhaps, too, she could not take his money because she also felt guilty of betraying him. She had drawn him into a perversion of justice by persuading him to fight for Dolph's acquittal. She parted from Markham without ever telling him about Dolph's confession to her.

As glad as she and Quinn were to be together, the problems they faced began to grind them down. Ladylike became for both the very embodiment of their hope to triumph over Dolph's effort to humble them and drive them apart. Desperately counting on such a deliverance, they managed for a while to ignore the logic and statistics that all but ruled it out. They grasped at the straws of promise given them by Ladylike's young trainer, who reported that the horse was coming back to condition, her speed steadily improving.

Toward the end of summer, the trainer said, 'I think she's ready to break her maiden,' and suggested shipping Ladylike south to run in the current meeting at Del Mar.

Taking even a small purse at Del Mar might make things easier, so she gave her consent to the trainer and took his recommendation for the jockey. She would have preferred to use Ramie, but her old friend had married Glenn Joye, settled into his mansion in Beverly Hills, and given up racing. Ramie was pregnant now — or, as she put it laughingly the last time she and Geri had talked, 'I am run the nine-month Derby carrying extra weight in my saddlebags.'

In Ladylike's maiden race at Del Mar, she came in seventh in a field of nine. 'She'll do better next time,' the trainer consoled. But there would be no next time, thought Geri. Not in the same place, with the same trainer. Perhaps she had already waited too long to implement her own plan.

On the following Saturday night, at an hour when she knew the regulars would be relaxing with a drink and a song after a day at the Saratoga race meeting, Geri put through a long-distance call to The Wishing Well. Someone located Oakie in the crowd around the bar and brought him to the phone.

She told him what she wanted. 'Only you can bring out the best, Oak. You could make this filly great . . .'

She had to confess that she had no money for the kind of fees Oakie was getting these days, nor enough to ship the horse, cover the skyrocketing cost of thoroughbred insurance, or even pay for a few weeks of stabling and feed. Billy couldn't contribute either — though in spite of Geri's insistence that he mustn't abandon the new direction of his painting, Quinn had lately been trying to ease the financial squeeze by seeking the lucrative commissions that had once come to him so easily. This time, though, he could find no takers. In part it was because once Quinn had severed his connections other painters had moved in to pick up the loose ends. The larger reason was that Dolph had pulled every string in the community of owners and breeders to keep Quinn from getting work.

'So you're askin' me,' Oakie said with a chuckle, 'to pay to ship your filly down to my farm, so I can start payin' to feed her and have her worked and walked, and puttin' in my valuable time to get her ready . . . so then I can pay to enter her in a race or two. A man'd have to be crazy to turn down an opportunity like that, wouldn't he?'

'Ladylike will pay her own way once she starts running. I know she will.' Geri told Oakie the full extent of her dream: with the proper training regimen, and the right early races for seasoning, by next spring Ladylike could be qualified to run in the classic stakes for three-year-olds, the Derby, the Preakness —

'Let's go one step at a time, darlin'. Send me your horse.'

When Ladylike was flown East to the Kentucky farm Oakie had bought with his recent winnings, Geri went along. In the trainer's first reactions to the horse and its initial workouts, Geri detected an absence of genuine enthusiasm, but it was a couple of weeks before Oakie stated his opinion openly. Ladylike was a sound horse, he said, but not a great one.

'She might take some claimers, but you can't be aiming for the Derby or anything like it. Even the best ladies would be in tough company there.' Only a couple of fillies had ever won the Kentucky Derby he reminded her, and there had been a sixty-five-year gap between those two — Regret in 1915, and Genuine Risk in 1980.

'Try her, Oakie,' Geri pleaded. 'The potential is there, I know it. If you could just see how far she's come from the condition she was in when I found her . . .'

Oakie's skepticism was not quelled, but Geri was content when the trainer agreed to continue making his best effort. Leaving the horse in his care, she traveled up to New York to meet a new challenge from Dolph. Markham had managed to clear her of involvement with Molly's extortion activities, and shift the case against her for misuse of stable funds from the criminal courts into the civil, but now Dolph was trying to strip away her very last source of hope. He had learned Geri had a horse in training, and, since her share of the filly had been purchased with funds from his breeding operation, Dolph was claiming Ladylike was the property of Justinean Farms.

Markham met the challenge head on. Charging into Lew Yancey's office, he declared that since Geri had never drawn a nickel of salary while she was running Justinean Farms, she was entitled to a substantial settlement not only for her labor, but for all she had done over two years to build up the equity of the breeding operation. In fact, Markham thundered, he was preparing to countersue for an amount far in excess of what Geri's share in Ladylike was worth.

Yancey didn't yield, though he knew that Dolph's desire to have the horse bore no relation to value, and came purely out of a need to inflict punishment. But because of his own affection for Geri, when the lawyer went to Glen Cove to report to Dolph, he couched his advice in a way that might resolve the matter quickly and painlessly.

'I've had some scouting done on this filly,' Yancey said. 'The horse shows no quality.'

'I still want it,' Dolph stated grimly.

'Think a second, Dolph. You've got some very promising horses that were bred while Geri was running the farm. One of the two-year-olds has already won some big stakes and looks like a contender for the top three-year-old events. If we lock horns with Markham on this, there's a chance he'll grab off some of those good horses in lieu of unpaid compensation. Aren't you better off leaving Geri with what she's got? Let her pour her sweat into this low-grade filly. She'll just be letting herself in for one disappointment after another.'

Dolph gave no sign of approving Yancey's logic, and for the next couple of weeks the lawyer continued to pursue the recovery of Ladylike.

Then Oakie sent the filly to race in the October meeting at Keeneland. Geri flew in from California with Quinn, and they watched together as Ladylike ran in a low-grade stakes for two-year-olds with a winner's purse of twenty thousand dollars. This time the filly moved up quickly into third position . . . before fading to finish last.

As soon as she found Oakie after the race, Geri told him that she wanted a change of jockey for any future event.

Oakie argued. 'That kid I had up in the saddle, is the number one bug-boy. He's won more races this season than any —'

'He didn't make it happen with my horse. I want someone else.'

Oakie warned her once more that there was a limit to what she could expect, but he agreed to race the horse again with a new rider after a few more weeks of training.

Once more Geri was called back to New York to give depositions in Dolph's civil suit against her, and Quinn went along. The constant shuttling from north to south and back and forth across the country was wearing them down, leaching the joy out of even their moments together. Still, there was no choice but to answer every charge that Dolph threw at them.

But this time they found Ed Markham waiting with news that Dolph's claim on Ladylike had been dropped. The horse's poor racing record, capped by the recent last-place showing, had persuaded Dolph it was pointless to pursue ownership.

After months of being under a constant legal siege, this victory injected a honeymoon mood into the few days Geri spent with Quinn in New York. They stayed at an inexpensive hotel, and walked the city from Madison Avenue to Soho holding hands; they ate meals from the carts of street vendors with gusto, and admired the rich displays in the shops and galleries without ever feeling an iota of regret or envy because the luxuries once afforded so easily were now out of reach behind the glass.

Quinn had freighted a number of his recent canvasses to New York, mainly sporting scenes, done with the distinctive flash of style that had first impressed Geri. Whenever she was occupied with her own legal matters, he took his work around to galleries. He would have gone first to Wagonner's because they had been so successful with his conventional scenes, but

his fling with Melinda Wagonner had ended on a sour note —
after he spent the night of his opening with Geri — and he
didn't expect she would renew their acquaintance, even if
purely for the sake of business.

But when he visited other gallery owners they offered little
encouragement. They knew his reputation, knew that as
'William Dane Quinn' he had carved out an important niche
in the market for traditional sporting pictures. But these new
paintings were so unlike his past work that the clientele he'd
built couldn't be expected to respond. Any why did he insist
now on signing his canvasses simply as 'Bill Quinn', in effect
rejecting his past trademark? That change alone somehow cast
doubt on Quinn's new work, causing dealers to suspect him as
an eccentric with whom it might be hard to do business.

At last, he went back to the Wagonner Gallery. Griffin
Wagonner wasn't there, unfortunately — Melinda was. She
greeted him politely, though, and kept their meeting
businesslike. When Quinn unwrapped the three canvasses
he'd toted along with him, she lined them up at the base of a
wall and spent a long time studying them.

'They're striking . . .' she said. 'But is that enough?' Her
clientele was attracted to the more conventional style, she
reminded Quinn, to artists with established marketability.
The rich didn't like to take risks on pure talent; whatever they
bought, they wanted to know it was a wise investment.

'Why did you have to change your style, Bill?' she asked
earnestly. 'Why did you have to change anything?' The
provocative glance of her pale blue eyes hinted that the
changes she regretted most had nothing to do with his
painting.

'I got tired of being someone else's invention,' he replied,
keeping the conversation on business. 'I wanted to be a
painter, not an actor playing a painter.'

She smiled with comprehension, then shifted her gaze back
to his new paintings and appraised them coolly for another
minute. At last she told him that the best she could do was keep
the canvasses, show them to her father when he returned from
London in a couple of weeks, and they would decide jointly

whether to exhibit them. There could be no promises.

The terms were no more than might have been granted to any struggling young neophyte, but it was still the best offer he'd had. Quinn swallowed his pride and left the paintings with Melinda Wagonner. He could only pray that the opportunity arose from a sincere if tentative interest in his new work, not out of a scorned woman's desire to tantalize him with false hopes.

Geri had been in constant contact with Oakie by phone, and for the first time the trainer displayed a burst of enthusiasm: the filly had shown excellent speed in recent workouts. If she could maintain the pace under race conditions, the potential was indeed there to beat the toughest competition. Oakie had entered Ladylike in a race to be run at Churchill Downs in the final days of autumn.

From New York, Geri and Quinn traveled to Louisville. On the day of the race, Geri joined Oakie to hear him give orders to the new jockey, a successful veteran who had flown down from New York for the day.

'There's a lot of speed in this animal,' Oakie said. 'The key is to know when to turn it on. I've tried holdin' her back, and I've tried savin' her for the stretch. But I've come 'round to thinkin' neither is right. The way to run this filly is to let *her* decide. Try to feel when she wants to make the move, then go with it. Don't ask *her*; she'll ask you!'

There was a ring of confidence in Oakie's tone. Geri felt certain that the tide was about to turn.

Just out of the starting gate in the third race of the afternoon, Ladylike moved into fourth place. She stayed there around the first turn and all along the backstretch. But even from her seat in the grandstand Geri could tell by the horse's loping motion that Ladylike was going easily, keeping plenty in reserve.

But as the leaders turned for home Ladylike still hadn't made her move. She was coasting, still holding the same position. The jockey kept waiting for the surge, but Ladylike stubbornly kept her pace and finished in fourth place — exactly where she'd started.

Hard as it was to watch the horse in which she had placed so much faith finish just out of the money, it was even harder to accept that the winner of the day's seventh race, the feature with a purse of $75,000, turned out to be a colt named Centurion which she had bred herself for Justinean Farms.

When Dolph didn't appear in the winner's circle to claim the trophy, Geri realized he wasn't there. Had he arranged to run this horse today merely to taunt her? No. It must be only coincidence. She was going to encounter Dolph's horses again and again, she told herself. She'd have to be prepared to bump into him, too, sooner or later.

'I'm sorry, princess,' Oakie said when they met at the stable at the end of the afternoon.

'She could have done it today,' Geri insisted. 'That jockey didn't —'

'No, Geri,' Oakie broke in forcefully. 'If you need a goat, blame me. I told him how to run it, and I was wrong. But maybe you're wrong, too. Maybe you've got to accept that the filly can't do it.'

'She's got the speed. You've clocked her!'

'That's only half the battle, darlin'. There's plenty of these critters who can win it on a Sunday, alone in the pasture, and just lose heart when they're out there with dirt flyin' up in their face from the pack runnin' in front.'

'Don't tell me she doesn't have the spirit!' Geri argued hotly. 'When I'm near that horse, I feel it as sure as if I was standing by a furnace.'

Oakie gave her a skeptical glance. 'You don't think you might be mistakin' plain ol' orneriness for spirit?'

'I might've done that once with a husband,' she snapped, 'but I know the difference now.'

Oakie laughed, defusing the argument. He agreed to go on with the training, and shouldering the burden of expense. But he urged Geri not to keep bouncing the jockey. When an owner blamed the riders unfairly for every loss, it became harder to find replacements.

She had thought that doubts about the horse were put to rest once Oakie granted his continued support. But later in their hotel room, it was Quinn's turn to take up the questioning.

'Don't we have what we want already? We're together. Why don't we enjoy every minute of that instead of running from one end of the country to the other, chasing a dream.'

'If you lose belief in that dream,' Geri said, 'then it means you've lost faith in me.'

'Don't make this a fight between us,' Quinn shot back. 'You know better than anyone this is a million-to-one shot. There isn't a racehorse born that somebody doesn't start out hoping will be another Man O' War —'

'Wrong sex,' Geri said flippantly.

Quinn didn't pause for a smile. 'That only makes the odds higher for Ladylike and you know it! Look, I ought to go where I can work. That means as long as you go on with this, we'll be apart.' He took her in his arms. 'And that seems like a bigger loss to me than a thousand silver trophies or anything else this damn animal can win.'

She let him gather her in, and rested a moment with her head against his. But she could not yield beyond that.

'I need this,' she said then. 'Whatever it takes. Lady's going to deliver more than anybody's seen yet. I can feel that untapped power in her as much as if it was a part of me . . .'

'And suppose that's *all* it is, something in you. You think Ladylike can perform the way you do — that she'll go on taking the knocks until a win finally comes in, take the punishment because it makes her stronger. But you've done it all your life, Geri. That doesn't mean she can!'

'She can,' Geri echoed with quiet ferocity, pulling away from him. 'She *will*.'

CHAPTER TWO

While Geri returned to Lexington with Oakie and stayed at his farm to watch over the training, Quinn went back to California. But they spoke daily by phone, sometimes twice a day. He didn't try again to dissuade her. He had never wanted anything but to save her from disappointments.

In workouts, the horse went on improving, shaving only fractions of a second each time — yet over two weeks this added up to speed that, if maintained, could beat track records. Oakie's enthusiasm began to bubble again, though he kept cautioning that the performance was meaningless unless it could be reproduced in a race. That would depend on a jockey, and they had yet to engage a new rider. They needed someone of proven experience at coaxing out the best from temperamental runners, and all the top men they approached turned them down in favor of other mounts.

All through December the training continued. Quinn flew in for Christmas and New Year, then went on to New York. The Wagonners were still dallying, and he hoped to pry out a decision about the show.

In January racing activity moved south to the warmer weather of Florida. Ladylike's season as a two-year-old had ended — no matter when any racehorse was born, for purposes of classification its birthday was the first of January — and for her debut as a three-year-old, Oakie planned to ship the filly south, along with other horses in his string, to run at Hialeah Park in Miami.

But only a couple of days before the move, as they sat in his kitchen after dinner, Oakie told Geri that it looked like the best jockey they could get would be one of the men who had previously ridden the horse.

'Anybody who's lost on this horse once,' Geri said, 'is going to lose again. If they haven't found the key to unlock what's inside her, they can't win.'

Finally, Oakie's patience was exhausted. 'If you don't think sheer riding skill is going to be enough, then you might as well throw the greenest bug-boy on her back and just hope for the best.'

'I might, Oakie,' Geri answered. 'I just might do that.'

The tension that had built between them over the months came to a head now. Geri felt she could no longer talk to Oakie. He was like Pa, she felt suddenly, stubbornly insisting that she had to curtail her expectations, stop reaching for more. Bolting from the kitchen table, she slammed out through the back door of the house.

Automatically, she aimed herself toward the stable area, propelled by the vain wish that some revelation might occur if she looked at Ladylike again. Or was there any 'key' to be found? Stalking angrily into the quiet barn, Geri faced the possibility that perhaps the stubbornness was her own — an inherited strain. Was it time to accept that this horse was just another also-ran?

Glancing ahead along the aisle of stalls, she pulled up short. Once again a haunting image of the past floated in obscure light, a ghost wavering beyond the row of overhead bulbs kept dim at night. As if he were there now, she could see Nickles standing in front of a corner stall — the young bug-boy as he'd been on the day they'd met on an evening years ago in Justinean's barn. She moved slowly toward the apparition . . .

It was still there when she came within a few feet, and the boy turned to face her. Only he wasn't a boy, small as he was. His face was deeply lined now, and gaunt, marked by all the adversity he had suffered since his suspension.

'It is you . . .' she said softly, slightly bewildered to see him.

He smiled shyly, and for a moment she saw again the face of the young jockey with a crush on her. 'Wasn't expecting you to come walking in here at this hour,' he said. 'I would've called tomorrow.'

'What are you doing here, Nicks?' She hadn't seen him, she realized, since that bitter parting where he had threatened her . . . the day after which, Heartbrakes had died suddenly and mysteriously. Now here he was again, lurking near her horse at an unlikely time. Her eyes darted to his hands, then over to the stall, looking for a hint of anything amiss.

He caught the suspicious glance. 'Wanted to see the horse, that's all. I've been watching from a distance 'til now, and I thought I'd take a look close up before I talked to you about it.'

'Talked to me? About what?'

He looked down. 'I want to ride for you.' It was almost a whisper.

The statement left her speechless. Could he really think she would let him?

In the silence, he lifted his eyes to find hers. 'Give me the chance, Geri. I'm reinstated now. I've been working again — only small tracks, I won't kid you, and the horses have been dog meat. But for you I could always win . . .'

'Nickles,' she sighed, only to stop his pathetic plea. She couldn't entrust her dream to him, even if she could believe he was ready to take it on. There was too much to forgive.

He went on, though. 'You need someone, don't you? The word was around. And I've been studying your horse, watched the last few races . . .'

'It couldn't work,' she said. 'I've got to have —'

'A winner!' he broke in. 'That's what you want. I can give it to you, Geri. They've thrown me on the garbage heap, but it's too soon.' He moved forward, and the dim rays from the overhead bulb caught the lines in his face, etching them deeper so it looked like his face was cracking apart. 'For God's sake, Princess, don't make me beg. Trust me. I can see what you've got there.' He glanced at Ladylike. 'Have you noticed the way she picks her head up slightly and swings a little to the

636

inside when she comes out of the gate passing the stand, and also when she turns for home? I think whenever she's near the stands, the noise spooks her, the crowd cheering. I think maybe her ears are extra sensitive. There's something holding her back, anyway. Because I know there's more to your horse than what she's shown anyone yet.' He clutched at Geri's hands. 'I'm not asking just for me. I owe you, Geri, don't you see? Please . . . give us both a second chance.'

Second chances. They were almost her religion.

And she was impressed by what he'd said. The horse's twitch wasn't anything she'd noticed — for all she knew Nicks had improvised that observation, made it up to impress her. Yet she needed a rider, needed an experienced jockey. When Nickles had been at the top, too, his specialty had been taking the temperamental horses and making them perform.

'Tomorrow's her last workout before we ship south,' she said. 'I'd like you to do that, too.'

It took a second before he caught the significance of her last word. Then he started forward as if to embrace her gratefully.

She stepped back. 'You better go now, Nicks,' she said. 'You've got to be here early in the morning.'

He went out quietly, like an obedient child.

A week later Nickles rode Ladylike onto the track at Hialeah for the seven-furlong allowance restricted to fillies and mares.

The choice of jockey didn't please Oakie, even if he hadn't registered more than a mild protest. But he didn't want to fight with Geri anymore. He had privately decided, however, that he would not go on sponsoring the horse if it lost again. In this resigned state of mind, he remained acquiescent even when Nickles offered the suggestion that some kind of special 'bonnet' might be fashioned to fit comfortably over the horse's ears and dampen the sound. The solution Geri eventually worked out with one of the saddlers at Hialeah was less obtrusive — separate leather muffs sewn to measure, then lined with foam rubber and secured to the racing bridle. It looked slightly ridiculous, but Oakie said nothing, even endured with quiet grace the ribbing from his fellow trainers. In fact, he was hoping to have the last laugh — but not on

Nickles or Geri. Unusual as he thought their idea was, he knew of stranger things that had turned a horse around, and he only hoped this one would work. The bettors didn't seem to think it would matter, though. Based on Ladylike's past record, and the dubious history of her jockey, the odds on the horse stood at 75—1.

At the cry of 'They're off', Ladylike got away from the gate behind a few other horses. But as soon as she was heading down the straightaway in front of the stands she began to dig in and move up. By the first turn, she had gone to the front — and she never stopped widening her lead. At the finish line, she was fourteen lengths in front.

That finish was only the beginning.

CHAPTER THREE

Up to the moment Geri dashed into the international arrivals terminal, all her thoughts had centered around the race to be run in a few hours at Belmont. But now she could only think of Quinn. Had his trip been successful? If not, then whatever victories awaited her couldn't be nearly so sweet. He was a partner in the horse, but that meant little to him measured against his own career.

Her heart lifted when she saw him emerge smiling from the customs clearance area, swinging his valise as if it were weightless. After he took her in his arms and kissed her, his first question was about the horse. That was a good sign, too, no trace of the resentment that had surfaced some months ago.

'How's it look for this afternoon?'

'Fine. But that can wait. I want to hear about you —'

He paused, a theatrical moment of suspense. 'They bought everything in the show!'

Thrilled and relieved, she kissed him again. Whatever happened this afternoon, she knew now, they would be all right.

The decision finally delivered by Melinda Wagonner had been negative. In her letter of explanation to Billy she had twisted the knife. 'Other dealers may have lower standards, but in our view these canvasses depart too much from the style and quality associated with the best sporting paintings.'

Quinn was steeled for such a response, but a depression took hold when he went to other galleries and continued to be denied an exhibition. His own sense of defeat was only heightened by the victories Ladylike had begun to reap. She had started by running in events restricted to fillies, but after winning a few by record-breaking margins, Oakie thought the horse could be tried in competition with colts. This had been Geri's idea all along; nevertheless it was unconventional. The rules of racing allowed three-year-old fillies to compete against colts in any major stakes, but so few had ever been successful against the best male horses, they were rarely matched in the same races. Prior to a filly winning the 1980 Kentucky Derby, there hadn't been another female horse in the race — or any other Triple Crown event — since 1959, and that had been a fifth-place finish. Yet Geri had always believed there was no inherent reason to separate horses by sex. If the colts ended up running faster as they matured, perhaps it was only because they were trained in a way that expected more of them, and were brought to peak performance by being tested in more demanding races against each other. It was the story of men and women all over again.

Ladylike was moved up in class to run against the colts and she beat them, too. By the end of March, she was being touted as a top contender for the Kentucky Derby.

Geri should have been walking on air. But Quinn's growing despair gave rise to friction between them. In April, when Ladylike was about to run in the important 'Derby preps' where she would meet other probable runners in the May event, Geri phoned Quinn and asked him to fly East and join her.

'I miss you,' he said, 'but I couldn't enjoy sitting at the track like a rich man with nothing better to do. I've got to get a handle on my own life . . .'

She said she understood, but within her was a growing fear that they might never be able to bridge the widening gap between them. The more she succeeded with her own dream, the farther it took her from him.

Ladylike went on winning. It wasn't until the Blue Grass Stakes at Keeneland, two weeks before the Derby, that one of

Dolph's horses finally showed up in the same race — the colt Centurion, which Geri had bred for Justinean Farms. After winning a couple of events in Florida, Centurion had spent the rest of the winter in California. The string of consecutive victories he had earned there — and the fact that he was the male of the species, made him the favorite in the Blue Grass and he went off paying even money. Because Geri's filly would be running against Centurion and a couple of other strong colts, her chances were discounted.

So when Nickles brought Ladylike first under the wire by half a length, she had paid off handsomely at six-to-one.

Making her way to the winner's circle after the race, Geri had kept looking for Dolph. If she could talk with him, then perhaps an armistice could be arranged. His evil appalled her, yet she would gladly deal with him if he could be persuaded to stop using his connections to keep the doors closed to Quinn's work.

But once again Dolph had stayed away. Like a puppeteer, he remained out of sight while forcing everyone else to dance to his tune.

On the next Monday morning, Geri was in the Keeneland backstretch, assisting as Ladylike was loaded into a van for the trip to Churchill Downs where the Derby would be run in two weeks. One of the stable grooms came out of the barn and shouted that there was a call for her on the office phone.

It was Ed Markham. He congratulated her on Ladylike's win and chatted about the outlook for the Derby, but the tightness in his voice told Geri that the smalltalk was masking some grave concern. At last she asked what was wrong.

'This is tough, Geri — particularly coming now. You've got so much you could be celebrating . . .'

She knew then what it was — the only one thing left for Dolph to use.

'I've just had a call from a friend,' he went on, 'an important news source who knows I represent you. He warned me to be prepared with a statement on a story that Dolph has just given out . . . that you instigated Diana's murder. It'll be on radio and television tonight, hit the papers in the morning.'

'How does he say I did it?' she asked.

'It would be laughable if it wasn't so damn serious.' Markham recounted the version of events Dolph had released — claiming his conscience had finally driven him to speak out.

The night of the murder Justinean had come back late from business in the city to find Geri already in the house. He had taken the presence of his mistress as an indication that his wife couldn't also be there, and he and Geri had gone to bed to make love. Later in the night there had been noises of someone entering the bedroom. Geri had prompted him to believe it was a prowler and to confront the intruder with a gun. It was true, Justinean allowed, that the shadowy figure in the bedroom had said nothing before trying to run, and so he had fired.

'I wasn't there, Ed,' Geri said flatly. 'I was at the clinic.'

'Got witnesses?'

'Sure, several of my associates would have seen me . . .'

'What about at night — between the hours of, say, eight p.m. and eight the next morning?'

It had been the period during her break from Dolph, she recalled, before the shooting had brought them back together. After a day at the clinic she would have spent a quiet evening. 'I think I was at home, alone,' she admitted.

'There's the rub. The distance between Saratoga and Glen Cove could be covered in a car in four or five hours. In theory, you could have arrived late; then, after Diana was shot, you could have driven straight back to the country.'

'Will anyone swallow that? If Diana was in the house, who'd believe she'd let me in and then creep quietly away — so that Dolph never realized she was there? Is that what a wife does when her husband's mistress shows up? Any anyway, if Dolph admits Diana tried to run and didn't speak when he held the gun on her, then I must be in the clear. That's what caused the shooting . . .'

Markham sighed. 'Listen, Geri, Dolph has this worked out to nail you and still leave him in the clear. Says he got all the facts from you of what really happened when you told him the story a few years after your marriage. It goes this way: after arriving at the house that night, you persuaded Diana to sit down to a little tête-à-tête over a drink — supposedly by telling her you and Dolph had broken up. You took the opportunity to slip her a drug, and while she was unconscious, you got her into the raincoat, and stuffed the jewels into a pocket. You made a reasonable assumption that she'd wake up a couple of hours later in the middle of the night and head for the bedroom. If she was still groggy, she might not even speak . . .'

'That's preposterous,' Geri said.

Markham agreed it was far-fetched, but pointed out that the story was carefully concocted. As a vet, Geri would be expected to have a degree of sophistication in administering drugs. And her supposed motive — to marry one of the world's wealthiest men — was certainly enough to drive some women to murder. 'I think you'd better fly up here, Geri. We've got to plot some strategy.'

Geri's heart sank. If it took no more than these wild lies to call her innocence into question, then how could she win once the old evidence Dolph had bought from Molly was used? Markham would have to be prepared. 'I'll be there today, Ed,' she told him. 'This strategy may be tougher than you think . . .'

Hearing of Dolph's press statements, Quinn had called at once offering to fly in and join Geri. She was eager for his moral support, yet she sensed there was something he was holding back. If there weren't, he would have turned up without calling first. 'If I could manage this alone,' she asked finally, 'would that be better for you . . .?'

He admitted then that he'd just had a lucky break. An English art dealer had been visiting Carmel and had sought him out. Unaware of the change of direction in Quinn's style, the dealer had come with the intention of purchasing the traditional work. But when he saw the new canvasses he was even more excited.

'This man has a top gallery and he's offered me a show. London, in June.' Quinn's voice fell. 'But that doesn't give me much time to prepare . . .'

'Then you've got to make the most of it.' She knew that

would mean staying home, in his studio, but she was truly happy for him. 'It's wonderful luck.'

'But why does mine turn good just when yours goes bad — or the other way around? I worry about us sometimes . . .'

She knew what he meant. 'Wait a little longer, love,' she said. 'We'll get our lucky stars synchronized.'

She had been at the eye of a storm of press attention before. But this was a cyclone. New elements made re-examining the death of Diana Justinean even more sensational than when it had been fresh news. For one, the woman accused of scheming to have him *unknowingly* murder his former wife was the owner of one of the favorites in the upcoming Kentucky Derby.

Yet the situation was not as bad as it could be. At least Dolph hadn't made public the information about Geri's past.

'He'll hold back until he can use it as a coup de grâce,' Markham had guessed correctly after Geri went through the history with him in his office. 'And the chance may come soon. Looks like a Grand Jury will be convened to hear new testimony and decide whether to hand down an indictment.'

That might happen soon in the next few weeks, he warned. Meanwhile, they should consider blunting the force of Dolph's bombshell by being first to tell the newspapers about the past murder case in Kentucky.

'I can't be the one to do it, Ed . . .'

He didn't press the point, he understood her reasons. Racing rules forbade a felon to own any thoroughbred that competed at the track. As long as Dolph restricted himself to allegations, Geri could only be a target for suspicion, while her rights were unaffected. However, if it emerged that she was a fugitive from the laws of the state — no matter how old the offense — Ladylike would have to be scratched. The Kentucky establishment was loath to have any negative publicity taking the shine off horseracing's most famous event. If Dolph had chosen, so far, not to hurt Geri this way she wouldn't be the one to do it herself.

While Markham maneuvered to minimize the damage, Geri flew back to Louisville, and worked with Oakie on Ladylike's training. With the reporters buzzing around her constantly, she kept up a bright facade and belittled Dolph's claims as meaningless sound and fury, a byproduct of the acrimony that might mark the end of any marriage. Except for the times it was necessary to be at the track, she kept out of sight, away from all the pre-Derby festivities.

On the day of the race, she held her breath right up to post-time, knowing that at any moment a steward might come to her and tell her the horse would have to be withdrawn.

But Dolph had kept silent. Geri could only assume that he expected Centurion to win this time, and relished the prospect of snatching the victory from her, rather than simply guaranteeing his win by eliminating her horse.

Knowing he would be there, she did not go to the clubhouse to watch. After conferring with Oakie and Nickles before the race, she went through the underpass to the infield and found a place at the rail along with thousands of other ordinary railbirds.

From the moment the gate burst open, the race was a two-horse duel. Centurion, running from an outside position, and Ladylike, near the rail, both went right to the front . . . and stayed there while the rest of the field fell back. Around the first turn, pounding down the backstretch, going around the far turn and then heading toward home, the two horses stayed neck and neck, matched each other pace for pace. Their battle on the track was like an allegory of the clash of wills in which their two owners were locked.

As the horses swept under the wire, they were still together. Instantly the word 'PHOTO' appeared on the totalizator boards, and a hush fell over the hundred thousand people who had been shouting at full pitch only a moment earlier. They had never seen such a close finish in the Derby.

Suddenly the illuminated word on the board winked off, and the order of finish was posted. A roar went up from the crowds, as the band always present on Derby day began playing 'My Old Kentucky Home', and a groom ran out on the track to take the head of the winning horse and guide it to the winner's circle.

Nickles, still astride Ladylike, saw Geri as she came running toward him. He blew her a kiss, then held his thumb up in the air and flashed a smile as the photographers started snapping pictures.

The Kentucky Derby has been run since 1875, but there are a number of famed races that date back even farther. Among these are the Preakness Stakes, which has been a fixture at Pimlico in Maryland since 1873, and the Belmont Stakes, which originated in 1867. These two races and the Derby, run three or four weeks apart, are known as the Triple Crown, and to win them all is to earn the greatest prize in the sport of horseracing, not merely in terms of money, but in terms of honor. The lure of the prize assures that a Derby winner will go on to race in the other Triple Crown events.

Geri had no intention of breaking with tradition. Ladylike was sent back to Oakie's farm to continue training before being moved to Pimlico for the Preakness. She couldn't stay with the horse, however. Markham had summoned her back to New York. The District Attorney had reopened the file and launched his own investigation. Now he was demanding to interview Geri.

On the rainy afternoon when she presented herself at the D.A.'s office on Long Island, Markham was unable to accompany her. Kept in Washington by a Supreme Court case, he had sent a young associate. The associate was able and knowledgeable, but he did not have the legendary stature of Edmund Grace Markham and the District Attorney was emboldened to take an aggressive line of questioning with Geri. Large and overbearing, with a strong deep voice that seemed to echo off the walls so as to drown out her replies, the prosecutor quickly cracked through layers of sophistication Geri had built up over half a lifetime, and put her on the defensive.

'Mrs Justinean, I'd like to believe that you're innocent. But on balance it's easier to believe that your husband is finally giving us the facts — that he kept your secrets for the years you and he were happy together, but it remained on his conscience and now a time has come when he no longer cares to protect you. Whereas you have a very strong motivation to deny everything.'

She felt as though no time had passed since she had sat in a small hearing room with Delbert Conroy. 'I have no "motivation",' she almost screamed, 'except to tell the truth.'

He leaned over her, smiling. 'The trouble is . . . both innocent people and murderers so often give that same answer.'

The District Attorney hammered at her for two hours, questioning her knowledge of drugs and her feelings about Diana Justinean, and wound up by saying he would recommend sending the case before the Grand Jury.

When Geri left the interview she was shaking. As soon as she got back to her hotel room she phoned Billy for comfort. Hearing how distraught she was, Billy announced that he was coming to join her.

She was relieved . . . for a moment. Then she thought ahead. What did she want most? 'Don't leave your work, Billy.'

'I can postpone what I'm doing. You shouldn't have to go through this by yourself . . .'

'I can manage *this* alone. It's later I may need you. And I'm afraid of losing you if I hold too tightly now — if you don't have a chance to fulfill your own dreams. Do that, Billy, do it for me, and I'll know we'll be together now and always.'

On the last Saturday in May, the Preakness Stakes was run at Pimlico Race Course. The thrilling head-on competition that had developed in the last race between Centurion and Ladylike made a potential replay the main attraction of this second classic. The battle between Geri and Dolph being reported on front pages of tabloids across the country, only added to the excitement of the contest. When Centurion emerged as the even-money favorite over Ladylike at odds of 3-to-2, the handicappers said the choice was based mainly on history: a filly had not won the Preakness since Nellie Morse in 1924. But for many who put money on one horse or the other, the bet was a symbolic vote on which of their owners was likely to win in court, which guilty of murder, or even a statement of personal philosophy — as to whether sheer power would always triumph over beauty.

Dolph was still holding back his file of old information on Geri. Nevertheless, she had become such a curiosity — pointed at by spectators, mobbed by television camera crews, trailed everywhere by the international *paparazzi* — that she could not bear to appear at the track in person. She took a room with TV at a motel near the track and instructed Oakie to accept the trophy if Ladylike won.

Once again, when the starting gate sprang open, there were two horses that surged straight to the head of the field. The second of the Triple Crown races was almost an exact copy of the first. From post-to-wire, Centurion and Ladylike ran side by side. Until, coming around the last turn, Ladylike faltered abruptly and dropped a stride. In an instant she was half a length behind. Through the last stretch she fought to recover, but Centurion was still ahead by a neck at the finish.

As the post numbers of win, place, and show horses lit up the tote board, the groans from the crowd almost drowned out the cheers. But a moment later a lighted word flashed on, too.

INQUIRY.

Then the track announcer's voice came through the public address speakers explaining that a protest had been lodged against the winner by the second-place jockey. The order of finish would not be official until the stewards had examined film of the race.

In Geri's motel room, the phone rang. She pulled herself away from the television screen.

It was Billy. 'Thought you might like to sweat it out together. Do you know what it's about?'

'Couldn't be sure from where I'm sitting, but there may have been interference from Dolph's horse on the turn.'

Through the television broadcast came the sound of a huge cheer. The inquiry had been settled, but Geri had missed the result. 'Did you hear it?' she shouted at Quinn.

'You were right. Bumping. Centurion's been disqualified.'

She had barely felt the first spark of a thrill before it was snuffed by a chill of fear. Dolph had lost again. She knew what had to happen next.

The Grand Jury convened three weeks later to consider the Long Island D.A.'s petition that an indictment be handed down against Geri for the murder of Diana Justinean.

The die had been cast the day after the Preakness when Dolph gave several newspapers photocopies of old documents relating to the Kentucky trial of Geri-Jo 'Lockely'. The next morning the story was headlined, earning even a lead column on the front page of the *New York Times*. What had been a crime of passion coupled to a top sports story was now laced with elements of another past crime covered up by corruption and influence-buying. It had everything.

This time Quinn arrived without calling. Though the paintings he'd planned for his London show were not completed, he could no longer be deterred from joining Geri. He wouldn't leave her side, he said, until they had fought the charges and won. Geri could no longer pretend that his support wasn't vital. Everything in her world, everything but their love, had collapsed in a matter of days.

Ed Markham had managed to keep her from being instantly jailed, or extradited to Kentucky. But when officials of the New York Racing Association ruled that Ladylike would be scratched from the Belmont Stakes — the third leg of the Triple Crown — there was nothing Markham could do to defer or reverse their decision.

As the air-conditioned limousine bringing Geri and Quinn to the courthouse with Ed Markham approached the front steps, a crowd pressed around the car. Reporters, their faces shining with sweat, photographers with heavy gear suspended from their shoulders mopping themselves with handkerchiefs. The weather reports had predicted that today's temperature would set a record for this date in June.

'I should have asked for a change of venue to Alaska,' Markham said.

'I won't wilt in the heat,' Geri said determinedly.

The lawyer turned to her. 'Weather like this puts everyone

on edge, Geri, makes them cranky. Even if it's cooler in the courtroom, there's always a few people who didn't sleep well the night before. Whatever happens you and Bill and I have to do everything to set a nice easy tone — help keep everyone cool.'

Geri smiled. 'Don't worry, Ed. I've spent enough time in hell over the years to make today feel like an arctic breeze.' Though she tried to sound jaunty — implementing his advice — his warning had scared her. He sounded even less confident today than on the day she had persuaded him to take Dolph's case.

Nothing that happened on the first day of the hearing or the next made her terror recede. The weather stayed hot, and no matter how imperturbable Markham appeared in court, the jury seemed impressed with the arguments in favor of indictment. Primary, of course, were the old Kentucky court records. If Geri had been guilty of committing murder in her youth — and wasn't fleeing from the charges a form of admitting guilt? — it wasn't hard to believe she might have done it again. Exposure of the old charges also raised the possibility of being extradited to Kentucky to face trial. The absence of a concrete alibi to cover her on the night of Diana Justinean's death also weighed against Geri, and her likely knowledge of drugs. Even her love of racing was turned against her. Involvement with thoroughbred horses, the District Attorney pointed out to jury members, was an expensive hobby. At a time when her clinic was failing, the only way Geri could have indulged such a hobby was to ensure her marriage to a rich man.

On the afternoon of the third day, Dolph Justinean finally took the stand. He looked suave and confident, his silver hair bestowing a suggestion of the wisdom that came with age. Listening to his lies, Geri marveled that she had once been in love with him. Had she been so blind? Or had each of them been such different people when they had met? For all her seeming indifference to wealth, her childhood had left its mark in a need for security. And perhaps the pursuit of wealth and power for their own sake had finally poisoned Dolph's soul.

While they sat twenty feet apart for several hours, and occasionally their eyes met, they were no more than the cold, grazing glances of strangers.

As Markham parted from Geri and Quinn outside the courthouse at the end of the hearing's third day, he ordered her to get as much sleep as possible. 'The D.A.,' he told her, 'will be putting you in the hot seat tomorrow.'

Before Ladylike's training at Belmont had been suspended, Geri had taken a room incognito at one of the old rooming houses near the track where many of the grooms and apprentice jockey lived. Proximity allowed her to monitor Oakie's training sessions easily, and the obscure rooming house also provided an escape from the press. By exercising extreme care in the way they traveled, Geri and Quinn had managed to keep their haven from being discovered.

Lying with Quinn in the furnished room the night before she would take the stand to plead her innocence, Geri had the sense of her life having come full circle. They had wanted to make love, but the accumulated tension of months had finally dulled them to the subtle touches of sex. They gave up trying to arouse each other, and the night passed lying naked in each other's arms, soothed only by the warmth and closeness.

Musing to herself, Geri thought of how very far she had come from her beginnings — only to be lying in a dingy room on a sagging mattress not so different from the one she'd slept on as a child.

'It's as if I've gone around the track myself,' she murmured to Quinn. 'I'm coming up to the wire, and I still don't know who'll win or lose, me or Dolph.' Or was Pa the one she'd really spent a lifetime running against — Pa, who'd told her she was crazy to try for too much, that it would lead nowhere and break her in the end.

'Tomorrow's not the end, love,' Bill said. 'Even if you're indicted, there's still a trial . . .'

'If I can't make those twelve people believe I shouldn't be tried, I can't convince the next twelve I shouldn't be convicted.'

'They'll believe you, Geri.'

'Truth doesn't always win, Billy. Dolph might carry the day just because he always has. Because . . . as folks in the hollow always said, "them as has, gets".'

'Don't give up, love,' Quinn said. 'Whatever happens, we'll get through it together.'

She turned her head and moved back slightly to look in his eyes. Together, he'd said. It struck her now that never before had there been anyone of her own to help her through the crises. Even Steve, kind as he'd been, had belonged to someone else.

'We are going to last, aren't we?' she said, with the simple awe of a child discovering some wonder of nature.

He knew what she was thinking. 'No mountain's going to fall on me, my darling. We're going to climb it and come out on top.'

'I love you,' she said softly, 'forever.'

All at once the urge to touch him, melt into him, overwhelmed her. What had seemed so difficult a minute ago was suddenly easy.

By the time the judge banged his gavel to reconvene the morning's session, Ed Markham had not yet appeared. The judge, a heavy man with a sallow face and impressive black eyebrows, shot a scolding look at the empty chair by the defense table, and asked Geri if she knew what had become of her lawyer. When she could not tell him, the judge irritably called an adjournment of fifteen minutes, and announced before disappearing again to his chambers that if Markham hadn't taken his place by the end of that time, he might be held in contempt of court.

Only a few minutes before the deadline, Markham bustled in.

'Where the hell were you?' Geri whispered furiously.

Markham had no chance to answer before the judge, alerted by the bailiff, returned to the bench. His first words were a rebuke to Markham.

Markham stood at respectful attention. 'I apologize to the court, Your Honor. But the business of this court is to find truth, and I needed to be at the airport to collect a parcel of truth you and the jury deserve to hear. Since I've caused you the inconvenience of waiting, perhaps you'd allow me to present what I've brought with me. It would make up for the lost time by helping to settle these proceedings sooner.'

The judge squinted dubiously at Markham but then gave his permission.

As Markham turned toward the back of the courtroom, Geri swiveled around, too. Now she saw the frail elderly man standing right by the door. He looked so familiar — tall, slightly stooped, with wispy strands of gray hair that hung over his eyes. Yet she couldn't place him.

'Your Honor, I call to the stand . . .'

As the name of the witness rang in her ears, Geri's hand started up, as though to grab Markham and pull him down, order him to retract his words. But then she stopped herself. She was no less curious than the other spectators in the room to hear what Hal Parker had to say.

CHAPTER FOUR

The crowds at Belmont were simmering with excitement. Even in the owners' enclosure, Geri had to push between thick clots of men and women exchanging opinions about today's runners. Many called out greetings as she passed — or congratulated her with pats on the back. She had been vindicated, and Ladylike was in the race. The stage had been set for one more round in a confrontation between two great horses heightened by the personal drama of the human interests they represented.

One other element had drawn the spectators in record numbers — the outside chance to witness a piece of unique racing history. In all the hundred-odd years that the Triple Crown races had been run, only eleven horses had performed the feat of winning all three. And not one of the eleven had been a filly.

Before going through a gate to the saddling area, Geri glanced over at the electric board that showed the betting odds, constantly changing as the sentiments of the crowd ebbed and flowed, and the experienced gamblers moved their money in search of the best potential pay-off. The odds on Ladylike were currently showing at 7-to-1, extraordinarily high for a winner of two previous Triple Crown events.

One reason, Geri realized, was the historical bias against fillies — especially over greater distances. At a mile-and-a-half, the Belmont Stakes was a full quarter mile longer than the

654

Derby. Handicappers obviously felt that Ladylike's strength and endurance were going to be pushed beyond the limit. Indeed, many racing fans thought that the natural superiority of the male horse had been demonstrated already in the recent Preakness. Centurion's loss on a technical ruling was unfair, they believed; at the end Ladylike had been tiring and she would have lost anyway.

But whatever doubts existed because Ladylike was a filly, these were magnified by the limited preparation the horse had been given for an even harder race than the last two narrow victories. During the time the filly had been suspended, neither Oakie nor Geri had imagined the decision would be reversed in time for the horse to run. Thus, for a crucial two weeks, Ladylike's training had been slack.

It was only four days before the race that Ladylike had been re-classified eligible.

The dramatic reversal had been the result of Hal Parker's surprise appearance at the Grand Jury hearing. Under Ed Markham's patient questioning, the retired auto-dealer had recounted the story of his own involvement with the Lockely family, from the day Garrett's jalopy had pulled up in front of his showroom, right through his wife's 'adoption' of Geri-Jo, and then Molly.

'But Geri-Jo, as you call her, was your wife's favorite,' Markham had prompted.

'Oh my, yes. Lettie loved that girl. Loved her too much, maybe, which was why I guess she went off her too fast . . .'

'Too fast?' Markham echoed, coaxing an explanation.

In a voice quavering with emotion, the old man had told of the renunciation that began when Lettie Parker thought that Geri had killed her father and made up stories about her sister in an attempt to clear herself.

'And what did your wife discover later about the stories she thought were made up?'

'That Geri-Jo'd been telling the God's truth. About a year after Molly moved in with us, she let it out one night in an argument with my wife. By then we'd discovered what a damn hellion Molly was — still, she wasn't quite fifteen, and we

655

couldn't bring ourselves to throw her out. Then came this argument. Lettie told the girl she was putting her foot down, and Molly just laughed and said she didn't mind leaving, there were plenty of men who'd take her in. And then to taunt Lettie, bring her right down, Molly said it was too bad she hadn't believed Geri-Jo . . . because then she could have ended up living with the kind of girl Lettie wanted, someone kind and sweet and innocent . . .' The old man shook his head as the memory came alive for him. 'And she didn't stop there. To rub it in, she went on and told Lettie the whole story of what really happened — shocking things, you know — how her Pa had . . . used her, and Geri-Jo tried to stop it, and so Garrett went out of his head and Geri-Jo had defended herself . . .'

'You mean . . . to keep her own father from killing her?' Ed Markham put in.

'That's correct, sir.'

Ed Markham went back and forth, drawing out every detail of the lurid story Parker had heard from Molly, making sure all the circumstances that had caused Geri to hurt her father were imprinted on the mind of each juror.

As Geri listened, the events of that terrible night had come so vividly into her memory that they almost seemed to be unfolding in front of her. Her body lived it as well as her mind, almost cowering by reflex as Parker testified that there had apparently been a chase, and Geri remembered hiding in the dark garage behind the oil drum . . . Pa stalking her . . . Throughout the testimony her heart had been pounding, and her skin was damp with perspiration even in the air-conditioned hearing room. When she remembered — as Parker told about it — striking her father, she bowed her head in shame, wishing as fervently today as she had in the moment after she saw Pa crushed, that she could have undone it, that she could have escaped him in some other way . . .

Parker came at last to describing his wife, mortified by having sheltered 'the town's busiest whore', and overcome with guilt at her unjust rejection of Geri, having taken her own life. At this point Hal Parker had broken down on the stand. There were few in the courtroom who were not deeply affected by the spectacle of the old man weeping, repenting of wrongs he had waited more than twenty years to right. Tears were seen to trickle down the cheeks of several women jury members.

When Ed Markham went to his seat at the defense table after turning the witness over for cross-examination, he scribbled a note on a slip of paper, folded it and slid it over to his client. Geri unfolded it and read two words: Home Free.

The District Attorney had made an effort to damage Hal Parker's testimony, but each barbed question only backfired.

'If you believed that Geri Lockely was innocent so long ago, Mr Parker, why would you wait until now to come forward?'

'Because I didn't think anything could be changed then. That was the pity of it. To escape being railroaded, the girl had run away and disappeared. As long as she seemed safe, I didn't see any reason to drag up a lot of dirt. A few years back I saw her picture in a paper, but from the story I could see she'd come out okay — married to a rich man — so I left it alone. Wasn't until I was watching Dan Rather last night and I saw about this hearing that I called Mister Markham and agreed to fly up here from Florida . . .'

Everything that had worked against Geri when she was thought to have a past record, now worked for her. If she had been haunted all her life because of past lies, there was every possibility that she might be innocent now, unfairly charged as an accomplice to murder by the man who had actually pulled the trigger.

When Markham brought Dolph Justinean back to the stand for cross-examination, his claims suddenly rang hollow. His willingness to use stolen court documents acquired from Geri's sister put his own motives under a cloud.

Late on the day that had started with Hal Parker's testimony, the Grand Jury retired to deliberate on whether to indict Geri on a charge of murder in the second degree.

'If they find against me,' Geri said to Markham as she watched the jury file out of the courtroom, 'I'll have to face the old charges, too, won't I? It'll mean they didn't believe Parker and —'

Markham placed a calming hand on her arm as he cut in. 'They won't find against you, Geri. Don't worry. That old case is dead.'

If only it could be, she prayed. If only she could feel at peace finally with what had happened so long ago.

The jury was out less than twenty mintues before filing back into the courtroom.

Geri stood to hear the verdict — so popular that a cheer broke out when it was announced.

Ahead Geri saw Oakie standing by Ladylike, waiting for Nickles to emerge from the jockeys' room. Glancing around, she saw Centurion, too, his jockey already up, the trainer giving instructions. But Dolph was absent. Had shame kept him from the track?

'How's Billy?' Oakie asked. He knew that Geri had picked him up at the airport this morning.

'On top of the world. His paintings sold out. I left him at the windows betting every penny he earned in London.'

'Guess it's a relief,' Oakie observed cannily, 'to have two winners in the family.'

Geri smiled and looked around. All the other jockeys had appeared, but not Nickles.

'What's keeping him?' she asked edgily.

Oakie shrugged. 'Hey now, sweetheart, somebody's got to be last. That's no cause to pop your springs.'

Moments later, Nickles came through the door from the jockeys' room and ran toward them. Other horses were already starting toward the paddock.

'Didn't leave much time for instructions,' Geri said crossly as the jockey came up.

He flicked her a smile so tight it looked more like a wince. 'My zipper got stuck,' he said. The lightness that would have made it funny was missing. Geri sensed Nickles' tension. Though, why wouldn't he be tense on a day when he was trying to make racing history and guarantee Ladylike's place as the most valuable breeding mare that had ever lived?

She stood by as Oakie conferred briefly with Nickles. The

huddle was a ritual they still went through, but there was little that needed to be said. The instructions hadn't changed since the time Oakie had determined that Ladylike should be allowed to set her own pace.

'Okay, I got it,' Nickles said hurriedly, moving from Oakie to mount up. 'Better catch the others . . .'

Geri had the sense he was rushing away to avoid her. 'Hey, Nicks,' she called to him as he started to steer the horse on the path to the paddock. 'Remember Saratoga? Do it like that.'

He turned and nodded, but there was no reply.

She was sure now, something was weighing on him. She ran to catch up. Walking alongside the horse, she demanded, 'What's wrong, Nicks?'

'Nothing . . .'

'Hey, we know each other better than that.'

'Forget it, Geri. It won't make any difference.'

'*What* won't make any difference?'

He let the horse walk another two steps, then reined her in. 'Shit . . . I don't know what to do. I don't want you to doubt me, Geri, that's the problem. You've got to believe, however it comes out today, that I tried my best . . .'

'I will. Of course, I will. Ladylike couldn't have come this far without you.'

Nickles hesitated another moment. Then he hunched over in the saddle to speak in a low voice. 'This morning, when I left my hotel to drive here, a car cut mine off on a street, made me stop. This guy got out, and came over to my window. I was scared, Geri, didn't know what the hell was happening. He put his hand inside his jacket and I thought for sure he was pulling a gun . . . but what came out was a long piece of green paper which he shoved under my nose. A cashier's check, drawn on some foreign bank. Five million bucks, Geri, payable to Nicholas Tennyson! "It's yours if you want it," he says, and then he stuck the check back in his pocket again, got in his car, and I went on my way.' He looked at her. 'At first I thought I'd better tell you right away. I knew it had to come from Dolph. But then . . . I got scared again . . .'

'Scared of what, Nicks?'

'A couple things. That . . . if anything went wrong today, I mean if the Lady just can't make it . . . that you'd always wonder.'

'And the other thing?'

It took him a second to reply. 'That sometime in the middle of the race, I might decide to take it.'

'How do you feel now?'

He pulled himself up in the saddle, and a smile spread slowly over his face. 'Tall,' he said. 'Very tall.'

She laid her hand over his where he gripped the reins. But she wasn't sure yet whether the gesture was one of reassurance or apology. Could she let Nickles ride? What temptation might take hold anywhere during those two fevered minutes? *Five million dollars.* Not so much to Dolph — if Centurion won today, the colt's breeding value would increase by twice as much — but for Nickles it surpassed the earnings of his whole career. He had sold himself in the past for far less.

There were rules to be considered, too. A bribe attempt ought to be reported immediately. But then Nickles would have to be replaced. There were substitutes to be had even on short notice, but could any control Ladylike as well as Nicks at his best? Dolph's horse, too, might be scratched from the race — and more than anything, Geri wanted the satisfaction of defeating Dolph again.

'Better get to the paddock,' she said quietly. 'I want to be there when you blow me a kiss.'

She reached the clubhouse box in time to see the horses being loaded into the starting gate. As she took her place beside Quinn, Geri was jolted by the awareness that an adjacent box which had been empty before was now occupied. Dolph was in one of the front seats, Sabine right beside him. Other places were occupied by Lew Yancey, Connie Fuller, and a couple of burly men in dark suits that Geri didn't recognize. Perhaps, she thought, one had a check for five million dollars in his pocket.

As she looked over, Dolph turned and their eyes met. He smiled at her in a way that made her shiver, not because there was any hint of danger in it . . . but because there *wasn't*. If she

660

had never known him, she would have been charmed by it. With all she knew now, she could only be terrified by his ability to take on the role of total innocence. When she turned away, she said a silent prayer that she would never have to see him again after today.

'. . . and they're *off*!' the track announcer's voice exploded through the amplifiers.

Over the next two minutes and twenty-five seconds, every tick of time was like a separate revenge exacted against Dolph. For with every stride, Ladylike left Centurion farther behind. By the time she crossed the finish line, the first filly ever to win the Triple Crown, Ladylike was ten lengths in front. Her time was only one-tenth of a second shy of equalling the track record.

At the moment of triumph, Geri forgot Dolph. He didn't exist at all. There was only Quinn, holding her, lifting her up to spin her around, and then pulling her away to ceremonies in the winner's circle.

She went without a backward glance.

The admiring crush of the winner's circle was followed by a steady tide of other top owners and breeders, jostling in line to say a quick word to Geri. They started with congratulations, though that was only the preamble to a more serious purpose: to let her know they were ready to pay almost anything if one of their best stallions could be promised a season. If Ladylike enjoyed an average career as a breeding mare, she might produce no more than ten foals, yet each one, if sired by a male champion, would be a unique commodity on the thoroughbred market — with the potential to sell for more than the record thirteen million dollars paid for a single yearling at the Keeneland summer sale in 1985. The whispers in Geri's ear as she shook hands with other breeders promised shares in ten, twelve, possibly fifteen million dollars for each time her great filly went to the breeding shed and delivered a live foal.

Geri made no promises. Ladylike's racing career wasn't even over. With breeding rights becoming so valuable that great colts were being syndicated for amounts of twenty and thirty million dollars, it had become common for champions to be retired as young as three years-old. No sense risking the sudden breakdown of such a lucrative investment in another race. But she wasn't thinking that way. She wanted Ladylike to go on running, to go on proving herself again and again — and she had a curiously certain intuition that it was what the horse wanted, too. Whatever came later would be a wonderful bonus. But the color of racing had been dulled and weakened by putting the lure of breeding rates, tax advantages, and auction prices ahead of the sport. Geri wanted to restore as much as she could of an older tradition. Ladylike would race until she could no longer win.

When the excitement finally died down, and after she and Quinn and Oakie had celebrated with champagne in the clubhouse, she visited Nickles and told him she was giving him a share of the horse, too. Then she told Quinn there was one final ritual she had to perform before they could leave the track.

'I think I can guess what that is,' Quinn said. 'Want me to go with you?'

She shook her head. 'If you don't mind . . . I want to thank her alone.'

The brilliant yellow light of afternoon was bathing the backstretch as she walked along its avenues, heading toward the barn where Ladylike was kept. The figures she saw everywhere looked like living statues of gold — a horse being washed under a tree, a group of stablehands talking in a doorway. The ghosts were gone.

As she neared the barn where Ladylike was kept, Geri saw at once that the security guard she paid to protect her priceless asset was not sitting in his chair at the entranceway. She was mildly peeved, but there were other workers around the barn who could be trusted to keep an eye on the horse, and she assumed the guard had only stepped away for a moment, perhaps to have a cigarette in some less precarious spot than a wooden building loaded with hay.

Her annoyance grew, though, as she walked through the barn toward Ladylike's stall and saw it was a moment when the grooms and stablehands were also outside, either attending to chores, or taking a break of their own.

Then all at once it struck her as unnaturally quiet. Alarm drove her to quicken her pace. She thought of the Aga Khan's valuable horse, Shergar, that had been kidnapped and held for ransom a few years ago — and never recovered when the ransom was not paid . . .

Arriving in front of Ladylike's stall, Geri saw the chestnut horse standing quietly. Relieved, she went forward unthinkingly, straight up to the horse, and reached out to caress the neck. She had already stroked the silky hide a few times before it occurred to her that it was the first time she had come so close without sparking the filly's mean disposition. Intrigued, she dared to go farther, rubbing the horse's velvety nose, bringing her hand right near the mouth. Ladylike's reaction, docile and friendly, encouraged Geri to open the stall door and enter. The horse remained passive.

'I think I understand, girl,' she said softly. Circling her arm under the animal's head, she held it next to hers as if to confide a secret. 'You've shown 'em all now, proven you're the best. You don't have to be on edge anymore.' Who was she really talking to? 'I guess we're both able to relax now . . .' she added.

The quiet moment was shattered by a rustling noise behind her. Her whole body tensed, skin sensitized as surely as if she had been brought within the perimeter of a charged electric field. Her instincts recognized the signals of a familiar danger even before she turned and saw Dolph standing in a corner of the stall.

She realized now why the barn had been left unguarded. The security man must have been offered more money than he could afford to refuse to give Dolph this chance alone with her.

But what did he want? Whatever his purpose, she had no doubt it was sinister. 'What do you want?' she said as he stepped closer.

He turned his hands up. Even the gestures were perfect in his practiced performance of harmlessness. 'I only wanted to talk to you . . .'

'There are other places to talk,' she said. 'Why here? Why did you send everyone away?'

'I thought it might help the mood. It used to, remember.

Being alone together used to be very romantic . . .' He advanced a step.

Romantic? Geri stared at him. Could he think there was any hope left for them?

'There's nothing for us to talk about, Dolph. You've done everything you could to hurt me — destroy me and everything or everyone I cared about —'

'Yes, I did,' he said without a trace of contrition. 'I wanted to destroy you because . . . you're the only person who's ever broken from me, and beaten me. But that's the magic of you, Geri. No matter what I've done, you've survived it all — proven your strength, forced me to accept defeat in every way. Do you know how hard it is for a man like me to accept defeat? To say at last that I haven't just met my match, I've met my conqueror? But I'm saying it now . . .' He kept moving closer, his voice lulling her. As much as she despised him, she was also reminded of why he had attracted her. 'I've never stopped loving you,' he went on. 'Whatever I've done, it was because of that desire. The more you proved your strength against me, the more I wanted you and hated you for leaving me. But at last I have nothing left to fight you with, and all I can do is surrender . . .' He reached out to take her in his arms. 'Come back to me, Geri . . .'

She dodged out of his grasp. 'No, Dolph,' she said, more in pity than in anger. 'You don't love me. You love yourself, only yourself. And now you want me because it's the only way left to justify that love, your right to be exactly the way you are — to go on living as you please even if it means being judge and jury . . . and executioner of those who dare to defy you. But I won't help you. There is no justification for who you are, and the things you do . . .'

Her attack on his ego had touched a nerve. His face twisted with fury, and he lunged at her. Geri tried to dart aside again, but there was little room in the stall, and as she fumbled urgently with the latch to open the door, he grabbed her and pulled her back. She made another effort to wrest free, but his strength was too great, and he pushed her so violently toward the rear of the stall that she fell backward. With a stride he was standing over her. Then he bent down and for a second, she thought the wave of insane rage had passed and he was going to help her up. But he swiped his hand in a savage arc, striking her so hard across the face that her vision momentarily blacked out. She hurled her arms around one of his legs and pulled, trying to topple him, but he kicked her mercilessly with his free foot, the hard toe of his shoe stabbing into her side. The pain caused her grip to loosen as she saw him lowering himself, his hands formed into claws. He was bent on murder, she realized without doubt. And it was possible, too, that she'd been wrong about her earlier prediction. He *would* get away with it. He would find a way to make power work better than justice.

His hands were at her throat, and though she tried to tear them away, his grip kept on tightening. She couldn't breathe. She felt consciousness receding, the light around her dimming.

All at once the filly, excited by all the movement in the stall, shied so that her flank bumped hard against Justinean. It was enough to distract him so his hold loosened, and Geri lurched free and stumbled toward the door, gulping painfully for air, her throat already raw from Dolph's stranglehold.

Immediately, he lunged, his arms reaching to grab her, maniacal rage clearly written across his features. Afraid to turn from him, Geri tottered backward into the door and fumbled at the catch, her hands behind her. He was almost upon her before she could maneuver it open.

Suddenly the prancing, skittish horse swung its head around, butting with full force against the advancing Justinean. Knocked off stride by what seemed to be the random collision, Justinean stumbled against the side of the stall. Quickly he started to right himself, but the horse reared back and flailed its front hooves, one striking Justinean in the shoulder, the other pummeling him in the stomach. He doubled over.

'No, Lady . . .!' Geri screamed automatically, not thinking what effect it would have on her own life to save Justinean's.

But the horse was beyond control. Rearing again, it brought

its hooves down again on Justinean's back, and as he collapsed to the ground, it stomped on him again and again. Justinean's body twitched, then lay still. Geri could only stare in shock as the horse struck once more at Justinean's head, lifting one leg and pawing down with the hoof. At last, the filly bent its neck to nuzzle at the body. When it remained limp, the horse backed off.

For a few more seconds, Geri watched the trickle of blood seeping from the wound in the back of Dolph's head into the hay. Then she dragged herself across the stall and felt Dolph's neck for a pulse. There was none.

She turned to look at the horse, now standing passively at one side of the stall. Getting to her feet, she moved slowly toward the filly. Ladylike waited, still and content as Geri reached out and stroked her neck.

'Okay, Lady, okay,' she said softly. 'Nobody's going to blame you. Nobody's going to blame either of us . . .'

BOOK IX: *THE CIRCLE*

One year to the day after Ladylike became the first filly in history to win the Triple Crown, Geri and Bill Quinn were married in the large landscaped garden of the horse farm they had bought in the Blue Grass country. The pillared red-brick mansion, surrounded by four hundred acres of prime pastureland, was one of the most beautiful of the historic homes situated on the northern fringes of Lexington. Geri couldn't remember well enough to be positive, but she thought it might have been the place that had first caught her eye — made her feel the magic around her — the evening she had made Pa stop the truck.

This time, the wedding was not a small simple ceremony. Laurette Wilkey had prevailed when she told Geri she intended to make it the social event of the decade. 'Face it, dear girl,' said Laurette, 'you're the Queen of Racing now. You've got to be married like a queen . . .'

Being called the Queen of Racing wasn't to Geri's taste, but there was certainly no one else who occupied the pinnacle she did. Not only was she the owner of the greatest thoroughbred filly in the world — running now as a four-year-old Ladylike had won every stakes she entered, and amassed record winnings of more than ten million dollars — but Geri had taken possession of the great breeding stable Dolph had assembled. Whatever drama they had played out in public, Dolph had evidently gone on loving her, for he had never changed his will, and the probate court had ruled it valid since

669

Geri was still married to Justinean at the time of his accidental death. The immense fortune he had amassed went to her, too. After making an amicable settlement with Sabine Delvaux, Geri had begun to set up a network of charitable trusts, several of them specifically geared to provide better health service and education to the poor of Appalachia.

Rich as she was, in accepting Laurette's offer to help make the wedding the grandest of occasions, it wasn't the social pomp and splendor that appealed to Geri. She was simply so happy that she wanted to share the feelings with as many people as possible. As she said to Laurette, 'Why not shoot the moon? After all, *this* wedding is going to be a once-in-a-lifetime occasion.'

So, on this golden afternoon, she wore a long blush pink silk gown sewn with thousands of seed pearls, and was trailed down the aisle by two little blonde girls of five and six holding the train — Charlie Hoyt's daughters.

A third little girl of eight in a dress of ivory lace, her bright red hair decorated with a spray of lilies of the valley, followed as ring-bearer. Carrying the golden ring on a silk pillow, she smiled shyly as she went down the aisle, yet it was still one of the brightest, steadiest smiles she'd shown in months. It was just seven months ago that a private detective had finally located Molly's daughter. For the past three years, she had been in a state welfare home in New Mexico, placed there after being abandoned in Albuquerque by the woman who had abducted her from Kentucky. With the wealth and prestige Geri now possessed, arrangements to take Molly's child into her own custody had proceeded swiftly. It would be longer before Tammy overcame the psychological effects of the abuse and abandonment that had marked so much of her childhood, but already Geri and Bill were making strides. Tammy laughed more these days, had begun to seem less fearful of everyone. One of the best therapies had been giving her a pony. At bed-time on the day she had received the gift, Molly's daughter had asked Geri if it would be all right to start calling her 'Mommy'.

'You know, honey, your real Mommy was my sister. That makes me your Aunt.'

'I know,' Tammy said. 'But don't you think calling you "Aunt Mommy" would sound kinda strange?'

So 'Mommy' it was for now, though Geri would make sure the memory of Molly was kept alive.

As she passed down the aisle between rows of chairs, Geri saw the elite of the world of owners and breeders to which she belonged assembled around her. And toward the front there were all the people who meant most to her, Ramie and Glenn, Oakie, Laurette, Charlie Hoyt and Sid Ross and their wives, Ed Markham and his wife, and Tony Novello who'd come from Philadelphia where he was a school principal.

Nickles was waiting at the altar. It had been Quinn's idea to ask him to be best man, and he had proudly accepted. He was engaged himself now to Faith Shannon, a beautiful ex-model who ran a successful public relations firm. Many people commented on her resemblance to Geri — though Faith was a couple of inches taller.

Nickles smiled and shook his head admiringly as Geri took the last steps toward him. When he winked in appreciation of the gown as she went by, Geri leaned over and whispered quickly, '. . . another Grade One entry by "Evening Saint" . . .'

When the judge performing the ceremony pronounced them man and wife, Quinn and Geri celebrated with a long kiss that brought applause from the many well-wishers.

As soon as their lips separated, Quinn started tugging Geri in a half-run toward a path that would lead them quickly out of the garden.

'Hey . . . where're we going?'

Quinn nodded to Oakie in the front row, who brought forth a large flat package from under his seat. 'You'll see,' Quinn said, as he took the package and tucked it under his arm.

Her hand clasped in Quinn's, she ran along with him, and a crowd of guests kept pace behind them, curious to see what would unfold as Quinn led the way to the front drive down an avenue of trees, to the entrance to their property.

Now she realized where he was heading. 'You finished it!' she burst out joyfully.

They started to run faster along the drive, Geri's lace bridal veil trailing behind her like a thoroughbred's white mane. Then she saw that Tammy was running close alongside her. Geri clasped Tammy's hand, too, and gave Quinn a little tug to slow down so they could all three run together.

At the entrance to the farm, a gate stood with a high portal above it. Beneath the portal a ladder had been placed, gaily decorated with colored silk ribbons. Arriving under it, Geri stopped, and Quinn unwrapped the package to reveal the shingle he had painted to hang from two hooks over the entrance to the farm — a gateway to the rest of their lives together.

'Will you do the honors or should I?' he asked Geri. 'This thing is pretty heavy.'

'Not too heavy for me, mister!' She slipped out of her white satin high-heels and started up the ladder. From the next to last step, she reached down and Quinn passed up the shingle. Geri admired it a moment, a background of golden light captured exactly as she had seen him do it on the morning they met. Lettered across the top was the name they had chosen for the farm.

'It's perfect,' she whispered, looking down at him. Then she took the last step up, and linked the two hooks on the shingle through the matching rings.

'Olé!' Ramie shouted, sparking a chorus of salutations from the watching crowd.

Back on the ground, even after the other guests had started drifting away to the mansion for champagne and dancing and a gala supper, Geri stood beaming up at the sign. Then, recalling the letter in which Steve had said he would always be looking over her shoulder, she glanced at the sky and sent a silent message to his spirit.

She looked back to Quinn. 'I love you, partner,' she said. 'I'll always love you.' At last, she reached out and swept Tammy into a hug. 'We've all got a family now.'

Above them, the shingle swayed gently with the gust of a faint summer breeze — or perhaps, she thought, it was a devoted ghost blowing her a kiss. She glanced once more at the two words on the sign, the name of her breeding and racing stables: Home Free.

And truly she was, Geri knew. Finally and forever, she was.

THE END